A Time to Love Anew
The William Barsh Roberts Trilogy

South Wind Rising
Honey from a Lion
The Winter is Past

Frederick W. Bassett

A Time to Love Anew: The William Barsh Roberts Trilogy

ISBN 978-0-578-28124-7

Cover art by Denise Smith Waldrep

Cover design by Lori Bassett

Author photo by Bill Lytell, IWL Photography

Published by Blue Haven Books

Printed and distributed by IngramSpark

Dedicated to the Memory
of
My Beloved Wife
Peggy Roberts Bassett
1936 - 2016

Author's Note

The first two novels of this trilogy were previously published by All Things that Matter Press. When I finished a draft of the final novel, the contracts with that press had expired and I did not renew them, having decided that I wanted to publish all three novels under one cover with the title *A Time to Love Anew.*

Contents

South Wind Rising

“Come, O south wind!
Blow upon my garden,
let its fragrance be wafted abroad,
let my beloved come to his garden,
and eat its choice fruits.”
— Song of Solomon 4:16

Chapter One

A boy carries with him, always, the experiences that shatter his innocence and set him on the road to stoical maturity—character tempered by fire and water. It's what some call the coincidence of opposites. Or as others say, no pain, no gain. Sometimes an unsettling event foreshadows those seminal experiences like a dark cloud looming on the horizon. That's just how it happened to William Barsh Roberts on the first Saturday of May, 1949.

Standing in his backyard with the sun well into the western sky, he changed his mind about returning to the swimming hole that he'd discovered that morning at the edge of an old forest. That forest was now calling him into her bosom, and he was eager to respond to that primal call of the wild.

School would soon be out for the summer, and he had been dreaming about a place in the wild where he could camp and learn to live off the land like the old woodsmen. In his mind he could picture the perfect place.

The vision came from his earliest memory of being in the forest with his father. They were beside a broad creek overshadowed by huge trees with the rays of the sun slanting through the lush foliage.

From the creek bank, his father pulled up a plant with a root clutching some dark dangling thing. There was a legend about the plant, but he could not remember the story that his father told him. The vision of the place, however, was fresh in his mind.

Now, he felt lucky to have discovered what he hoped was a deep forest within walking distance. If he could roll time back on its heels, he would start the day anew and spend it exploring those woods. But the day was almost spent, once and forever.

He might as well be wishing that he could be in two places at once, and he knew it. He would have to wait for time to roll him another Saturday, the best day of the week for a schoolboy.

Down the road, Thomas Wade was working in the open-sided, tin-roofed shed that was the center of his family's junk business. Barsh liked to hang out at that workshop. He especially liked to watch them use their acetylene torch. It was magical to watch metal turn red and melt into big drops as the flame ate its way through some piece of junk.

With nothing better to do, he set out for a short visit before supper. Thomas was stripping copper wire from an electrical generator, and Barsh remembered why. Scrap copper brought a better price than scrap iron.

"Hey, Thomas. You're working mighty late."

"Can to can't, as they say. Daddy says I'll make enough money on my first boxcar shipment to pay him back for buying my truck and have some left for myself."

"Where will you ship it?"

"Birmingham, the iron city."

Thomas started talking about the new preacher they had at the Pentecostal Holiness Church. What a God-fearing man he was. How hard he preached against sin and the ways of the world. Barsh picked up a ball-peen hammer and tapped it on the steel anvil just to hear it ring and to show his lack of interest in the Pentecostal Holiness Church.

Becky Wade came bounding across the yard, but the shrill voice of her older sister Ruth called her back. Five minutes later, Becky came running to the workshop.

She was such a pretty girl with dark eyes and long black hair, and Barsh felt a tinge of sorrow that she wasn't allowed to enjoy the things that most girls took for granted. The youngest Wade, she was the only one who had not dropped out of school or bought into the Pentecostal Holiness faith.

Soon after Barsh moved into the neighborhood, she began to look up to him, and he felt close to her, almost as if he were a big brother looking out for a needy sister.

"Hey, Barsh. What exciting things have you been doing?"

"Swimming and diving."

"Where?"

"Turtle Creek beyond the railroad. There's a good swimming hole washed out below the culvert. I just discovered it, this morning, and I've named it Turtle Creek Swimming Hole."

"I wish you would teach me how to swim, there."

"Becky," Thomas broke in, "you know mixed bathing is a sin."

"I don't think it's a sin for girls and boys to swim together. Do you, Barsh?"

"How could swimming together be a sin?"

"It brings out the lust in you, just like dancing," Thomas said.

Barsh watched two boys walking down Britton Road. They turned up the Wades' long driveway.

"Y'all got company coming," he said.

"That tall skinny one was at church last Sunday night," Becky said. "Kept hanging around Ruth, afterwards, trying to get her to talk to him. But she wouldn't have nothing to do with him. He gives me the creeps. There's something about the way he looks at you."

"They call him Root. Root Riddle," Barsh said.

He was a mean fellow from the mill village, a school dropout who was nearly grown, maybe eighteen or nineteen. The other boy was Doug Conyers, one of Barsh's classmates, who lived at the edge of the mill village. He was almost a midget and never talked or had anything to do with the other students. Even at recess, he stayed at his desk and drew cartoons with characters robbing and killing people.

"Is this where Ruth Wade lives?" Root asked.

"Why do you want to know?" Becky snapped back at him.

"Well, Doug and me were over this way, and I thought it would be nice to drop by for a social visit with her. Get to know her better. I do like the way she can play a piano. If you'll let her know I'm here, I just might give you a quarter. See if she'll come out here where we can talk by ourselves. No adults listening."

"Ruth don't want to see you. I can tell you that for a fact, so why don't you go on back where you came from. You're not wanted here."

"Oh, we got a little smart mouth, don't we? What's your name?"

"I don't have a name when it comes to you."

"Is that a fact? Well, I'll tell you what. Let's me and you take a little walk into the feed room of that barn and I'll give you a name you won't never forget."

Barsh picked up a large ball-peen hammer and started ringing the anvil with measured blows. The sharp sound of steel against steel shut Root's mouth for the moment.

Becky drifted over next to Barsh as his eyes searched for something to hammer with furious blows. He found an iron rod and began to pound it with all his might—sparks flying from each hard blow of the hammer.

"Who's the blacksmith we got there?" Root asked.

"I'm Barsh Roberts."

"Yeah, I've seen you before in town. What you doing here?"

"These are my friends."

"Then maybe you ought to go tell Ruth I want to see her. Or am I gonna have to teach you a lesson the next time I catch you on a side street somewhere?"

"You heard Becky. Ruth doesn't want to see you. You better leave before Mr. Wade sends you packing."

"Well, Becky, you do have a name. And I won't be forgetting it, neither."

"What does that mean?" Becky asked.

"That's for me to know and you to find out."

"You were told to leave, and that's what you better do," Barsh said.

"Boy, you better watch your manners. The next time I run up on you, I may just cut your little dick clean off and feed it to my dog."

"If you ever cut me, it'll be the last time you use a knife."

"And how's that, you little piece of shit. What do you think you could do about it?"

"Do you know what a twelve-gauge shotgun can do to you?"

"Oh, but you ain't gonna be carrying no shotgun when I get my hands on you."

"I'm talking about payback. You know what the word *ambush* means, don't you? It's what Indians used to do to people they didn't want around. You'll be walking down some street not expecting a thing to happen, and I'll step out of the bushes and blow your guts out with Dad's shotgun.

"You know that old saying, if you take one of my eyes, I'm going to take both of yours. Double payback. That's the only answer for people like you."

"And what's the answer for a woman like my mama?" Doug Conyers asked.

That was like a bolt out of the blue. The boy hadn't said a word since they walked into the yard. Not even a "Hello" to Barsh, his classmate.

"I don't know your mother, Doug. What do you mean?"

"She's the sorriest woman who ever lived. My daddy went off to fight the Japs and left Mama to run his store while he was gone. We live upstairs, and there was hardly a night that she didn't have some man sleeping with her. I wanted to take a butcher knife and cut her throat.

"Then Daddy came home paralyzed from the waist down. He runs the store in a wheelchair and sleeps in a little room he had built on the side. Mama's gone nearly every night.

"I told Daddy he ought to kill her, but he said he'd done enough killing for one lifetime. Now, since you think you're so smart, what's the answer for my sorry mama?"

"I don't have an answer, Doug."

"Jesus Christ is the only answer for her," Thomas said.

"She scoffs at that name," Doug said. "Her preacher raped her when she was twelve years old."

"I do know the answer for her preacher," Barsh said, recalling a story he had overheard at Clark's Store before they moved to town. "Her daddy should have castrated him and left the bloody evidence on the altar of his church. But I don't know what you do with a sorry mother. She's still the one who brought you into this world."

"Jesus is the only answer," Thomas said. "Don't y'all believe the Bible is the Word of God?"

"You're a fool," Root said. "I believe every word in the Bible, and that ain't changed me one bit. I've got a front-row seat reserved in Hell. Some people are just naturally bound for Hell. I'm one and Doug's mama is another."

"Sometime I wish I'd never been born," Doug said. "Come on, Root. We need to get going."

"Hell, you're right, my little cunning fox. We might as well make us a social call on Joe Crawford. He's always open for business. But I'll tell you this, Becky Wade, I've got something special in mind for you that'll cure your sassy mouth. But then you won't be telling nobody about it, when I'm done with you."

Without another word, they turned their backs and left. Doug stopped after a few steps and took a backward look at Barsh. At that moment, Doug looked more like a whipped dog than a cunning fox.

Barsh didn't know what to make of his lingering look. Nor did he know what to make of Root's remark about Joe Crawford. As far as he knew, Joe Crawford didn't have a business. He was a grown man who lived with his old parents in their big house on Crawford Street.

The three of them watched in silence until Root and Doug turned up Britton Road. Thomas resumed his work of stripping copper wire from the generator. Barsh tossed the ball-peen hammer on the table beside the anvil and walked away from the workshop with Becky following him.

"What do you suppose Root meant, when he said that to me?"

"Maybe he was just trying to scare you. He's threatened me before. Anyway, be on the lookout for him and don't let him get close to you."

"How did he threaten you?"

"If he was standing on the sidewalk in front of the pool hall, downtown, when I passed by, he'd call me bad names. Then he'd say if he ever caught me alone somewhere, he'd beat my head to a bloody pulp with his lead knuckles or he'd cut me good with his hawksbill knife.

"He has a bad reputation, so I took him seriously. That's one of the reasons I run up and down the road from the house to Britton's Dairy. My feet are my best defense until I get big enough to take care of myself, one on one with the likes of Root Riddle. If he can't catch me, he can't hurt me."

"But I can't run like you."

"You should tell Ruth that he was here asking about her. If she keeps giving him the cold shoulder, maybe he won't come back. And you never go downtown by yourself, do you?"

"No, Ruth won't let me. Barsh, please be careful with the likes of him in town. What would I do if something happened to you?"

"Don't you worry about me. See you later. I've got to go."

Walking home, he couldn't get Root's leering face out of his mind. The way he had looked at Becky. He knew, even if she didn't, what Root was thinking when he said he had something special in mind for her. And he would do it if he got a chance. But would he kill her afterwards? That's certainly what he wanted her to think.

Chapter Two

Barsh hurried from the side door of the schoolhouse, empty-handed and ahead of the pack. No homework for him. It was Friday, and he had two days of freedom from school, freedom to explore a forest that was calling him into her wild bosom.

As always, he stopped at the sidewalk to wait for Amy Burdette. His eighth-grade classmates trickled out of the redbrick building, but Amy was not among them. She was lagging again. What had gotten into her of late?

Dark clouds were drifting in from the west. A restless energy pulsed through him. He could hardly stand still as he waited for her. For the first time, he thought about striking out for home, alone.

Rayford McKay, a neighborhood boy but not a friend, exited the building. Typically, he would angle across the yard and head downtown, but he kept to the walkway, striding straight toward Barsh. Then he stopped not ten feet away.

His face was softer than usual. His lips parted as if he were going to say something, but he swallowed the notion, whatever it was, with a slight shrug of his shoulders.

Their eyes were steady, warm, but neither boy would speak. Barsh raised an open hand, the safest gesture he could offer. Rayford lifted his hand and smiled at him for the first time. Still neither spoke. Then Rayford turned and walked away, toward town.

Barsh knew he was likely headed for work at Colonial Food, where his older brother managed the meat department. The last time his mother sent him to that store, Rayford was wrapping fatback in cellophane and sealing it with a hot iron.

Now pacing on the sidewalk, he was thinking that maybe he and Rayford could become friends. They had gotten off to a bad start, a hard fistfight, when Barsh moved into the neighborhood.

School would soon be out for the summer, and he wanted to camp in the wild for days at a time. He could do it alone, but it would be good to have a friend to share in such adventures.

Amy Burdette ambled up with an armload of books. A sullen

mood enveloped her, dampening his desire to tell her about Rayford's apparent gesture of friendship.

"No school for two whole days," he said instead.

"Yeah."

"We better hurry. It's going to rain any minute."

They walked in silence on a course that they had followed since fourth grade. On Crawford Street, his eyes followed a green Buick. It turned into the Crawford estate, which took up one side of the whole block.

He had seen the Crawfords creeping in and out of the driveway in their black Hudson but knew little about them, except that they were ancient and that strange people visited them and their bachelor son from time to time. It was no surprise that he did not know the middle-aged man driving the Buick.

As he watched it ease up the driveway to the Greek revival mansion, he thought about what Root Riddle had said last Saturday: We might as well make us a social call on Joe Crawford. He's always open for business. What did he mean? Barsh couldn't figure it out.

He looked at Amy, as they walked side by side. So atypically from her old ways, she had not spoken a word since they left school, and they were halfway home. What was going on in her head?

Looking again at the Crawford estate, he remembered how, on several occasions, Amy and he had slithered among those trees and shrubs to marvel at the fading grandeur of the old mansion and to steal a few apples.

Once they were startled and ran away, when Joe Crawford came out of the carriage house and invited them to visit awhile with him. But as they walked by that Friday, Amy didn't even glance at the place.

They had been best friends since the day he moved to town from the country. By the time his dad backed the truck to a good spot to unload their things, Amy wandered over from her yard next door.

She was a spunky, slender girl with beautiful red hair, and for the next four years, she had returned almost daily to play with him. Things had changed, however. Their playdays had ended.

Almost home, they turned onto Barkley Street, where Amy

lived. Shifting the books to the other arm, she stopped on the sidewalk in front of her house and looked deep into his eyes as if she were trying to figure out who he was.

"What are you doing this weekend?" she asked.

"Tomorrow, I'm exploring a forest beyond the railroad. I'm looking for a place to camp that's away from everything except nature."

"What a great idea! I wish I could go with you. You know I would if Mama would let me. But she won't."

"What will you be doing?"

"Reading my latest library book."

She pulled the school books against herself with both arms. His face flushed as he caught himself staring at her breasts, swelling gently above the books.

He glanced quickly into her eyes. Yes, those bright green eyes had noted his gawking at her breast. He turned and looked up at the threatening sky.

As he turned back to Amy, he saw a new look on her sweet smiling face. Her eyes were soft, yielding. There was a stirring within him that took his breath away.

"Barsh, you be sure to think about me, tomorrow. You should know that I'd like to be exploring those woods with you, but the best I can do is start working on my tan. If it's not cloudy, I'll be sunbathing behind the garage, tomorrow afternoon.

"With all the tall hedges, nobody can see me on my quilt, unless you happen to come crawling through our secret passage like you did last summer. Please meet me there tomorrow afternoon if it's not too late, when you return from exploring the forest."

"Oh, I'll make it a point to get back in time to give you a report," he said as big drops of rain began to fall.

"See you then," she said and ran toward the house.

He watched until she entered the house. He had felt the sexual tensions of a growing boy but never before with his friend Amy. He had always thought of her as his best friend. She could have been a boy for all he cared.

In a moment, his world had changed, again. This was definitely a new season of awakening for him—the call of the wild was pulling him into her bosom and now Amy was pulling him into hers.

He was almost home and could beat the downpour if he made

a run for it. But what did he care about rain? He was in love.

At the corner of Amy's yard, he turned down Britton Road, which wasn't a regular town street. It was a dirt road that started at Barkley Street, sloped gently past his house, crossed Turtle Creek, curved up a hill, and descended through the pastures of Britton's Dairy, where it came to a dead end at the railroad.

The pastures of that dairy were the only places in the neighborhood that were specifically off-limits to Barsh. His father had warned him never to cut across any of those pastures, because Mr. Britton had a Jersey bull that could gore him to death.

Seven families lived on Britton Road—four white, three colored. They lived halfway in town and halfway in the country. They had city mail, electricity, and running water, but no telephones or sewer lines. They had septic tanks for their toilets or they had outhouses, and they all owned milk cows.

Barsh lived in the first house on the right. Its two-acre lot included a pasture for their cow and a vegetable garden that his dad tended with a push plow and a hoe. There was also a small barn.

In no hurry to get home that Friday afternoon, he walked with his head down, watching big drops of rain pepper the dusty road. Stopping in the front yard of his house, he looked up at the dark sky. The rain was coming hard. Eyes closed, he let the rain wash over him until he was soaking wet.

In his room with a big window onto the front porch, he changed clothes, knowing exactly what he intended to do that afternoon. He loved books but only read at night or when the weather was too bad to be outside.

He was eager to finish *The Eyes of the Woods* in his favorite reading place, the loft of their small barn. He tucked the book in the waist of his pants and put on his raincoat.

His mother was cooking supper. Smiling, she turned from the stove and asked about his day. As usual, he reported that he'd had a good day. She kept to her business at the stove, knowing by the raincoat that her only living child, who loved the outdoors, would soon be leaving the house.

There was a glass of milk and a peanut butter and jelly sandwich on the kitchen table. He ate the sandwich, drank the milk, and told is Mother that he was going to his treehouse in West Woods, although his final destination was the loft of their barn.

The little barn was set back against a grove of mixed trees that

Amy had named West Woods. It had a large stall on one end and a feed and storage room on the other. Above these, there was a loft that he had taken over for a hideout.

The loft was gabled on the north and south ends. He could see out through a few knotholes, but no one could see him. And he had never shared it with anyone except Amy.

He entered West Woods and walked to his treehouse, the destination that he had told his mother, and then worked his way to the backside of the barn. He believed that action kept him from lying.

There on the back side of the barn, at the north corner, he had created a secret entrance by pulling the nails from three broad boards and hinging them back in place. He always took that entrance to his hideout.

He lifted the hinged boards and crawled through the opening into the stall. From the stall, he entered the feed room on the south end, through a door that was always secured by a chain. The sweet aroma of molasses mixed with crushed corn and hay followed him up the ladder to the loft.

On the north end of the loft, overlooking Amy's backyard, he had spread an old quilt over a bed of oats, a residue of hay from the past. It was a good pallet for reading.

He stretched out on the quilt, waiting for his eyes to adjust to the dim daylight that crept through the cracks. The rain was playing its lonesome music on the tin roof.

His mind took him back to the sidewalk at Amy's house, a space in time he had just left. That moment when he looked into her bright face and saw her dreamy eyes yielding to him was the most wonderful moment of his life. Through the miracle of memory, he lingered with that magical moment.

He got up and looked out the north end of the gabled loft to the spot where Amy did her sunbathing behind their garage, a separate structure that set back from their house. At the back corner of the lot, there was a bit of an opening in the tall hedge row that separated their yards.

On returning from exploring the forest beyond the railroad, Saturday afternoon, he would slip through that space and join Amy sunbathing on her quilt. Never in his life had he felt so invigorated by two such compelling expectations—exploring a new forest and sharing Amy's blanket behind their garage.

Stretched out on his back, he began reading the final section of *The Eyes of the Woods*, one of a series of books by Joseph Altsheler that followed the exploits of five young men who had shunned frontier settlements to roam the vast virgin forests of eighteenth-century North America. Time stood still as the story carried him to the final word.

He closed the book and stared at a nail hole in the tin roof that was shining like a distant star. The rain had stopped and the sun was out, but the magic of the book held him in the barn loft.

He envisioned himself walking beneath giant trees where no white man had ever walked. And like every good woodsman, he carried a trusted rifle in his hand. That time had come and gone, however.

The forest he would be exploring in the morning was not a virgin forest, but he needed a rifle to take with him. His father had a .22 caliber, single-shot, bolt-action Remington and had given Barsh shooting lessons in the backyard on several occasions, always with dire warnings against using the rifle without his supervision.

He had to find a way to talk his father into letting him take the rifle into the forest, all by himself. Too proud to beg, he did not want his first attempt to fail. So, he lay there on the quilt, strategizing about how to approach his father about the rifle.

He had heard his father's truck pull into the driveway. Perhaps, it would be a good time to talk to him about the rifle.

Leaving the loft, he stopped, as always, to fasten the door of the feed room with the chain. He knew his father's warning. If their cow ever got in there, she would overeat, swell up like a blimp, and die. The image of Molly, dead and bloated, caused him to be extra careful about rechaining the door.

His parents had just started eating super, when he got to the kitchen, where they always ate. He exchanged greetings with them, washed his hands in the sink, and took his place at the table.

It was unusual for him to eat supper with his parents, except in the foulest of weather. He was free to go and come in the neighborhood as he chose, and he did.

His mother would fix him a plate before she cleaned up the kitchen, and he would eat whenever he decided to come home. His parents never fussed about his not eating with them.

There was little extended conversation at the table. His parents never engaged in gossip or idle talk in his presence, and they kept their worries to themselves. Still, the three of them were very happy with each other.

"Dad, how old were you when you got your .22 rifle?"

"Fourteen. I remember it well. Took me two years to save up the money. Rode to town with Papa in his Ford T-Model, when I finally had enough. Bought it at McMillan Hardware."

"How much did it cost? I'm saving my money for one."

"It wasn't much, but money was hard to come by back then. Everything costs more now. I don't know what a new one would cost."

"A used one would suit me just fine. I was hoping you would sell me yours. I've saved up thirty-six dollars, and I plan to make more this summer."

"I'd never sell that rifle, but I plan to give it to you when you're older."

"Why can't I have it now? You wanted one when you were twelve, and I'm already fourteen, almost fifteen."

"I know but we lived in the country. It's different living in town. We got too many close neighbors here. There could be a dreadful accident. Maybe next year."

A deep silence settled over the table. His mother, who as usual had deferred to his father's judgment without comment, tried to comfort him with a smile. His father's face was pleasant but unyielding to his slumping despair.

"Barsh!" Thomas Wade yelled from the front porch and began banging on the door.

Joining his neighbor on the porch, he learned that their cow was out, again, and Thomas wanted him to help find her, something he was good at.

"I'm going with Thomas to find their cow," he yelled from the front door.

"Where should we look, first?" Thomas asked.

"Let's try the south side of Turtle Creek toward the railroad."

Barsh took the lead and cut through their small pasture toward Turtle Creek. To cover more ground before dark, he jogged at a steady pace, cutting back and forth in broad sweeps with Thomas huffing and puffing to keep up.

Reaching the railroad without finding the cow, they stood in the middle of the track. Barsh searched both sides of the right of way. No cow.

He surveyed the forest that lay beyond the railroad. He could not tell how deep the forest extended, but he hoped it stretched for miles. In the morning, he would find out.

Taking a different route back, they found the cow eating kudzu that had been planted to stop the erosion of a gully that cut through the red clay. The cow was never a problem to catch once they found her. Thomas tied a short rope to her halter, and they headed for the barn.

As they passed through the yard of Auntie Dee's place, she cracked the door and watched them without speaking. The old colored woman's one room hut, which had been painted a barn red many years ago, now faded, was located in the middle of an old cotton field that had grown up in bushes and small trees.

She rarely left the place, but Barsh would see her, from time to time, working in her garden or boiling things in a big black pot in the yard. On many occasions, his father had sent him to her door with a bag of groceries. Occasionally, she gave him a tea cake that was dark as gingerbread.

What had once been a driveway from Britton Road to her place was now little more than a footpath, that was overshadowed by trees. The two boys took it.

As they passed Sam's hut, built like Aunty Dee's but painted white, the colored man was sitting under a big oak, smoking a pipe. He worked at Britton's Lumber Company and typically rode there and back with Barsh's father who was the foreman.

"Hey, Barsh, you done found that cow, again."

"Yes, sir. She was eating kudzu in that ditch below Auntie Dee's."

"Well, Thomas knows who can find a cow. He's gonna be a junk man like his daddy. I can't imagine what you gonna be when you grows up. But it won't likely be a lumber man like yo' daddy."

They crossed Britton Road and soon had the cow in the barn. Back at the workshop, Thomas resumed his task of bursting car batteries with a sledgehammer to salvage the lead.

Rayford McKay, on his way home, saw them at the workshop, stopped in the road for a moment, and, to Barsh's surprise, turned up the driveway to join them, something he had never done before.

"You been working at Colonial Food?"

"Yeah. What you been doing?"

"Just got back from finding their cow. She was out again. Rayford, you ever been back in those woods across the railroad over yonder?"

"Not yet."

"Me neither, but I'm going in the morning. I'm looking for a campsite, deep in the woods. I'm tired of camping in my tepee. You want to go with me?"

"I've got to work tomorrow. But if you want to go back next Saturday, I'll plan to get off and go with you."

"If you can go next Saturday, I'll wait for you."

"Yeah, I'd like to do that. My brother Joe used to hunt squirrels in those woods before he joined the Navy. Well, I've got to go. See you at school, Monday."

Rayford cut through the pasture, taking the shortcut home. The two boys were a matched pair. Tall for their age, they were lean and tough, not an ounce of fat on them. Barsh's hair was blond, Rayford's a dark brown. Both had crew cuts.

"Thomas, I'll see you later. I've got to go."

"Barsh, you're headed for trouble if you start camping out in the woods."

"How could that be?"

"Can't nothing good come of it. It's just another kind of loafing that's bound to lead to some kind of trouble."

"I don't see it that way. See you later."

He left the workshop and started down the driveway, delighted that Rayford would be exploring the forest with him, Saturday week. He would gladly wait a week to have him along.

"Wait up, Barsh," Becky Wade yelled as she ran from the back porch. "I didn't know you were here. Please don't leave now. I haven't had a chance to talk with you all week."

"I'm sorry, Becky, but I've got to go."

"Can you come back tonight? It's Friday, so we'll be singing those old gospel songs around the piano. I hate it unless you happen to come over."

"I can't tonight, but I will soon."

"Well, bye. I hope *soon* means tomorrow night."

Striding straight and tall, Barsh whispered to himself, "This is my lucky day."

Chapter Three

After spending most of Saturday morning at his newly discovered swimming hole, Barsh ate a late lunch and spent about an hour on the back porch with his parents. Then he left the house, again.

The sky was clear, and the sun was well into its journey westward. It was time to check on Amy. She had said she would be sunbathing behind their garage. But would he find her there? The question trembled through his whole body.

Taking the circuitous route into West Woods and doubling back behind the barn where no one could see him, he squeezed through the tall hedge that separated their lots, and there was Amy stretched out on a quilt. The shoulder straps of her blue swimsuit were under her arms.

They greeted each other, she sat up, and he kneeled on the edge of the quilt. She leaned back, bracing herself with her arms, her legs stretched toward him. She was absolutely gorgeous.

"Been sunbathing long?"

"About thirty minutes. Did you find a good campsite in your exploration of the forest?"

"I decided to wait until next Saturday, so Rayford can go with me."

"When did you two make up?"

"Late yesterday. I was at Mr. Wade's workshop, talking with Thomas, and he came by on his way home from work. I asked him if he would like to go with me. He had to work today, so we're going next Saturday."

"I wish girls could be free like boys. Me and you would ramble for miles until we found a beautiful place deep in a forest beside a big creek. We'd camp out just me and you."

"If wishing could make a difference, I'd place that at the top of my wish list," he said and a silence hovered over them for a moment.

"Amy, I found a good swimming hole last Saturday. It's just beyond the railroad. I was wading down Turtle Creek looking for a turtle. You know how Dad loves turtle soup.

“When I got to the railroad culvert, I decided to keep going. Right under that railroad I went, bent nearly double, and there on the other side was a big swimming hole that had washed out below the spillway.

“I spent most of the morning there, and I’m going back later this afternoon. I’m learning how to dive from the spillway without jarring against the bottom.”

“I'd go with you if I could, but as you know, Mama won't let me. Remember last summer when you went to Panama City Beach with us? That's the only time we ever got to swim together. I can't believe this town doesn't have a public swimming pool.”

“What a trip! I can see the ocean now and all those shore birds.”

“You went crazy over those birds.”

“That's because it was my first time at the beach. I guess y'all will be going back again this summer.”

“Yeah, we take the same vacation every year,’ she said and closed her eyes.”

He watched her chest rise and fall with each sweet breath. Nearby, a mockingbird trilled the glories of spring, but it was only background music for him. She opened her eyes, breaking his spell, and then started rubbing baby oil on her arms and chest.

“Will you do my back?”

He took the oil and watched as she stretched out on her stomach. He had oiled her back last summer, but now she was a woman, opposite flesh. Her skin was soft and sensuous and his heart was pounding. Rubbing ever so gently, he covered her back and shoulders with the oil.

“That felt so good. Now, do the back of my legs.”

They were long and lean. His eyes moved slowly, deliberately over her body, admiring her beauty. His hand seemed to have a mind of its own, rubbing, rubbing. He wondered if she could feel the trembling in his hand, in his whole body.

She raised up on her arms, rolled over, facing him. The swimsuit had slipped lower over her breasts.

“While you're at it, do the front of my legs. Your hand is so soothing.”

She settled back on the quilt, extended her arms above her head, and closed her eyes. Starting at her feet, he inched his oily hand up her legs toward the pronounced crease that split the gentle swell beneath the tight swimsuit.

He had seen the outline of that crack through her panties, many times, as they sat cross-legged on burlap sacks before the tepee that he had built in the meadow near West Woods. In those days, it was just another part of her like the freckles on her face. Now, it held him with a power of its own as he rubbed the oil on her thighs.

"That was so relaxing," she said and sat up. "I wish we were on an island somewhere, just me and you. We'd swim in the surf and lie in the sun."

"Amy! Oh, Amy!" Her mother's voice rang from the back porch.

"What do you want, Mother?"

"I need you in the house."

"All right, I'm coming."

But she wasn't in any hurry. She gazed straight into his eyes, but he broke the contact and looked past the corner of the garage toward the house, fearful that he would see Mrs. Burdette coming around the corner at any moment.

Without stirring, Amy sat there, studying him. The tension was more than he could stand.

"Bye, Amy."

"Have a good swim."

He stood to exit their yard at the corner of the hedge, the one place he could squeeze through.

"Wait," she whispered.

She pulled herself against him and kissed him on the mouth. Then letting him go, she walked slowly toward the house and her mother. He slipped through the hedge into his domain—a boy relishing, for the first time, the ecstasy of a girl's kiss.

Chapter Four

As planned, he got to Mr. Wade's workshop at seven that Saturday morning, but Rayford was nowhere in sight.

Time seemed to drag, and he began to wonder if something had gone wrong. He had waited a whole week for this outing, just so Rayford could go with him. Now, he was ready to go, with or without his new friend. He would give him a little more time, but only a little.

The air was crisp and the sky was clear. Jittery blue jays squawked in the pecan trees. Three robins hopped about on the lawn, stopping every few feet for that head-cocked search for a worm.

Velma Wade, singing to the Lord in a strong voice, came out the back door of their house with a milk bucket. Seeing Barsh, she veered by the workshop.

"Good morning! You're up mighty early."

"I'm waiting for Rayford. We're going to explore those woods beyond the railroad."

"Well, you'd better watch out for snakes. They're already crawling about. Daddy killed a big rattlesnake over there by the woodpile on Wednesday. If a rattlesnake bites you down in them woods, you might not make it home."

"That's why I've got my hunting knife. I know how to take care of a snake bite."

"Well, you be careful."

He milled around the workshop, worried that Rayford would not show. A flock of crows jarred the sky with loud cawing as they winged hard across the way toward the railroad track.

Footfalls. It was Rayford, running down the hill through the Wades' pasture with a single shot, bolt-action .22 rifle.

"Well, I'm glad you made it. Is that a Remington?"

"Yeah. My brother Joe gave it to me last year when he joined the Navy. It was his squirrel rifle. I target shoot with it behind our house, but Daddy uses it to kill blue jays. He hates blue jays and niggers."

"Dad has a rifle just like yours," Barsh said and suddenly, his mind was racing down a course that surprised him. "Rayford, I'm going back home and get Dad's rifle, but I don't want Mother to know I'm taking it. She'd worry about an accident.

"You go back through the pasture to the top of the hill and cut through the woods to the railroad. I'll meet you there as soon as I can."

He felt lucky that his dad had just left in his Ford pickup not more than ten minutes earlier. His mother was in the kitchen straining the morning's milk into a big jug.

He wasn't worried about sneaking the rifle past her, but he made a ham biscuit to explain his return home. Then he was in and out of his dad's closet without a moment's delay, while his mother was busy in the kitchen. With rifle in hand, he left by the front door, walked down the road past Turtle Creek, and cut through the old field, where Auntie Dee's hut was located.

As he jogged toward the railroad, he counted four shots that cracked the morning air. When he climbed up the railroad bed to the tracks, Rayford was standing on the far side, examining the tin can he had riddle with the four bullets.

"You're a good shot."

"Like I said, I practice a lot behind our house."

Barsh was not so accomplished, having shot his dad's rifle only a few times, but just having it in his hand made him feel six feet tall.

"Rayford, there's a good swimming hole just down the railroad. You want to take a look before we head into the forest?"

"Yeah, I like to swim."

Barsh led the way. A colored boy, about seventeen, was fishing from the opposite bank.

"You catching anything?" Barsh asked.

The boy held up a stringer with three bluegill bream. Rayford stood back without speaking.

They climbed back up to the railroad and walked south several hundred yards. Then they entered the deciduous forest.

Barsh's spirit soared as he walked beneath tall red oaks and old hickory trees. His eyes were everywhere.

"This is a squirrel's paradise," he said, pointing to chipped shells of hickory nuts scattered among the leaves.

"This must be where my brother Joe used to squirrel hunt."

Deeper in the forest, they came to a trickling branch. Barsh stopped to savor the mingled odors of lush new growth and musty decay. Proceeding westward, they ran into heavy undergrowth that soon opened onto a cluster of shanties.

A colored woman was hanging out clothes in the backyard of one of them. Next door, three colored children were playing under a shade tree.

"Let's go back to that little branch we crossed and turn south," Barsh said. "Maybe the forest runs deeper that way."

"That suits me."

Back at the branch, Barsh led the way south on a course he hoped would be more productive. After a few minutes of steady walking, he stopped to focus his senses on the sights and sounds of the forest. A pileated woodpecker swooped down on long arching waves and attacked a dead tree in a thunderous display of beak-hammering.

He looked back at the trail they'd left in the soft leaves. There were no human tracks ahead of them and that pleased him. This is a good forest, he thought, and set out with great expectation.

They soon came to a barbed-wire fence. Barsh paused a moment, wondering what a fence was doing in the woods. Then he remembered that was the way country people often marked the boundaries of their farms. Without saying anything, he climbed over the fence. Rayford followed.

Before long, they came to a grassy field that sloped down to what appeared to be a creek, shaded by a line of trees and bushes. Barsh could see that the woods started again at the top of the hill beyond the creek, so he led off in that direction.

The creek had cut a broad bed into the soil. The shallow water flowed gently around big rocks, making it easy to cross by jumping from rock to rock.

He climbed up the opposite bank and made his way through some bushes to the edge of a meadow, where he stopped dead in his tracks. Upstream, a herd of Jerseys grazed peacefully on the lush spring grass. He searched for the bull among them.

"Thank God," he said with relief.

"What is it?" Rayford said.

"They're just cows. We're lucky there's no bull with them."

Still frozen, Barsh heard a snorting behind him, upstream. He turned quickly, hoping his mind had played a trick on him.

The Jersey bull was coming up from the creek, maybe thirty yards away. It stopped, lowered its head, and began pawing the ground. Barsh quickly looked for a tree to climb and saw several sweet gums just up the creek.

"Run for those trees," he shouted, and they raced for them with the bull charging after them.

"God, that was close," Rayford said. "Hey, how did you climb that tree with your rifle? I threw mine down."

"I don't know. Thankfully, this tree has lots of big limbs within easy reach."

The bull paced back and forth, snorting and pawing. Then it lowered its head and charged into the tree that Barsh had climbed, striking the trunk with its broad head.

Shock waves shot up the tree and set it swaying. The bull backed up for a second charge, changed its mind, turned toward the smaller tree that held Rayford, and rammed it. Rayford let out a yell from hell.

"Oh, God! He's gonna kill me."

"Just hold on tight. The bull can't topple these trees. It'll give up after a while. Uncle Edward told me this happened to him one time. The bull gave up and left. We got to wait it out."

The bull was soon torn between them and the cows, that were grazing farther and farther away. Finally, it turned and walked up the creek. Then it stopped about twenty yards away for another look at the boys before joining the cows.

"We can go now," Barsh said.

"I don't know. What if the bull sees us and comes charging after us, again?"

"It's not that far back to those woods near the fence we crossed. From where the bull is now, we can outrun it."

They climbed down, crossed the creek, and raced for the fence. There, they stopped to catch their breath.

"You forgot to get your rifle, Rayford,"

"I don't care. I'm ready to go home."

"That's a good rifle. You can't leave it. Come on, let's go get it."

They walked slowly toward the creek, pausing occasionally, half expecting to see the bull come charging through the trees along the creek. They found the rifle and raced away from the place.

Headed for home, they trudged back through the forest in silence. Back at the railroad, Rayford took a shortcut home.

Alone, Barsh walked north on the railroad tracks. The crossties, old and bleached, yielded a faint scent of creosote. He walked with his head down, taking them two at a time.

He soon stopped and looked back down the tracks. His thoughts were alternating between the Jersey bull that he had just escaped and his father whom he would soon face.

The angry bull had turned him back from the journey he'd planned for the day, but he wasn't ready to go home. For the first time, he felt a strange anxiety about facing his own father, since he had deliberately disobeyed him by taking the rifle without his permission.

He felt the weight of the rifle in his right arm. Shifting it to both hands, he turned the rifle before his eyes. Satisfied with its simple elegance, he glanced about until he found a target, a female cardinal perched in a nearby bush.

Easing the rifle to his shoulder, he drew a fine bead on the bird with his father's voice alive in his head: Don't pull the trigger, Son. Squeeze it. Pleased with his steady aim, he lowered the rifle. With it or a similar rifle, he would become a crack shot and a skilled hunter of small game, not a killer of songbirds.

He had already made that mistake with a Daisy air rifle. Playing like a hunter, he had killed a cedar waxwing only to discover that a dead songbird is a worthless thing.

He ejected the .22 long cartridge and set out for home, carrying the rifle across his shoulder, taking the crossties two at a time. At Turtle Creek, he left the railroad and entered West Woods.

In the middle of West Woods, he had built a wooden platform in the branches of a huge water oak. His original plan was to build a treehouse, but the platform with a railing and a tarpaulin for a roof turned out to be all he needed for a place to observe the birds.

He had spent many hours on that platform, alone and with Amy, watching the birds that lived in those woods and those that migrated through them each fall and spring. To help him identify new species, he would typically have Peterson's *Field Guide to the Birds*, one of the gifts his Uncle Edward had given him.

He leaned the rifle against a persimmon tree and climbed the slats that he'd nailed into the trunk of the oak and sat on the platform, his mind active as usual. He had no idea where he could find a piece of wilderness big enough to meet his needs, but he was not going to give up the quest.

Shifting thoughts, he pondered a more immediate problem. How would he get the rifle back in the house without being seen? His father would likely be home, so he decided to leave the rifle in his hideout in the barn loft for the time being.

A small bird with bright yellow feathers fluttered in a hickory tree twenty-feet away. It was a prothonotary warbler, the first of the summer warblers he had spotted that year. He watched it as it quickly foraged the branches of the tree for insects and moved on.

Rested, he left the treehouse to practice his diving skills at Turtle Creek Swimming Hole. The sun was high overhead, when he took his last dive, dressed his naked body, and headed home.

Approaching the back side of the house from West Woods, he looked for his dad's truck. It was parked in the driveway. Now he would have to face his father with a guilty conscience for having disobeyed him.

He had often done things that he knew his father would disapprove, like climbing the tower of the town's water tank. But taking the rifle was different, and he could feel the difference. Taking the secret way into the barn, he stashed the rifle in his hideout and left.

His mother and father, having finished lunch, were still sitting at the kitchen table. A brooding silence seemed to hover over them. Did they already know? His dad broke the silence.

"You look tired, Son. What you been up to?"

"I've been exploring those woods beyond the railroad."

His parents didn't know that he and Rayford had finally become friends, so he let them think he had been by himself.

"That's good," his father said. "You're a lot like me when I was your age."

"Dad, I found a good swimming hole on Turtle Creek just below the railroad."

"Did you take a dip?"

"I did on my way back from exploring the forest."

Country-fried steak, creamed potatoes, and a big pot of English peas were on the counter. Barsh helped his plate and sat down at the table, feeling easier with each passing moment.

"You know to watch out for snakes," his dad said. "Water moccasins like to hang around places like a swimming hole. They're aggressive and very poisonous."

"Yes, sir, I'll be on the lookout for them."

His dad left the table to go work in the garden. His mother sat watching him clean his plate.

"That was good, Mother. I was starved."

"Please be careful at that swimming hole, Barsh."

"You know I will, Mother."

Bash went to his room and stretched out on his bed for a while. Then he left the house and worked his way to the back side of the barn to check on Amy. He had promised her that he would join her behind their garage.

He squeezed though the hedge, but she wasn't there. He entered his hideout by the secret route and stretched out on the quilt.

During the course of an hour, he looked down, several times, through a knothole in the gabled end of the loft to see if Amy was sunbathing. She never showed.

Puzzled and disappointed, he left his hideout and returned to his swimming hole. There he practiced his diving until he was weary. Then he dressed and sat at the top of the spillway until supper time.

His parents had already eaten when he got home. His father was listening to the radio on the screened back porch. His mother was milking.

After eating, he joined his father. The barn door opened, and his mother walked out carrying the evening milk in a shiny bucket.

Remembered the rifle he'd left in the loft of the barn, he looked at his dad and wondered how he would respond if he discovered the rifle was missing.

He didn't believe his father would treat him harshly but he would certainly be disappointed in him—something that he didn't want to happen. Maybe, he could sneak the rifle back in his father's closet after school on Monday before his dad got home from work.

His mother greeted him and eased into the kitchen, where she strained the milk into a big jug and refrigerated it. Then she joined them on the porch.

Restless, Barsh soon excused himself and left by the back porch door for his tepee. Playing Indians with Amy had been their favorite game for a while. Often as the day was dying, they would build a fire in the rock-lined pit beside the tepee and sit until nightfall without a worry in their heads.

He had camped there many times by himself. Amy often

wanted to, but her mother never let her.

Of late, he had lost interest in the tepee as a place to camp and used it only as a place to take refuge and think about things, usually at night. He crawled through the tent flap and stretched out on a burlap sack.

Deeply disappointed that Amy had failed to meet him in her sunbathing place behind their garage, he brooded over that. Then his mind shifted to his and Rayford's failed quest that morning. He was far from defeated, however. There was a place somewhere still wild enough for him to live off the land, and he was determined to find it.

Footfalls. Someone was running toward the tepee from the road. He sat up and watched Becky Wade loping toward him in the twilight.

Dark-featured, she was the prettiest of the Wade sisters. Her long black hair was striking. Once, he'd heard her threaten to cut it, just to spite her sister Ruth, who was always telling her what she could and could not do, according to the teachings of the Pentecostal Holiness Church.

"Hey, Barsh," she said as she entered and then sat before him. "I saw you when you came down here. I was looking out the living room window. You don't come here much anymore."

"I've outgrown this place. Sometimes I think it's time to tear down this tepee."

"No, please don't. I love this place. I've started coming down here, whenever I can slip off. I like to sit and think about things. Please promise me you won't tear it down."

"Well, no, I won't. Not as long as you want it to stay up. Besides, I still come here, usually at night, to think about things. Sometimes I build a little fire here in this small firepit."

"Oh, that's what I want to do. Let's come back tonight when everybody goes to bed. You can build a fire, and we'll talk for hours, just the two of us.

"Ruth says it's dangerous for me to come down here, so I've started coming after everyone goes to sleep. Except I had to come just now when I saw you come here. But I can't stay long."

"What does Ruth think is dangerous about this place?"

"I don't know. She's always saying that somebody's gonna get me if I'm not careful. Ruth's scared of her own shadow. She tries to boss me around like she was my mother. But she ain't. Velma's the closet thing I've got to a mother. Anyway, I ain't afraid to be here by myself."

Barsh was suddenly jolted by the image of Root Riddle. It was indeed dangerous for her to be there by herself with the likes of him coming into the neighborhood.

"Becky, Ruth is right. Remember Root Riddle's threat. If he saw you coming down here, he would hurt you for sure. I beg you, stop coming here."

"But I'll be safe tonight if you're here."

"I'm not coming back tonight. I've had a tiring day and need to go to bed early. We're leaving at daybreak to visit Granny Roberts in the country."

"Well, I'm coming, anyway."

"Please listen to me. You must never come here again by yourself. It's just too dangerous."

"I can't stop myself, and I'm not afraid of that creepy Root Riddle. Bye now. I've got to go before Ruth misses me."

Alone once more, he was overcome with a sense of dread. He should do something. But what? Tell her father? No, he couldn't do that. Maybe, he should come back, as she had begged him to do, so she wouldn't be there alone. No, that would only encourage her. Perhaps, he should break his promise and tear the thing down. No, he couldn't do that.

A whippoorwill was calling to its mate. His thoughts turned to Amy. How he longed to see her, to feel her warm embrace. But he could not sustain his longing.

Root's leering face was soon back in his troubled mind and he found himself wondering why some people were so evil. Girls should not have to worry about the likes of Root Riddle.

As twilight had faded to darkness, Barsh remembered the new library book he had checked out on Thursday. Maybe he could read his troubles away in his bedroom.

Chapter Five

When Barsh opened the front door on his way to school, Monday morning, Rayford was waiting for him at the edge of the yard, something he had never done before.

"I came by twice yesterday but no one was home."

"We left early to visit Granny Roberts out in the country and didn't get back until late. It was her birthday."

As usual, Amy was waiting on their front porch. She was wearing an off-white dress with little blue and pink flowers. He didn't know if the dress was new or if he simply hadn't noticed it before. They exchanged greetings and were on their way to school.

"Did y'all find a good place to camp, Saturday?"

"No, that forest is too small. So, we cut through a pasture to explore another forest, but a bull chased us up two sweetgum trees."

"How did you get out of the mess?"

"The cows moved on down the pasture and the bull eventually followed them. Feeling safe, we climbed down and ran for the fence as fast as we could."

"Barsh, after I got home, I thought of the perfect place for us to camp."

"Where?"

"Not too far from where my cousin Wesley Workman lives. Last summer he took me fishing at an old campsite on this big creek way back in the woods beyond their pasture. The trees were huge and the creek was full of fish.

"We caught a mess of red-eyed bass. Man, that was fun. Then Wesley cooked them for our supper that night."

"Sounds perfect. Can we hike there?"

"It's about four miles to Wesley's house and about four more through the woods to the campsite."

"Good, we can hike that far. When can we go?"

"If I work after school every day, I can get off Saturday. We could leave early Saturday morning and come back late Sunday."

“Then let’s do it. Do you know the way?”

“Yeah, Wesley lives on the Lafayette Highway. We can't miss it. All we got to do is look for Workman’s Garage. Uncle Horace built his own garage next door to their house.”

“Do you think Wesley will go with us?”

“I don’t know. He’s changed a lot. He dropped out of school to work full-time at his daddy’s garage, and now he’s got a new Harley-Davidson. Came by to see me on it about a week ago. You should have seen him when he left. Man, he roared off on that motorcycle like a speed-demon.”

“I did see him. Saw him coming and going.”

They all turned inward as they neared the school. Barsh was thinking about Wesley.

He had never seen anyone quite like him. His black hair was flying in the wind, and he was wearing tall black boots. The sleeves of his shirt were cut off at the shoulders, and his arms were rippled with muscles.

Just before they got to school, Barsh noticed that he and Rayford were walking side by side. Amy was trailing behind them. He stopped for her to catch up.

“I’ll wait for you after school.”

“Well, it would be the first time if you didn’t.”

***

The day wore on, class after class, but Barsh could not concentrate on a single lesson, which was unusual. He was too much of an outdoors boy to be studious, but he was always eager to learn.

He tried to make up for the fact that he rarely studied at home by carefully listening to whatever his teachers had to say. But not that Monday.

The day washed over him like a dense fog as he drifted about on the currents of his own mind, which ebbed and flowed between Amy and the camping trip that he and Rayford were planning for the weekend.

When the final bell rang, he made a quick exit and waited for Amy. Rayford joined him and then Amy joined them. They chatted briefly on the sidewalk. Rayford left for work at Colonial Food. Barsh and Amy took their usual route home.

“How was your day, Amy?”

“Same old stuff,” she answered.

“It was a total waste of time for me. I spent most of the day thinking about the camping trip this weekend.”

She didn't respond. He dropped back into silence and replayed once again the scene with her sunbathing on the quilt. How he oiled her back and legs. How boldly she had kissed him. Did that kiss mean the same to her as it did to him?

The sun was too far in the western sky for her to start sunbathing after school, but it wouldn’t be long until that would happen. He could hardly wait. He longed to be alone with her again.

“I like your dress.”

“Thanks. It's new. Mother took me shopping in Auburn, Saturday afternoon. Sorry I wasn’t able to meet you behind the garage.”

“I understand. I’ve been thinking about how we used to go to the picture show almost every Saturday morning. Do you think we’ll ever be able to do that again?

“Maybe we could go a week from Saturday if you're not camping again with Rayford.”

“No, I won’t be, not if we're going to the picture show.”

“I’ll have to meet you there. I’ll tell Mother I’m going with Laura Underwood. She’s not my friend, but lately, she’s been trying to be. Mother knows they live just down the street. Hopefully, she’ll think that it’s safe enough for me to walk by myself to her house.”

“I certainly hope so,” he said as they turned onto Barkley Street and paused in front of their house.

“I best get inside or Mother will want to know what we were talking about. Bye, now.”

“See you in the morning,” he said and headed home.

His mother was in the kitchen, cooking supper. There was a platter of freshly baked tea cakes on the table. He sat down and began eating them. She poured him a glass of milk.

“I got a letter from my sister Catherine this morning. She's looking forward to your visit this summer. You can come anytime and stay as long as you want.”

“Rayford and I are now friends, and we’re planning to do a lot of camping this summer. But I do want to visit Aunt Catherine before school starts back.”

“Well, I'm sure she’ll understand. She's expecting her own

child now."

"That's good news."

Finished with his snack, he left the house for his hideout in the barn, eager to make a list of things he would take on his camping trip that weekend. He entered the barn through his secret entrance and made his way to the loft.

His Dad's rifle was propped against the southwest corner where he'd left it. He picked it up, drew a bead on a knothole at the far end of the loft, and leaned it back in the corner.

The rifle was at the top of his list of things he wanted to take, so he decided not to sneak it back into his father's closet. If his dad discovered it was missing, he'd have to tell him the truth and face the consequences.

He sat down on his old quilt and began making a list of things to take. It was four miles to Wesley's place and another four to the campsite, and he and Rayford would be hiking. What would he need? What could he carry?

The list began to grow—rifle, sleeping bag, his sheathed knife, fishing line, fishhooks, sinkers, matches, skillet, mess kit, and canteen. As he thought about food, he decided to take only a can of sardines and a few crackers for Saturday lunch, assuming that he and Rayford could catch enough fish to cook for their other meals.

Having completed the list of the things, he looked thought a knothole in the gabled end of the loft into Amy's backyard to see if perchance she was sunbathing behind their garage. She wasn't. The afternoon was slipping away, but there was time for a quick swim in Turtle Creek Swimming Hole.

Chapter Six

Barsh woke to the aroma of fried bacon, ten minutes ahead of the alarm clock he had set. His stuffed backpack and sleeping bag humped in the chair beside the door. He dressed quickly and eased into the kitchen, where his mother stood before the stove.

"Good morning," she said. "Fix your plate. The biscuits are almost done."

"Thanks for cooking breakfast for me, but I wish you would have let me fix cereal for myself."

"I can't protect you while you're camping, but I can send you off with a good breakfast," she said and poured him a glass of milk.

"Don't worry about me, Mother. I'll be extra careful."

With a helping of scrambled eggs and bacon, he took his place at the table and studied his mother. She was a petite woman with a smooth, creamy face and dark eyes. Her silky black hair draped down her back to her waist. She would put it up in a bun before she milked their cow.

She set the platter of steaming biscuits on the table and sat down across from him. She would eat later with his dad.

"Do you know how excited I am about this trip?"

"It would be hard to miss it."

"I hope it doesn't rain."

"Your father says it will be fair."

"I wish I could read the signs like Dad. How did he learn about so many things?"

"Your father is a smart man. He won the math prize every year in high school. His teachers wanted him to go to college, even helped get him a scholarship to attend Auburn University."

"Why didn't he go?"

"He was planning to go. Then his father broke his leg that summer. After that, he told me he was needed at home to run the farm."

"But Uncle Edward went to college."

"Yes, and your father helped make that possible."

Finished with breakfast, he left the table to get his camping gear. Returning to the kitchen, he noticed a grave concern etched in his mother's face.

"Yes, I'm a bit overloaded, but I'll make it fine. We'll stop and rest from time to time."

"I hope you will and do be careful."

He exited the backdoor, entered West Woods, and walked toward the railroad, until he was sure his mother could no longer see him. Then he set his things on the ground and doubled back to the barn, where he slipped through the secret entrance to get his father's rifle from the loft.

With the rifle in hand, he returned to the camping gear, loaded up again, and walked to the railroad. There, he turned south. His father had told him the best way to hike to Workman's Garage was down the railroad that paralleled the Lafayette highway.

Rayford was to meet him on the railroad behind Britton's Dairy barn at seven, but he wasn't there. Barsh set his things on the side of the track and waited.

A cow lowed behind him, but he couldn't see it for the thick bushes beyond the railroad. He walked down the trail that opened to a clear view of the pasture. The sight stopped him dead in his tracks.

Inside the barbed-wire fence not forty feet away, Britton's Jersey bull loomed over the cows. The very bull that had chased Rayford and him up two trees. The bull had caught wind of him and was looking dead at him.

Just the sight of the bull set off a trembling in his body and got him to thinking. Why would Jersey bulls want to gore people? What made them so different from Jersey cows like their Molly? You could walk right up to a strange Jersey cow, even touch her, and she wouldn't mind at all. So why would the bull want to kill you?

"Barsh," Rayford called from the railroad.

"I'm coming," he answered and rushed up the trail. "Guess what I just saw. The Jersey bull that spoiled our outing last Saturday. It's a good thing those trees were close by or it would have gored us."

"So, we were in Britton's pasture."

"For sure."

"Hey, Barsh. Look at that buzzard. I'm going to kill it if it circles this way."

“Why would you kill a vulture? They're scavengers, you know.”

“Yeah, but I want to kill one, just so I can say I killed a buzzard.”

The vulture drifted out of range, and they headed down the railroad track.

“That was a turkey vulture,” Barsh said.

“I was a buzzard to me.”

“Uncle Edward gave me a book about birds. That’s how I learned there are two kinds of buzzards around here, turkey vultures and black vultures.”

“What’s the difference?”

“They’re both black-feathered, but turkey vultures have red heads. That’s how they got their name. Black vultures have gray heads. The undersides of their wing patterns are also different. A black vulture has some white feathers near the tip of its wings, turkey vultures don’t.”

***

When they entered Workman's Garage, the place appeared to be empty. Then someone let out a string of curses from the back corner. Rayford dumped his gear on the concrete flood and headed toward the curses. Barsh followed him.

“Hey, Wesley,” Rayford called to a pair of legs sticking out from under an old car that was jacked up on one side.

Wesley scooted out on a flat mechanic’s gurney, grinning in a devilish sort of way.

“My god, Rayford. What the hell are you doing down here?”

“Me and Barsh are going camping. Want to go with us?”

“Where you going?”

“That creek where we fished last summer.”

“Yeah, I’ll join y'all late this afternoon. I got to work till noon. Then I got something to take care of, but that won’t take too long. Hell, I need a coke. Looks like y'all could use one, too.”

A large glossy calendar, advertising Genuine Motor Parts, hung on the wall above the cooler. It displayed a beautiful woman with blond hair and a golden tan. She wore wide-legged white shorts, and her breasts rode high in a low-cut halter.

“It’s good to meet you, Barsh. Didn't I see you the other

week?"

"Yeah, I was in the front yard when you came by on your motorcycle."

"God, that's a fine piece of machinery. There's only one thing in the whole world I'd rather ride than my Harley."

"What's that?" Barsh asked, in all innocence, without the slightest notion of what it could be.

"A hot woman who's aching for a hard banging."

Blushing, Barsh walked over for a closer look at the motorcycle, that was parked just inside the big rolled-up door, where they drove the cars in and out of the garage. A breeze whispered in through the door. It felt good against his sweaty body. Wesley and Rayford joined him beside the Harley-Davidson.

"Ever rode a motorcycle, Barsh?"

"No, I've never had a chance."

"Hell, we'll fix that. I'll take you for the ride of your life."

Another Genuine Motor Parts calendar hung over a workbench nearby. Barsh stole a quick glance at the pinup, who was in a side pose with her thumb out like she was hitch-hiking. She had a sassy face and red hair that matched her skintight shorts. The yellow halter was loaded with bulging breasts.

"God, what a woman," Wesley said when he caught him looking at the pinup. "What about it, Barsh? Wouldn't you like to pound her with every inch you got?"

He blushed again but didn't say anything.

"She wouldn't tilt that ass out but one time around me. I'd pop her a hard one, quicker than a bull can jab it in a cow, which you know is damn quick if you've ever seen the action."

"Hell, y'all need another coke," Wesley said noting that their Royal Crown Cola bottles were empty.

They walked back to the cooler. Barsh got a Nehi Orange this time. Rayford took a Nehi Grape. Wesley opened another Coca-Cola and drained it in two long pulls.

"Wesley," Barsh said, "how do we get to the creek where you took Rayford camping?"

"Go down through the pasture behind our barn to that little branch and follow it till you come to the creek. Then go up the creek about a mile. You can't miss it."

"Y'all don't have a bull in that pasture, do you?" Barsh asked.

"No, we don't even own a cow, anymore."

"Wesley, we'll need some worms," Barsh said. Can we dig some down by the barn?"

"Yeah, but I'd wait till I got to the campsite. There's an old hoe hanging from a tree limb right there. Cane poles too, all fixed for set hooks, but you can redo a couple if you want to fish for red-eyed bass. I'll see y'all sometime before dark."

***

They followed the little branch toward a thicket of scrub pines at the edge of the old pasture that briars and bushes were taking over. Deep in their own private worlds, they had said little since leaving the garage.

Barsh was thinking about Wesley, not the red-eyed bass he had hoped to catch before the day ended. His mind was stuck in a groove that kept repeating Wesley's comment about the red-headed pinup woman.

A briar ripped into his arm and broke off. He stopped to pull it out. Watch where you're going, he said to himself and looked up to take his bearing.

High in the lazy sky, a black vulture drifted in a wide circular pattern. Barsh refocused his thoughts on the role of vultures in the scheme of things, relieved to have something other than Wesley comment's stirring around in his head.

"Rayford, how often do you suppose some animal dies around here?"

"Huh?"

"I was just thinking about vultures. Wouldn't you hate to have to wait for something to die before you could eat? You couldn't hunt something down and kill it. All you could do was search and search until you found something that was already dead."

"I've never thought about it. But that is a strange way to have to live."

"There must be days when vultures don't eat at all. You know there are a lot more vultures than dead animals on any given day."

"Yeah, that seems reasonable to me."

At the end of the pasture, they climbed over the barbed-wire fence and continued following the little branch through the pine thicket which soon gave way to a second-growth forest.

Then they entered an old-growth forest of mixed trees. Barsh stopped to survey the trees, that were bigger than any he had ever seen. The air was spiced with mixed odors that rose from the multi-layered carpet of decaying leaves and damp humus.

"I've never seen such a forest," he said. "I've read about virgin forests, but this is my first time to be in one. It's more beautiful than I ever imagined a forest could be."

Spotting an enormous poplar, he walked to it. Even if he and Rayford joined hands, they could not begin to reach around its massive trunk. Dwarfed by the giant, he touched the gnarled bark as if the tree were a sacred monument.

"Rayford, this is, by far, the biggest tree I've ever seen."

"We'll see more just like it before we get to the creek."

Eager to get to the creek and make camp, Barsh pressed on, keeping close to the bank of the little branch they were following. The undergrowth was scant and the walking was easy.

A covey of quail exploded before them and rocked them back on their heels. Rayford threw his rifle to his shoulder and fired into the whirling mass as it veered off to the right.

"Damn, they ought to give you some warning," he said as he reloaded his rifle.

"But they never do," Barsh said and they set out, again, for the creek.

Then they were there, standing on the bank, which rose about five feet above a large pothole of blue water. From where he stood, he could see another pothole created by a shaft of bedrock that crossed the creek like a dam.

"This is just what I've been looking for. What's the name of this creek?"

"I don't remember, but it's some Indian name. What I do know is I'm dying to go for a swim."

"Me too, but let's find the campsite first. Wesley said it wasn't far from here."

"I can't wait. The last one in is a rotten egg."

Butt-naked in a flash, they leaped into the cool water, Rayford a split second ahead of him. They breast stroked around and about. Tiring of that, they took turns leaping from the bank to splash like cannonballs into the water.

***

It was late morning, when they got to the campsite. Barsh stopped beside an old beech tree to survey the place. The rock-lined fire pit was in the center of a small open space, as if the trees had stepped back from each other to create a campsite. A crystal-clear branch trickled into the creek just above the camp.

"Perfect," Barsh said. "This is just perfect. I plan to spend a lot of time here this summer."

"Me too, but right now I'm starving. Let's eat."

Rayford sat on his sleeping bag, eating Vienna sausage and crackers. Barsh settled down beside the fire pit, studying the charred ends of burnt tree limbs. He opened a flat can of sardines that he ate slowly, savoring each one with a saltine cracker.

When he finished, he lay back on the soft leaves, using his sleeping bag for a pillow. Rayford seemed to have drifted off to sleep.

Overhead, soft white clouds sailed high in the sky on a slow breeze out of the south. The trees were stone still, not a leaf stirred. And no bird sang. The forest had taken a quiet nap. Only the creek murmured its endless tale.

The day ticked on, minute by the minute, as Rayford napped and Barsh planned the things he'd like to do before the day ended.

Nearby a Carolina wren belted out one of its sharp refrains. He sat up, his eyes searching for the wren. He couldn't spot the bird in the thick foliage, but he smiled with pleasure at the image that came to his mind. Such a perky little creature with a bold voice.

It was time to wake Rayford and he did. First, they each rigged one of Wesley's set hooks with a longer line. Next, they dug worms, and then set out to catch a mess of red-eyed bass for their supper.

Chapter Seven

Long shadows fell across the camp. Rayford lay on his back, eyes closed. He had not stirred for some time.

Barsh sat on the ground beside the campfire. Smoke curled past his face on the shifting breeze, burning his eyes, stinging his nose.

His mother's cast-iron skillet sat on a flat rock beside the fire. His father would have already cleaned it with sand from the creek, but Bash was so entranced by the events of the day that he could not force himself to move.

Various sensations pulsed through his body. Surreal images drifted in and out of his mind like dreams.

At the sound of rustling leaves, he refocused his attention on the moment. Someone or something was tramping through the woods, toward the camp. A dead limb snapped, sharp and ringing. Rayford sat up.

Wesley Workman huffed through a tangle of bushes with backpack and sleeping bag.

"Damn, it's a long way back in here. What in the hell was I thinking when I told y'all I'd come? It's Saturday night, and they ain't no women in these woods."

He shed his camping gear and sat down.

"You the fire tender?"

"You can call me that. This is a special place, and now that I know the way, I plan to spend a lot of time here when school's out for the summer."

"Well, that won't be long. What grade are y'all in?"

"We're both in the eighth," Rayford said.

"The tenth was as far as I got. God, I'm hungry. Y'all had supper?"

"Yeah, we caught a mess of red-eyed bass and Barsh cooked them."

"I got Vienna sausage, and extra cheese and crackers. Y'all want some?"

"I'll take some cheese and crackers," Rayford said.

"What about you, Barsh?"

"No, thanks."

"How many red eyes did y'all catch?"

"Four," Barsh said. "We could have caught more, but that's all we needed for supper."

"This is the best fishing creek I know of," Wesley said. "It's full of red eyes and yellow catfish. I like to catch the catfish with set hooks. Y'all want to try it tonight?"

"Yeah," both boys answered.

"Damn, I'm tired. I worked my ass off this week. I never seen so many people with broken-down cars. And Daddy telling them all that we'd get to them right away. Shit! A week like this makes me wish I was still in school.

"I don't miss the books or the teachers. But I miss being around a bunch of girls all day. Flirting with them. Undressing them in my mind's eye.

"Yeah, sometimes I miss those old school days. But I'm doing all right. As a matter of fact, I got me a goldmine right now in Lurlene Pullen.

"I can get it any night, except Saturday and Sunday, which is all right with me. Frees me up for something different on the weekend.

"Truman, that's her husband, works the second shift at the cotton mill. That gives me and Lurlene all the time we need. Then I got the weekend to hook up with somebody new."

"You're telling us that you're doing it with a married woman," Rayford said.

"Hell, yes. Married, single, divorced. It don't make no difference with me."

"But what about her husband?" Barsh asked. "Put yourself in his place. How would you feel if you were married and somebody was doing that to your wife?"

"Barsh, you don't know nothing about women. There are only two kinds of women. The same holds for girls. Them that will and them that won't, unless they're married to you.

"I wouldn't marry a girl who'd let me get it before we got married. So, I wouldn't have to worry about my wife. And besides, Truman ain't nothing but a whore-hopper himself. What do I care about him?

"If it wasn't the weekend, I'd take y'all to see Lurlene before you go home. You ain't never seen nothing like this woman. She's got a mouth you won't believe. It's big as a saucer for one thing and dirty talking like you never heard. Yeah, if it wasn't a weekend, I'd show you boys a woman that's got the hots for yours truly.

"Believe me, I'm doing all right these days. But I've always got my eyes open, looking for a new piece. You never know when you're gonna need it. Hell, sometimes it dries up so quick you don't know what happened.

"By the way, y'all getting any? Damn, I've got to piss."

Wesley walked off to the edge of the camp and took a leak. Barsh was dumbfounded that Wesley would ask such a question. No one had ever asked him that before. But Wesley would not be the last to ask him.

Other boys and even grown men would ask him that same question with some frequency as he made his way toward manhood. But he would never ask anyone such a question. Nor would he ever tell anybody if he were having sex with a girl.

Wesley walked back and sat down. Barsh, still sitting by the fire, stretched out on his back as if to disappear from the scene.

"Well, what about it, Barsh? You getting any?"

"No," he said and then added, "not hardly."

He wanted to take back the "not hardly" immediately, but it was too late.

"What do you mean *not hardly*? You got your eyes on some?"

"No. What I meant was I wouldn't even know how to ask a girl."

"Hell, it's not a matter of asking, unless she's a whore. You got to feel your way into it. Once you know how to read girls, you can tell, nine times out of ten, if they will or won't.

"While you're getting to know a girl with just regular talk, you're always sizing her up, looking for little signs—how she's standing or sitting, the way she looks at you. You can't rush it, and you can't hang back either. But you never ask. You just do it, when the time's right, one step at a time.

"What about you, Rayford? I bet you're still looking for your first piece, right?"

"I tried to do it with a girl, once, but she wouldn't let me."

"The best thing for y'all to do is to find yourself an older girl who's already putting out. Sometimes they'll help a young boy out. That's how I got started. I was fourteen that first time. I'd been beating the juice out of Jack for about a year but was still looking for my first piece.

"We'd gone to visit Daddy's brother up at Big Springs. After Sunday dinner, I rambled about the yard and outbuildings till I saw a horse across the way beside a neighbor's barn. I walked over there and tried to pet the horse, but every time I got close, it would trot off out of my reach.

"Christine Brewer was swinging on the porch of their house. We didn't know one another at the time, but she came out to where I was and told me that I could catch the horse with some corn. So, we headed for the barn to get some corn.

"We started talking, just small stuff. By the time we got in the barn, I wasn't interested in the horse anymore.

"What surprised me, she wasn't either. You want to climb up in the hay loft? she asked with a devilish look on her face.

"Up the ladder she went with me staring straight up her dress. As soon as we got up the ladder, she stepped out of the panties and fell back of the hay, her legs spread and her dress pulled up. You want to wrestle? she said.

"There it was staring me in the face. That's when I learned my first lesson about how to get it. If a woman will let you see it, she'll let you have it. Oh, it might be an accident once in a while, but they know what they're doing. If you ever see it, that's because she wants you to see it.

"I jumped on her quick as a chicken on a June bug. In no time flat, I was finished. But she grabbed me and said, Don't quit, Wesley. Back then, I didn't know that girls could ejaculate like boys."

A silence settled over the three of them. Barsh reflected on Wesley comments about girls ejaculating. He had no way of knowing that he had equated orgasm with ejaculation.

Then he reflected on Wesley's discourse on a girl letting you see it. He had never seen the amazing it, but he'd seen the crack of it through Amy's panties when they play as friends as well as more recently through her swimsuit.

He had also touched Karen Phillips's it. For the last two summers, he had spent two weeks, visiting his aunt Catherine and uncle Oliver on their farm in the Woodland community, where Karen had spent both summers with her grandmother who lived on the adjoining farm. Almost daily, Karen came over and spent time with him during his two weeks.

Last summer, Karen's Uncle Jim took them swimming in Bear Creek. It was their last day, together, before his parents came to take him home. Her uncle, who was sitting on a nearby log, had given them five more minutes in the swimming hole.

She wanted to play diving through the others spread legs. Much to his surprise, she squeezed his dick, through his swimming trunks, on her second dive. On his next dive, he returned the favor by touching her though her swimsuit.

Next, she pulled her swimsuit aside and put his hand on it. Then her uncle ordered them out of the swimming hole, and they left.

"We better get moving if we're gonna put out any set hooks," Wesley said.

***

Twilight was fast fading to darkness, when the they got back to camp. Rayford dropped on his sleeping bag with a groan. Wesley moved his sleeping bag closer to the smoldering remains of the campfire and sat down.

"I'll build up the fire," Barsh said.

"Good," Wesley said as he stretched out on the ground with his sleeping bag for a pillow.

Barsh added a few twigs to the coals and fanned them into a blaze. Gradually, he added more wood to the crackling fire. Intent on keeping the fire going till bedtime, he had collected a pile of dead limbs before supper.

As he sat beside the dancing flames that pushed back the darkness from the camp, his thoughts drifted home. His dad was likely sitting on the back porch, listening to the Grand Ole Opry on the radio. His mother was either working in the kitchen or sitting with him.

Next door, the light was likely be on in Amy Burdette's bedroom. He envisioned her lying on the bed in her white shorts, reading a book and pausing occasionally to think about him.

"God, this is a fine night," Wesley said breaking the silence. "I've been wanting to do this all spring, but camping by yourself ain't no fun. I can hunt by myself and I can fish by myself, but it's just too damn lonesome to camp by yourself."

Wesley raised up and looked straight at Barsh.

“So, you like this place.”

“I can't imagine a better place to camp. It’s got this big creek filled with fish. And all these giant trees.”

“I've heard this is one of the last forests around here that was never logged. No telling how old some of these trees are. They’ve got to be hundreds and hundreds of years old.”

“That's what I was thinking,” Barsh said. “My father knows timber. He can walk through a forest and calculate how many board feet of lumber you can saw from the trees.

“I've heard him tell how he watched the last of the old-growth longleaf pines on their place being cut, when he was a boy. I never thought I would see one, but now I have. And these giant hardwoods. It's hard to stay on the ground when you're looking up at such trees.”

“So, you're an old tree climber,” Wesley said.

“Yeah, there's something in my bones that makes me want to climb things. I climbed a water tower once, but that was easy compared to some of the trees I’ve climbed.”

“I used to like to climb trees myself,” Wesley said. “Then my dick started growing and I took a liking to girls. Now, Jack's my pride and joy. Shit, I don't know how big my dick would be if the doctor hadn't cut the end of it off.”

“Why would the doctor do that?” Rayford asked.

“Here’s all that I know. I was pissing in the barn. I had a morning hard on, and I was spraying the wall like Jack was a water hose. I looked up, and there was daddy.

“Hell, Wesley, he said, the doctor did some more job on your dick. You’re lucky he didn’t cut the whole thing off.

“He didn’t say why, and I sure wasn’t gonna ask him. I must have been a baby when it happened, since I don’t remember anything about it. Anyway, me and Jack can get the job done.”

Barsh tried to imagine what Wesley's dick must look like with the end of it cut off. He’d seen his mother cut off links of stuffed sausage. That image came to his mind, a dick as blunt as a sausage link.

“Why do you call your dick Jack?” Rayford asked.

“Because he’s got a mind of his own, although Jack ain’t too smart. I can fool it any time I want to jerk off.”

“What do you mean?”

“Don’t you know? I'll be talking to Jack, in my head, about

some hot woman. Then he'll stand up, raring to go."

Barsh sat there in dead silence, amazed that Wesley would talk about jerking off.

"Listen to that whippoorwill," Wesley said. "When I hear one calling like that, it makes me lonesome for a woman to love. I mean somebody special, a sweetheart you'd want to marry.

"There was a girl like that when I was in the seventh grade. I would have given my life for her. She moved away with her family that summer. Never saw her again. But I still think about her. Someday I'll meet a woman like her and we'll get married."

A hush had settled over the three boys. Wesley unrolled his sleeping bag and stretched out on top of it, staring into the heavens. Perhaps he was still thinking about true love.

Rayford had rolled over on his side facing the fire. Maybe he had a girlfriend and was thinking about her.

Wesley and Rayford soon drifted off to sleep. Barsh poked the fire with a stick, added more wood, and sat watching the dancing flames. Then he began to think about Amy.

***

"Hell," Wesley said sitting up with a start, "I must have dozed off. How long did I sleep, Barsh?"

"Not long. Thirty minutes, maybe."

"Rayford, wake up," Wesley yelled.

"What's wrong?"

"Nothing. It's time to check our set hooks. Y'all get your flashlights and follow me."

"You want my stringer?" Barsh asked.

"You're all right, Barsh. Be prepared. Ain't that the Scout's motto?"

Chapter Eight

Back at the campsite after checking the set hooks, they settled into their places. Rayford and Wesley lay on their sleeping bags. Barsh sat tending the fire.

"Wesley, are we gonna check the set-hooks again tonight?"

"No, we'll check them again in the morning. I about ready to call it a day, but first I got to tell y'all about Lurlene Pullen.

"She lives just down the highway from our place. About a month ago, she walked up to the garage after Truman had left for the cotton mill, something she'd done occasionally to buy a coke.

This time, Daddy had gone to town to get some auto parts. I stopped my job and drank a coke with her.

"Finished with her coke, Lurlene leaned back against the cooler, giving me the once over, and told me she had a motor that needed tuning up. Wanted to know if I'd come by after work and tune it. Wouldn't take but one tool if I knew how to tune it.

"I told her that I had that tool and would be there as soon as I could leave the garage. I could hardly wait till quitting time.

"I cleaned up as quick as I could and raced off on my Harley. Before I could knock, she said, Come on in. That screen door ain't latched.

"She was slouched back on an old couch, fanning herself, and I could tell she was ready for me, but just for the hell of it, I asked her about the motor she wanted me to tune up. It's right here, she said, pulling up her dress and spreading her legs.

"God, there's no way to describe that sight. I'd never seen one that would match it—a red bush all glowing in the light like she'd been using three-in-one oil on it."

Wesley proceeded to give Barsh and Rayford a detailed description of the whole act without the slightest inhibition, as if he were tuning up the engine of a car.

"Are you in love with Lurlene?" Barsh asked.

"Hell, no. Love is kind of like religion to me. The problem I have with both is that neither one understands the way my dick works. A man like me can't be satisfied with just one woman.

You'll know what I'm talking about when you get older. I'll tell you what, boys, I'm ready for the sack. See y'all tomorrow."

"I'm calling it a day, too," Rayford said.

Barsh sat beside the campfire long after his new companions were fast asleep. He couldn't help himself from musing over Wesley's unbridled narrations about his sexual conquests. He had never met anyone like him, didn't even know they existed.

The doing it was one thing. The telling about it was another. Why would he want to spill his guts about Christine Brewer and Lurlene Pullen? How would they feel if they knew he had talked about them that way?

The fire had almost burned itself out. Darkness was creeping back over the camp as the last flames flickered. He was weary but not the least bit sleepy. He slipped off his Keds tennis shoes and crawled into his sleeping bag.

Turning off the world for sleep was usually a simple matter for him. He could jump in bed and be gone in ten minutes. What was wrong? It was not the hard ground under his sleeping bag nor any anxiety about things lurking in the dark woods that kept him awake long after his two new friends had fallen asleep.

He welcomed the rigors of life in the forest and found deep satisfaction in shunning the comforts of home. It was his own unruly mind, that kept thrashing about among the varied experience of the day that deprived him of sleep.

Weary of tossing and turning, he sat up in his sleeping bag. In the faint light that fell from the sky, he could make out two dark mounds where Rayford and Wesley slept, pushing their heavy breath into the night air.

He sat there in the darkness, focusing his senses on the world outside his mind—the now, the present moment. The immediacy of tuning in as many different sounds of the wild as he could stopped his thinking mind for the first time since he crawled into the sleeping bag.

He stretched out, again, in his sleeping bag, pleased that he was camping in the wild, in an incredible old-growth forest. Now that he had found such a special place to camp, he would return often.

As he searched the clear night sky, his emotions of the day began to drift away with the current of the gurgling creek. At last, the awaited sleep seized him, and he went under.

He went down, down into that mysterious void of deepest sleep. There on those currents of nothingness, he drifted as mindless as a water-soaked log.

Before daybreak, a nightmare from his earlier boyhood pulled him up from mindlessness into that nether realm of dark dreams, where he was caught again in a world of horror that was so vividly real that it had become a part of his long-term memory.

Alone, he was walking down a dirt road that snaked through a dense forest. He was a barefooted boy, wearing short pants. The trees rose like walls on both sides of the road. There wasn't a house in sight in either direction. Shadows of the waning day stretched before him, tensing him with their foreboding patterns.

From the woods on his left, the faint rustle of dry leaves seeped into his head. He stopped. Something was afoot in the forest. A squirrel? No, too loud. Maybe a fox or racoon. It was coming toward the road, its feet peppering the leaves in a steady flow. The sound of those pattering feet grew louder as they neared the edge of the forest.

Suddenly, an ominous notion gripped him. Too scared to look back, he listened intently for the faintest sound of paws striking the dusty dirt road. Nothing. He hurried on, his heart pounding in his throat.

A low guttural growl pricked his ears, stopping him dead in his tracks. He leaned forward, head cocked ever so slightly, listening. He could not look back. He could not move forward. He was frozen.

Then louder, unmistakable, the snarling started. He whirled to face the fangs of the slobbering mongrel, bigger than any dog he had ever seen, its brownish fur bristling on its neck, its red eyes glowing like hot coals.

Run! Run! His father's voice rang in his head, but the hypnotic eyes of the rabid dog held him fast. He strained with every ounce of his being trying to run, to flee to the nearest tree, but not a single muscle in his body would respond.

The rabid dog crept toward him, crouching low to the ground, its snarling, upper lip curled above its red gum. Hot-blooded terror surged through him, but it didn't thaw his frozen muscles. Then, as always, he bolted upright from the nightmare.

Disoriented by its intensity, he did not remember where he was for a moment. He searched the camp, bathed now in soft light, and found his bearing. The moon, almost full and glorious, had drifted overhead during his sleep. Rayford and Wesley had not moved as far as he could tell.

Barsh was surprised that the old reoccurring nightmare had returned. He could not remember the last time it had troubled him, nor could he remember the last time he had thought about a rabid dog. Why had the nightmare returned? He couldn't figure that out, but he knew why it started years ago when they lived in the country.

***

A six-year-old boy, Barsh was eating supper with his father and mother when a truck, with its horn blaring, whirled into the yard. His father ran to the door and he followed. It was Jack Anderson, their nearest neighbor.

"Bill," he shouted from the truck, "there's a mad dog in the community . . . came by our place earlier this afternoon . . . killed one of our chickens then headed down the road this way. Get your shotgun. Maybe we can catch up with it before dark."

His dad got his twelve-gauge shotgun, a handful of shells, and headed out the door. He stopped and turned to his wife.

"Elizabeth, y'all stay inside. Don't worry about milking. I'll do it when I get back. That mad dog could be lurking about."

"Can I go with you, Dad?"

"Yeah, come on. Time you learned about mad dogs."

Barsh sat between the two men as they rode down the dirt road.

"What kind of dog was it, Jack?"

"Essie said it was a big cur, with long shaggy hair, a brownish color. She heard the chickens squawking, all stirred up, and went to the door. There it was, chasing a hen. Caught it with her yelling as loud as she could.

She picked up a piece of stove wood and started toward it. Didn't realize it was a mad dog till it lowered its head and started toward her, creeping along in a half crouch, slobbering at the mouth like a calf sucking its mama.

"Essie ran back in the house and shut all the doors. She watched it out the window while it ate part of the chicken. Then it wandered off down the road toward your place."

"What time was that?"

"Essie said it was about four this afternoon."

"Barsh, did you see a dog like that this afternoon?

"No, sir, but I did hear the calf bawling about that time."

"Jack, was Essie sure it was a mad dog?"

"She's dead certain, and she was worried sick cause she couldn't warn Barsh. In her mind, she could see it attacking him, knowing how he liked to play in the yard and up and down the road. She was about crazy when I came in."

"How would you know it was a mad dog, Dad?"

"You can't always tell. Sometimes they foam at the mouth and act crazy. They're just regular dogs until they get infected with a disease that makes them go mad. Rabid, they call it.

They're more dangerous than a rattlesnake. If one bites you, you'll go mad and die unless you take a bunch of shots in time. If you ever see a dog that looks like it's mad, slobbering at the mouth and acting strange, run to the house as fast as you can."

"What if I'm off somewhere?"

"Then climb a tree. Run to the nearest tree and climb up out of its reach."

They never caught up with the mad dog, but his dad did discover a gash on their calf's hind leg, when he went out to milk for his mother that evening. He thought the mad dog might have done it and fastened the calf in the garden, that was fenced with chicken wire. They would wait and see if the calf went mad.

Barsh checked it every day, looking for signs. When it went mad, his dad killed it with his shotgun. He had quit farming a bought a sawmill, so he borrowed a neighbor's mule to drag it off in the woods with a rope, where he buried the calf and the rope.

Several weeks later, Barsh's nightmare about the mad dog began. He soon became a good tree climber, could scoot up a tree, with or without limbs near the ground. But in the recurring nightmare, he was always frozen in his tracks as the mad dog crept toward him.

***

Breaking from his musings about the dream, Barsh sat in his sleeping bag, wondering how long it was until daybreak. A breeze stirred overhead in the trees. There was a damp chill in the night air, and he wanted to build a fire but decided against it.

His thoughts drifted down the creek to the set hooks they were fishing, wondering if they had caught anything else. He could see the one that had hooked the big catfish they planned to eat for breakfast, the bamboo pole dancing up and down, the taut line quivering.

He eased out of the sleeping bag, put on his Keds tennis shoes, and quietly left the camp without waking Rayford or Wesley. He set out to see if there was any action on the set hooks.

He searched the edge of the creek with his flashlight, looking for the fishing poles. The first three stretched lifeless over the creek. The fourth was alive, being tugged about by a fish caught on its hook. He stood watching the action with no intention of landing it.

This would be a good way to feed himself in the wild, he thought. With growing confident that he could live off the land for days in that deep forest, he headed back to camp to await the coming daylight.

It was the first time he had camped with Rayford and Wesley, so the dynamics of the trio was yet to be established, although one thing was clear. Wesley would be the camp narrator.

He didn't know what they had in mind for the morning, but he would not wait for them to take the lead. In his mind, he was ordering the day as he wanted it to go.

After breakfast, he wanted to target practice with his father's rifle. Then he wanted to explore more of the forest along the creek. Upstream or down? Up, he thought. He wanted to see what was upstream first. On some later trip, he would follow the creek's course toward the sea.

Barsh stopped at the edge of the camp and stood there as though he needed to reorient himself to the presence of his new friends. Some un-nameable apprehension swelled in his chest.

He looked again at the dark bundle that enveloped Wesley and recognized the source of his apprehension. There was a different kind of wildness in his new companion, the likes of which he was experiencing for the first time. It was his new discovery about unbridled male sexuality that was as unsettling to him as the truth about mad dogs.

Snuggled deep in his sleeping bag, he began to think about Amy Burdette. How wonderful to be in love. He envisioned his return home, eager to share with her the pristine beauty of the old-growth forest with its wonderful creek.

She would understand what the wild place meant to him. But what would he tell her about Wesley Workman? Nothing.

Did she know there were boys like him, always looking for pretty girls like her to seduce? Probably not. She was so young, so innocent. He could not believe that she realized the dangers she faced as a beautiful girl.

In spite of his unsettled mind, he drifted off to sleep, again.

Chapter Nine

The first light of day was shifting through the tall trees into camp when Barsh woke. Rayford and Wesley were still sleeping.

He checked the sky, which was clear. No need to worry about being driven from the forest by rain.

Early that afternoon, they would break camp and hike home. Until then, he would live the self-sufficient life of a woodsman.

He started the morning fire by lighting a small stick and gradually adding other sticks and dead limbs until the flames leaped higher and higher. He would need a lot of hot coals to cook the big yellow catfish for breakfast, a task he had volunteered to do. The fire crackled and roared as he sat beside it and stared into the flames.

“Hell, Barsh, what you doing up so early?" Wesley said.

“No need to waste time sleeping, not in a place like this. We’ve got to break camp after lunch. Then it's back to school, tomorrow."

"What time is it?" Rayford asked.

"It's time for breakfast. Soon as I get enough good coals to fry the catfish that we caught last night.”

"Wake me up when it’s done.”

"You ever cleaned a catfish?" Wesley asked.

"No, but I've watched Dad. I know which cuts to make before I can pull the skin off."

"You got a sharp knife?"

"Yeah, I keep it razor sharp with Dad’s whetstone."

Barsh cleaned the fish and cooked it to a golden brown in his mother’s cast iron skillet. Then they sat around the dying fire, eating the fish with pleasure.

“That was as good a fish as I ever ate,” Wesley said. “You’re a good camper, Barsh. I could do this again next weekend. What y’all say?”

“I can’t,” Rayford said. “I got to work all day, next Saturday.”

“Soon as school’s out, I want to camp from Monday until Saturday,” Barsh said.

"Then I'll join you that Friday night," Wesley said.

"Let's check the set hooks," Barsh said without telling them he'd already checked them during the night. "Then I want to do some target shooting."

"Sounds good to me," Wesley said.

They caught two more yellow catfish, took out the set hooks, and carried them back to the camp. Wesley had a good plan worked out for catching catfish with set hooks. Use them and leave them at the camp for the next time.

That gave him an idea for the cast iron skillet. He'd hang it up in a tree. That would save him from carrying it back and forth. He'd buy his mother a new one if she needed it.

He got a box of .22 long cartridges from his backpack and picked up his rifle. What could he use for a target? Ah, an empty Vienna sausage can. He picked it up.

"Okay, I'm challenging you both to a shooting contest," Wesley said. "I'll bet you a dollar I'm the best shot, and I haven't practiced since last summer."

"Count me out," Rayford said. "I've seen you shoot."

"I just want to practice," Barsh said. "I'm practically a beginner with a .22 rifle."

"It takes a lot of practice to get good," Wesley said. "Here's my test for a sharpshooter. Take an empty .22 shell, stick it in the bark of a tree, and drive it in with the first shot from ten paces.

That's a perfect shot and hard to make, but I could do it most every time last summer. I'll show you what I mean. First, I'll see if I can still hit a tin can in the air.

Barsh, let me borrow your rifle. Now throw that can, straight up, as high as you can."

He threw the can. At its highest point, Wesley aimed and fired. A direct hit sent the can careening off to the left. Both boys complimented him.

He took the empty shell from his rifle, tapped it into a tree trunk with his pocket knife, and stepped off ten paces. His first shot missed, just below the shell. The second shot drove it into the tree.

Rayford tried the same shot but after several misses he quit. Barsh was contented to riddle a Vienna sausage can, shooting from different distances, while Wesley, grinning like the Rifle King, sat with his back against a tree.

"What y'all want to do now?" Wesley asked.

"I'd like to hike up the creek," Barsh said.

"That's okay with me. There's a waterfall about a mile from here, and just below it, there's a great swimming hole, the best I've found on this creek."

"What's the name of this creek?" Barsh asked.

"Wehadkee. At least that's what Coon Peters told me."

"Coon Peters. Who would name somebody Coon?" Rayford asked.

"If you were coon hunting in the woods as often as he did before he got too old, people would start calling you Coon McKay," Wesley said.

"But I'd never do that."

"Yes, but Coon Peters did. Fished and hunted other game too. This is his old campsite. He's too frail to get back in here now, but he taught me how to fish and hunt. Anyway, if you can believe Coon Peters, this is Wehadkee Creek."

"Then we ought to name this place Camp Wehadkee," Barsh said.

"That suits me," Wesley said and they set out for the waterfall with Barsh taking the lead.

***

"Well, here it is," Barsh said as he stood there absorbing the beauty of the place—the water cascading over a rock formation, the deep blue pool of water below it, giant trees on both banks.

"Anybody ready for a swim?" Rayford said.

"Hell, this water will freeze your balls off," Wesley said. "It's cold, even in the middle of summer."

"It ain't too bad," Rayford said. "We swam in it yesterday. Come on, I double dog dare you."

As they started undressing, Barsh remembered what Wesley had said about the doctor cutting off the end of his dick. In spite of himself, he had wondered several times what it looked like. Time was about to put his imagination to rest. He looked around at Rayford who was already butt naked.

"The last one in is a rotten egg," he said and dashed for the creek, his normal dick dangling from brown pubic hair.

Barsh had stripped naked, but before he jumped for the enticing pool of water, he cut his eyes for the dreaded sight of Wesley's butchered dick. And there it was, dangling from a mass of black pubic hair. To his astonishment, it was just a bigger version of his own dick, except for a decided upward tilt of its head.

All three boys had been circumcised but didn't know it. Barsh was in college, taking a course on the Bible, when he first figured it out. He never knew if Wesley ever realized that he had misunderstood his father's comments about his dick. What he meant was the doctor had done a lousy job circumcising him.

***

It was around two o'clock Sunday afternoon, when the boys walked into the backyard at Wesley's.

"Hell, I got to have a coke," Wesley said, striking a straight line for the garage. "You start drinking cokes and you can't live without them. They do something to your blood."

Wesley turned toward a picnic table beside the garage, where he dumped his camping gear. Barsh and Rayford did likewise.

The big rollup door on the side of the garage was padlocked. Wesley pulled out a ring of keys and opened it. There sat the Harley, facing them, poised for flight. Inside, Wesley took a Coca Cola from the cooler.

"Help yourself." He gestured toward the cooler with his coke, threw his head back, and drained the bottle before taking it down.

Barsh and Rayford helped themselves. Wesley took a second Coca Cola. They walked back to the picnic table, that was shaded by a huge water oak. A deep silence fell over them as they sat around the table, each boy going to some secret place in his head.

"Why don't I take y'all home on my Harley, one at a time?"

"Now you're talking," Rayford said. "I been dreading that hike back."

"You can take Rayford, but I want to walk home. I saw something on the way down that I want to check out."

"And just what would that be?" Wesley asked.

"A lake below the railroad near the fertilizer plant. I want to check it out. That's the only lake I've seen around town. It looked good for swimming."

True, he did see that lake and he did make a mental note to check it out on the way home. But the real reason he decided to walking home was his father. He couldn't come riding home in broad daylight with his dad's rifle for everyone to see. He'd have to slip through West Woods and hide it in the loft of their barn.

"Okay, Barsh, if that's what you want. But I'll tell you what. I promised you a ride on my Harley and I'm a man of my word. I'll take you for a spin down the highway, then I'll take Rayford home. How does that sound?"

"I'd like that."

"Then let us up and be going."

Barsh rose from the picnic table, his heart racing with anticipation, since he had never ridden a motorcycle.

"I might as well change into my riding boots if I'm gonna be sporting you guys around."

The tall back boots transformed Wesley into a young man with a slight swagger. He cranked the Harley, revved the engine a few times, and motioned for Barsh to get on behind him.

"Just lean with me. I don't want to lose you."

Wesley eased the Harley out of the garage and down the driveway. A lumber truck was barreling down the highway, headed south toward Lafayette. The Harley roared after it with Wesley shifting gears with the fluid ease of a man pumping a hydraulic jack.

At full throttle, they were closing the distance on the truck. A car was coming toward them, filling the other lane. Barsh's silent mind was begging Wesley to slow down, but he kept gunning it.

They shot around the truck just in time to avoid a collision—the driver of the oncoming car blaring his horn. Wesley raised his fist, pumped it twice, and then they were alone, leaning left, leaning right as they took the curves of the winding highway.

Slowing for the railroad crossing at Stroud, Wesley said, "I hit this rough crossing going way too fast, once. Almost crashed. Now I know to slow down for railroad crossings.

"A dog, however, can wreck you quicker than anything. It's not like hitting one with a car. Then there's a dead dog. But you hit a dog, going flat out on a motorcycle, it's you and the dog. Dead! Dead!

"A damn dog came within inches of wrecking me right after I got this Harley. Best to slow down if you see a dog on the side of the road. They don't have sense enough to know when not to cross a highway."

After crossing the railroad track, Wesley shifted down two

gears, and off they roared again.

At Five Points, Wesley stopped at the country store with a single gas pump.

"I'm out of rubbers. Truman's just got Lurleen pregnant, so I don't need them with her. But I'm counting on needing them tonight.

"Once, I got caught without one, when Jack was ready to go. That's a hell of a place to be, because there's no stopping Jack when that happens. I could have fathered a kid. Fortunately, I didn't. But that ruined my relationship with the girl, and she was mighty damn sexy.

"You got any rubbers?" Wesley asked.

"No."

Barsh stood beside the Harley, as he waited for Wesley. He could hear him bantering with someone in the store. Their voices were loud, jovial, coarse. Then Wesley came striding from the store.

"Here, I bought this three-pack for you. Keep them handy. You never know when you're gonna need your first rubber.

Barsh pocketed the condoms without a response. He'd seen the dispensing machines in gas station restrooms, but he had never bought any. Now he had three in his pocket.

"How old are you, Barsh?"

"Almost fifteen."

"Yeah, it's definitely time. I may have to fix you up."

"Thanks, but I don't need your help."

"That's good. If you learn how to take charge of girls like you've mastered camping, you'll be a hell of a man. Girls will fall at your feet. But I can see that you're a different kind of boy. Maybe one girl is all you'll need.

"Sometimes I wish I was that kind of man. But hell, my blood's already boiling with images of all the hot girls that'll be waiting for me at Panama City Beach this summer.

"I ain't never been yet but it's now on my list. A traveling salesman from Birmingham stopped by the garage last week. He told me Panama City Beach was the place to be in the summer if you wanted to hook up with cock-loving girls. Women, too, he said."

They raced back to Workman's Garage on the Harley. Rayford took his place behind Wesley, and they roared off. Barsh got his camping gear and started the hike home.

Chapter Ten

Barsh trudged down the railroad, too weary to lift his eyes from the crossties except for an occasional check on his whereabouts. At the back of West Woods, he stopped, trying to decide whether to head on home or cool off in Turtle Creek Swimming Hole.

The sun was well into the western sky, and he was eager to get home, but there was no need to alarm his parents with the toll the camping trip had taken on him. He planned to make that journey on a regular basis, once school was out, and he would need their approval. Thus, he decided to cool off and refresh himself in his new swimming hole.

Rested and refreshed by the cool water, he walked through West Woods to the backside of their barn and took the secret passage to the loft, where he left his father's rifle.

Exiting the barn as he had entered it, he approached the house from West Woods. His dad's truck was gone. His mother, who was sitting in her rocker on the back porch, rose to greet him at the screened door.

"Welcome home. It seems like a week since you left."

"It was too short for me. Where's Dad?"

"He left early this morning to appraise a track of timber for Mr. Britton. It's somewhere along the Tallapoosa River above Malone. He said he'd be late getting home."

"I can't wait until I get old enough to explore that river. I wish Dad would take me camping there this summer. It's been a long time since he last did that."

"Maybe he will but don't worry him about it. Put your camping gear in your closet and then wash your face and hands. I made a banana pudding especially for you."

"Thanks. I love your banana pudding."

When he stashed the camping things in his closet, he noticed his winter jacket hanging on one side and decided to hide the rubbers that Wesley had given him in one of its pocket.

Back at the kitchen table, his mother waiting patiently, until he finished eating the pudding. She was such a sweet, gentle woman.

"Did you have a good time?"

"Yes, ma'am. I found the perfect place to camp. It's deep in an old forest beside a big creek that's filled with fish. I've never seen anything like those giant trees."

"How did you and Rayford get along?"

"We didn't have a bit of trouble. He enjoys camping as much as I do. We caught enough fish for our supper, breakfast, and lunch. I fried them in your big skillet.

"Oh, I left it at the camp, so I wouldn't have to lug it back and forth. I'll buy you a new one if you need it."

"Consider it yours. I don't need it. It's good to hear you had a good time.

"You're a lot like your father when he was a young man. He used to come to see me before we got married, and we'd sit in the front room and talk until bedtime. He would tell me how he liked to camp and fish on the Tallapoosa River."

"Where did you and Dad first meet?"

"Rock Stand School. We were in different grades but you knew everybody there. It was a small country school."

"How old were you when you fell in love with Dad?"

"I was twelve when I started going to school there, and I noticed your father right away. He was different from all the other boys. I guess I was about fourteen when I knew I loved him."

"Was he in love with you?"

"If he was, he didn't tell me."

"Did you tell him you loved him?"

"You know me better than that. I waited for him to show me some attention."

"When did that happen?"

"Oh, it wasn't very long until he started giving me sweet smiles. But that was all for about a year."

"Did you ever have any other boyfriends?"

"Your father is the only man I've ever loved."

"How old were you when you got married?"

"I was nineteen and your father was twenty-two. He asked me if I would marry him, when I was seventeen.

"Those were hard times for everybody. It took him two years to save enough money for us to start out on our own. Why are you asking me so many questions about your father and me? Do you have a sweetheart?"

"I think Becky Wade is in love with me, but I'm not in love with her," he said, avoiding her question.

"Well, while we're talking about such things, there's a story I want you to read. You know how Mrs. Aubrey brings me her magazines after she reads them. There's a story in one of them that you need to read. I'll leave it on your bedside table."

"Okay. I'll read it tonight."

***

When Barsh was in the forest with Rayford and Wesley, there was no sense of Saturday or Sunday, only day or night, and both were good. Standing in his own backyard, he felt the weight of another waning Sunday settling upon him.

The sun was dropping fast. Monday would soon shake him out of bed for another week of school. The thought filled him with an urgency to do something. But what?

He longed to see Amy. He knew it was too late for her to be sunbathing, but he checked anyway. He was right. Amy was not in her backyard.

It struck him that Amy had always been the one who sought him out. Until last year, she had always come to him. She would walk into his house, calling his name, without so much as knocking. Now, he wanted to go knock on her door, but he knew he would not be invited in.

Maybe, it would be a good time to keep his promise to Becky Wade and sit in on their gospel singing. She had begged him several times, lately. He left the backyard and walked down the dirt road toward their house. As he climbed the steps to the front porch, Becky came out to greet him.

"Hey, I was hoping you would come over. I been watching for you out the window. How was your camping trip?"

"It was great. Rayford and I found the perfect place to camp. I plan to spend a lot of time there this summer."

"Why do you like camping so much?"

"I don't know. There's just something about being in the wild that makes me feel good."

"Come on in before Ruth comes looking for me."

Mr. Wade was in his big chair, slowly nodding his head like he was in deep thought. Thomas sat next to his father. Velma, standing beside the piano, greeted him warmly as always.

"Well, look what the cat drug in," Ruth said, twisting around on the piano bench.

He sat down on the empty couch. Becky picked up her songbook by the window and sat beside him.

"Let's do number thirty-four," Ruth said. "I'll get me a drink of water, while y'all find it."

She pranced out of the room in clacking high-heel shoes, swishing her dress, like she was wanting to be noticed. Returning, she sat down on the piano bench, swaybacked, with her butt sticking out over the back of the bench.

He could hear Wesley Workman's response to the vision before him: She wouldn't tilt that ass out but one time around me. I'd pop her a hard one, quicker than a bull can jab it in a cow.

Ruth started playing the lead in to the upbeat song. Velma, keeping time with her right hand, led them into the first verse. Becky was expected to sing along with them, but she sat as silently as he, for the first time.

They finished the song and started another. Barsh began thinking about their religious behavior. Every Sunday, morning and night, the whole family attended the Pentecostal Holiness Church across town near the mill village. With the exception of Becky, they were always talking about religion, praising their beliefs and scoffing at those of others.

The Holy Ghost was one of their favorite subjects. The Holy Ghost could sanctify you. The Holy Ghost would give you the ability to speak in tongues or to interpret them. But woe to you if you ever spoke a single word against the Holy Ghost. That was the unforgivable sin. Not even God the Father could forgive you, and you were damned to Hell for eternity.

Even as a boy, Bash knew the difference between talking about religion and living it. Velma was the only one that he had any confidence in. She talked plain, dressed plain, and looked plain. She lived the holiness faith as far as he could tell.

Ruth was the worst of the lot. She was always boasting about her goodness and condemning others. But she didn't dress or carry herself like a Pentecostal. True, she did not cut her hair and she did not wear makeup, but she wore pretty dresses and flaunted her sexy body like she was some worldly woman.

"That was mighty fine singing," Mr. Wade said. "I thought once or twice the Holy Ghost was gonna give me a tongue. Since it didn't happen, I feel sure it will happen tonight at church. Is it supper time, Velma?"

"Yes, sir. If we don't hurry, we'll be late for church. Barsh, can you stay for supper?"

"No, I've got to go."

Becky followed him onto the front porch. The sun was dropping low over West Woods. He looked toward his house to see if his father's truck was there and it was.

"I wish I didn't have to go to church tonight," Becky said. "I wish we could sit together in your tepee and talk, just me and you, with nobody to bother us."

"Becky! Oh, Becky!" Ruth called as she came breezing down the hall, her high-heel shoes pounding the wooden floor. "We're late, Becky. You're gonna miss supper if you don't get to the table right now."

"I'll be right there," she yelled. "Barsh, can you meet me in your tepee after we get back from church? I'll have to wait till everybody is asleep. Then I'll sneak out of the house."

"I can't, Becky. I'm going to bed early tonight. You can't imagine how tired I am from the long hike home today."

***

After supper, Barsh sat on the back porch, telling his father about his camping trip. How awed he was by the old-growth forest. How they fed themselves with red-eyed bass and yellow catfish that they caught in Wehadkee Creek. He did not tell him about Wesley Workman, however.

He then questioned his father about his experience of appraising the track of timber along the Tallapoosa River. Specifically, he wanted to know if he'd discovered any new fish camps.

"The road leading to the track of timber I appraised ended at a campsite on the riverbank. A beautiful place. Deep, quiet water stretched upriver and downriver from the camp. Nearby, there was also a big creek, flowing into the river."

"Sounds like the campsite at the mouth of Corn House Creek."

"Somewhat. But it's more remote. More difficult to get to."

"Why don't you camp and fish anymore, Dad?"

"That's a good question. My boyhood fishing friends have all moved away, looking for jobs, and you know that Mr. Britton expects me to come to the company office on Saturday morning to go over work orders for the next week. Then I have to check to be sure we have everything we need to get them done.

"Well, I often think about the times you used to take me on camping and fishing trips with your friends. Those were good experiences for me and I miss them."

"Truthfully, I also miss them. Now that you've got me thinking about them, I'll try to work out something with Mr. Britton, so I can take you a few times, this summer."

"I'd like that a lot. Could one of those include a trip to Jay Bird Creek on Lake Martin?"

"Yeah, that would be my first choice if I can work it out."

They soon said their goodnights and retired to their bedrooms. Barsh picked up the magazine his mother had left on his bedside table, and as he'd promised her, he read the story she had marked."

It was about a girl who fell in love with a boy who said he loved her but only wanted to take advantage of her. When he got her pregnant, he would have nothing to do with her. It broke her heart when he said he had never loved her.

Her parents sent her to a special home where she lived until she gave birth to the baby, a beautiful boy. She loved the new baby with all her heart, but she had to let a married couple, who couldn't have children, adopt it. Twice betrayed, he thought as he closed the magazine.

As he turned off the light and settled in his bed, he realized why his mother wanted him to read the story. It wasn't to admonish him to use a rubber if he did it with a girl. Her intended message was simple: Don't have sex until you're married.

She would be horrified if she knew that Wesley Workman had shared graphic details of some of his sexual experiences, that he had given him his first rubbers, that they were stashed in the pocket of his winter coat hanging in his closet. Yes, she would be horrified to know those things. But surely, she knew that, whatever he did, he would take full responsibility for his actions. That was the way she lived, the way his father lived, and that would be the way he lived.

He shifted his thought to Amy. Saturday morning, she was

meeting him at the picture show, and that anticipation was enough to get him through the week with a sense of wellbeing. Moreover, the sun would still be bright enough for her to sunbathe behind their garage after school. What joy that would be for him to meet her there, more often.

Chapter Eleven

Saturday morning, Barsh waited for Amy outside the Martin Theatre. How different it felt from the old days, when they walked there together, almost every Saturday morning.

"You been waiting long?"

"Just a few minutes. I like your green dress."

"Then maybe you'll like my new swimsuit. It's a bright green. Mother took me shopping, last Saturday while you were camping. I bought this dress, two more dresses, and the green swimsuit."

"You should know I'll like the green swimsuit. Can't wait to see you in it."

He bought two tickets, a first for him.

"You want to sit in our old place?" he asked as they entered the lobby.

"Let's sit near the back corner."

"Yes, I'd like that," he said and they did.

People were talking, here and there, with no concern about being overheard. Amy took his hand and didn't let go of it. That had never happened before. When the movie started, she leaned her head against his shoulder, and he put his arm around hers.

***

As always, it took the immediacy of broad daylight to jar Barsh out of the movies setting and back into reality. They turned up the sidewalk, walking side by side, but they were not holding hands.

"I want to walk with you to Barkley Street, then I'll take a different way home."

"If that's what you want."

"You know it is. What are your plans for this afternoon?"

"It's Aunt Mary's birthday, so we're going to Lafayette and won't be back until late afternoon. Tomorrow, I'll go to Sunday school and church as usual. Then I'll work on my tan if it's a clear day. Will you come by to see me?"

"You can count on it."

"Then I'll be waiting for you. Barsh, what do you think about Laura Underwood?"

"I know who she is but that's about all."

"She wants me to spend the night with her as soon as school is out for the summer."

They ambled along in no hurry. Amy started talking about how she hated living in *this* town.

Everyone knew her father, who was a reporter for the local newspaper and had been for years. She had one sibling a brother who was nineteen years older than she. He lived in Huntsville. Some of her teachers had also taught him, and they were always telling her what a wonderful student and model citizen he was as if she weren't.

"I wish I lived somewhere far away from here, somewhere exotic. Don't you?"

"Britton Road is a junky place to live, for sure," he said. "If I didn't live next to you, I'd like to live in the country, where I could have a horse."

"You can't help where you were born. But why would anybody want to stay in a town like this after they grow up? My brother got out as soon as he could. Mother says he was in college at Auburn when I was born. As soon as he got his degree, he was out of this town for good."

The sound of a motorcycle broke his musing on Amy's feelings about getting out of her hometown. It was Wesley Workman. He recognized Barsh and stopped.

"Good to see you, my friend. Who's that pretty girl?"

"Amy Burdette."

"What y'all been doing?"

"Just got out of the picture show."

"Well, I've got a day and a half, all my own, and I'm headed to Panama City Beach. You want to go with me? We'll be back late Sunday night with a smile on our face."

"No, I can't go."

"What about you, Amy? We'll burn the roads up on my trusty Harley. But I promise not to lose you if you hold on tight."

"No, I've got other plans."

"Well, I hope they'll give you as much pleasure as I'll be having. Barsh, when you going camping again?"

"As soon as school is out. Monday week, I'll be headed for Camp Wehadkee with plans to stay until Saturday."

"Okay, I'll join you late that Friday afternoon. Good to see you both."

Wesley roared off. Silently, Barsh and Amy resumed their course. She was staring straight ahead with a frown etched on her face. They stopped at Barkley Street where they would split up.

"Barsh, did Wesley think I might go to Florida with him?"

"No, he was just teasing you, maybe flirting. That's one of his favorite things to do."

"Is he the cousin that Rayford was talking about?"

"Yeah, he camped with us last weekend."

"Well, I hope you'll join me when I'm sunbathing tomorrow afternoon."

"I'll definitely join you. And I hope we can see another movie, soon."

"I'll be counting the days. Bye now."

***

Barsh was walking six-feet tall as he made his way home. Being in love was the most wonderful thing in the world. But why did Wesley have to come by and lay his dirty eyes on Amy?

Now, he'd have to put up with his crude teasing. The next time they camped together, he'd surely ask him if he'd been in her panties, yet. Always a fly in the ointment, as he'd heard people say.

Chapter Twelve

Sunday afternoon finally came. Amy had asked him to join her behind their garage at two o'clock. He squeezed through the tall hedge in the corner of their lot, and there she was in her new green swimsuit, spreading baby oil on her arms and upper chest.

"Hey, just as I knew I would, I love your new swimsuit. I've been eagerly waiting to see you in it."

"And I've been eager for you to see me in it. Pull off your shirt, and I'll oil you. We'll sunbathe together."

He slipped out of his shirt.

"Lie down so I can do you better."

She was generous with the oil, and he loved every stroke of her hand.

"Now, you do my back and shoulders."

She stretched out on her stomach, and he oiled them. How wonderful to touch and be touched by someone you loved.

"That feels so good. Now do my legs."

He oiled them tenderly. Nothing in all the world could compare with the sensual beauty of his dear Amy.

"Thanks. Lie down beside me. Close your eyes and dream your sweetest dream. That's what I do, and the blazing sun makes it even sweeter."

They lay on their backs, side by side. She reached for his hand and held it. What was her sweetest dream? He was too excited to dream, too absorbed in her nearness.

"Amy! Oh Amy! Laura Underwood is here," Mrs. Burdette called from the back porch.

Amy jumped up and rushed past the corner of the garage.

"Hey, Laura. Come join me."

"I thought I'd walk up the street and see what you were doing. Hope you don't mind."

"No, I'm just working on my tan."

Barsh was standing when Amy turned the corner of the garage and gave Laura the shush sign.

“Mother doesn’t know we’re sunbathing together,” she whispered.

“Hey,” Laura whispered. “Amy told me about your camping trip with Rayford. I wish I could get to know him better. Maybe the four of us could go to the picture show sometime.”

Now, there were three on the quilt. Amy and Laura were talking in muted tones. It was obvious that Laura, who was directing most of the conversation, was trying hard to forge a friendship with Amy and seemed to be succeeding.

They could not wait for the school year to end so they could start spending the night with each other. Amy would spend Saturday nights with Laura, and Laura would spend Wednesday nights with her.

“Amy!” Mrs. Burdette called from the back porch. “I’ve made lemonade for you and Laura.”

“We’ll be there in a minute, Mother.”

“I’ll see y’all later,” Barsh said as he stood and put on his shirt.

“No, wait. We’ll be back in a few minutes.”

“I have to take care of something, but I’ll see you in the morning. Our last Monday to walk to school for a while.”

Amy followed him to the hedgerow, where they paused for a moment, each searching the other’s eyes. She stepped against him and kissed him without the slightest concern that Laura was watching. After she pulled back from the kiss, he slipped through the hedge.

***

On returning from Turtle Creek Swimming Hole, Barsh joined his parents on the back porch. They had finished supper and were listening to the radio.

Hank Williams was singing “Move It on Over.” The man came home late and his woman had changed the lock on the door and wouldn’t let him in.

“Mother, would you ever do that to Dad?”

“Do what, Son?”

“Lock Dad out of the house?”

“You know better than to ask me that.”

“You’re right. I was just teasing you.”

"Dad, what kind of music did you play when you were growing up?"

"Old ballads, mostly. Songs Papa taught me. And some I learned from records. We had a windup Victrola player. Papa swapped a man his best fox hound for it."

"How did your banjo get broken?"

"I don't like to tell that story, but I guess you're old enough to hear it. I was playing with a group for a dance one night.

"People used to have dances in their homes. Word would get out and folks would come from all over. They'd move all the furniture out of two rooms, and people would dance late into the night.

"Sometime, boys from another community would come. One night, a boy that I didn't know got out of hand. I told him to calm down before he got himself in a fix. He grabbed my banjo and broke it."

"What did you do?"

"I had to whip him. That was the last dance I ever played."

"Were you there, Mother?"

"No, I've never been to a dance in my life, but your father would occasionally bring his banjo, when he was courting me. He could pick a banjo better than anyone I ever heard. And he could blow a harmonica at the same time.

"Bill, why don't you buy yourself a new banjo? Barsh has never heard you play one, and I'd love to hear you play, again."

"I don't know. But I've still got a harmonica. I'll have to play it sometime."

"I'd like that," Barsh said.

"Aren't you hungry, Son. I fixed your supper."

"Thanks, Mother. I am hungry."

After eating supper, he was too restless to sit on the porch with his parents, so he wandered down to his tepee. Alone, he sat cross-legged on a burlap bag inside the tepee.

The day was yielding to twilight that crept in on noisy feet. A horde of tree frogs in West Woods held center stage, telling their old story. In the distance, a mourning dove sang its sad tale to the dying day.

He stared at the small firepit in the center of the tepee. For him, sitting beside an open fire was almost like being with a companion. The fire seemed to reach out to him like a living thing, giving comfort yet demanding little in return.

Tired, he lay down, and as twilight deepened to darkness, he drifted off to sleep.

He woke to the sound of a truck rattling down Britton Road. A bit disoriented, he followed the sounds of the truck until they faded away.

Joe Tucker, the colored man who ran Britton's Dairy, he thought. Then the only sounds were those of nature—an owl hooting in West Woods, two bullfrogs bellowing on Turtle Creek.

Someone was running toward the tepee.

"Barsh," Becky whispered as she approached the open flap.

"Wait. Let's sit outside in the moonlight beside the old fire pit."

"Thank goodness you're still here. I saw you come down here just before we left for church. I couldn't wait to get back home. I slipped off as soon as everyone went to bed."

"I just woke up from a strange dream."

"Can you tell me?"

"I dreamed a Jersey bull was chasing me through a swamp filled with water moccasins. I've been chased by a bull before, but not in a swamp full of water moccasins. That part of the dream doesn't make sense."

"Guess what I dreamed about the other night."

"You were in church speaking in tongues."

"You know I would never do that."

"True, I was joking. But maybe we dream about the things that worry us."

"You could be right. I've had nightmares about things I'm afraid of. But sometimes, I dream about good things, like the other night. Me and you were all alone here in your tepee. We had built a little fire. We talked about what we wanted to do when we grew up. That was the best dream I've ever had."

"I haven't figured out what I want to do when I'm a man. Do you know what you want to do when you grow up?"

"I'd like to be a schoolteacher."

"Then I hope that happens. You'd be a good one."

"What are your plans for the summer?" she asked.

"The only things I've planned so far is a camping trip. A week from tomorrow, I'm leaving early for Camp Wehadkee and won't come back until Saturday afternoon."

“Is Rayford going with you?”

“He has to work, so I’ll be going by myself.”

“Won’t you be afraid to be way down in the woods all by yourself?”

“Not at all.”

She questioned him about what he would do during the days and nights, and he told her the things that he planned to do. He also noted that the place itself would inspire him to do other things.

“Becky, it late and I have to go. I’ll walk you home. I won’t be able to sleep if I know you’re down here by yourself.”

“Okay, if you’ll walk me home.”

Chapter Thirteen

The last week of school was uneventful. Barsh was consumed with two things—Amy and Camp Wehadkee.

Laura Underwood had latched onto Amy and walked home with them every afternoon. That was somewhat troubling to him, although he couldn't quite figure out why.

Early Saturday morning, Amy left with her parents to visit her brother in Huntsville. She'd promised to meet him behind their garage when they returned Sunday afternoon, and that had animated him with high expectations.

As soon as he finished Sunday dinner, he went to his hideout in the loft of the barn. It was too early for her projected time of return, but he didn't mind the wait. It would be his last chance to see her before he left for Camp Wehadkee, early Monday morning, and he wanted to join her as soon as she left the house with her quilt.

Stretched out on his back on an old quilt, he opened his latest library book, *The Last of the Mohicans*. Miss Pruitt, the venerable librarian, had tried several times to get him interested in James Fenimore Cooper. In her judgment, Cooper was a much better writer than his favorite author, Joseph A. Altsheler.

He had looked forward to reading the book, and the hideout was his favorite place to read, when the weather forced him from the outdoors. But there was no magical rain peppering the tin roof to settle him into the book. It was Amy's magic that held him captive on that bright Sunday afternoon.

He was glad to have a book to read while he waited for her return, but his mind kept grasping at things other than the story of the last Mohicans. He caught himself turning a page without any recollection of what he had just read. He marked his place and laid the book beside him.

He had already packed for Camp Wehadkee and felt good about his preparation. Many times, he had spent the night alone in his tepee, but that was only playing at living in the wild.

He planned to spend five nights in an old-growth forest, miles from home, and he was taking no food, just some shortening to fry the fish he anticipated catching. He was also confident that he could supplement the fish with wild blueberries that he could pick on the forest ridges.

There were different kinds of mushrooms near the campsite. He did not yet know which ones were edible, but finding someone to teach him was on his agenda.

On the way, he would stop at Workman's Garage, since he had promised Wesley that he would. Now he was hoping that Wesley would not join him at the campsite, Friday, as he had promised. If he did, Barsh felt certain that he would be in for crude teasing, now that Wesley had seen Amy and him together.

The very fact that he would have to tolerate such dirty talk about her would be, in itself, a kind of dishonoring her. Again, he concluded that girls like her likely had no idea how boys like Wesley talked about them.

Love, however, was a wonderful thing, even when circumstances frustrated one's deepest desires. He thought about how his father, a grown man, had to wait years before he could afford to marry his mother.

Did his dad feel about her the way he felt about Amy? Longing a dozen times or more every day to be near her.

Barsh was already aching to be a man in charge of his own life. But he had four years of high school and then college. Maybe Amy and he could go to the same college.

A truck rattled down Britton Road and past his house. He went to the south end of the loft to see if he knew who it was. It was Joe Tucker headed back to Britton's Dairy.

The .22 rifle was propped in a corner of the south end of the loft. With the passing of time, he worried less about his father discovering that the rifle was missing. He could not imagine himself setting out for Camp Wehadkee without it.

Two days ago, he made a special trip to McMillan Hardware to buy a box of .22 long cartridges for the trip. Just as casually as if he were a seasoned hunter, he told Mr. McMillan what he wanted.

Back on his quilt, he thought about Rayford's father who used his rifle to kill blue jays. Thomas had said he would occasionally go on a drinking binge and stay drunk for a week in the little shed behind his house.

That made no sense to Barsh. What would make anyone want to get drunk? And why were people so different?

You didn't even have to study people from different countries to see how different human beings were. There were only three white men who lived on Britton Road, and they were as different as possums, racoons, and foxes.

Why was that? He had no idea but thought someone must have figured it out. Why didn't they teach that kind of thing in junior high school? Hopefully, they would in high school.

Of all the men he knew, Barsh judged his father's character to be the very best. He certainly wanted to be like his father, but he didn't want to be a lumber man.

He wanted to go to college like Uncle Edward, but he didn't want to become a high school history teacher. But what? How would he support himself and his family? He couldn't figure that out either.

He opened *The Last of the Mohicans* and started reading, again, better focused now than before. Miss Pruitt was right. Cooper was a better writer than Altsheler, but he liked Altsheler's main characters as well as those of any book he had ever read.

He got up at the sound of a car. He couldn't see the car, but he knew the sound. Mr. Burdette was riding the clutch with the engine racing as it eased along and stopped inside the garage.

He moved to the knothole in the gabled end of the loft for a glimpse of Amy. One door slammed, then a second one. Mr. and Mrs. Burdette crossed the yard and disappeared through the back door.

Where was Amy? Perhaps, she was engrossed in a book in the backseat and wanted to finish the scene before going inside. He waited thirty minutes, but Amy did not emerge from the garage.

He had to conclude that she had not returned with her parents. But where was she? Perhaps, she'd gotten out at Laura Underwood's house. Or maybe, she didn't even go to Huntsville but had spent the night with Laura.

Those were the only conceivable answers that made any sense to him. She had obviously changed her mind about meeting him behind the garage.

Disappointed, he left the hideout and set out to visit Rayford at his house, a first for him. Taking the shortcut through the Wades' backyard, he was stopped by Becky, who ran from the back door to meet him.

"Hey, Barsh. I've been watching for you out the front window. Rayford went looking for you about two o'clock, but you wasn't at home."

"I'm on my way to see him. I'm hoping he'll go swimming with me in Acid Lake."

"Acid Lake?"

"Yeah. It's down the railroad on past Britton's Dairy Farm. The water's so green I named it Acid Lake."

"Won't it be dangerous for y'all to swim in a lake? I heard about a boy getting drowned in a lake. He got the cramps and couldn't make it back to the bank. I'll be worried about you if I know you're swimming in that lake."

"I've never had the cramps, so don't worry about me. Becky, I've got to go before it gets too late. I'll see you later."

"You know we'll be singing before church tonight. Will you come over?"

"I don't know when I'll get back."

"What about after church? Will you meet me at your tepee?"

"No, I plan on getting to bed early. I'm leaving first thing in the morning for Camp Wehadkee and won't be back until Saturday."

"Well, have a good camping trip if I don't see you before you leave."

"I'm sure I will."

"Oh, I forgot to tell you. Root Riddle was back at church this morning. Not to worship. You know that. All he did was stare at Ruth. Whether she was at the piano or in her pew, he stared at her with that sick grin on his face.

After church, he walked by me and said that he hadn't forgotten his plan for me. He's crazy."

"One thing for sure, he's mean as they come. You be on the lookout for him. And stay away from my tepee."

"You know I can't do that. Bye now."

Barsh knocked at the open front door. Mrs. McKay, who was sitting in the front room, came to the door holding a worn Bible that was closed on her finger to hold her place. She seemed hesitant and withdrawn. It was the first time he'd seen her up close. She was older and frailer than he had imagined her.

"I'm Barsh Roberts, Mrs. McKay. Is Rayford home?"

"He's in his room. You want me to call him?"

"Yes, ma'am."

"Rayford, you got company."

He came rushing to the door, and the two boys ambled away from the house.

"I was by your house, earlier this afternoon, but you weren't home. What you want to do?"

"You remember that lake we saw hiking down to Wesley's? I checked it out, when I hiked back. The water is so green I named it Acid Lake. Let's go swimming there."

"Yeah, let's go. You didn't see any posted signs, did you?"

"No, I walked all over the dam. It's not posted."

They set out for Acid Lake and were soon standing in the middle of the dam. They undressed and swam naked to a concrete overflow shaft about thirty feet from the dam.

The open cement shaft was about four-feet square and rose about a foot above the water level. It was a good base to swim and dive from. There would likely be no good outcome, however, if one of them slipped and fell down that shaft.

They swam up the lake and back, twice, then they took turns diving from the shaft. The goal was to swim to the bottom of the lake and come up with a handful of dirt.

Before either reached that goal, a man at the fertilizer plant, that was located at the top of a slopping hill several hundred yards away, spotted them. Shouting and waving them out of the lake, he left the plant, coming toward them.

Heeding his alarm, they swam to the dam, dressed quickly, and disappeared into the woods below the lake. From there, they rambled about until they ended up at Turtle Creek Swimming Hole, where they sat beside the concrete spillway and talked, until the sun dropped low in the western sky.

Chapter Fourteen

His father was sitting in his rocker on the screened back porch, when Barsh got home from his outing with Rayford, that Sunday. He sat down beside him in his rocker.

"Are you all packed for your camping trip, tomorrow?"

"Yes, sir. This will be my longest camping trip ever, and I can't wait to get back in that forest with all those huge poplars and virgin longleaf pines."

"I don't think I've told you about the last of the virgin longleaf pine trees on our farm that were cut and sawed into lumber. They didn't have chainsaws back then, just a long straight saw with a handle on each end, called a crosscut saw.

"Daddy had a man helping him. They'd saw awhile and stop and start a wedge. Saw awhile and drive the wedge some more. Finally, the tree would come crashing down, and they'd cut off all the limbs with axes.

"The logger, who Daddy had hired, had a rig with two big wheels that he'd put astraddle the butt-end of the log and winch that end off the ground. Then he'd hitch his yoke of oxen to the rig and drag it to Grandaddy Brown's sawmill.

"That's a sight to see. Oxen don't get excited about a heavy load like horses, jumping and jerking till they're likely to tear something up. That team of oxen would lean into their yokes and slowly pull those heavy logs to the sawmill, one at a time, the butt-end riding free and the other dragging the ground."

"How far did they have to drag them?"

"You know where Uncle Jim Brown lives. It's that big white house on the left side of the road about a mile before you get to Mama's. That's the Brown home place, first settled by my great-grandfather Samuel Brown. My grandfather, William Brown, got the place when his daddy died."

"That's where Granny Brown Roberts was born, right?"

"The very same house. It's made out of heart pine, just like the one Daddy built for us from the lumber cut from the virgin longleaf pines on our place, when I was just a child.

"That lumber has so much resin in it that it will last for ages unless it catches on fire. If that should happen, you're in big trouble. I know that from experience.

"All the farmers in our community used to have dinner bells like the one Mama has. They'd ring it only two or three times to call people from the fields, when dinner was ready.

"If somebody was in trouble, needed help, they'd ring and ring the dinner bell. Their neighbors would stop what they were doing and go see what the trouble was. Well, John Staples' house caught on fire, when I was about ten, and they started ringing their dinner bell.

"Papa headed for his T-Model to go see what was wrong, and I went with him. When we got there, black smoke was billowing out from under the eaves.

"The fire was in the attic, and they assumed that it started from a bad stove flue.

"They were carrying things from the house, trying to save what they could. Daddy and others joined them, but they were just setting everything about thirty feet from the house.

"Soon, that house was one big ball of fire. It was so hot we had to keep backing away. Then to everyone's surprise, their household things burst into flames. They lost all their household things as well as their house.

"I can't imagine that kind of fire." Barsh said.

"It was awful. John Staples was never the same after that. All he wanted to talk about from then till he died was that fire and Hell.

"Here's his summation: If Hell is seven times hotter than that fire, nobody could burn in such a fire, forever. So, Hell don't make sense to me anymore, and I can't believe in something that didn't make sense.

"The old man never did go to church, much, even before the fire. Afterwards, he never darkened the door of the church, until they carried him there in a pine box."

"Do you think he was right about Hell?"

"In a way, I do. There's a deeper side to spiritual things that the mind can't understand. Things like God and eternity.

"We know that we exist, but we had nothing to do with our coming into existence. And the same holds for our parents, and their parents, and as far back as you can go.

"So, we believe that an immortal creative force, that we call

God, is responsible for everything. Yet, the idea that God or anything, for that matter, has always existed is beyond our understanding.

"I remember the first time it dawned on me that we live in a mystery. It was the summer after I finished high school.

"I was standing in the yard that night, looking up at the stars, and I began to wonder what was beyond the visible stars. More stars without end? If not, there would have to be something enveloping the universe even if it was nothingness. And that nothingness would be something that would have to keep going forever or there would have to be something else beyond it.

"How could that be? How could it not be? Either way you think about it, you come up with a problem that's beyond your understanding. It'll drive you crazy, if you think about it too much."

"I've never thought about things that deep," Barsh said. "But now that you've got me started, I'm afraid I can't quit. I can see it could drive you crazy."

"Son, it's a matter of keeping things in balance. You can't live in your mind all the time. Somebody has to work to put food on the table. If you don't eat, you're not going to live long."

"But, Dad, how do you decide what you want to do to make a living? Uncle Edward is a high school teacher, and you're the foreman of Mr. Britton's lumber company."

"When I was in high school, my math teacher wanted me to go to college and become a math teacher or maybe a civil engineer. I could see myself being a civil engineer, and I wanted to be one.

"Miss Pinckard helped me get a scholarship to go to Auburn, but Daddy broke his leg, and I had to take over his work on the farm. So, when your mother and I got married, I became a farmer like my father."

"But you didn't like farming, did you?"

"Oh, I liked farming, but it didn't like me. It got to where you couldn't make ends meet by farming. The land in this county is better suited for growing timber than farming. I don't know anybody that I grew up with that's still trying to make a living by farming.

"Some moved away to get work. Others started working in the cotton mill in town. I couldn't stand the thought of working in a cotton mill, all shut up in a building with all that lint.

"Before Granddaddy Brown sold his sawmill, he taught me

how to operate it. So, I bought a sawmill and ran it for a few years. Then I sold it to Mr. Britton who hired me to run it and his planner mills on alternating schedules."

The screen door opened, and Barsh's mother step up on the porch, carrying a pail of milk. It was almost dark, well past her usual milking time.

"Have you had your supper, Barsh?"

"No, ma'am."

"Well, it's ready. Can I get you anything, Bill?"

"I'd like a glass of ice tea, please."

Barsh got his plate from the cupboard and sat down at the table. His mother fixed his father's tea and joined him on the porch, where he was searching for the latest news on the radio. Finding no news, he stopped at a station where Bill Monroe was singing a woeful gospel song, "What Would You Give in Exchange for Your Soul."

Finished with supper, he joined his parents on the back porch and watched darkness fall upon the place. Restless, he left the house by the front door.

Standing in the front yard, he looked into the night sky and began thinking about *nothingness* without end. How could it be? How could it not be?

Next, his thoughts shifted to Rayford. What were his habits between supper and bedtime? Did he spend his time inside or outside the house? Did he have a special place for thinking?

He did not want to go back inside the house, or to Rayford's or to his tepee. But where else was there to go? The Wades were at church.

He wandered down to his tepee and lay down on a burlap sack beside the firepit. He closed his eyes and tried to still his mind. But as soon as he got one thing out of his head, something else would creep in.

A car turned onto Britton Road. He sat up and watched it, until it stopped in the Wades' backyard. They scrambled toward the house—Thomas yelling at Becky, Velma scolding Thomas, Ruth singing at the top of her voice, Mr. Wade hobbling along.

The windows of the house began to light up. It would be a while before that bunch settled down for bed. Would Becky slip off, again, and come to the tepee? Surely, she knew it was dangerous. At least he had warned her.

Barsh left the tepee, troubled of soul. His parents had retired to their bedroom. He turned off the light on the back porch and made his way to his room in the dark. Stretched out on his bed, he tried to lift his spirits by thinking about Camp Wehadkee and all the things he would be doing there for five days and five nights.

Soon his thoughts refocused on Amy, arousing the disquietude he'd been experiencing because she did not meet him as promised. What did the future hold for them?

Chapter Fifteen

Alone, Barsh took his time hiking through the old-growth forest, stopping whenever he wanted to admire some giant tree, veering off course whenever he saw something of interest. The natural world was so inviting to him.

Near the bank overlooking Wehadkee Creek, he stopped to admire a patch of violets. He recalled how Amy loved to wear wild daises in her hair, back in the days when they were just playmates.

How he loved her and the forest. It was like he was two different people—a boy happy to be in the forest and a boy eager to be a grown-up man, making his way in the world with Amy beside him.

With a growing eagerness, he set out to make camp and catch a red-eyed bass for lunch. Having packed no food, he would have to catch a lot of fish in order to spend the week there, and he was confident that he could.

Trekking up the creek bank, he began to notice set hooks in the best fishing holes. He checked one for bait. Live nightcrawlers were wiggling on the hook.

Someone was already at the campsite, he thought. As he neared the camp, a dog barked, signaling his approach.

Barsh paused at the edge of the camp. An old man sat beside the fire, cooking something on a skewer. A frisky hound was tethered to a nearby sapling.

"Come on in, boy."

"I didn't think about anybody camping here."

"They's plenty of room for both of us. Come on over and dump all that gear."

Barsh propped the .22 rifle against a tree, picked out a spot for his backpack and sleeping bag, and dropped them.

"Come join me for dinner. This skewer of catfish is about done. I'll give it to you. I done ate my fill. I was cooking this one for Blue but he can wait."

"Are you sure you have enough for me?"

"They's plenty for you and my coon dog."

"I wish I knew how to cook fish this way."

"Somebody left a skillet hanging on that tree, but you don't need no skillet to cook in the woods."

"That's my skillet. I left it so I wouldn't have to lug it back and forth. It's a long hike from town. Maybe you'll teach me how to cook your way."

"You bet I will. First, you got to get a good bed of hot coals. You see how I'm cooking these, a few small pieces at a time, close to the coals but not too close. It don't take long to cook fish this way.

"Here, you take this skewer. Then I'll cook you some more. I caught two big yellow catfish on set hooks last night."

Barsh took the skewer and sat down near the fire, studying the old man. His eyes were dark. His hair thin and grey. His face stubbled with hair. He was wearing rumpled khaki pants and a green shirt. His boots were old and cracked. But there was something appealing and trustworthy about the man.

"This fish is good," Barsh said. "I'll be cooking mine this way from now on."

"Say you camped here before."

"Once, several weeks ago."

"I been camping here for more'n fifty years. What's your name?"

"Barsh Roberts."

"Who's your daddy?"

"Bill Roberts."

"Don't know him. What does he do?"

"He's the foreman at Britton's Lumber—runs the sawmill and the planer mill on alternating schedules."

"Then he works for J. P. Britton. He tried to buy my farm once. I got two-hundred-and-forty acres that's been in the family for generations. Most of it's woodland.

"Old J. P. wants to own all the timber land in the county. He reminds me of a man Paw used to tell me about. Said he didn't want all the land in the world, just all that joined his.

"By the way, I'm Coon Peters. Call me Coon. Everybody else does."

"Wesley talked about you when I was here before."

"I guess he gave me a bad name."

"No, nothing like that. He said you taught him how to hunt

and fish."

"Well, I did that, for sure. I used to wish I had me a boy like Wesley. But that was when he was a young fellow. He's changed now. Got nothing on his mind but sorry women. Who'd you say you were?"

"Barsh."

"That's different. Never heard of nobody named Barsh. A family name?"

"My mother was a Barsh. They named me William Barsh Roberts, but Dad has always called me Barsh. So, I'm Barsh and I like it. I know who's being called when I hear the name."

"You look like a good boy. I always wanted me a boy, but all I got was a houseful of girls. Now they're scattered everywhere. Don't hear much from them, except my last-born girl.

"She's the best one of the lot. Just like in a litter of dogs, they's usually one in a family that turns out real good. That was my baby."

"I didn't know you still camped here, Mr. Peters. Wesley said you couldn't get back in these woods anymore."

"Call me Coon. I'm proud of my name. Took me a long time to earn it. People will tell you that I would rather sleep in the woods with my coon dog than in the bed with my own wife. But that ain't so. A man can love his wife and the woods. Come on, let me hear you call me Coon."

"Coon."

"That's better. You'll get used to it after a while. Wesley was right. I'm all crippled up in my knees, and there's something wrong with my lungs. This is the first time I've been here since my last coon dog died, three years ago.

"A year ago, that youngest daughter sent me a hundred dollars. Said I had to buy me something special. Well, that set me on fire to buy myself a new coon dog. That's him over there. Name's Blue. Raised him up from a puppy.

"I decided to hobble in here, yesterday, and find out what kind of coon hound I got in Blue. As I expected he has a lot to learn about the tricky ways of coons.

"Last night, he sniffed out the trail of a coon and tracked it into the hills beyond the creek and back. Then the coon outsmarted him when it got back to the creek.

"Blue'll get another change, tonight. If he's a good coon

hound, he may even tree one."

The old man threaded several small pieces of catfish on the skewer, roasted them, and gave them to Barsh, He ate them with pleasure and gratitude for the happenstance that brought Coon and him together.

"Coon, this is such an ideal place to camp. How lucky I am to be sitting here with you in the old forest."

"I don't know of another forest like it anywhere. But I guess it's just a matter of time before somebody logs it. Then all the old trees will be gone."

"There should to be a law against cutting these trees," Barsh said. "The first time I saw them, I was thinking that the Indians must have walked beside these same trees."

"You're right about that. When I first stepped on the ground here at this campsite, I thought the Indians must have camped in this same spot. And I know for sure they were here. I once found an arrowhead on a sandbar in that little branch there."

"I'd like to see it. I have a few I found on my uncle's farm near Woodland."

"You stop by the house anytime, and you can see it. I got a syrup bucket half-full of them, turned most of them up, plowing my fields. But the one I found here is different. It looks more like a spear than an arrowhead. Barsh, I got to get me a little drink of corn whisky. You don't mind, do you?"

"No, go right ahead."

The old man hobbled over to his knapsack, unscrewed the lid of a quart Mason jar, and took a drink. The hound began frisking about, again.

"I ain't forgot you, Blue. Hang on a bit, and I'll feed you."

"Why do you have him tied?"

"He'd wonder off and start hunting during the day, otherwise. Probably jump a rabbit and trail it all over the place. Coons don't come out until night. Do you know about coon dogs?"

"No, sir."

"Blue's what they call a bluetick hound. Some coon hunters like redbone hounds and some like black-and-tan hounds. But I always had me a bluetick. Some like to hunt with a whole pack of hounds, but I liked it best with just one good bluetick.

"Barsh, you look mighty tired. Why don't you take yourself a little rest while I roast the rest of this catfish for Blue? He'll need a lot of energy tonight."

Barsh stretched out on his back. White fluffy clouds drifted out of the west in a steady stream. A red-tail hawk sailed out of the north and disappeared. He closed his eyes but wasn't about to take a nap. Feeling refreshed after about thirty minutes, he sat up.

"I don't know anything about hunting racoons," he said. "What's the point of it? You don't eat them, do you?"

"Yeah, I've ate many a coon. And in the olden days, I'd tan their hides and sale them for a few dollars. But that wasn't the main reason I hunted them.

"It was the hunt itself that I enjoyed the most. Who would win the chase, my hound or the coon? As I got older, that was the only reason I hunted them. Haven't killed a coon in years.

"My grandfather Roberts was a fox hunter. There's a picture on Granny's mantle of him with his hunting horn strung around his neck and his hound reared up with its paws on his chest."

"My father was also a fox hunter. Coon hunting is somewhat like fox hunting. At least the way country people, like my father and his friends, used to fox hunt around here.

"Their foxhounds would chase a fox till they'd lose its trail or it would take shelter in its den. Either way, the hunt was over at that point and they'd call their hounds in with hunting horns.

"Like me, they enjoyed the chase. Unlike me, they like to hunt together, a group of men just being in the woods, talking and telling tales, when the dogs weren't trailing a fox.

"Coons are smart creatures, Barsh. They'll swim across a creek, get out on the other bank like they was heading straight away, then double back to the creek, swim up or down it apiece, and head off in a different direction.

"They'll also mark a tree by climbing up it a ways. Then they'll double back on the trail, and head off in a different direction.

"An inexperienced coon dog will chase one to a marked tree and set there, howling like it had treed the coon. The old coon will be off laughing at the hound it had fooled. Even the best hound won't be able to tree one every time."

"How do you know when your dog has treed one? It's barking all the time it's trailing, right?"

"A hound has got a different voice when it's trailing than when it's treed something or thinks it has."

“And you can tell the difference?”

“Oh, yeah. You’ll likely get to hear the difference tonight if you want to stay up with me.”

“Yeah, I’ll stay up with you. I’m always interested in learning something new. But now, I want to catch some red-eyed bass for supper. I’ll use the cane pole I rigged to catch them with when I was here before.”

“Let me tell you what’s the most fun. Get yourself a rod and reel. A short rod is better, so you won’t be hitting no tree limbs, while you’re casting.

“You wade up the creek, casting a Hawaiian wiggler. Red-eyes can’t stand a Hawaiian wiggler. You cast it close to one, and it’s gonna hit it.”

“That does sounds like a fun way to fish. I’ll have to buy me a rod and reel.”

“Look, I’ll never be able to use mine again. I’ll give it to you.”

“That’s a generous offer but I can buy my own.”

“Please, I want you to have mine.”

“Okay, if that what you want, I’ll gladly take it.”

“Barsh, if you’ll let me borrow your rifle, I’ll kill us a squirrel while you’re fishing for redeyes. Then I’ll show you how to roast a squirrel. It’ll make us a fine breakfast.”

“That sounds good. The rifle is loaded with a .22 long. I’ve got a box of them in my backpack. I’ll get it for you.”

***

Coon Peters was sitting with his back against a tree, when Barsh walked back into camp with four red-eyed bass. On a flat rock near the fire pit, there was a red squirrel, gutted but not skinned. It was the biggest squirrel he had ever seen.

“I see you killed a squirrel. What kind is it? I’ve never seen one like this before.”

“That’s a red fox squirrel. You don’t find them everywhere, but I’ve killed lots of them in these woods. I could have killed three or four common grey squirrels, but I waited for that one to come jumping through the trees and stop at the big hickory tree near where I was sitting.”

“Is that what they call still-hunting?”

“Yeah, you find a good hickory tree, set off a ways, and wait for the squirrels to come for the hickory nuts."

"Then I'll have to try that."

"How many red-eyes you got there?"

"Four. I thought they would be enough for our supper, since you said you had another yellow catfish. I caught them in no time at all. Then I spent most of the afternoon exploring the forest on the east side of the creek.

"I followed a little branch to a deep hollow with a rocky bluff. The top of that bluff was covered with be blueberry bushes. I ate a few, and I'll be going back for more later this week."

"I know exactly where you were. And you won't find a better blueberry anywhere.

"While we're talking about wild fruit, I'll tell you where the best wild grapes are if you come back this fall. You go down the other side of this creek till you come to the third branch and then follow it back up in those hills. You'll find more wild grapes than you can imagine. I call them fox grapes."

"My father taught me about fox grapes. They were small and sour, but they suit me just fine."

"These are the same, and they go good with broiled fish. This fall, you can also find muscadines scattered all over this forest.

"I'm getting hungry. You want me to cook those red-eyes for supper?"

"Yes, sir, I want to see how you cook them."

"Since they're small, it's best to roast them whole, after you clean them, of course. Barsh, in all my days, you're the first person I've met who has any interest in these old ways of living in the forest."

"Learning about your ways of living in the forest is like a gift from Heaven to me, and I'll be putting them to good use."

"How long you staying?"

"Until Saturday if it doesn't rain."

"I was planning to go home tomorrow, but maybe I'll stay till Wednesday. My old lady knows to expect me when she sees me. She don't care when I go or when I come, and I'm the same with her. She's a good-hearted woman. We both know what we got in each other, and it works out just fine.

"I just wish I could get about better, so I could camp with you, again this summer. I'm sure this will be my last time in these woods. Now, let me clean those red-eyes, and I'll show you how I cook them.

"After I scrape off the scales and gut them, I'll run a forked hickory skewer down the mouth, through the stomach, and into the body. This way, I can turn it from one flat side to the other against the hot coals."

"You want me to build the fire?"

"Yeah, start it with small limbs so we'll get a good bed of coals, real quick."

***

With daylight slowly fading from the camp, Barsh sat by the flicker fire. A sense of good fortune swelled in his chest, because Coon Peters happened to be camping there. The old man sat up from his quilt, where he had been resting on his back, since supper.

"Barsh, you want to build up the fire. We'll come back here, once we get Blue started. Let me get me a swig of whisky, and we'll get going. You got a flashlight?"

"Yes, sir."

With the corn whisky down his throat, Coon released Blue, and the three of them started up the creekbank with the hound running ahead. After hobbling a short distance, the old man stopped.

"We can go back now," he said. "Blue'll keep right on hunting till he picks up the trail of a coon."

Back at the camp, they sat beside the fire. Barsh had decided that he would tend the fire and had collected a pile of dead limbs to feed the flames deep into the night.

It started with a long howl, then rapid short barks that fell into a steady pattern. The chase was on. Coon's face was one big grin. His eyes sparkled in the firelight.

"Barsh, that's music to my ears. You're hearing Blue's trailing voice, and it's a good one."

"It sounds to me like they've crossed the creek headed east," Barsh said.

"No doubt about it. But that coon will come back to the creek after a while. I'd bet a dollar on it."

And that is exactly what happened. The racoon doubled back to the creek. There, Blue lost the trail twice but managed to pick it up. Then the racoon headed west away from the creek—Blue's trailing voice letting them know he was on its trail.

Before long, Barsh noticed that the old man was watching him intently, and he refocused on the sound of Blues's voice which, at the moment, was more like a howl.

"Has Blue treed the racoon?"

"He's barking treed. But I ain't believing that coon has give up and taken to a tree this soon. It's likely marked the tree and doubled back to the creek by now, having a good laugh on Blue.

"I'm hoping Blue will soon realize they ain't no coon up that tree and try to pick up its trail.

"If he can't figure it out, soon, I'll call him in with my horn.

The hound kept barking treed. Barsh's focus shifted to some of the things that he would like to do, tomorrow, until the silence pulled him back into the moment.

"Just as I hoped, Barsh. Blue has finally realized they ain't no coon in that tree, but he ain't likely to pick up the trail, again. If he don't in about twenty minutes, I'll call him in with my horn.

Blue didn't pick up the trail. Coon stood up and started blowing his hunting horn in a pattern of short and long blasts. After a few minutes he stopped and sat down by the campfire.

Blue soon made his way back to camp. The old man tethered him, and then he rolled up in his Army blanket for the night.

Barsh sat by the fire, thinking about Amy. He was still distraught that she had not kept her promise to meet him behind their garage, Sunday afternoon.

Chapter Sixteen

Tuesday was filled with new experiences for Barsh. Coon Peters showed him how to roast a squirrel over hot coals and then taught him how to still-hunt for squirrels. Barsh bagged his first squirrel, a common gray one.

Back at camp, the old man wanted to talk about how things had changed in his lifetime. When he was a boy, farmers worked hard every winter cleaning new ground to plant more crops. Now people were planting their fields in pine trees or turning them into pastures. He had turned his fields into pastures and started raising Black Angus cattle.

"Are Black Angus beef or dairy?" Barsh asked.

"Beef, and the best breed of beef if you ask me. I wouldn't have a dairy farm if you gave me one. It's nothing but work, seven days a week, fifty-two weeks a year, year in and year out."

"What about horses?" Barsh asked. "If I lived on a farm, I'd have a saddle horse."

"My daddy was crazy about saddle horses, always kept a good one. I'd ride occasionally when I was a boy, but I never cared much for horses. If I wasn't working back then, I was camping and fishing or I was afoot with a good hunting dog."

"Coon, I want to explore more of this old growth forest today. Maybe follow the creek on its journey for a while."

"Well, if you stick with this creek, it'll take you to the Chattahoochee River."

"How far is that from here?"

"Hard walking can get you to the river and back by night fall."

"Then that's where I'm headed, right now."

"Wait up. Let me cook you some catfish to take with you."

"Thanks, but I won't need any more food until supper. I'll see you before dark."

Just so, Barsh set out immediately and followed Wehadkee Creek all the way to the Chattahoochee River. Here, he sat on the bank, watching the currents rush toward the sea.

A hawk's lone cry fell from the distant sky. For one pure moment, he was totally absorbed in nature. He and the hawk and the river and the forest were one.

He emerged from the oneness, thinking that some things, like a hawk's cry, had not changed for eons, while elsewhere there were radical changes. He imagined that in the not-too-distant past, some Creek Indian boy sat beside this river with that same magnetic cry of a hawk falling upon his ears. The hawks were still here, but the Creek Indians had been forced from their native lands in Alabama to Oklahoma.

Pleased with his hike to the Chattahoochee River, he left for Camp Wehadkee, eager to rejoin Coon Peters.

***

Twilight had settled on the camp. Barsh sat beside the campfire. Coon Peters was stretched out on his Army blanket.

"Barsh," he said as he sat up, "are you staying up with me tonight? I'm hoping Blue learned his lesson last night."

"Oh, yeah,"

As darkness fell upon them, Coon set his hound hunting again, this time down the creek. The chase started about like it did the first night, but it went on and on for a much longer time.

"Blue's done it this time, Barsh. He's treed that coon, for sure, and he knows it just as sure as I know we're setting by this fire."

"How can you be so certain?"

"Just think about it. Blue's barked treed once already tonight but not for long. He knew that coon had marked the tree and moved on, so he left the tree and picked up the trail, again.

"Now he's been barking treed for a sometime. He'll stay there all night if I don't call him back with my horn, which I'm gonna do right now."

The old man stood and blew his horn, until Blue went silent.

"That's good. He's on his way back to camp. Barsh, I've got myself a fine coon hound. We'd make a good pair if I wasn't so old and crippled. But I'm satisfied. Everything comes to an end in its time. I'll be happy just to have him around the house to keep me company."

"People used to say I stayed out all night camping and coon hunting just so I could get drunk. But they didn't know a thing about why I liked to do that. Truth is I can't explain it myself.

"Take yourself, Barsh. Why did you walk all the way back in these woods to fish and camp out? I bet you can't put it in words, can you?"

"No, I can't explain it. I read a book, *Call of the Wild*, by Jack London. The title of that book kind of describes how I feel. I don't really hear a voice calling me, but it's like there's something drawing me here."

"Yeah, that's got to be part of the answer. But there's got to be more to it. There's something in me that needs the wild. I know this for a fact.

"Think about this. Sometimes, I just flat out need a woman. I guess all men do, unless they're a queer like Joe Crawford. I couldn't believe there were such men when I first heard about him.

"Anyway, when I need a woman, I can feel it in my blood. Maybe, there's something in my blood that needs the wild.

"Now, that I think about it, it must be the same thing with a queer like Joe Crawford. You know who the Crawfords are, don't you?"

"I pass by their place nearly every day."

"They're the richest people in town. With that kind of money, Joe Crawford could have just about any woman he wanted, but they tell me that he don't care a thing about women, that all he wants is to suck off boys and men.

"So, here's what I think. It just ain't in his blood to want a woman. His blood has got to be different.

"I guess it's the same thing when it comes to the wild. It's either in your blood or it ain't. I don't know how it got in my blood, but it's there. And it must also be in yours."

The old man and the boy sat silently by the campfire, each absorbed in his own inner world.

So, Joe Crawford sucks off boys and men, Barsh thought. That would explain Root Riddle's strange remark about making a *social call* on him.

The old man's comments were the first he'd heard about queers, and that news was quite puzzling, although his thoughts about people having different kinds of blood made sense to him.

He knew, for certain, that Root Riddle was a sorry excuse for a human being. He would certainly be back on Britton Road, driven by a need to connect with Ruth Wade, and that would increase the possibility of horrid trouble for Becky.

There was no doubt in Barsh's mind that great harm would come to her if Root ever saw her going to his tepee. Maybe, he should just go back on his word and tear it down.

Unable to resolve that dilemma, his mind jumped to Wesley Workman, who was different in most respects from Root, and yet both seemed to be driven by vulgar sexual desires that frightened him.

There was also something disturbing about the fact that Wesley started flirting with Amy the first time he saw her, and it didn't matter that Barsh was standing beside her. He told Amy that Wesley was only teasing her, but he took note of the way he sized her up.

Quite disturbed about that, he pulled off his Keds tennis shoes and crawled into his sleeping bag. Sleep, however, was slow to come.

Chapter Seventeen

After breakfast on Wednesday, Barsh and Coon Peters sat beside the campfire. The old man was dreading the long hike back home. He would have to take it easy, stopping often to rest and get his breath.

Working in the cotton mill had ruined his lungs. But he was going home a happy man, and Barsh was going to walk with him to make sure that he had a safe return. To help him, Barsh volunteered to carry his backpack.

They left the camp and finally made it out of the forest. On reaching a barbed-wire fence, the old man held on to a fence post, wheezing again.

Beyond the big pasture, a farmhouse was nestled in a cluster of oak trees. There was a big barn and a scattering of outbuildings behind the house.

"Those are my Black Angus grazing down there. I had forty-three when I left for the woods. Could have more now. The cows are calving. Give me another minute, and we'll cut right through the pasture to the house."

"Is that a bull I see with the cow?"

"That's Willard but he won't bother us. Now a Jersey bull is something else. You don't never want to get in a pasture with a Jersey bull."

"I know about Jersey bulls. I've been chased up a tree by one. Scared me to death."

"You can trust me about Black Angus. Goring ain't in their blood. Willard don't care about nothing but eating and putting it to the cows."

"I trust you're right. There are no trees to climb in your pasture."

"I think I can make it now, but I'll have to take it slow."

They crossed the pasture and walked to the back of the well-built house that had never been painted. The weathered boards had bleached out but still looked solid. It was obviously an old house, but there was no sagging to it.

With an invitation to come in and rest awhile, Barsh propped his rifle against the screened back porch and climbed the step behind the old man. The well-curb rose through the floor on one side of the porch. There were two rocking chairs and a work table on the other side. The door into the kitchen was open.

"Edna, I'm back. And I brought us some company. Come meet Barsh."

A fine-featured woman came to the door. She was a good ten years younger than Coon and seemed to be puzzled by Barsh's presence on her porch, as if something might have gone wrong.

"This is Barsh Roberts. We been camping together down on Wehadkee Creek. I was cooking some catfish at noon on Monday, and here come this boy, walking into my old camp. Wesley Workman had told him about the place, and he'd hiked all the way from town to spend the week there by himself."

"Well, I'm mighty pleased to meet you, Barsh. You're a good-looking boy if I ever saw one. Who's your daddy?"

"Bill Roberts."

"Don't know him. Does he work in town?

"He's the foreman at Britton's Lumber."

"He must be a good man to put up with old J. P. Britton. Y'all rest, while I put some dinner on the table. I got a pot of black-eyed peas with a lot of ham in it. And there's turnip greens and cornbread. Barsh, you can have your choice of sweet milk or buttermilk. I know Coon will have his buttermilk."

"I can't stay for dinner, Mrs. Peters."

"Why, of course, you can. I'll have it on the table in five minutes. You can't be in that big of a hurry."

"Any other time, I would join right in, but I made a bet with myself that I could live off the land all week. And that's what I want to do."

"Well, I'll let you by this time. But I won't take *no* for an answer next time. And you be careful by yourself in them woods."

"He ain't going yet, Edna. I got some things that I want to show him."

The old man led him to a bedroom where he rummaged about in a closet, until he found the syrup bucket with his collection of arrowheads. Barsh was eyeing a shotgun on a rack above the bed. He'd never seen one like it.

"What kind of gun is that, Coon?"

"That's a twelve-gauge pump shotgun made by Winchester. I've had it forty years and it's still good as new. Bought it at McMillan Hardware. You know the McMillan brothers, don't you?"

"I've seen them in their store."

"Their daddy bought the first Winchester pump shotgun when it came out in 1897. Paw used to let old man McMillan hunt quail here on our place. Anyway, when I saw what he could do with that Winchester pump shotgun, I was determined to get me one, and I did. It's rapid fire when you need it."

"Dad has a single shot twelve-gauge shotgun, and I've seen a double-barrel shotgun but never a pump."

"If you're gonna be a hunter, you need a pump shotgun. If you miss the first or second shot, you can even get off a third shot."

"Dad used to like to hunt rabbits. What kind of game did you like to hunt?"

"I hunted squirrels, quail, and rabbits, but I like hunting rabbits with a pack of beagles, best of all."

"How does that work?"

"When you take to the fields and forests, the beagles will spread out, sniffing around in brush piles, honeysuckle vines, places where rabbits bed down. When they jump one, they'll trail it around and about, until it circles back toward its bed.

"That's where you'll be waiting for that to happen. Then you'll get a good shot to kill it."

"I'd like that."

"Now that I think about it, I'm gonna give my Winchester to you. I can't hunt no more, and I don't have a son to pass it on to. You're just the boy I always wanted. So that's what I'm gonna do. Give my Winchester to you."

"I'd like to have a shotgun like yours, but Dad doesn't even want me to have a .22 rifle. He thinks I'm too young. But maybe I could buy it from you when I get older."

"It's as good as yours. It'll be right here when you get ready for it. I'll tell Edna I want you to have it, just in case I happen to die in the meantime.

"Now, let me show you these arrowheads. You'll take them, won't you? Maybe I'll keep a few just for a remembrance."

"I'd love to have them. Are you sure you want to give them to me?"

“Yeah, I want you to think about old Coon Peters every time you look at these arrowheads.

“My rod and reel are in the toolshed by the old cotton house. Let me get them for you and you can be on your way back to Camp Wehadkee. I like the fact that you’ve named the place, something that never occurred to me.”

Barsh followed him to the toolshed. He gave him the rod and reel along with two Hawaiian wigglers. Then he showed him how to break the reel with his thumb so it wouldn’t backlash when he cast it.

“I hate to see you go, Barsh. Can you find your way back?”

“Yes, sir. I won’t have any trouble finding the camp.”

“Well, tell me this. How did you get there from town?”

“I hiked down the railroad until I saw Workman’s Garage and then I cut through the woods behind their place.”

“That’s what I thought. It’s actually shorter to come by here. This dirt road by the house crosses that railroad about two miles before you get to Workman’s Garage. All you got to do is cross the Lafayette Highway and come right on down this road to the house here.

“This way you can stop and visit with me before you head into the wild for Camp Wehadkee. Will you do that?”

“One way or another, I’ll see you again on my next trip to Camp Wehadkee. If I don’t come by on my way in, I’ll come by on my way out.

Chapter Eighteen

Late Friday afternoon, Barsh sat alone beside the campfire as he roasted catfish over the hot coals. Pleased that he could now trust his eyes and sense of timing, he lifted the skewer from the coals and waited for the fish to cool. It was cooked to perfection.

Just as he had planned, he had sustained himself all week on the flesh and fruit of the wild.

Overhead, the leaves danced with a gentle spring breeze. Behind him, the creek sang a timeless refrain.

He remembered the saying of an old Greek philosopher that his Uncle Edward had once taught him: You can't step in the same river twice. That provoked him to apply its underlying truth to people: You can't interact with the same person twice.

When Amy kissed him the first time only two weeks ago, she was not the same girl that he had played with all last summer. Nor was he the same boy. Yes, a lot had changed in him, and yet there was something deep within him that seemed unchanged and unchangeable.

He had not seen another person since he left Coon Peter's house at noon on Wednesday. Never before had he gone twenty-four hours without interacting with another living person.

Now, he had lived alone for two days and two nights. There was something profoundly satisfying about the experience of being by himself in the deep forest and living off the land. Even so, he had also learned that he did not have the heart of a hermit.

From time to time and always at night during those two days, he was thinking about someone or creating an intimate fantasy.

True, it was good to be by himself at times, but that was not enough to keep him happy. Camping in the forest was a special retreat from living at home, not a permanent way of life.

He felt a deep need to connect to others, and Amy Burdette was now at the center of that need. Time and again, he had thought about her with the deepest longing.

Wesley Workman had promised to join him that evening. But why would he? He seemed to have outgrown camping. What was in it for him? Maybe he needed a male friend to share his stories with. He certainly had a need to talk. But did Barsh need him as a friend?

Wesley's vulgar way of talking about girls and women was unsettling to him. He had never before heard anyone give a detailed description of doing it.

He remembered Wesley response to Rayford's questions about his unbridled womanizing: Married, single, divorced. It don't make no difference to me. How could Barsh respect someone like that?

Ah, but Wesley's skills with that Harley-Davidson and his cocky independent spirit. Those Barsh admired greatly. He didn't know the word for it, but he knew that he would never be totally relaxed around Wesley.

He sat up at the sound of someone or something crunching through the dry leaves toward the camp. It was Wesley with backpack and sleeping bag.

"Hey, Barsh. I was hoping you would still be here. Daddy said you stopped by the garage, Monday morning."

"It would have taken a heavy rain to have sent me home."

"Have you had your supper?"

"Ate some catfish a little while ago. You want me to cook you some?"

"I brought some stuff, but that sounds good. You sure you don't mind cooking, again?"

"Not at all. I cooked mine on a skewer. Want me to do yours that way?"

"How did you learn to cook catfish on a skewer? Coon Peters is the only one I ever knew who cooked like that."

"He was here when I walked into camp, Monday. We camped together until Wednesday, and he taught me how to cook without a skillet."

"Then roast me some catfish if you don't mind. I'll see how good you are."

"I'm still learning. But I like cooking this way."

"How many yellow catfish you got?"

"Three. I'm sure we can catch more tonight."

"Good, I want to take some to Mama. I got in a cussing fight with Daddy this morning, and she took my side for a change."

"Let me build up the fire, and I'll roast you some catfish."

With the campfire roaring again, Barsh walked to the creek bank, took a catfish from the stringer, that was the right size to feed one person, and sat down on a log to clean it. Wesley sat on the other end of the log watching.

"Tell me about Coon Peters. I didn't think he could get back in here anymore."

"He's got a new coon dog. That's why he took the trouble, and it was hard for him, coming and going. I walked home with him. He barely made it back. But I was glad he was here. He taught me a lot about living in the wild."

"You're getting to be a true woodsman. That's more than I want out of life, but I got to have more time off from work. I told Daddy this morning that I was taking off every other Saturday, starting tomorrow."

"So, you don't have to work tomorrow."

"That's right. I've got two whole days off, Saturday and Sunday, I ain't had this in a long time.

"Daddy's mad as hell, but I told him he could take it or leave it. The people at Ford Motors have been trying to get me to work for them, so I don't have to work for him."

Back at the campfire, Barsh roasted the catfish on a skewer a few pieces at a time. Wesley ate them with pleasure as each batch came off the fire.

"Barsh, you're a hell of a cook, but I believe you lied to me the other week."

"What you mean?"

"Last time we camped here, you told me you weren't getting any," he said grinning. "I can't believe that, now that I know you got a girl like Amy following you around. She is one hot piece of ass, and you can't tell me you ain't done been in her panties. Tell me the truth?"

"Amy's not that kind of girl."

"So, you've done tried to get her cherry."

"No, I haven't tried that."

"How do you know she ain't that kind of girl if you ain't tried?"

"I just know her. We've been best friends a long time, and now that we're in love, I plan to marry her when we grow up."

"Well, buddy boy, I hate to tell you but things don't usually turn out like you plan them. I've lived long enough to know that.

"Amy's ripe for the taking, and if you don't do it soon, somebody's gonna beat you to it."

"You're wrong about her."

"Well, time will tell. It always does."

Barsh welled with anger. Amy had been as loyal a friend as anyone could be, and now they were in love. He needed to cool down. Wesley knew nothing about Amy.

"We need to bait the set hooks before it gets dark," Barsh said.

"Then let us up and be going."

***

The campfire had almost burned out, nothing left but some coals and the ends of a few smoldering limbs around the edge of the pit. Occasionally one would flare up for a moment and then die down. Barsh tossed them into the center of the coals and watched them light up the camp. Wesley stirred from sleep.

"How long have I been sleeping, Barsh?"

"An hour, maybe. I'm ready to turn in as soon as the fire burns out. There's no need to check the set hooks, again, is there?"

"No, we already got a good mess of catfish for Mama, and there'll probably be more in the morning."

"That's what I was thinking."

"Hell, I'm wide awake now. I didn't know where I was for a minute when I woke up. Guess who I was dreaming about."

"Lurleen Pullens?"

"No, I don't dream about her anymore. She's big in the belly, and I hate to think of her gonna be a mama. When that baby's born, it's gonna mess my mind up."

"How's that?"

"It ain't a sexy sight to see a woman nursing a baby. You know how you can put a governor on a car or truck, and it'll cut off the gas at a certain speed. Well, that's what I'm talking about.

"When I walk in a room with a woman nursing a baby, it wilts my dick every time. Otherwise, if I saw a woman with her tit hanging out, it would ignite a lustful fire in my body."

Barsh could hardly see Wesley's face through the dying fire, but he looked serious for the moment. Perhaps, he was trying to figure out why the sight of a baby nursing at a woman's breast would shut down his sexual desire.

"But I'll tell you what. Lurleen is one clever woman."

Once again, Wesley began narrating a sexual experience with Lurleen. This time, he gave all the details about the first time she asked him to do it to her like a bull. Then he lay back on his sleeping bag, staring into the heavens.

"Look at that starry sky. Not a cloud up there. Just stars upon countless stars. And here I am talking about a woman's hot flesh. But I didn't invent the stuff. It's as natural as the stars when you think about it."

"I'm going to turn in," Barsh said, slipped off his tennis shoes, and crawled into his sleeping bag in his clothes.

"Well, I guess I will too, but I want to tell you about my trip to Panama City Beach the other week. I met a girl from Birmingham. Sexy as they come. Her name was Gail. She was there with her college roommate.

"They were looking for jobs as bar waitresses. Anyway, she was jitterbugging at the pavilion with her girlfriend, and I cut in on her. Hell, man, you should have seen us. We were the star attraction for a while."

"I didn't know you were a dancer."

"Oh, yeah. If you want to meet girls at a night spot, you got to be a good dancer. You know how to dance, don't you?"

"They taught us how to do the two-step for our junior high dances. But that's all. I never wanted to learn how to jitterbug."

"But that's how you pick up girls. You go to a night spot where there's dancing, and you'll find all the women you want. They're there looking for a man. You wouldn't believe the number of women you'll see in any bars with a dance floor around Phenix City.

"They flock in those places, knowing those soldier boys from Fort Benning will be there. Everybody is looking for a good time. If you can hit it off dancing with a good-looking woman, you got it made."

"That doesn't interest me. I guess I'm looking for something more in a girl."

"Well, I hope you find it. Back to Gail from Birmingham. That's who I was dreaming about before I woke up."

Wesley pulled off his shoes and burrowed into his sleeping bag. Then he narrated all the details of doing it with Gail from Birmingham.

“Have you ever been to Panama City Beach, Barsh?”

“Once, last summer.”

“You need to go back with me. I saw all kind of good-looking girls your age. They’ll go dreamy-eyed over you.”

“What I’d like to do is go deep-sea fishing with Captain Anderson. He takes you out all day on his boat. They say you can’t even see the land.”

“We can do that. But tell me this. What would you like to do tomorrow? We can spend the day here or we can take a trip on my Harley. I’ve been wanting to go to Atlanta, again. Roar in and out of the big city, just for the hell of it. Is there any place you been wanting to go?”

“I wouldn’t mind going to Atlanta with you if that’s where you want to go. I’ve never been, but I know someone who lives there. I’ll have to be home before dark, though. That’s what I told my parents.”

“Oh, we can get back before dark. Let’s do it.”

“Okay. I like riding with you on your Harley. You’ve got me wanting one.”

“Yeah, you’re gonna need your own Harley before long.”

Chapter Nineteen

Barsh could not believe his eyes as they rode through downtown Atlanta and then up Peachtree Street. He thought about his friend, Karen Phillips, who lived somewhere in that big city but had to spend her summers on a farm next to his aunt Catherine and uncle Oliver.

He wondered where she lived. Wherever it was, he was amazed that she and her friends would venture downtown on a trolley, but that's what she had told him.

Wesley eased the motorcycle into a gas station and stopped at the gas pump. They dismounted the Harley.

"What do you think about Atlanta, Barsh?"

"It gives me a strange feeling, like I'm in a movie. Why would anyone want to live in a place like this?"

"So, you've seen enough of Atlanta?"

"Yeah, I'm ready to head back."

"Let me fill up with gas, and we'll hit the road toward home."

Barsh paced about scanning everything in sight. A trolley eased to a stop at the street corner with sparks flying from the electrical connector. Four people got off and scattered in different directions.

The most glamorous woman he had ever seen came clacking down the sidewalk in high-heel shoes. She could have been a movie star for all he knew.

Captivated by her stunning beauty, he was obviously gawking, until Wesley shattered the moment with a loud wolf whistle. To Barsh's surprise, the woman didn't ever turn her head to see who had whistled. She didn't frown. She didn't smile. She just kept staring straight ahead.

"Good God in Heaven, Barsh. The fires of Hell couldn't thaw out that woman. She could have cursed me if she didn't want to give me a smile.

"Let's get us a coke, then we'll head home," he said and swaggered into the gas station, smiling like he was on top of the world.

Barsh followed his black boots, lost in thought about the

woman who had just walked by them. He had observed her for just one brief moment, and then she was gone forever from his sight. But he could not get her out of his mind.

In that single moment, Wesley had assaulted her with a wolf whistle. How often did such an unwanted advance happen to her in a day? A week? A year? A lifetime?

***

The ride out of Atlanta was breathtaking. Wesley zoomed in and out of traffic, stopping for red lights, roaring off again on green, and then racing flat out on the highway toward Alabama.

In Newnan, Georgia, they stopped at Sprayberry's Barbecue for a sandwich and onion rings. Wesley flirted with the waitress. Nothing crude. Just gentle banter.

To Barsh's amazement, she seemed to enjoy it. At least, she returned the banter.

On the road again, Barsh thought about Amy. How disconnected he felt from her. Even when he was home next door to her, he had no access to her, unless they had prearranged a time and place to meet. They had agreed to meet next Saturday at the picture show, but that was a week away.

Wesley stopped at a gas station in Franklin, Georgia, a small town built on a high bluff overlooking the Chattahoochee River. Barsh stayed with the motorcycle, while Wesley stepped inside to get directions to Mayhayley Lancaster's place. He'd heard she lived on a dirt road near Franklin.

Old Mayhayley, as people called her, was known far and wide as the best fortune teller in the South, if not the whole world. Promoting her own fame, she called herself the Oracle of the Ages.

Barsh, who had been influenced by his father's doubts about the woman's ability to see the future, was even more skeptical and wanted nothing to do with her.

Wesley, on the other hand, was looking forward to having his fortune told by her. He hadn't said whether he believed in her powers or not. What he said was that he wanted Old Mayhayley to tell his fortune, just for the hell of it.

Wesley had no difficulty finding her place. Cars of every description were parked across the road from the house in what had once been a cotton field. People of all ages and social standing were milling about in the dusty yard.

Barsh couldn't imagine why the Oracle of the Ages, said to be a very wealthy woman, would live in a sagging old house that looked like it was about to cave in.

All eyes were on the two boys as they crossed the road and entered the yard. A wrinkle-faced man with no front teeth drifted over and gave them a squint-eyed once over

"You boys come to get your fortune told by Old Mayhayley?"

"Yeah," Wesley said. "But I had no idea there would be so many people here. How long you been waiting to see her?"

"Got here about midmorning. But Old Mayhayley don't have no set order to see people. That's her sister Sally, coming down the steps, she picks out who gets to go next. It don't matter when you come.

"They's a woman here from Birmingham, just drove up in a new car about five minutes ago. You can take my word for it. She'll take her next. Look at her sister Sally heading straight for that rich woman. See what I done told you."

"Hell, I ain't got all day," Wesley said.

"She might take you next, being as you're the only ones here on a motorcycle. Then again you can't tell what she'll do. But they's a red-headed girl here that will sell you a co-cola if you got the money."

"Go tell her to bring all three of us cokes if you don't mind."

Delighted to have the offer of a free coke, the old man hurried off in a halting gait. A young girl, obviously pregnant, strolled over to take his place.

"What kind of trouble are you in?" she asked, staring Wesley dead in the eye.

"Me? I ain't in no trouble. You got trouble?"

"Big trouble. The boy who got me this way has run off some place. They don't know where he is or when he's coming back. Some say he's done run off to Texas. He's got an uncle out there. I'm going to him if Mayhayley can tell me where he is."

"Good luck," Wesley said.

"Why you here, if you ain't got no trouble?"

"Just for the hell of it. I want to hear what Old Mayhayley sees in my future."

"That ought to be easy. I can see your future myself, and I wasn't born with no caul over my head.

"You may not have no trouble now, but you're too damn good looking to stay out of trouble for long. And besides, I can see that you got a devilish way about you that spells trouble.

"If some man or another don't kill you in the next year, they ought to, cause you ain't gonna leave their women alone. I can tell you that myself."

"Well, hell, Barsh. We might as well go on home. I done got my fortune told for free."

"I'm ready."

"I was joking. But if you're wanting to go, we can leave. I can come back to see Mayhayley some other time."

"As long as I get home before dark, I don't mind waiting."

"Here comes old Snag and that red-headed girl with our cokes. Soon as we drink them, we'll hit the road. We could be here all afternoon."

Wesley paid for the drinks and offered to buy the pregnant girl one, but she was too proud to accept his offer.

Mayhayley's sister Sally was back on the porch, sizing up the crowd again. This time she heads straight to Wesley.

"You boys wanting to see Mayhayley?"

"Came all the way from Alabama for that single solitary purpose, but we're fixing to leave you in a trail of dust. Looks like the Oracle of the Ages has got too much trade to fit our plans."

"Now hold on a minute. What about you, young fellow? You wanting to see her?

"No, ma'am. I'm just along with him."

"You ain't got no money?"

"That ain't it."

"Oh, you're one of them skeptics," she said and faced Wesley, again. "Mayhayley can see you next. What's your name?"

"Wesley Workman."

"Come on up on the porch with me."

The two walked away, leaving Barsh with the pregnant girl and the old man.

"You wanting to know if the baby's been marked, ain't you?" he said.

"I'm wanting to know where its daddy run off to."

"Why would you want to go live with someone who ran away without telling you where he was going?" Barsh asked.

"You don't understand how it is. Tommy got word that Paw

was laying for to kill him, which he was. He had to run off and didn't have no way to let me know where he was going. I've got to believe he wants me to come to him."

Another car turned into the parking area. It looked brand new. Four well-dressed women got out, laughing like someone had just told a funny joke. All eyes were on them as they crossed the dirt road into the yard. The Coca Cola girl headed straight for them.

Barsh wandered off to the edge of the yard away from the crowd. Anxious to get on the road, he kept watching for Wesley to emerge from his time with Mayhayley. Instead of Wesley, the pregnant girl joined him.

"Even if Mayhayley can tell me where Tommy is, you don't think I should go to him, do you?"

"I can't tell you what to do."

"But you would wait for him to contact me, wouldn't you?"

"That's what I would do, but you got to figure it out for yourself."

"Well, here comes your friend," she said as Wesley came striding toward them, cocksure of himself.

"Enough of that woman. Let's get on the road, Barsh."

"What did she tell you?" the girl asked.

"Same thing you told me. I'm headed for a dark downfall. That's one haughty woman to be so damn ugly. And self-righteous as hell.

"As I was leaving, she said, If your hand offends, cut if off, like she was Jesus Christ himself. And believe me, I'd do just that if she was the only woman left in the world."

"Why would she want you to cut your hand off?" the girl asked.

"Surely, you're worldly enough to know she wasn't talking about my hand. You know how they turn a bull into a steer, don't you? But that'll be the day Hell freezes over.

"I'm a natural man just like a bull. And I ain't never heard of a bull wanting somebody to castrate him."

"Oh, I see. You think you're like a bull who has a right to every cow in sight, just for your own sinful use."

"Well, ain't you a fine one to be preaching—knocked up to hell. Come on, Barsh."

"Why do you run with somebody like him, Barsh?"

"He camps with me. Anyway, I hope things turn out good for

you."

***

Back on the Lafayette Highway, less than five minutes from Workman's Garage, Barsh leaned with Wesley as the motorcycle passed one car after another. It seemed so effortless to Wesley who knew how fast the motorcycle could take each curve. A bat out of hell could not keep up with him on that stretch of highway.

Wesley stopped the Harley beside his father's garage, and Barsh jumped off.

"Well, you can now say you've been to Atlanta."

"And what a trip it was. Thanks for the ride. I sure wish I could handle a motorcycle like you."

"Then I'll teach you how to handle my Harley. Let's get us a coke before you head home."

Barsh kicked out a Nehi Orange. Wesley, who drank only Coca Colas, finished two while he drank his.

"Wesley, can I use your telephone. No one on Britton Road has one. We're out of their service area."

"Sure, who you calling, Amy?"

"Yeah."

"I guess you know her number?"

"No, I've never called her."

"I'll look it up for you. What's her Daddy's name?"

"Herbert Burdette," he said realizing he'd made a mistake.

Wesley called out the number, he dialed it, and Mr. Burdette answered. Barsh had already decided he would not identify himself if one of her parents answered.

"May I speak to Amy, Mr. Burdette? . . . . Bye."

"He wouldn't let you talk to her?"

"She's spending the night with Laura Underwood."

"Laura Underwood? Does she have an older sister named Jo Ann?

"That's her."

"Jo Ann was in my class before I dropped out. They live on Petty Street, don't they?"

"Yeah. Wesley, I got to head home."

"I wish you'd change your mind and let me take you home."

"I'll have to walk back. Dad doesn't know I've got his rifle.

He thinks I'm too young to handle it, safely. I sneaked it out of his closet, so I'd have a rifle when Rayford and I started looking for a place to camp. I keep it in the loft of our barn."

"Here's an idea. Let me take you back to where the highway crosses over the railroad. That'll get you almost home."

"That's a good idea."

"Here's another idea. Leave your sleeping bag here in the garage. That'll save you some energy."

"Where's a good place?"

"Put it on top of this cabinet."

It was midafternoon, when Wesley dropped him at the overpass. He descended the steep bank to the railroad, that would take him to West Woods.

He did a lot of thinking, especially about Amy and her new friendship with Laura Underwood. For some reason, that was causing him a new anxiety.

He also found himself regretting that he had called Amy in Wesley's presence. That had to be one of the dumbest things he had ever done.

Chapter Twenty

When Barsh returned home late that Saturday afternoon, he found a note from his mother on the kitchen table. They had gone to Granny Roberts' for the day.

He poured a glass of milk and helped himself to the fried chicken and vegetables his mother had cooked for him. Sitting alone at the table, he sensed a strange loneliness, something very different from the experienced of being by himself in the wild.

His thoughts shifted to Amy. Her father said she was spending the night with Laura Underwood. What would happen if he showed up at her house and asked to speak to Amy? The only way to know was to go and find out.

Bathed and dressed for the occasion, he set out for Laura's. The big Victorian house was a perfect fit for the large corner lot with its massive oak trees. There was a balanced beauty about the whole place, which was well maintained. What a contrast with everything on Britton Road, where Barsh lived.

He climbed the front porch steps, rang the doorbell, and stepped back from the screen door that opened onto a hallway. Laura's mother answered. She was a grownup version of Laura—tall and thin with dark eyes, a quick smile, and black hair cropped just above her shoulders.

"Hello, there. You're Barsh, aren't you?"

"Yes, ma'am. Is Amy here?"

"She's back in Laura's room. They're having the best time. Come on in. Laura! Amy! I've got a surprise for you."

Mrs. Underwood led him into the living room, where the two girls joined them.

"Hey, Barsh," Laura said.

"I hope it's okay for me to stop by."

"Oh, yes. We've been talking about you."

"Excuse me," Mrs. Underwood said. "I've got to finish supper. It's about time for John D. and Junior to close the store. Can you stay for supper, Barsh?"

"No, ma'am. I can't stay but a few minutes."

“I’m glad you came by,” Amy said.

“Hey, y’all, let’s go out on the back porch,” Laura said. “Barsh can tell us all about his camping trip.”

Amy took his hand, as they followed Laura to the screened back porch. Amy chose the wicker settee for them and sat against him still holding his hand. Laura sat across from them in a wicker chair. Both girls were dressed in shorts and strapless tops.

“Barsh, tell us all about your camping trip.”

“It was good. There was a man camping there, and he taught me how to cook fish and squirrel over hot coals with a hickory skewer like the old woodsmen.”

“Did he camp with you all week?” Amy asked.

“No, he left Wednesday morning.”

“Well, did that Wesley Workman camp with you?” Laura asked. “Amy told me about him. I can’t believe he asked her to go to Panama City Beach with him on his motorcycle. My sister, Jo Ann, says he has a reputation.”

“He came Friday night, but I was by myself for two days and two nights.”

“Well, I hope Wesley didn’t take you off somewhere on that motorcycle,” Amy said.

“Actually, he took me to Atlanta this morning. But we didn’t do anything there. Just drove through downtown and then turned around. We did stop outside of Franklin, Georgia, on the way back. He wanted Old Mayhayley to tell his fortune.”

“I’ve heard of her,” Laura said.

“Did you let her tell your fortune?” Amy asked.

“No, that’s not something I would do.”

Jo Ann appeared in the kitchen door, dressed in black shorts and a white halter top. She had the same features as Laura and her mother.

“Barsh, did I hear you say you’ve been camping with Wesley Workman?”

“He camped with me Friday night.”

“Wesley was in my class before he dropped out of school. A good-looking guy who can’t keep his mind off girls. When he would look at you, you knew what he was thinking. But can he ever dance!

“None of the boys at school could jitterbug like Wesley. You need to get him to give you some lessons, Barsh. Then you could teach Laura and Amy a few things."

"Amy and I are going to teach Barsh, and we don't need any help from Wesley Workman."

"But you haven't seen him dance," Jo Ann said.

Mrs. Underwood burst onto the porch from the kitchen, her pocketbook looped over her shoulder.

"I'll be back in a minute, kids. I've got to pick up John D. and Junior. Their old car is in the shop again. I don't understand why John D. won't spend some of his money and buy them a new car. That money's not doing him any good in the bank.

"It's just making more money for me to spend when he dies. That's what I tell him, but it doesn't do any good."

Mrs. Underwood exited the porch and left in her new white Cadillac. Jo Ann returned to the kitchen.

"Amy has invited me to go with them on their vacation at Panama City Beach, and we can't wait to get to there. She told me how they dance all afternoon and into the night at the pavilion.

"Come on, Amy. Let's show Barsh how you can jitterbug."

Laura dashed for the record player on a table in the far corner of the porch. Amy joined her in the middle of the floor and they danced the fire out of the music.

"What do you think?" Laura asked.

"You are both good, very good," he said, surprised to see how excited Amy had become about dancing.

Mrs. Underwood drove into the backyard and stopped the Cadillac in front of the free-standing garage. She was out and headed for the back porch before the two men even opened their doors.

"Back again. Hope y'all are having fun. I'll have supper on the table in five minutes. I wish you would stay and eat with us, Barsh."

"Thanks, but I've got to go."

"Well, you must come back. You're welcome anytime."

She was in the kitchen before Barsh could respond, but he was overjoyed that she had welcomed him into their home. She wasn't the least bit anxious that he, a boy with love pulsing in every fiber of his flesh, was in her house with Amy and Laura.

What would the men think? Laura's father opened the screen door and waited for his father.

"Papa! Daddy! This is Amy's friend, Barsh Roberts. He lives around the corner from her on Britton Road."

Laura's introduction made Barsh acutely aware of where he lived. He felt a twinge of embarrassment. People like the Underwoods must see Britton Road as an unsightly blemish on their little town.

"Good to meet you, Barsh," her Papa said and kept walking toward the kitchen.

He was a short little man who couldn't quite straighten up. Laura's father stopped to shake hands with him.

"I remember you, Barsh. I sold you a fine suit of clothes back in the fall. Your mother was with you. She's such a sweet lady."

"That was for church. I'd outgrown my old suit."

"Well, y'all picked out a good one. Where do you go to church, First Baptist?"

"Yes, sir."

"Y'all have got a fine minister. I think everyone would agree that Dr. Franks is the most learned man this town has ever seen. Can you stay for supper, Barsh?"

"No, sir. I've got to go."

"By the way, what does your father do?"

"He's the foreman at Britton's Lumber Company."

"I've never met him, but if Mr. J. P. Britton thinks that much of him, he must be a good man. What's his name?"

"William Roberts, but people call him Bill."

"You tell him to come see me, when he needs a good suit of clothes. I'll give him a good price, and the same goes for you. I can also fix you up in some good-looking sports clothes."

"I've got to go," Barsh said when Mr. Underwood entered the kitchen.

"Wait a minute. I'll see you off."

Amy took his hand and led him out the screened door. On the far side of the house, she stopped and pulled him against her, hugging him ever so tight.

"Do you really love me, Barsh?" she asked, pulling back enough to look into his eyes.

"With all my heart. You would be surprised at how often I thought about you this week."

"And I love you," she said and kissed him hard and long. "Sorry, but I've got to get back inside. What are you up to?"

"I'm going by Colonial Food to see Rayford. When can I see you again?"

“Laura’s coming home with me after church tomorrow. If the sun’s shining, we’ll be sunbathing in my usual place behind the garage most of the afternoon. Will you come by to see us?”

“Yes. But what if it’s raining?”

“We’re back and forth almost every day now. If she’s not at my house, I’m at hers. She plans to spend the night with me every Wednesday, and I’ll be at her house Saturday nights.”

“I promised Thomas that I would help him all next week. We’ll be collecting scrap medal from all over the county from early morning until late afternoon. Just in case I don’t get to see you tomorrow, will you meet me at the picture show, Saturday?”

“Here’s a better plan. Come by Laura’s first. I’ll be spending the night with her. We’ll go together from her house.”

“Okay,” he said and they parted ways.

Chapter Twenty-One

Barsh turned up Petty Street with a lot on his mind. He'd never felt so close to Amy, and yet he was unnerved by the changes he could see taking place in her.

Last year, at Amy's begging, the Burdettes had taken him to Panama City Beach with them for their summer vacation. He and Amy would go to the pavilion from time to time and watch the wild dancing.

Golden-tanned girls in shorts, weaving and bobbing and shaking with the pulsing music. Boys with crew cuts and t-shirts with the sleeves rolled up as high as they would go, trying to out-rhythm the girls.

At the time, neither Amy nor he had any interest in learning to jitterbug. Now, Amy was looking forward to joining the dancers at that same pavilion.

Who besides Laura would she dance with? He knew how girls, without dates, would dance by themselves or with another girl, hoping some boy would cut in on them. They would be all over Amy. One after another wanting to dance with her.

That unwanted vision was stuck in his head. He definitely needed a distraction and hoped that Rayford would stop by for a visit as soon as Colonial Food closed.

He turned down Main Street. Most of the stores had closed. The grocery stores would be closing next.

He walked past the pool hall without an anxious thought, until he heard someone scream, "God damn it, Root. Don't you try to pull that shit on me."

Barsh wasn't thinking straight. After his last encounter with Root Riddle, he had decided the safest course was to stay out of his way. And there he was walking right past his favorite hangout. He would be sure to take the opposite side of the street, going home.

A few people were still shopping in Colonial Food. Rayford was weighing a baking hen for a woman. He waited back in the aisle until Rayford wrapped it, and the woman left the meat counter.

"Hey, Barsh. I'm glad to see you're still alive. How was your camping trip?"

"It was good, very good. Wish you could have been with me."

"Me, too. Maybe I can get off work the next time you go."

"I was hoping we could get together tonight. Can you come by the house later?"

"I'm going to the picture show with Grace Wilkinson. This is my first date with her."

"I hope it goes well. See you later."

"Yeah, we'll get together next week."

"I'll be working with Thomas Wade during the day."

"Then we'll get together some at night."

"That'll be good."

***

His parents were talking on the back porch when he got back from town. He had a lot to tell them. There was also a lot he could not tell them—the motorcycle trip to Atlanta he took with Wesley and the squirrel he killed with his father's rifle.

"Hey, Mother! Dad! How was Granny Roberts?"

"Mama's fine. Your Uncle Edward came by last night for a short visit. He was visiting Mama, so we spent the day there. He's driving back to Birmingham in the morning."

"Well, that explains it. I was surprised that you had gone on a Saturday. You usually visit her on Sunday. I wish I could have seen Uncle Edward. Did he talk about his bird dogs?"

"No, you're the one he likes to talk to about his bird dogs. He asked about you. Wished he could have seen you. He thinks you're going to be a college professor. But he can't figure out whether you'll teach history, like him, or biology."

"Why would he think I'm going to be a college professor?"

"I don't know. He's just pleased to see how curious you are about everything, especially nature and the old ways that people used to live. I guess you remind him of himself when he was a boy. Young people today don't seem to care about nature or the past. Tell us about your camping trip."

"It was good. I was able to live off the land like I planned. I also learned how to roast fish over hot coals with a hickory skewer. That was the best part. That and just being in the forest. I brought your cast iron skillet home, Mother. I don't need it now that I know how to cook without it.

"Dad, I told you that the trees there have never been cut. That is such a wonderful forest, and Wehadkee Creek brims with yellow catfish and red-eyed bass. It's paradise to me."

"Yes, you told me. I'd like to see that forest myself. I hope Mr. Britton doesn't hear about it. He'd want me to do an appraisal. Then he'd try to buy the place or the trees and cut them for lumber."

"I don't think anybody should be allowed to cut those trees," Barsh said. "That forest should be preserved in its original state."

"You're right about that. We need to keep what's left of the virgin forests as they are."

"Thanks for leaving us a note," his mother said. "Did you see Rayford at Colonial Food?"

"Yes, ma'am. He's going to the picture show with his new girlfriend, but we'll get together some after he gets off from work next week."

"You know I expect you to stay out of trouble," his father said.

"Yes, sir. I know your expectations."

"I'm confident about that, but I'm less certain about Rayford. Friends can lead you don't the wrong road if you're not careful. I've seen it happen too often. Just be aware of that fact."

"Thanks for pointing that out to me. I need to talk to Thomas to see if he still wants me to work with him next week. He'll be collecting scrap medal out in the country, and this will be a new experience for me."

"It'll be hard work, but you can do it. I'm pleased with the way you're building up your strength with all your exercises."

Leaving the house, he walked down the dusty dirt road toward the Wades' house. The neighborhood needed a good rain to settle the dust, and it looked like it might soon get one. Rows of tumbled-up clouds were moving in from the southwest. The under sky was all aglow with red hues of the setting sun.

He was halfway to the Wades, when he stopped in the middle of the road. The gospel music was pouring out of the house in full force. He was too restless to sit in on their singing. He could talk to Thomas, Sunday afternoon. No, he would stick with his plan.

Get it over with and then excuse himself.

He stood at the foot of the front steps, waiting for the song they were singing to end. Becky rushed through the door, smiling sweetly.

"Hey, Barsh. I'm glad to see you. I've been looking out the window, hoping you would come."

"I need to ask Thomas if he still wants me to help him next week."

"Oh, please stay for a while."

"Okay, but I can't stay long."

"Well, look who's here, the woodsman," Thomas said from the couch, where he was sitting with a girl, whom Barsh had never seen.

"Thomas, do you still want me to help you next week."

"You bet. Be here at seven o'clock, Monday morning. Wear some old clothes. You'll need work gloves. And bring your own lunch. We'll be out in the country, all day, picking up scrap medal."

Barsh sat down on the floor next to the door with his back against the wall. Becky sat down beside him.

"Who's got a number picked out?" Mr. Wade asked

"I like number 149, the girl said. "It's one of my favorite songs, and we hardly ever sing it at church, except during funerals."

"I like that one, too," Thomas said.

"Barsh, do you know Thomas's girlfriend?" Velma asked.

"No, I haven't met her."

"This is Sally Stillwell. She's a member of our church and soon to be a member of our family."

"Pleased to meet you, Sally."

"Barsh is our neighbor," Velma said.

Sally nodded her head at him but didn't say anything. She was a skinny thing with big eyes and a tight little mouth. Curley brown hair draping down her back and across her shoulders.

She was old enough to put it up like Velma and all the other Holiness women he'd seen. But he could tell that her hair was her glory by the way she kept shaking it about with her head movements.

Ruth played the opening bars of the song on the piano with

Velma beating the time. Then they joined voices, in perfect harmony: They are going down the valley, one by one . . .

What a woeful song about people dying. Barsh tried to remember where he had heard the song. Then it jumped into his mind. It was at Mrs. Wade's funeral in the Pentecostal Holiness Church.

How could he ever forget that service? He looked at Becky, who was not singing, but the song didn't seem to affect her. Did she not remember?

They finally finished the song. Mr. Wade, sitting in his big stuffed chair, tilted his head back as if he were looking into Heaven for a vision of his departed wife.

Then he broke forth in a loud guttural commotion, sounds the likes of which Barsh had never heard. It was over in a few seconds. The old man's face was drained and vacant. The room was silent as death for another moment.

"Hallelujah!" he shouted with renewed energy. "Hallelujah! Hallelujah! Praise the Lord God Almighty. Thank you, Jesus! Thank you, Jesus!"

"Amen and Amen," Thomas said.

So that was speaking in tongues, Barsh thought. Was it just him or did everyone in the room feel the strange tension?

"I'm going to bed," Mr. Wade said. "It's been a hard week, and I'm about wore out. Y'all carry on with the singing."

"Papa," Velma said, "Sally is doing a solo for the morning service. I'm gonna let her and Ruth practice while I finish my work in the kitchen."

Velma followed her dad out of the living room and disappeared into the back of the house.

"Thomas, I'll see you at seven Monday morning," Barsh said and stood to leave.

"I'll be ready for you. Becky, will you bring me and Sally some ice tea?"

"Only if you'll let me work with you and Barsh, next week."

"You can forget about that. You'd just be in the way. Bring us some ice tea like a good little sister."

"You can get it yourself if that's the way you feel about me." she said and followed Barsh out the front door. "Let's set on the steps here. I do so want to talk to you."

"I really have to go, Becky. Maybe we can talk next week."

"I'm counting on that, and I'm working with y'all. You wait and see if I don't.

***

Barsh sat on the back porch with his mother and dad. The three of them listening to the Grand Ole Opry until his parent's bedtime.

Restless, Barsh left for his tepee and crawled through the flap into the dark tent, where he lay on his back on a burlap sack. The bullfrogs were bellowing along Turtle Creek.

He thought about Rayford and his first date with Grace Wilkerson. Since they were going to the picture show at seven, he assumed that her parents knew about the date. Would they walk to the Martin Theatre and back? Or would one of her parents drop her off and pick her up?

Again, he wished that Amy's parents would approve of her dating him. That, however, was not going to happen.

Then a somber spell descended upon him, as his mind took him back to Mrs. Wade's death and the funeral.

When they moved next door to the Wades, she was already sick and spent most of her time in bed. He had only seen her a few times before she died.

Before she took to bed for good, Mr. Wade called Dr. Gay to come examine her. He found a large growth in her stomach. They took her to Birmingham for surgery.

After cutting into her stomach, the doctor sewed her up and sent her home to die. She was full of colon cancer.

It was the Holiness prayers that he remembered most about her dying. Day and night, they wailed for God to heal her. Sometimes a group would all be praying at the same time, their voices mingling and drifting over the neighborhood.

Barsh refused to go about the place, but he could hear them when he was in his tepee or back porch.

He had watched his grandfather Roberts die after a long illness. The whole family was there, sitting or standing quietly in his room. They wanted him to live, but they let him go, grieving with silent tears and soft words.

He was too young, at seven, to feel the full sting of death. That thought reminded him of Becky. How quiet she had been at the funeral.

Except for her, the whole family wailed inconsolably. Ruth fainted at the opened casket at the end of the service, during the viewing of her mother for the last time.

Becky paused, looked at her mother, and returned calmly to her seat. She was pale and forlorn, but she kept her feelings locked inside herself. He could not remember her crying at any time.

A distant thunder, awakening his senses to the moment. Someone was running through the pasture toward the tepee. He sat up, assuming that Becky had slipped off again.

"Barsh," she whispered, "are you in there?"

"I'm here."

"Thank goodness," she said and crawled through the tent flap. "I was afraid you had gone home. I came here several times last week while you were camping. One night, I built a fire in this little firepit, so I could pretend I was camping with you. Can I build one now?

"I think there's a thunderstorm headed this way."

"But I'll have time to see your face across from the fire. That's what I need."

"Okay, but be prepared to leave quickly if I'm right about the thunderstorm."

Soon a small fire flickered between them, filling the tepee with a soft light. Becky's face was bright and hopeful. He was filled with compassion for her, but he could not return her smile, when he glanced occasionally into her eyes, which were always studying him.

"Becky, I've been thinking about your mother. When they were singing that song, tonight, about going down the valley, one by one, it carried me back to her funeral. Do you remember that was one of the songs?"

"No, I don't remember what songs they sang."

"Mother said your mother suffered something awful. And all that praying. We never talked about it."

"I didn't know how to talk about it."

After a moment of silence, Becky started singing that old death song, ever so softly.

Her singing turned into a whimper, which was followed by deep sobbing. As if to mute the sobbing, she curled up on the burlap sack. He wanted to take her up in his arms and hold her tight, until the sorrow eased. Instead, he moved beside her and began rubbing her back, ever so gently.

"It's all right, Becky. Cry all you want to. I can still see the tears on Dad's face as he looked at his father for the last time."

The sobbing gradually stopped and Becky sat up.

"You are such a comfort, Barsh. Without you, there wouldn't be any point in living."

Such a passionate outpouring deserved a response. But what could he say? The truth would be too harsh. Stick with friendship, he thought.

"It's always good to have friends, Becky. I don't think you can have too many."

Lightning struck nearby, cracking through the night like a giant whip.

"Becky, we've got to get out of here. Run home. I'll put out the fire and do the same."

Barsh scraped up dirt with his hands and put out the fire. Standing outside by the tepee, he watched Becky run up the steps to the front porch and disappear into the house.

Chapter Twenty-Two

The sky was overcast all day Sunday with an occasional shower. No sunshine for Amy to do her sunbathing and no chance for Barsh to see her. It was a frustrating day for him but redeemed in part by a good book.

Monday morning, he started working for Thomas Wade. Becky, who was angry because Ruth wouldn't let her go, waved them off as they left in Thomas' truck.

Beyond town, they chugged down one county road and up another, stopping at each farm house to buy any scrap medal the occupants were willing to sell.

Often, during that long workday, he thought about Amy. That night, he hung out with Rayford.

Late Tuesday, as Barsh walked home after another tiring day of working with Thomas, his father called him to the garden where he was hoeing a row of cabbage.

"Barsh, I've got a job for you in the morning. Mr. Wade's taking their cow to be serviced by Mr. Britton's bull. It's time to take Molly, and I have to work. So, I'm depending on you. Just follow Mr. Wade's lead, and you won't have any trouble. He plans to leave around seven-thirty."

"Okay, I'll be ready. I think I'll cool off in Turtle Swimming Hole before it gets dark."

Cooling off, however, was now secondary to him. He was thinking about the task of taking Molly to be serviced by Mr. Britton's bull. Never having gone with his father, he didn't know how the middle part worked, but he knew how it started and how it ended.

His father would leave home, leading Molly down the road by a short rope tied to her halter. Returning, he would put her in the pasture as if nothing had happened.

Barsh had seen bulls mount cows in various pastures, but they were part of the herd. He was puzzled about how it worked when you took a cow to visit the bull. How did you get them together and then separated without being gored by the bull?

Tomorrow, the task would fall on his shoulders, and he was worried about having to deal with Mr. Britton's Jersey bull. After much anguished thought, he concluded that he and Mr. Wade would likely turn the cows into the pasture and wait outside the fence. But then he couldn't imagine how they would get the cows out of the pasture. It was too much for his mind. He would have to trust his father and just follow Mr. Wade's lead.

***

Wednesday morning, Barsh woke to the aroma of cooked bacon. His father, who had finished breakfast, was sitting at the table drinking a second cup of coffee.

"Morning, Barsh. How's my boy?"

"Good! How are you?"

"Just fine," he said, staring at the coffee cup like he was in deep thought.

"Fix your plate, and I'll pour your milk," his mother said.

A silence overshadowed them, as she sat across for him in her usual place. She seemed worried.

He assumed his father had told her about the task he had assigned him, although it didn't seem like something to concern a woman with. On second thought, it did make sense. She would probably see him going and coming with the cow.

Barsh tried to hide his own anxiety, but he kept thinking about Mr. Britton's Jersey bull, how the angry beast had chased Rayford and him up nearby trees. Now, he had to take Molly to that same bull.

He studied his father's face, which was calm. His dad didn't seem the least worried, and there was some comfort in that.

It was also obvious his dad wasn't going to mention the subject at the table. Perhaps, there would be some lastminute instructions for him if they left the house, together.

He followed his father out the back door, but there were no additional instructions. His father just drove off for work.

Molly was easy to manage. He tied a short rope to her halter, and she seemed eager to be going.

He waited for Mr. Wade in their driveway, until the old man came leading their cow. He offered a gruff greeting and set out for Britton's Dairy. Barsh followed their broad-hipped red cow, her sagging udder squeezed between her hindlegs.

The Wade's cow had her tail cocked up and tilted to one side. her swollen sex was cracked open just a bit. That wasn't normal. So, he concluded, that's how you knew when it was time to take a cow to the bull.

Barsh kept pace with the old man. One minute, it seemed like it was taking forever to get there. He'd been up and down that road hundreds of times, running and walking. Why was it taking so long to lead a cow down it?

The next minute, he felt like the old man was walking too fast. Molly was practically pushing him down the road with an apparent eagerness to get there. He wanted to amble along. Anything to delay the encounter with the bull.

They walked past the tenant house, followed the trail out past the barn to the railroad, and then down to the pasture on the other side of the railroad. They were at the gate and there was no turning back.

Barsh quickly scanned the pasture, looking for the bull. Neither the bull nor the cows were anywhere in sight. The old man opened the gate and led his cow into the pasture.

"Close the gate when you're in," he said.

A slight trembling had overcome Barsh. He breathed deeply, trying to relax, but to no avail. Why was he trembling? His father would have never assigned him this task if it was dangerous. He knew the right thoughts, but he was still shaking with fear.

He knew the source of that fear—Mr. Britton's bull. How it chased him, gaining on him as he ran as fast as he could. Fortunately, he'd reached the tree first and scrambled up it before the bull could hook him with its horns. Then the bull tried to topple the tree as it rammed the trunk with sufficient anger to gore a boy lifeless just for being in the pasture.

It was hard to believe that he was heading into the same pasture with an old man and two cows to meet the same bull. It didn't make sense to him, but he kept following Mr. Wade and the red cow. He did not know the word *surreal*, but he was experiencing its meaning.

The cow trail that they were following led them through a small grove of trees to another large pasture. There was the herd of Jersey cows and the massive gray bull, grazing down by the creek.

Mr. Wade kept walking, straight toward them. Barsh paused for a moment and then set out after the red cow.

He wanted some distance between them, but not too much. He remembered his father's words: Just follow Mr. Wade's lead, and you won't have any trouble. How could he believe that? It contradicted everything he had experienced.

The bull had spotted them and was loping toward them. Not charging but loping. Barsh stopped. Mr. Wade stopped. The bull kept closing the distance. His head was high in the air, his upper lip curled back, his nostrils flared.

The sight of two new cows and that special scent that only the bull could smell had already pushed his blood-red rod from its hairy sheath. The jarring gait of alternating hooves striking the ground had it swinging from side to side.

The bull stopped behind the red cow and gulped her readiness through his nostrils. The cow waited, motionless, tail still arched to one side. The bull reared on it hind legs, its pointed ramrod jabbing until it found its target, its hips then thrusting, buckling the cow's back.

Barsh had been so focused on the bull that he didn't see the bull-yearling until it loped past the bull that was now dismounting Mr. Wade's cow. The bull-yearling was headed straight for Molly. As he tried to mount her, the bull charged and struck it in the side with a blow that knocked it side-winding away from Molly.

The bull-yearling stood watching as the bull prepared to mount Molly. It was as if Barsh and Mr. Wade were invisible to the bull and the bull-yearling. Neither one paid any attention to them. With his cow already serviced, Mr. Wade had turned and started home.

"Follow me when the bull finishes its business."

It didn't take long, and Molly seemed as eager to leave as Barsh. Ahead, the bull-yearling had caught up with Mr. Wade's cow and was trying to mount her.

The bull loped past Barsh and chased the bull-yearling away. This time the bull fell in line behind the red cow, the old man leading them all. The bull-yearling, now following Molly.

Back at the fence, Mr. Wade cracked the gate enough to slip through and waited outside for the bull to service his cow once more.

Barsh had to stop twenty yards from the gate. There was nowhere for him to go. The bull dismounted and turned toward Molly. The bull-yearling had just finished its job on her.

While the bull chased the bull-yearling away from Molly, Mr. Wade pulled his cow through the gate and closed it. Barsh hurried Molly toward the gate, but the bull was on them again before they could exit. He climbed over the gate, still holding the rope.

The bull soon serviced Molly a second time, dismounted, and turned on the bull-yearling, again. Barsh opened the gate, pulled their cow through, and closed it.

The ordeal was over. He could calm down now. His dad had told him the truth. But why didn't he spell the whole thing out for him? It would have been easier for him to get through it, if his dad had told him exactly what would happen.

On second thought, there was no way he would have believed his dad or anyone who told him any such thing. Not after his experience with the bull. And he still would not believe it if he had not experienced it first-hand.

He followed the red cow back to the Wades. The old man turned up his driveway. He continued on Britton Road, eager to finish the task his father had given him. He'd had enough of cows and bulls for a while. Working with Thomas would be a welcomed change.

As he put Molly in their small pasture, he assumed his mother was watching from her bedroom window for his return. She knew he had been given a man's job, and now that he was back, she could stop worrying. He also knew she would never say a word to him or his father about what he had done. It was time to join Thomas for another long day of collecting scrap metal in the country.

***

Barsh worked hard and long that Friday, helping Thomas on a job that should have taken another half-day. He had promised him that he would help him with his junk business between his camping trips. But he would only work Monday through Friday, never on Saturdays.

After supper, he read in his room, waiting for Rayford to come by on his way home from work at Colonial Food. Then they would hang out until bedtime.

***

"Barsh," Rayford whispered through the window screen of his bedroom.

Revived and ready to go, he was at the front door in a moment.

"Hey, you got off early."

"Yeah, they ran out of things for me to do. Let's go to my house. I haven't had supper. Then we'll do something."

"I'm going home with Rayford," he shouted from the front door.

The boys set out down Britton Road at a fast clip. Near the top of the hill, they passed Sam's little hut.

"Is that you, Barsh?" the colored man asked from his bench under a big oak.

"Yes, sir."

"How did you get along with Mr. Britton's bull. Your daddy told me you was taking Molly to see Dingo. Told me he knew you were worried since you'd never done it. I forgot to ask him how you made out. But I can see you must of did all right."

"I was scared to death, the whole time."

"I knows what you mean. Well, don't you boys get in no trouble."

They hurried away and turned up the long driveway to Rayford's.

"Barsh, you don't say *sir* to a nigger."

"Why not?"

"You just don't. It ain't right. Daddy would knock the fire out of me if he ever heard me do that."

They walked in silence. Barsh had been taught to respond to grownups with "sir" and "ma'am." His parents had not told him to treat colored people any differently, so he would stick to his rearing. Rayford could do the same.

Mr. McKay was in the shed behind the house, slurring an old mountain song.

"Daddy must be drinking again. Let's go in the front. I don't want him to see us."

They walked through the house to the kitchen. There was no food on the table or the stove.

"I guess Mama's in her room, too upset to cook supper since Daddy's drinking."

Rayford got a bowl from the cabinet, filled it with Shredded Wheat, and covered the cereal with milk. They sat at the kitchen table, Rayford crunching down the Shredded Wheat.

"I've got an idea, Rayford."

"What's that?"

"Let's go swimming in Acid Lake, tonight. Even if they're working at the fertilizer plant, they won't be able to see us and run us off."

"That suits me."

Rayford's mother appeared in the kitchen door, hesitant and a bit confused by Barsh's presence.

"You want me to cook you some supper, Rayford?"

"This is all I need. You remember Barsh, don't you?"

"How are you, Barsh?"

"I'm fine, Mrs. McKay."

"Mama, I'm hanging out with Barsh's for a while."

"Your father's drinking, again, and he's got his pistol."

"Don't worry, Mama. He won't leave the shed. After he goes to sleep, I'll slip out there and get the pistol before I go to bed."

The plan of swimming in Acid Lake at night worked out well. The moon was bright, and the water was refreshing.

Chapter Twenty-Three

Early Saturday afternoon, Barsh set out for Laura Underwood's house. What a great feeling to know that he could walk up on the porch and be welcomed inside. Would the day ever come when he would be able to visit Amy at her own house? Laura answered the doorbell with Amy on her heels. They were wearing bright sundresses and bubbling with energy.

"Hey, Barsh. Come on in," Laura said.

"Am I ever so glad to see you," Amy said taking him by the hand.

"It's good to see you. Y'all ready to go to the picture show?"

"Mama is driving us," Laura said, "so we've got some time. Let's go out on the back porch."

Laura's older sister, Jo Ann, was sitting at the kitchen table eating a slice of apple pie. Mrs. Underwood looked up from the sink where she was washing dishes.

"You're looking good, Barsh. What about some apple pie? I baked it myself this morning."

"No, thank you, but it sure looks good."

The three of them sat in the same places they had last Saturday. Laura was about to burst with some nervous energy.

"Did you have a hard week working with Thomas?" Amy asked.

"It was hard work, for sure, loading and unloading tons of scrap medal, but I didn't mind. You know I'm playing football this fall, and this will make me stronger."

"Did you and Rayford get together any?" Laura asked.

"Most every night, he'd stop by when he got off work, and we'd do different things."

"Like what?"

"Well, Wednesday night we went swimming in Acid Lake."

"Acid Lake? Where's that?" Amy asked.

"If you walk south on the railroad past Turtle Creek a mile or so, you'll see it, just below the fertilizer plant. The water is so green that I named it Acid Lake.

The first time Rayford and I swam there, a man from the fertilizer plant ran us out. So, we decided to try swimming there at night. It was fun and no one ran us out."

"Hey, I got an idea," Laura whispered, huddling over them. "Let's slip off some night and the four of us go swimming there. Does Rayford have a girlfriend?"

"Maybe."

"Maybe? Don't y'all talk about such things?"

"Not really. I know he went to the picture show with Grace Wilkinson after he got off from work, last Saturday. But we're not like Wesley Workman. He'll tell you everything."

"Guess what, Barsh. Wesley called Amy, Tuesday."

"What did he want?"

"He just wanted to aggravate me. He's planning another trip to Panama City Beach and wanted to know if I'd changed my mind about going with him. I told him I had my own way of getting there."

"And we'll be leaving tomorrow," Laura said. "I can't wait to get there. Amy and I are heading straight for the pavilion. Just think, we'll have a whole week of dancing."

The news that Wesley had called Amy hit an unnerving note with Barsh, and he realized he was guilty, in part, for revealing her number. He'd made a stupid blunder by calling her in his presence. But surely, she didn't tell him that they were going to Panama City Beach, next week.

"Okay, kids. It's time to go," Mrs. Underwood said as she exited the kitchen door and kept walking toward her car.

Laura led the way into the back seat of the Cadillac, Amy followed, and Barsh sat against the door with Amy snuggled against him.

What a strange feeling to be riding in that car. Who hadn't seen Mrs. Underwood, countless times, cruising around town as if she had nothing else to do? Well, there goes Mrs. Underwood in her new Cadillac, he'd heard people on the street say to nobody in particular.

She stopped the car in front of Martin Theatre. Two older boys, probably from the country, stood on the sidewalk, gawking at Laura and Amy as they got out. Barsh insisted on buying Amy's ticket.

"Let's sit in the same place we did last time," Amy said.

"That's good."

He led the way with Amy and Laura following. He sat against the left wall. Amy held his hand and draped her head against his shoulder. She kissed him twice during the movie.

Even though Amy was bolder in her affection, it wasn't quite the same with Laura sitting next to them. Maybe it would be a good thing if she and Rayford could get together to make it a foursome.

After the movie, the threesome went to City Cafe for sundaes. Amy reminisced about their last vacation at Panama City Beach, all the things she and Barsh had done. But that was last summer.

Things had changed. This year, they were taking Laura, and he was anxious about her new influence on Amy.

Laura was distracted. He could see the wheels spinning in her mind, but he had no idea what she was working on. She left the booth and came back with a telephone book.

"Amy, do you know Grace Wilkinson?"

"She's in my class. Long blond hair. She looks kind of sickly to me, like she would break in a hundred pieces if she fell down."

"That's who I thought she was. Do y'all know where she lives?"

"No, but at school, she hangs around Ann Bowman," Amy said. "Ann lives on Cannon Street. Maybe Grace lives near her. They don't seem to have anything else in common."

"There's a Harold Wilkinson listed on Cannon Street. I'll bet you that's her daddy. Are y'all ready to go back to the house? I'll call Mama to come get us."

They stood on the sidewalk in front of City Cafe, waiting for Mrs. Underwood to pick them up. Barsh tensed at the sight of Root Riddle and Doug Conyers.

Root, pants tucked in his brown cowboy boots, quickened his pace when he spotted Barsh. Doug's short legs were double-timing just to keep up.

"Well, looky who we got here, Doug. Chicken Shit Barsh. Well, well, well. What's warped your mind, boy, thinking you can handle two girls?"

"Root, you better get on back down to the pool hall and mind your own business," Barsh said.

"And what are you gonna do, if I don't? You ain't got no ball-peen hammer in your hand, today, to make you feel like a man. I think I'll just cut your ears off and give these girls one apiece."

"Police, help! Police, help!" Amy began screaming and Laura joined her.

The two hoodlums darted across Main Street and disappeared up a side street, running toward the mill village.

"Who was that," Amy asked.

"Root Riddle."

"Why was he picking on you?" Laura asked.

"He's just mean. Hates all the town boys. But me in particular, for some reason."

"What ball-peen hammer was he talking about?" Amy asked.

"Thomas, Becky, and I were talking at Mr. Wade's workshop the other day, and he and Doug came by. When he threatened to violate Becky, I picked up a ball-peen hammer and started pounding an iron rod on their big anvil. Just to let him know I could hurt him with that hammer if he started anything."

"Doug is in your class," Amy said. "Why is he running around with somebody like him?"

"I don't know, but he's headed for trouble if he keeps hanging out with Root Riddle."

"Here's Mama."

Laura scrambled in the back seat. Amy followed and then Barsh.

"Mama, do you know where Cannon Street is?"

"Of course, why?"

"Drive us there. I want to see where Grace Wilkinson lives. Do you know her folks?"

"I don't believe so. Why are you interested?"

"She may be Rayford McKay's girlfriend. He went to the picture show with her last week. I want to see where she lives."

"Oh, I see. You're gonna steal him away from her, right?"

"You know what they say about love and war?"

***

Back at Laura's house, the two girls demonstrated their progress at jitterbugging. It was hard for Barsh to believe that one of the girls dancing before his eyes was his dear Amy, who used to ridicule girls for the same thing she was doing with such abandon. Why did it bother him that jitterbugging had become so important to her?

He was not like the Wades who believed that dancing was sinful. Two-stepping could be quite nice. He would love to be on a dance floor, lost in a crowd of classmates, shifting with Amy to the beat of a slow song.

There was no spectacle to the two-step. It was a moment of closeness for two people, but there was always an audience at the pavilion when people were jitterbugging.

The music ended. Amy plopped down on the settee beside him. Laura turned off the record player.

"Hey, y'all want some ice tea?"

"Goodness, yes," Amy said.

"And you, Barsh?"

"Sure."

Laura left to fix the ice tea. Amy embraced him and kissed him.

"Well, look at you two love birds," Jo Ann said from the kitchen door.

She took Laura's chair and sat studying Barsh, who was feeling a bit uncomfortable under her unyielding eyes.

"What you reading?" he asked glancing at the book she was holding.

"Oh, it's just a love story. That's mainly what I do every summer. I can't wait until school starts back."

"Yuck!" Amy said.

"Barsh, when are you going camping again?" Jo Ann asked.

"Monday."

"How long will you be camping?"

"Until next Saturday."

"That's the same time we'll be coming back from Panama City Beach," Amy said.

"Will Wesley Workman be joining you?" Jo Ann asked.

"He said he would join me Friday night."

"Tell me what it feels like to ride Wesley's motorcycle."

"It's like racing on a powerful horse, except ten times more so."

"He rode by here Wednesday, late in the afternoon. I heard a motorcycle coming down Petty from town, but it turned up Barkley and was gone before I could see who it was. I thought it might be Wesley going to see you or Rayford. Then I heard it coming back down Barkley.

“It was Wesley. He turned up Petty and roared away toward town. I thought that looked like a lot of fun.”

“It is. I’m going to get my own Harley-Davidson when I get older,” he said as Laura returned with the ice tea.

“What’s all this talk about motorcycles? You never told us that Wesley came by here on Wednesday.”

“He didn’t stop, but he did slow down and look at the house before he roared away. He may be wild as a buck, but he sure is good-looking.

“Barsh, you have a good time next week and don’t let Wesley get you in any trouble,” Jo Ann said and left.

“Amy, let’s teach Barsh how to jitterbug.”

“I’m not much of a dancer, Laura.”

“I used to be the same way,” Amy said. “I never dreamed it could be so much fun, until Laura taught me. It’s really not that hard. Come on. I’ll show you the steps without the music.”

“Maybe later. I’ve got to go.”

“Oh, I wish you could stay longer. But if you’ve got to go, I’ll walk you halfway home. You don’t mind, do you, Laura? I’ll be right back.”

“Not at all. Time for a little private talk, right?”

They left by the back porch, holding hands, and headed up Barkley Street. There was a lot of sweet talk between them until they stopped at Wright Street, which was halfway.

Wright Street, like Petty Street, came to a dead end at Barkley. But unlike Petty, there was an unpaved cutout that extended about a hundred feet beyond the sidewalk to the edge of West Woods.

The city at one time had obviously intended to extend the street. Now the cutout was something of an eyesore, which accounted, no doubt, for the vacant lots on both sides, which had grown up with bushes and trees.

“Remember how we used to slip off from your house, cut through West Woods, come out here, and walk to town and back with our parents never knowing?”

“I remember,” he said, also remembering that it was always her idea.

“Let’s make a quick visit to our favorite magnolia tree in West Woods.”

They crossed Barkley Street and entered West Wood through the cutout and hurried to the large magnolia that was located near the backside of the barn and Barsh's secret entrance to his hideout.

"I used to love to climb this tree with you. It was so easy with all the limbs from the ground to the very top. The leaves were so thick, it was almost like being in a tent. Barsh, you were my first true friend, and West Woods was our last playground."

"And you were my first true friend," he said.

"From the very beginning, we were so close. Those were good days but these are even better. Why didn't I want to kiss you back then?"

"I guess we were too young for this kind of love."

"Just think, someday we'll be grown. Nobody to answer to but ourselves. I can't wait."

"I know what you mean. Right now, I'll be glad when your parents will let you date, so we don't have to slip around."

"Thank goodness Laura's parents aren't afraid to have boys around," she said. "If I could follow my heart, right this minute, I'd ask you to take me to your hideout in the barn.

"We'd crawl through the secret entrance and no one would know we were there. We would kiss and kiss and kiss, right there on your old quilt."

"That's a dream to die for, Amy."

"Maybe, that day will come, but now I've got to hurry back to Laura's."

She kissed him. Then they walked back to Barkley Street, where he stood watching her until she entered the back porch of the Underwood's house.

Chapter Twenty-Four

Barsh sat in his treehouse in West Woods. A tufted titmouse was calling nearby in a loud repetitive voice, but he was not interested in his feathered friend. His thoughts were focused on Amy. Perhaps, he should learn how to jitterbug, even though he didn't want to.

He could see Amy's new interest in dancing was going to wedge them apart if he didn't follow her lead. The jitterbug looked easy enough, and both Amy and Laura were eager to teach him.

A gunshot, loud and powerful, turned Barsh's head toward Britton Road. Then a second shot rang out.

Mr. McKay was likely shooting his pistol, again. Rayford had obviously failed to get it away from his father.

Mrs. McKay must be beside herself, he thought. What must it be like to live with a man who goes on week-long drunks that take another week to recover? Rayford had said that it would be days before his father left the shed behind their house, that he would eat little, just drink whisky.

Carolina chickadees were foraging a poplar nearby. He liked the sound of their thin voices and the way they foraged, often hanging upside down.

They would soon be beyond the range of his hearing, but for the moment, they graced him with their presence like a fresh breeze. Something would be dreadfully wrong with the world if there were no songbirds to enjoy.

It would be a while before Rayford got off work. What could he do until then? He did not want to go home nor to the Wades. He decided to practice his diving at Turtle Creek Swimming Hole.

On reaching the top of the steep concrete spillway, he watched the steady stream of waters slide into the shallow pool below. His goal was to glide into that pool from the top of the spillway without jarring against the bottom, and he believed he could if he perfected the angle of his dive. With that goal, he had started near the bottom of the abutment and had already worked his way past mid-point.

He stripped naked, descended the spillway, and dove into the pool, which was only chest deep. Energized by the cool water, he breast-stroked back and forth for a few minutes before practicing his dives.

He had worked himself almost to the top of the spillway with dive after dive, each one being a little more challenging. Again, he sprang for the water. This time his hands slammed hard against the bottom, breaking the force of the dive but his head still jarred against the bottom. He surfaced and breast-stroked back to the abutment.

A colored boy with a fishing pole and a can of worms was standing at the top of the spillway. Turtle Creek Swimming Hole was a secluded area, and Barsh thought nothing about swimming there naked.

From time to time, he had to take cover in the water when a steam locomotive came churning down the track, pulling a few passenger cars. Twice, people on passenger trains had actually spotted him and waved.

This was the first time a stranger had caught him swimming naked. The colored boy sat down at the top of the spillway.

"Hey," Barsh said.

"You can sure ′nough dive. Wish I could do that, but I'm scared of the water. I can't so much as swim a lick."

"The water here ain't deep. Look, I'm standing on the bottom. Come on in. I'll teach you how to swim if you want me to."

"You do that?"

"Sure. Ain't nothing to it. My dad taught me in his boyhood swimming hole out in the country."

"Let me see you make that long dive again. That sure was something else. You can dive like Tarzan. I do like to watch Tarzan at the picture show."

Barsh heaved himself up on the spillway with his arms. He was butt naked but so what? He was glad to have someone who was interested in his new diving skills.

He would try the last dive again, pulling out sooner this time. It worked. He cleared the bottom and came up smiling.

"Come on in. The water's just right."

"How do I know you ain't fooling me? They could be a step-off, way over my head. I heard tell of a boy that got drowned like that.

"He waded out in a creek and all of a sudden, he was gone.

They was people standing on the bank. Couldn't nobody swim to save him."

"This is the deepest place. Look, it's just chest deep on me, and you're taller than me. Watch me."

"You walking with your feet on the bottom?"

"Yeah, come on in. Why would I lie to you?"

The boy pulled off his shoes and stood up to take off his shirt and pants.

"Can I jump in from here?"

"Yes, but look out for that abutment. See how the concrete slants down under the water. Be sure you jump past that."

The boy leaped well past the end of the abutment, lost his footing on landing, and tumbled under the water. He came up sputtering and gasping.

"Don't worry about that. You just lost your balance. Welcome to Turtle Creek Swimming Hole. That's what I named this place. I'm Barsh Roberts. What's your name?"

"Toby Turner. Everybody calls me Toby."

"Where do you live?"

"I stays out on the Antioch Highway. It ain't far from here. Didn't you come by here some time back with another boy? Y'all both had guns. I was fishing on the bank over there."

"Yeah, that was me and my friend Rayford. Toby, let me show you how Dad taught me to swim. Squat down until your head is just above the water. Cup your hands like this. Then stretch your arms straight out and pull them back like this. Let me see you do it."

"Like this?"

"Yeah, that's good. Now lean straight out into the water, breast-stroking as fast as you can, but keep your toes running along the bottom."

"What if I starts sinking to the bottom?"

"That's okay. Hold your breath so you won't get strangled. Then stand up and start over. Let me see you try it."

"Watch me now. Here I go."

"Good! Good! That was good, Toby."

"You think so?"

"Yeah, you keep doing that till breast-stroking is as natural as walking. What you do then is shove off with your feet and start kicking and breast-stroking at the same time.

"You probably won't get far, at first, before you sink. But keep trying until you can swim as long as you want to. Then you can learn to swim like Tarzan with an overhead stroke."

***

Dressed, Barsh and Toby sat on the bank at the top of the spillway, silently gazing into the western sky, where a solitary turkey vulture circled high above the earth. For the moment, a contented peace had settled over Barsh, who was in no hurry to leave Toby.

It felt good to be able to help someone learn how to swim. Moreover, he was almost fifteen, and this was the first occasion he'd had to be with a colored boy. There was something satisfying about that too, although he didn't know exactly why.

"Toby, I've got to go."

"Barsh, I knows your friend Rayford. He works at Colonial Food, don't he?"

"Yeah, his brother manages the meat department. Rayford works most every afternoon until they close. Then we hang out until bedtime."

"He don't like colored folks. I be waiting on the stoop out back of McGilvray's and here he come, walking right past me. He won't even speak to me.

"I gots me a little job at McGilvray's. When they close the doors, I sweeps up the store and takes out the trash. It ain't much of a job, but it's better than nothing. I needs me some daytime work."

"I work part-time for Thomas Wade, helping him with his junk business. He might give you a job if you don't mind working with junk."

"No, I don't mind no kind of work if it pays. Where can I find Mr. Wade? I be sure to ask him for some work."

"He lives on Britton Road. You know where that is?"

"Yeah, it's a dirt road, ain't it?"

"That's right. Thomas lives in the second house on the left. You can't miss it with all that junk. I'll see him sometime tomorrow. You want me to tell him you're looking for a job?"

"Oh, yeah. Do that for me if you will. Tell him I'll be by to see him early Monday morning. Will you be working?"

"No, I'll be camping on Wehadkee Creek all next week. But

I'll be working with Thomas the next week."

A steam locomotive was churning in the distance, coming northwest. It soon rumbled past them, whistled a warning before it got to where Barkley Street crossed the track, and then stopped at the water tank near Britton's Lumber Company. Next it would head off for Birmingham. Barsh knew the terrain, well.

On leaving Turtle Creek Swimming Hole for home, he decided to go back to Laura's house and let them show him how to jitterbug before they left for Florida. The best way to get there was to walk up the railroad to Barkley Street, turn right onto it, and he would soon be there.

As he approached the Underwood house, he was jolted by the sight of a black motorcycle, parked on the street near the back porch. There was no doubt about whose motorcycle it was. Music was coming from the porch.

He continued up Barkley with no intent to stop, since Wesley was there, but he had to check out the scene. There was Amy, as he feared, jitterbugging with Wesley. Jo Ann and Laura were sitting in the wicker settee, watching their performance.

Damn you, Wesley, he whispered. You know I'm in love with Amy. Do you have no honor?

Seething with anger at Wesley and disappointed beyond words at Amy, he hurried home.

Chapter Twenty-Five

Early Monday morning, Barsh set out alone for Camp Wehadkee. He would stop at Workman's Garage to pick up his sleeping bag, but he dreaded seeing Wesley in the worst kind of way. Would he be gloating about dancing with Amy on Saturday or would he keep it to himself, not knowing that Barsh already knew about it. And what would he say if Wesley did bring it up?

Anxiously entering Workman's Garage, he scanned the place for Wesley but did not see him or his motorcycle, which was usually parked just inside the big rollup door. Mr. Workman saw Barsh and started toward him.

"Good morning, Mr. Workman. I stopped by to pick up my sleeping bag. Wesley said it would be all right if I left it. Is he around?"

"No, he should be here, but he didn't come home last night. He got in late Saturday night and then left early Sunday morning. I haven't seen him since. Have you seen him?"

"I saw him in town late Saturday afternoon."

"Did he tell you what he was planning for Sunday? He always goes off somewhere on that motorcycle."

"No, sir. We didn't talk. I just saw him in passing."

"Well, there are two possibilities. He went off somewhere and had a wreck on that damn motorcycle, or he's shacked up with a sorry woman somewhere."

"My sleeping bag is on that cabinet over there. I'd better get it and be on my way."

"I'm gonna drink me a co-cola. You want one?"

"No, thank you. I'm camping on Wehadkee Creek this week, and I need to get going."

As Barsh left Workman's Garage, he was thinking there was another possibility of Wesley's whereabouts and a very troubling one. He had likely gone to Panama City Beach to hang out at the pavilion with Amy and Laura.

It was worrisome enough that Wesley had stopped at Laura's on Saturday. Barsh had tried to explain it away and had half convinced himself that Wesley was just passing by, saw them dancing on the back porch, stopped, and Jo Ann, who had shown an obvious interest in him, had invited him in. She was on the porch with Amy and Laura. If so, Wesley was likely taking turns, dancing with the three girls.

While he was there, he could have learned about the Panama City Beach trip. If Wesley had followed them to Florida, Barsh felt certain it was because Amy would be there.

Jo Ann did not go to Florida with Amy's family, and, of the two girls, Wesley would definitely be more interested in Amy than Laura. And Amy would undoubtedly be impressed, if not seduced, by his good looks, swagger, dancing skills, and sweet talk. Not even a self-deceiving fool could explain that away.

He tried to forget about Amy and Wesley by thinking about what he planned to do when he got to Camp Wehadkee. The first thing he wanted to do was catch a red-eyed bass with the rod and reel that Coon Peters had given him.

He had left the rod at the camp, tied to a sapling, so he wouldn't have to carry it back and forth. The reel and Hawaiian wigglers were in his backpack.

Once he got to the old-growth forest, his spirits began to rise as he became absorbed in the wild beauty of the place. It was such a wonderful forest, so unlike any other he had ever seen. How unfortunate that most of the old forests in his native state had been logged.

He stopped beneath a giant poplar and gazed, with awe, at its towering height. And to think, he would never have experienced such a wonderful tree if he and Rayford had not become friends, and if Rayford had not gone fishing with Wesley on Wehadkee Creek, and if, and if, and if.

You'd have to go back to the beginning of time to explain anything fully. What a scary thought. But there he was in an old-growth forest, suddenly consumed with a powerful urge to break forth into a song of joy to the forest itself.

Where did that come from? he wondered. And what was holding him back? He could answer neither question. But some controlling force in his mind won the moment, and he moved on toward Camp Wehadkee.

The camp was just like he had left it. No one had been there, since he last camped on the site, and that pleased him very much. He changed into a pair of cutoff pants, assembled his rod and reel, and waded out into the creek, ready to catch a red-eyed bass.

Just up the creek, he came to a deep pothole with a rocky ledge on one bank. His heart was already revved up in anticipation. That first strike was always such a rush.

The reel backlashed on his first cast, leaving him with a tangled mess of line to straighten out. He remembered Coon Peters' words: You got to control the speed of the reel with your thumb or it'll get ahead of the lure. Then you got to strip the line down to the end of the tangle and rewind it.

He would like to see Coon. Maybe he would take him a mess of catfish later in the week.

A red-winged blackbird started trilling its distinctive notes nearby. Ah, he thought, maybe that's where his urge to break forth into a wild song had come from. Maybe the songbirds had found the right pattern for living in the forest.

Sometimes they sang and sometimes they were silent. Why should one spend his days in the forest as silent as a possum that never gives voice to anything?

He cast the Hawaiian wiggler again, and he reeled it with a slow steady motion just like Coon Peters had instructed him.

Wham! A red-eye struck it hard. Barsh set the hook and played the fish with a tight rod.

Since he didn't have a net, he waded to a sandbar and pulled the exhausted fish from the creek onto dry land. It was just the right size for roasting whole and all he would need for lunch.

Wow! A redeye on the first good cast. What a creek. He would worry about supper later. His stomach was calling for food.

After broiling the fish over hot coals and eating it, he focused next on digging worms and placing a few set-hooks along the bank of the creek. He already knew the best holes for catching yellow catfish.

He wasn't dependent on just one source of food, however. In addition to the fish, there were blueberries to pick and squirrels aplenty that he could kill with his Dad's .22 rifle.

***

Darkness had swallowed the forest, except for a small circle of space around the campfire. Sitting idly for the first time all day, his thoughts kept going back to Amy. What was she doing that very minute in Panama City Beach? Dancing at the pavilion? Could she be dancing with Wesley Workman that very moment?

He tried to get his mind on something else. Why worry yourself with questions you couldn't answer? But he was losing the battle. He needed to get up and do something before he drove himself crazy. But what?

Up and down the creek, bullfrogs were baring their souls to the forest. Barsh focused his attention on their bold bellowing, which seemed to be proclaiming a simple fact: I'm here! I'm here! Soon there was a stirring within his own soul.

From his memory of Saturday westerns, he could hear the plaintive chants of Indians as they danced in circles. Were their chants composed of real words? Or were their chants more like the *unknown tongues* that the Wades talked about?

Whatever the reason, they danced and they chanted as if it were a natural thing to do, and he decided to follow their practice. Alone in the forest, there was no one to judge him. He could follow his own inner voice.

He stood up and began to circle the campfire in a slow stomp, self-conscious about every step he took. Gradually, he let his body go, until it found its own pace and rhythm. Round and round he silently danced until that first phrase rose from his throat. Ah yah, yah, yah.

He chanted the phrase over and over with rising and falling pitch. Ah yah, yah, yah. Ah yah, yah, yah. Then new chants began breaking forth of their own accord. Into the night, he danced and chanted around and around the campfire until at last he dropped exhausted on the ground.

He lay there for what seemed like a long time, conscious only of his breathing. Then the sounds of the wild began to rouse him—the boisterous bullfrogs, an owl's lonely hooting from some distant tree, the ever-murmuring creek.

He sat up. The fire had burned itself out, but the moon and the stars bathed the camp in a soft light. He crawled into his sleeping bag in the open air and drifted into deep sleep.

***

Wednesday Morning, he left the camp to take Coon Peters a mess of catfish. Although they had shared the campsite for only two nights, he felt like they were true friends, who would never turn against each other, and he was eager to see him.

The old man had wanted to give him his twelve-gauge pump shotgun, one of the first that Winchester made, and Barsh was highly honored by that gesture. That was the kind of gun most men would never give to a new acquaintance, and yet the old man had said that he wanted him to have it.

At length, he reached the backside of the pasture. The herd of Black Angus were grazing at the south end of the pasture. Although Mr. Peters had assured Barsh that his Black Angus bull would not hurt him, he was still anxious about cutting across the pasture. The bull, however, paid him no attention.

"Well, hello, Barsh Roberts," the old man said from the back porch. "You're a sight for sore eyes. Join me and tell me what you've been up to, other than catching some good size yellow catfish."

"I thought you and Mrs. Peters might like a mess."

"Well, thank you. Just leave them in that tub of water there by the steps. I'll clean them after a while."

He dropped the catfish in the tub, propped the rifle against the porch, and climbed the steps onto the porch.

"Get yourself a drink of water. I just drawed a fresh bucket not more than ten minutes ago. Then we'll set in these rockers, awhile. I got some bad news to tell you about a murder Sunday night, just up the road."

The water was good. Barsh drained the aluminum dipper and filled it again, wondering about the murder as he drank his fill. The man's face had turned solemn.

"You know Sam Floyd, don't you? If you've seen Floyd's Taxi, you've seen him."

"I know who he is."

"Somebody killed him Sunday night. Shot him in the back of the head. I'd gone to bed and was just laying there, thinking about a trick I once pulled on a boyhood friend, who was later killed in World War II.

I could hear Edna fingering with something in the kitchen. Other than that, they wasn't no noise about the place. Then I heard a car rattling down the bumpy dirt road, coming this way.

"This is a dead-end road, but we get a fair amount of traffic, mostly at night, on account of the Homebrew Sisters, who live in the last house down there. They do a good business in that old house, whoring and selling bootleg whisky.

"The car stopped just up the road, maybe two-hundred yards before it got down here. There ain't no house there, but I didn't think nothing about it. I thought somebody needed to take a piss before tangling up with one of them Homebrew Sisters.

"Then a loud shot rang out like a .38 pistol. I jumped out of bed and ran out on the front porch in my underwear. Two car doors slammed. I heard some talking, more like shouting, but I couldn't make it out. That was the last I heard for a while. I sat down in the swing, awaiting to see if they would drive on down this way.

"Maybe ten minutes passed, and I heard another car coming down the road. It wasn't in no hurry, just bumping along. Then it stopped. I heard two car doors slam. The next minute, the car took off, heading back the way it come.

"I thought to myself that somebody had just got murdered. And I was right. I hadn't seen nothing yet, but it all stacked up in my mind like they'd planned it all out, ahead of time.

"I slipped in my clothes, put on my shoes, and walked up there. Floyd's Taxi was parked on the side of the road. Old Sam Floyd was slumped over in the front seat, dead as a door knob.

"Edna drove me to town so I could call Sheriff Horton up in Wedowee. Then we came on back there.

"When I heard Sheriff Horton drive up to where Floyd's Taxi was, I walked back up there and told him what I'd heard. How I heard the car stop. Then the shot, the slammed doors, the voices, the second car. He thanked me and said he'd take care of everything. So, I came on back home and went to bed.

"As soon as it got daylight, I was back up there and noticed two sets of tracks on the edge of the dirt road, running away from Floyd's Taxi.

"One was made by a long-legged guy. They was two-yards apart. The heels dug down deep in the dirt like maybe he was wearing boots. The other set was flat and close together like he was a short little fellow."

"I'd like to see those tracks," Barsh said.

"Then let's go. They moved Sam Floyd and the car last night, but those two sets of tracks are still there.

"Here's what I think. Somebody paid them two fellows to kill him, and my mind keeps going back to Bud Drake. You know he runs Drake's Taxi, the only other taxi business in town, and he just added a second car and driver. I'd say Bud Drake wants all the taxi business for hisself.

"Most of that is connected to bootleg whisky. This is a dry county, you know, but if you want some whisky all you got to do is call Bud Drake. It was the same way with Sam Floyd before he got murdered."

"Well, I hope they catch whoever did it," Barsh said.

"Oh, they'll catch them, all right. Sheriff Horton is a good lawman."

Barsh hadn't thought about a connection with Bud Drake, whom he knew only as a sinister figure, but his mind had gone straight to Root Riddle and Doug Conyers, the first time Coon described the tracks leading away from the car.

Root, who always wore cowboy boots, was tall and lanky. Doug, who was short and tiny, wore Keds tennis shoes just like his. Both had dark criminal minds.

"Look at this," Barsh said as he stooped over his own shoe print next to one left by the little guy. "This one was wearing Keds tennis shoes, just like mine."

"Well, I'll be damned. I wonder if Sheriff Horton realized the short one was wearing Keds tennis shoes. I know he had his deputy taking pictures and measuring the tracks the next morning. The next time I go to town, I'll give him a call and tell him."

Barsh was certain his hunch was right. In his mind, Root Riddle and Doug Conyers had no doubt made those tracks. He wanted to tell Coon the connection he was making with those tracks, but something was holding him back. He would wait and talk with his father, who would know what to do.

"Barsh, them fellows ran about fifty yards up the road and waited there beside the road till somebody picked them up. The killing was definitely planned by whoever was driving that second car, and I'd bet a hundred dollars it was Bud Drake.

"He's the one that'll profit by Sam Floyd's death, and he's the one who paid them to kill him. There ain't no doubt in my mind about it."

"Did you tell Sheriff Horton that?"

"I ain't told nobody but you. If word got back to Bud Drake that I was accusing him of hiring somebody to kill Sam Floyd, he'd be looking for revenge. Bud Drake is lowdown wicked. Hell's too good for a man like him."

"Well, if Bud Drake is behind it, I hope Sheriff Horton can make a case against him. Maybe he can track down the two boys who made these tracks. They're likely buddies who're always hanging out together."

"You got a point there, Barsh. I'll bet you that's exactly what Sheriff Horton's thinking. But why do you think they're boys?"

"I don't know. Maybe they were men. But I was just thinking they could be young hoodlums."

Barsh noticed Coon's short shadow on the dirt road. It was almost noon, and he should be heading back to Camp Wehadkee. He'd left a nice yellow catfish on a stringer in the creek, which he planned to broil for lunch.

"Coon, I better be heading back to Camp Wehadkee."

"Oh, that reminds me. I got some bad news about the camp. A timber company over in Georgia is gonna start logging down there any day now.

"That'll be the end of the only old-growth forest that I know of. I wouldn't sell them a right-of-way to get in and out, but them Homebrew Sisters jumped at the chance to make some easy money."

"That is bad news," Barsh said.

What he wanted to say was God damn them. The words had welled up in his mouth, needing to spring forth, but he restrained himself since he had not picked up the habit of cursing, publicly.

"They'll bulldoze a road, likely along Wehadkee Creek, and set up a sawmill inside those woods. As they cut the surrounding timber, they'll keep moving the sawmill deeper, until all those old trees are gone.

"It's just as good that I can't get back there anymore. But I sure hate it for you. I've had my time, but you're just beginning to enjoy that forest."

"At least I got to see how this country used to be," Barsh said. "That means a lot to me. But that also makes it hard to bear, since I've seen those trees and now know they'll soon be gone, forever.

"This will probably be my last camping trip there. I don't want to see what they're doing to that old growth forest."

"I hate to see you go, Barsh. You be careful down there all by yourself."

Chapter Twenty-Six

Barsh broke camp early Saturday morning, never to return, and hiked to Coon Peters' place. After a short visit, he was on his way home, troubled by two pressing concerns, neither of which he had shared with Coon.

Wesley had not joined him at Camp Wehadkee on Friday, and Barsh was relieved that he didn't have to put up with him. But it also left him thinking that Wesley had spent the week in Panama City Beach, where Amy was vacationing with her parents and her friend Laura.

Perhaps, this was the day of reckoning. They should be on their way home. Hopefully, Amy would spend the night with Laura, and he would be able to see her. The question in his mind, however, concerned her response. Would she be glad to see him?

The Sam Floyd's murder was also distressing him. He felt certain that Root Riddle had pulled the trigger. The scoundrel had no conscience.

He also thought Sheriff Horton should know that Root Riddle and Doug Conyers wore the same kind of shoes as those that left the prints at the murder scene. In all likelihood, his father would want him to stand up and get involved. If so, he would probably take him to the sheriff's office that afternoon.

Back and forth, Barsh fretted about Amy and Wesley and then about Root and Doug. All he was doing, however, was going over the same ground.

He shifted his thoughts to football. During spring practice, the coach had promised him that if he set his mind to the task, it would give him a ticket out of the small town and into a new world. Now, he was more committed to this objective than ever.

By late morning, he was back at their barn, where he stashed the rifle in his hideout and walked into the backyard from West Woods, as though he had not detoured by the barn. His dad's truck was not in the driveway. His mother rose from her rocker on the back porch and waited for him at the screen door.

"It sure is good to have you back home. I hope you had a good time."

"Yes, ma'am," he said and stashed his camping things in the corner of the porch. "Where's Dad?"

"He went to town to get some things. He should be back any minute. We'll eat lunch as soon as he gets back. I bet you're starved."

"No, but I sure would like a glass of cold milk."

"Sit down at the table, and I'll get it for you."

His mother handed him a large glass of milk and sat down at her place across from him. She was the dearest of mothers and such a sweet, gentle woman. She never grumbled or complained about anything.

His dad was a lucky man. Barsh could not imagine that his mother had ever looked at another man with lust or longing.

"Excuse me," he said. "I'm going to take a bath while we're waiting for Dad."

Soon he was bathed, dressed, and ready to tell his father about visiting the scene where Sam Floyd was murdered and how he had connected Root Riddle and Doug Conyers with it.

***

It was only fourteen miles to the county seat, but it seemed like a long ride. Neither he nor his dad had much to say on the way. His dad parked his Ford pickup behind the courthouse and led the way straight to the sheriff's office. The door was open.

Sheriff Horton got up from his desk to greet them. He was a big a man. He wasn't fat, just big. He was well over six-feet tall with broad shoulders and long arms, and he had a fierce face with dark eyes and black hair. The two men shook hands and exchanged friendly greetings.

"Robert, this is my son Barsh."

"Glad to meet you, Barsh," the sheriff said grasping the boy's hand for a few manly pumps. "Your daddy and me went to school together. Are you as good at math as he was?"

"No, sir."

"What brings you up this way, Bill?"

"Barsh thinks he might be able to help you with the Sam Floyd murder if you ain't solved it, yet."

"I ain't arrested nobody, but I've got a good suspicion. Tell me what you know, Barsh."

"I was camping earlier this week on Wehadkee Creek. Wednesday morning, I took Coon Peters a mess of catfish. He told me about the murder and showed me the tracks of two people running away from Floyd's Taxi.

"As soon as I saw them, I thought about Root Riddle and Doug Conyers. Root is tall and wears cowboy boots. He stuffs his pants down in them, so you'll be sure to notice them. Doug is short and wears Keds tennis shoes like mine, only mine are bigger. The treads are the same. They hang out together at the pool hall a lot.

"Several weeks ago, I was talking with Becky and Thomas Wade at the shed where they sort out junk, and they came by. Root wanted to see Ruth Wade. He was talking ugly, so we told them to leave.

As I was going home, I noticed the kind of tracks they left in the dirt road. As soon as Mr. Peters showed me the track, I thought about them."

"I don't know them boys, but one of my deputies told me about them. We're already watching them. And now with your information, I'm rather sure they did it.

"If they killed Sam Floyd, someone paid them to do it, and I've got a good idea who that might be. Anyway, if they're the culprits, they'll start spending the money.

"And here's something else I'm looking out for. They may buy an old car and leave town for a while. That's what them Kelley boys did after they robbed the Commercial Bank here.

"They laid low for a while. Then they bought a used car and ran off on a wild adventure, robbing two more banks on the way. But they came back home after a while, bragging about what a wild trip they'd made. Of course, they never mentioned robbing no banks.

"Thanks for bringing Barsh by to see me, Bill. Y'all have a good day and don't be surprised if you hear them boys are in jail on murder one charges, along with the man who hired them to kill old Sam."

Driving back from the sheriff's office, Barsh's dad decided to go by and see his mother, which wasn't much out of the way, but it was another frustrating delay of his plan to see Amy.

He felt sure she would go home with Laura Underwood as soon as they returned from Panama City Beach. If that happened, he would be able to see her there, and he needed to find out if she still loved him.

It was late afternoon when his dad turned the corner of Petty and Barkley, and there was Wesley's motorcycle, parked next to the Underwood's house. Jo Ann, Laura, Amy, and Wesley were all on the back porch.

"What's wrong, Son? Are you worried about them two boys? Sheriff Horton's not going to mention your name to anybody. And if he hauls them into court for the murder of Sam Floyd, you won't be asked to testify. Don't you worry."

"I'm all right, Dad. I just got a little upset thinking about my situation."

"I understand. And if those boys come back over to the Wades', you let me know. I'll talk to Mr. Wade. He can get a warrant against them. They ain't got no business over here."

His mother was in her rocker on the back porch when they drove into the backyard. She rose to meet them at the back door.

"Is anything wrong, Bill? I was getting worried."

"No, all's well. I had a longing to go by and see Mama. Her sister Leona was there, and I stayed too long. As you know, Leona's got the latest news on everybody."

"Supper's ready. I'll put it on the table if you're ready to eat."

"I'm hungry and I'm ready," his dad said. I didn't see Molly in the pasture. Have you milked, already?"

"I was so worried about y'all that I went ahead and milked early."

His dad sat down in his rocker on the back porch. Barsh followed his mother into the kitchen.

"Sorry you were worried about us, Mother."

"That's part of the duties of a wife and mother. What did Sheriff Horton say about your observations?"

"He said he was already watching those two boys. But he was glad I came by. He didn't know about the kind of shoes they wore."

"Are you worried now that you are involved?"

"A little, but Dad says Sheriff Horton knows how to handle the situation."

"Well, you stay clear of those two boys."

"Don't worry, Mother. I'll keep my distance. You know I can run like a jackrabbit. Coming home from my camping trip, I decided it was time for me to spent more time on the football field, preparing for this fall.

Coach Walker thinks I have the potential to be the fastest boy on the team if I work hard on sprinting this summer, so I'm starting today. I still have time to get in a good workout.

"First, I'll stash my camping things in the feed room. Like I told you, I have no intention of camping on Wehadkee Creek, again, now that a sawmill with be cutting those giant trees."

"Don't you want to eat before you go."

"No, it will be best if I wait until I get back."

***

Passing by Bradley High School, he recalled spring practice back in April. Coach Walker had challenged the rising ninth-grade boys to come out for practice with the varsity team. Barsh had taken the challenge, along with about a dozen other classmates.

Bruised and battered after his first experience of scrimmaging with the high school players, Barsh was leaving the gym, when Coach Walker called him into his office.

***

"Roberts, come in and have a seat. I want to talk to you a minute. How you feeling after scrimmage today?"

"Okay."

"You just passed the test of fire this afternoon. You took some hard blows from the big boys and jumped right up. How old are you?"

"I'll be fifteen in September. The year I turned six, I missed the deadline for first grade."

"I thought that might be the case. You're definitely the strongest boy in your class. Even so, you're still a boy, but you've got a fearless heart. And you got speed and talent to go with it. In another year, you'll have an even stronger body that will equal your fearless heart.

"By the time you're a senior, every university in the state will be trying to recruit you with a full scholarship if you stick with me. I'm just gonna scrimmage you rising freshmen a few plays every day. Enough to give you a little experience. Here's what I want you to do.

“Watch the older boys who know how to play the game and learn from them. Then this summer, I want you to work on your running. Jog a few laps around the track at the football field to warm up, then work on flat-out speed from twenty yards to a hundred yards. Sprint and rest, sprint and rest, until you drop.

“If you’ll work hard like that, you’ll get to play some this fall. I got a special play I’m gonna put in just for you. You’ll be a starter your second year. Do we have a deal?”

“Yes, sir.”

***

The football field was rather isolated on the edge of town. He had just left West Point Street and turned down the driveway for the football field, when he heard a motorcycle.

He stopped to see if it was Wesley. It was and Amy was sitting behind him. They roared down West Point Street without noticing him.

Barsh had never felt so betrayed, but he had no intention of confronting Amy. If she wanted Wesley, she could have him. If she didn’t want him, she’d have to find a way to let him know.

He could not believe she knew what Wesley had in mind for her. Nor did he know how she would respond.

Disheartened, he walked on to the football field. He had intended to warm up with a few slow laps around the track and then work on sprints. Instead, he began to run at half-throttle. Round and round the track he sped, pushing himself harder each lap until he dropped on the side of the football field, exhausted. It was time to go home, as soon as he recovered a bit.

After supper, he would sit on the back porch, listening to the Grand Ole Opry with his parents. Then he would go to bed and pray for sleep.

Chapter Twenty-Seven

His mother's voice, calling his father in a near panic, pulled Barsh from troubled sleep.

"What's wrong, Elizabeth?"

"Molly's dead. What could have happened to her? She was fine when I milked her last evening."

"Sometimes cows just die like other living thing."

Barsh dressed quickly and followed his parents to the barn. Molly was stretched out on her side—eyes wide open, belly swollen, both left legs stiff and suspended in the air by the bloating.

"Now I see what happened," his father said. "She got in the feed room last night. Cows don't know when to quit eating crushed grain. It'll kill a cow nearly every time.

"Barsh, you must have left the door open, when you put your backpack and sleeping bag in there, after Elizabeth milked last evening."

The door to the feed room was wide open. No question about that, but Barsh felt certain that he had fastened it, securely. Even so, he struggled for a response.

"I'm sorry, Dad. I thought I fastened the door. You can have the money I've saved. It won't buy a new cow, but you can have it and whatever I make the rest of the summer."

"No, I wouldn't take your money even if we needed to buy a new cow. We don't. It's time for us to get on the milk route. Your mother has been milking way too long."

"Well, I'm sorry about Molly," Barsh said. "This is a bad way for her to die."

"Don't worry about it. We all make mistakes, and you got a lot on your mind of late.

"Today is Sunday. I'll get Joe Tucker to drag her off in the woods behind Britton's Dairy, tomorrow."

"Will he bury her?"

"No, he'll leave her in the woods for the buzzards. They are nature's way of taking care of death in the natural world, and they're glad to help us with the death of domesticated animals."

"Bill, maybe we better not go see Catherine and Oliver, today."

"There's no reason not to go. I know you're wanting to see them and their new baby, again. How old is he now?"

"He'll be a month old this Tuesday. Barsh, don't you want to change your mind and go with us?"

"No, ma'am, I have plans to keep, but tell her that I'll be coming for a visit before school starts back."

"You'll go to church this morning, won't you?"

"Yes, ma'am."

"Catherine wants us to get here in time to eat dinner with them, but I'll cook something for you before we leave."

"Don't do that, Mother. I'll make myself a sandwich."

"This will be your Sunday dinner. I'm fixing some country-fried steak with onions, creamed potatoes, and green beans. Help yourself to it, and we'll eat the rest for supper."

***

There wasn't a sound in the whole house as Barsh sat at the kitchen table. The only light in the room seeped in through the one window on the north side and the door that opened onto the back porch. He had not bothered to turn on the overhead light.

Having finished his Sunday dinner, his thoughts were focused on their dead cow. At first, he felt certain that he had fastened the door to the feed room. Now, he was having doubts.

He was beside himself at the time, having just concluded that he had lost Amy to Wesley Workman. Maybe he had been too preoccupied to remember to fasten it.

It was a beautiful Sunday afternoon. He would like to practice target shooting with his father's rifle in the woods beyond the railroad. He had already made a lot of progress, but he wanted to get better. Maybe Rayford would go with him.

He decided to take the rifle from the barn loft to his treehouse and leave it there, before checking with Rayford. He wasn't ready to reveal his hideout to him.

He opened the barn door, stepped into the stall, and studied Molly. A green blowfly was already buzzing about one of her big eyes. Death was an ugly sight.

He entered the feed room and climbed the ladder to his hideout. Someone had moved the rifle. It was propped against the south wall, not in the southwest corner where he always left it.

He walked to the north end of the loft. Someone had rumpled his quilt. Someone had been in the barn loft after his mother had milked Molly and didn't fasten the door to the feed room on leaving. But who could it have been?

From his rocker on the back porch, his father had watched him enter the barn and return. He would have also seen anyone else who might have entered the barn through its door between then and nightfall.

Amy was the only one who knew the secret entrance from West Woods. She was the likely one who had entered that barn that evening. And if so, she was not alone.

He could see the whole story unfolding. Amy had shared the place with Wesley as a safe place for them to smooch, and they had decided to take advantage of it during their motorcycle excursion late Saturday afternoon.

At Amy's suggestion, Wesley had eased the motorcycle down Wright Street, crossed Barkley Street into the cutout, and stopped at the edge of West Woods. Then she led him to the back of the barn, and they entered through the secret passageway.

She had expressed a desire to do that with Barsh, just a week ago. Now she had done it with Wesley, and they had failed to chain the feed door, when they left. They were responsible for Molly's death. There was no doubt in his mind.

He left the barn through the secret entrance to check for tire tracks of the motorcycle in the cutout. There they were as well as the mark that the kickstand had made in the dirt. That evidence confirmed his conclusion.

He could not undo what had been done but he could stop their smooching in his hideout. He left for the house to get a hammer and nails. Returning to the back side of the barn, he nailed the hinged boards to the studs, so no one could enter the barn that way.

Having no further use of the hideout, he decided it was time to burn the old quilt in the firepit before his tepee. Up the ladder he climbed, gathered the quit, and hurried to his tepee.

As he dropped the quilt in the firepit, he noticed that it was soiled. On close examination, he took it to be semen.

Now he knew there had been more than just smooching. The only thing he didn't know was whether or not Amy had consented. It was possible that Wesley had force himself on her.

The semen reminded him of what Wesley told him, when he gave him a packet of rubbers: Once, I got caught without one, when Jack was ready to go. That's a hell of a place to be, because there's no stopping Jack when that happens. I could have fathered a child. Fortunately, I didn't. But that ruined my relationship with the girl.

The lack of a rubber would account for the semen on the quilt. It could also prove damnable for Amy. In spite of his disappointment, Barsh did not want her to get pregnant at her age.

With those ponderous thoughts, he struck a match and set the quilt on fire. The small flame took hold of the quilt and began to consume it.

As the flames rose higher and higher, he wished Amy could see the quilt disappearing in smoke, not that it would have provoked any regret in her. But she would know the symbolic meaning of the flames. They were consuming his dreams of a future with her.

For some reason the story of Samson and Delilah came into his mind. Just a few Sundays ago, Dr. Franks had preached on the dangers of paganism.

The ancient Philistines were the pagans for that day's lesson. Barsh was especially interested in the story of how the Philistines had invaded Palestine and conquered five coastal cities with superior weapons made of iron. They drove the Hebrews, who were still living in the bronze age, back into the hill country.

The chief god of the Philistines was Dagon, depicted as half man and half fish, a grand symbol of pagan philosophy.

Their most famous woman Delilah, a symbol of pagan sex, was the very flesh that doomed Samson, the strongest man among the Hebrews.

Woe to anyone who turns aside to a woman like Delilah. Virtuous women, however, lead men to light and redemption or so Dr. Frank had proclaimed.

Barsh understood the powers a woman could have over a man. But Amy was no Delilah. Her heart was not evil.

She had no way of knowing what kind of person Wesley really was, that he was not the right person for her, that he was just using her for his own pleasure. She would likely pay for her mistake of trusting Wesley.

The memories of friendship and first love were woven into the very fabric of who Barsh was and what he would become. Amy would always be that special friend of his boyhood, but above all she would be his first love.

Beyond that, she would play no role in his imagination of the future. But where would his imagination take him now? How could one live without a dream?

He stirred the fire with a stick. He did not want a single fragment of the quilt left unburnt.

Sick of people, Barsh realized he didn't even want to see Rayford. What could he do? He would go to the football field and run himself to exhaustion, again.

He had solved the puzzle of the unsecured feed room, but he could not tell the story. In his father's eyes, he would always be responsible for Molly's death.

As soon as the flames had totally consumed the quilt, he would return the rifle to his father's closet. But he did not know whether or not he would tell his father that he had deliberately disobeyed him by taking it.

He knew his father would not punish him, but he would be disappointed in him—even view it as a mark against his character. That would hurt him more than any punishment.

"Hey, Barsh," Becky said. "What you burning?"

"It's an old quilt that I don't need anymore."

He had been so engrossed in his thoughts that he did not hear Becky coming. How pretty she was all dressed up in her Sunday best, a light green linen dress that highlighted her dark features. Her long, black hair, that had never been touched by scissors, fell over her shoulders, as she leaned to examine the last fragments of the quilt that had flared up.

"Becky, our cow is dead. Last night, she got in the feed room and ate too much."

"Where is she?"

"She's still in the stall."

"Can I see her?"

"If you want to, but it's a horrible sight. She's got that death stare in her eyes, and she's bloated like she's about to pop."

"I want to see her anyway."

They walked to the barn and he opened the door. Inside the stall, they stared long at the dead cow without saying a word. Then Becky broke the silence.

"What are y'all gonna do with her?"

"Joe Tucker is going to drag her off in the woods, tomorrow. Let get out of here, Becky. I've got plans for the afternoon."

"What are your plans?"

"A hard workout at the football field. Coach Walker says that if I work hard on my running this summer, I'll get to play some this fall."

"I've never seen a football game. But if you're playing, I'm gonna be there. I don't care what anybody says about sin and foolishness. I'm gonna watch you play. What are you doing when you leave the football field?"

"Rayford and I are supposed to get together. I don't know what we'll do the rest of the afternoon, but we'll probably go for a swim in Acid Lake sometime after dark, so we won't get run off."

"Will you stop by your tepee on the way home? I was there last night and nobody missed me. They were all sleeping. I'm doing it again tonight, so please come by."

"I don't know when I'll get home, Becky, but I'm sure it will be late."

"I don't care how late it is. I fell asleep there last night. Wake me up if I'm asleep."

"All right, I'll stop by just to check on you. But you've got to stop this. I'm telling you Root Riddle could really hurt you if he sees you going down there."

"Root Riddle don't scare me."

"Well, he does me. Anyway, I've got to go. I've got some hard running to do. See you later."

"Bye, Barsh. Be careful if you and Rayford decide to go swimming in Acid Lake."

The quilt was ashes and he left to get his father's rifle. On the way, he was thinking how fickle love can be. Becky loved him but he didn't love her. He loved Amy but she had thrown him away.

Back in the loft, he took a last look through the knothole into Amy's back yard. Never again would he do that. Never again would he stretch out on the old bed of oats.

Then taking the rifle, he left the loft for the last time and replaced it in his father's closet. Then he left for the football field.

Chapter Twenty-Eight

At the north end of the football field, Barsh set his mind on speed. He wanted to be the fastest boy at Bradley High, and he would if hard work and determination could make it so.

During spring practice, Coach Walker had described him as fearless. Now, something had changed within him, driving him toward a new goal.

Amy had been the only thing of exceptional worth he had found in his small hometown. Now, that he had lost her, he was ready to bid the place goodbye. If that took a football scholarship, that's what he would get.

The sun was scorching hot, the worst possible time of the day to be working out, but better to run than explode with rage that was swelling in his chest against Wesley. Crouching in a halfback stance on the twenty-yard line facing the goal, he imagined Wesley defending the goal line, imagined himself running with all his might straight at him, knocking him flat as he crossed into the end zone.

He could hear David Dunn, the quarterback, barking the signals. Hup one. Hup two. Barsh was off, racing as fast as he could. Just so, he sprinted up and down the field, varying the distance—twenty yards, thirty yards, fifty yards, one-hundred yards, until he fell, exhausted, onto the grass.

He lay on his back, his eyes burning with sweat. His mind was calm, empty. At length the outside world began to creep into his consciousness—a small plane droned overhead, a car horn blared in the distance.

Sitting up, he looked around. The place was still desolate. He would find Rayford and kill the rest of the day with him. But first he would go home, bathe and change clothes.

***

It was late Sunday night, when he and Rayford split up and headed for their separate homes. All the lights in the neighborhood were out except the one on his back porch. His parents always left that light on for him to enter the unlocked house.

He hoped that Becky had come to her senses and stayed away from his tepee. But he would check on her as he promised.

The flap to his tepee was open. He knelt in the pale moonlight, listening for her presence. Not a sound.

"Becky?" he whispered and waited. "Becky, are you here?" he asked and waited a moment.

"No, no," she moaned.

"Becky, what's wrong?"

"Oh, Barsh, you woke me out of a horrible nightmare. You were backed into a corner, and Root Riddle was coming at you with a big knife. You wanted to run, but he had you trapped."

"It's all right now, Becky. Dreams can scare the devil out of you, but they're still just dreams."

"That was the worst one I've ever had. Oh, I remember the one you had where a Jersey bull was chasing you through a swamp filled with water moccasins. Was that your worst dream?

"No, that one was about a rabid dog. I'll tell you about it sometime but not tonight. How was your day?"

"Not good. Root Riddle and Doug Conyers came by late this afternoon. Ruth and me were home by ourselves. Thomas was off courting, and Daddy and Velma had gone to the country to put flowers on Mama's grave.

"Ruth didn't want to go, so she acted like she was sick, so I got to stay with her. I was setting in the front room looking out the window, when this old car, that I didn't recognize, turned up our driveway. Doug Conyers was setting in the passenger seat and Root Riddle was driving.

"He commenced to blowing the horn. I ran to tell Ruth who it was. She made me go tell them to leave.

"I left by the back door and told them to leave and never come back. Root got out of the car and said he wasn't leaving till he talked to Ruth.

"I didn't know what to do. Then I thought about your daddy. His truck was in the driveway, so I knew your folks were back from Woodland.

"I made a dash across the yard toward your house, but Root took off after me. The long-legged devil caught me and started dragging me toward the car.

"I started screaming and hollering for help. Your daddy came running down the road, yelling for Root to let me go. He turned me loose, ran for his car, and gunned it back up Britton Road."

"It was a good thing that Dad was home. Root could have dragged to into that car and taken you off somewhere. If he comes back, don't leave the house.

"Please listen to me, Becky. You must never come down here again. Root's as sorry and mean as anyone can be. That's what I was trying to tell you this afternoon. It's dangerous for you to hang out in this tepee."

"But it's the only place we can talk, just me and you. You're the only friend I have. When I'm aching to see you, it helps to come here and curl up on your old burlap bag. You may not believe this, but I get this peaceful feeling, even though you're not here.

"Sometimes I think about the things I want to do when I grow up. I want to cut my hair, wear lipstick, dance, and go to the picture show."

"Yes, you can and should do those things. I've got to go, but first I'll walk you home. Then it's bedtime for me. I'm weary down to the marrow of my bones."

"Okay, if you'll walk me home."

***

Headed back up Britton Road, Barsh noticed that a light was on in Amy's bedroom, although it was past her typical bedtime. Perhaps she was sick. No, if that were the case, there would be other light on. She was likely reading late into the night. But why?

Maybe, she was deeply troubled, having realized that Wesley was not the one for her, that he had taken advantage of her, and she had turned to reading to ease her mind.

If so, he wondered, would she come back to him, declaring her true love for him. Could the magic ever return?

Back in his room, he stripped to his shorts and stretched out on top of the bedcovers. After tossing and tumbling with mounting disquieted, he left his bedroom and exited the front door to see if the light was still on in Amy's room. It was out. He returned to his bedroom and lay down in darkness, once again.

Chapter Twenty-Nine

Barsh woke after a fitful night of strange dreams. The morning light had filled his room. The house was quiet. He could smell the aroma of fried bacon, and then he heard his mother's soft voice in the kitchen. His dad was still at home.

It was Monday and he remembered the dead cow. Had his dad made arrangements to have her taken away?

He had not seen his parents since Sunday morning when they left for Woodland. Such a short time, and yet so much had happened to burden him down, things he would have to keep hidden in his own heart.

He felt like a stranger in his own house, as he dressed and then entered the kitchen.

"Good morning, Mother! Dad! I almost slept through breakfast."

"You got in so late last night, I was going to let you sleep this morning," his mother said.

"Barsh," his dad said, "Joe Tucker is coming around ten o'clock this morning to get Molly. I want you to stay here at the house until he comes. He'll be driving a tractor. After he drags Molly off, you can be about your business."

"Yes, sir."

"Fix your plate and I'll pour your milk," his mother said.

He sat down at his place and quickly ate his breakfast. His father sat looking out the back door. His face looked unusually serious. An urge welled up in Barsh to come clean with him.

"Dad, I've been thinking about what you said about making mistakes. I've certainly made my share. There's one I need to tell you."

"What's that?"

"I disobeyed you about your rifle. I knew I could handle it, safely, so I've been taking it on my camping trips. Between trips, I kept it in the loft of the barn. While you and Mother were in Woodland, yesterday, I returned it to your closet."

"That's what I assumed, when I found it missing. I was upset, when I first discovered you had taken it, but by the time I next saw you, I'd had a change of heart. You may not believe it, but I can still remember what it feels like to be a boy.

"I went against Papa more than once before I left home. You trusted yourself to handle the rifle, safely. And I misjudged you. So, I share in the blame. Does Rayford have a rifle?"

"Yes, sir, he has a Remington just like yours, otherwise I wouldn't have disobeyed you.

"I intended to tell you that I'd taken it, but I kept putting it off, because I knew you'd be disappointed in me."

"Well, I'm not disappointed that you disobeyed me. You can now consider the rifle yours and keep it in your closet."

"Thanks, Dad. I will and I'll pass it on to my son if I'm blessed with one. I'll tell him it once belonged to his grandfather."

"Well, I hope you'll have a son that will make you as proud as you do me."

"Then my challenge will be to become as good a father as you."

After a brief moment of silence, his mother shifted the conversation.

"Barsh, those two boys came back trying to see Ruth Wade yesterday, and they grabbed Becky when Ruth wouldn't talk to them. Your father had to run them off."

"I'm sorry to hear that, but I'm glad you were home, Dad," he said deciding not to tell them that he already knew. "Do you think they'll come back now that you ran them off?"

"I don't know. That tall one seems to have his mind fixed on the Wade girls."

"Well, I hope Sheriff Horton will soon arrest them."

"I'm confident that he's making a good case against them."

"How was the trip to Woodland?" Barsh asked shifting the subject.

"Very good," his mother answered. "Catherine and Oliver were disappointed that you weren't with us, but they were pleased to learn that you will be visiting them before school starts back.

"Karen Phillips came by. She's very lonesome and would like to be back in Atlanta with her friends. She said to tell you to please come, soon, that you would love Uncle Jim's new saddle horse."

"It's a quarter horse, the kind cowboys ride," his father said.

"I would like to have my own saddle horse, someday. Dad,

why don't we move back to the country?"

"I thought you liked living here in town. You'd have to ride the bus to school if we lived in the country."

"It would be worth it if I could have a saddle horse."

"I wouldn't mind moving back myself. Your mother and I will talk about it. Well, I've got to go to work."

***

Midmorning, Barsh heard the John Deere tractor putt-putting down Britton Road and went outside to meet Joe Tucker. The colored man whirled in the driveway and hit the clutch with one foot, the brake with the other, as he idled the tractor with the hand lever.

"Where's the cow?" he shouted over the John Deere.

"In the barn. Follow me."

Barsh opened the stall door as the colored man backed the tractor in place and shut it down. He was a tall strong man, wearing faded overalls and black rubber boots that almost reached his knees.

"You Mr. Bill's boy?"

"Yes, sir. I'm Barsh."

"Yeah, I done seen you, up and down Britton Road, and now I knows you by name. Call me Big Joe. That's what my people calls me.

"Let me git my chain out of this here box, and I'll drag that cow out of there and into the woods. She'll soon be stinking. I knows all about dead cows. I done drug off another one, last week."

"How long have you been running Mr. Britton's Dairy?"

"Lord, I can't even remember. I was just a young man when ol' man Britton moved me from the country. I remember when y'all moved here, and it was a long time before that. I likes doing the dairy. It's a lot better life than what I had in the country."

"Big Joe, can I follow you when you leave? I want to see where you take the cow."

"Oh, yeah. I be glad to have you with me. You can stand on this here tow bar and hold onto the seat. You don't want to be afoot in that pasture across from the railroad. That's where old Dingo stays. That bull will gore you to death. But he won't pay us no mind as long as we're on this here tractor."

Big Joe wadded the chain in his arms and jumped down from the John Deere.

"This here chain ain't long enough to reach her. I gots to drag that cow this way some."

He grabbed a curled horn in each hand and dragged Molly past the door.

"That'll do. Now, I'll hook this chain around them horns, and we'll be on our way to the cow graveyard. The buzzards be glad to see us coming."

Barsh stood on the tow bar behind Big Joe, holding onto the seat, watching his every move, as he eased the tractor forward. Out on the dirt road, Big Joe revved the tractor up a notch, and they chugged along in first gear.

Auntie Dee, her head tied up in a red kerchief, was boiling something in the big black pot beside her little hut. She looked up and waved to Big Joe, who stopped the tractor on the side of the road.

"Be right back. I needs to tell Auntie Dee something."

He jumped down and ran toward the old woman in long, slow strides, his black rubber boots pounding the ground.

Barsh looked back at the skid mark the cow was making in the dirt road. Blue Jays were chattering in a tall oak beside Sam's hut.

They reminded him of Rayford's father. How he hated blue jays and niggers. Big Joe was on his way back, walking now.

"Barsh, you knows Auntie Dee, don't you?"

"Dad sends me over there with groceries from time to time, but I don't know much about her. I used to wonder how she made a living."

"Sam ain't done told you about Auntie Dee and ol' man Harold Britton?"

"No, sir."

"He's long dead, but he was Mr. J. P. Britton's daddy. Well, Mr. Harold Britton was how she made a living. She was his woman.

"He moved Auntie Dee to that little hut way back when she was nothing but a young gal. Sam done told me the old man fixed it so she could live there till the day she dies."

"I never heard it mentioned."

"Auntie Dee ain't showed you her fancy bed?"

"Never been inside her house."

"They say it's from the old Britton home place in the country. Four big posts with a high headboard. Ain't no hardworking colored woman be sleeping in a bed like that.

"Along after dark here come Mr. Harold Britton, parking his new automobile out of sight behind her house. Lord help me, here I am done running my mouth about Auntie Dee. But you can't help but like Auntie Dee.

"Old as she is, she got a mind that will keep you laughing. You take her a mess of something to eat, and she make you glad you done took the trouble."

The John Deere was off again, the cow dragging along behind. Barsh was thinking about Auntie Dee and her bed. He had assumed that his dad had bought the groceries for her, as an act of charity.

"Now he was thinking that Mr. J. P. Britton must have sent them as a part of his father's arrangements. Grownups were much more complicated than he had ever imagined. What else was there for him to learn about the ways of the world?

Big Joe didn't even slow down when he passed the tenant house at the dairy—yard chickens scattered all over the place, some clucking and squawking to get out of the way. The John Deere putted on up the cow trail to the railroad crossing. Big Joe cut the throttle back and eased across the tracks.

At the pasture fence, Barsh opened the gate, then closed it, when the dead cow cleared. His memory took him back to the morning he led Molly through that same gate to be serviced by Dingo. Now, Big Joe was dragging her to the cow graveyard.

Barsh saw the herd off to the right on the side of the hill. It was easy to spot Dingo. He threw up his head and trotted away from the herd toward the tractor. Then he stopped and watched them as they moved on toward a grove of trees where the hill got steeper.

Big Joe followed a twisting trail through the trees and stopped the tractor near a barbed-wire fence. Sun-bleached cow skulls and bones were scattered all around.

"This is it, Barsh. The final resting place, as they say. Ain't gonna be no resting for this cow for a while though. The buzzards be here before the sun goes down."

Big Joe jumped down and unhooked the chain from Molly's horns.

"Have you ever been back in those woods on the other side of that fence?" Barsh asked.

"Mr. Britton's pasture ends right here, and this is as far as I've been. I don't know what's back in there."

"I'm going to find out starting right now. I'm looking for a new place in the woods to camp out."

"You ain't going back with me?"

"I'm checking out those woods, while I'm over here."

'How you gonna get back through this pasture, past old Dingo?"

"If I follow this fence, won't I come out at the railroad?"

"Oh, yeah. I didn't think about that. You can go either way, left or right. Just follow this here fence, and it'll take a turn back to the railroad. That'll git you by old Dingo, but you gots to look out for snakes in these woods."

***

It was a seasoned second-growth forest, mostly hardwoods with a sprinkling of pines. The trees were large but nothing to compare with those at Camp Wehadkee. There was little undergrowth, which made for good walking. Hiking south, Barsh took his time, noticing the lay of the land.

He crossed two dry hollows then came to a branch, where he stopped to study how the water trickled over a series of flat rocks from one small eddy to another. In the crystal-clear water of each little hole, he saw two or three minnows and a few crawfish.

He was sure he could catch the crawfish with his bare hands. There was no place for them to go. A dozen crawfish tails, roasted over hot coals, would make a good meal.

He decided to hike down the beautiful little stream. Maybe it would soon lead him to a big creek with a good campsite.

Passing a number of large hickory trees, he noticed numerous shell fragments scattered among the leaves, a sure sign that squirrels abounded there. He would have no trouble killing a squirrel when he wanted one for a good meal.

At length he came to a big creek, flowing southwest. A beautiful old beech tree stood beside the creek on the south side of the branch. Jumping the branch, he walked straight to the tree and carved his initials in the light gray bark with his Barlow pocket knife.

This will be Camp Beech, he thought. The very act of naming the place reminded him of Amy. That was something she had taught him.

It was the first time he had thought about her since Big Joe drove into their driveway on the John Deere tractor. Keep busy, he said to himself. That's the only way to live without her.

It was an easy trek back to the railroad. Once on the railroad, he decided to go by Turtle Creek Swimming Hole for a few dives from the spillway.

***

After a few dives, he sat down at the top of the spillway. Soon two bitter visions were back in his head—one of Amy giving herself to Wesley in his hideout and the other of him forcing himself on her. Would he ever know which one was true?

Whatever the truth, Barsh had to find a way to get over Amy, and he would with time. He also had to learn how to deal with the new Amy. They were still neighbors, living in a small town. He was bound to run into her from time to time.

Chapter Thirty

After lunch Wednesday, Barsh left the house for the library to return a novel and check out another.

It was Laura's turn to spend the night with Amy if their pattern of visitation had not changed. He thought they might be sunbathing behind the Burdette's garage, but they were nowhere in sight.

Striding down Crawford Street, he saw them walking toward him. They had likely been to town and were headed back to Amy's house.

It has been almost two weeks, since he had talked with Amy. Now, they would soon meet on the sidewalk. He had never felt such strange emotions. How would she greet him? Would she stop and talk to him? In a flash, his questions were answered.

As soon as the girls saw him, they stopped and huddled. Then they crossed the street to the other sidewalk and hurried past him, their blank faces staring straight ahead.

Man, did that hurt. He would never have imagined in a thousand years that his old friend would deliberately shun him like that.

Nothing Amy could ever do would make him act that way. He would never forget the sweetness of their past relationship, even if love had withered and died.

The good days of the past, alone, would require a courteous response to her presence, always. How could someone's heart change so radically in such a short time?

Her behavior was beyond his understanding. In a way, the shunning hurt him more than the fact that she had stopped loving him.

Troubled and confused, he kept walking toward the library. Then he stopped, no longer interested in the library. What could he do? Home was the only place he felt like retreating to, and there he trudged.

***

It was early afternoon on a clear day, and he was indoors,

stretched out on his bed doing nothing, not even reading. When had that ever happened?

His mother was concerned about his behavior and asked him to come sit with her on the back porch. He tried to set her mind at ease by insisting that he was just tired and need to resting up before he and Rayford got together that night. She accepted his explanation and decided to bake him some teacakes.

Alone again, he remembered Karen Phillips' thin letter that came in Tuesday's mail, fetched it, and started reading it, again.

Dear Barsh,

When are you coming? I'm going crazy on this farm. All I can do is ride Uncle Jim's new quarter horse and skate in the empty cotton house, which, as you know, ain't big enough to do much skating in. How I miss the skating rink in Atlanta.

Hurry and get here. Uncle Oliver's horse has a bad hoof, but you'll love Uncle Jim's quarter horse. We'll ride him together to Bear Creek every day for a good swim. Can't wait to see you. I'm desperate.

Karen

Maybe, it was time for him to visit Aunt Catherine and Uncle Oliver. He was also desperate and needed a change. Something new to keep him busy, to help him get over the pain of being dumped and shunned by Amy. The more he thought about a week in the country, the more appealing it became.

There was a new quarter horse to ride, and he looked forward to experiencing the difference between it and Uncle Oliver's five-gaited horse. And there was Karen Phillips. Never a dull moment with her on the scene.

An only child, Karen was a feisty city girl, whose father had left the family farm as a young man to find work in Atlanta. There he met and married a city woman.

When Karen was twelve, her mother went back to work. Instead of hiring a sitter, she cut a deal with the manager of the neighborhood skating rink, where Karen loved to roller skate.

After school, she would hang out there until her mother could pick her up. Summers, she was sent to Granny Phillips' to while away the days until school started back.

Granny Phillips, long widowed, lived on the old home place. Her oldest son, Barsh's Uncle Oliver, owned a farm that joined hers. Her youngest son Jim, a bachelor, had stayed at home and farmed the place after his father died.

In recent months, he had turned the place into a cattle farm and taken a job in Anniston, where he boarded Monday night through Thursday night. Weekends, he came home.

On his past visits, Barsh and Karen were back and forth between the two farms every day. He imagined that would be the same if he decided to go again this summer.

In her letter Karen had promised him that they would ride Uncle Jim's quarter horse to Bear Creek for a good swim, every day. The Bear Creek swimming hole was in the backwoods, maybe two miles from Granny Phillips' house.

When they first heard about it, last summer, they started begging Uncle Jim to take them. He promised he would but kept putting them off.

Finally, the morning of the afternoon that Barsh's parents were coming to take him home, he took them. It was a spectacular place below a waterfall. Now, Barsh was wondering if he and Karen would be allowed to go by themselves, since her Uncle Jim was working in Anniston during the week.

Soon he was reliving their experience at Bear Creek. How they touched each other, while diving through the others legs. But that had happened last summer. What would Karen be like now? Could this be the summer of another new first for them?

"Barsh," his mother called from the kitchen, "the teacakes are ready. Come get them while they're hot."

"I'm on my way," he said and left for the kitchen."

"What would you like to drink?"

"Milk."

She poured the milk and sat across the table, smiling in her caring way.

"Mother, I've decided to visit Aunt Catherine and Uncle Oliver, tomorrow if that's possible. Does the bus still run every morning?"

"As far as I know. You can walk up there and check."

"What time is it?"

"A little after three."

"That's good. I'll check their schedule when I finish the teacakes."

The bus schedule had not changed, and he bought a ticket for Woodland. On leaving the bus station, he stopped in the Gulf Service Station, bought a candy bar, and then in the privacy of the outside bathroom, he dispensed two packs of rubbers from the vending machine. He had decided to trash those that Wesley had given him. It was time for him to look out for himself in that department. He did not know if he would need one during his visit to Woodland, but he honored the Boy Scout Motto: Be Prepared.

Chapter Thirty-One

Walking down the dusty dirt road, Barsh was thinking about Karen Phillips. It had been a year since he last saw her. Like him, she had likely changed a lot, but he could not imagine how.

At least from her recent letter, he knew some things had not changed. She was still big into roller skating, and she had not lost her love of horseback riding.

The thing that stuck in his mind from the letter was her promise that they would ride Uncle Jim's new quarter horse to Bear Creek every day for a good swim. Surely, she knew that would evoke the memory of their last swim in that creek.

Rounding a curve, he could see his aunt and uncle's farmhouse beyond the cotton field that stretched all the way from the main road to the edge of their front yard.

The two-mile hike from the bus stop in Woodland had seemed like a breeze to him. What a difference a year could make in one's ability and perspective. Only last summer, the packed suitcase had taken a toll on him.

He shifted it to his left hand and turned down the narrow road that ran past the edge of the cotton field. The cotton had been plowed clean for the last time, laid-by as they called it.

In past visits, Barsh typically visited before that happened. He liked to follow behind his uncle, when he was plowing, and look for a flint arrowhead that the plow occasionally turned up.

Uncle Oliver had given him a few from his collection, but there was nothing like finding a flint arrowhead. It gave him such a deep satisfaction, knowing that his were the first white hands ever to touch the remains of an arrow that some Indian had drawn and let fly from his bow, hundreds or even thousands of years ago.

It would be good to be back in the country, again. The tin-roofed, clapboard house was so familiar that it would almost seem like coming home.

A porch stretched across the front of the house. It was furnished with two rocking chairs and a two-seat swing, hung from the ceiling.

The porch on the back of the house had a well-curb rising through the floor on one side, a worktable and straight chairs on the other side. Nothing was better for one's thirst than water just drawn from that well.

He loved to open the hatch on top of the curb and drop the galvanized bucket down the hole, breaking its speeding fall with the palm of his hand against the smooth oak windlass. When the bucket hit the water, he would wait for that slight tug on the rope after it filled and began to sink. Then he would crank it up and drink his fill of fresh, cool water.

From the front door, you entered a large sitting room with an open fireplace. Behind it, opening onto the back porch, there was a big kitchen-dining room with large walk-in pantries on both sides.

In one pantry, there were pots and pans and pressure cookers and meat grinders and the like.

The other was filled with all kinds of preserved food to help get them through the winter. Wooden shelves were lined with home-canned vegetables in quart and half-gallon Mason jars. Bags of dried fruit and long cloth casings of pork sausage hung from hooks in the ceiling.

There was a bedroom on each side of the house, both opening onto the front room.

There was no bathroom in the house, only a two-hole privy near the hen house.

On his first extended visit, Barsh started off sleeping in the guest bedroom on the west side of the house. After he and Karen Phillips became good friends, he slept on the couch in the front sitting room and she slept in the guest bedroom.

Barsh turned up the driveway, leading to the house. The front yard, just dirt no grass, had been recently swept with a brush broom. Aunt Catherine was sitting on the front porch, shelling beans. He hoped they were speckled butterbeans, a favorite of his. Their baby boy lay on a quilt next to her.

"Great day in the morning," she cried and rushed into the yard to embrace him. "Welcome, welcome, dear Barsh. I'm so glad you finally decided to pay us a visit."

"You knew I'd come before school started, didn't you?"

"Well, I was counting on it, but boys have a way of changing as they get older. My, oh my, you are growing into a young man.

Look at those strong arms. I bet the girls are already after you, ain't they?"

"No, ma'am."

"Now, don't be modest like your mother. She's such a pretty lady and always so modest. You know she got all the beauty in the family and most of the goodness. You hold out for a woman like your mother and you'll live a happy life.

"On second thought, I can see you're not as modest as you mother. Who taught you how to cut the sleeves off your shirt?"

"Wesley Workman who camped with me a few times."

"I guess he has strong arms like you that he wants to show off."

"I've only cut off the sleeves of a few shirts. I like to wear them when I'm helping Thomas Wade with his junk business. It's cooler this way. When I dressed this morning, I was thinking about the walk from the bus stop and having to carry my suitcase."

"Well, I don't blame you. It makes you look healthy."

"Oh, by the way, Karen was here again this morning, wanting to know if I'd heard when you was coming. Wait till you see how she can ride Jim's new quarter horse.

"I'm to ring the dinner bell twice and then twice again. That's my signal that you're here. Come on and meet your cousin Jacob."

With suitcase in hand, he followed his aunt onto the front porch, where she picked up Jacob with a beam of pure joy on her face.

"Oh, Barsh, I didn't know what I was missing. Jacob is such a blessing. You know your mother and I have had a hard time carrying a baby to full term. But thank God she got lucky with you and I now have Jacob."

"We were happy to hear the good news when Jacob was born. That's all that Mother talked about for days."

"Here, you take Jacob, and I'll draw you a fresh bucket of water."

"I'll hold him, but I want to draw the water myself."

"Then I'll let you. Come on to the back porch. You can hold Jacob while I ring the dinner bell to let Karen know you're here.

"My Lord, she'll be glad to see you. She's been awful lonesome out here in the country this summer.

"I think her parents should let her stay at home, next summer. She's old enough to take care of herself, while they're working.

That's what I'm gonna to tell them, when they come for her this time. Good God, I wasn't much older than her when I got married."

His aunt hurried to the cast iron bell beside the garden and rang it as planned to announce his arrival.

"Barsh," she called, "you still like hot pepper, don't you?"

"Yes, ma'am."

"Well, we got some, this year, that'll set you on fire. It's way too hot for me. Oliver can hardly eat these pods, and that's telling you a lot. It'll make good pepper sauce, though. You want to try some for dinner?"

"Yes, ma'am."

"Okay, I'll pick a few pods, while I'm out here. But I'm warning you, this is the hottest pepper that we ever raised."

Shaking the cropped brown hair out of her pleasant face, the little woman rushed up the porch steps, carrying several long pods of red pepper in her apron.

Hard working and generous to a fault, Aunt Catherine was a good woman to have in your corner. She was fair and reasonable in her dealings, and she had always given Barsh the run of the place. How could he not think she was a special woman?

"I'll take the baby now, so you can draw you a fresh bucket of water. I know you must be thirsty."

She sat in a chair, goo-gooing to Jacob, while Barsh drew the water.

"Oliver will be back soon. He took some corn to the gristmill at Tin Shop. We were getting low on cornmeal, and you know how he has to have his cornbread every day for dinner and supper.

"I hope you're hungry. I'm gonna cook you a big dinner."

"You always do."

"Well, I've got a good piece of pork that's done cooked, so it won't take me long to finish up. If you'll bring me Jacob's quilt and those speckled butterbeans from the front porch, we can set right here, while I shell the rest of them. Then I'll finish dinner.

"Karen will come racing up through the short cut on Jim's quarter horse any minute now. Y'all will have to double up on him. Oliver's horse has got a bad hoof, and he don't want anyone to ride him."

Barsh got the quilt and Aunt Catherine place Jacob on it. She paused often, as she shelled the speckled butterbeans, to offer him a few goo-goos, which seemed to make no impression on him.

"I believe I hear Karen coming," Barsh said.

"Your ears are better than mine if you do."

He walked to the edge of the porch and could see Karen's head rising and falling above the tall rows of corn as the horse cantered up the dirt road from her grandmother's place. Soon she was in the lane leading to the back of the house.

"Whoa," she cried, as she reined him to a stop near the porch, but the horse kept prancing about on quick short steps, blowing and tossing it head up and down.

"Whoa, Jake, whoa," she repeated in a calm voice, waiting for the horse to settle down.

Barsh could not help noticing Karen's tanned legs as she raised up in the stirrups and dismounted in one quick motion. Her blond hair was cut short as usual. She was wearing baggy black shorts and a white blouse that rippled over her breast.

"Hey, Barsh. Come say hello to Jake."

"Man, this is one more fine-looking horse."

"Wow, you're now taller than me," she said.

"Yeah, I guess I am. Jake is a quarter horse, right?"

"According to Uncle Jim. You ready to try him out?"

"You bet! Can I race him?"

"Oh, yeah. Give him the rein and let him go, when you get on the road."

"Do you neck-rein him?"

"Yeah, and you got to rein him back, as you mount. He'll take off before you get on good if you don't."

Karen took a cloth bag that was looped over the saddle horn, and Barsh mounted with ease. He turned Jake down the lane toward the dirt road.

It felt good to be back in the saddle, a western one, which was a first for him. Uncle Oliver had an English saddle for his five-gaited horse.

Reaching the dirt road, he urged Jake into a canter. What a pleasure to be riding high on such a powerful horse. With a yell, he dug his heels into Jake's sides and raced him all the way to the main road.

A few minutes on Jake, and he was longing once more to move to the country. He was sick of living on Britton Road, but he didn't just want to move away from something he didn't like. He wanted to live in a place where he could own a horse. But not just any horse.

He had always wanted a five-gaited horse like his Uncle Oliver's. Now, he was thinking about a quarter horse. He'd like a horse with Jake's spirit.

The flat-out run had winded Jake. Barsh knew the feeling from his sprints on the football field and let the horse walk back toward the house, until he stopped blowing. Then he cantered him into the backyard.

"How was that?" Karen asked and jumped from the porch to join him.

"Great! Now I'm wanting a quarter horse."

"I like a spirited horse like Jake," she said. "Let's tie him to the hitching post."

He dismounted and led Jake toward the barn lot with Karen walking silently beside him. He had many things to tell her about his summer, but he didn't know where to start.

"It's good to be back, Karen. We've had our share of good times here."

"I hate having to stay here, except when you're here. Oh, Mama and Daddy are driving over tonight. Daddy wants to go fishing with Uncle Oliver. That's the one thing he has to do every summer—go fishing with Uncle Oliver on the Little Tallapoosa River."

"I hope they'll let us go," Barsh said.

"You know they will, I don't care anything about fishing. But I know you do. I'll go just to be with you. I can sunbathe on that big flat rock. They always go to the same place."

"Aunt Catherine said she was going to tell your parents that you were old enough to stay home next summer."

"I know, and she will. She speaks her mind and I like that about her. But Mama is so stupid, when it comes to me."

"What do you mean?"

"Oh, it's a long story. Anyway, Mama thinks she can keep me from doing the dirty deed by making me go straight to the skating rink after school.

So that's what I do, and I'm there when she picks me up. But that don't mean I've been there the whole time."

They stopped at the barn lot, and Barsh tied Jake to the hitching post. Without either saying a word about what to do next, they left for the shade of a large oak beside the blacksmith shop, one of their favorite places to hang out and talk.

Karen sat on the old wooden bench against the side of the shop. He sat cross-legged on the ground facing her.

"What's the most exciting thing you've done this summer?" she asked.

"Camping in an old growth forest and learning how to live off the land."

"By yourself?"

"Most of the time. And with two boys, occasionally. Once with an old man who taught me how to cook fish and squirrels over an open fire with a hickory skewer."

"Didn't you get bored camping by yourself?

"Not at all. I'd hunt and fish, so I'd have something to eat, and I'd swim in Wehadkee Creek, that flowed by the campsite. Some days I'd explore the forest. The trees are the biggest that I've ever seen. One day, I hiked all the way down the creek to the Chattahoochee River.

"I don't have the words to tell you how satisfying it was to camp there. But now that a lumber company is going to cut all of those old trees, I have no plans to camp there, ever again."

"Speaking of swimming, let's you and me go in Bear Creek, this afternoon. I brought my bathing suit and stuff in my cloth bag."

"Yes, let's go."

"Okay, we'll ride Jake."

Karen drew up her legs, wrapped her arms around them, and rested her chin on her knees. What was she thinking about? The fun they had last summer at Bear Creek?

"What did you think about at night when you're camping by yourself?" she asked.

"Wait a minute. It's my time to ask a question. Tell me the one thing that you think about most often at night."

"That's easy. Boys. I think about all the different boys I'd like to date. What it would be like to be alone with this one or that one."

"Can you date now?"

"Not officially. Mama says I can start this fall, but there's a lot she doesn't know about me."

"Does that mean you have a boyfriend?"

"Not now, but I've had a few. My best girlfriend stole my first one. We would skate every afternoon, until she got her claws in him.

"After that, they'd head straight to her house as soon as school was out. Like mine, her parents were both working.

"I didn't really care though. And besides, I learned from her that I could do the same thing.

"I had fun with my second and third boyfriends. Then I dumped the third one to get my claws in a new boy. That hasn't happened yet, but I was making progress with him before Mother sent me over here for the summer.

"Tell me about your love life. I bet you and Amy have been doing it all summer."

"No, she's got a boyfriend. We're not even close anymore. There's a girl who would like to be my sweetheart, but I'm not interested."

"So, we have no commitment to anyone, right?"

"I certainly don't."

"Nor do I."

An automobile rattling down the road. It was Uncle Oliver in his Ford pickup. Barsh stood and waved as he pulled into the yard.

"Karen, I want to greet Uncle Oliver."

"I'm with you. I'll bet you Aunt Catherine will be calling us to dinner any minute now."

Chapter Thirty-Two

The four of them sat around the kitchen table, happy to be together, again. Already stuffed, Barsh was trying to clean his plate. Everyone else had already finished.

He'd have to remember to take smaller servings next time. It wouldn't do to leave anything on his plate. Aunt Catherine would think he didn't like it. She took great pleasure in watching her guests enjoy themselves at her table.

Uncle Oliver leaned back in his chair and rolled his own cigarette with Prince Albert tobacco. A tall lanky man, he was an old-time farmer who took pride in farming with a mule.

"Barsh, go with me, if you will, to Uncle Quincy's when you finish eating. I'm taking them some fresh cornmeal. He and Aunt Sally sure would like to see you.

"The last time I was there, they ask if you was visiting us this summer. Uncle Quincy says you're the only boy he knows who likes to hear about the olden times."

"Sure, I'll go. Are they doing all right?"

"Yeah, considering their age. He's ninety-six now and she's eighty-two.

"You won't be gone long, will you?" Karen asked. "Barsh and I are going swimming in Bear Creek, this afternoon, and we're riding Jake. I been waiting all summer for this."

"No, I don't plan on staying long. You're going with us, ain't you?"

"I was there yesterday. I'll stay with Aunt Catherine and get dressed for a good swim in Bear Creek."

***

On the way back from Uncle Quincy's, Barsh assumed that Karen and he would be allowed to go to Bear Creek by themselves, since no one had questioned her plan, when she mentioned it at dinner.

He knew the general direction and was confident that he could find the place. He had developed a good sense of direction and took pride in his ability to get about in the forest without getting lost.

Even so, Barsh entered the front door with anxious anticipation. Aunt Catherine was nursing Jacob. Karen was slumped on the couch. She had changed into a black, one-piece swimsuit, which she wore under her baggy black shorts and white blouse that was unbuttoned and hanging loose.

"Barsh, I put your suitcase in the guest bedroom," Aunt Catherine said.

He closed the bedroom door and placed the suitcase on the bed. Why was his heart racing so? Calm down, he kept telling himself. He slipped out of his blue jeans and briefs, pulled on his swimming trunks, and put back on his pants.

He took one of rubbers that he had stuffed in a sock and put it in his pocket. He might not need it, but best to be prepared. Karen seemed even wilder than she was last summer.

"I'm ready," he said on joining the group.

"Catherine, they'll need a quilt to ride double. I'll hold Jacob if you'll find them one."

Aunt Catherine was back in a minute with an old quilt.

"This one has seen its best days. A few horse hairs won't hurt it. Do y'all need towels?

"I've got one in my bag," Karen said. "We can share it."

"Y'all be careful now and be sure to get out of them woods before dark."

"We'll be back way before dark," Barsh said and took the quilt. "Uncle Oliver, last summer we walked through the woods behind your mother's place to the creek and then walked up it to the swimming hole. Is that the best way to go?"

"No. Don't even go by Mother's, since you're riding Jake. Take the road past Uncle Quincy's, till you cross over a little bridge. Turn right and follow that branch to Bear Creek. The swimming hole ain't too far up the creek. Just look for the waterfall.

Barsh led the way to the horse. There, he folded the quilt to the right size and placed it behind the saddle.

"You take the saddle," Karen said.

***

Barsh reined the horse through the forest, picking the best course around fallen trees and underbrush. Karen had been quiet for some time. What was she thinking?

An alder thicket stretched out before them from the branch to the side of a hill, blocking their way along the bank of the little stream. He thought about the woodcocks he'd flushed from such thickets, how their wings whistled, when they took flight.

"You better hold on, Karen. We need to get on top of that ridge."

Instead of grasping the saddle, she locked her arms around him—her breasts jostling against his back, as Jake lunged his way to the top of the hill. He turned the horse down the ridge. Karen unlocked her arms and rested her hands gently on his hips.

Barsh stopped the horse. The ridge was now falling off toward the creek.

"There's Bear Creek."

"Good. I'm ready for some fun, ain't you?"

"You're backing up, as they say, if you're waiting on me."

He eased Jake down the hill and turned him up the bank of Bear Creek, that was a delightful sight for the human eye. With Jake clopping along at a steady pace, they were soon at the waterfall.

"At last," Karen said.

He gave her the left stirrup and she dismounted. He followed.

"I guess I better water Jake, and then I'll tie him to a nearby sapling."

"Give me the quilt, and I'll spread it on the bank next to the swimming hole."

Finished with watering Jake, he found Karen stretched out on the quilt, sporting her black swimsuit. Her shorts and shirt were flung to one side. She was well tanned and had obviously been sunbathing in that swimsuit.

Barsh stripped down to his swimming trunks and sat beside her. Unlike her, he was two-toned. His arms and face well-tanned, his body and legs only slightly tanned from lying naked after diving and swimming in Turtle Creek.

"My goodness, Barsh, your stomach looks like a washboard. And your arms. How did you get all those muscles?

"Sit-ups for my stomach. I do hundreds every day. Pushups

and a chinning bar for my arms and chest. They're part of my conditioning routine.

"I'm playing football with the varsity team this fall. Coach Walker says I can get a scholarship to college if I give it everything I got."

"You want to go to college?"

"Yeah, don't you?"

"Heavens no. I hate school. You know what I've been thinking?"

"What?"

"Two different things. This will be our last summer together. I'm sure I'll never see you again after we separate this time."

"Not everything about getting older is good, is it?" he said.

"No, but you will always be a special part of my memory. Nothing can ever take that away."

"Nor will I ever forget the good times that we've had out here in the country."

"Yes, and one of those good times from last summer was the other thing I was thinking. You want to guess what it was?"

"I'm no good at guessing," he said. Although he thought he knew, he didn't want to be the first one to mention it.

"I was thinking about me and you swimming here last summer, how I touched you and you touched me back. That was the first time I'd ever touched or been touched that way."

"Me, too."

It was both the first and the last time that Barsh had touched and been touched that way. He was certain, however, that Karen had a different story.

"I was so excited I could hardly stand it," she said. "And I wanted to do it for the first time with you, right then and there."

"So, did I. But there was Uncle Jim sitting on a log, thirty feet away. Then I had to go home later that afternoon."

"We can do it now if you want to," she said. "If you don't have a rubber, I do. Here's why. My best girlfriend gave me this advice: Whenever you're ready to offer yourself to a boy, be prepared, because he may not be. Otherwise, you may find you belly bulging with a baby."

"I've got a rubber and I'm ready to use it."

They stripped naked, and with a common desire, they consumed the erotic passion that their young bodies had sparked on that summer afternoon.

For Barsh, there was no sense of conquest or exploitation, only the mutual sharing of their erotic sensuality. It was also his surrender of innocence for experience, and he had done so without guilt or regret.

The experience was imbedded in a special chamber of his brain. The truth was the truth even if it was a private truth to be confined to his memory, for there would be no telling. From the very first, he had deplored the *telling* that Wesley Workman seemed compelled to do.

Chapter Thirty-Three

The weekend was slowly dropping into the pages of time that was, and Barsh would be glad to see it go. There were too many adults on the scene.

Aunt Catherine had cooked Sunday dinner for the whole clan. Afterwards, they all sat on the front porch. The grownups chatted and told stories—some sad, some tragic, others funny.

Karen and Barsh listened with their quick glances telling the other what they were thinking. About mid-afternoon, the guests scattered. Karen's parents took her with them to Granny Phillips before they headed home to Atlanta.

As the sun dropped low in the West, Barsh helped with the evening chores. Then they ate supper and talked on the front porch. By nine o'clock, the three of them were in bed.

Barsh wasn't a bit sleepy, as he lay there in the dark. He had expected Karen to come back, when her parents left, even if she didn't spend the night like she used to. She did not return, however, and that puzzled him. Could she have talked them into letting her go home with them?

Even though there was no way to answer the question, before tomorrow, it kept bumping around in his head. He wished that he had brought a book to read, but wishing did him no good. His mind took its own course and jumped about from one thing to another, until a severe thunderstorm rolled in.

It started with fierce lightning that lit up his room and cracked the silence with harsh booming thunder. Then the rain came pounding down upon the tin roof.

Once, his aunt came to the door to see if he was all right. She knew that some people were terrified to be in a thunderstorm.

As the lightning and thunder moved north, the rain turned to a sweet drumming on the tin roof, and that calmed and soothed him into a deep sleep.

***

Early Monday morning, he sat at the kitchen table, talking

with Uncle Oliver. Aunt Catherine was cooking breakfast. Karen rode into the backyard on Jake, and Barsh left to greet her.

They walked together toward the lot, Karen leading the horse, he thinking about Bear Creek. He was hoping they would go back that afternoon, although he was not going to bring it up. He would wait for her to say what she wanted to do.

"What did you do after we left yesterday?"

"Just killed time mostly. And you?"

"The same. I wanted to spend the night, here, like I used to, but Granny wouldn't let me. She was obviously afraid you would come crawling in the bed with me in the middle of the night, when everybody else was asleep. But she don't know you or me.

"I'd be the one crawling in the bed with you. Anyway, don't say anything around her about us going to Bear Creek. What she don't know won't hurt her."

She tethered Jake to the hitching post, and they left for the kitchen.

"How long do you plan to stay?" she asked.

"A week."

"Oh, no, you got to stay longer. I can make it through the rest of the summer if you will stay two weeks. Please reconsider."

"Well, I guess I could stay two weeks."

"Great! You don't know how much I need your company."

Back in the kitchen, they ate a hearty breakfast. Barsh was surprised that Karen drank coffee for breakfast, something she had started since last summer.

Aunt Catherine, who drank two cups every morning along with Uncle Oliver, had asked him if he wanted coffee or milk. He had chosen milk.

At home his father was the only one who drank coffee. His mother didn't like it, and he had never switched from milk to coffee.

Finished with his second cup of coffee, Uncle Oliver rolled a cigarette, as he always did. Barsh liked to watch how he tapped the can of Prince Albert tobacco with his forefinger to get just the right amount in the paper, that he held in the other hand. With both hands, he would roll the paper around the tobacco and then run his tongue along the edge of the paper to seal it.

"Y'all know you can't go swimming in Bear Creek, today, don't you?" Uncle Oliver said.

"No, sir," Barsh answered, his heart racing for fear that Granny Phillips had already heard about their trip to Bear Creek and had laid down the law for her son to enforce.

"Why not?" Karen asked.

"It's way too dangerous. All that rain we had last night has got Bear Creeks flooded out of its banks. But don't y'all worry. It should be back to normal by Wednesday or Thursday if it don't rain anymore."

***

Tuesday morning, he woke at daybreak to Rooster Tom's loud crowing. In his mind, he could see the cocky Rhode Island Red, ready to do his daily duty to the hens in his flock.

No one was stirring in the house. It was too early to get up, so he lay in bed.

He had to find time to run each day, during his visit, and decided on early morning. Then he could spend the rest of the day with Karen.

As soon as Aunt Catherine got up, he would ease out of the house and do some hard running. He would be ready when football practice started.

Aunt Catherine was soon up and in the kitchen. He eased out of bed, dressed, and joined her.

She understood his commitment to training for football and promise to wait and eat breakfast with him, although Oliver would want to eat as soon as she finished cooking it. Barsh urged her not to wait for him, noting that he often ate alone at home, but she stuck with her intent to wait for him.

After a few minutes of calisthenics in the front yard, he jogged to the main road beyond the cotton field. There he pushed himself hard, sprint after sprint, some short and some long.

Pleased with his workout, he walked back to the house. Stopping on the back porch to draw a bucket of water, he heard Karen talking at the kitchen table. She heard him drawing the water and joined him on the porch.

"Hey," she said.

"And hey to you."

"Man, you're soaked through and through."

"Barsh, your breakfast is ready," Aunt Catherine called from the door.

"I got to cool off first, and then I got to take a bath."

"Well, I'll get you a foot tub, and you can bathe in your room."

***

Barsh and Karen left the house midmorning, riding double on Jake, to take some okra to Uncle Quincy and Aunt Sally. At Barsh's insistence, Karen was riding in the saddle. He sat behind her on the quilt, holding the bag of okra.

As they approached their house, a flock of guineas darted across the road and scattered in the woods. They were noisy, odd-looking creatures, but they fascinated him.

He liked the way they would forage for their own food in the fields and forest surrounding the house. That made them ideal for Uncle Quincy and Aunt Sally, since he no longer raised any feed.

Barsh had never eaten a guinea egg, but he would if he had a chance, although he'd heard others say that they, unlike chicken eggs, had a disagreeable taste.

Uncle Quincy's original clapboard house had only one big room with a fieldstone fireplace and chimney on the back side. He built it for himself, when he was a young man.

Behind the house there were several outbuildings, notably a privy and barn. The forty-acres that his father had given him included a small pasture, a patch for tobacco, a patch for vegetables, and a field to raise enough corn to keep himself in cornmeal and to feed his stock—a horse, a cow, and a few hogs.

There was also an orchard with various fruit trees and a scuppernong arbor. Most of the scuppernongs were destined to become homemade wine.

In his youth, Uncle Quincy was considered the best sharpshooter in the county, and he supplemented the food he raised and the fish he caught with the game he killed.

Since leaving home, he had never planted a row of cotton, the best cash crop in the county, back them. Occasionally, he would hire himself out for odd jobs to get a little money to buy the other things he needed to get by.

Never married, he cooked, ate, slept, and lived in that one room house, until his youngest sister, an old maid, moved in with him. She had lived at home until her father died, her mother already long dead.

The other children forced a sale on the home place, leaving her with no place to live, so Uncle Quincy built her a small room on the back of his house. It was a good thing he did, since he was ninety-six-years old and could no longer take care of himself.

Karen walked right in the door without even knocking, and Barsh followed her.

Uncle Quincy was sitting by the far window in his rocking chair, smoking a pipe. He had a full beard and hair that draped down over his shoulders, both as white as cotton.

Aunt Sally was sitting at the table, stringing and snapping green beans. She was wearing a long dress, it's blue dye long faded, and her gray hair was put up in a bun on the back of her head.

"Come on in, children," she said.

"Aunt Catherine sent y'all some okra," Barsh said.

"Put it on the table here and be sure to thank Catherine for me. I don't know what we would do without her and Oliver."

She pushed the green beans aside and reached for her pipe. Barsh knew a few young women who smoked cigarettes and a lot of old women who dipped snuff, but Aunt Sally was the only woman he'd ever seen smoke a pipe.

"Barsh, come here," Uncle Quincy said. "Y'all was in such a hurry the other day that I didn't get a good look at you. My goodness, you're about grown. Make me a muscle."

As requested, Barsh flexed the bicep of his right arm. The old man's hand trembled as he grasped it, but his blue eyes still had a lot of fire in them.

"Hard as a rock! Make good use of your strength, Barsh, before the days come when it will fail you. See how my hands tremble. When I was your age, I could hold a rifle as steady as any man who ever lived."

Barsh looked at the old muzzle-loading rifle above the bed. He would like to buy it someday, just to have as a piece of the old man's life.

***

Riding back, Barsh was in the saddle with Karen pulling herself against him, as Jake cantered down the dirt road. At the edge of the yard, he pulled the horse back to a walk, reined him to the lot, and tethered him to the hitching post. Aunt Catherine was sitting on the back porch, when they approached the house.

"Y'all wash your hands. Dinner is on the table."

Black-eyed peas with slices of streak o' lean were heaped up in a big bowl. Supplementing that was fresh creamed corn, fried okra, sliced tomatoes, and a pone of golden-baked cornbread.

At home, Barsh's father always graced the food before each meal with a short rote prayer. Here, they passed the food and started eating. Everyone ate heartily without a lot of conversation. They were eating the apple cobbler when his aunt remembered the letter.

"Oh, my, I forgot to tell you, Barsh. You got a letter from your mother in the morning mail."

"I wonder what the news is," he said. "Mother never writes this soon."

"I hope nothing is wrong," his aunt said. "I'll be right back with the letter."

All eyes were on Barsh, as he opened the letter, and began silently reading it.

Dear Barsh,

It's Monday morning, and I have bad news. Becky Wade is missing. Thomas came over to see if we had seen her.

Velma thinks she has run away with somebody. She said all Becky had talked about for the last week was Nancy Magby, a sixteen-year-old girl from the mill village who ran away to Detroit, Michigan, with a twenty-year-old boy. The girl was missing for three days before her best friend told her parents that they had planned it for some time.

I know this will trouble you, but I also know you would want me to let you know. I'll write again as soon as I know something. I want to get this letter in the mail before it runs.

Love,
Mother

"What's wrong, Barsh?" his aunt asked as soon as he looked up from the letter.

"It's my friend, Becky Wade. She's missing. She was gone when her family woke up Monday morning. Her oldest sister Velma thinks she ran away with somebody."

"I've known that to happen," Uncle Oliver said.

"It just did on the mill village, according to Mother's letter. A sixteen-year-old girl ran away with an older boy. According to her best friend, who told her parents three days later, they had been planning it for some time.

"Velma said that was all Becky wanted to talk about ever since she heard the story. I'm confident, however, that Velma is wrong. Something bad has likely happened to her, and if so, I know who's behind it."

"How old is Becky?" Aunt Catherine asked.

"She's almost fifteen. Uncle Oliver, will you take me home?"

"Sure, whenever you're ready."

"I'll have my things together in five minutes."

"Well, I'm going too," Aunt Catherine said.

"And I'm going too," Karen said.

"Karen, go unsaddle Jake and turn him in the pasture. It may be late before we get back."

Chapter Thirty-Four

The five of them chugged along in the old Ford pickup. Barsh sat between Karen and Uncle Oliver. Aunt Catherine held Jacob on her lap.

Karen wanted to know more about Becky Wade. Barsh expressed his need for time to think through some things before he got home, and she respected that.

As soon as he had read the words, *Becky Wade is missing,* the image of Root Riddle leaped into his mind. That devil is mixed up in this, he thought, and there would be no happy ending.

Then he thought that maybe nothing bad had happened to Becky. Maybe she had fallen asleep in his tepee and slept there, until after his mother had mailed the letter.

Becky could be safe and sound in her own house. His mother's letter telling him about the good news could already be in the mail. His mind could not stick with that account, however, and soon refocused on Root Riddle.

He remembered the first time Root walked into the Wades' backyard where Thomas, Becky, and he had congregated. The rascal wanted Becky to tell Ruth to come out and talk to him without any adults present. When she refused, he threatened her with words that Barsh understood as rape and murder.

Now, he could see how the current situation might have started. After dark Saturday night, Root could have parked his recently purchased used car on the side of Britton Road next to Sam's little hut and slipped into the Wade's yard, like a peeping Tom, to lust after Ruth through her bedroom window.

Becky could have been reading a book, as she waited for the rest of the household to fall asleep. Then she could have eased out of the house for Barsh's tepee, hoping he would be there or would come by. She did not know he had gone to Woodland.

Root could have seen her leaving the house and followed her to the tepee. What then?

His imagination kept trying to write the next scene, but he refused to let it carry him there. At this point in the story, he would refocus his thoughts on some pleasant memory of Becky or switch back to the story with the happy ending. Then he would try to close his mind down altogether.

As they drove into town, Karen touched his arm and he looked at her.

"If Becky didn't run away, what do you think happened to her?"

"I can't figure that out. My mind keeps going around in a circle. But I confident that she didn't run away."

They passed the schools on West Point Street, turned onto Crawford Street, then Barkley, and finally Britton Road. Cars were parked everywhere at the Wades.

That sight wins the case for bad news, he thought. He knew how people gathered when there was a death in the family.

The pickup squeaked to a stop in Barsh's driveway. Somber, somber was the mood as they entered the house through the backdoor. His mother was sitting alone on the porch, gently rocking her sorrow. With tears on her face, she rose to greet them.

"I have very sad news, Barsh. Let's sit around the kitchen table and I'll tell y'all what I know."

His mother looked frail, even fragile, as they moved into the kitchen. She knew the bitter taste of sorrow. Her mother died of Spanish influenza when she was eleven. Then her father died the following year of the same illness. She knew the pain of four miscarriages and the stillbirth of a daughter, mangled by the doctor's forceps.

"After Thomas came over early Monday morning with news that Becky was missing, your father walked home with him and talked to Velma and Mr. Wade. Then he went to work, but he kept thinking about Becky.

"Late Monday morning, it came to him what might have happened to her. We had an awful thunderstorm Sunday night. It woke us up as it kept getting closer. Then a bolt of lightning struck just below the house near your tepee."

Barsh could see where the story was going, and he knew the sad ending. His hands were trembling. He gripped the bottom of the chair, trying to steady himself.

"When your father shut down the planner mill for lunch, he came home to check for Becky in your tepee. He knew she had been going down there at night. I guess you know the rest of the story."

"Where is she now?"

"In a casket in their front room. People have been coming and going all day. The funeral will be tomorrow afternoon at their church.

"Why don't you go to your room and rest awhile. Maybe take a nap."

"I couldn't possibly go to sleep. But I would like to go to my room."

"Can I sit with you?" Karen asked. "I'll be quiet."

"If you want to."

***

Barsh lay on the bed with his eyes closed. After a while, he sat up on the side of the bed. Karen sat in a chair near the bed, and true to her word, she had not spoken.

"This is the worst day of my life, Karen."

"Becky must have been very special to you. I can't imagine a friend grieving so over me."

"You don't know the whole story. Becky's dead because of me. If it weren't for me, she'd still be alive."

"The lightning killed her, Barsh."

"True, the lightning killed her, but she wouldn't have been in that tepee if it wasn't for me."

"What do you mean?"

"I built it. If I hadn't built it, she couldn't have gone there."

"But it was her choice. She didn't have to go."

"She was there because she loved me, and she was hoping that I would join her. She didn't even know that I was visiting Aunt Catherine and Uncle Oliver. I didn't love her, but I did meet her there from time to time."

"Did y'all—"

"No, that would have been wrong. I couldn't do that with someone who loves me if I don't love her. That would be taking advantage of her."

"What about us?"

"I assumed that we just needed a good tumble."

"Yeah, that's a good way to put it."

"I loved Becky but only as a friend and that put me in a bad place. She needed me and believed that I understood her. She wanted to get away from that junkyard and be somebody. She wanted to go to college and become a teacher.

"Now she's dead at fourteen. I don't know how to deal with this."

"Maybe you should talk to your parents. Unlike my parents, they seem to be wise and loving."

"You're right, but I haven't figured out how to do that, yet. I feel like I've betrayed Becky by telling you. So please don't tell anyone."

"You have my word of honor."

***

Around four o'clock Uncle Oliver announced they had to get on the road. Karen wanted to go view the body before they left. She needed a mental picture of Becky to take away with her.

Uncle Oliver agreed to allow it, but Aunt Catherine spotted a problem.

"Karen, you can't go over there wearing shorts."

"Why?"

"It's just not done when there's a death. And besides, the Wades are Holiness people. They believe it's a sin to wear shorts, anywhere at any time."

"That's true, Karen," Barsh's mother said. "Come with me. I have a skirt I believe will fit you. It may be a little big, but I think it will be all right."

In short order, Karen was fixed up. Barsh was not ready to view Becky's lifeless body or to face the Wades. But he put on a stoical face and went with his friend.

He was somewhat relieved that the Wades were not in the front room with the casket and assumed that they were in the back of the house.

Strangers had taken the couch and every chair. Others were standing. Most were uttering prayers with up-stretched arms that trembled to God as if He needed some motion to attract His attention.

The two young friends stood at the open casket. To Barsh, Becky looked as sweet as an angel, lying there like she was asleep. But undertaker's presentation was a lie. She was dead.

He felt like crying but the tears would not come. His eyes were moist but not a single tear trickled down his cheeks. Karen, who didn't even know Becky, was sobbing.

***

Alone at last in his room, Barsh lay on his bed, staring at the ceiling. His mother was cooking supper. How could he eat at a time like this?

His dad would be home any minute. Unlike his mother, he would surely say something to him about the tepee. But what? Would he blame him for building it? For Becky's being there? How could he explain her presence in the tepee to his father?

His Ford pickup turned in the driveway. The door slammed. Barsh knew that he would enter through the back door. Should he join him in the kitchen or wait for him to come to his room?

"Oliver brought Barsh home. He's taking it hard."

"I knew he would. Is he at the Wades?"

"He's been but he's back in his room."

"This is so sad, Dad," he said, standing in the kitchen door.

"I need a hug, Son."

His dad pulled him to his chest and held him tight in his strong arms.

"Let's sit on the porch, while your mother finishes supper. We need to talk. Elizabeth, will you bring us some ice tea?"

They sat in their rockers, his father's kind face studying him, as if he didn't know where to begin. Barsh broke the silence.

"Dad, it wouldn't hurt nearly as bad if Becky hadn't been in my tepee. I should have torn that thing down a long time ago, but she begged me to leave it like it was.

"It was a good place for her to slip off and think about things other than Holiness doctrines and the restrictions they placed on her life. She wanted to cut her hair and go to movies like other kids. She wanted to go to college and become a teacher."

"Listen to me, Barsh. You can be a part of something that goes wrong without an evil intention in your head. I know a man that lost control of his car and killed his wife and only child. If he could have done it over, he wouldn't have made that same mistake. But you can't change *what was*.

"Even when you do your best, you can come up short. Sometimes you just have to forgive yourself."

"That's hard to do, Dad."

"The older I get, the easier it is for me. Oh, the pain is still there, but you can get on with things. People who've been there, and me and your mother have, will tell you that time is the best medicine for sorrow."

"I know one thing for certain," Barsh said. "I'm tearing down that tepee, even though it's too late for Becky. I would do it now, but that would probably cause the Wades even more pain if they saw me. I'll wait until after the funeral and do it late at night, when they are asleep."

"I think that's a good idea. About the wake tonight, do you want to go with me?"

"I don't know. Let me think about it."

"I'll take a nap after supper and go to the wake around eleven. People begin to go home before midnight. I'll stay the rest of the night. I doubt there'll be more than two or three people sitting with her when morning dawns."

"If that's the case, I want to go with you."

Chapter Thirty-Five

On Wednesday, Barsh managed to get through the funeral and burial of his friend Becky Wade. That alone would have been an ordeal to endure, even without all the Pentecostal hysteria and the guilt that linked him with Becky's death.

The combination of those factors left him so burdened that he could not focus on a single constructive idea that Thursday. It was almost midnight. Time for him to do what he knew he must do.

He eased out of the house and made his way to the cursed tepee. There wasn't a light on in a single house in the neighborhood, but the moon, almost full, hung in the eastern sky.

Standing before the tepee, he remembered the day he built it. How he and his dear friend Amy had played in it and beside it, all in childhood innocence. How he had outgrown those days of pretention. How it became a deathtrap for Becky, who loved him, who needed him. How he had failed her.

Amy and Becky, the first two girls to love him, had both shared the tepee with him in different ways. The bond between him and them now broken forever in different ways.

With as little noise as possible, he tore down the tepee and piled it on the old fire pit. With unresolved guilt, he struck a match and watched it go up in flames.

***

He had spent most of Friday brooding in his room. There was nothing he wanted to do, nothing he felt he could do. Earlier his mother, desperate to get him up and going, had asked if he planned to work out at the football field that afternoon.

Football seemed as far removed from his life as China. He didn't even want to see Rayford, actually hoped his friend would not stop by on his way home from work.

Time dripped like a leaking faucet.

"Your father is late," his mother said as she entered his room. "It's way past time for him to be home. I'm worried about him. I don't know why I'm so anxious. Becky's untimely death, I guess.

"Death can be so unpredictable. I don't know what we would do without your father. And obviously, it troubles me to see you grieving so."

"I'm beginning to feel better, Mother," he said knowing he had to perk up. "You probably won't see me more than thirty minutes during daylight tomorrow."

"I never thought I'd say such a thing, but that would make me very happy. Supper's ready if you'd like to eat something. I made you some banana pudding."

"I'll wait for Dad."

"I wish you would come sit on the porch with me, until he gets here," she said and they moved to their rockers on the porch.

"I thought Amy would be at the funeral. Have you talked to her lately?"

"Not in several weeks. She and Laura Underwood have become best friends. They spend a lot of time together."

He picked up his father's Bible from the small table beside his rocker.

"Mother, why does Dad read the Bible so much? He doesn't go to church, since we moved to town."

"You'll have to ask him yourself. He has studied the Bible ever since I've known him. And he was active in church before we moved to town. Thank goodness, here he is."

"There's a boat in the back of the truck," he said and hurried out the back door to examine it.

"Whose boat is this, Dad?"

"Take a guess."

"Where did you get it?"

"A man at the cabinet shop on Johnson Street builds them. This one is built with marine plywood, which makes it lighter than the old bateaus we used to have. We got an outboard motor, too. Bought that at McMillan's Hardware. You want to go with me to the backwaters in the morning?"

"You know the answer to that. Where on the backwaters?"

"Jay Bird Creek! You remember those big rocks we saw scattered about in the river, just up from the mouth of the creek?"

"I even remember that you told Uncle Edward you'd give a dollar bill to be sitting on one of those rocks fishing for a big yellow catfish."

"Well, that's what I aim to be doing tomorrow. With this boat and motor, we can fish anywhere we want to on Martin Lake."

"Can we spend the night?"

"That's my plan. We'll pack everything tonight. I want to leave by daybreak."

***

After supper, the three of them returned to their rockers on the back porch.

"Bill, can you explain to Barsh why you read the Bible so much? He asked me this afternoon if I knew."

"There are lots of reasons, Son. For one thing, it gives me a lot to think about. And I learn a lot of interesting things.

"Here's something I bet you didn't know. If your mother and me had lived back in the days of the Old Testament and I had died before you were born, my brother Edward would have been obligated to take Elizabeth and father a son for me. What do you think about that?"

"You telling me that's in the Bible?"

"I read it again last week."

"What if Mother didn't want that?"

"Well, she would be obligated to do it as a way of giving me a son. That was the way they did things back then."

"That doesn't seem right to me, Dad."

"Well, I wouldn't want to live by those laws, either. I used that as an example to show you that there are a lot of interesting things in the Bible that cause me to think about different things."

"I bet you and Dr. Franks would have a good time talking about the Bible. You've never heard him preach, have you?"

"No, I'm just a country man. I don't think I'd fit in at First Baptist. But I'm glad you like Dr. Franks."

"I've learned a lot from him, but nothing like you just told me."

"There are a lot of things in the Bible you won't hear about from the pulpit. I'll tell you what. Let's me and you pack our things for tomorrow and turn in early?"

"Sounds good to me."

***

The truck bounced along the dirt road, the air rushing through the open windows. They had to be getting near the Tallapoosa River.

Barsh was thinking about the time he had camped at Jay Bird Creek with his father and Uncle Edward, who was home on leave after finishing basic training. They fished from the bank with long cane poles and caught largemouth bass and crappies with live minnows.

He would never forget that experience and the things he had learned from Uncle Edward, who was the only member of his father's family who had gone to college. Before being drafted into the Army in World War II, he graduated Auburn University with a major in history.

On the way, Uncle Edward told them about basic training and the army's plans for him. He would be sent to Iceland. Then he changed the subject.

***

"Barsh, do you know about the Battle of Horseshoe Bend?"

"No, sir."

"Well, it's time you heard about the people who first lived in this part of Alabama. Bill, let's stop, just ahead, at the sign about Jackson's Oak."

His father stopped the Ford pickup beside the sign. They walked up the bank to the top of the hill and stood beside the gnarled oak, where Andrew Jackson had issued final orders on how they would attack the Creek Indians who had gathered at Horseshoe Bend on the Tallapoosa River.

There beneath the branches of that tree, Barsh listened as Uncle Edward told him the story of how Jackson's forces massacred the Creek Indians in March, 1814, how the river ran red with the blood of those who tried to escape by swimming the Tallapoosa.

Like his uncle, he took sides with the Creeks in their struggle against the advancing white settlers.

"You know we have Creek Indian blood," his uncle said. "It all goes back to Wilfred Roberts who came over from England just before the Revolutionary War. He was an indentured servant to a man in Augusta, Georgia, who had paid his ship fare from England.

"Then he became a patriot and fought for our freedom and independence. They say he was an expert marksman with a long rifle.

"When the War of Independence was over, he traveled west into Indian territory and took up with the Creek Indians. He lived in a number of different villages, before he settled down near Talladega Mountain in what is now the State of Alabama.

"Meantime, he'd married a Creek woman. Paw-Paw Roberts, your great-grandfather, is Wilfred Roberts' grandson. That makes Paw-Paw Roberts one-fourth Creek. Your daddy and I are one-sixteenth. You are one-thirty-second, and I hope you never forget it."

"No, I won't. I know Paw-Paw Roberts is proud of his Indian blood. Every time we visit him, he tells me about the Creek Indians and how the government forced them out of Alabama and settled them in Oklahoma."

"That was in the 1830s when Andrew Jackson was President."

***

Barsh glanced at the father who was staring straight ahead, trying to dodge the roughest places in the dirt road.

"Dad, I was just thinking about the time we drove down this road with Uncle Edward on the way to Jay Bird Creek. He told me about the Battle of Horseshoe Bend. Are we getting close to the sign about Jackson's Oak?"

"It won't be long now. It's on your right."

"Did you ever spend much time with Paw-Paw Roberts when you were growing up?"

"No, not really. Why?"

"Every time we've visited him, there was always a crowd of people there. I'd like a chance just to sit and listen to him before he dies. He was ninety-four his last birthday. I'd like to hear his stories, especially about his grandmother and grandfather."

"Well, he would be glad to tell you all about them. Like his grandfather, he was an expert marksman. They say he was the best deer hunter in Clay County. We were there one Saturday, when he came home, carrying a deer across his shoulders."

"I remember that. He was wearing buckskin clothes."

"Yeah, he always hunted in buckskin clothes. He made them himself out of hides he'd tanned the old Indian way. He's kept a lot of the Indian ways.

"He's an honorable man and his word is his bond. He's got a strong mind, but he's the only member of the family who never learned to read and write. Says it would be useless to him.

"He rejects Christianity and holds to the spiritual teachings of his Creek grandmother. He wants to be buried beside a big cedar on a hilltop near his house.

"Bury me with no preacher, no reading of scripture, and no singing. I've heard him say these very words."

"Did he ever talk to you about the spiritual teaching he learned from his grandmother?"

"No, Granny Roberts was a Christian and is buried at Mount Lebanon Church. They honored each other's beliefs. I never heard them talk about religion, except she let it be known that he followed the Indian ways, when it came to religion and that was good enough for her. She didn't want the preacher trying to convert him."

"I'd like the hear what his grandmother taught him. Do you think he'd talk to me about them?"

"I'm sure he would. I'll take you for a visit this fall."

"I'd like that. Well, you were right about the sign. There it is"

"Do you want to stop?"

"No, I'm too excited about getting to Jay Bird Creek."

"It won't be long now. After we cross the covered bridge over the Tallapoosa, that's coming up soon, we'll look for an old logging road that'll take us to the backwaters of Lake Martin right at the mouth of Jay Bird Creek."

The truck rumbled on down the dirt road, with father and son deep in their separate thoughts.

***

They sat beside the campfire on the bank of Martin Lake, where Jay Bird Creek flowed into it. Just above the place, the Tallapoosa River came rushing down through rocky shoals. They had experienced a mighty fine day on the water.

Barsh had gained his first experience of operating an outboard motor and was brimming with the expectation that he would soon be able to take command of the new fishing boat, with or without his father. His father had even commended him for being a fast learner with good judgment.

Fishing had been good. They caught crappies and largemouth bass in the backwaters, moving from place to place with ease. They also caught several big yellow catfish in the Tallapoosa just below the shoals.

Barsh was roasting the last skewer of one of the catfish. He wanted to show his dad how he could cook over hot coals without a frying pan. His dad had made a pot of coffee and fried a skillet of potatoes and corn fritters.

"You want a cup of coffee? I brought two cups."

"Yes, sir, I'd like to try some. This will be my first, you know."

"Well, it's time to see if you like it."

'This last skewer of fish is just about done. I hope you can eat my roasted catfish."

"I'm going to salt mine."

"I'll salt mine, too, since I'm eating with you. But I like to rough it when I'm by myself."

Darkness had engulfed the place except for a circle illuminated by the campfire, but they ate with a sense of unusual contentedness.

His first cup of coffee was unexpectedly bitter. Nothing like he thought it would taste, but he drank it to the very last drop.

"Thanks for bringing two cups, Dad. It's good to drink coffee with you."

"You want to join me for a second cup?"

"Thanks, but not tonight. It's going to take me awhile to develop a taste for coffee."

"Well, the fish you roasted was better than I expected. Barsh, you really want to live in the country, don't you?"

"More than anything I can think of. I just don't feel good living on Britton Road. I don't belong there. Plus, I really do want a horse. I had a great time riding Uncle Jim's quarter horse."

"I've been talking it over with your mother. We feel the same way that you do. We don't belong on Britton Road. I'm going to find us a place at Broughton. I think I can buy Grandfather Brown's farm where Mama was born."

"That would be great."

"What about football? We played basketball when I was growing up, so I don't know much about football. It looks mighty rough to me. Are you sure you want to play football?"

"Yes, sir, I do."

"You know you'll have to practice after school. That could be a problem if we move to the country. The school bus leaves when school's out."

"Maybe I could get a ride with somebody."

"Well, now that I think about it, you can ride home with me. I'll still be working for Mr. Britton. I'll pick you up at the gym after work. One of us may have to wait on the other some days, but I won't mind."

"Neither will I."

"Here's an idea. You'll turn fifteen next month and can get your driver's license. When that happens, I'll buy a new car and giving you the old Ford pickup."

"You'll give me the pickup?"

"As soon as you get your driver's license."

"Wow. I never dreamed I might have my own pickup anytime soon. Then I can drive myself to school and back. I can also hunt and fish on the river. Could I take the new boat and motor?"

"Just as soon as you get a little more experience."

"Things are looking up for me, Dad, especially if you can buy your grandfather Brown's farm."

"I just learned it's for sale. Uncle Windsor, one of Mother's brothers, owns it. Hopefully, I can make a deal with him. That would be a good place for you to grow up."

"Sounds ideal to me."

"I know it's been a hard summer of you, but you've learned a lot. You won't be fifteen until next month, and you're already becoming a man. Just know I'm proud of you."

Yes, it had been a hard summer for him, and yes, he had learned a lot. But his father knew little of the true story of his fourteenth summer—stories he would never hear from Barsh's mouth. Both father and son knew, however, that they were sharing a night to remember with deep pleasure.

His dad made a pallet and rolled up in an old quilt. Barsh crawled in his sleeping bag, and focused his attention on the brilliant night sky.

What glories adorned the heavens! And on earth, the night was alive with the sounds of the wild.

Chapter Thirty-Six

Barsh's father bought his grandfather's eighty-acre farm and moved the family back to their roots at Broughton, Alabama. There was a good house with indoor plumbing and five outbuildings—a large barn, a cotton house with sheds that were filled with four generations of farming implements, a brooding house of chickens, a smoke house for curing and storing meat, and a hen house with a three-hole privy attached to its backside.

The acreage contained a well-fenced pasture with a branch running through it, a ten-acre cornfield, a fenced garden, and several patches for peanuts, sweet corn, potatoes, cantaloupes, and watermelons. There were pecan trees, peach trees, apple trees, pear trees, and fig bushes.

The old cotton fields had all grown up in pine trees. There was also a good stand of second-growth deciduous trees with a creek running through it.

As he had dreamed of doing, Barsh bought a spirited quarter horse named Thunder, and he made two special friends, who rode horses with him.

Susan Henry and John Marshall had lived all their lives in the country but had never ridden a horse before Barsh moved into the community. Following his lead, they both got a horse so they could ride with him on the dirt roads that crisscrossed the countryside. They rode together almost every Sunday afternoon.

Susan, who was only twelve, had latched onto to Barsh, and he loved having her as his little riding pal. Frequently, she rode with him at night when his daily duties were done. But there were nights when he rode alone.

Barsh loved everything about living in the country, especially being close to nature. He could walk, east or west, from his house for ten minutes and be in a deep forest.

The transition to high school that fall had gone well for him. His father had bought a new car and given him his old Ford pickup.

No one worked harder during football practice, and it was paying off. People were noticing him, talking about him and his potential.

He, on the other hand, had taken notice of April Morehouse, a demure classmate of exceptional beauty and delicacy, who had moved to town that summer. The girl's very presence in his classes had rekindled his romantic heart. Their circumstances, however, could not have been more different.

She and her parents had moved in with her grandmother who lived in a grand house on Main Street. April's father was a pharmacist and owner of the newly opened Morehouse Pharmacy.

In October, Sheriff Horton arrested Root Riddle and Doug Conyers along with Bud Drake. All three were tried and convicted of the murder of Sam Floyd.

Barsh could not understand their behavior. What had gone wrong to turn them into murderers?

There were days when he felt the loss of Amy, his first love. But they were less frequent after the Burdettes moved to Huntsville. Laura Underwood told him that Amy was living in a home for unwed mothers in Birmingham and that she would give up the baby for adoption.

Sometimes he wondered if he would ever hear from her or see her again. He could only hope that he would and that the circumstances would be amicable. Her gifts to him were locked in his soul, and often in quiet moments of introspection, he would pull one out in remembrance of their good old days as best friends or their short time of being sweethearts.

At times, a smoldering anger would blaze up within him, and he would feel compelled to find Wesley Workman and try to beat the devil out of him for what he had done to Amy. Although he knew he would end up with the worst part of the beating, he thought it would make him feel better, just to get in a good lick or two. But that didn't seem right either. What would it change?

In early November as he was leaving the field after a football game for the bus ride back to the gym, Wesley tried to get him to go camping with him as if nothing had happened between them.

"No, Wesley. I won't be camping with you, ever again."

"Well, ain't you a sore loser?"

"This has nothing to do with losing or winning, and you should know it."

"Well, if that's the way you want it, then so be it. I warned you that Amy was ripe for taking. That if you didn't . . ."

The anger boiled over. Barsh whirled into him with both fists flying and knocked Wesley to his knees.

Wesly cursed him and righted himself. Barsh stepped back and took a defensive position, expecting Wesley lay a beating on him. Instead, he slowly shook his head and walked away without raising his fists—a surprising move that Barsh understood as a confession of remorse. That was their last encounter as boys.

Having registered the depth of his antagonism, which seemed beyond reconciliation, he was able to get beyond the anger. Still, he wondered if old Mayhayley, The Oracle of the Ages, got it right when she predicted a dark downfall for Wesley.

At quiet moments, Barsh would find himself grieving for his friend Becky Wade. She deserved so much better than she got, and he had been profoundly affected by her death. Among other things, that early awakening to the tragic sense of life had matured him beyond his age.

The year that Barsh turned fifteen had come and gone, leaving in its wake the first of the winnowing experiences of youth that would soon start him on a long spiritual and intellectual journey.

Honey from a Lion

“[Samson] turned aside to see the carcass of the lion: and behold, there was a swarm of bees and honey in the carcass of the lion. And he took thereof in his hands and went on eating.”

— Judges 14:8-9

Chapter One

William Barsh Roberts pulled into his driveway, parked in the garage beside Debbie's Buick, and lingered in his Audi for a few moments. It was late, and he hoped that his wife had already gone to her bedroom for the evening.

Try as he would, he had not been able to make her happy. She had endured the first four years of their marriage in Atlanta, while he earned a Ph.D. at Emory University, and contrary to his promises, things did not improve for her after he accepted a professorship at Cooper College.

Although she owned a successful accounting firm, she hated living in Ashland, a small town in Upstate South Carolina. Moreover, she was miserable around academics.

But things were looking up for her. Her old boss in Louisville, Kentucky, had offered to make her a partner at Dugan, Johnson and Bennett, Certified Public Accountants.

Barsh had given up all hope of revitalizing the marriage, but because of their eleven-year-old daughter Hannah, he felt dutybound to keep the family under one roof and offered to move the family to Louisville. He could find work there. It didn't have to be a professorship.

Debbie, however, rejected his offer and asked for a trial separation for one year. That left him wondering what she really wanted, although he felt rather certain about what her old boss wanted.

Henry Dugan definitely had an eye for Debbie, when she worked as his assistant before she married Barsh. And she certainly held him in high esteem. It was years before she stopped talking about *Henry* on a regular basis.

Based on Debbie's uncompromising decision to move to Louisville with Hannah, their only child, he had concluded that if things worked out for her during the trial separation, which he had agreed to, she would insist on a permanent separation, rather than a divorce.

According to the teachings of Saint Paul, that Debbie believed to be the word of God, a woman could separate from her husband but a man could not divorce his wife. She had referenced that passage in Saint Paul's first letter to the Corinthians more than once in defending her decision to move to Louisville without him.

He closed the garage door with the remote and entered the dark den, a good sign that Debbie had gone to her bedroom. He turned on the overhead light and quietly made his way to Hannah's room.

She was sleeping peacefully with the nightlight gently bathing her sweet face. Another day had slipped away, and he had not spent any time with her. Poor child, she had no idea that she and her mother would soon be living in Louisville without him.

Down the hall, the door to the master bedroom was closed and would not be opened by him. He had moved into the guest bedroom after Debbie insisted on a trial separation.

He went to the basement for his regular workout and managed to complete it in spite of his troubled mind. Afterwards, he thought about going to bed but realized that would be foolish. It would likely be midnight before he settled down enough to sleep.

He was reading a brilliantly written book about Baruch Spinoza. Thinking that it might take his mind away from his troubles if he could get back into the world of the extraordinary philosopher, he went to his study to resume reading the book.

The walls of the study were lined with floor-to-ceiling bookshelves, except the outside one with the big windows onto the backyard. Beyond the yard, the remnant of a hardwood forest dropped to Coleman Creek and then rose to the top of a hill. That connection with a bit of nature had sold him on buying the house, and he had never regretted the decision.

Settled at his desk, he noticed that someone had moved *Spinoza*. He picked up the book and smiled at Hannah's bookmark on page five. This was not a book for an eleven-year-old, but it pleased him that she was already developing a critical mind.

He set the book aside and reached for the photo of his parents that was taken by a traveling photographer during the first year of their marriage. His mother had told him the story, when he asked about it as a boy.

Later, when he asked why he was an only child, she told him about the miscarriages and the stillborn daughter.

How often he had wished his parents could have lived to see Hannah. They would have doted on her, and in time, they would have wondered why she was an only child, although they would never have asked.

He returned the photo to its place, anguished by the memory of their death. An eighteen-wheeler had crashed into their car and killed them, instantly. His mother was fifty-two, his father fifty-seven.

They were so pleased when Barsh finally got married. From their point of view, the marriage was made in Heaven. If they had lived to learn that Debbie was leaving him for a trial separation and would probably never return, they would have been terribly distraught.

He thought about a passage from the Book of Job on how the dead are utterly cut off from the living: Their children come to honor, and they do not know it; they are brought low, and it goes unnoticed.

At least he could take solace in the fact that they would never know his marriage was a failure. No, *failure* was not the right word. How could a relationship that brought Hannah into the world be a failure? He would not judge the marriage by what it had become.

Barsh was a tenured Professor of Religion and Philosophy at Cooper College, but he had serious doubts about his future there after Debbie moved to Louisville.

On several occasions, the conservative trustees and the majority of the ministers of Ashland had launched efforts to get him fired for his liberal views, especially those based on an empirical critique of the Bible.

Now he was certain that they would take the news of the separation as an opportunity to renew their effort to get him fired. He could imagine them ranting: His own wife could not live with him.

Although Catherine Thompson, the academic dean, and Georgette Wingo, the wealthiest trustee, had managed to foil previous efforts to get him fired, he was tired of being in the middle of that fray.

He had considered looking for a professorship at another college, but he knew that would be hard to find, given his age and status as a full professor. Colleges look for new teacher in his field typically hired those who had just completed their graduate studies.

For weeks he had pondered the possibility of an appropriate career shift, but the vision he sought would not come.

In spite of his concerns about his own future, he had made Hannah's wellbeing his first priority. She was deeply connected to him, and he had to find a way to prepare her for the separation.

Debbie had given him a little time to work on that. She knew, all too well, the trouble she would have with Hannah if he could not ease her into accepting the separation.

Tomorrow would be another long day with no time to spend with Hannah. In addition to his regular duties on campus, he had to drive to Charlotte, North Carolina, to pick up Angela Kundera, who was flying down from Providence, Rhode Island, for a job interview. Her flight was scheduled to land at 6:20, and he was responsible for taking her to dinner before checking her in the Ashland Hotel.

Dr. Kundera was currently teaching in a non-tenured track at Brown University, where she had recently earned a Ph.D. in Southern Literature. The search committee had placed her at the top of the list of candidates to interview for the opening in the English Department. Due to conflicts, however, she would be the last candidate they would interview.

As chair of the search committee, Barsh had no doubt that she was well credentialed and highly qualified for the position, but based on her resume, he could not see her moving to a small Southern town like Ashland. Even so, he had kept his feelings to himself and submitted to the will of the English faculty to invite her for an interview.

When he called to invite her for an interview, he was surprised that she seemed to be genuinely enthusiastic about the visit. But what puzzled him, even more, was the fact that her animated voice had been buzzing in his head, ever since.

There was a stirring down the hall. Hannah's feet were pattering toward him, and he turned the swivel chair toward the door.

"Daddy," she cried in alarm and ran for his embrace.

"What's wrong, my sweet girl?"

"I just had a horrible dream. You were lost in a forest and I couldn't find you."

"Oh, my dear Hannah, nightmares can seem so real. I had lots of them when I was a young boy. Some of them kept recurring, but those went away, when I got older."

"What kind of nightmares?"

"Things that a boy my age would be afraid of."

"Like what?"

"Are you sure you want to hear about my boyhood nightmares?"

"I want to know what they were about."

"Well, snakes for one thing."

"But you're not afraid of snakes. You told me they have their place in the scheme of things."

"Yes, but I was scared of them when I was a boy. Dad had warned me that I might die if a poisonous snake bit me. Since I was too young to know which were poisonous, he told me to run away as fast as I could when I saw a snake of any kind. Thus, I grew up hating snakes and later began killing them.

"Now, I give them their place in the world. We should be open to change. There's always something new coming our way, challenging us to deal successfully with it."

"I know. You've taught me well."

"Let's get you back in bed. We should both be sleeping the night away."

"Can't I stay up a little longer?"

"Sure, but just a little longer. You want some milk?"

"No, I want to talk."

"Okay, what do you want to talk about?"

"I want you to take me hiking in the mountains this Saturday."

"Would you like to go to Table Rock State Park and hike to the top of the mountain?"

"Yeah, and this time I'm going to make it all the way to the top without having to stop and rest."

"I don't doubt that you can do that, but stops are good when you're hiking in the mountains. They give you a chance to listen to the sounds of nature and take a closer look at things along the way."

"Daddy, I hope you don't have to work late tomorrow."

"I hate to tell you, but tomorrow and Friday are both going to be long busy days for me. I probably won't get home before your bedtime either day.

“If it would do any good, I would complain. Speaking of which, I haven’t heard you complaining lately about school. Are things going better?”

“Like you said, what good would it do me to complain? My classes are mostly boring. I can’t wait to get to college.”

“I see you started reading *Spinoza*. I like old Baruch Spinoza. He was way ahead of his time and that got him in deep trouble. Could you make any sense out of what you’ve read?”

“A little. You’ll have to tell me about his philosophy. I can understand you.”

“Not tonight. You have to get some zzzz’s. We’ll talk about Spinoza on the way to Table Rock.”

***

With Hannah back in bed, Barsh sat at his desk, wondering about the underlying anxiety that had caused her nightmare. Had she overheard any of Debbie and his conversations about the separation? He didn’t think so.

She did know that he had started sleeping, alone, in the guest bedroom. Was that troubling her? Should he broach the subject with her? No, that didn’t seem like a good idea. He would leave it to her to query him. She had never been hesitant to question him about anything.

His first reaction to the impending separation was to draw his daughter closer to him. Perhaps that was a bad strategy. Maybe A. E. Housman get it right: Train for ill and not for good. If so, he should be pulling back to prepare her for the separation.

He picked up *Spinoza,* flipped to his marker, and started reading. After a few pages, he gave up and decided to go for a walk. He checked on Hannah, who was fast asleep, and then left her a note on his desk, just in case she woke up again.

On leaving the house, he stopped in the driveway and studied the heavens—a simple act, which often transported him into that infinite realm of awesome wonder. The sky was clear, but he was too earthbound for the flight.

The new moon spoke to him of earthly things. Like the phases of the moon, the seasons of his life were changing. But unlike the recurring phases of the moon, he was on a journey that would never repeat itself. The best he could hope for was to live until he was an old man, stilled at last to face the sting of death.

He left the driveway with the intention of walking through the neighborhood at a fast pace. Most of the houses were dark. He wondered how many of them held secrets that the inhabitants were hiding.

People were unpredictable. Who could have imagined the problems next door, that caused John Young to knock his wife's brains out with a frying pan?

Barsh could not imagine himself ever hitting a woman. So, why were men prone to violence in marital conflicts? That question got him thinking about one of Robert Frost's poems.

What he remembered about "Home Burial" was the husband's callous response to his wife's despair over the death of their child. On some level, the man understood that he had failed his wife, but rather than taking responsibility for contributing to her despair, he threatened to bring her back by force if she left him, which she intended to do.

Barsh knew that he had failed to meet Debbie's deepest needs, and his only moral response had been to support her plan for a trial separation. He could live alone, and he could deal with any challenges that he might face if he had to shift into a new career. His major challenge was to find a way to prepare Hannah for the separation, and he was desperately searching for one.

Chapter Two

Barsh waited for Angela Kundera at the Charlotte Airport. The room was filled with chatter and movement, but he was deep within himself, as he struggled to regain his stoical equilibrium and rise to the demands of duty.

A raspy voice announced that her flight was arriving, and people gathered their belongings and started forming a boarding line. He joined several individuals who were waiting for their party to disembark, but unlike them, he held a manila folder with Barsh Roberts printed in bold black letters.

As he waited, he wondered if he could identify Dr. Kundera from the impressions of her that had formed in his mind. Why not give it a try? She would never know.

The passengers streamed out of the plane. Several business men. A few older folks. A handsome couple with two small girls. Then a petite woman with a brief case came bouncing through the door. That's her, he thought. His eyes followed her as she hurried across the way, but she didn't even look at him.

"Dr. Roberts," a woman called as she made her way toward him.

She was tall, willowy, with dark eyes, long black hair, and a pleasant face that was adorned with dangling silver earrings. She was wearing black slacks and a white, silky blouse.

"Welcome, Angela," he said taking her extended hand, as her perfume struck his nostrils. It was an enticing fragrance that he had not previously experienced.

"Thank you, Dr. Roberts. What a pleasure to meet you."

"Please call me Barsh. We're informal at Cooper as you can see by the way I'm dressed."

"Barsh. A family name I presume."

"My mother's maiden name. Needless to say, I know who's being called when I hear it."

"Yes, I can imagine that. Don't ask me why, but it seems a perfect fit for you.

“I am so excited to be here. There’s something about Cooper College that intrigues me.”

“That’s good to hear. Do you need a restroom before we get on the road?”

“I’ll be right back.”

There’s something sweet about this woman, he thought, as he watched her walk away. He had known she was intelligent and sophisticated. But sweet? Was that a Southern expression?

He could not imagine her being flattered by such a tag. He’d met too many cynical women at academic conferences who would consider it male condescension.

Waiting for her return, he felt strangely energized. He had been so emotionally devitalized by Debbie’s decision to leave him that duty, alone, had kept him going in a perfunctory way.

Now, he was thinking about the Cooper students. The English majors would love Dr. Kundera.

In spite of his belief that it was unlikely that they would be able to bring her on board, he decided to make every ethical effort to sell her on the college. It just might be his last chance to do something significant for the students.

***

With her suitcase in hand, he led the way to the airport exit with the heels of his boots clanking against the floor and Angela gliding along as if she were walking on air. He liked the fact that she wasn’t wearing high heels.

“Angela, would you prefer to wait here, while I get the car? It’s about a block away.”

“No, I prefer to walk with you.”

Finding he car, he deposited her luggage in the trunk and turned to face her. A breeze lifted her glossy black hair across her face. She brushed it aside and glanced at his boots.

“I’ve been admiring your boots. What kind are they?”

“Durango harness boots. I wore boots like these all through high school. I had a polished pair for school and a scuffed pair for riding my horse. I always chose brown to match the saddle leather.

“These are the first I’ve had since I left home for college. Bought them earlier this year, and I’m sticking with them for the foreseeable future.”

"Good decision. They go well with your broad shoulders, height, short highflying pony tail, and well-trimmed beard.

"Please take it as a compliment, but if you hadn't been holding the manila folder with your name written in bold letters, I would not have imagined you to be the Chair of the Division of Humanities at Cooper or any college."

"Then I will accept it as such."

A bit apprehensive that she would think him too patronizing, he opened the passenger door and held it for her. He had been taught to open doors for women, always, but to shake hands only if the woman offered hers.

He was all for women's liberation, but he was never sure about what a new woman expected of him. So, he followed his old habits but with some hesitancy.

Angela gracefully eased into the leather bucket seat and looked up at him with an engaging smile. Okay, she's easy to be with, he thought as he walked behind the car. Then settled in his seat, he buckled up, keyed the ignition, and turned to face her.

"Angela, there's a first-rate steakhouse near Ashland. We can stop there for dinner or we can dine here in Charlotte. Your choice."

"The steakhouse suits me."

"Good. I think you'll like the place."

Leaving the airport, he was constantly shifting the gears of the five-speed Audi 5000, as he stopped and started in the traffic. Then the traffic thinned out.

"I'm looking forward to introducing you to Jackson's Steak House—a rustic place overlooking the Broad River. It's my favorite restaurant around Ashland. Sometimes we leave early and drive along the back roads of the river to Cherokee Falls and then make a loop back through the rolling hills to the restaurant."

"Sounds like a picturesque drive."

"It is, but there's something haunting about it. The sharp contrast between the natural beauty of the woodlands and the crude houses and ramshackle barns that are scattered along the way."

"Barsh, you have the soul of a poet."

"How I wish that were true, but I'm far too analytical."

"Have you ever written poetry?"

"I wrote a few poems during my freshman year in college. But when I shared them with the Academic Dean, who was an honored poet, he gave me such a cold critique that I trashed them, and I have never written another poem."

"How unfortunate. I don't praise poor work, but I always find something positive to say about a student's effort before I start making constructive comments.

"I believe anyone who has good eyes, feels deeply about things, and loves language is capable of writing decent poetry. With that bag of tools, which you undoubtedly have, all you need to do is read and write, until you find your own creative voice."

"Angela, our English majors will love you."

"Thanks for the compliment. Will I get to meet some of them tomorrow?"

"Definitely. Would you like for me to go over the agenda?"

"Maybe at the restaurant. Right now, I'm trying to visualize Cherokee Falls. My parents took me to Niagara Falls, when I was nine. They were awesome."

"These falls are quite ordinary. It's just that I love waterfalls, so I like to drive down to see them when we're out that way. We do have splendid waterfalls in our Carolina mountains, and many are within easy driving distance from Ashland."

"That's a definite plus for Cooper College," she said. "If I get the job, I'll be checking them out."

"Well, now that I know you like waterfalls, I could take you to Cherokee Falls before dinner if you'd like. They're not far from Jackson's Steak House."

"Yes, I'd like that."

"Good. We might even get there in time to watch the sun paint the western sky with its weeping descent into the netherworld."

"Ah, an intellectual who can still envision the world mythopoetically. I like that about you. Among other things, I should add."

He did not respond to her comment as he concentrated on taking I-85 South. Spotting an opening, he gunned his way into the heavy flow of traffic.

"This is a fun car," she said breaking the silence. "Watching you shift gears brings back memories of my first efforts behind the steering wheel, long before I was old enough for a license."

"Actually, this straight shift is part of my nostalgic jag. When I was in high school, Dad bought a new car and gave me his Ford pickup.

"I loved that truck. It had a long stick-shift mounted in the floor. By my junior year, it had a blown muffler, and I would leave school every afternoon, double-clutching each gear just for the racket I could make."

"You were a hellion in those days, right?"

"No, no. I was never a hellion, although I did have my own distinctive country style. An outdoors boy in those days, I was not studious, but the teachers liked me because I respected them and listened intently to what they had to say.

"Angela, you can relax and rest in silence. Or you can ask me any questions that come to mind about Cooper. Or you can tell me about yourself. I'll take my cue from you."

"Actually, I'm surprisingly relaxed after all the hassle of getting to Charlotte. What do you mean, you had your own distinctive country style? Tell me about your youth."

"Okay, but I must warn you that my roots strike deep in an old agrarian culture that will likely bore you or else put you on the warpath. First and foremost, I loved hunting, fishing, and camping in the wild. Next, I loved riding my quarter horse Thunder.

"That's the difference I was talking about. None of my schoolmates had that combination of interests. There was also football. And my senior year, I was the only one in our school who owned a motorcycle, a black Harley-Davidson."

"Well, now that you have aroused my interest, please tell me where you grew up."

"Central East Alabama. I was born on a farm, but before I was old enough to know anything about farming, Dad bought a sawmill and got in the lumber business. When I was nine, we moved to town. Then we moved back to the country the summer before I started high school.

"I loved living in the country. I could walk ten minutes, east or west, from our house and be in a forest with my shotgun and hunting dogs."

"Do you still hunt?"

"No, and the hunting days of my youth were not what you're probably thinking. It was never a sport for me but a way to put food on the table. I've always abhorred hunting as a sport, especially big game hunting. Actually, hunting was a part of my agrarian heritage.

“I regret the fact that my paternal grandmother’s people once owned slaves, and so did my mother’s people on both sides. My grandfather Roberts’ people were the exception. They were both unionists and abolitionists, which was very rare for Southerners.

“No one in my extended family talked about slavery or segregation, when I was growing up. Those topics were too controversial for good conversation in my family.

“I never knew about the slaves until a few years ago, and that discovery really hit me hard. Having slave-owning ancestors was one burden I didn’t think I’d have to bear as a Southerner.

“Segregation, yes. I was a part of that system and was far too insensitive to its cruel injustices before my fourteenth summer.

“In broad daylight one Saturday, a neighbor brutalized a black man on Main Street, with total impunity, because he would not step aside for him when they met. That was my wakeup call, and I started taking note of the horrors and inequities of our Jim Crow society, but it took me four more years to take a stand against my South.

“Sorry to have digressed. I was trying to tell you how my hunting days were tied to my agrarian roots before I got sidetracked.”

“No apology needed. I’m interested in your story.”

“Well, the status of my ancestors had declined over the years from successful farmers, most of whom had owned slaves, to farmers who barely scratched out a living from the land. When my father was growing up on a hundred-and-twenty-acre farm, hunting was an important element in their agrarian life. It was an additional way of putting food on the table.

“That’s the hunting culture my father introduced me to, and I felt good about being a skillful hunter, who could contribute something to the table. I also liked being a part of what was left of the wild.

“I would occasionally spend days, often alone, camping in the forest and living off the land. But that was another life.”

“You were definitely different.”

Focused on telling his story, he had gotten stuck behind an eighteen-wheeler slowly whining up a steep grade of the Interstate. The left-lane traffic was flashing by in a steady stream.

“Sorry,” he said. “I’m usually a better driver than to get caught this way.”

“It happens to me all the time.”

"Angela, please tell me about your youth? I'm embarrassed that I've been talking so much about myself."

"No, don't be embarrassed. I'm intrigued by your stories. I've never known anyone like you.

"Yes, I want to tell you about my youth, but before I get started on that, I'd like to know where you did your graduate studies and what your specialty was."

"Regarding my graduate studies, I earned a Ph.D. at Emory University. My specialty was separated from yours by two to three millennia.

"You focused on Southern literature. I focused on Biblical literature, which spans almost a thousand years and is written in two totally different languages. Hebrew, as you probably know, is Semitic, and Greek is Indo-European."

"Did you work from translations or did you have to learn those languages?"

"I could use translations as an aid, but I had to work from the Hebrew and Greek texts. I've spent years studying both languages."

"I'm impressed."

"Don't be. I've lost most of my ability to translate them. Here at Cooper, I have to teach a wide range of courses in religious studies and philosophy. So, I soon chose to set aside my interest in Biblical research and thus I've neglected both languages."

"Well, I'm impressed. I'm also surprised, I should add. I assumed you were a member of the English faculty."

"This search is atypical. The Chair of the English Department is leaving under unpleasant circumstances. There are two contenders who want to become the new chair, and Dean Thompson didn't want to indicate which one she will likely select by appointing one of them to chair the search committee. So, she asked me, Chair of the Division of Humanities, to oversee the search, but I won't be voting on the candidates. My job is to keep the committee on task until the position is filled."

"I wasn't questioning your role in the search. I was just surprised. Pleasantly surprised, I should add. Unfortunately, I've never taken any religion or philosophy courses, but I've recently found myself interested in the subjects. Maybe you could tutor me if I get the position."

There was a break in the left-lane traffic, and he gunned the Audi past the eighteen-wheeler.

"Yes, of course, I'll recommend some great books for you, and we can discuss them."

"That will be another plus for Cooper. Barsh, I'm truly impressed by the breadth of your teaching. Would you prefer to be a specialist at a major university?"

"No, I actually prefer teaching a wide range of courses. Something they would not let me do in a major university. Three years ago, we changed the academic year to include a January Interim. Each faculty member had to design a new course specifically for the Interim. The students then choose one of those courses to study.

"The first year, I taught Perspectives in Black Literature, the next year Death and Dying, and this year Sexuality in Contemporary Fiction.

"I've also developed two interdisciplinary courses for the Humanities curriculum: 1) The Future of Mankind and 2) Faith, Knowledge, and Selfhood. They are now my most popular courses for non-majors. This is one of the things I like about teaching at Cooper."

"I can understand that. I'd also like to broaden my teaching."

"Then Cooper just might be a good place for you. Dean Thompson will let you develop your special passions into new courses, and only you will get to teach them."

"That's certainly another plus for Cooper."

"Speaking of our Academic Dean, I think you'll like her. Catherine Thompson is a very special woman. Over the years, she has become my closest and dearest friend. The two of us have wide-ranging discussions on a regular basis."

"You're lucky and I'm envious. I've never had a friendship like that."

"Based on what I know about you, I'm confident Catherine will welcome you into her inner circle if your next move brings you to Cooper.

"Okay, you're on. Take me into the world of Angela Kundera, while I drive us to Jackson's Steak House by way of Cherokee Falls."

"I was born in Peekskill, New York. It's on the Hudson River not far from New York City, and I have always lived near the Big Apple."

They were headed south on I-85. Angela was sharing stories about her youth, and Barsh was processing every word. For the moment, he had forgotten his own troubles.

Chapter Three

The visit to Cherokee Falls went well and so did dinner at Jackson's Steak House. They were approaching the outskirts of Ashland, and he had not glanced at Angela since she last spoke, which could not have been more than a few minutes, although it seemed like a long silence.

"Angela, do you need to make any stops before I check you in the Ashland Hotel?"

"I don't need anything, but I like to experience a place at night. Could we stroll around the campus before you drop me at the hotel?"

"Your wish is my command," he said, a bit surprised with his response to a woman whom he had just met.

"No sarcasm, please," she said with a playful slap to his upper arm. "Wow, you are solid. Are you a bodybuilder?"

"No, but I work out with weights as part of my effort to stay in shape."

"I've never worked out with weights or any of those new exercise machines, but I walk a lot to help with staying fit."

"One of my favorite activities is hiking various nature trails in our Carolina mountains. There are a lot of good ones within easy driving distance from Ashland."

"Another plus for Cooper. I told you in our phone conversation that I was fascinated by James Dickey's novel *Deliverance*, especially its wilderness setting and the primal yearnings of the protagonist. Do you know the river where they filmed the movie?"

"The Chattooga River. And I'm pleased to tell you that Congress recently designated it a Wild and Scenic River, thus protecting it from damming, logging, and development. There are wonderful trails along the Chattooga, and I've hiked most of them."

"I would love to have that experience."

"Then I promise to take you hiking on one of those trails if you accept the position at Cooper."

"Accept it? First, I have to get an offer."

"I don't want to jinx you. Let me just say, that part is not worrying me."

"Then what part is worrying you?"

"You haven't seen the campus. Cooper is as different from Brown as night is from day."

"Good. I need something very different from Brown, and thanks to you, getting a deeper connection with nature is now a part of that need. Will you really take me hiking along the Chattooga River if I get the position?"

"Most definitely, and if you like that, I'll take you to one of my favorite places—the Joyce Kilmer Memorial Forest, which far exceeds the aesthetic power of Kilmer's poetry.

"That marvelous forest, however, would have been logged years ago if it were not for his poem 'Trees' and the devotion of his friends and fans.

"A timber company was about to cut those giant trees when Kilmer's friends discovered the place and bought it. Believe me, they could not have chosen a better forest to honor the man."

"I've never heard of the place."

"It's one of last major old growth forest in the South. Giant yellow poplars that will take your breath away. And huge hemlocks."

"For that and the Chattooga excursion, I'll make a special trip back down here if I don't get the job, unless your promises were contingent on my getting it."

"Absolutely not. They are based on nothing other than your desire to experience them. I'm always looking for friends to join me on my hikes in the Carolina mountains. Fortunately, Hannah is already taking short hikes with me on some of those trails."

"What about your wife?"

"Hiking through the forest is one of the last things in the world that Debbie would be interested in doing."

"Well, please count me in. I never dreamed my interest in James Dickey's novel would lead me to this exciting moment.

"Oh, I just thought of something that should interest you. You were asking me about contemporary Southern poets. Dickey is one of the finest poets writing today. Have you read his poetry?"

"No, only his debut novel *Deliverance*."

"In literary circles, he's better known as a poet than novelist. He has served two terms as Consultant in Poetry to the Library of Congress or Poet Laureate as most people say. You likely know that he grew up in Atlanta with a connection to the mountains of North Georgia. There's an earthy quality to much of his poetry."

"Thanks for sharing that. We just turned onto College Drive. I'd better prepare you for your first viewing of Cooper if that's possible.

"Old Main is older than the college. It was built in the 1830's as a resort hotel that catered to planters from Coastal Carolina, who brought their families to escape the summer heat and mosquitoes of the Lowcountry. But whatever you think of the buildings, the campus trees are magnificent. Some of them are at least three-hundred years old.

"Here's the college. That's the Quad, straight ahead."

He turned left, skirting the east side of the campus, and parked in his usual place beside Kimberly Hall. Someone was practicing on one of the grand pianos.

"Listen to that music," she said. "How wonderful. I already like the feel of the place."

"There are benches on the Quad. Would you like to sit awhile and listen to the music?"

"Yes! Yes!"

"This is Kimberly Hall. The first floor has large studios for music profs and a number of practice rooms for students. Some faculty offices, including mine, are upstairs."

"Will my office be there if I get the job?"

"Most likely. After I pick you up at the hotel in the morning and take you to breakfast, we'll come here to my office. That will give you some idea about office space at Cooper."

They sat on a wrought iron bench beneath a dogwood tree in front of Kimberly with the music pouring from the open window. The piece, which he could not identify, ended with a flourish, and the pianist rose to close the windows of her studio.

"That's Margaret Glenn. Students, faculty, and town folks adore her. She's practicing for her concert next week. Shall I show you more of the campus or have you seen enough for tonight?"

"More, please. I want to get a feel, at night, for the whole place."

They strolled around the Quad, which seemed unusually quiet. He gave a brief history of each building and its current use. The back campus, however, was much alive with stereos blaring and students scurrying from dorm to dorm. He and Angela kept ambling along until they ended up on a bench by the lake.

"Barsh, I didn't fully understand my expectations when I flew out of Providence this afternoon, but I had a strong feeling that something good was in store for me in South Carolina. Please know that feeling is burning brighter than ever."

"That's good to hear. But take your time evaluating everything. Culturally, Ashland is about as far from the Big Apple as you can get in the States."

"But aren't you happy here?"

"Only because my interests and goals have changed as I told you earlier. When I left Emory, I had big ideas about making a name for myself in the world of Biblical scholarship and teaching in a graduate program at a major university or theological seminary.

"I got off to a good start by reading a paper at the national meeting of the American Society for the Study of Religion. I felt confident that I had solved the textual problems in the Biblical story of Noah's nakedness and the curse of Canaan that had plagued scholars for more than two thousand years, but even so, I was surprised that my paper was so well received by so many distinguished professors from across the states. The next year it was published in an international journal and is now generally accepted as the best solution to those problems.

"Here's my point. I believe that I had the potential to actualize my earlier goals, but now I have no interest in spending my life studying more and more about less and less, which is what one has to do to become a nationally known Biblical scholar. It's all about specialization.

"I care deeply about the students at Cooper. The most satisfactory aspect of my tenure here has been the positive response of the students, most of whom have had little or no introduction to critical thinking.

"I'm confident that I've made a greater contribution at Cooper than I could have at a major university. I'm also confident that you will be wonderful for our students if you can make the adjustments."

"If you're worried about me, please know that one of the things I'm looking for in this move is a Southern experience."

"Well, there's nothing more Southern than South Carolina."

"I know. Look. The moon is rising."

They watched the crescent moon rising above the distant trees. As it cleared the horizon, a silver wake shimmered across the lake, straight into their eyes as if it were bringing some special message just for them.

"I've never seen a more beautiful moonrise," she said. "It's a new moon, and I'm taking that as a good omen. Honestly, I need a change of luck."

"Then I shall also take it as a good omen," he said thinking how desperately he needed a change of luck. "Angela, I hate to say so but I need to check you in the hotel and get on home."

"Then reluctantly I will go."

Silently, they drifted back toward the Quad. Back at Kimberly Hall, they met a couple strolling, hand in hand, toward the dorms.

"Ah, to be young and in love," she said. "Do you ever long for your old college days?"

"Heavens, no. I might as well have been a monk. All I did, day and night, was study during the whole school year. Then for two months every summer, I worked hard during the day with a construction company that built houses in the suburbs of Birmingham. After work each day, there was more serious reading, usually late into the night. I don't remember having a single date during the whole four years of college.

"My only break from studying was the month before the fall semester when I toured the country with Uncle Edward, my father's only brother. I was his driver, and we took in most of the United States and parts of Canada during the four summers that I lived with him.

"From Key West to Nova Scotia in the East and from San Diego to Vancouver in the West. And lots of interesting places in between."

"I'm surprise that you can't recall a single date during your college years."

"In high school, I had a lot of balls in the air. In college, I was a dull young man. Serious as hell and dull as dirt."

"No, I'm not going to believe that."

"Okay, but it's the truth. For me personally, however, it was a time of tremendous intellectual and spiritual growth. And I should add that the travels with Uncle Edward were very special and rewarding.

"Unfortunately, I've had only one summer of extended travel since then. The summer before Hannah was born, I toured Europe in a two-seater Fiat convertible, all by myself."

"Well, there's nothing dull about you now," she said. "And I should add that I'm envious of your travels. Extensive travel is something that I have longed for but have not yet had a chance to experience."

"Then Cooper could be the place to get you started on that. We have a strong Faculty Development Fund, thanks to the generosity of our alumna and devoted trustee Georgette Wingo, who is Ashland's wealthiest citizen.

"Each year a number of faculty members enjoy study and travel with grants from this fund. Just know that you would be a candidate for grants from this fund."

"I'm pleased to hear that. Another plus for Cooper."

"This may also interest you. Georgette spent most of her adult life in New York City before returning here to the house she grew up in, and she still maintains her apartment there. Catherine, the Academic Dean, is her closest friend and usually spends time with her at that apartment every summer.

"Thanks to Catherine, Georgette is also one of my close friends and has invited me up several times to enjoy New York with her and Catherine. I've yet to accept her invitations because of Hannah, who still enjoys daily interactions with me. Call it parental duty, but I love it.

"There aren't many cosmopolitan women in Ashland, and I'm sure Georgette will be eager to draw you into her circle of friends. Catherine and I will certainly make the introduction if you're interested."

"Yes, the possibility of a friendship with Georgette does interest me. I also hope that you and I can become friends. Could we correspond even if I don't get the job? I'm at a place in life's journey where I need to converse with a good theologian and philosopher."

"I promise you that I will not be the one to break any correspondence. If you write, I will answer."

"Then you will soon be getting a lot of letters."

They left the campus for the hotel. After checking her in, he carried her suitcase to her room and placed it on the luggage rack. When he turned around to leave, there she was searching his eyes.

"Barsh, this has been a magical day for me, and I hate to see it end."

Astonished by the statement and her yielding eyes, he wished her a good night, which she returned, and left the room with that sensual movement shivering through his body.

Chapter Four

Debbie and Hannah were both asleep, when Barsh got home. Typically, he would head for the basement for a workout, but there was nothing habitual about this day. Even the house seemed oddly strange to him after spending four hours with Angela Kundera.

After going to the bathroom off the den, he went to his study to settle down, but that was impossible. Angela's voice had followed him into his sanctuary: Barsh, this has been a magical day for me, and I hate to see it end.

What was happening to him? He had trained himself not to get carried away with women, even those who aggressively pursued him.

Why then was he responding so to this woman? As he analyzed his situation, he had to concede that she had awakened him to the fact that he needed a woman like her, but he felt boxed in.

Based on Saint Paul's teachings, Debbie's faith allowed her to separate from him but it did not allow him to divorce her, and he could not imagine himself divorcing her without her consent, which he did not believe she give him.

What recourse did that leave him for intimately sharing life's journey with a woman like Angela? The answer was none within his range of acceptable behavior.

As he tried to put Angela out of his mind, he found himself thinking about his adulterous entanglement with a married woman, twenty-seven years ago. It started on a day like no other.

***

It was the last period of the day at Bradley High. Barsh walked into the school library for what was labeled study hall and sat down at his usual table with his back to an open window.

After finishing his math assignment, he glanced at April Morehouse, two tables away. As usual, she was absorbed in a book, that he assumed was a novel.

He remembered her amazing confession, earlier that year, in their English class. She had gotten so engrossed in a novel that she fainted at a terrifying moment in the story.

She was the granddaughter of the late Dr. Albert Norton, one of the most distinguished families in town, and Barsh knew he was a fool for loving her. What chance did he, or any country boy, have of winning her love?

At least he had not humiliated himself with awkward advances like a couple of classmates. He was always courteous and reserved in her presence. Forwardness had no place in his code of honor.

He had not dated anyone since Amy Burdette betrayed him during his fourteenth summer. At first, he thought he would never again experience that wonderful feeling of being in love, but he had already learned that a romantic heart is as strange as a phoenix.

From the ashes of first love, his heart had flickered to life and was soaring again on the wings of his fantastic imagination. In reality, he had found a love in April Morehouse but not a lover.

A cool breeze caught the back of his neck, and he turned to check the weather. The sky was clear, not a cloud in sight. It would be a good night to ride his quarter horse Thunder.

Once again, he looked at April. She had closed the book and was intently studying him. She held her gaze for a moment before dropping her eyes.

Twice now in one week, he had observed her studying him. Based on her responses in class, he knew she was smart, but he had no idea what went on in her head. What did she dream about? And why had she started studying him?

It was the last week of the school year, and he would not likely see her during the whole summer break. He lived five miles out in the country and rarely came to town, during the summer.

His town friends came to see him, but he never visited them. There was too much to do in the country, and he enjoyed it all.

April lived on North Main Street in a big house with expansive grounds. It was known as Dr. Norton's house, although he was long dead.

Her mother had grown up in that house and then attended to the University of Alabama, where she met and married John Morehouse. Two years ago, they moved into the big house to help care for Mrs. Norton. April's father opened Morehouse Pharmacy, and she joined Barsh's freshman class.

From the first day she appeared in class, he registered her as special. She was slight, almost frail. Her skin was so fair you would think she rarely went outdoors, and her long blond hair was striking.

To his knowledge, she did not have a boyfriend. Nor did she seem to have any close girlfriends.

The bell rang ending study hall and the school day. He knew April would go to her homeroom and pack her things. If her mother was not there to pick her up, she would sit on the steps near the sidewalk and wait for her.

He looked out the window. Mrs. Morehouse's Buick was nowhere in sight.

He lingered in his homeroom, until April settled on the top step of the stairs to the sidewalk. With his heart racing, he descended those stairs and turned to face her.

"April, your book report, this week, was very good. I always enjoy your reports."

"Well, thank you."

"I never thought I'd say such a thing, but I hate to see this school year end. Miss Little is the best English teacher I've ever had."

"She's the very best," April said. "I don't have the words to tell you how much I'm going to miss her class. I'm like Miss Little. I'd die if I didn't have good novels to read."

"I wish I had more time to read, but there's just too much to do in this world."

"Barsh, that was the most fun the other day when you and Miss Little were discussing a story. You think about things that would never cross my mind in a million years. I like that about you. I hope we get the same English class, again, next year."

"I'd like that, too."

"I'll probably have a good cry when school ends, Friday."

"I won't cry," he said, "but I'll miss seeing everybody. Anyway, I hope you have a good summer. Do you have any special plans?"

"Summer is always a sad time for me. I'll stay home, except for our vacation at Panama City Beach. What about you? What will your summer be like?"

"Work for the most part. I have a farm to take care of. I'm building up a herd of Black Angus cattle, which means raising corn and hay and taking care of the pastures. I'll also be working at a sawmill, Monday through Friday."

"That's why you have such muscular arms, all that hard work. And all I ever do is sit and read."

"Give me the outdoors, any day, for work or play. The only time I read is late at night or when I'm stuck indoors on a rainy day."

"Oh, I just thought of something," she said. "I recently read the most wonderful novel about this girl and her horse. Someone said that you have a horse. Is that true?"

"Yes, that's one of the good things about living in the country. In fact, I'm riding my horse tonight."

"You ride at night?"

"That's about the only time I have to ride this time of the year, other than Sunday afternoons. It's also a good time, especially on a stary night with a good moon. But we ride in all kinds of weather, up one dirt road and down another, sometimes until midnight or later."

"We? Who rides with you?"

"A couple of neighbors. One is just a kid, but she has a special way with horses. She usually rides with me a night."

"Do you have a picture of your horse?"

"No, but Thunder is special."

"Thunder! Does that mean he's spirited?"

"Very spirited. He's a quarter horse and loves to run."

"Oh, darn, here's Mother. I'll see you tomorrow. Have a good ride, tonight."

"I'm sure I will."

As she started toward her mother's car, she turned back and looked intently into his eyes. What a contrast they posed at that moment! He was almost six feet tall. She barely reached his broad shoulders.

She was the essence of refinement in her pale blue dress. He, rugged as the old West, was dressed in a tan cotton shirt, faded blue jeans, and brown harness boots.

"I must say I like the way they cut your hair. That flattop looks good on you. That's the first thing I noticed about you when we moved here. That and your strong arms."

She yielded her eyes and then walked away. There he stood for a moment with that magical shiver surging through his body. Then he hurried across the schoolyard to his Ford pickup.

The truck was nothing to brag about, but he was proud to have it. It kept him from having to ride the bus to and from school, and it met his transportation needs for camping, fishing, and hunting.

Man, did he feel good, as he drove toward home. April Morehouse had just talked to him with real interest.

There was no way to get pictures of Thunder developed before school ended on Friday, but he would have some before school started in the fall.

Fall. That was a long time to have to wait to see April's sweet face.

He was almost home before he remembered the sacks of crushed grain that he was supposed to pick up for Joe Foster's cattle. He turned around and headed back to town.

After his father died, Joe had taken over the family farm and started raising Black Angus cattle to supplement his income as a clerk at Randolph Farm Supplies. Then the Korean War broke out, and he was obsessed with the notion of fighting for his country on foreign soil.

His older brother, a decorated World War II hero, had filled him with stories about the glories of war. Now it was Joe's time to fight the Communists in Korea, and he volunteered for service in the Army. Off he went, leaving behind his wife Rachel, a four-year-old son, and a feeble mother.

Before leaving for basic training, he hired Barsh to look after his cattle until he returned. He had to bush-hog the pastures whenever they needed it, put out hay for the cattle during the winter months, and see that the bull had extra feed when it was servicing the cows.

At Randolph Farm Supplies, Barsh charged four one-hundred-pound sacks of crushed grain to Joe Foster's account and set out to deliver them. The old farm was on a back road about a mile from where Barsh lived.

Driving up to the old farm, he was surprised to see Rachel's car. She worked as a teller at First Commercial Bank, and it was too early for her to be home.

He backed the Ford pickup to the barn, threw a hundred-pound sack of crushed grain on his shoulder, and carried it to the feed room. Returning to the truck for another sack, he saw Rachel coming toward him.

"Hey, Barsh. Thanks for bringing the feed."

"Glad to do it. I didn't expect you to be home. Is Lewis or Mrs. Foster sick?"

"Mrs. Foster hasn't been feeling well lately, so I took her to the doctor, this morning, and decided to stay home for the rest of the day."

"I hope it's nothing serious."

"Her blood pressure is way too high. That's the main thing. She should be all right if she'll take the medicine the doctor prescribed. She can be contrary at times. Barsh, do you know what I'd like to do this afternoon?"

"What's that?"

"Go swimming at the Boy Scout Lake. Joe and I used to swim there a lot. I'm afraid to go by myself. Could you meet me there in about thirty minutes?"

"Yes, if that's what you want."

"Thank you, thank you. You don't know how much this means to me. I never get to do anything anymore, except work and look after Lewis and Mrs. Foster. I'll meet you at the lake in thirty minutes."

She returned to the house and he finished unloading the feed. As he drove away, he was thinking about Rachel. Why hadn't it occurred to him that she was having a hard time while Joe was in Korea?

It was a bloody war, and he could be killed any day. Just worrying about that possibility would be enough to drive her crazy.

He parked the pickup in the backyard and rushed into their old farmhouse to get his swimsuit. His Mother was working in the kitchen.

"I was getting worried about you, Barsh."

"I had to pick up some feed for Joe's cattle, and now I'm going swimming in the Boy Scout Lake. I haven't been since last summer and I need a good swim."

"Well, please be careful."

"You know I will."

He got his swimming trunks and a towel and left for the lake, that was less than three miles from his house. Driving down the bumpy dirt road, he wished he was on his way to meet April Morehouse. Then he reminisced about the wonderful moments he had shared with her before leaving school.

He turned off the main road onto the dead-end drive that curved up a steep grade to the Boy Scout Lake, that was nestled in a hardwood forest. After parking near the dam, he ran up the path to the lodge to change into his swimming trunks.

Back at the lake, he dove into the blue water and swam hard to the upper end and back to the dock, where he stretched out on his towel to await Rachel's arrival.

He sat up at the sound of a car. Rachel parked next to his pickup and got out. He assumed that she would be wearing her swimsuit, but she was still dressed as she had been at the barn.

"Barsh, come over this way and watch out for me, while I change into my swimsuit."

"Okay," he said and started toward her.

"That's good. Stand there and give a yell if you see anyone coming."

She slid into the back seat and closed the door. It was impossible for him to keep his eyes on the road when she began taking off her clothes.

God, he saw her breasts when she stretched against the seat to pull up the one-piece swimsuit. Out of the car, she adjusted the swimsuit and then hurried toward him with a tote bag.

"Thanks for coming. I want to sunbathe for a while on the dock and then take a swim before I have to go. I don't have a lot of time, today."

Rachel settled on her towel and started oiling herself. The sight of her spread legs, that were surprisingly athletic, aroused him in spite of his efforts to control himself. She was a married woman. Well oiled, she stretched out on her towel.

"Lie down beside me and talk to me. Is Susan Henry your sweetheart? Tell me the truth. She practically lives with you."

"No, I don't have a sweetheart. Susan is just a friend. We like to ride our horses, together. That's all."

"Well, you've certainly changed things around here. Nobody rode a horse before you moved out here. You and Thunder were a sight for sore eyes as you rode by our place. It wasn't long until Susan got a horse and then John Marshall.

"Now you've got me wanting to ride double with you some night. Just you and me. Is that possible?"

"Sure."

"Okay, I can't wait."

"Just let me know when you're ready."

"I will and soon. I don't want Mrs. Foster to know about it, but that won't be a problem. I can slip off and meet you at the barn after she and Lewis are asleep. We can ride in our pasture. No one will ever know about it but us."

Rachel was nine years older than Barsh. He had always admired her and thought Joe Foster was a lucky man to have her as a wife. But he would never again think of her in that same innocent way. He had seen her breasts and trembled in her presence. And now she wanted to ride secretly with him on Thunder in their pasture, at night.

He did not know what she had in mind for them, but she had given him the most important rule. Whatever the two of them did, it should remain a secret.

Before two weeks passed, he was entangled in an adulterous relationship with Rachael, that lasted almost a year. It ended abruptly when she received word that Joe would be coming home from Korea without his left arm.

The night she told Barsh, their relationship immediately reverted back to what it was before, without either of them having to verbalize the new reality.

As acts within themselves, he could accept their sexual liaisons without guilt. When Joe came home, however, he could no longer isolate them.

Every time he saw Joe, he felt guilty for betraying his neighbor. Thus, his guilt was chronic because Joe still needed his help with the farm.

Sundays were the worst of days for him when they attended the same country church. Rachel would joyfully sing with the congregation, while Joe, by her side, was mute as stone. Barsh knew the source of his own silence but could only wonder about Joe's.

Whatever the affair had given Barsh, it cost him double. When school started back that fall, April Morehouse was definitely interested in him.

She frequently sought him out and flirted with him, but it was too late. How could he court her in good conscience, when he was secretly meeting a married woman for sex?

Too artless to untangle himself from Rachel, he never asked April for a single date, even though he loved her above every girl in the world. Before the school year ended, a prominent town boy made a move on her, and she became his girlfriend.

***

The crescent moon had crept into view through the big windows of Barsh's study, and his mind jumped back to the scene with Angela by the campus lake at Cooper.

Although he had responded in harmony with her about taking the rising new moon as a good omen, he knew better. He could not envision a path to a happy life for himself in the foreseeable future.

Regarding her confession, he had no idea what change of luck she needed. Yet, he whispered a wish that it would come her way.

It was almost midnight, and he had to get to sleep. Tomorrow would be another long day for him.

Chapter Five

Angela was waiting in the lobby of the hotel with her suitcase, when Barsh got there Friday morning. She was dressed in a black skirt and a green silky blouse that rippled over her small breasts with the fluid elegance of a brook. And there was her perfume enticing his nostrils. They exchanged greetings with solicitations of each other's well-being and left the hotel.

He took her to breakfast at Ashland Cafe, a local landmark. Their conversation was light with moments of silent reflection, as they studied each other with approving eyes. Finished with breakfast, they left for the college.

"Are you ready for today's agenda?" he asked.

"Truthfully, I'm getting anxious. I definitely want this position."

"Just keep a positive focus. You'll impress everyone. I know Dean Thompson and the English majors will love you.

"Play yourself down a little with the English faculty. They already know you're highly qualified for the position. Your major task is to convince them that you're a team player who's looking for a role to play in the English department."

"Thanks for the advice."

"Well, here we are back at Cooper."

"You're right. The college does look different in the daylight. Even so, I like it. That's because you like it. But I'll keep that between you and me."

"Yes, that would definitely be to your advantage with the search committee."

He parked in his usual place and led the way to his office, upstairs in Kimberly Hall. He opened the door, flipped on the light switch, and motioned for Angela to enter.

"These are handsome floor-to-ceiling bookshelves."

"Thank you. I built them myself."

"May I see the photos on your file cabinet?"

"Yes, of course."

"Debbie and Hannah, obviously. Both natural beauties as I would have imagined."

"They're as fair as the flowers of May, to use Grandmother Roberts' expression."

"And this is you and your horse Thunder," she said picking up the photo. Ah, your hair was blond, and the flattop cut looks so becoming on you."

"I was a towheaded boy. Then my hair turned blond. Now it brown, and hopefully I'll live until it turns white, again."

"Just so you know, I like the way you wear your brown hair in a short high-flying ponytail. I also like the way you trim your beard."

"That's kind of you to say so. Neither are popular around here. I think I was the only man in Ashland with a beard and long hair when I first grew them several years ago."

"That doesn't surprise me. You are obviously your own man."

"Please have a seat," he said gesturing toward two comfortable chairs in front of the desk.

"First, let me take note of some of your scholarly books. Oh, here's an interesting one, *The Denial of Death*. Tell me about it."

He pulled it from the bookshelf, and they sat facing each other.

"This is Ernest Becker's seminal treatise on the various ways humans attempt to escape their mortality. Strong meat as they say."

"Then I must read it. Is it still in print?"

"Probably. Would you like to borrow mine? If you join us this fall, you can return it by hand. Otherwise, you can mail it to me.

"I should tell you that it's marked up. I have a habit of making notes of notable passages in my books. That makes it easier for me to find them if I need to reference them."

"Yes, I'd like to borrow it, all the more now that I know you've marked it up."

"My current reading is focused on modern novels. I'd like your recommendations on some of the books I should read."

"I'd love to do that. Would you like to start with Southern novels?"

"Definitely. Let's talk about Southern novels on the drive back to the airport this afternoon."

"Your wish is my command, if I may quote you," she said with a smile.

"Then I'm looking forward to our conversation. I have time to show you Old Main before your appointment with Dean Thompson. Shall we head that way?"

As they walked leisurely to Old Main, students were criss-crossing the Quad on the way to their classes. Everyone they met sized Angela up with approving smiles.

In Old Main he gave her a brief tour of the formal parlors with their portraits of past presidents and other Cooper dignitaries. He showed her the parlor where the faculty came for morning coffee and light banter.

Then they were off to see Dean Thompson, a Cooper alumna from Charleston, who had earned a Ph.D. in American history from the University of North Carolina at Chapel Hill. A slender woman in her early sixties, she was the epitome of Southern grace, which, in her case, was gilded with an intellect that gave her a special power that she wielded wisely.

She was one of the reasons Barsh had stayed at Cooper and probably the major force that had kept him from being fired by the predominately conservative trustees because of his liberal theological views and empirical analysis of the Bible.

He introduced the two women and left to teach his nine o'clock class. As soon as the bell ended the class, he rushed to the library conference room to chair Angela's meeting with the English faculty. Dean Thompson, who had walked Angela over, excused herself. Barsh introduced everyone and moderated the session, that went exceedingly well.

At eleven o'clock, Dr. June Hurst took Angela to her American Literature class where she led a discussion on Faulkner's *As I Lay Dying*—a task she had been asked to prepare for.

The other members of the English Department were invited to sit in on Angela's presentation and two of them did. At twelve Barsh and the English faculty took her to lunch in the cafeteria's private dining room.

After lunch, she met with a group of English majors and talked about her philosophy of teaching as well as some of her special interest. Afterward, two English majors, who were almost beside themselves with excitement, brought Angela to his office.

He was pleased to see that they were so taken with her. She embraced each of the girls, as they were leaving, and told them she hoped to see them in the fall.

"Well, I certainly called that one right," he said and motioned for her to have a seat, as he came around the desk to sit next to her.

"The students are just as excited about you as I predicted they would be."

"They definitely want me to get the job, and I do want to be here this fall."

"Then let's talk about housing. Do you plan to rent or buy?"

"I'll have to rent for a while."

"The College owns several rental houses near the campus. They're adequate and the rent is reasonable. My favorite one will be available later this summer. Would you like to check it out?"

"Yes, if you don't think it would jinx my getting an offer."

"I hope you won't think I'm too presumptuous, but to expedite matters, I just talked with the Business Manager about this house. If you get the position and want to rent it, he'll send you a lease.

"I also called Elizabeth Campbell about a possible visit this afternoon. She's moving back to West Virginia to care for her ailing mother. We can drop by this afternoon if you're interested. No need to call."

"Yes, thank you. This is exciting. I've lived in dorms and apartments ever since I left home for college. I'm ready for a house."

"Then let's check out this one."

Chapter Six

The visit with Elizabeth Campbell was pleasant. They wished her well on her move back to West Virginia and left.

"Thanks for arranging the visit. I really like the house. And I was taken with that big backyard."

"That backyard would be a good place for bird watching. Are you a birder?"

"No, but I wish I were."

"All you'll need are field glasses and a field guide to the birds."

"What would you recommend?"

"I have extra field glasses, and I don't know how many field guides. I'll be glad to get you started."

"Then I'll take you up on the offer if I get the job."

"Assuming you do, let's think ahead to a time when you might want to buy a house," he said still trying to promote Cooper. "The mortgage for a modest house in Ashland is quite manageable on Cooper salaries. Would you like for me to show you some of the neighborhoods where faculty members live?"

"I'd like to see where you live if you don't mind."

"We'll be there in five minutes."

He drove through Fern Meadows and stopped in front of his house. She was pleased to learn that she would be able to manage a mortgage on a similar house.

"Barsh, could I use your house to change from this skirt back into slacks for the flight home? I much prefer to travel in slacks."

"Yes, of course," he said and pulled into the driveway.

He carried her suitcase into his bedroom, which he described as the guest bedroom, and went to his study. After a few minutes, the toilet flushed. He rose from his desk and waited for her in the hall near the foyer.

"Thanks. This is much more comfortable."

"Here, let me carry your suitcase."

"I like your house," she said shifting the suitcase to him. "Do you have a study? I've never had that luxury in my one-bedroom apartments."

"It's just off the kitchen. I think it was built as a sunroom, but it works just fine for my study."

"I'd like to see it if I may."

"Sure," he said setting the suitcase on the floor. "Right this way."

"Whatever they built it for, you've turned it into a lovely study. If I get the job, I'll probably turn the second bedroom of the college rental house into my first study."

"Sound like a good plan."

"Your parents?" she said picking up the framed photo from the desk.

"That was taken by a traveling photographer soon after they married. Mother and Dad were killed in a traffic accident, two weeks after I received my Ph.D. from Emory."

"How sad to lose both parents so suddenly. How did you deal with that?"

"With much grief, although not so much for my own loss as for their loss. They deserved many more good years. I've never known a couple more devoted to each other than they were.

"I didn't want to lose them, but I could let them go with eternal gratitude, because they had given me the things I needed when I was growing up. I never once doubted that they loved and treasured me. That's a great gift, you know."

"I wish I could say the same about my parents. Not a good scene. I have no patience with them, especially Mother. Oh, well, that's a boring story."

"Angela, I was just thinking about what you said last night about looking for a Southern experience with this move. I could take you to Kings Mountain National Military Park on our way back to the Charlotte Airport. We'll be traveling within a few miles of the place.

"This is a major Revolutionary War site where the Southern Patriots won a critical battle against the British. Some historians consider it the turning point in the War.

"There's a visitors' center and a good trail around the battlefield. If we leave now, we'll have time for a short visit before your flight back to Providence."

"Yes, I'd like that experience."

"How are those shoes for walking?"

"Quite good. I always wear comfortable shoes, never high heels."

"I certainly approve of that. Here's an idea. When I'm on an outing like this, I take a canteen of water as well as some dried fruit and roasted nuts. Whatever I have on hand. I like to take a break somewhere along the trail to think about things."

"Then I'd like to follow your practice."

"I've got a special place in mind for us to take a break—Colonel Patrick Ferguson's grave."

"I assume Colonel Ferguson was killed in the battle. Whose side was he on?"

"The British. A citizen of Scotland, Ferguson was a Colonel in the British army, but the men who fought under his command were all South Carolinians who had remained loyal to the King. Are you familiar with the Southern strategy that the British developed after the war bogged down in the North?"

"No, I'm ill-informed about the Revolutionary War. You're good at summarizing things. Give me a synopsis."

"I'll tell you on the way. Let me get my backpack and take care of our snack. I'll be right back."

She was browsing his books when he returned all prepared for their excursion.

"Shall we go?"

"Ready! Ready!"

They left Fern Meadows with Angela telling him how lucky she felt that he was overseeing the search. She had never experienced such genuine hospitality.

"I feel good about your visit, Angela. As for as I can tell, everything went super well. The search committee will meet Monday at one o'clock. It's possible you'll hear from Dean Thompson, early next week."

"Believe me, I really want this job. And I want your friendship even if it's long-distance."

"The question of friendship is settled as far as I'm concerned."

"Okay, I'm banking on it. Now give me the background for the Kings Mountain battle."

"In 1778, the British decided to focus their efforts on conquering the Southern States, and they believed they could because there were so many Loyalists among them. If they were successful, they would then refocus their efforts on capturing the Northern States.

"The British Navy transported a large force, commanded by Sir Henry Clinton, to Savannah, Georgia. They soon captured Savannah and then Augusta, the two major population centers in Georgia.

"From those bases, they moved into South Carolina and captured Charleston in May of 1780. George Washington sent continental forces under the command of General Gates to stop the British advance through South Carolina. Gates and his army, however, were routed by Lord Cornwallis and his British forces at Camden.

"By the end of that summer, the British had captured all the important forts and outposts in Georgia and South Carolina. The only forces of resistance left in these two states were local militia who waged a kind of guerrilla warfare against the British. Are you still with me?"

"Oh, yes."

"Okay, this is where Colonel Ferguson comes in. His orders were to recruit and arm his own force from the citizens of South Carolina, and being a man of passionate persuasion, he was able to recruit and arm a force of over a thousand Loyalists. Their mission was to subdue the backwoods Patriots.

"Those who lived over the Blue Ridge Mountains were especially independent minded, and Ferguson had threatened to march his force over the mountain and burn them out if they didn't pledge allegiance to the King.

"As a response to that threat, these Over-Mountain Men, as they were called, marched into South Carolina in October of 1780 to take the battle to Ferguson. Joined by other Patriot forces, they surrounded him on Kings Mountain. Within a few hours, Ferguson was dead and the rest of his men were killed or captured."

"Well done," she said. "This is a bonus I never expected on this trip. My own expert tour guide to a major Revolutionary War site."

"Please, I'm far from an expert on this war, but Cooper does have an expert, Bobby Morrison, who's a member of the History Department. He tells me there were more Revolutionary War battles in South Carolina than any other State."

"You sound like an authority to me, and I thank you for the synopsis. Now, I'm looking forward to walking the battlefield with you."

***

Kings Mountain was always a good outing for Barsh, and he had never enjoyed being there more than with Angela. Back in the car on the drive to Charlotte, they conversed about the Southern Literary Renaissance. He had never heard about the group of poets and critics from Vanderbilt University known as the Fugitive Poets.

They were a new breed of Southerners, and he was eager to read Angela's favorite Fugitive Poet—Robert Penn Warren, who became the first Poet Laureate of the United Sates.

Next, Angela informed him about Caroline Gordon, who had been pulled into the literary scene by her marriage to Fugitive Poet Allen Tate. What a turbulent marriage it turned out to be.

Nevertheless, Gordon managed to become a successful novelist. Based on Angela's discussion of Gordon and her novels, Barsh could see why she chose to write her Ph. D. dissertation on her.

He also learned that Gordon had taught, as a visiting author, at Emory University during the spring of 1965. He was there, but so deep into his studies of Biblical literature that he knew nothing about her presence. He felt an affinity with Gordon just from the way Angela had cast her, and he wished he had met her.

Angela had suggested that he might like to start with Gordon's novel *Aleck Maury*, since she knew he would appreciate the protagonist's love of nature. But he had set his mind to start with Angela's favorite novel by Gordon, *The Women on the Porch.* He didn't need Aleck Maury to show him the value of nature.

On arriving in Charlotte, they dined at Emile's Restaurant, and he managed to keep her talking about Southern literature. At one point, she shared with him the major points of a graduate paper she had written on Carson McCullers' *The Heart is a Lonely Hunter,* and at his request, she promised to send him a copy.

On leaving the restaurant, he drove straight to the Charlotte Airport. They checked Angela's luggage, found her departure gate, and sat side by side. At the first call for boarding, they stood for their parting words.

"Barsh, I don't know how to thank you for making this such an extraordinary visit in every way."

"It's been my pleasure."

"I trust you know that I'm hoping, with all my heart, that we'll be colleagues this fall."

"I'm also hoping that happens."

"Whatever happens, I'm claiming you as my dear friend. There's something about you that allows me to be myself without pretense. You bring out the best in me. I feel like I'm entering a new stage on life's journey."

Looking into her eyes, he nodded slowly as if he knew what she meant. An attendant announced that all passengers should board, immediately.

Barsh extended his hand, and she took it in both of hers. Then she moved against him with a tight embrace that he returned.

"Goodbye, Angela, and do take good care."

"Goodbye for now. Have a safe drive home and double-clutch the Audi, just for me, when you leave the parking lot."

She tossed her hair over her shoulder and eased into the short boarding line. At the door, she waved and disappeared. He moved to the widow onto the runway and waited until her plane was airborne.

Chapter Seven

As Barsh had promised, he took Hannah to Table Rock State Park that Saturday. After stopping at the Visitors Center, they headed up the Carrick Creek Trail, stopping occasionally to examine a shrub or a tree.

He was pleased that she had taken an interest in wild plants and knew the distinguishing features of rhododendron and mountain laurel. She could identify several major deciduous trees. Among the evergreens, she could differentiate pines, hemlocks, and cedars.

A little before noon, they stood on the mountaintop and looked down on the valley. She was tired but all smiles.

He spotted a moss-covered oak that the wind had toppled, and they sat, face to face, astraddle its trunk. There they ate their picnic lunch, while discussing environmental issues. Then they descended the trail and left for home.

"That was fun, Daddy. I want to start hiking different trails with you."

"It's always a joy to hike with you, my sweet girl. I have several trails in mind for us to hike this summer. I also have plans to hike a few trails that are too remote and difficult for you. But they'll still be there when you get older. Then we'll hike them. Okay?"

"That's fine."

"Here's my plan. I'll save my difficult hikes for this fall, so you and I can hike together this summer. How's that?"

"Sounds good. Do you mind if I take a nap?"

"Sleep well and I'll do some thinking."

She reclined her seat and was soon asleep. As he drove the first leg of the route home, he worried about how he might prepare her for Debbie's move to Louisville but made no progress on solving the problem.

Shelving that unresolved issue, he reminisced about the time he had spent with Angela Kundera on Thursday and Friday. He didn't have a category that would adequately describe the experience. It almost bordered on the surreal, but in other ways, the whole experience seemed to flow so naturally.

He remembered her words at the airport as she was leaving: Whatever happens, I'm claiming you as a dear friend. There's something about you that allows me to be myself without pretense. You bring out the best in me. I feel like I'm entering a new stage on life's journey.

He wanted to believe that they would become close friends, something he thought he could manage. He wasn't confident, however, that would happen.

He knew that she could have been playing him for a fool. He had only spent portions of two days with her and had no way to judge her integrity. Only time would tell if she had shown him her true self.

There was no doubt in his mind that the search committee would recommend her for the position and that the college would offer her the job, probably sometime next week. If she did not accept the offer, he would know she had been playing him. If she accepted the offer, he would be traveling in a new country without a map.

Hannah woke from her nap in a chatty mood, and he shelved his thoughts about Angela Kundera. But he knew his mind would not leave them there for long.

***

After dinner that evening, Debbie went to the den to watch television, Hannah to her room to work on a new poem, and Barsh to his study to resume reading the Spinoza biography. His mind, however, frequently shifted to Angela—sometime focusing on her visit and sometime wondering what she was doing that very moment.

Just before her bedtime, Hannah read him her new poem. He liked the conceit and told her so. Then he offered her two suggestions to consider.

While she reflected on his suggestions, he reflected on the progress she had made since her fifth-grade language arts teacher turned her on to writing free verse poetry.

Then he remembered Angela's surprising response to his description of the landscape along the Broad River to Cherokee Falls: Oh, my, you have the soul of a poet. That had awakened the memory of his first attempt at writing poetry when he was a college freshman.

Hannah accepted both of his suggestions and reread the poem. As he praised her sensibilities, it occurred to him that he had never told her about his first attempt at writing poetry. And so, he did.

"Daddy, could I see those poems?"

"When I showed them to the Academic Dean, who was a respected poet, he gave me such a cold critique that I trashed them, and I've never written another poem. But here's something I trust will interest you. I've decided to give it another try.

"This time, I'll be more inspired by your achievements than classical poets. I'll definitely choose free verse. Who knows? Maybe, I can become a third-rate poet, but first, I need to start reading more modern and contemporary poetry."

"Let's do it together, Daddy."

"Okay, we'll make it one of our summer projects. I'll start by reading you a couple of Carl Sandburg's poems.

"His last home, named Connemara, is at Flat Rock, North Carolina, not far from Table Rock. I thought about taking you this afternoon, while we were up that way, but decided to make that a separate trip. I bought Sandburg's *Collected Poems* on my first visit to Connemara."

Barsh found the book and read "Fog" and "Chicago." She especially enjoyed "Chicago" and laughed as he bellowed out the lines with such bold force: Stormy, husky, brawling, City of the Big Shoulders . . . Fierce as a dog with tongue lapping for action.

Next, he gave her a brief history of Connemara. Then he talked about Sandburg's habit of writing through the night and about the dairy goats his wife kept.

"When can we go? It sounds like an interesting place."

"We'll find a Saturday for that outing before long. We can also visit Chimney Rock, again, since it's not far from Flat Rock. But right now, it's your bedtime."

She left for bed without asking for a single extension. He resumed reading *Spinoza*.

Debbie turned off the television and left the den for her bedroom. The toilet connected to the master bedroom soon flushed, and he followed the sound of her steps as she came back down the hall and turned toward the study.

"Can we talk?" she asked.

"Here or the den?"

"The den if you don't mind."

He followed her into the den. She sat in her swivel rocker, and he sat across from her in a big stuffed chair.

"I had another call from Henry Dugan at work, yesterday. He's pressing me to let him know when I'm moving to Louisville. He wants me there right away. You can't keep dragging your feet on this. It's time you told Hannah."

"I'm sorry, but I'm not ready for that. In fact, I'm worried about her."

"What do you mean?"

"Thursday night, she came running down the hall to the study. She'd had a bad dream in which I was lost in a forest. She was searching for me but couldn't find me.

"I've never seen her so upset. I talked to her about nightmares, but she was still clingy and didn't want to go back to bed."

"Why are you just now telling me this?

"I don't know. Maybe I was afraid that I was reading too much into the dream because of my own anxiety."

"Barsh, you know that I would already be in Louisville if I wasn't concerned about Hannah's wellbeing."

"Yes, and I'm desperately looking for a way to make that move easier for Hannah. Hopefully, I'll find one if you'll give me more time."

"I'm trying to be patient. Surely, you understand my situation."

"I fully understand your situation, and I hope you understand mine. If you want it done now, you'll have to tell her yourself."

"Okay, I'll give you more time," she said standing to leave. "We both know she'll take it better coming from you, but please find a way, soon."

"Believe me, it's my top priority," he said and watched her leave for her bedroom.

Ever since he had known her, Debbie had always been conscious about her looks and had kept a trim figure. She was an attractive woman with beautiful blond hair, but her natural beauty was overshadowed somewhat by her sad-eyed countenance. He had never seen her bubbling over with joy or passion about anything.

A true professional, she dressed the part and played it well, Monday through Friday. Saturday was her day—shopping, relaxing, whatever she wanted to do. Sunday, she faithfully attended church in the morning and then rested at home.

On a typical evening, one of them prepared dinner on a somewhat rotating basis. After dinner, she usually changed into her pajamas and watched television, more often than not by herself.

There was no doubt in his mind that those days were doomed, forever, and that he would soon be living alone.

Chapter Eight

The search committee met Monday afternoon at one o'clock. With much praise for Angela Kundera, they unanimously recommended her for the English position and quickly dispersed.

Barsh walked across campus to tell Dean Thompson. As he topped the stairs of Old Main, he could hear her chatting with her receptionist.

"I didn't expect you so soon," she said and ushered him into her office. "What's the verdict?"

"They voted unanimously for Dr. Kundera."

"My gracious, when have they ever voted unanimously on anything? Have a seat and visit with me.

"I'm pleased with the committee's choice. Do you think she'll accept our offer?"

"Truthfully, it doesn't make sense to me that she would come here. On the drive back to Charlotte, I learned that she has an offer from Bennington. She got the offer three days before her visit with us.

"We can neither match the salary they've offered her nor the prestige of teaching there. Yet, she told me, several times, that she hopes to be teaching here this fall."

"My intuition tells me she will accept our offer. She told me she was looking for a Southern experience, and we can give her that. I assume she also told you."

"She did. That could be the deciding factor for her if she was sincere with me."

"Let's hope she was. Once again, I thank you for your excellent leadership. You're the best at chairing committees. You always keep them on task until they get the job done.

"As soon as I get the President's approval, I'll call her, hopefully this afternoon."

"Please let me know her response. I'll be in my office until five."

"I'll call as soon as I get off the phone with her," she said looking straight into his eyes with a worried face. "Forgive me, but something seems to be troubling you of late."

“Unfortunately, you’re right. Things are not good at home. It’s serious but I can deal with it. I’ll share the situation with you before long. Meantime, don’t worry about me.”

“That’s a hard order, but I’ll do my best. And I will take a hug, now, if you don’t mind.”

He tenderly embraced her and left—his emotions as entangled as a plate of spaghetti.

Halfway across the Quad, he remembered Angela’s discussion of Caroline Gordon’s novel, *The Women on the Porch,* and changed course to see if the library had it.

“Ah, Dr. Roberts, I presume,” Amanda McGee said. “Are you looking for me or some rare book?”

“Wouldn’t that be one and the same?” he said with a smile and she laughed.

“Changing the subject, are we getting that English professor from Brown?”

“We should know soon.”

“Then she’s being offered the position.”

“That’s a reasonable deduction. Amanda, have you read Caroline Gordon’s novel, *The Women on the Porch?*”

“No, but I assume you came by to see if we have it.”

“Your assumption is right.”

“Do you want me to check the files for you?”

“No, I will. I’m also looking for poetry books by James Dickey.”

“Then you’re in luck. I’ve ordered all of his poetry books for the library. You know he teaches at the University of South Carolina, don’t you?”

“I do.”

“I wouldn’t attempt to judge his poetry, but James Dickey is, without doubt, the most colorful professor at USC. I went to one of his poetry readings, while I was a graduate student, and he clearly had more fun than anyone in the audience.”

Although the library didn’t have any of Gordan’s novels, that didn’t concern Barsh. He would order them through the college book store.

He checked out an arm load of poetry books and hurried to his office. He didn’t want to miss the Dean’s call. After brewing tea, he began reading Dickey’s first book of poems. Just after four o'clock, Catherine called to tell him that Dr. Kundera had accepted the position.

"You won't believe how excited she is about our offer. She wants to rent the house that Elizabeth Campbell is vacating. She said that you had taken her by to look at it."

"Well, your intuition was correct. There's no doubt that she will be a tremendous addition to the faculty. I just hope it's the right move for her."

"Time alone will tell, but I'm confident of one thing. You and I will go out of our way to make this a good Southern experience for her. Again, I thank you for your help with the search."

***

The rest of the week slipped into *time that was* in the same old academic rhythm for Barsh, except for those quite moments when he found himself thinking about Angela.

After teaching his last class that Friday, he headed for the college post office. Angela had promised to write him as soon as she heard from Dean Thompson, and he was hoping to find a letter from her in his box.

No letter from her, but a puzzling one from Crescent Moon Literary Review, 1978 Future Lane, Providence, Rhode Island.

He had never heard of Crescent Moon Literary Review, but Providence, Rhode Island, caught his eye and so did 1978 Future Lane. He smiled, realizing that Angela had created a false address to keep anyone working in the college post office from knowing that she was corresponding with him.

Back in his office, he read the letter with great anticipation. After explaining the disguised return address, she raved about how the visit to Cooper had energized her beyond her wildest imagination.

She had already modified her agenda for the rest of the semester and summer. It included a return to her creative writing, more vigorous walking to prepare herself for hiking with him in the Carolina mountains, and teaching two courses in Summer School. She needed the money.

She thanked him again for the way he had managed her visit and for lending her his copy of Ernest Becker's *The Denial of*

Death. She had been deeply engrossed in reading it and found it challenging and informative.

In late August, she would be on her way to Ashland and a new life in the South. She promised to write often and signed off with *Affectionately yours, Angela.*

He labeled a manila folder Crescent Moon Literary Review, inserted the letter, and locked the folder in his file cabinet.

Like most of Cooper's faculty, he did not typically keep office hours on Friday afternoons. But this was not a typical Friday.

He ate lunch in the college cafeteria and returned to his office. The task before him was to respond to Angela's letter and that turned out to be a bit challenging.

He didn't want to dampen her enthusiasm about joining the Cooper faculty, but he needed to be careful in his response because of the uncertainty of his own future at Cooper.

Finished with the letter, he came up with his own creative return address. Even so, he decided to mail the letter and future correspondences at the town post office.

Chapter Nine

The bell rang, and Barsh concluded his last lecture for the semester. The students scrambled for the door, except for Laura Buck who stepped from her front-row seat to his desk.

"Dr. Roberts, I don't have words to tell you how much you've helped me this semester. I'm amazed at your ability to analyze things so clearly. You're the best. I have a whole new perspective on life and my own existence."

"I appreciate your kind words, Laura. And thanks for your engaging participation. Your comments stimulated several lively discussions that I enjoyed."

"Will you be in your office at one o'clock this afternoon? I need to talk to you about a serious matter."

"Yes, I'll sign you up."

He gathered his lecture notes and went straight to his office. The phone rang. It was Dean Thompson.

"Barsh, do you have plans for Saturday morning? I'd love to have you over for breakfast and a good discussion. It's been too long since your last visit."

"I'm sorry, Catherine, but I've promised to take Hannah to Connemara and then Chimney Rock. I can come next Saturday if that works for you. Our breakfast discussions are just as important to me as they are to you."

"Yes, that's a good time for me. Have a great day with Hannah, tomorrow."

"Have you had lunch? I have a student appointment at one, so I'm eating in the cafeteria today."

"Then I shall join you."

It being Friday, the faculty table was empty, which pleased them. Catherine inquired about his situation at home, but he wasn't ready to share Debbie's plan for a year-long separation. Instead, he simply reported that things were manageable and urged her not to worry about him.

He had just finished reading Catherine Gordan's *The Women on the Porch* and shifted the conversation to the novel. The Dean remembered that Angela did her dissertation on Gordan and asked to borrow the novel. He promised to bring it to her, Monday.

Finished with lunch, they walked back to Old Main, both pleased to have shared a few moments.

Next, he checked his mail, which contained a large manila envelope with the fake return address, Crescent Moon Literary Review.

Back in his office, he began previewing the rest of the mail, which was mostly junk. Ah, something from an old classmate, he said to himself without voice.

It was an invitation to the twenty-fifth anniversary of Bradley High's class of 1953. There was a handwritten note apologizing for the late invitation. They had just tracked down his address.

The reunion was scheduled for two weeks from tomorrow. How fortuitous, he thought as he began to think about his classmates. Yes, he would definitely be there.

He looked at his watch. It was time for Laura Buck's appointment. She had dropped by a few times during the semester, always lavishing him with praise. She admired his intellect, his compassion, and wanted to tell him so.

Other than what he could see, which was an attractive woman, probably in her early-thirties, all he knew about her was that she was a registered nurse in Spartanburg, who had decided to earn a bachelor's degree. It would open more professional doors for her.

"Hi, Dr. Roberts," she said standing in the doorway.

"Come in, Laura," he said and rose to greet her.

She closed the door and extended her hand, which was firm. There was nothing wilted about the woman. He gestured for her to take a chair and then sat facing her.

"I don't know where to start."

"Start anywhere. You'll find your way as you go."

"I told you I'm a nurse, but I don't think I told you that I'm married to a doctor. Mark is a highly respected surgeon and has a good practice.

"The problem is he's lost interest in me. He works hard and then he drinks with his buddies.

"I assume he has a woman or more likely several women. The point is he does nothing with me, and I can't take it anymore.

"He won't agree on a divorce, so I need help. Should I pursue a divorce, anyway?"

"I'm not a marriage counselor. You need to find a good marriage counselor. I think that's the first step."

"You're an enlightened philosopher and professor of religion, and I want your opinion. Do I have moral grounds for seeking a divorce?"

"Have you told Mark the current situation is unacceptable?"

"Yes, but he doesn't take me seriously."

"I suggest that you demand a serious discussion with him. Then you can hold him responsible for his reaction and take it from there."

"Then you don't condemn divorce outright."

"Definitely not. People often make grave mistakes in choosing a spouse. People also change after they get married, sometimes for better and sometimes for worse. Relationships can become destructive, unbearable, unredeemable. Divorce is clearly the best response in those cases.

"My advice is to find a marriage counselor who can help you sort things out, preferably with Mark. If you can't fix the marriage, get a divorce."

"Okay, I'm taking your advice. Do you know how much I admire you? You are so intelligent without a hint of arrogance. You would not believe how arrogant Mark is. He has contempt for almost everyone he meets."

"I'm sorry to hear that."

"I was so disappointed to learn you're not teaching summer school. Do you plan to travel?"

"I'm still working on summer plans."

Laura fished a pen from her pocketbook and wrote her name and phone number on a piece of paper.

"Please call me the next time you're in Spartanburg. I'd love to take you to lunch or dinner. We'll dine high or low. Your preference, my pleasure."

"That would be nice. But I seldom get to Spartanburg."

"I don't blame you. Anyway, I can't thank you enough for your understanding and advice. See you in class next week for the final exam. Hope it's not too hard."

"You're a good student and should have no difficulty with the exam. Please know that I wish you the best with your marital problems."

He opened the door for her, and she reluctantly left. Alone, he picked up the large manila envelope from Angela and opened it with much anticipation. There was another letter and a copy of the paper on James Dickey's poetry that she had promised to send him.

He started with the letter and savored it from the opening *My Dear Barsh* to the final *Affectionately yours, Angela*. The letter was the most excessive yet in expressing her devotion to him.

Praise was nothing new to him. Students often flattered him and, occasionally, flirted with him, but he had never taken advantage of any student advances. A few women had also attempted to allure him into their lives without success.

Angela, however, was a new experience. Her words were like manna from heaven for a weary pilgrim. He began rereading the letter but stopped to reflect on one special sentence: Barsh, you didn't hear the typewriter stop clicking, but it did while I, alone in this apartment, lifted my glass of wine to you in deepest affection.

He was out of wine, but he would get some on the way home. Angela, my friend, he said to himself without voice, when all the house goes quiet tonight, I'll lift my glass to you.

He locked Angela's letter in the file cabinet with her other letters and put her paper on Dickey's poetry in his briefcase. He would read it after Hannah's bedtime.

***

With a bottle of wine that he considered expensive, he left the store for home but was soon haranguing with himself. He'd never bought expensive wine before. And to toast a woman in Rhode Island. Had he lost his senses?

Shifting thoughts, he focused on the invitation to his class reunion. Twenty-five years ago, he had marched through those final exercises at Bradley High without a backward glance and then pursued a spiritual and intellectual life that none of his classmates could have predicted in a thousand years.

In spite of his position at lowly Cooper, his teaching had remained lively and engaging, but he could not see himself teaching at Cooper after Debbie left him. For three months he had searched for a new vision for his life, but all in vain.

He needed a diversion, and the notice of his class reunion could not have come at a better time. How good it would be to reconnect with his old classmates.

Chapter Ten

Barsh counted down the days, until the anticipated day of his high school reunion dawned. Early that morning, he set out alone for the small Alabama town that he had forsaken twenty-five years ago.

As he traveled south on I-85, various memories of his youth kept streaming into his consciousness. His experiences growing up were rich and diverse, sad and joyful, and he reminisced about them, off and on, until he approached his hometown in early afternoon.

He thought about checking into a motel to rest awhile before visiting some of his old haunts but decided to drive straight to the cemetery of the country church where his parents and stillborn sister were buried.

On arriving, he sat in the Audi in the church parking lot, gripping the steering wheel, as he tried to calm his emotions. Then he walked to the cemetery.

Standing beside their graves, he stepped out of his stoical shoes for a moment. The tears were flowing, and then he began to sob.

Never in his life could he remember actually crying, to say nothing of sobbing. A tear may have trickled down his face on the day his parents were buried, but nothing more.

As he took control of his emotions, he realized that the salty sobbing was more about the breakup of his family than the loss of his parents. Their deaths were just the catalyst that set him bawling.

From the churchyard, he drove by their old farm. The new owners had done a good job of keeping the place up. The pasture was well maintained and filled with Hereford cattle.

Down the road and around the bend, he was pleased to see that the Henry place had been turned into a horse farm. The old cotton fields and corn fields were now well-fenced pastures, and the horses grazing the bright green grass were first-rate saddle horses. The old wooden house with its tin roof had been demolished and replaced by a stately brick home.

God, he would love to see Susan Henry, his little riding pal from those days of yore. Perhaps the horses and other changes were a good sign that she was still connected to the place. He stopped but found no one at home.

Disappointed, he headed for the back road where Rachel and Joe Foster lived. He had no intention of stopping, but he needed to drive by the place. The house had a new coat of white paint. Joe's Black Angus cattle were grazing across the way in the back pasture near the forest.

There was a cow trail through those woods that led to a large creek where the cattle went for water. Farther up the creek, there was a waterfall and a small bottomland pasture. The very thought of that place took him back to one of the most astounding nights of his youth.

***

He had camped and fished for two nights on the Tallapoosa River to celebrate the end of his sophomore year at Bradley High. Early Sunday morning, he broke camp to honor his mother, who did not approve of fishing or hunting on the Lord's Day. Fortunately for him, she did not object to horseback riding on Sunday afternoons.

As usual, he and Susan Henry rode their horses for miles along three different dirt roads that afternoon. As they passed the Foster farm, he saw their bull mount one of the cows and made a mental note of what he needed to do before the day ended.

He had agreed to look after Joe Foster's Black Angus cattle, while he was fighting the communists in Korea, and that included giving the bull a good measure of crushed grain and hay on those days when it was *servicing* the cows.

After super, Barsh drove his Ford pickup to their barn to fulfill his duty. As he was filling the grain bucket, Rachel appeared at the door of the feed room.

"Hey," she said and stepped into the room, "thanks for staying on top of things. Raymond's had a busy day with the cows."

"Just following Joe's instructions."

Barsh was surprised that Rachel would call attention to what the bull had been doing. He thought all women played blind to the bull's business. At least he had never heard a woman comment about it, even when it was going on before her eyes.

"I'll be right back," he said and took the grain to the feed trough in the bull's stall.

Rachel was sitting on a sack of grain with her skirt hiked up above her knees when he returned.

"Have you given him any hay?" she said.

"That's next."

He climbed the ladder to the loft, forked the hay down the chute into the bull's trough, and returned to the feed room.

"I saw you and Susan riding by on your horses this afternoon. Did y'all have fun?"

"We always have fun when we ride our horses."

"You remember promising me that we could ride double, don't you?"

"All you need to do is tell me when."

"What about tomorrow tonight?"

"Uh . . . okay."

"Can you meet me here around nine? Lewis and Mrs. Foster should both be sound asleep by then."

"Sure, if that's what you want."

"Please wait for me if I'm late."

"I'll wait until you get here."

"You are so dear."

True to his word, he waited for Rachel on the side of the barn that shielded him from any traffic on the road. The lights were out in Mrs. Foster's bedroom. Soon the lights in the living room went out. The whole house was dark.

The night, however, was well lit by the stars and moon, that was just a few days past its majestic fullness. Rachel slipped out the back door, carrying a blanket, and hurried across the yard.

"Barsh," she called as she approached the barn.

"I'm here," he said.

"I'll ride behind you on this blanket."

"Don't you want the saddle?"

"No, I want to hold on to you."

"You still want us to ride in the pasture?"

"That's safer for me. A neighbor might pass us on the road. I don't want any gossip. Let's ride up the creek to the waterfall."

They crossed the pasture and followed the cow trail through the woods with Rachel snuggled against his back to shield herself from tree branches. Even so, he felt the erotic pull of her tight embrace. It had been two years since the opposite sex had pulled herself against him.

"Here we are," he said as he reined the horse to a stop at the edge of the small bottomland pasture between the woods and the creek.

"Gracious," she said. "Look how bright the moon's wake is on the creek. Let's sit on the bank and talk."

"Okay," he said and dismounted first so he could help her down.

"I'll spread the blanket while you tether Thunder to one of these trees."

He tied the reins to a sapling and walked to the grassy bank of the creek, where Rachel was stretched out on the blanket.

"Lie down beside me and let's study the stars. Have you ever seen a more brilliant night sky? All those distant stars make me feel so small and worthless. What does my life matter in the scheme of all this vastness?"

"You're a wonderful person, Rachel. Everyone respects and admires you."

"A few people seem to like me, but I need more than that. I'm sure you have no idea how lonely I get in that old house at night."

"I know you must miss Joe."

"You're right. But this will surely shock you. I don't allow myself to think about Joe, anymore. It's as if there was nothing connecting us, not even our letters. When I answer his, I seem to be writing what's expected of me, not what I feel.

"At first, I could hardly stand it when I knew he was on the frontline in Korea. Nothing I did seemed important. My world seemed like one big waiting room—at work, at church, at home. I seemed to be waiting for word that Joe had been killed. At one point, I thought I was going crazy. Now all I feel is emptiness."

Barsh was shocked as she had warned him that he would be. He did not know what to say. Everything that came to mind seemed trivial. But her silence was more than he could bear.

"I'm sorry. I didn't know. You're living in hell."

"I knew you would understand. A woman I work with at the bank is always trying to get me to go out with her. There's a place on the Wadley Highway where she goes to dance and meet men on Saturday nights.

"I can't do that, but I'm dying for your companionship. Do you know how good it feels, just being here with you, tonight? I need you to be close to me. And I mean intimately close."

Not knowing how to respond, he sat up and looked into Rachel's face, shining in the moonlight. She lifted her arms to him and he filled them. Body to body and soul to soul, they rocked gently in a tight embrace.

"Do me," she said, and he did her with all his passion as the moon slipped slowly into the western sky.

Never again did she have to ask him to *do* her. He could not count the nights he had waited for her at their barn. They soon had a pallet in the hayloft. Sometimes they didn't make it to the loft but used the sacks of crushed grain as a love-bed.

Their secret rendezvous ended, however, the day Rachel got word that Joe would be coming home without his left arm. Barsh thought she would avoid him, once Joe returned, but she didn't. At church, she joked with him, teased him, and inquired about his activities as if their adulterous affair had never happened.

***

Those bitter-sweet memories followed Barsh all the way back to town. He could not repudiate what Rachael and he had done, but he could not think about Joe without feeling guilty for betraying him.

He checked into a motel on the edge of town. After he showered and dressed for the class reunion, his thoughts shifted to various classmates. He was especially eager to see April Morehouse, the second girl who had captured his heart, and Rayford McKay, his best friend during high school. He wondered how they had changed? What had they done with their lives?

They were both there with their spouses. April had married the banker's son, whom she had dated during their junior and senior years. Rayford, who had also married his high school sweetheart, was now the town mayor.

They seemed glad to see him, but the brief conversations with them were most unsatisfactory. He seemed to have nothing in common with them.

After dinner, the class president presided over a vacuous program that included a reminder of the class superlatives. He had been voted best looking boy by his classmates.

Then there was a report on the latest class superlatives. The most kids, the most divorces, and so forth. Barsh was recognized for having earned the most academic degrees, four, an achievement no one who had known him in high school could have imagined.

The reunion was over in less than two hours. Then everyone faded into the night, leaving him so disappointed that he felt betrayed by his expectations.

Chapter Eleven

Leaving his hometown Sunday morning, Barsh stopped for gas at Bonner's Texaco. There, challenging his eyes, stood Wesley Workman jesting loudly with a tall black man. The voice was unmistakable.

The year he turned fifteen, he had formed an unlikely friendship with Wesley—a high school dropout, a skilled garage mechanic, and an accomplished womanizer. It was their common interest in camping that had brought them together. But that was another life.

More than a quarter of a century had coursed its way through the marrow of Barsh's bones since those days. The memories, however, were as vivid as ever.

Wesley had once filled the night air with explicit narrations of his sexual exploits as they sat around a campfire by a creek in an old-growth forest.

There were other memories, the dark ones of Wesley's seduction of Amy Burdette, Barsh's first love, that ended in an unwanted pregnancy.

Wesley, dressed in khaki work clothes, was gaunt but still handsome in a rakish way. The black man, probably on his way to church, was wearing a gray striped suit with an orange tie and a tan hat. Wesley broke out in loud laughter, reeled on his heels, and headed toward a battered pulpwood truck.

"Wesley," he called and walked toward him with deeper emotion than he could have imagined before seeing him.

"Yeah," he said trying to figure out who had called him.

"Barsh Roberts."

"God a' mighty, Barsh, you're the last person in the world I expected to see today. What you doin' back in this hellhole?"

"Our class reunion, last evening. First time I'd been back for one. I couldn't wait to see everyone, but I was terribly disappointed."

"What did you expect from this god-forsaken place?"

The sun, climbing higher in the sky, shimmered on Wesley's truck.

“How long you been hauling pulpwood? The last time I heard, you were still working at your daddy's garage.”

“I walked out of that damn garage in a fit of anger for the last time . . . God, it's been twenty years,” he said and eased into a guttural laugh. “You know how Daddy was always ridin’ my ass. I could out mechanic him, but I could never please him. It was bound to happen.”

Wesley searched his eyes with unyielding intensity. Barsh wondered what he was looking for. A renewed acceptance? It was finally there. He had a better understanding of that old saying: The flesh is weak. But neither man would ever give further voice to Wesley’s betrayal that shattered their friendship.

“How's Jenny?” Barsh asked. “Rayford told me you married her. I knew her brother. He used to go rabbit hunting with me.”

“She's fine. And a good woman. She puts up with me, and I sure as hell ain't changed. Well, I guess I have changed some. I drink a lot now, and I don't take on as many women as I used to. Most of the time I'm too drunk to give a damn. What about you? Did you ever get married?”

“I married Debbie Whalen, a Kentucky woman."

“I bet you ain't been campin’ since you got married, have you?”

“Actually, we did camp for one night in a state park in Georgia, during my first year of graduate studies at Emory University. Debbie had a miserable time.”

“For God's sake, Barsh, who ever heard of takin’ your wife campin’? The whole idea is to get away from home for a spell.”

“I thought it was to get back close to nature.”

“Well, I guess you would. You liked trees better than people back in our old camping days. Sorry, but I’ve got to go. I’m closin’ a deal on a track of timber that I’ll be cuttin’ for pulpwood, and I’m already late. Where you headed? Home?”

“As soon as I gas up.”

“And just where would that be?”

“Ashland, South Carolina.”

“Well, you take care of yourself.”

“And you, too. It's good to see you, Wesley.”

“Yeah, it’s good to see you. I’ve thought about you a million times.”

There was a tinge of regret in Wesley's eyes. Then he cocked his head, grinned in his special way, and climbed into the truck.

The loud muffler roared in Barsh's head until it merged with the memory of Wesley's throaty Harley-Davidson. The two of them were flying down the Lafayette Highway on that black motorcycle, flat-out on the straights and backfiring into the curves.

With a full tank of gas, Barsh left the Texaco station for home. Although he was disappointed with the class reunion, he was glad he had made the brief trip.

It had awakened a lot of boyhood memories, and he was soon reveling in those days when he had found strength and grace in the wild. How satisfying it had been for him, in his teens, to be able to live off the land by his gathering, hunting, and fishing skills.

At forty-three, he had forgotten how it felt to kill a rabbit and roast it over an open fire, to live wild and unfettered in the forest for days at a time.

Energized by those memories, he decided it was time to experience, once more, that primal essence of life, and he set his mind to camp, alone, for two weeks in some remote forest. Purged by the solitude of the wilderness, he just might find the new vision for his life that he had been searching for.

Then a radical thought began to take hold of him. It was an idea that had first occurred to him after reading *A Modern Utopia* by H. G. Wells. The samurai, who served the new world order that Wells envisioned, were expected to spend time alone in the wilderness each year to renew and purify their spirit.

Reflecting on that notion, Barsh had wondered if he could learn the old earth skills and live alone in the wild, through the seasons of one year, by only the tools and products that he had made with his own hands from the raw materials of the earth. At the time, it was only a whimsical thought.

Traveling north on I-85, he turned that whimsical thought into a commitment. That would be a worthy challenge for any man in the postmodern world. Strip yourself of ten-thousand years of material culture and live in the wild by your own strength, wit, and handmade equipage. Do or die.

The vision filled him with an irrepressible resolve, as he drove toward his fractured home. If he took a sabbatical, which he was due, he could use it to experience his vision of a year-long sojourn in the wild.

Moreover, he could postpone the decision about resigning from Cooper College, when Debbie left him for a year-long separation. Who knew what a year might bring forth? Things might not work out the way Debbie had envisioned them, and she might be ready to bring Hannah home.

At whatever price, he wanted Hannah to grow up under the same roof with him. Even if that didn't happen, he would have a year to find a way forward.

The plan was not worthy of an academic sabbatical, so he would take one without pay. Once he shared his crisis with Dean Thomson, she would undoubtedly approve his request.

He also assumed that Hannah would support such a sojourn as an appropriate response to Debbie's move to Louisville if he presented it to her as something that he had often dreamed of doing. He could tell her that it was now or never for him, and he was confident that she would give him her approval.

***

Late that Sunday evening, as Barsh sat in his study reviewing his plan for a sabbatical, a devious notion occurred to him. If he told Hannah about his plan for a wilderness sojourn with no reference to the separation, Debbie could then recast her move to Louisville as a reaction to his plan.

Could he pull such a devious scheme on his daughter? Yes, he could swallow the deceit in order to shield her from the truth for at least a year, possibly forever if things didn't work out for Debbie.

This approach would have definite advantages for Debbie. She could justify the move to Louisville in order to be closer to her parents, while he was doing his thing in the wild. Thus, she would get her trial separation without having to take the blame for it.

There was one negative consequence for Debbie, however. She would have to give him time to learn the old earth skills and make the things he would need to survive. That was the only aspect of his vision that concerned him. She was already jumping at the bit to move to Louisville.

He checked on Hannah, and she was sound asleep. It was time to lay out the plan for Debbie, who was watching a movie on television. She gave him a quizzical glance as he entered the den and sat in his chair.

"How's the movie?" he asked at the first commercial break.

"It's okay. Are you watching the rest of it with me?"

"No, I have something to discuss with you, but it can wait until after the movie."

"Let's discuss it now," she said and turned off the television.

"I think I have a way out for us with Hannah, but it's complicated."

She listened carefully as he explained the strategy, and she accepted it. He returned to his study, overwhelmed by the daunting tasks before him.

The absolute critical task for him was to learn to make flint arrowheads. Without them, he would not be able to kill deer for their hides, which would be essential for the clothing, bedding, and other things he would need.

He would have to find someone who could teach him flintknapping. This would likely be his most challenging quest, and he decided to make it his first priority.

The elderly members of the Eastern Band of the Cherokee in North Carolina were always eager to tell him about the traditions of their people. Thinking that they might still know how to make flint arrowheads, he decided to drive to their reservation that Monday morning and query the curator of their museum.

As he thought about the trip, he realized that Hannah would likely want to go with him, and that would work out well. He would let her think his new quest was just a hobby, until it was well underway. Then he would take her to Alabama and work his deceptive scheme on her.

It was also obvious that he would need his own place in the country with a deep forest, where he could stealthily hunt and kill the deer that he would need to make his buckskin necessities. He could not wait until hunting season opened. It was time to buy a place in the country.

Chapter Twelve

Early Monday morning, Barsh called the realtor who had sold him the house in Fern Meadows and asked him to be on the lookout for a farm with the specifications that he needed. Then he and Hannah were on the road to Cherokee, North Carolina.

They were both in a good mood and happy to be headed for the mountains. Beyond Asheville, he decided it was time to tell her about his goal of learning the old earth skills of Native Americans.

"Hannah, I've been thinking about Paw-Paw Roberts. I told you how he decided on his ninety-fourth birthday that he'd lived long enough and then refused to eat or drink until he died, but I don't think I told you about his burial."

"No, you never told me that."

"He had already chosen his gravesite on a forested hillside overlooking the homeplace. He had also built his own wooden coffin.

"Following his instructions, there was no church service with a preacher speaking over him, just a graveside gathering of family and friends. When they lowered him into the good earth, his only surviving son stepped up to the open grave and talked to his father as if he could hear him. Then other people did the same.

"I wanted to say something, but no young people spoke, so I held my tongue. After all these years, I'm going to visit his grave, later this summer, and tell him the things I wanted to say that day. Would you like to go with me?"

"Yes, I want to go."

"That's what I was hoping you would say. There are a lot of things in Alabama that I want to show you."

"Do you know what I'm really looking forward to seeing?"

"I don't have a clue, my sweet girl."

"The Tallapoosa River. You always describe it as the river of your youth. It's like a mythical place to me."

"Then, I'll definitely show you the Tallapoosa."

"When can we go?"

"I don't have a date. But you and I will be in Alabama sometime before school starts this fall. You know how proud I am of the Creek blood that flows in my body even if it is only a few drops. In honor of that heritage, I've decided to learn the earth skills they once lived by.

"You and I have our poetry project and a few mountain trails to hike. Beyond that, I'm devoting most of my energy this summer to this project.

"Paw-Paw Roberts made his own hunting clothes out of deerskins just like his Creek grandmother taught him. That's on the list of things I want to learn to do.

"Here's something you probably don't know about me. When I was a boy, I made my own bow and arrows. I don't know where I got the idea, but I cut the arrowheads from a piece of heavy tin. Fashioned them like an Indian arrowhead and filed them sharp.

'Now I want to learn how to make flint arrowheads. But finding someone who knows the art of flintknapping will probably be a big challenge."

"Knowing you, I believe you'll find someone."

"That's my intention and I'm starting today by asking the curator of the Cherokee Museum if he knows anyone who makes flint arrowheads."

***

The curator at the museum, a full-blooded Cherokee, didn't know anyone who made flint arrowheads, but he told Barsh and Hannah about Moon Man, who lived at Big Cove, the most traditional section of the Qualla Boundary Band of the Eastern Cherokee. His first language was still Cherokee, and he was the only person the curator knew who tanned deerskins to make buckskin clothes.

After several wrong turns, they found Moon Man's place. Barsh explained his mission, and the old man welcomed them. Yes, he knew how to tan deer hides, which was traditionally a woman's task. Before his mother died, young, she taught him brain tanning.

He knew nothing, however, about making flint arrowheads. He had always hunted with a rifle, just like his father before him, and like his father, he only wore his buckskin clothes when he was deer hunting.

"My Paw-Paw Roberts followed the same practice of deer hunting," Barsh said. "His full-blooded Creek grandmother taught him how to make buckskin clothes. And like you, he hunted with a rifle."

"Bad blood between Cherokee and Creek after white man get between us."

"I know the story well."

"Andrew Jackson no good President. Trail of Tears for most Cherokee. But my people stay here in these mountains. No go to Oklahoma. Where Paw-Paw Roberts live?"

"He's dead but he lived at the foot of the Talladega Mountain in Alabama. My biggest regret is that I didn't get him to teach me how to tan deerskins."

"I teach you like son."

"Mr. Moon Man, can I ask you a question?" Hannah said.

"What, child?"

"How did you get your name?"

"When young man, I study moon every night. Need answers. One night, moon study me. I Tell Uncle. He name me Moon Man."

"That's a good name for you," Barsh said. "Have you ever visited the Cherokee in Oklahoma?"

"No leave these mountains."

"If you'd like to go, I'll take you. It won't cost you a dime."

"No like Oklahoma. I teach you brain tanning. No cost you dime."

"I'll be honored beyond words."

"Come back with deerskin. Bring brain."

They left Moon Man's place and visited Oconaluftee Village, a reconstructed Cherokee village like those of the eighteenth century. It was Hannah's first visit, and she thoroughly enjoyed it. He promised to bring her back at a later date for the outdoor drama "Unto These Hills."

Leaving Cherokee, Barsh felt lucky to have found Moon Man. Now he had to find someone who could teach him how to make flint arrowheads. Tomorrow, he would call the Department of Anthropology at the University of South Carolina. Maybe they could put him on to someone who knew that skill.

***

On Tuesday, Barsh learned that Don Crabtree, an archeologist from Idaho, had almost singlehandedly revived the art of flintknapping. In the 1930's, he was giving demonstrations at the University of California at Berkley. Since then, the number of flintknappers had significantly increased across the country. They made various types of flint points as a hobby.

Barsh also learned that one of the Park Rangers at the Ocmulgee Mounds National Historical Park near Macon, Georgia, gave demonstration on flintknapping, and he arranged a visit to begin taking lessons that Wednesday.

The trip to Ocmulgee was a good experience for him. He enjoyed experiencing the huge Indian mounds and learning about their history. But more importantly, he quickly learned the technique of flintknapping and was soon making crude arrow points.

On his return home late that Friday, he was pleased to learn that his realtor had found a farm for sale and was eager to show it to him that Saturday.

The farm turned out to be perfect for Barsh's needs. Overjoyed with the find, he signed a contract to purchase the property at the earliest possible closing date.

After leaving the real-estate office that afternoon, he drove to the college to check his mail, which included another large manila envelope from Angela. Eager to open it, he hurried to his office.

It contained another letter and two chapters of a new novel that she had started. He read the letter and then reread the good news section:

> I have good news. I've started another novel, and I'm writing with more joy than I've ever known. I used to write desperately longing to be that new voice that literary critics were waiting to discover and herald to the world. That never happened, however, and I grew more despondent about my fiction with each rejection letter I received.
>
> The enclosed chapters are for you, my dear friend. They are somewhat autobiographical as you will no doubt recognize.
>
> I've gone back to my youth, searching for a protagonist, and I found her there, awkward and vulnerable. That's something I had avoided in all my previous fiction.
>
> My female protagonists were always so smart, so

sophisticated. They just popped on the scene that way. They had no history, no roots, no family.

You helped me find my true voice. The way you claim your own roots. You are so comfortable with your journey, and that was liberating to me.

Remember the drive from the Charlotte airport to Jackson's Steak House by way of Cherokee Falls. On our way from the falls to the restaurant, I told you about the trauma of my thirteenth summer. How an older boy had raped me.

That was the first time I had ever talked about that summer to anyone. You made it easy for me to tell you.

I would love to read the enclosed chapters to you, face to face, but I can't wait for the day I can look you in the eye. I need to share them now.

Barsh, you are my muse! And what a wonderful muse you are.

Never in a thousand years would he have ever imagined the day coming when a writer would claim him as her muse. He had sparked fire in a few women, during the course of his life. Sometimes, it was the other way around, and he was the one feeling the heat. But after his adulterous entanglement with Rachel Foster, he had kept a strong hand on the rudder of his passion.

He did not presume to know the ramifications of Angela's affection for him. Perhaps her feelings were purely platonic.

He certainly felt intellectually connected to her. He also felt the pull of romantic intimacy. But there was no place in his life for romance in the foreseeable future.

He began to read the two chapters of her new novel and relished each sentence to the very last word. She was an excellent writer, and he would like to pick up the phone and talk to her about the chapters she had shared. But he would have to respond by letter with great care and caution. It was difficult for him to steer a steady course of collegial friendship in his letters to her, but that was always his objective.

He locked Angela's letter and the two chapters of her novel in the file cabinet and drove home. Debbie was fixing supper and seemed to be in a good mood, which was a major change of temperament. When he left to check out the farm, she had even expressed her appreciation for his determined efforts to master the old earth skills, so he could experience a year-long sojourn in the wild.

"Do you like the farm?" she asked with a hopeful look on her face.

"It's the perfect place for me to pursue my project, and I signed a contract to buy it. Believe me, I'll be prepared to live in the wild before the Christmas break."

"That's good news," she said as Hannah came running down the hall to join them.

"Did you buy the farm, Daddy?"

"I have a contract to buy it. We're closing the deal as soon as they can do a title search and a new deed to the property."

Chapter Thirteen

Barsh left the lawyer's office with the deed to the property that Jeremiah Keeble first settled in 1792. The current heirs had sold the place to him, as it was, and that included all the household furnishings, the farm tools, and an old Ferguson tractor with a bush-hog mower used to keep sprouting trees from taking over the pastures.

With an elevated spirit, he drove toward the farm, eager to explore the woodlands, more thoroughly. Passing Horton's Store, he took note of the fact that it would be a good landmark if he needed to give anyone directions. The farm was about a mile past the store.

He was especially pleased that the property was fenced with barbwire. It was also posted with no trespassing signs, and there was a lockable gate that would give him total privacy as he worked to master the old earth skills.

He turned off the county highway and stopped to unlock the gate. Then driving past the gate, he stopped, relocked it, and drove down the long lane that curved through a strip of woods, cut through the eastern side of two pastures, and ended at the old farmhouse that, to his delight, was not visible to traffic on the highway.

He parked at the edge of the yard and retrieved his hiking boots and backpack from the car. There was an old bench beneath a massive white oak in the front yard, and sitting here, he changed into his boots. He checked out the farmhouse and left for the forest beyond the two pastures.

His property stretched all the way to the Pacolet River. He had hiked there before buying the place, but he had not explored the whole forest that belonged to him, nor the length of the riverbank that marked the southern boundary of the property.

There was little underbrush, and he hiked with a new vitality that emanated from his connection with a mixed hardwood forest that now belonged to him and his heirs. Well into the forest, he stopped to take in the beauty of the rolling woodland.

As he set off again, he caught sight of a Cooper's hawk darting through the canopy of the trees. It was hard on the tail of a small brown bird, probably a sparrow.

He did not see how the chase ended, and that suited him just fine, because he could not take sides. The fate of the wild was the fate of the wild.

At length he stood on the north bank of the Pacolet River, where its headlong rush from the mountains of North Carolina had slowed to a languid pace. How good it felt to be standing there.

He walked upriver until he came to a bluff with a large granite ledge overlooking the river. He climbed onto the ledge and sat thinking how lucky he had been to find this particular property. He could not have dreamed up a better place for his needs.

A lone turkey vulture circled gracefully overhead. He lay back on the warm granite and watched the vulture until it drifted out of sight.

His mind was soon drawing the sharp contrast between the vulture's placid search for carrion and the fierce thrashing of the Cooper's hawk as it chased a live bird. The vulture and the hawk, scavenger and hunter, each filling its niche in the biosphere.

He recalled the claim of anthropologists that scavenging for carrion had been a critical step forward in mankind's becoming a hunter. How ironic that the ancestors of the deadliest hunters on earth had once scavenged for carrion.

Like most civilized people, he had moved beyond hunting, which he only did for food, never sport. He was always mindful, however, that slaughterhouse workers did the dirty work of processing all the meat he had consumed since his youthful hunting days.

He was soon wondering if he could turn his own cultural clock back and stoically wash the blood of a kill from his hands without guilt or sentimentality. He would have to make that adaptation in order to live in the wild for a year.

As he mused on that, his mind turned back to the idea of scavenging. It was common to see vultures eating roadkill, including deer. Occasionally, he would see a dead deer on the side of the highway before vultures got to it.

With those images in mind, he decided to work out an agreement with the highway department to acquire such kills for their rawhides. That would limit the number of deer he would have to kill.

All he needed to do in order to prove himself capable of creating his buckskin necessities was to kill one deer with bow and arrow that were made by his own hands. If he could kill one deer, he could kill more.

The parts of his plan for a sojourn in the wild were coming together much faster than he had imagined. It was time to talk to Dean Thompson about a sabbatical.

***

Late that afternoon, Barsh climbed the stairs to Dean Thompson's office. Her secretary was nowhere in sight, and for a moment, he watched Catherine reading some papers. He tapped on the side of the open door.

"Barsh," she said and rose to greet him. "I haven't seen you in two weeks."

"I've been busy with a new project."

"I'm sure it's an interesting one. Please bring me up to date."

As they took their regular chairs, he heard the Dean's secretary talking with someone and looked at the open door before answering.

"Catherine, could I stop by your house for coffee in the morning? I've got a lot to share with you."

"Yes, and I'm fixing breakfast just like it was one of our regular Saturday morning discussions. I'll walk out with you. I need some fresh air."

He knew he had set off an alarm and would have to clue her in before he left campus. As they walked onto the Quad, she broke the silence.

"Okay, Barsh, give it to me straight. What's going on?"

"It hurts me to tell you, but Debbie is leaving me. She has asking for a trial separation for a year, but I fear it will become permanent."

"I don't know what to say. I knew she was often depressed. I can't believe she wants a separation. I thought she depended on you."

"No, no. In spite of her bouts of depression, she is a determined woman with her own goals and needs. Her old boss in Louisville has offered to make her a partner in his accounting firm. She was his assistant when I first met her.

"She tells me that the only time that she's ever been happy was when she lived in Louisville, so I can't blame her for going. She has not been happy with me, and she deserves happiness."

"I am so sorry, Barsh. How is Hannah taking this?"

"We haven't told her. Debbie will be taking her to Louisville, and that's going to be a real problem for Hannah and me. You know how close we are. But I have a plan I think will make the separation easier for her."

"Well, that's a small relief. Can you share it with me?"

"It's quite complicated. I'll explain everything in the morning. I can tell you that I'd like to take a sabbatical after the fall semester.

"I've talked Debbie into waiting until Christmas break before moving. That will give me more time to prepare Hannah for the separation.

"A sabbatical will hopefully give me time to work through some critical issues, just in case the separation becomes permanent."

"You know I'll support your plan for a sabbatical."

"Thanks, Catherine. What would I do without you in my corner?

Dean Thompson proceeded to the library, and he left for home to tell Hannah that he'd closed the deal on the farm and would take her there the next day.

Chapter Fourteen

During breakfast with Dean Thompson that Saturday, Barsh filled her in on everything, and she promised her full support for his sabbatical plan. Leaving the breakfast table, they moved to the den.

Catherine shared with him the highlight of an article she was writing about Winnie Davis—the daughter of the Confederacy as she was often called in the Old South. He was surprised to learn that she was not a traditional Southern belle.

She was a mere baby when the Civil War ended and her father Jefferson Davis, the deposed president of the Confederate States of America, was imprisoned by Union forces for two years.

Later she was sent to school in Europe and returned to the Gulf coast of Mississippi to live with her parents.

As a grown woman, she spent her last years in New York City after being befriended by Kate and Joseph Pulitzer. She also wrote for Pulitzer's newspaper.

While living in New York City, she became engaged to a Northern man, whose father was a prominent abolitionist, and that cause such a Southern reaction that she broke the engagement. Never marrying, she died at the age of 34.

Barsh shared with Catherine the poetry project he and Hannah had undertaken. Then he told her about buying the Keeble farm and left for home where Hannah was waiting for him in the den.

"Daddy, can we go to the farm, now?"

"As soon as we load up. Did you pack us a lunch?"

"Lunch is prepared."

"Good girl. Do you have a book and a blanket?"

"I have everything I need."

"Just checking. You can read in the hayloft of the barn, while I work at flintknapping in the feed room. After lunch, we'll hike through the woods to the Pacolet River and watch the currents drift by, as we soak up the sun on a granite ledge."

"Sounds like a fun day to me," she said as Debbie entered the den.

"When will you two be home?"

"Probably late afternoon. You want to eat out?"

"Maybe, I know I don't want to cook."

"I'll cook something if you don't want to eat out."

"We'll see how I feel."

Barsh and Hannah gathered their things and left for the farm. She was chatty, but he was thinking about Debbie.

"Hannah, maybe we can get Debbie to the farm, tomorrow afternoon, just to show her the place."

"I wouldn't count on it. You know how Mother feels about farms."

"Do you know your mother's favorite place in the whole world?"

"I have no idea."

"Louisville, Kentucky. That's where she lived after finishing college. She worked at Dugan, Johnson and Bennett, the foremost accounting firm in the city. She was Henry Dugan's assistant, and she hated to leave Louisville after we got married.

"She was the primary bread winner during my graduate studies at Emory, although I did have a scholarship and a stipend as a Teaching Assistant. It was a great time for me but not for Debbie. She hated living in Atlanta.

"After I finished my Ph.D. program at Emory, I applied to every college and university that advertised an opening in religious studies. The only offer I got was from Cooper College.

"Then a marvelous wonder happened in Ashland. You, Hannah Marie Roberts, made your grand entrance into the world."

"Well, I'm glad to be here."

"I was as proud as any father who ever lived, and I still am."

Hannah quietly observed the scenery as he drove down the county road. He glanced at her every few minutes and gave her a big smile if she returned his glance.

"Do you know what I'm thinking?" he said.

"What?"

"Just how much you remind me of Mother. Did I ever tell you that you have her features? Your hair, eyes, and complexion are so like hers."

"You never told me, but I learned it on my own. I used to wonder why I looked so different from you and Mother. Then it hit me one day as I was studying a photo of your mother."

“Well, I should have told you myself, long ago. Of course, it would not have mattered to me who you favored.

“Here’s an awesome truth that you should never forget. You are uniquely you. There’s never been another you and there never will be.”

“Do I have your mother’s personality?”

“No, your grandmother Roberts was not a critical thinker like you. She was all about love and compassion.”

“Are you saying it’s wrong for a girl to be a critical thinker?”

“Heavens, no. I love you just the way you are. And there’s nothing in the world more important to me than your wellbeing and happiness.”

“That’s what I thought.”

“Look to your right. Our farm begins there with that barbwire fence. I’m really pleased that this grove of deciduous trees, stretching along the highway, blocks people from seeing the house from the road.”

“What do these signs mean?”

“They prohibit people from lawfully entering without an invitation. For the most part, they were intended to keep people from hunting on the property. But I like the privacy that the gate and the posted status of the property give me.”

A minute later, he turned onto the dirt lane and stopped to unlock the gate.

“This is the entrance to the old Keeble farm, which now belongs to me and my heirs. I just had an idea. After I pull through the gate and stop to relock it, I’d like for you to drive us to the farmhouse. This private lane will be a good place for me to teach you how to drive.”

“Great. I’m ready.”

After several demonstrations of clutching, accelerating, and braking, he turned the car over to Hannah, who drove all the way in first gear.

“You did just fine, my sweet girl. Next, I’ll teach you how to shift from first to second gear. This will be your job from now on. I’ll unlock the gate, you’ll drive through and wait for me to relock it, and then you’ll drive us to the house.”

“Job accepted. Driving is fun.”

He gave her a tour of the old farmhouse and led her to the screened porch that faced the west sides of two pastures and the forest beyond. There was a gate near the house that the previous owners used for moving their cattle from one pasture to the other. There was also a gate in the south pasture that opened into the woodland.

"Let's sit in this porch swing," he said. "You have no idea how excited I am to own this place."

"Daddy, can we spend the night here, soon?"

"I'd love to do that. Which bedroom do you want?"

"I like the one with the blue walls."

"Then that will be yours. I plan to redo the kitchen and bathroom. Of course, I'll buy new mattresses for the beds, and I'll buy a few pieces of furniture to go with this old stuff. Okay, I'm ready to show you the barn."

"And I'm going to read in the hayloft, just like you used to do when you were a boy."

"By the way, the hayloft is also a good place to daydream about the things you want to come your way in life.

"I was just about to ask you to tell me about your daydreams, and then I realized that I never shared my boyhood dreams with anyone. I held them close to my heart, and I guess that's the way it should be."

"Yeah, daydreams are private."

"But anxieties and troubles are different. You should be able to talk openly about these with Debbie and me, right?"

"Don't worry, Daddy. I know I can talk to you about anything."

"That's the way I want it to be between us."

She got her book and blanket, and they headed for the barn.

"Hannah, there's nothing like a barn for a country man. This one has never been painted, and I have no plan to paint it. I like the way the old boards have weathered. I do plan to replace the rusty tin roof with new tin, and I'm doing the same for the house.

"Let me show you the feed room. Unlike the stables, it has a wooden floor. Look at this old table. It's made out of oak. Weighs a ton. No telling how old it is. I found it in the tool shed. This is a perfect place to do my flint-knapping and some of my other projects.

"I plan to work on them, out here, most days this summer, but I don't expect you to come with me. It's going to get sweltering hot, and you'll be better off staying home with Davis.

"You and I will have the evenings for our poetry project, and we'll do our hiking on Saturdays."

"I understand. Can I come when I want to?"

"Of course. Guess what I'm buying next week?"

"Some cows?"

"Good guess, but, no, I'm buying a new Ford pickup. A man with a farm needs a truck. I haven't decided how I'll use the pastures.

It turned out to be a good day at the farm. Hannah seemed relaxed and pleased to see him pursuing his new quest with such determination, and she enjoyed the experience of reading in the hayloft and hiking to the Pacolet River.

Chapter Fifteen

As the summer rolled by, week after week, Barsh worked hard preparing for his wilderness sojourn, and his determined efforts had paid off. He was ahead of his original target to be prepared by the middle of December.

He had made a fine hunting bow out of hickory, something he had made as a boy. This one, however, was stronger and well suited for killing a deer. With his newly acquired flintknapping skills, he had also made a good collection of arrows with flint points, something essential for killing a deer.

He had formed a friendship with a Catawba Indian near Rock Hill, who taught him their traditional method of making pottery. Crude though they were, he had made the pieces of pottery that he would need.

Having been taught by Moon Man, a traditional Cherokee, he was in the process of brain-tanned enough deer hides from road-kill to make his clothes and footwear, a sleeping bag, a quiver, a gathering bag, a hunting bag, and a few pouches.

As soon as he killed a deer and tanned its hide, he will have completed the task of acquiring buckskins. With this one, he planned to make a poncho type cloak.

Using his own ingenuity, he had built two fish traps out of split bamboo that were modeled after wire fish traps his father once made and used. After successfully testing the bamboo ones in the Pacolet River, he was confident that he could sustain himself, primarily, on a diet of catfish from the Tallapoosa River.

A good archer, he was also confident that he could supplement his fish diet by killing rabbits and ducks as needed.

With each meal, he would also add various species of edible mushrooms that he would gather on his daily treks through the forest. An old woman, who lived on the backside of their farm, during his high school years, had taught him which ones were edible.

By the second Sunday in August, he was ready to kill a deer. In preparation for the kill, he reread parts of Leslie Silko's novel *Ceremony,* including the chapter where Tayo, the Laguna Pueblo protagonist, performed a ceremony over the deer he had just killed.

Barsh had been deeply moved by that scene and wanted to emulate it over his kill.

He spent the first part of that Sunday evening with Hannah. She read him her latest poem, which was about their latest hike on a mountain trail near Caesars Head and the joy of being close to nature with her father.

Then they read to each other several poems they had selected from the anthologies they were reading. As the hour of her bedtime approached, he prepared himself to tell her about his plan to kill a deer.

"Hannah, when we visit Paw-Paw Roberts' grave, I want to tell him that I've developed proficiency in the earth skills that enabled his Creek ancestors to live a good life. But there's one thing I have yet to do. Kill a deer. That skill was essential for their way of life."

"You're going to kill a deer."

"Yes, but unlike Paw-Paw Roberts, who annually killed deer for food, I'm only killing one. I need to prove to myself that I could survive in the wild just like the Creek Indians did before the Europeans came and drove them from their expansive native land onto restricted reservations.

"I'm well aware that this will be a selfish act, since I don't need the food, but it's something I have a deep need to do."

"I couldn't kill a deer, Daddy, but I'll take your word that it's something you need to do."

"Thanks for understanding. I'm setting the alarm clock, tonight, so I'll have time to drive to the farm about two hours before dawn and make my way into the forest to a place I've picked out as a deer stand.

"There, I'll wait for dawn, hoping a deer will come by on its way to bed down for the day. I'll do this, day after day, until I kill one.

"Hunting season for deer hasn't yet opened, so I'll be breaking the law. If the game warden catches me, I can deal with that."

"What does that mean?"

"I'll have to pay a fine and I'll gladly do that. I bought a hunting license and can kill the season limit on deer, when the season opens. I'm just pushing up the timetable to kill only one, so I can tell Paw-Paw Roberts when we visit his grave.

"Of course, the law doesn't care about my reason and it shouldn't. If I'm caught, I'll plead guilty and take the consequences.

"I've made a deal with a deer hunter to butcher the deer. I'm paying him for doing that and I'm giving him the meat. He has a deep freezer and will store most of meat there. It'll feed his family, as they choose to eat it, over a course of several months.

"I'll tan the hide and make a poncho type cloak from it. Like the days of old, nothing will be wasted.

"As soon as I kill a deer, I'll be ready to take you to Alabama. Are you still interested in going?"

"No reason to change my mind."

"Want to guess whose bedtime it is?

"I know."

"Good night, my sweet girl."

***

Fortunately for Barsh, a buck came within striking distance on the second morning. He stoically pulled the bowstring and released the arrow that struck its mark. The deer jumped and ran off a short distance before falling.

He sat on the ground and waited for the hemorrhaging wound to drain the lifeblood from the deer. When that occurred, he stood over it and performed his own version of Tayo's ceremony. Then lifting the deer across his shoulders, he carried it to the barn and left to get the neighbor who had agreed to butcher it.

Late that afternoon, Barsh drove home from the farm and parked the Ford pickup, as usual, on the side of the driveway. Debbie's space in the two-car garage was empty. Davis exited the den with Hannah following her.

"How was your day, Dr. Roberts?"

"I had a good day. How was yours?"

"Every day with Hannah is a good one. Well, I better get going. I need to stop at the grocery store on the way home. See y'all tomorrow."

He opened the car door for her and watched as she drove away.

"Daddy, Angela Kundera called. She wants you to call her. The number is on your desk."

"She's our new English professor. When did she call?"

"About an hour ago," she said and followed him to the study, where she sat watching him as he dialed the number.

"How good to hear your voice, Barsh. I'm leaving for Ashland this Thursday. The movers will be here at eight, and I'll get on the road as soon as they finish loading my things.

"I should be there sometime Friday afternoon. The movers said they will be there by nine o'clock Saturday morning. They have a side delivery in western Pennsylvania."

"We're all set for you. I checked with the business office last week and the house is ready."

"I'm so excited about having my own house. No more apartments."

"What can I do to help with the move? Have you contacted Ashland Public Works to have the water and electricity turned on?"

"I thought I'd have to do that in person."

"Let me do it for you. Then you'll have water and electricity when you get here. If they want a deposit, you can pay me back."

"That's a kind offer. Thank you. One more thing. Would you pick up the keys from the business office just in case they close before I get there Friday?

"Consider it done. I'll be working at my Cooper office."

"Good, I'll come straight to your office. I can't wait to see you. Bye."

"Bye. And do be careful driving down."

"Hannah, as you know, I always offer to help new members of the Division of Humanities when they move in. Some have accepted my offer, some haven't. Dr. Kundera has, so I'll help her move in this Saturday. Then I'll be ready to take you to Alabama, Sunday morning."

"So, you killed a deer."

"Yes, luck was on my side this morning."

"How long can we stay?"

"I have meetings at the college next Thursday, so we'll have to drive home on Wednesday. But we'll have two full days and three nights.

"I wonder what's keeping Debbie. I guess I should start dinner. You want to help me?"

"I always want to help you."

They worked as a team preparing dinner, but all the while, he kept thinking about Angela.

Chapter Sixteen

Standing at his second-floor office window in Kimberly Hall, Barsh looked down on the parking lot, that was empty except for his Ford pickup. The shadow of a huge white oak was taking a lazy afternoon stretch across the asphalt pavement. He remembered how Angela had embraced the stately tree before she left campus back in April.

Now she was on her way to join the Cooper faculty. He tried to envision her driving south and realized he didn't know what kind of car she owned.

The phone rang. It was the Academic Dean.

"Barsh, I need a break."

"Can you come over? I'm waiting for Angela. I thought she would be here before now. I'm getting a little worried."

"I'm on my way."

At the sound of her shoes tapping on the hardwood floor, he rose to greet her.

"Well, it looks like we've got the place all to ourselves."

"Margaret Glenn was the last to leave."

They sat opposite each other in the two comfortable chairs with their eyes trying to read the other's face. She looked at the open book on his desk.

"Am I to assume that you and Hannah are still working on your poetry project?"

"Yes, and she always amazes me by her analytical abilities. I find it hard to believe she's only eleven."

"Hannah is amazing, and you deserve most of the credit for her development. You're such an extraordinary father."

"I don't know about that. Sometimes I think I've done it all wrong. Maybe the inaccessible father is the best model for the child."

"No! No! I know about the distant father. It's a joy to see how you two relate to each other."

"This Sunday, I'm taking her to Alabama to share my sabbatical plan with her, and I'm having doubts about the deceptive slant

I've worked out in order to shield her from the truth about the separation."

"I understand your concern."

"You haven't told anyone about the sabbatical, have you?"

"The President. And I only told him that you wanted to take a sabbatical without pay, starting in January, and that I approved it. Without any questions, he signed off on it."

"Let's keep that plan to ourselves. I may have to do something else."

"As you wish. I'd better get back to the office and finish my work for today. Call me tonight and let me know if Angela likes my offer of ham biscuits and coffee for breakfast."

After walking her to the stairs, he picked up the anthology and began reading the editor's selection of poems by Richard Eberhart. He did not remember Eberhart from his year-long sophomore lit class at Samford until he got to "The Groundhog."

The sentiment of that poem had followed him across the years. He even remembered the opening lines:

In June, amid the golden fields,
I saw a groundhog lying dead.

He also remembered the lines about the angry stick, perhaps because he, as a boy, had done the same thing to a bloated dead dog.

Half with loathing, half with a strange love,
I poked him with an angry stick.

A car whined into the parking lot and stopped near his truck. He closed the book. The car door slammed.

"Hello, Ford pickup."

There was no doubt about the voice. He hurried to the window to wave a welcome, but Angela was on her way to the front of Kimberly Hall with her long black hair dancing with her stride.

He waited for her at his office door. Up the stairs, she bounded and broke into a broad smile when she saw him.

"Welcome to Cooper, Angela."

"I'm glad to be here," she said taking his hand in both of hers and looking deep into his eyes. "I'm sorry I've kept you waiting. I pushed the Volvo as hard as I dared."

"I didn't mind the wait. I've been reading. But I was getting a little worried. Actually, I was afraid you might have had car trouble.

"It's a male thing, I guess, worrying about women on the road. Anyway, it's something I can't seem to slough off in spite of the women's movement. Would you like tea?"

"Yes, please, I'll be right back. The bathroom's downstairs, right?"

He nodded and watched her walk away. Having already filled the kettle with water, he turned on the hotplate. He had also broken out a new Japanese tea set for the occasion.

She was soon back, and it was obvious that she had refreshed her lipstick and perfume.

"Do you take sugar with your tea?"

"No, thanks."

He poured the tea, and they sat facing each other in the two comfortable chairs in front of his desk.

"Barsh, I've never been so excited about a move."

"You should know I'm glad you're here, and I do hope it's the right move for you."

"Have no worry. This move seems so right for me. I've never felt so good about myself. I'm trusting my intuition like never before."

"That's good to hear. Do you still want me to help with the move in, tomorrow?"

"Yes, I'm looking forward to your presence and your help."

"Then I shall be there to help. Catherine would like to bring ham biscuits and coffee for breakfast. Is that okay?"

"Yes, please tell her to bring them. Can you come at eight? The movers will be here at nine."

"Eight is fine. As you requested, I picked up the keys from the business office and checked out the house. The water and electricity have been turned on.

"While I was there, I set up a card table and three folding chairs in the kitchen, just in case you accepted Catherine's offer. There's a bottle of Chardonnay and a basket of fruit in the refrigerator. You'll also find two small gifts on the card table."

“That was super nice of you. But rest assured that I’ll find a way to pay you back.”

“Your office is across the hall. Well, actually it’s not a typical hall but a huge room as you can see. Your office is number 203.”

“Splendid! Let’s check it out.”

He handed her the key and followed her. She unlocked the door and gestured for him to enter.

“After you,” he said.

“I like this location,” she said sitting behind the desk. “I can see your office door across the way. I’ll be able to keep track of the goings and comings.

“Barsh, I have a special request. Could you join me for a glass of the Chardonnay? I want to welcome you as the first guest in my new home.”

“Okay. Do you remember the way or do you want to follow me?”

“I’ll follow you, and thanks for everything.”

***

After taking the driveway into the backyard, he parked near the porch steps. Angela stopped beside his pickup and jumped out.

“I love being able to park here. Please call on me at the back-door,” she said and led the way through the screened porch into the kitchen.

“Oh, you remembered the binoculars and the field guide to birds. Thank you! Thank you! I do want to become a birder.

“Okay, it’s time to toast our friendship. How interesting. We’ll have to drink from the same glass.”

“I didn’t anticipate your invitation, but I’m pleased to share the glass with you.”

She opened the refrigerator, took the wine, and picked up the corkscrew that he had left on the card table. Normally, he would have offered to open the wine, but she seemed intent on doing it herself, so he hesitated a moment.

“I’ll be glad to open that for you,” he said.

“Thank you.”

He opened the wine and she poured it.

“You’re my guest, so you must drink first, which means you get to make the first toast.”

Raising the glass, he said, "To friendship as true as the North Star." Then he drank and handed her the glass.

She drank, lifted the glass, and said "To friendship as true as the North Star." Then they drank in turn.

"Here's a confession," she said. "I now know why one side of me trusted you from the day I met you, even though the other side kept calling me a fool."

"Caution in a new friendship is usually a good policy in my estimation. I will never deliberately betray you as my friend, but I have unintentionally failed more than my share of good people."

"I'll take my chance. I'm here, happy and expectant."

"Angela, I don't know how to say this without sounding like a presumptuous fool, but I need to tell you that true friendship is all I can offer you."

"Then we're on the same page. During my graduate studies at Brown, I fell for the advances of the English professors who would become my dissertation advisor. He was married with grown children and told me that he and his wife were estranged and soon to be divorced.

"Like a fool, I believed him. The affair ended traumatically for me, and I made a vow never again to get romantically involved with a married man."

"Please forgive me. Sometimes people misread the motives behind my gestures of friendship. Now I feel totally ridiculous."

"No, please. I appreciate your honesty. All is well."

Silently, they studied each other until he looked at his watch.

"Yes, I know you have to go."

"Where are you staying tonight?"

"The Ashland Hotel."

"Sleep well. See you tomorrow morning."

"Yes, tomorrow morning."

She followed him to the back porch steps and waved as he drove away.

Chapter Seventeen

The moving van pulled away from the house, headed north, and Barsh joined Angela in the living room.

"I can't believe how wonderfully well this went," she said. "Having you really made a difference, and I can't thank you enough. I've never been welcomed anywhere so warmly."

"My pleasure. We stacked the boxes you marked *Cooper office* on the back porch. Mostly books, I assume. Let me carry them to your office, and you'll be finished with that."

"How could I refuse such an offer? Yes, they're books and a bit heavy for me. But first, let's sit in my new living room for a few minutes. I'd like to hear about the Alabama trip you mentioned earlier this morning."

She motioned for him to take a big stuffed chair and then sat on the couch next to the chair.

"You're leaving early in the morning and will be back Wednesday afternoon, right?"

"Yes, and this will be Hannah's first trip to Alabama. Earlier this summer, I promised to take her before school starts back. But the summer slipped away, as I got involved in several projects at the farm. This is my last chance to keep my promise."

"Ah, a man who keeps his promises. I look forward to meeting Hannah."

"She'll be pleased to meet you. I told her you were a poet and novelist, and she was impressed. Angela, I like the way your furniture fits in this room. It's very pleasing."

"Yes, I'm pleased with the way it's shaping up. I can envision how it will look when I get the paintings hung and all the accents in place.

"I'm also pleased to have this log-burning fireplace. I've never had one before, and I can't wait to start a fire this fall."

"As the proud owner of a farm with woodland, I've already cut more firewood than I'll burn this winter. I have split oak and small hickory logs that are just the right size to sizzle the evening away.

"I also have an abundance of rosin-rich lighter wood. Strike a match and it flames up. No need for lighter fluids. I'll bring you everything you need to build delightful fires."

"How generous of you. Will you show me how you build a fire?"

"Yes, of course."

"Your joy over buying the farm jumped from the pages of your letters."

"I was there almost every day this summer. I've made a lot of progress on several projects that I'm excited about."

"Like what?"

"For one thing, I've made pottery according to the traditional method of the Catawba Indians."

"How did you get interested in that project?"

"Last year, I visited the Catawba Reservation near Rock Hill, South Carolina, and learned that they still make pottery. So, when I bought the farm this summer, I got one of the potters to teach me their technique. My pieces are not as beautiful as theirs, but I'm pleased with what I've made."

"I trust you know the farm is on the list of places I'm eager to visit."

"I'll take you as soon as the weather cools down a bit. We'll hike through the forest to the Pacolet River."

"Speaking of my list, do you have any idea when you might introduce me to the Carolina mountains?"

"Unless something comes up, I can take you on our first field trip to the mountains as early as two weeks from tomorrow. Will that work for you? Or do you need more time to get settled in?"

"That date's good for me."

"Do you like surprises?"

"Good ones, yes."

"Then I think you'll enjoy this one."

"Could I prepare a picnic lunch?"

"Sure. Without giving away the detail, I can tell you that we'll share your picnic lunch high on a mountain top in North Carolina."

"Sounds divine."

"Okay, let's move the books to your new office."

***

In less than an hour, they had finished that task and returned to her backyard.

"Angela, if you need help with anything, while I'm in Alabama, call Catherine. If she can't help you, she'll know who can. I'll see you Thursday morning at the faculty meeting."

"Yes, Thursday morning. Have a good time with Hannah in Alabama, and please be safe."

Standing on the porch steps, she waved as he drove away.

Chapter Eighteen

Sunday morning, Barsh and Hannah were packed and ready to leave for Alabama. Atypically, Debbie followed them to the car.

"Bye, Hannah. I hope you have a great trip."

"I will, Mother."

"Barsh, please be careful."

"Don't worry. We'll be just fine."

He backed out of the driveway and looked back at Debbie, who was drooping with anxiety. She was counting on him to sell his sabbatical plan to their daughter. He, however, was having doubts about it, although he had not shared them with his wife.

Hannah was unusually subdued, as they left the neighborhood. He turned to smile at her, but she was looking straight ahead with a book in her hand.

"I hope that's an interesting book. We've got a long drive ahead of us."

"I want to talk."

"You name the subject and we'll have at it."

"You and Mother."

"What about us?"

"Why did you stop sleeping with her? That's been worrying me for months, and you said we should talk about anything that was bothering me."

"Yes, we definitely need to talk. I assume you know that my new sleeping arrangement means that Debbie and I no longer have an intimate marriage."

"That's what worries me. What's wrong?"

"I'll give you my perspective on what has happened. You can also ask you mother."

"Your account is all I need."

"As you well know, Debbie and I hold very different beliefs about a lot of things. For example, she does not believe in evolution because it contradicts the Biblical account of creation. For me, evolution is totally evident and should be for anyone who will study the evidence.

"This kind of difference has been there since we first started dating, but rather than our views on various topics converging over time, the gulf between us has grown wider. She has remained conservative and traditional, and I have become much more liberal.

"At first, I tried to share my intellectual and spiritual journey with her, but it was too threatening for her to embrace. I don't know for sure, but I think Debbie found it more and more difficult to be intimate with me as the gulf between our worldviews continued to grow.

Back in March, I decided that having my own bedroom would be less complicated for both of us. She approved my decision, and she will never invite me back into what was our bedroom.

"I'm the one who has progressively changed. If anyone is to blame, I guess it's me, although I don't think it does any good to assign blame. I certainly don't blame Debbie for being who she is. She's a good woman, just traditional in so many ways.

"The truth is that Debbie and I are no longer lovers in the romantic sense of the word, but I love and honor her as your mother. And I always will. I also respect her needs as she does mine, which means we often go our separate ways.

"The summer before you were born, I wanted the two of us to take an extended tour of Europe, but she had no interest in traveling in Europe. She insisted, however, that I go by myself, and I spent most of the summer traveling alone over Europe.

"Debbie never complains when you and I do things that she doesn't enjoy. And she never complains when I leave for some hiking trip or any other trip I choose to take."

"Okay, I understand."

"I trust you know that we both love you, unconditionally, and we always will, no matter what our relationship is now or may become in the future."

"I know that. I think I'll read. Do you mind?"

"You read and I'll drive. And between us, we'll rack up the miles."

There was another factor that had impaired the intimate bond between Barsh and Debbie, but it was something that he would never share with Hannah.

After she was born, Debbie had a long bout of depression that left her terrified by the idea of a second pregnancy. He had wanted a second child but honored her position on the subject.

She gradually lost interest in sex for pleasure and blamed it on her lack of confidence in condoms and birth control pills. For Hannah's sake, he had borne that burden with controllable resentment and remained a loyal family man who found great joy in parenting their daughter.

***

As Barsh drove south on I-85, he did a lot of thinking, while Hannah did a lot of reading. Occasionally, she would take a break from reading and they would talk.

As they approached Atlanta, he exited the Interstate to show her Emory University. He just drove around the campus pointing out things without stopping.

Back on course, they stopped for lunch at Sprayberry's Barbecue in Newnan, Georgia. As they enjoyed barbecue sandwiches and onion rings, he reminisced about his old friend Wesley Workman.

As teenagers, they once roared in and out of Atlanta on Wesley's Harley-Davidson, just for the hell of it, and then stopped at Sprayberry's on the way home. He could still envision Wesley flirting with the sassy waitress.

Barsh was soon thinking about Amy Burdette, his first sweetheart and victim of Wesley's seductive powers. She had such potential as a young girl, but there she was pregnant just before she turned fifteen.

He had never told Hannah about Amy, because he was not ready to tell her about how their relationship ended. On leaving the restaurant, he decided it was time to tell her. Perhaps it would be helpful to her when she started down love's treacherous pathway. He had not been lucky with love. Hopefully, she would be.

"Hannah, I've told you that we moved from the country to town when I was nine, but I don't remember telling you about Amy Burdette who lived next door?"

"No, you never told me about her."

"I was a month older than she, and from the day we moved in, she started coming to our house, almost every day. We played in the house, under the house, and in the yard."

"You, played under the house?"

"Oh, yes, one side of our yard was sloping, so that side of the house rested on brick pillars, and that left plenty of space under the house for us to play. There, we build roads and a make-believe village. We called it playing cars."

"I've never heard of such a thing. Was it fun?"

"We were in a world by ourselves for hours and as contented as you can imagine. But we soon outgrew playing cars under the house.

Then we played in and around a tepee that I'd built in the meadow below our house. Again, we were as happy as larks in our own imaginary world.

"Adjacent to our backyard, there was a grove of mixed trees, mostly hardwood, where we developed our climbing skills. We especially enjoyed climbing this big magnolia tree. Its foliage was so dense that no one could see us when we were hanging out in that beautiful tree.

"For almost five years, Amy was my best friend. She could have been a boy for all I cared.

"Then her parents stopped her from coming over to hang out with me, but I didn't care. I'd started rambling beyond our neighborhood, all by myself.

"We continued to walk to school and back each day, however. Then this astonishing thing happened one spring afternoon. Standing on the sidewalk in front of her house, I looked into her yielding eyes and mysteriously fell in love with her.

"Soon I was crazy in love with her. She was the girl I wanted to marry when we grew up, and she seemed to be just as committed to me. But things don't always turn out the way you expect them to.

"Before that summer ended, she became infatuated with Wesley Workman, one of my camping buddies who had made a move on her. She then dumped me without the courtesy of telling me that she had fallen in love with him.

"She just started avoided me, completely. Being shunned by a girl, who once loved you, is almost harder to deal with than being rejected by her.

"Then the family moved away that fall. There were no goodbyes or explanation. I later learned from her friend that Wesley had gotten her pregnant and her parents put her in a home for unwed pregnant girls."

"Why?"

"That was a way of protecting girls in her predicament as well as their families. When the baby was born, it would be put up for adoption, and when that happened, the girl would return home to grow up."

"What a sad story."

"A sad story, indeed, and a painful experience for me. In spite of my broken heart, I have always wished her the best, and I hope she's had a good life."

They both fell silent. Hannah began writing on a notepad and he continued to think about his parental responsibilities.

***

They checked into a motel on the edge of his hometown. After a short rest, they left for a brief tour of the small town. He pointed out the places that he had frequented and noted how shabby they looked, especially the once glorious Martin Theatre where he had spent many Saturday mornings as a boy.

From Main Street, he drove by the cluster of schools he had attended and then headed for his old neighborhood. In spite of his effort to point out all the changes that had occurred, he knew there was no way Hannah could envision the place as it was when he lived there.

"I'm sorry, Daddy, but it seems strange to me that you once lived here."

"That's understandable. It now seems strange to me. Well, my sweet girl, let's have an early dinner at the Galley, and we'll call it a day. I have a busy scheduled planned for us, tomorrow."

Chapter Nineteen

After breakfast Monday morning, Barsh drove through town and headed north on the old U.S. 431 and then turned west on State Highway 22. As a high school boy, he had taken that route countless times on the way back to their farm in his Ford pickup. It was a beautiful day, and he was full of memories.

"Hannah, we're coming up on High Pine Creek. Look to your right as we cross the bridge and you'll see its rippling currents. About two miles up the creek, there's a cave in the side of a bluff that's known as Coot's Cave.

"My elders used to tell me about Coot Pitman, who lived in that cave when they were children. He would tramp the roads, near and far, and people called him a boogeyman. Parents would tell their kids that they'd better look out or old Coot Pitman would get them."

"Daddy, I thought I'd heard all of your boyhood stories."

"No! No! I have a good stock of them, and I'm not near the bottom of the barrel."

A mile past High Pine Creek, he turned right onto a county highway.

"Okay, we're ascending the hills to the sacred soil of Broughton Community, where I spent the happiest years of my youth. Before we leave the community, we'll visit the cemetery where Mother, Dad, and my stillborn sister are buried.

"First, I want to drive by our once-upon-a-time farm. Then we'll stop at the Henry farm to see if anyone is home. You know the stories of Susan Henry and our horseback-riding days."

"Do you think she still lives there?"

"I don't know but I hope to find out in a few minutes."

"Have you seen her since you moved away?"

"Not a single time."

He turned right at King Marshall's Store onto another county highway. They were almost there.

"Hannah, look to your left."

"Is that where you lived?"

"That's it. I lived there during my high school years. Not much to brag about, but I would not have traded it for a royal palace.

"I'm pleased that the current owners are keeping the place up. They're raising Hereford cattle. We raised Black Angus.

"That fence running away from the road up ahead is the property line between this farm and the Henry farm. Susan lived there with her mother and grandparents."

Barsh was pleased to see a late model Buick parked in front of the garage and turned into the driveway. A strange feeling came over him as he headed for the door with Hannah following. He rang the doorbell, and Mrs. Henry soon opened the door.

"Lord o' mercy, it's you, Barsh," she said and rushed into his arms. "For a moment, I couldn't believe my eyes. And who's this pretty girl?"

"My daughter Hannah."

"She's sure got your mother's features. Hannah, you are a beautiful child. Barsh, you don't know how glad I am to see y'all. Come on in."

She led the way to the spacious den. There, above a well-crafted stone fireplace, was a large oil painting of Susan wearing a classy riding outfit and tall brown boots. She was sitting astride a magnificent black stallion.

Following Mrs. Henry's directions, he sat in a big stuffed chair and Hannah sat beside her on the couch.

"Barsh, I ain't married no rich fool if that's what you're thinking. Papa left this place to me, and I sold it to Susan after she married Terry Halford, a doctor up in Nashville.

"They live on a big horse farm out in the country. She built this house for me and turned Papa's old fields into pastures for some of her broodmares."

"Well, I'm pleased to hear she's doing well. I know you must be proud of her."

"She's done good for herself. If you met her for the first time, you'd think she was born with a silver spoon in her mouth. Look at that painting. Does that look like the Susan you knew?"

"Her outfit is definitely an upgrade and so is the horse. But there's a good resemblance to the girl who once rode a Palomino horse named Dan, back in our day. Susan was beautiful then and she's beautiful now."

"She owes her love of horses to you. When y'all moved out here and you got Thunder, nothing was ever the same with Susan. She was driving us all crazy until I bought her that horse. Then she didn't care about nobody or nothing but you and y'all's horses.

"When you went off to college, all she talked about was going to college herself and becoming a horse doctor. Nobody ever believed she could do it, but she did. Susan was a spunky girl. You got to give her that.

"Oh, my Lord, she about went crazy when your parents moved to Georgia, and she lost you. It was her love of horses and her dream of being a horse doctor that pulled her through."

"Susan was a natural with horses," Barsh said. "Sometimes she would curry Thunder and Dan, while waiting for me to finish some chore. She would talk to them like they could understand everything she said."

"Daddy, how old was Susan?"

"She was about your age when we moved to this community. The last time I saw her, she was fifteen."

"Hannah, I'll tell you something else. Susan would have followed Barsh to Hell if he'd a-wanted to go there."

"Don't believe that. True, we were very close friends. Susan was my little riding pal, and I was determined to look out for her. I always believed she would do well in life, and I'm pleased to learn she has excelled."

As a hush settled over them, he studied Susan's portrait and had a renewed longing to see her.

"Barsh, tell me about yourself. Do you still hunt and fish? Lord, I missed all the fish and game you used to bring us. You was so good to share with us."

"I gave up hunting and fishing when I went off to college. I don't camp anymore either, but I still love the wilds of nature. I do a lot of hiking in the Carolina mountains."

"What about a horse? I can't imagine you without a horse."

"Thunder was my one and only horse. I married a girl from Kentucky. She was born on a big tobacco farm, but she hated living in the country. Horses and country living were out of the question for her and thus for me."

"That's a pure shame."

"Daddy, you could have a horse now that you bought a farm for yourself."

"Hannah's right. You, of all people, should have a horse. And Hannah should also have one. She could be your little riding buddy. Susan would love to fix you both up with a horse. You should go see her. It would do her a world of good."

"Yeah, Daddy, let's visit Susan and buy us a horse. You can teach me how to ride."

"Well, maybe we could visit Susan and check out her horses."

"I can't wait to tell her that y'all are coming to see her."

"Hold off on that until I call her."

"Then promise me you'll call her."

"Okay, I'll call her."

"That will tickle her to death. She's won about every prize there is when it comes to Tennessee Walkers. Let me show you some pictures of her and her horses."

Mrs. Henry retrieved a thick photo album, and he and Hannah sat beside her on the couch as she narrated the photos. He was most impressed.

"I'm giving you this picture. It's like the painting up there."

"Thank you. I'm delighted to have it."

"Can y'all spend the night with me?"

"We'd enjoy that, but we have a reservation for tonight on Cheaha Mountain."

"Well, I hope you can spend the morning with me. I'll fry some okra and cook y'all some cornbread and black-eyed peas."

"Thanks, but it's time for us to get on the road. There are lots of places I want to take Hannah, and we don't have much time.

"It's so good to see you and learn about Susan. Please tell her that I love the painting of her and the black stallion. Tell her that she's as beautiful as she was when I last saw her and I'm proud of all her accomplishments."

"I'll tell her for sure. Now let me give you Susan's phone number."

They exchanged phone numbers, said their goodbyes, and promised to stay in touch. Hannah was beaming with joy as they left.

He would call Susan about a visit, but he would not be buying horses for Hannah and himself within the next year if he stuck to his plan for a year-long wilderness sojourn. Still, he wanted to see Susan, and if Hannah wanted a horse, he would buy her one as soon as he returned form the wild.

As he drove around the community, he shared a bit of information about the people who had lived on each of the farms, when he lived there. Then he stopped at the church cemetery. He did not break down this time but talked about his mother and father until Hannah started crying.

"What's wrong, my sweet girl," he said and took her in his arms.

"I don't know, Daddy."

He felt sure she was crying because of his and Debbie's estrangement, but he decided not to go there. As soon as she ceased crying, they left the cemetery.

"It's time for me to show you the Tallapoosa River. We'll cross the river in about fifteen minutes, just before we get to a little town named Wadley. I've camped at a dozen or more places upriver and downriver from that bridge. We're going to a place called Horseshoe Bend, that is downriver.

"In 1814, General Andrew Jackson's forces massacred an aggregation of Muscogee Creek Indians at this site and ended their last uprising against the whites, who were illegally settling on their traditional land. It's now a National Military Park, but when I camped there, it was just a wild place on the Tallapoosa River, where I liked to camp and fish.

"When we leave Horseshoe Bend, we'll head for Cheaha Mountain, the highest place in Alabama. Hopefully, we'll have time to do some hiking on one of the nature trails. We'll dine at Mountaintop Restaurant, that has a spectacular view, and then spend the night in one of the lodges."

"Daddy, I'm glad to see where you grew up. But you know what? I don't know how to say it. How did you get to where you are from here?"

"That's a good question. We'll talk about that tomorrow when we visit Paw-Paw Roberts' grave. Okay?"

"That's fine with me."

It was a good day for both of them. Hannah seemed to enjoy it all. She went to sleep at her regular time. Unable to sleep, he pondered the task of selling his sabbatical plan to her the next morning.

Chapter Twenty

Barsh drove to Paw-Paw Roberts' old homeplace, and with rising anxiety, he turned up the lane that led to the house. There was neither car nor truck in sight.

As he stopped at the edge of the yard, a redbone hound scrambled from beneath the house and announced their arrival in a husky voice. Hannah, who was silently taking it all in, also seemed anxious but for a different reason—she over the strangeness of the place, he over the task of selling her on the sabbatical.

"Don't worry, my sweet girl. If anyone's home, they'll come to the door to check out the dog's announcement that we're here."

A stooped woman with gray hair in a bun opened the front door and stepped onto the porch.

"I don't know this woman. You stay in the car and I'll talk to her."

Exposing the palm of his hand, he talked calmly to the barking dog as he walked toward the house. The woman, who had moved from the door to the porch steps, shouted for Jaw Bone to hush up and get back under the house. Instead, the dog accepted Barsh's friendly overture and followed him to the steps.

"Good morning. I'm Barsh Roberts. My great-grandfather Roberts used to live here."

"Lord o' mercy, Barsh, I remember you when you was a boy. Never knowed another boy named Barsh. You're Bill Roberts' boy, ain't you?"

"Yes, ma'am."

"You don't likely remember me, but we're kinfolks."

"No, I don't remember you."

"I'm Arrie Roberts. Call me Cousin Arrie. I was a Hammell before I married George Johnson Roberts. We bought this place after Paw-Paw died.

"My husband up and died on me six years ago. Dropped dead without a warning. But I ain't complaining. Momma lost Daddy when she was just forty-seven. Besides, my youngest son keeps a regular check on me. Those are his beef cows grazing down yonder by the creek. Who's that in the car, out there?"

"My daughter Hannah."

"Well, you git that girl, and y'all come on in this house and talk to me."

Thankful that relatives still owned the property, he hurried to the car.

"We're in luck. She's a distant cousin who remembers me. Let's visit with her for a while, and then we'll be on our way to Paw-Paw Roberts' grave."

He opened the car door and she followed him to the porch.

"Hannah, this is Cousin Arrie Roberts."

"My Lord, you're the prettiest girl I ever laid my eyes on. Y'all come on in."

She led them through the house to the back porch, that had been screened in since Barsh was last there. They sat patiently answering the questions that she threw at them, as her eyes shifted back and forth.

"Cousin Arrie, we'd like to visit Paw-Paw Roberts' grave if that's alright."

"Lord, yes, and I'd go with you if I was able. Do you know the way?"

"I remember walking to the top of that hill," he said pointing. "The grave was between two big cedars."

"That's right. You won't have no trouble finding the grave. Look for those two cedars. The others have been logged and sold to a furniture company."

***

On finding the grave, they spoke their chosen words to Paw-Paw Roberts and sat down on the thick bed of cedar needles. Hannah seemed calm and pleased to be there. Barsh searched for a good segue to the task before him.

"Did I ever tell you about the time I camped for a week in a cave?"

"No, sir."

"This is how that came about. The summer before my senior year at Bradley High, I discovered a cave in a high bluff about five miles up the Tallapoosa River from where I was camping. Following my habit of naming places, I named it Bluff Cave.

"On my way back to camp, I was excited to see deer tracks on a sandbar in a creek. They were the first I had ever seen.

Over-hunting had killed most of the deer in the county before I was born. So, I started making plans to camp at Bluff Cave during Christmas break with the goal of killing a deer.

"The day after Christmas, I left for that cave, prepared to camp until New Year's Eve. Each morning, I'd get up before dawn and hike to a different deer stand where I'd wait for one to come by on its way to bed down for the day. I think I told you that they forage at night and bed down for the day soon after daybreak."

"I remember."

"I did that for five mornings and never saw a deer."

"Didn't you get discouraged and want to go home?"

"Not at all. I knew the chance of seeing one was small. That camping trip remains one of my cherished experiences.

"During the day, I'd kill a rabbit or duck and gather a few edible mushrooms. An old woman, who lived on the back side of our farm, had taught me which mushrooms were edible. In late afternoon, I'd butcher whatever I'd killed and roast it and the mushrooms over hot coals, using a hickory skewer.

"I'd eat half for supper and the other half for breakfast, and that worked well for me.

"Every evening, I would sit on the bluff above the cave and watch the sun set in the distant horizon across the river. I did a lot of thinking about a lot of things. I was confused and bewildered about what I wanted to do with my life.

"While working with a logging crew, back in the summer, I witnessed senseless racism that caused a black man to kill a white man with an ax. He killed him in self-defense after the white man shot him three times with a semi-automatic .22 rifle.

"The black man survived the shooting, only to be unjustly convicted of murder and executed by the State of Alabama. I testified that the black man acted in self-defense, but the jury refused to believe me and convicted him of murder.

"The racial bigotry and legal injustice that I experienced firsthand shattered my trust in our social system, and I started thinking seriously about going to Alaska to live in the wild.

"I soon realized that I couldn't do that to Mother and Dad. They wouldn't know what was happening to me, and I wouldn't know what was happening to them."

To his dismay, Hannah seemed shaken by his narration. She was so young, so innocent, so dependent on him. At that moment, he knew his sabbatical scheme was dead. How could be abandon his daughter to Debbie's care for one year with no way of communicating with her? To hell with that plan.

Debbie could take Hannah to Louisville but not under false pretense. At an appropriate time, he would tell her the truth, and he would remain an integral part of her life.

"Well, my sweet girl, I guess you know I'm glad I decided against Alaska. Otherwise, I would not be the father of the best daughter I could ever imagine."

"What happened to cause you to want to be a professor?"

"Before witnessing that racial injustice, I'd decided to attend Auburn University and major in civil engineering—a degree that would give me a career I could follow outdoors.

"During my senior year at Bradley High, however, that plan no longer appealed to me. After graduating, I had a profound religious experience, that left me with a clear sense of calling to be a voice for justice and righteousness as well as a servant to broken humanity.

"With that new goal, I enrolled at Samford University to major in religion. During my freshman year, I decided that I could best carry out my mission by becoming a college professor of religious studies. That led me to philosophy and all the other branches of knowledge. And you know the story from there."

"I like your story, Daddy."

"I'm glad you do. Okay, it's time for us to take leave of this place. We're spending the night in Birmingham with Uncle Edward, who had a big influence on me as a young man. He gave me my first field guide to birds, when I was ten.

"We'll get to Birmingham in time for me to show you Samford University and the colossal statue of Vulcan standing on a tall pedestal on Red Mountain. You and I will climb the stairs to the top of the pedestal and cast our eyes down on the old iron city.

"Uncle Edward wants to take us out to a nice restaurant. He's a great story teller, so you'll get to hear some of his tales before bedtime. Then we'll head home, tomorrow morning."

Chapter Twenty-One

Back in Ashland Wednesday afternoon, Barsh left Hannah at home with Davis and drove straight to Debbie's office to give her a report on the trip. She was with a client, and he waited in the reception area. The door to Debbie's office opened, and she exited with the client, who thanked her for her help and left.

"Thank God, you're back," she whispered as he entered her office. "How did Hannah respond to your sabbatical plan?"

"I changed my mind and didn't tell her."

"Why?"

"I realized that I could not leave her for a whole year. She needs me to stay involved in her life. That was a bad idea, and I'm ashamed I ever thought about such a deceptive scheme.

"On the drive to Alabama, she asked why I started sleeping in the guest bedroom. I told her that as our intellectual differences continued to grow, it become difficult for us to be intimate with each other. I also told her that whatever our relationship might be, now or in the future, we would always love her unconditionally."

"How did she respond?"

"She seemed to take it in stride. So, I believe she's going to be able to handle the separation if I can assure her that I will continue to be a major part of her life."

"Of course, that's what I want. You can call and visit her at any time. She can visit you during holidays, and she can live with you during the summer."

"That's a fair arrangement," he said. "Let's give Hannah a little time to process the things I shared with her during our trip, and then I'll tell her about the separation in a way that supports you."

"Okay, I'm feeling better about this approach." she said.

"Debbie, I've decided to take a break from church. I feel hypocritical sitting in the sanctuary with you and Hannah with things as they are between you and me. In the months ahead, I plan to spend most of my Sundays hiking various nature trails."

"Then I'll leave that between you and God."

***

After dinner, he worked on a presentation he was giving at the faculty meeting the next day. Hannah was in her room, working on a new poem that she had started that afternoon. Just before her bedtime, she read him the poem that praised the Tallapoosa River for all the joy and pleasure it had given him during his youth.

"What a beautiful poem, my sweet girl. Do you know what literary critics call this kind of poem?"

"No, sir."

"A poem that addresses an inanimate thing like the Tallapoosa River or a person who is absent is called an apostrophe."

"You just gave me an idea. I'm going to write an apostrophe addressed to your horse Thunder about the sorrow you experienced when your father had to sell him."

"That was a sad experience. The owner of the big lumber company, who had hired Dad as his new foreman, wanted him to move quickly. So, he sold Thunder and the rest of our livestock at an auction before I could come home from college. I don't even know who bought Thunder.

"I was able to come home the weekend they moved. That Friday was the last time I slept in that old farmhouse—another sad experience to lose the place where I'd spent the best years of my youth.

"Saturday, I got to say goodbye to my riding pale Susan, and that was a very sad experience. I hope my sad stories don't trouble you."

"I can deal with them. I'm glad I got to see where you spent the best years of your youth."

"Do you know what I kept thinking about on the drive home from Alabama?"

"What?"

"Camping again at Bluff Cave during Christmas break. This time, I want to test my survival skills for two weeks, using only the things I've made with my own hands."

"Knowing you, I bet you can do it."

"You won't object if I'm not with you this Christmas, will you?"

"Not as long as you're doing something that's important to you."

"Good. This is definitely important to me."

***

The house was quiet when Barsh came up from the basement after a hard workout. He went to his study to cool down. As he sat at the desk, he felt more optimistic about easing Hannah into accepting the separation.

Now, he had to come up with a new plan for his sabbatical. The obvious thing would be post-doctoral studies at some university. But what would he study?

As he thought about it, the answer became obvious—contemporary novels and poetry. Taking graduate course in these subjects would certainly expand his expertise in the humanities and improve his chance of getting an appointment as a Professor of Humanities. Feeling better about his situation, he left the study to shower and go to bed.

Chapter Twenty-Two

Just before four o'clock Thursday afternoon, Angela appeared at Barsh's office door.

"Can I join you for tea?"

"You're just in time. The water is hot."

He fixed green tea and they sat facing each other in the two comfortable chairs.

"It's been a long day," she said, "but the meetings were helpful. I got my course schedule for the semester, and I'm pleased with it."

"That's good news. How are you adjusting to your new house?"

"I couldn't be happier. It's such a joy to be living in a house."

The phone rang and he answered it.

"That was Catherine. She wants me to stop by her office before I leave campus. She's eager to hear about Hannah and our Alabama trip."

"I'd also like to hear about it."

"It was a good trip for both of us. One of the highlights was a visit with Susan Henry's mother. Susan was my little riding pal, back during my horseback-riding days.

"I learned that Susan is a veterinarian but she limits her practice to houses. Eleven years ago, she married a physician who owned a horse farm near Nashville, and they raise Tennessee Walkers."

"Tell me about Tennessee Walkers. Clydesdales are the only breed I can identify."

"They're excellent saddle horses that are known for their high-stepping gait. In recent years, Susan has won most of the big riding competitions in Tennessee."

He retrieved the photo of Susan astride her black stallion and showed it to her.

"And this woman was once your little riding pal?"

"For almost five years. Before I went off to college, I doubt there was a week that we didn't ride at least once.

"Hannah was fascinated by all the photos of Susan and her horses. Now, she wants a horse."

"I have never touched a horse, but as a young girl I wanted one more than I can tell you. Maybe I was just in love with the idea of having a horse."

"That's probably the case with Hannah. When Mrs. Henry suggested that Susan would love to fix each of us up with a horse, Hannah was ready to go for a visit."

"Are you going?"

"I promised Mrs. Henry that I'd call Susan about a possible visit."

"Changing the subject, is our trip to the mountains still on for a week from this Sunday?"

"Oh, yes, I'm all set for that field trip."

"Great. I've decided what we're having for our picnic lunch. Can you forget about surprising me and tell me where we're going?"

"The top of Mount Mitchell, the highest place in the United States east of the Mississippi River."

"Wow! Now I'm even more excited if that's possible. Will there be a lot of hiking?"

"Just the last few steps to the observation tower. There's a good road up the mountain and a visitor's center. I've also adding two nearby attractions that I'd like to share with you."

"Great! But surprise me with those."

"Sorry to rush off, but I have to give Catherine a report and then head home."

"Off with you, then. I'll clean the tea set."

"Thanks, but I'll swing by and clean up after I see Catherine."

***

Barsh gave Dean Thompson a report on the Alabama trip, including the fact that he had abandoned his goal of experiencing a year-long sojourn in the wild. Now, he intended to make it a two-week excursion, during the Christmas break, something he felt like he owed himself. It was now or never.

"Well, I agree that you owe yourself the experience. Do you have a new plan for your sabbatical?"

"I'm working on one that I'm excited about. It focuses on improving my credentials to become a humanities professor. I'll share it with you as soon as I get a few details worked out.

"Catherine, I have a strong premonition that Debbie will never move back, once she gets to Louisville. If she doesn't come back by the end of my sabbatical, I'll probably resign from Cooper, unless you can get me an appointment as a Professor of Humanities. I'm tired of dealing with the hostile trustees and ministers who keep trying to get me fired as a Professor of Religion because of my liberal views."

"Then I'll shake heaven and earth to get you that appointment. Truthfully, that's what you are now."

"I trust you know that I would hate to leave Cooper, but I don't want to put a heavy burden on you."

"Working to keep you here will not be a burden. And you know that Georgette will join me in this endeavor."

"I've said it before, and it's ever so true, without you two I would have already been fired."

"And we intend to keep you here. You are the best Cooper has. Changing the subject, do you have any new ideas about how to prepare Hannah for the separation?"

"I will soon tell her the truth. Debbie is on board with this. She has also agreed that I can call or visit Hannah any time. She can visit me during holidays and she can live with me during the summer. With this agreement, I'm a bit optimistic for the first time."

"That is good news. Please keep me informed."

"Be assured that I will keep you informed." he said and left.

Back at Kimberly, he took the stairs two at a time and hurried to his office. Angela had cleaned the tea set. He got his briefcase, locked the office, and stopped at her office door to thank her for cleaning up.

Chapter Twenty-Three

As they had planned for that Sunday, Barsh drove into Angela's backyard. She was sitting on the porch steps with a cloth tote bag hanging from her shoulder and a picnic basket resting beside her. They exchanged greetings as she hurried to the Audi. He took the basket and opened the door for her. She eased into the seat and looked up at him with that winsome smile. He stashed the basket in the trunk, and they were on their way.

"What a beautiful day for our first field trip to the Carolina mountains," she said. "I am so excited about experiencing Mount Mitchell, the highest mountain east of the Mississippi River."

"There's an interesting story about the man for whom the mountain is named. He's buried there. I'll tell you about him when we visit his grave."

They were relaxed, chatty, and playful. They were also mindful of the scenery, both natural and manmade, and commented on it from time to time.

"Barsh, please tell me about the other two places you're taking me."

"First, there's Linville Caverns inside Humpback Mountain. It's a relatively small but interesting cave."

"Sounds like another good experience to me. The New York City subway is as close as I've been to experiencing a cave."

"Next, we'll drive north on the Blue Ridge Parkway to Grandfather Mountain. The last time I took Hannah, several people were hang-gliding. It was quite exhilarating to watch them launch from the mountain top and glide into the valley far below."

"That will be another new experience for me, but I can't imagine myself ever doing it."

"In my youth, I would have been eager to try it, but not now. There's a swinging bridge that will take us to a beautiful overlook with an expansive view of things, including hang-gliding if it's happening. Are you up for that?"

"Yes, I'd love that experience."

"Good. When we leave Grandfather Mountain, we'll head south on the Blueridge Parkway to the exit for Mount Mitchell, that is a part of the Black Mountains. They form a relatively short range of about fifteen miles, but six of the ten highest peaks in the Eastern United States are found there, including the highest."

"Truthfully, I don't know when I've been as excited as I am about this day."

"A day in the Carolina mountains is always good medicine for me, and I'm pleased to be introducing you to them."

A lone vulture, drifting in from the west, caught his eye, and he leaned forward for a better view through the top of the windshield. It was a turkey vulture. As he righted himself, Angela was quizzically looking at him.

"I was just identifying a vulture that was drifting into view. A habit I've carried with me from boyhood. Whenever I see a vulture riding the air currents, I keep eyeing it until I can identify it as a turkey vulture or a black vulture, our two species in these parts. I know that may sounds pointless to you."

"I can't deny it's a rather strange habit. Yet, somehow it doesn't surprise me that you would do that. I must confess that I have such negative feelings for vultures that I turn away as soon as I see them scavenging roadkill."

"The connotations of *vulture* have all turned negative, but I've grown to admire the feathered ones. I think of them as the Jains of the bird kingdom."

"The Jains?"

"You know those totally passive people of India who have such reverence for every form of life, plant and animal, that they will only eat food that was prepared for someone else. The leftovers if you will. The analogy isn't perfect. It's just that I've learned to give vultures their place in the scheme of things."

"I can see that you would, and I'll try to be more understanding and less repulsed by them. You have a way of changing my perspective on things if you haven't noticed."

"Beware! Beware! I'd hate to corrupt a good Northern woman."

"Like I've said before, I'll take my chance with you. Shifting subjects, I brought music to share, as you requested. Is this a good time?"

"Sure," he said and she fished a cassette from her cloth tote bag.

"I'll start with James Taylor's 'Carolina in My Mind.' Do you like him?"

"I'm not familiar with him or the song, but I like the title."

"I'm a big James Taylor fan. I remembered this song on the way home from the job interview back in April and played it when I got back to the apartment.

"If you want to know the truth, I played it throughout the summer, always singing along. Even when I wasn't playing it, I'd break forth with the refrain: In my mind I'm going to Carolina."

"Then play the song for me," he said and she did.

"What do you think?"

"I like the song, and I like James Taylor's voice."

"Good. I'll save the rest of the cassette for later. Do you like Bob Dylan?"

"Truthfully, I don't know much about him."

"He's one of my long-time favorites. Bob Dylan is his professional name. I've heard that he took the Dylan part from the Welsh poet, Dylan Thomas. But who knows?"

"Certainly not me. Nor would I have recognized the poet's name before this summer. The poetry anthology I'm reading has three poems by him."

"What do you think of them?"

"There's something quite moving about the poems I've read, although I was often confused by the lyrics. I knew he was using language figuratively, but even so, some of the words made no syntactical sense to me. I couldn't make a connection with the title and various phrases and similies, but the poems always aroused certain emotional feelings in me."

"You're right on target about their emotional impact. His poems evoke a certain mood that you can't miss. That and the music of the lyrics are what I admire most about his work.

"Poetry critics talk about *sound and sense*. Both have their place, although not equally so in most poems. Dylan Thomas usually gives a bigger nod to sound or music. You don't have to make sense out of every expression to get the essence of his poems."

"Well, that's helpful. I thought I was supposed to make sense out of every word. I'll reread his poems tonight and listen for the music and feel the emotions. Okay, I'm ready for Bob Dylan."

He shifted down a gear for the gravity of the rising highway. Angela inserted the cassette, and they settled back to let Bob Dylan take over.

Barsh listened attentively, but he had a hard time understanding some of the lyrics because of the way Dylan mumbled the words. Yet, there was something appealing about the music. Good instrumentation and a distinctive voice to say the least.

Angela paused the cassette.

"The next song, 'I Want You,' always reminds me of a crush I had on a new boy who joined my sophomore class in high school. Oh, did I ever want him but that never happened."

Again, Barsh had a difficult time catching all the lyrics, and some of those he did understand seemed to have no logical relationship with the refrain—I want you.

She paused the cassette when the song ended.

"You look puzzled."

"I couldn't make out a lot of the lyrics."

"Some of his words are difficult to catch and some of the lyrics are somewhat disjointed, even corny. But I learned them all. Want to hear about my high school heartthrob?"

"Yes, of course."

"I was too tall, too awkward, and I desperately needed someone to love me. When Joe Snyder joined my class, I fell for him like half the girls. I'll bet you've never known unrequited love, right?"

"Wrong. A new girl joined our freshman class in high school and immediately captured my heart. I had just been dumped by my first love, who shunned me at every turn until her family moved away that fall. I think the shunning hurt worse than the rejection.

"Anyway, I fell for the new girl, although I knew I didn't have a chance to win her love. I was a country boy, and she belonged to the town elite. Even so, I loved her for four years without ever asking her for a date."

"Why? What did you have to lose?"

"My pride, I guess, at least at first. By our junior year, she was definitely interested in me and often flirted with me. I, however, had gotten entangled in an adulterous relationship with a married woman.

"Her husband was in Korea, and she was lonely. She was nine years older than I. At first, it was all about companionship. Then she added sex.

"I yearned to respond to the overtures of the girl whom I loved so dearly, but there was no way I could in good conscience, as long as I was involved with a married woman. I wanted out of that relationship, so I could follow my heart, but because I had willingly entered it, I felt honor bound not to be the one to end it.

"The woman immediately ended our sexual rendezvous when she got word that her husband was coming home from the war, but it was too late for me. One of the prominent town boys had won the girl's affection by then. Believe me, I know the depths of unrequited love."

"Well, I never dreamed that Bob Dylan's music would lead us to this moment. If it's okay with you, I'd like to save the rest of the music until later."

"That's fine with me. Angela, I've never before told anyone about that adulterous affair, and now I'm regretting it."

"Why? Do you think I'm untrustworthy?"

"No, I consider you very trustworthy. It just seems wrong for me to talk about this experience as if I were dishonoring the woman as well as myself.

"Wesley Workman, an old camping friend from my youth, used to spill his guts in graphic detail about his sexual exploits. He wanted just one thing from a girl or woman, and he didn't care what the ramifications might be.

"I was both intrigued and repulsed by his erotic rants. I actually knew some of the girls that he had seduced. After experiencing his rants, I vowed that I would never share my sexual experiences."

"I honor that vow, Barsh, but what you told me was quite different from what your friend was doing. You weren't bragging about a sexual experience. You were explaining a dilemma."

"That's true. Thanks for your understanding."

"I have the highest respect for you and I trust you implicitly. I surprise myself at the things I want to share with you."

"You'll never guess what my monkey mind just latched onto with a willingness to share," he said.

"Then please tell me."

"Remember our conversation about Caroline Gordon on the way back to Charlotte for your flight home in April. I didn't know about the woman, but I felt a deep connection with her as you told me about her and how her novels became the subject of your Ph.D. dissertation.

"That Monday I checked the Cooper library for her books. Finding none there, I ordered four, including *The Women on the Porch*, which I had moved to the top of my reading list.

"As I read the novel, I felt the same close affinity with the protagonist Catherine Chapman that I had when you were telling me about the author. You did tell me the novel was somewhat autobiographical, right?"

"Would you like to read my dissertation? It will give you a better idea of its autobiographical dimensions."

"Yes, I was going to ask if I could."

"I'll bring it to you tomorrow. Barsh, I'm intrigued that you felt such a strong connection with the protagonist Catherine Chapman. Let's take a look at her.

"After she discovered her husband's infidelity, she fled New York for Swan Quarters, her ancestral home in Tennessee. That was also the home of the women on the porch.

"I like Gordon's symbolism of that porch as the portal to the land of the dead. It was obvious that the women living at Swan Quarters were idling their lives in relative disjunction from the world as they waited for death."

"I also found that interesting. But I knew Catherine Chapman had too much fire in her bones to choose that porch for her final destination. I did not know, however, if she would leave Swan Quarters with Tom Manigault, the neighbor who wanted her, or with her husband Jim, who came seeking reconciliation. Good literary suspense."

"Yes, I agree. Which man did you think Catherine would choose? And did she make the right choice in your opinion?"

"I felt like she would go back to her husband and she did, although I could not see that choice working for her in the long run."

"That's interesting because Caroline Gordon made the same choice. She actually divorced Allen Tate because of his infidelity, remarried him, and then divorce him for good because of his repeated infidelity."

"Did Gordon ever find her true love?"

"I think Tate was her true love, meaning she truly loved him, but unfortunately for her, he was not a true lover. And to my knowledge she has never found a true lover."

"That's sad," he said.

"Yes, very sad. Let's refocus on the ending of Gordon's novel. She doesn't tell us how Catherine Chapman's reconciliation with her husband Jim worked out. Why did you think it would not lead to a happy ever after for her?

"Her husband regretted having lost her and wanted her back, but I didn't see any transformation of his character that would keep him faithful to her."

"Well, that was certainly the case with Gordon's own husband. Do you think Catherine should have rejected her husband's efforts for reconciliation and stayed with Tom, her new lover?"

"I could not see that working either. They matched up well in the department of lovemaking, and they both shared a love of horses and the land—both a Southern thing. But Tom was not an intellectual, and I think Catherine needed an intellectual man who was also a true lover.

"I saw her as a woman with a questing mind, so I understand why she would give her husband another chance. He was her door to a circle of intellectuals.

"Truthfully, I did not see a man in the story who was both capable of and willing to meet her needs. In my opinion, life did not give her the choice she needed. Unfortunately, I've known a lot of people with Catherine Chapman's dilemma."

"I totally agree with your analysis. I've spent my adult life bonding with men that were not good for me or choosing to live by myself. You just helped me see that the man I needed was never available for me."

"Finding the right mate is definitely complicated," he said, "and, in my judgement, includes a bit of happenstance."

They fell silent as the Audi hummed over the rolling hills. Barsh knew that he had not been lucky in love, and now Angela had confessed that she had struck out in love.

He looked at her and she turned to meet his eyes. What a pleasure for him to watch her face light up with that winsome smile.

"Look, Angela, we're getting close to the Blue Ridge Mountains. Let's enjoy the scenery?"

Chapter Twenty-Four

He parked near the Visitor's Center on the top of Mount Mitchell. Angela, animated by the drive up the mountain, scrambled out and shouted, "Hello, Mount Mitchell."

"I need a pit stop," he said.

"The same here."

At the urinal in the Welcome Center, the refrain of one of Bob Dylan's song kept spinning around in his head. Yes, he wanted Angela. How could he deny it? But there was no way he could envision himself taking that road. Control yourself, he murmured in his head and left the restroom.

When Angela returned, she raised her hand for a high five that he rejoined.

"Let's take the trail to the observation tower. After we take in the view, we'll pay our respect to Elisha Mitchell at his grave. Then we'll pick out a good place to eat lunch and come back for our things. I'd like to sit on a blanket somewhere off the trail if that suits you."

"Yes, lunch on a blanket any day."

A few other visitors were going and coming as they made their way up the trail and ascended the tower. The various views were spectacular—the Blue Ridge Mountains to the east and range after range of mountains to the west.

"I am so taken with the beauty of the Carolina mountains. Flying home after the interview in April, I was so afraid I would never get to experience them with you. But here I am with you on top of Mount Mitchell."

"Being here, even alone, is good for the soul but far better with a friend."

"That's what I was thinking," she said with a shiver and rubbed her arms with her hands.

"You're chilled. Let's head for the car. I have a jacket in the trunk."

“I’m okay but I’ll take the jacket when we go back for the picnic basket and the blanket, that I assume you packed. I want to hear the story of Elisha Mitchell.”

“Back to the car, my friend. I’ll tell you the story on the way. I got my account from Wilmar Dykeman’s excellent book *The French Broad,* which is part of the *Rivers of America Series.* Dykeman covers the basin of the French Broad River and that included the Swannanoa River that drains the east side of this mountain.

“The French Broad actually starts way south of there and runs north to Asheville where the Swannanoa flows into it. Then it wanders west past Asheville until it’s joined by the Holston River at Knoxville to form the Tennessee River.

“In case you haven’t concluded, I have a fondness for our rivers. The Tallapoosa River was the river of my youth. You’ll likely be hearing tales about my experiences there, during my boyhood, if you stay at Cooper.”

“In case you haven’t concluded, I’ve settled in for the long haul, and I eagerly await the tales of your Tallapoosa River experiences. Now take me back to the story of Elisha Mitchell.”

“He was a multi-talented intellectual who taught in the science department at the University of North Carolina at Chapel Hill in the first half of the nineteenth century. One of his many accomplishments was the measurement of the height of this place.

“Afterwards, he declared this mountaintop to be the highest point in the United States east of the Mississippi River. Prior to his measurement of this peak, Mount Washington in New Hampshire held that honor.

“Soon after Mitchell established this place to be the tallest, Thomas Clingman claimed that he’d discovered an even higher peak in the Great Smoky Mountains. His claim, which had disturbed Mitchell, was later proved to be incorrect.

“To double check his work, Mitchell set out, alone and afoot, for the top of this mountain to remeasure it and was never again seen alive. That was before there were any roads in this area. His son persuaded some of the mountain men to form a search party to look for his father.

“Big Tom Wilson, an old bear hunter, tracked Mitchell from here to a thirty-foot waterfall, and there was Mitchell’s body floating face down in the pool, below the waterfall. Some think he was trying to hike down from here at night or in a thunder storm when he fell from the cliff. They buried him first in Asheville and then here."

"Thanks for sharing that. I'm so impressed by your knowledge of local history."

"Most people are bored by such stories, but they always interest me. I'm grateful for people like Dykeman who record them. She also wrote a novel, *The Tall Woman,* and I'm quite fond of it."

"I'm not familiar with any of her work. What's the novel about?"

"It's set in the French Broad Basin just after the Civil War. The protagonist is a mountain woman—strong of body, mind, and heart. Someone I could have loved if I had lived in her time. I like the fact that Dykeman's main characters are multidimensional people, not Appalachian stereotypes.

"Here, let me get the jacket. You are definitely chilled. I forgot to tell you that the temperature is much cooler up here."

"Thanks," she said as he held the jacket for her. "This is much better."

"Now let's break our daily bread. I saw the perfect place for us to enjoy the lunch you prepared."

***

They had finished eating and were sitting cross-legged on the blanket in a moment of golden silence. Barsh felt vivacious and whole.

The feeling, however, was too good to last. How could it hold against the reality that awaited him back in Ashland?

"This is a day to die for," Angela said. "Halcyon is the only word that does justice to it."

"As always, the mountains have renewed my spirit, but you've added good music, delicious food, and interesting conversation. I join you in declaring this day halcyon. And now I think I'll try a little ground therapy."

He stretched out on his back and closed his eyes as if he could retreat from the truth.

"You look so peaceful lying there," she said.

"In spite of the chilled air, the sun feels warm on my face, and grounding one's self like this is great therapy for the soul. You should try it."

She lay down on her back so near him that he could hear her breathing.

"Angela, I like to still my mind, shut it down to a blank page for a moment after relaxing this way. Then after the first image or thought creeps into my consciousness, I try to figure out why that particular thought or image emerged out of all the possibilities. Consciousness is such an astonishment."

"What a novel thing to do. Let's both try it."

After a minute of concerted effort to keep his mind blank, the image of an Italian woman, whom he had once encountered on Palatine Hill in Rome, emerged in his consciousness. Why that experience? he wondered. Did Angela's presence trigger it? If so, what was the connection?

He sensed a dimming of the sun's brightness and opened his eyes to check the sky. A grey cloud was shading the sun. He sat up to check the horizons. Darker clouds were drifting in from the west.

"Angela, sorry to disturb you, but rain clouds are moving in from the west. We have a few more minutes, however, before we have to scramble."

"I'll take them," she said and sat up. "In spite of the tranquility of the moment, I could not still my mind. I kept having all these pleasant thoughts. What about you?"

"I had a strange experience and don't know what to make of it."

"Was it good or bad?"

"I don't know how to categorize it."

"Is it something you can share?"

"The year before Hannah was born, I spent most of the summer traveling by myself in Europe. Debbie had no interest in Europe but insisted that I go without her. Late one afternoon in Rome, I wandered about among the ruins of Palatine Hill in a state of total enchantment.

"Actually, the experience was so mystical that I don't have the words to describe it. I was in the past and the present at the same time.

“As twilight began to settle over the place, I started up a pathway and met a woman coming down. There was something magnetic in our eye contact that turned me around after we passed. And there she stood, a dark-featured woman looking back at me.

“I expressed my amazement at the place, and she responded with something in Italian that I didn’t understand. Afraid to face the possibilities of the moment, I turned and walked on up the path. End of story.

“Well, guess what? An image of that woman was the first thing that came into my consciousness after I had stilled my mind. I’ve had that experience at least twice but not recently. The last time, I was sitting in my study, thinking about various things, and all of a sudden, an image of that woman surfaced.”

“Did you regret the lost possibilities of that moment on Palatine Hill?”

“Truthfully, I don’t know. I would not have been unfaithful to Debbie. But there was something unnerving about the experience.

“We’re about to get caught in a heavy downpour. Let’s pack up and head for the car.”

They gathered their things and made it to the car just as the rain moved in.

Chapter Twenty-Five

They left Mount Mitchell and drove south on the Blue Ridge Parkway with the rain sweeping across the road from the west.

"Before the rain," he said, "I thought we would exit the Parkway at Tunnel Road and drive through Asheville. Now I don't think that's a good idea.

"We'll stay on the Parkway until we get to the I-26 East ramp and take it to Spartanburg. Then we'll take I-85 North to Ashland."

"How far is it to Ashville?"

"About thirty miles."

"I think of Thomas Wolfe when I think of Asheville. What an interesting novelist."

"If you'd like, we'll plan a field trip that will include a visit to The Old Kentucky Home in downtown Asheville. It's quite an experience for anyone who likes Wolfe.

"The place will come alive in your imagination. You'll think about young Tom taking note of all the people who boarded there."

"Yes, please take me."

"The first time I visited the place, the guide read the scene from *Look Homeward, Angel* in which Ben Gantt is dying. We were in the very room where Wolfe's brother Ben died."

"What an experience that must have been. Do you think they're still doing that?"

"Probably. But I'll take the novel, just in case they don't. We'll linger in the room, and I'll read the scene to you."

"I'd like that even better. And please take me anywhere else you can think of that will fill the day."

"Okay, I'll include a visit to Connemara, Carl Sandburg's last home that's located in Flat Rock, North Carolina."

"Super! But I think of Chicago when I think of Sandburg. I didn't know his last home was in the South."

"Oh, yes, I'll show you the I-26 exit for Flat Rock in about fifty minutes.

"The place was once known as Little Charleston of the Mountains, because so many wealthy planters from the Lowcountry had built summer homes there in the early nineteenth century. Entire families, along with their house slaves, would spend the summer at Flat Rock to escape the mosquitoes and the oppressive heat of the Lowcountry."

"That reminds me of my first visit to Cooper. You told me that Old Main was built as a resort hotel that catered to Charleston and coastal planters during the summer."

"That's true, and they also built summer homes in Ashland. Flat Rock was more difficult to reach, because they had to cross the Blue Ridge Mountains, but the cooler mountain air was more desirable."

"Tell me about Sandburg's last home."

"It was built in the 1830's by Christopher Memminger, who later became the first Secretary of the Confederate Treasury. He named his property Rock Hill. The next owner changed the name to Connemara to honor his ancestral home in Ireland. Sandburg bought the place in the 1940's if I remember correctly."

"How ironic, Barsh, that a major biographer of Abraham Lincoln would spend his last days in a house built by a member of the Confederate Cabinet."

"I hadn't thought about that but you're right. The place is now a National Historic Site. I could spend hours just reading the titles of Sandburg's books.

"I think there are more than 10,000. I once noticed books about the Ku Klux Klan on the same shelf with works by prominent black writers, including Richard Wright and Zora Neale Hurston."

"I'd like to find that shelf," she said. "Was there a copy of Hurston's novel, *Their Eyes Were Watching God*?"

"A first edition. I had to hold it in my hands for a minute before moving on."

"That book," she said, "was required reading for one of my college courses that focused on strong women in novels. I found myself totally engrossed in it. After I got the hang of the black English, I even enjoyed the way everyone spoke. Before reading the book, I had no idea there was an all-black town in the South."

"Yes, Eatonville, Florida, was a real place. It was founded in the eighteen eighties if I remember correctly.

"There was also an all-black town on Hilton Head Island named Mitchellville with its own mayor, town council, and school.

It was founded during the Civil War after the Union Army captured and occupied the Island."

"Is it still there?"

"No, it gradually disappeared after the Union Army left the Island."

The rain seemed to be falling in sheets as the wind whipped it across the road with the windshield wipers marking the silence that had overtaken them.

"How long will it take us to get back to Ashland?" she asked breaking the silence.

"About two hours. You want to talk or listen to music?"

"If you're leaving it to me, I say, let's talk."

"Then talk we will. I even have a subject. Your mother. You said things were not good between you and her. Are you up to talking about that?"

"This is intriguing, coming on the heels of our discussion about Thomas Wolfe and The Old Kentucky Home. Wolfe got it right: You can't go home again."

"That may be so, but you can keep in touch with your parents and visit them from time to time. I'm a firm believer in that."

"Even if your mother drives you crazy."

"Only if you have control of your life. Sometimes you have to be the mature one and cut your parents a little slack. You don't have to like who they are, just understand them and what their needs are. Give them what you can in the way of filial love without letting them control your life. It's the strong ego that can give freely, even go the extra mile, without compromising itself."

"You are right, of course, but I'm still lagging in that department. The problem is primarily a religious one. Mother is a devout Catholic. When I would go home, she pressed me to go to Mass with her and that made me feel hypocritical, since I no longer believe in the Catholic doctrine of transubstantiation.

"During my last visit home, I refused to go, and she made the rest of my stay miserable. That was more than two years ago. Our phone conversations are not much better. As soon as she asks how I am, she wants to know if I've recently been to Mass."

"Believe me, Angela, I understand the difficulty of your situation."

"But you still think I should go home, right?"

"Only if you can manage it."

"And go to Mass with Mother?"

"Not if it makes you feel hypercritical. You know what underlies your mother's behavior—fear and love. She believes you will end up in Purgatory or worse if you don't hold steadfast to your childhood faith. Put yourself in her shoes. She loves you and yet fears for your soul. Forgive her, if you can, for the trouble she causes you."

"But I don't have to go to Mass with her?"

"No, not in my judgment. I agree with you that the Catholic doctrine of transubstantiation is untenable, like a lot of other Christian dogmas, both Protestant and Catholic."

"Then you wouldn't go to Mass with your mother if you had grown up Catholic."

"Actually, I would. The Catholic Mass has evolved into a holy sacrament with divine benefits for those who are allowed to take it. For early Christians, however, the partaking of the bread and wine was a symbolic act of remembering the crucifixion of Jesus.

"The New Testament Gospels ground the practice in the Jewish Passover Feast that Jesus shared with his disciples just before he was crucified. The Gospel of Luke even quotes Jesus as saying, Do this in remembrance of me.

"In my Protestant tradition, we call it communion, and I do participate. The partaking in itself has no merit, and at our church, everyone is invited to partake. Yes, I could go to Mass if I were in your shoes, but I would take my own understanding of the bread and wine.

"We have an obligation to think for ourselves, regardless of the official doctrines of the religion we grew up in. The Catholic Church can ex-communicate you, but it can no longer burn you at the stake. Fortunately, the Inquisition is over.

"Yes, thank God, the Inquisition is over. And thanks for the theological lesson. I'll think about following your practice."

"Regarding the Inquisition, have you ever read the recantation that the Pope forced Galileo to sign after he wrote his book on the heliocentric view of the known world of his day?"

"No, tell me about it."

"It's a damnable document of horrendous abuse. That was in the early 1600. I don't know if the Catholic Church has officially acknowledged that Galileo was right and it was wrong. They did remove his book from the Church's Index of Forbidden Books about two-hundred years later. Better late than never as they say.

"Of course, no educated person still believes that the sun revolved around the earth or that we live in a three-story universe in which Heaven is the upper-story where God and other immortals dwell, the earth is the middle-story where mortals live, and Sheol is down below where the dead linger in a devitalized state.

"As you know, *up* in modern cosmology is a very relative term. Pointing up is pointing in a new direction every split-second. How astonishing to know that we're rotating daily with the earth as it circles the sun, while the sun and billions of sister stars spin, round and round, with our Milky Way Galaxy as it and billions of other galaxies, each with billions of stars, expand with astonishing speed from some theoretical center."

"How astonishing, indeed!" she said.

"Even so, most Christians, as well as most people of other religions, have yet to demythologize their faith. But I don't despise these people or put myself above them. It's a long journey from where they are to scientific enlightenment, so I love them just as I love those who have made the journey. Hypocrisy, however, I judge harshly.

"Since liberal arts colleges are supposed to aid people on this journey. I share with my student the critical issues that they need to deal with in order to embrace spirituality and modern science. I don't demand that they end up where I am. I grade them on their conversance with the critical issues."

A strong wind rocked the Audi as it crested a ridge on the Blue Ridge Parkway.

"This is a hard, wind-driven rain, and it may follow us all the way to Ashland. I hope you're not anxious."

"No, I'm fine. I've yet to experience a moment of anxiety when I'm with you, and I'm enjoying this conversation."

"Okay, let revisit the subject of attending Mass before we shift to something else. I think the question for you is a simple one. Is there anything about the historical Jesus or the Jesus of faith that you honor?"

"There are many things about Jesus that I honor, but I don't understand your distinction between the historical Jesus and the Jesus of faith."

"It's a rather modern notion that has caused a lot of consternation among Christians. But every legitimate Biblical scholar, living today, knows there's a difference between the historical Jesus, the man from Galilee who lived and taught and died on a cross, and the Jesus of faith. Do you know about Albert Schweitzer?"

"Somewhat. I'm familiar with his reverence for life philosophy."

"What a man! Brilliant scholar . . . acclaimed concert organist . . . compassionate physician . . . bright star of Europe who humbled himself to become a medical missionary in Africa.

"Among his scholarly achievements is an extraordinary book, *The Quest of the Historical Jesus.* First, he shows how allusive the early quests for the historical Jesus were by demonstrating that those who had been involved in the search for the real Jesus behind the Gospels of the New Testament typically found the Jesus that they needed to find."

"What do you mean?"

"Well, the rationalist, for example, found the historical Jesus to be a rationalist, who rejected the irrational laws and rituals of Judaism and redefined religion with two commandments: love God and love your neighbor as yourself."

"That's interesting."

"Schweitzer, however, gave us a totally different view of the historical Jesus. With his scholarly acumen, he constructed a portrait of Jesus based on the messianic scriptures of the Hebrew canon and the messianic expectations of the Jewish people.

"Thus, he claimed that Jesus believed that he was the long-awaited Messiah chosen by God to establish the Kingdom of God on earth. But that didn't happen. Jesus died on a cross, disillusioned and crying to God, Why have you forsaken me."

"Wow! Do you think Schweitzer was right?"

"I don't think we have enough empirical evidence to know what the historical Jesus thought about himself. Most contemporary Biblical scholars believe that his teachings focused on the imminent coming of the Kingdom of God. They are divided, however, on whether or not Jesus thought he was the Messiah who would establish the Kingdom of God here on earth.

"Perhaps he did. Perhaps he only thought of himself as a prophetic teacher whose mission was to proclaim its imminent coming, along with the requirements necessary to enter the golden age in which all the imperfections of the world will be perfected.

"There's a lot we don't know and have no way of knowing about the historical Jesus. We do know, however, that his disciples, at some point, believed that he was the Messiah.

"It is also obvious to me and other Biblical scholars that in order for Jesus' disciples to proclaim him as the Messiah after the crucifixion, they had to change the mission of the Messiah as defined by Old Testament prophets and Jewish tradition."

"Why? You'll have to help me here."

"According to the sacred scriptures of Judaism, the primary role of the messiah was to reestablish the Davidic Kingdom. By the time of Jesus, that role had morphed into establishing the Kingdom of God on earth. Since Jesus did not do that, the first Christians had to redefine the mission of the Messiah.

"Thus, they believed that Jesus the Christ (the Greek word for the Hebrew word Messiah) was ordained by God to die on the cross to redeem us from sin. But they didn't abandon the traditional mission of the Messiah. They simply pushed it into the future, and thus we have the doctrine of the second coming of Jesus the Christ.

"They believed that after Jesus was crucified, God raised him from the dead and transformed him into an immortal being. He then ascended to Heaven, where he sits at the right hand of God and waits for his time to return to the earth. When he comes back, his mission will be to establish the Kingdom of God on earth."

"So, that's the Jesus of faith that the early Christians have given us," she said.

"Yes, and we can now trace the history of messianic ideology from the royal ideology of the Davidic Kingdom of ancient Israel to New Testament Christology. It's an integral part of what scholars call Jewish and Christian eschatology."

"Eschatology? That's a new word for me."

"It comes from the Greek word *eschatos,* meaning *last*, so eschatology is the doctrine of the last things. Increment by increment, Jewish prophets of old proclaimed that at some future date the Messiah would establish a radically new world order—one in which all the imperfections of the current world are perfected.

"If you want an in-depth study, I'll lend you one of my treasured books, *He That Cometh,* by Sigmund Mowinckel. Or at a later date, I'll lay out the various ways these beliefs developed and changed over time if you're interested."

"I'd like for you to narrate them for me."

"Well, I hope I didn't overload you with my perspective on religion."

"Not at all. It was just what I've been needing. You know that I applied for the position at Cooper because I was looking for a Southern experience. After my job interview, I desperately wanted to get the position because of you.

"I'd never met anyone like you, and I believed you could help me untangle my confused life. I'm now confident that my intuition about you was right."

"That's kind of you, but never forget that you are enriching my life with your literary expertise, etc. I need your friendship as much as I can imagine your needing mine."

"I can't believe that's true, but it's most gratifying to hear those words."

"Well, I assure you that it's ever so true. Let me add this before we move to something else. Sometimes I read the Bible critically with scholarly objectives and sometime I read it devotionally.

"When I'm reading devotionally, I'm looking for something that speaks to me about my daily life. For example, if I'm reading the Gospels devotionally, I'm not concerned about whether or not the historical Jesus actually gave us a particular saying or if a story about Jesus actually occurred as it has been recorded. As you know, parables and fictional stories can teach us profound truths."

"Yes, and you should also know that I'm interested in your story. I'd really like to know how you got from being a nature-loving boy in Alabama to such a scholar. Will you share that story with me at some appropriate time?"

"I'm not sure I know myself. But for you, I'll give it a try, one of these days."

"Oh, I'm confident that you can show me how it happened. Would you like more music?"

"Yes, please."

"I brought a John Denver cassette with 'Rocky Mountain High' which seemed appropriate for our first field trip. I've never been to the Rocky Mountains, but I have now experienced those same feelings about the Carolina mountains that Denver experienced about the Colorado mountains."

With the rain pouring down, they listened to the song. When it ended, she paused the cassette.

"When next I play this song, which will be before I go to bed tonight, I intend to sing along, but I will transpose Mount Mitchell High for Rocky Mountain High. I always sing along when I'm by myself. Do you?"

"Not often, but sometimes the mood strikes me. Okay, we're fast approaching the exit to Flat Rock and Carl Sandburg's last home."

"I don't suppose you know when we might take our literary field trip that includes Connemara."

"No, but I'll find a way to schedule it before Thanksgiving."

***

A graceful silence settled over them as Barsh exited I-85 for the little town of Ashland. He felt a tinge of disquietude that such a special day with Angela was about to end. And yet, he was anxious to get home to spend time with Hannah. As they approached Angela's house, she broke the silence.

"Barsh, this has been an extraordinary day in every way. I've been to the mountain top in more ways than one. Even the rain seemed to have played a role in enhancing the drive back. The cozy comfort of the Audi with you driving.

"Honestly, I don't have the words to express my true feeling. Don't be surprised if you find your ears burning this evening. I will be journaling with my heart brimming with gratitude for all I've experienced."

"It was also a good day for me. You know that I have family duties in addition to my Cooper responsibilities, but whenever we can manage a field trip, I want to expose you to the interesting things around Ashland."

"And you know me. I'll be ready to go."

He pulled into Angela's backyard and parked beside her Volvo. The sky was still overcast, but the rain had finally stopped.

"You can come in, can't you?"

"I'll take the picnic basket for you, but I can't stay."

He got the basket from the trunk and followed her into the kitchen.

"Could we have a drink before you go?"

"Sorry, but I have to get on home. Hannah will be looking for me to come rolling in any minute now."

"Do you two have something planned?"

"Just our poetry project that I wrote you about."

"I'm impressed that you are so devoted to helping her with her writing. Please know that I'm available if you'd like for me to help her."

"Are you serious?"

"Yes, I'd love to tutor her."

"I can't speak for her, but I would like that. I do my best to help her, but I'm not a creative writer."

"Could you bring her by one afternoon this week? We'll talk poetry. If she would like for me to work with her, we can work out a schedule for that."

"I'm picking her up after school, Wednesday. Davis, who usually does that, has a doctor's appointment. Would that work for you?"

"Yes, please bring her by. I've decided to keep office hours from 1:00 to 5:00, Monday through Friday. If I'm not helping students, I grade their papers or prepare for my classes. This way, I'll be free to work on my novel, evenings as well as weekends."

"That sound like a good plan."

"Yes, it's working well. Last Friday, Catherine and I ate lunch together in the cafeteria. On learning that I would be in my office until 5:00, she come over at 4:00. We had a good time, sharing stories and discussing things. I invited her to come again and she promised she would. Now, I'm looking forward to meeting Hannah on Wednesday."

"Of course, I'll pay you if you start tutoring Hannah."

"No way. This is something I want to do on my own."

"But I insist on paying you."

"Please do not mention money to me. We'll call it a tradeoff for field trips like today if you insist on some kind of exchange arrangement."

"Okay, I'll look at it that way. Regarding office hours, I'm cutting back on mine, this semester. Starting next week, my posted office hours will be from 1:00 to 4:00 on Tuesday and Thursday.

At 4:00 on those days, I'll make tea. My friends know they can join me and they periodically do. The other afternoons, I'll be working on my projects at the farm."

"Then I'll look forward to sharing tea with you, occasionally."

"Good. See you at Cooper, tomorrow."

"Yes, tomorrow," she said and followed him to the back steps where she waved as he drove away.

Chapter Twenty-Six

The new academic year was going well for Barsh. He was lecturing with his old intellectual vitality, and he admitted to himself that Angela was the inspiration behind his renewed vigor.

It was late Friday afternoon, and as usual, he had worked on his earth skills project at the farm. He checked the time and realized he would be late for his four o'clock meeting with Angela if he didn't leave immediately.

Thursday morning, she had asked if she could join him for tea at four that afternoon. He had a conflict, but he invited her to join him at four o'clock on Friday. He had planned to return from the farm early to take Hannah out for dinner, so it would be no problem for him to come by the college on his way home.

When he got to Cooper, her Volvo was the only car left in the Kimberly parking lot. With long strides, he headed for his office. As he reached the top of the stairs, he heard Dean Thompson and Angela conversing.

"Speaking of the devil as they say . . . We were just talking about you. I'm taking Angela out for dinner this evening. Any possibility that you could join us?"

"Debbie's working late on a special account she manages, and I promised Hannah we'd eat out."

"Then you must both join us."

"We'll join you if you'll let dinner be on me."

"Okay, if that's what it takes. I'd planned to take Angela to the Ashland Hotel which, as you know, has the best restaurant in town. But I'll now defer to you."

"How about Antoine's in Spartanburg?"

"Sounds good to me. Is that alright with you, Angela?"

"I'm happy just to be going anywhere with friends on a Friday night."

"Good," he said. "I'll drive. Is six too early to pick you up?"

"That's fine with me," Angela said.

"Me too," Catherine said. "Now if you two will excuse me, I have phone calls to make before I leave campus."

He walked with her to the stairs. When he turned back, Angela was standing in her office door.

"What an exciting turn of events. Can we still have tea?"

"Sure."

She followed him to his office and sat in her usual chair as he turned on the hotplate.

"I hope Hannah won't be disappointed with the new dining arrangement."

"I assure you that she will be jubilant over this development. She idolizes you and talks about you all the time. You've made a huge impact on her writing since you started tutoring her. I can't thank you enough. You are just the mentor she needs."

"That warms my heart. Hannah is special, and you two are so lucky to have each other."

The kettle started whistling and he fixed the tea.

"Just in case you didn't notice," she said, "I had a wonderful time at Georgette's cocktail party last Saturday evening. She's a fascinating woman. And what an art collection. I've never known anyone who owned an original Picasso."

"As I expected, Georgette was pleased to meet you. She called to tell me. She will definitely include you in her circle of friends.

"Here's something that might interest you. Tomorrow, I'm taking Hannah for the annual Hawk Watch at Caesars Head. Do you have plans?"

"No, and the answer is yes if this is an invitation."

"Let's call it the setup for an invitation if you're willing to play along."

"What do I need to do?"

"After dinner, I'll take Catherine home, first. On the way to your house, ask if we have plans for the weekend. I'll tell you that I'm taking Hannah to Caesars Head for the annual Hawk Watch, and you can express an interest. That will give me an opening to invite you to join us."

"How clever of you. Please tell me more. What's a Hawk Watch and where is Caesars Head?"

"Caesars Head is an escarpment on the eastern rim of the Blue Ridge Mountains with a breath-taking view. It's a flyway for hawks this time of the year. They use the thermal drafts of the mountains on their migration to warmer climates for the winter, so it's an excellent place to count them on their journey south. This is a crude way of trying to keep up with how the hawk populations are doing.

"I usually help with the count on the weekends, but I wanted to take Hannah this year, just to watch for them an hour or so, not all day. And now that you will be joining us, we could work in a little hiking on a mountain trail if you'd like that."

"Yes, please pack as much as you can into the outing. I'm hoping for a full day with you two. Will my Nike shoes be okay for mountain hiking?"

"Sure. And bring a jacket. There are wonderful hiking trails in Caesars Head State Park. My favorite is the one to Raven Cliff Falls, but I don't think Hannah is ready for this hike.

"I'll save it for another field trip with you. I think we'll hike the Carrick Creek Trail at Table Rock State Park, which is near Caesars Head. Hannah likes to hike this trail. I'm also thinking a morning hike before we join the hawk watchers at Caesars Head."

"Both will be new experiences for me and I'm eagerly looking forward to them. Could I bring a picnic lunch?"

"Thanks, but Hannah and I have already planned one. Angela, I'd like to share something with you."

He retrieved a flint arrowhead from his pocket and leaned toward her with it hidden in his hand.

"You want me to guess what it is?"

"I want to tell you that it's something I made," he said and opened his hand.

"You made that arrowhead?"

"It and others with my own hands. The arrowheads and the Catawba inspired pottery, that I told you about, are part of my effort to learn the old earth skills of Native Americans. This is why I spend so much time at the farm. I want to finish the different tasks before Christmas."

"Then I trust you will. Did your Catawba friend teach you how to make the arrowheads?"

"No, but I found a good teacher. Actually, the lithic technology of Native Americans was all but lost by the beginning of the twentieth century.

"Here's a story about a man named Ishi, who is thought to be the last of the Yahi tribe. He was still following the Stone Age way of life of his people in California, when he was discovered in the early1900's.

"An anthropologist from the University of California at Berkeley brought him to the university, where he worked as a janitor while teaching them about his culture. He made excellent flint arrowheads.

"When he died a few years after coming to Berkeley, they said the Stone Age in California came to an end. For most Native Americans, it had ended long before, when they started trading for rifles and metal tools. Ishi was a rare relic from the past.

"Fortunately for me, Don Crabtree learned the technique from Ishi. Crabtree is now credited with reviving the ancient earth skill of flintknapping in the U.S.

"Today, there are quite a few people who make beautiful flint arrowheads and spearheads as a hobby. This summer, I spent three days taking lessons from a park ranger at Ocmulgee Mounds National Historical Park near Macon, Georgia."

"I like your story about Ishi, and I'm fascinated by your efforts to learn the old earth skills of Native Americans. You are a different kind of man, and I love the difference.

"Thanks for returning from the farm to have tea with me on a Friday afternoon. Who could have imagined the wonderful way it has turned out? I have a new dress I'm wearing, tonight. You can call me Miss Delighted."

"Then we'd better get moving, Miss Delighted. I'll get Catherine and then come by for you a few minutes after six."

"And I'll be ready and waiting with high expectation for a special evening."

Chapter Twenty-Seven

Barsh and Hannah were up early Saturday morning. Debbie was sleeping in, so they prepared breakfast together and ate leisurely. After they cleaned up the kitchen, Hannah went to her room and he went to his study, where he reminisced about how well the dinner at Antoine's had gone that Friday night.

He had deliberately picked up Catherine first and seated her up front with him. Hannah had the best time riding in the back seat of the Audi with Angela. The two of them chatted with ease, going and coming. Back at Angela's, his plan to invite her to join Hannah and him for the hawk count at Caesar's Head went so well that his daughter had no idea that he had orchestrated it.

"I have chosen two poems I want to read you," Hannah said interrupting his musings. "What have you selected?"

"I've marked several. I'll read two of them this morning. The others this evening."

"You read first and then I'll read."

He read Henry Reed's "Naming of Parts" and Randall Jarrell's "The Death of the Ball Turret Gunner." She liked both poems and made several perceptive comments about them. Then she read "Harlem" and "Dreams Deferred" both by Langston Hughes.

"Daddy, I'm working on a new project that Angela recommended."

"When did you start calling her Angela?"

"When you were walking Dr. Thompson to her door last night, she asked me to call her Angela."

"Okay, if that's what she wants. Tell me about your new project."

"She wants me to write short pieces of prose about experiences that have had an emotional impact on me. Things like awe, surprise, compassion, fear, dread, anxiety.

"I've already started a piece about our visit to Paw-Paw Roberts' grave. It's based on the story you told me about wanting to live in the wilds of Alaska because you'd lost confidence in Southern society. That really shook me up. I also want to write about other things from our trip to Alabama. Angela says this type of writing will open up ideas for new poems, and I can already see that."

"Well, I like your new project. It's time for us to get on the road, but first, I'll let you in on a little secret. One of the reasons Angela took the position at Cooper was to get a firsthand experience of the South.

"She's an expert on Southern literature, but she'd only spent a few days in the South before moving here. With that in mind, I'm packing a lot into this outing. I love our Carolina mountains, and I want to share them with her. Are you with me?"

"Yeah, let's show her a good time in our Carolina mountains."

He had decided to drive the Ford pickup, so the three of them could sit together on the wide seat. Angela was sitting on the porch steps, when he drove into her backyard. He got out and opened the door for her. Hannah slid to the middle of the seat. Then they were off.

"For your information, Angela, we'll soon be on State Highway 11, that was recently designated the Cherokee Foothills Scenic Highway. It's a fine route through Western South Carolina that eventually winds its way back to I-85 just above Lake Hartwell near the Georgia State line. A few miles down the highway, we'll pass the entrance to Cowpens National Battlefield."

"I trust you haven't forgotten you promised to take me."

"No, but we'll save that for another day."

"Can I go with you, Daddy?"

"Sure. We'll make it a threesome. Here's an idea. Let's take turns talking about different people that we admire. Angela, tell us about a woman of national or international fame whom you admire?"

"Okay, give me a moment. So far, I'm thinking about literary women."

"That's fine. Who was the first woman who came to mind?"

"Emily Dickinson. I definitely admire her."

"What specifically do you admire about her?"

"The fact that she stuck with her poetry project with little or no public recognition during her lifetime, and thus, she left us such a splendid collection of poems."

"That's exactly what I admire about Dickinson, but would you trade places with her? I mean would you settle for that kind of reclusive life?"

"No, I need more from life than she seems to have gotten."

"Like what?"

"A lot of things. A professorship at Cooper College to name an obvious one. I need the ongoing interaction with students and colleagues that I'm now experiencing. I need the joy of mentoring a super special girl named Hannah. And I also have other special needs, like sharing this day with you and Hannah."

With that said, she embraced Hannah and rocked her in her arms for a moment.

"Hannah, do you want to go next?" he asked.

"I don't want to play. I want to listen to you and Angela. This is interesting."

"Okay, Barsh," Angela said, "tell us about a woman of fame whom you admire. Maybe a Southerner."

"I'm thinking about a Charleston woman. Coincidently, you share a version of her given name. Do you know about Angelina Grimké?"

"No, I've never heard that name."

"She was born in antebellum Charleston, the daughter of a wealthy judge and planter who owned several plantations. He was thus a major slave owner.

"Angelina was deeply disturbed by the slave culture of her native South and took refuge with the Quakers of Charleston. Later, she and her sister Sarah moved to Philadelphia to seek the quiet peace of the Quakers.

"Angelina soon became known as a powerful voice for the abolition of slavery with her book, *An Appeal to the Christian Women of the South.* She also took to the lecture halls in the North as a forceful abolitionist, one of the first women to be given such a public platform.

"Although she is known primarily for her activism against slavery, she was also a strong advocate for women's rights. In fact, she insisted on making women's rights a part of her activism. And guess what?"

"The abolitionists wanted her to focus solely on slavery," Angela said.

"You are exactly right."

"My kind of woman. I must learn more about her."

"You should talk with Catherine. She's something of an authority on Grimké and the later suffragettes."

"Then she probably knows about Matilda Joslyn Gage, one of my favorite suffragettes and a New York woman."

"I'm sure she does, but I'll have to plead ignorant about her."

"In one of my courses on Women's Rights, I had to digest and report on Gage's informed book *Woman, Church and State*, that was published toward the end of the nineteenth century.

"The book has been out of print for years, but fortunately, the library at Brown has a copy. I can tell you that she documented a horrific history of how women have been treated by both Church and State through the ages."

"I'm well aware of that story in general, but I'd like to see Gage's documentation."

"If I can find my notes, I'll share them with you."

"Here's a suggestion. Catherine frequently invites me for Saturday breakfast, and we always have a lively discussion about something that interests us. Would you like to join us some Saturday morning and share your notes on *Women, Church and State*?"

"Just get me an invitation and I'll be there, eager to spend time with you two."

"That won't be a problem. Catherine has already said she wants to invite you to join us."

"Daddy, I want to go, too?"

"Then I'll see that you are invited. Look, there's a good view of the Blue Ridge Mountains. Let's enjoy the scenery as I drive us to Table Rock State Park."

"Good idea," Angela said, and pulling Hannah into her arms, she hugged her. "I hope you don't mind my hugs."

"You can hug me anytime. I told Daddy that I want to be like you when I grow up."

"You are so dear to say that, but you will exceed me in every way—beauty, charm, intellect, creativity."

"I just want to be like you."

"You'll be like me and more."

***

The hike up the Carrick Creek Trail and back was a huge success. Angela exclaimed, several times, how exhilarating it was to be hiking the nature trail. Hannah was excited to be with them, and Barsh was pleased to observe his daughter bonding with Angela.

By noon, they were back at the Visitors Center where they ate a light lunch that he and Hannah had prepared. Then they were off in the Ford pickup.

***

Caesars Head was crowded with hawk watchers, but he found an open spot with a good view, and in less than an hour, they had identified four species of hawks. Satisfied with that experience, they left Caesars Head for Brevard, North Carolina, where they stopped for coffee and hot chocolate. Then he took Angela and Hannah to a nearby art gallery.

"Ah, here's a painting of Raven Cliff Falls. Angela, these are the falls I told you about. I love this artist's work."

"Yes, that's a beautiful painting."

As they checked out several more paintings, Barsh spotted a painting of Carrick Creek by the same artist.

"Here's another good one," he said. "Anybody recognize the place?"

"Carrick Creek Falls?" Angela said.

"The very ones."

"That's such a beautiful scene and I love how large and bold the painting is," she said and checked the price. "As soon as I save a little more money, I'd like to buy it for my study to commemorate my first nature hike with you two."

"It's an excellent painting and would be a wonderful addition to your collection. Let's see if I can negotiate an agreement that will hold it for you."

"I can't let you do that. But thanks for the offer."

"Why not, Angela? That's what Daddy wants to do."

"Yes, why not? Why take a chance on letting it get away?"

"Well, okay, I'd really like to have the painting."

"If you and Hannah will check out the pottery next door, I put my negotiating skills on trial."

Barsh bought the painting on the condition that the owner of the gallery would hold it until he came back for it. His plan was to pick up the painting the following week. Then he would store it at the farm until he had an appropriate occasion to give it to her.

Joining them in the pottery shop, he reported a successful transaction. Angela bought each of them a mug, and they left downtown Brevard in a happy mood.

"I'm taking a short detour through the campus of Brevard College. We just might see a white squirrel. Brevard is known for its population of white squirrels, and they're not albino squirrels."

He drove slowly around the campus, but they didn't see a white squirrel. Then he headed for U.S. 276 that would take them up the mountain to the Blue Ridge Parkway.

Shortly after he began the ascent, he stopped to let Angela experience Looking Glass Falls. Further up U.S. 276, he stopped at a popular recreation spot known as Sliding Rock.

He described the scene on a typical summer day when there would be a crowd of swim-suited people sliding down that rock into the large natural pool. He also noted that Hannah and he had experienced the slide on two separate occasions.

At the top of the mountain, he drove north on the Blue Ridge Parkway. It was a gorgeous drive. The leaves of the deciduous trees were beginning to show their fall colors, and he stopped at three overlooks before taking the Tunnel Road exit for Asheville.

As he drove through the downtown area, he renewed his promise to Angela of a literary field trip that included The Old Kentucky Home. Hannah wanted to join them, and Barsh promised her that she could.

Then they had an early dinner on the Terrace Restaurant at Grove Park Inn. It was the perfect place to cap off their day in the mountains.

"You were so right in describing this place as a must experience," Angela said as they drove away from the hotel."

The distant sound of a train whistle caught Barsh's ear.

"Angela, that lonesome train whistle remined me of *Train Whistle Guitar*. I finished the novel last night, and it was a good read. Thanks for putting me onto Albert Murray. I'd never heard of him, and I'm an Alabama native. There are still a lot of holes in my knowledge of African American literature.

"The thing I like about *Train Whistle Guitar* is that it's not a black protest novel. We obviously need protest novels like Richard Wright's *Native Son,* but Murray gives us an interesting portrait of a black boy's largely positive experiences of growing up in a black community in Mobile. He rarely mentions the white community."

"You're absolutely right," she said, "and that's also the thing I enjoyed about it. There's an earlier black novelist from Alabama. I can't remember his name, but I do remember the title of one of his novels that I read in graduate school. *Ollie Miss* is written in the black folk tradition, although the author had moved north and was a part of the Harlem Renaissance. It's also about blacks interacting with each other in rural Alabama. You can borrow my copy if you'd like."

"Yes, I'd like very much to read *Ollie Miss*. I've been trying to become conversant with African American novels for some time. Lately, I've been thinking that I should also read more Native American novels.

"Last year, Amanda McGee, our wonderful librarian, put me onto Leslie Silko's *Ceremony.* Have you read it?"

"No, tell me about it."

"The setting is the Laguna Pueblo Reservation after World War II. Silko grew up on that reservation, and she took me inside the heads of her Laguna characters in a transformational way. I truly felt for the first time how deeply tragic the loss of *this land* was to Native Americans. I wish I were more informed about their novels, but I have no idea what's out there."

"Neither do I, but I've read one major novel, *Waterlily,* by Ella Deloria.

"That sound interesting. Tell me about it."

A Sioux, Deloria was sent to an Indian boarding school as a young girl, and as you probably know, those schools were designed to strip them of their native language and ways.

"She ended up attending Columbia University. That's how I learned about the book.

"She wrote *Waterlily* in the 1940's, but it was published posthumously only recently. It's set in the early nineteenth century before the Sioux had a lot of contact with whites. Deloria does an excellent job of depicting traditional Sioux life, including the sun dance which the U.S. government later outlawed.

"It's also written from a woman's point of view. Otherwise, it would not likely have been on the reading list of one of my courses about strong women."

"That's exactly the kind of novel I'm looking for. I especially want to learn more about the Sioux.

"Last year, I read Stephen Ambrose's dual biography, *Crazy Horse and Custer.* Of the two men, I would take Crazy Horse over Custer as my friend."

"Yes, I would have guessed that, just from the short time I've known you. Like you, I'm interested in reading more Native American and African American authors. We could make it a joint goal if you'd like."

"Let's do it. No other ethnic group has been as horrendously abused as African Americans and Native Americans."

A pleasant silence settled over them as Barsh took I-26 East for Spartanburg.

"Angela, can I assume that you brought music?" he asked.

"Yes! Hannah, what kind of music do you like?"

"I don't listen to music that much. Play something you like."

"Okay, I'll start with some folk songs."

They shifted back and forth between listening to music and conversing on various topics, until Barsh parked in her backyard.

"I can't thank you two enough for inviting me to join you for this extraordinary outing. The whole day was so exceptional."

"It was a pleasure to have you with us," he said.

"Yeah, it was more fun having you with us," Hannah said.

"I hate to see this day end. Can you come in for a while?"

"We would enjoy that, but we have to get on home. I'll see you to the door."

He stood beside her at the kitchen door as she unlocked it.

"Thanks again for working out a deal for me on the painting. I'll pay you back."

"Forget the payback. That was the least I could have done. I'm indebted to you for tutoring Hannah without compensation, so I'm looking for ways to reward you for that."

"You already have, my friend."

"Not to my satisfaction. See you tomorrow."

"Yes, tomorrow."

Driving away, he looked back, and she was waving from the steps. God, she was special. He could not deny that she had awakened his romantic heart. What he could not figure out was how that could have a happy ending.

Chapter Twenty-Eight

The days eased by until it was time for Barsh and Hannah to visit Susan and Terry Halford in Nashville. They left early that Saturday morning, and to his delight, Hannah was in a talkative mode. First, she wanted to talk about his boyhood in Alabama that focused on his horse Thunder. Satisfied with a few new stories about those days, she changed the subject.

"Daddy, I can't believe how lucky I am to have you to help me with critical thinking and Angela to help me with writing."

"Well, I count my lucky stars because I have this amazing daughter named Hannah."

"Guess who else feel lucky."

"Give me a clue."

"I'll just tell you. During our meeting this week, Angela talked about how lucky she was to have you as a friend. Among other things, she said that you had already helped her work through a major problem that was bugging her big time."

"Angela is an impressive woman, and I'm glad that we both have her as a friend. Okay, you read or write and I'll focus on getting us to Nashville. It's a six-hour drive, but we'll break it up with at least one stop. More if you need them."

It was a lovely morning, and he was pleased to be on the way to the new domain of his boyhood friend. His mind, however, kept shifting back and forth between Susan and Angela.

Occasionally, Hannah would start a brief conversation stimulated by what she was reading and then get lost in her book for a while. Thus, the miles rolled by until they were definitely in horse country.

Hannah read aloud the last of Susan's directions. Then Barsh saw the gateway to Halford Horse Farm. He slowed, turned up the lane, and drove toward the big house.

"This is too rich for my taste," he said.

"I'm with you, Daddy."

He rang the doorbell and took a deep breath. The maid answered and welcomed them in. Susan, dressed in a riding outfit, came running down the hall and threw herself into his arms.

"Oh, my dear Barsh!"

"What a joy to see you, Susan," he said pulling back from her tight embrace to look into her brown eyes.

"God, I thought you'd never get here. I've been wild to see you, ever since you called. I tried several times to tell Terry what our days together in Alabama mean to me, but they are really beyond words. Finally, he said, I get it. Please calm down. But I couldn't as you can see."

"It's been a long time, Susan, far too long."

"Yes, far too long. And this is Hannah. You are just beautiful. I love your long black hair. Speaking of hair, the last time I saw your father, he had a flattop? But I like his short high-flying ponytail, don't you?"

"I like everything about Daddy."

"That doesn't surprise me. I liked everything about him when I was your age. Lord, I can't believe you're here. I'm eager to show you my horses, but that will have to wait. The spotlight will be on you two this afternoon and evening.

"Barsh, I'm counting on you to dance with me at the Country Club."

"Okay, but I'll likely embarrass you. I've never been much of a dancer."

"There's no way that will ever happen. I know two snobs who will be green with envy when they see me on the dance floor with you. Come on. I want y'all to meet Terry."

The distinguished man rose to greet them as they entered the huge den. A good fifteen years older than Susan, Terry Halford looked rather delicate compared to her vigor, but he was confident and self-assured without a hint of arrogance. Barsh liked him immediately for his wit, intelligence, and grace.

***

Late Saturday night, Barsh and Susan sat in the den, alone for the first time. Terry had excused himself and retired for the evening after Hannah went to bed, well past her usual bedtime. Susan had just made coffee, after insisting that they stay up late.

Without a hint of phony airs, she had added a lot of hard-earned polish to the girl he had known back in Alabama, and she was definitely the queen of Halford Horse Farm. Terry seemed to adore her, and she was clearly devoted to him.

"Barsh, you filled me with joy and pride at the Country Club. Those snobbish lady friends of Terry's ex-wife are still trying to find out who you are and what our connection is."

"It was a delightful evening, and you should know that if we had been dancing back in Ashland, you would have doubled my status as a man in that little town."

"You're sweet to say that. I hate to think where I might have ended up if you had not come into my life, all those years ago. I owe you so much for everything I've accomplished."

"You're giving me way too much credit. You had the right stuff as they say. You were a beautiful girl, and you had determination and integrity. I never doubted that you would do well. Do you remember the last thing I told you that fateful day my parents moved to Georgia?"

"Those parting words kept me going during the hard years. And I still hold them close to my heart."

"Just know the vision of you riding Dan, alongside of me and Thunder, has never faded. I've thought of you so often through the years. I truly regret that it has taken so long for this day to come.

"I was so pleased when your mother told me that you were a successful veterinarian, trophy-winning horsewoman, and breeder of champion Tennessee Walkers. My little pal has become quite a woman."

"Barsh, we have never talked about the depth of our relationship back then, but I knew we were close. You made me feel special. And, God, were you special to me. From the day I met you, I looked up to you. By the time your parents moved away, I was desperately in love with you, and I thought I would die without you.

"Eventually, I came to understand that being your little pal, as you called me, was something to cherish and that you were destined to move on without me. That realization was finally enough for me.

"Knowing that you could have taken advantage of me, I treasure those days even more. I would never have said *no* to you about anything, whatever the consequences might have been."

"Don't think I wasn't tempted by your sensual beauty as you matured. Fortunately, I knew my conscience would give me hell if I'd tried to take advantage of you.

"You knew, of course, that I was in love with April Morehouse. I didn't get her out of my system until the second semester of my first year at Samford University. You and I have both known the anguish of unrequited love."

"I probably shouldn't tell you this, but John Marshall did try to have his way with me after you left for college. I kicked him in the balls and that was the end of that. You taught me to set the bar high."

"Susan, tell me more about your journey since our horseback-riding days."

"Terry and I have been married eleven years. This is my first marriage. He was divorced when I started doctoring his horses. Before long, he invited me out for dinner. That went well, so we quickly moved toward steady dating and then marriage.

"He has two daughters and a son by his first wife. I've never wanted children, and that suited Terry just fine. He loves his three children, and the five of us get along very well

"His ex-wife had already remarried when I met Terry. She was the one who filed for divorce to marry the man she was having an affair with. Rumors are that she's running around on her current husband."

"Terry seems like a good man. I like him a lot."

"He is so good to me and I truly love him."

"That's good to hear."

"Barsh, I'm amazed when I look at Hannah. She reminds me so much of your mother, the sweetest and kindest woman I've ever known. I so admired your parents and couldn't believe Mother didn't tell me about their death. I flew into a rage when she finally told me. I would have attended the funeral to honor them and to see you. I trust you know that."

"Honestly, I was afraid you wouldn't want to see me. I did wonder, however, if you would be there, and I was disappointed, because I needed to see you."

"I finally figured out why Mother didn't tell me. She was afraid that if I saw you, it would send me to my knees, again. She never could understand me because she was always looking for a good time, not love. Do you know who my father was? I'm sorry to say he's dead now."

"I knew who people said he was."

"Then you knew. John Marshall told me that you beat the devil out of Howard Bowen for calling me a bastard. Tell me about that."

"I'd never wronged Howard, but he resented me for some reason. One day he accused me of . . . I can't say it. Anyway, he referred to you as that little bastard. I demanded that he take it back. Otherwise, I was going to make him wish he had never said it. That's how it happened."

"Well, it made me feel good when I heard about it. Now tell me about your wife. Where did you meet her? What kind of woman is she?"

"During my studies at the theological seminary in Louisville, I was the student pastor of a country church about fifty miles away. Debbie's parents were members. We met one weekend while she was back home. She had finished college and was working at a prestigious accounting firm in Louisville. The rest is history."

"And you're now a professor at Cooper College. That's impressive."

"A professorship at Cooper College is far from an academic prize, but I'm proud to be a part of any institution devoted to higher learning."

"I'll bet your students love you."

"They seem to like me. They're always telling me how much I've helped them."

"I couldn't believe it when Mother told me that Thunder was the only horse you ever owned. Why? I can't imagine you without a horse."

"After getting a professorship at Cooper, I wanted to buy a place in the country where I could own horses, but Debbie wouldn't consider living in the country.

"This past summer, however, I bought a place in the country. It's a wonderful place for me to get away. I'm thinking about buying horses for Hannah and me, but I'll have to wait awhile. I'm planning to take a sabbatical after this semester."

"I would love to fix you both up with a horse if you're interested in Tennessee Walkers."

"I've wanted to own a Tennessee Walker ever since I first saw one. After Mother and Dad moved to Georgia, I lived on campus at Samford during the school year and with Uncle Edward in Birmingham during the summers.

"That first summer, he took me to the horse country of Tennessee and Kentucky. I don't remember where, but somewhere on that trip, I got to see Midnight Sun, the most amazing saddle horse I'd ever seen. I think he was the World Champion at one time."

"He was the World Grand Champion twice, 1945 and 1946. My stallion is out of his line from the Harlinsdale Farm in Franklin, Tennessee.

"That is most impressive."

"Okay, I'm going to give you and Hannah each a horse whenever you're ready. That's the least I can do after all you've given me."

"I can't let you do that, but I'll buy each of us one of yours after my sabbatical."

"No, I'm giving them to you. Do you know what I'm dying to do?"

"What's that?"

"I'd like to jump in some jeans and go for a ride, just me and you riding in the night, once more, like we did in the good old days."

"You think we could pull that off?"

"Give me two minutes, and I'll lead the way."

***

Wide awake, Barsh lay on his back staring into the darkness from the four-poster mahogany bed that Susan had all but tucked him in. How good it felt to be reconnected with her on such a wholesome footing of mutual admiration.

It was late, and he had to get to sleep. Susan was getting him up early so that they could spend time with her horses. Then he and Hannah would leave after lunch for home.

He tried every method he knew to still his mind. Finally, it happened and sleep took him down.

Chapter Twenty-Nine

When Barsh got to Cooper a little before eight Monday morning, Angela's car was parked in her usual place beside Kimberly Hall. He hurried upstairs with briefcase in hand and stopped at her office door.

"Welcome back. I've been waiting for the sound of those boots."

"It's good to be back."

"What time did you and Hannah get home last night?"

"It was after ten o'clock. We didn't leave Susan's until late afternoon. Sleep deprived and weary, I went straight to bed. I'm ill prepared for my classes, but this won't be the first time I've had to fly by the seat of my pants, as they say."

"How did the visit with Susan go?"

"Wonderfully well. I'll give you a report, later. How was your weekend?"

"Friday evening, I built my first fire in the fireplace and sat on the couch with a glass of wine, reminiscing. I toasted you for bringing me the wood and showing me how to build a fire.

"Saturday and Sunday, I wrote my heart out on my novel, and I'm pleased to tell you that it's the best writing I have ever done."

"That's good to hear. You can't imagine how deeply moved I was by the chapters you sent me back in the summer. I'm especially intrigued that the novel is somewhat autobiographical, and I'd like to see more whenever you feel like sharing."

"Believe me, I want to share everything with you, but I prefer to wait until I've completed the first draft."

"That's fine. Well, I'd better get ready for my nine o'clock class."

"Are you going to the farm this afternoon?"

"No, Catherine wants to talk to me about something."

"Could I join you for tea at four? I'd like to hear more about your visit with Susan."

"Sure."

"Then I'll see you at four," she said and looked at her watch. "Time for me to head for my eight o'clock class."

***

Just before four o'clock, Laura Buck came sashaying into Barsh's office and closed the door. Since they last talked, she had filed for divorce and wanted to bring him up to date.

There was no residue of love for the surgeon, who had swept her off her feet when she was a young nurse. That was a discarded chapter of her life, and she was moving on in high gear.

She was clearly making a play for him. He had no interest in any kind of intimacy with her, however, and tried to signal that without being rude.

As soon as she cleared his space, he hurried to Angela's office door.

"Sorry that I got delayed by Laura Buck. Do you still have time for tea?"

"Yes, but I wish you'd join me at home for a glass of wine. I need to talk to you about something that's very personal."

"Uh . . . what time?"

"What about now?"

"Let me go to the hardware store before it closes, and I'll stop on my way back. It shouldn't take more than thirty minutes."

"Take your time. I'll be waiting for you."

He got his briefcase and left for the hardware store, feeling a bit unsettled. What did she need to talk to him about that was very personal?

***

Angela opened the back door with a bright smile. She had changed into a soft lavender dress that hugged her body, curve by curve. Sleeveless, the dress had a plunging neck line and the hem fell short of her knees.

She welcomed him graciously, poured two glasses of Merlot, and led the way to the living room. He took the stuffed chair at her gesture. She sat next to him on the couch with her dress riding up her thighs.

"First off, what's the story with that Laura Buck? I've never seen you close your office door before."

"I didn't close the door, Angie."

"Wait. Do you realize you just called me Angie?

"No, I wasn't aware of that. I trust you didn't mind."

"No, please call me Angie. Okay, Laura Buck closed the door. What did she want?"

"Have you met her?"

"No, but you obviously know her well."

"She's taken two of my courses as electives and has stopped by the office on several occasions to discuss things that concerned her."

"She's not a traditional student. Who is she?"

"A nurse from Spartanburg who's working on her bachelor's degree. Cooper has an excellent program for nurses like her."

"And what did she need to discuss if I may ask?"

The question put him on the spot. As a rule, he did not discuss a student's personal conversation with anyone. Always perceptive, Angela immediately noticed his reticence.

"I'm sorry," she said. "My curiosity got the better of me."

"That's okay. I can tell you that she has just filed for divorce and wanted to give me an update."

"Looks like she wants to get her claws in you. I saw the way she looked at you as she left."

"That will never happen."

"Are you sure? She looks rather seductive, and I've heard that men have a special weakness for red hair."

"You can bet your virtue and your fortune on my word about Laura Buck."

"Okay, but I'll still have to watch her closing your office door, right?"

"Possibly. I'm empathetic with students who share their personal problems. But I keep my distance. I have never gotten romantically or sexually involved with a student. I won't deny that Laura would be fun, but with my conscience, the buck wouldn't be worth the entanglement. I have a hard time walking away from connections."

"Buck . . . entanglement . . . connections . . . you've giving me new connotations for those words."

"Sorry, I did get a bit carried away."

"Don't be. Now please tell me about your trip."

"It was a remarkable visit. I could not have asked for a better outcome. Susan and I are both pleased to be reconnected as friends, and we do not intend to lose contact, again.

“I was also pleased to meet her husband. I like him and they seem to adore each other.”

“How did the visit go for Hannah?”

“Just fine. She was taken with Susan’s horses. My intention was only to explore the possibility of buying horses for Hannah and me. Now, Susan is determined to give each of us a Tennessee Walker.”

“She’s giving you both horses?”

“She wouldn’t even let me discuss money. She credits me with putting her on the road to becoming a veterinarian and horse-woman.”

“Well, I’m impressed by her devotion to you.”

“We were very close during our youth, but that ended after Dad and Mother moved to Georgia. A sad day for me. I lost my horse Thunder and the farm where I’d spent the best days of my youth. But there was a very different sadness for Susan and me.”

“Would you share that sadness with me?”

“Later if you’re still interested.”

“Later is fine. Have no doubt that I’ll still be interested.”

“Changing the subject, I was not surprised to hear the joyful voices of several students coming from your office this afternoon. Nor was I surprised to detect Dr. Tanner’s voice?”

“This was his second visit. He’s trying to connect with me, but that will never happen. As you said about Laura Buck, you can bet your virtue and your fortune on my word about Dr. Tanner.

“You were right about the students. They do like me, and it’s a joy to have them stop by.

“They’re all excited about the school dance that’s coming up. What’s it like to chaperone their dances? They said they always count on you, and now they’ve asked me.”

“It’s not too bad. We have a faculty table to ourselves and try to make the best of the evening, although it can be vexing for me at times.”

“Why?”

“One of the coeds usually drags me onto the floor at least once, when there’s a slow number. Then the students start cutting in on each other. It’s a game they play, and everyone knows it.”

“How did that get started?”

“Early in my tenure here, a moon-struck coed from Charleston asked me to dance with her. I was embarrassed but took it in stride.

Then it became obvious to everyone that she had lost her senses when she asked me for a second dance. But how do you say *no* to a girl who asks you to dance?

"One of my all-time favorite students saved me by cutting in on her, during the second dance, and that started a chain reaction. Now the coeds do it just for fun."

"I can't wait to see the show. Can I join in the fun this year?"

"If you don't mind getting your toes stepped on."

"No worry here."

An easy silence settled over them. The evening traffic buzzed by on the street. He looked at his watch.

"Do you have to go so soon?"

"Before long. You said you needed to talk with me about something very personal."

"Sorry, but I've lost my courage."

"That's okay. Trust your feelings."

"Thanks for understanding and thanks for coming by. I wish we could do this every week?"

"I would like that, but it's more than I can manage. If I came again next week, a dozen people would be gossiping about it within twenty-four hours."

"I'm sorry. I'm not sensitive enough yet to small-town life. I hope this doesn't mean we can't do any more field trips."

"No, I promised that I would help you get a Southern experience, and I intend to keep my word. I even have an idea that will make it easier for me if you approve."

"That's a relief. Out with it."

"Would you be willing to meet me at the farm for our field trips? We can leave your car there and be off in my Ford pickup or Audi."

"You should know that's acceptable. I will do anything to protect your reputation. Just give me directions and a time and I'll be there, whenever you arrange our next field trip.

"Could you meet me at the farm, Sunday morning? I have a historical field trip in mind if you're free."

"Yes! I'm excited about another field trip, and I'm eager to see your farm."

"Good. I'll give you directions, tomorrow. Dress for some hiking. But I also have other things in mind. Sorry, but I do have to go."

“I know,” she said as he stood.

“I’ll see you at Cooper, tomorrow,” he said.

“Yes, tomorrow.”

She followed him through the screened porch and stood on the steps. When he started the engine and looked back, she waved and blew him a kiss.

Saluting her, he drove home, quite conflicted. He needed Angela’s friendship, something he thought he could manage. In truth, he needed her love, something he knew he could not manage. Even so, he was already in over his head.

Chapter Thirty

As Barsh sat in the den of the old farmhouse with a fresh cup of coffee, it occurred to him that he didn't have a backup plan in case Angela couldn't find the place. There was still time to call before she left her house, so he dialed the number.

"Good morning, Angie."

"Oh, I hope nothing's wrong."

"No, I just realized that we don't have a backup plan in case you have trouble finding the farm."

"Don't worry. I drove out there, yesterday. Your directions are perfect. Can I come now?"

"Sure. The gate is open."

"See you soon."

Having decided that he would show her the old farmhouse when they returned from the activities he had planned, he locked the door and ambled about in the front yard.

Several blue jays were squawking, back and forth, in the huge while oak. He knew they could mimic the sweet cry of a hawk. So why do they prefer that noisy clamor? Were they typically disgruntled or did they enjoy such strident racket?

In response to the thought of a hawk, he searched the southern sky where he occasionally saw one soaring above the forest. No hawk there, but a lone turkey vulture was drifting high on the wind currents.

As he meandered around to the backyard, he spotted a red-tail hawk, circling above the north pasture, and took delight in knowing what it was likely looking for in the grass below—a rat or snake. As a boy, he had watched them take such prey from open pastures.

Back in the front yard, he sat on the porch steps. The blue jays had vacated the white oak. At the sound of a car, he stood and watched Angela's Volvo rumbling up the gravel lane. She parked beside his Ford pickup.

"Welcome to the farm."

"What a joy to be here. I love the seclusion of this rustic place."

"I was afraid it might be too isolated for you."

"No, the privacy is wonderful."

"If you don't mind, I'll wait until we get back to show you the old farmhouse."

"That suits me just fine. This is a huge tree. What kind is it?"

"A white oak. I'd say it's at least three hundred years old."

"Well, it certainly has character."

"This white oak is the sole survivor of numerous old-growth trees when Jeremiah Keeble cleared this parcel of land to build a log cabin. That was back in 1792. Would you like for me to point out the components of a small farm like this?

"Yes, please lay it out for me. I've never been on a farm like this."

"After building the log cabin, that was later incorporated in this house, he cleared land for corn and cotton fields. Those old fields have since been turned into two pastures. I call them the north pasture and the south pasture.

"I'm very pleased that most of the acreage was never cleared. The woodland stretches all the way to the Pacolet River."

"Which way is the Pacolet River?"

"South," he said pointing that way. "Before long, I'll take you to my favorite place on that river."

"And I'll be jumping to go."

"Fortunately for me, Jeremiah Keeble left this oak in the front yard for shade. The front yard is also enhanced by the beauty of hollyhocks and hydrangeas. Both bloomed most of the summer, as did the crape myrtles at the edge of the front yard.

"The rest of the yards were put to practical use. There are pecan trees on the north side, and on the south and west sides, there are peach, apple, and pear trees. There's also a scuppernong arbor and a garden on the west side.

"I didn't plant the garden this year, but I did enjoy the fruit. My plan is to plant the garden next summer.

"For two weekends this summer, I opened the gate for neighbors to help themselves to the fruit. I left word with the owner of Horton's Store to spread the invitation, and they came. I don't like to see good things wasted.

"Regarding outbuildings, there's a barn, a cotton house with toolsheds, a smokehouse for curing meat, and a chicken house.

Built onto the back of the chicken house, there's a privy, something I'm sure you have never experienced."

"You're certainly right about that."

"Don't worry. The house has a bathroom."

"Oh, I'll likely want to use the privy just so I can claim the experience."

"Angie, I'm pleased to tell you that the pecans have started falling. You can have as many as you want. I'll gather them for you or you can do it yourself. Later, I'll open the gate for the neighbors."

"I want to gather them for myself. That's something I've never done."

"Okay, shall we head out for today's field trip."

"Ready, ready. What's first on the agenda?"

"Musgrove Mill Revolutionary War Battle Site. It's less than an hour's drive from here.

"Wilfred Roberts, from whom I'm directly descended, was in that battle. The British shot his horse from under him. Fortunately, he wasn't injured.

"That story was handed down to me by Uncle Edward. He'd heard it from my great-grandfather Paw-Paw Roberts. Wilfred Roberts was Paw-Paw's grandfather.

"Before the Revolutionary War, he was an indentured servant to a man near Augusta, Georgia. I like to think it was the lure of the vast wilderness beyond the settlements of Georgia that enticed him to sell his services for several years in order to secure passage from England.

"After the Revolutionary War, he traveled west from Augusta deep into Creek Indian Territory. Eventually, he took a Creek wife and settled down at the foot of Talladega Mountain in what is now Alabama.

"When I was a boy, Musgrove Mill was just a legendary place somewhere in South Carolina. I never dreamed I would someday walk the battlefield."

"What an interesting family you have. How did you find Musgrove Mill?"

"I told you that Bobby Morrison is an expert on the Revolutionary War. I told him the story about Wilfred Roberts, and the next weekend he took me to Musgrove Mill.

"I've been back several times by myself, and to my delight, Hannah went with me on my last visit.

"On the nature trail to the battle site, we'll pass Horseshoe Falls on Cedar Shoals Creek. Hannah and I ate a picnic lunch on the exposed bedrock above the falls. I'm thinking that will be a good place for us to enjoy a midmorning snack after we explore the battle site."

"Did you pack us some dried fruit and roasted nuts?"

"That I did. As a rule, I'm very predictable."

"Then I assume you have a canteen of water. Today, I want to drink straight from the canteen, no paper cups like we drank from at the Kings Mountain Battle Site, during my first visit to Cooper. Let's drink directly from the canteen, okay?"

"As the woman wishes," he said and they left in his Ford pickup, stopping at the gate to lock it.

***

Their conversation was spirited and wide-ranging, as he drove through the countryside. The miles rolled by and they were there. He parked at the trailhead that led to the battle site, and they hiked through the forest to the north side of the Enoree River, where the battle took place.

Angela seemed genuinely interested in his narration as they walked the grounds. On leaving, she thanked him for sharing the place with her and noted that he was lucky to know so much about four generations of grandparents. She knew nothing about her great-grandparents who never left Czechoslovakia.

On the way back to the trailhead, they stopped at Horseshoe Falls where they sat on the flat bedrock above the falls and ate dried figs and roasted pecans. As she had requested, they drank water directly from his canteen—he always conscious of the fact that his lips were touching where her lips had been.

Before they left, she wanted to turn the pool below the falls into a wishing well. He fished a coin from his pocket and gave it to her. She insisted that he join her in making a wish. Complying, he wished for an enduring friendship with Angela that would include Hannah.

"That was fun," she said as they left for the parking area. "Are you willing to share your wish with me? I'm obviously curious."

"I thought a wish had to remain a secret in order to come true."

"Then I will hold mine within my heart, forever. What's next, my dear friend?"

"The British Star Fort at Ninety Six."

"Now that's an interesting designation for a place."

"The little town of Ninety Six was originally a trading post. Some say it got its name because it was located ninety-six miles from Keowee, the nearest Cherokee town. During the Revolutionary War, the British built a fort there in the shape of a star and thus its name.

"General Nathanael Greene and his Continental Army lay siege to the fort in 1781. They had completed the parallel trenches and were digging a tunnel to blow a hole in the wall when they got word, that British reinforcements were on the way from Charleston. Knowing that he didn't have time to complete the tunnel, General Greene ordered a frontal assault on the fort.

"The assault was a bloody failure, and Green ordered a retreat before the British reinforcements arrived. Ironically, the British almost immediately abandoned the fort.

"The grounds and what's left of the fort are now a National Historical Site. Are you with me?"

"All the way. And I hope there's more on the agenda after Star Fort."

"There's more. Something quite different, I might add. The Greenville County Museum of Art with lunch somewhere in between.

"I think you'll enjoy the museum. In my opinion, it's exceptionally good for a place no larger than Greenville. It has a fine Southern Collection, an excellent Andrew Wyeth Collection, and a strong Contemporary Collection.

"Among works by other nationally known artists, the museum has paintings by Jasper Johns who, as far as I know, is the only South Carolina artist with paintings in New York's Museum of Modern Art.

"During my one and only visit, I saw his paintings of the American flag. You, no doubt, have visited the museum and may have seen them."

"I don't remember that name, but yes, I've visited MoMA. On several occasions, my best friend and I would take the commuter train from Peekskill for a good visit. I was fascinated early on by the impressionists and surrealists, and now you're making a naturalist of me."

"Well, you can still love the impressionists and surrealists. I also appreciate them. As noted, I've only visited MoMA once, but a return visit is on my list of things I'd like to do."

"Then I'm adding that to the dream list of places I'd like to take you in the Big Apple to pay you back for giving me these Southern field trips."

"I'd like that," he said although he doubted it would ever happen. "I also have a dream list."

"Then please share it with me?"

"For one thing, I'd like to take you to Charleston, but given the driving time involved, we wouldn't be able to do much in one day. And I can't manage an overnight field trip."

"I understand. Just know it pleases me that you would like to take me to Charleston."

"Would you consider going with Catherine? She would like to show you the old city, and you must visit the place. When I told her that I'd promised to introduce you to the Carolina mountains, she said that she would like to introduce you to Charleston.

"Her sister still lives in the family's antebellum house. It's what they call a rowhouse with an enclosed garden, and it's located South of Broad. That's where the old aristocrats lived.

"Once when we were vacationing on Hilton Head Island, Hannah and I drove up for lunch with Catherine and her sister. If you're interested, Catherine will likely arrange a weekend visit for you. Of course, that will just be an introduction. There's a lot to see down there."

"Then please tell her I'd like an invitation."

"Will do. Okay, we'll be at the British Star Fort in about forty minutes. What about a little music?"

"I have just the music for this moment."

***

At the Welcome Center, they enjoyed the exhibits and a movie that depicted the battle. With that orientation, they leisurely hiked the forest trail to the battlefield and the earthen ramparts of Star Fort.

Next, Barsh took Angela down a trail to the old Cherokee Path that once came down from the Cherokee town of Keowee to the trading post at Ninety Six and then continued to Charleston. She especially enjoyed the experience of walking on that path where countless Cherokee had once trod.

On the way back, they stopped to explore the old stockade. Then they visited an authentic two-story log house and left. It was past noon.

"We'll be in Greenwood in about twenty minutes. I suggest we eat lunch there, since it's more than an hour's drive from here to the Greenville County Museum of Art.

"I was in Greenwood with Catherine a few years ago, but I don't know anything about the restaurants. You'll have to help me look for a suitable place to eat as we drive through."

"Why were you and Catherine in Greenwood if I may ask?"

"For the inauguration of Larry Jackson as the new president of Lander College. She was the official representative from Cooper and participated in the academic procession. I was there to meet Dr. Benjamin E. Mays, who was receiving an honorary doctorate.

"It was a wonderful day for both men. Catherine predicts good things for Lander under Dr. Jackson's leadership. She also claims that Dr. Mays is one of the most significant men to come out of South Carolina. I can't speak to that, but I can say that I hold him in highest esteem."

"Sorry, but I don't recognize the name."

"I learned about him from Catherine, who knows most of the prominent people with ties to South Carolina. She recommended his autobiography, *Born to Rebel,* and I found his story quite compelling.

"Both of his parents were born in slavery. It's hard for me to believe that the parents of someone living today were born in slavery."

"Yes, I agree. It's actually shocking when you think about it. Tell me about Dr. Mays."

"He was born on a tenant farm near Greenwood before the turn of the century. When he was about four years old, a mob of armed white men on horseback rode into their yard and humiliated his father. They made him bow down to them. That mob scene is Mays' earliest memory."

"What an awful first memory! Why did they do that to his father?"

"Mays had no idea at the time but later learned that those men were one of several white mobs roaming the county after an incident knows at the Phoenix Riot. A white man had just been killed in the Phoenix community, presumably by a black man.

"The whites took that and several other activities to be a black uprising. White mobs took the law into their own hand and lynched several blacks before things calmed down.

"Blacks outnumbered whites three to one in the county, back then. The fear of a black uprising appears to have been a common phenomenon from emancipation until recent times.

"There were a few uprisings during slavery, notably the one led by Nat Turner in Virginia. Have you read William Styron's *The Confessions of Nat Turner*?"

"No, do you think I should?"

"It was a difficult read for me. I'll tell you about it sometime and you can decide for yourself."

"Okay, I'll look forward to that. Now take me back to Dr. Mays."

"At an early age, he realized that education was his only chance for a better life. Against his father's admonitions, he took matters into his own hands and eventually graduated Bates College in Maine. Then he earned M.A. and Ph.D. degrees from the University of Chicago.

"He became such a highly influential minister and educator that he served as advisor to Presidents Kennedy, Johnson, and Carter. He is especially honored, however, for his long and successful presidency at Morehouse College in Atlanta.

"There, he mentored numerous black men who went on to distinguish themselves in various fields. Martin Luther King Jr. was one of those *Morehouse men* as they are frequently called.

"King entered Morehouse at age fifteen with plans to become a lawyer. It was Mays' influence that led him into the ministry and helped prepare him for his role in the Civil Rights Movement."

"Now I understand why you and Catherine hold Dr. Mays in such high esteem."

"Fortunately, the culture down here has changed dramatically since his childhood. Catherine claims that Greenwood is now one of the most progressive small towns in South Carolina.

"After the activities at Lander University, she and I visited the Greenwood Genetic Center, a wonderful place dedicated to medical genetics. Their mission includes genetic research, diagnostic testing, clinical services, and education for the people of South Carolina and beyond.

"I was most impressed by the visit. The fact that the founders of the independent Genetic Center chose to locate in Greenwood speaks well for the town, so I take Catherine's word that it's one of the most progressive small towns in South Carolina.

"Okay, we're approaching the outskirts of Greenwood. Help me look for a place to eat lunch."

"I've got my eyes wide open."

She soon spotted the Inn on the Square, and they stopped for a fine lunch.

Chapter Thirty-One

When Barsh stopped at the farm gate, his mind was wrestling with whether to relock it on entering.

"Angie, I always lock the gate when I'm out here, not for security but to insure my privacy. If you don't object, please slide over and drive though when I open it. I'll lock it again and you can drive us to the house."

"No objection here. And I get to drive your Ford pickup."

He unlocked and relocked the gate, and she drove slowly down the gravel lane.

"I've been reveling in our experience at the Greenville County Museum of Art. I especially enjoyed the Wyeth exhibit."

"Yes, it's wonderful. I wish the collection included 'Soaring,' an aerial view of three turkey vultures mastering the air currents high above a farmhouse and outbuilding. You're looking down on the vultures that are looking down on the farm.

"I bought a large print of it at the gift shop back in the spring and had it framed. When I bought the print, I didn't have a place for it. But guess where it's hanging?"

"The farmhouse. I'm looking forward to seeing it."

"This old farmhouse is a patchwork of additions that have been built onto a log cabin, that now serves as the den. I've made several improvements, starting with a new tin roof. I also had someone tear out the bathroom and build a larger one. The floors are all made of pine boards, and I had them sanded and finished with a clear sealer.

"Then I replaced all the kitchen appliances and had a central heating and cooling system installed. Even with the improvements, it's still an old farmhouse."

"If you're worried about me, I assure you I'll love the house."

"It's like I enter a different time zone when I come out here, and I'm not talking about measuring the time of day in different parts of the world.

"One of the happiest days of my life was when we moved back to the country the year that I turned fifteen. Twenty-nine years later, I own my own place in the country and I'm very pleased with it."

She parked the Ford pickup beside her Volvo. From the front porch, they entered the big room, which was both kitchen and dining area. She exclaimed about its country charm and examined some of the old furnishings. Next, he showed her the view from the screened back porch off the west side of the big room.

"Ah, a porch swing," she said. "Come, let's swing together."

As they sat, swinging gently, a bird landed at one of the feeders near the porch.

"What bird is that?"

"A purple finch."

"I do so enjoy watching the birds in my backyard, but I haven't seen that one. It's beautiful. I want to become a good birder like you. That was such fun identifying the hawks at Caesars Head."

"Hannah and I also enjoyed that. She's pushing me to schedule our field trip to the Cowpens Battle Site. Would you be up to that, two weeks from yesterday?"

"You should know by now that all you have to do is mention the word *go* and I'm ready."

"Here's a proposal. After visiting Cowpens, we could work in the literary field trip I promised you."

"Sounds wonderful to me."

"Good. Let me show you the rest of the house," he said and led her back through the big room to the den.

"We're standing in what used to be Jeremiah Keeble's one-room log cabin. Look how the logs have weathered to a pewter shade of gray. I just have to touch them, occasionally. The stories they could tell if they could talk.

"I'm also very fond of the old fireplace. The original mortar between these fieldstones was clay, not the concrete you see. You can also tell that the hearth was raised when someone added the wooden floor. The original floor was dirt."

"This room is definitely special," she said scanning the walls. "Ah, there's the Wyeth print. Now I see why you like it."

"The original is on the list of paintings I'd like to see. According to the information on the back of the print, it's in the Shelburne Museum in Vermont."

"I trust you know that I'd like to be with you when that happens."

"I'd like that but I can't imagine it happening."

"But a woman can dream, right?"

"Dreams are good as long as we control our expectations."

"That's a good point."

"Angela, this is my old stereo. The couch is new. The rest of the furniture belonged to the previous owners."

"I like the way it's furnished," she said and moved to the stereo. "What kind of records do you have?"

"Just a hodgepodge of this and that. No serious collection of anything. Well, I guess I do have decent collections of early Mississippi blues and old mountain songs. Uncle Edward gave me most of them."

"Am I expecting too much to think I might get to listen to some of them with you before too long?"

"Not at all. You've been good to share your music. Would you like to see the bedrooms? There are only two."

"Please lead the way," she said and followed him.

"Hannah has claimed this room, although she has never slept in it. We call it the blue bedroom. I left all the old furniture. Of course, I replaced the mattress with a new one."

"Wouldn't it be interesting to know the people who have slept in this bed?" she said.

"Or maybe died in this bed. Forgive me. That's too somber."

"Or made love in it."

"That's better," he said.

He opened the door to the green bedroom and waited for her to enter.

"This room had an iron bedstead that I knew Debbie wouldn't like, so I put it in the toolshed and built a box frame for a queen-size mattress set, just to keep things simple. Everything else is the same.

"I'm especially fond of this antique armoire, and this cedar chest is full of hand-sewn quilts. I have no idea why the heirs didn't take them. I feel certain their mother or grandmother made them.

"Okay, this is my old farmhouse that has grown over the years from a one room log cabin. First, someone added the big room with the small front porch on the south and a larger one on the west.

Next, someone added the two bedrooms, and finally someone added a bathroom."

"How interesting. New generations adding onto what they inherited."

"Now I think it's my turn. I've been thinking about adding a complex to the southside. A foyer to replace the front porch and branching out from that a study, master bedroom, and bathroom."

"Sounds like a good plan."

"Let's get something to drink. I have red wine and cranberry juice. I can also make coffee."

"I'd like a glass of wine to celebrate another good field trip."

She went to the bathroom while he poured the wine. Then they settled in the den where she sat on the couch and he in an old rocker angled toward her.

"I trust you know I don't take your friendship and our field trips for granted. What can I do to show my gratitude?"

"Your tutoring Hannah is more that compensation. Moreover, I enjoy our field trips as much as you."

"I hope that's true."

"Trust me."

"Then can I ask when we might hike the Chattooga River Trail?"

"I'll be free to take you two weeks from today, but that would mean back-to-back outings if we stick to our field trip that Saturday. Or I can take you three weeks from today. Your choice."

"I'm free and ever so ready for the first option."

"Then Hannah and I will pick you up at your house that Saturday morning for our Cowpens and literary field trip. But I'd like for you to meet me here for our Chattooga River trip. Just you and me and the Ford pickup if that's okay."

"I'll be here eager to take to the road with you and then the trail. You can't imagine the times I've dreamed about this trip."

"It's a favorite of mine and I trust you won't be disappointed."

"Have no worry. Barsh, your story about Benjamin Mays reminded me of your promise to tell me how you got from a boy who loved the wilds of Alabama to the most distinguished professor I've known. I can't think of a better place for you to share that with me than in the privacy of this old house. Is this a good time for you?"

"I have to get home, soon, but I have time to share some of the obvious factors behind that transformation. I'll start with the traumatic ones. The year I turned fifteen, several disturbing things happened that caused me to raise some challenging existential questions, although I had never heard the word existential.

"The first was the death of my neighbor and friend Becky Wade. She was fourteen when she was killed by lightning. A lesson about the tenuous nature of life and what, I would learn later, the Spanish philosopher Miguel de Unamuno called *the tragic sense of life*.

"To make matters worse for me, Becky was killed in the tepee that I had built in the meadow below our house. I had outgrown the tepee as a plaything, but I'd go there at night just to think about things.

"Unfortunately, Becky had fallen for me, which was troubling enough, because I was not in love with her. Knowing my habit of spending a lot of time in the tepee at night to think about things, she would slip off, occasionally, hoping to find me there. If she did, we would talk until I made her go home.

"I warned her that it was dangerous to be there by herself, but without a thought of lightening. I was thinking of a scandalous older boy, who occasionally came into our neighborhood. He had actually threatened to violate her. But that's another story.

"One night during a thunderstorm, Becky was there by herself when lightning struck the tepee and killed her. As soon as I knew what had happened, I realized that I had played a role in her death. If it had not been for me and my tepee, she would not have died that night. Consequently, I experienced a strange, yet deep, guilt over her death."

"Barsh, your penchant for philosophy and theology was already manifesting itself when you were only fourteen. That amazes me."

"Well, I had a lot of profound questions but no answers. I also wanted to get out of that neighborhood for good after Becky's death, and Dad knew it. He bought his grandfather's old farm and moved us back to the country in late August of that year.

"That was the best thing that happened to me growing up. It's what some philosophers call the coincidence of opposites.

"Of course, you know that by the time I was seventeen, I was sexually involved with a married woman, an experience that shattered what was left of my innocence.

"The guilt I experienced here was not over what I had done with the woman. It was what I had done to her husband. He was my neighbor and friend, and I had betrayed his trust and violated my own sense of honor."

"I remember you said she was lonely. Since her husband had volunteered to fight in Korea, I think that makes him responsible for her loneliness. Maybe, you did him a good deed by keeping her out of a relationship with someone who wouldn't have been as caring as you."

"She said I had saved her from going crazy, but that didn't relieve me of the guilt."

"I find it interesting that your guilt stemmed from what you did to the husband, not what you did with the woman. Would you share your personal philosophy of sex with me?"

"Evolution has programed us, unlike most species, for both sexual reproduction and sexual pleasure with no intention of reproduction. Obviously, I did not know that during my youth.

"Even so, my first experiences would fall under the concept of pleasure fairly exchanged for pleasure with no other expectation. I have never forced myself on anyone. Nor have I tried to seduce anyone. Truthfully, the girls and the one woman I coupled with in my youth initiated the action.

"Oddly enough, I soon evolved into what I call a hopeless romantic, and sex became intrinsically tied to my need for intimacy with the woman of my heart. Thus, my heart became my guide for sexual pleasure. The desire or lack of desire for children was a totally separate issue."

"Then whoever holds your heart is one lucky woman."

"That is debatable."

"I'd like to take that debate up some time. Okay, please take me back to your youth in Alabama, and I'll try not to sidetrack you. I need the rest of your story."

"Since Dad was in the lumber business, he would get me a summer job in some aspect of the business, after I turned sixteen. The summer after my junior year of high school, he got me a job with a logging company. The workers were all black men, except the truck driver Echols and me.

"Before the summer ended, I watched a black man, whom we called Knox, slam a double-bladed ax into Echols' chest. Knox actually killed him in self-defense. Echols had shot him three times with a semi-automatic .22 rifle, before Knox threw the ax."

"What a horror. I can't imagine you working with such violent men. Were you ever in personal danger?"

"I got along well with all the men, and I desperately wanted to defuse the situation with Echols and Knox as the tensions kept building. I didn't have a clue, however, about how to head off the impending fight that I knew would likely be deadly. Wanting to save them both, I was unable to save either, and that left me reeling."

"Of course, it would leave you reeling. What happened between them that led to such violence?"

"Let me tell you about the two men. Echols had previously worked for my father, and I had known him since I was sixteen. Aside from his womanizing and racism, there was a kind of primitive honor about the man.

"He was as good as his word, and he actually got along just fine with all the black men in our logging crew, except Knox. That was because they never challenged him with their blackness. He was even kind and generous to them and often went out of his way to help them.

"Knox was an angry black man in his early thirties. He had been stationed in France at the end of World War II, and according to him, the French women were glad he was there. He loved to talk to me about his experiences with the French women.

"After France, he had a difficult time accepting the place that had been assigned to him in the segregated South. I understood his anger, but I could see he was headed for trouble with Echols.

"About mid-morning that day, Echols drove back into the woods for another load of logs, and we all stopped what we were doing to load the truck. We were a small crew, and it took us all to roll the logs onto the truck, using skid poles.

"The two antagonists were sparring verbally when Knox began bragging about his success with the French women. That was more than Echols could take.

"He told Knox that he would kill him if he ever saw him so much as looking at a white woman with sex on his mind. Knox came back, saying he would do it to Echols' wife if he got a chance.

“Without another word, Echols went for the rifle that he kept behind the seat of the truck. With rifle in hand, he walked within ten feet of Knox, who had picked up a double-bladed ax. Echols raised the rifle and started shooting. In response, Knox threw the ax into his chest.

“I could not stop the flow of blood. In less than five minutes, Echols was dead. I drove Knox to the hospital and the doctor was able to save him.

“In spite of my explanation of what had happened, Knox was charged with first-degree murder, convicted, and executed. I was a witness for the defense, but the all-white jury refused to believe my testimony.

“The prosecutor also badgered the black men who were on the scene into admitting that Knox had threatened Echols by picking up the ax. It was a horrible miscarriage of justice.”

“I can’t believe you had to endure such a horrible experience. You, of all people, who are so caring and compassionate.”

“I have to admit I had a hard time dealing with it. The racial violence, bigotry, and legal injustice that I experienced firsthand that summer had shattered my trust in our social system. I started thinking seriously about going to Alaska and living in the wild. Okay, I’m almost finished.”

“Please, take your time. I’ve been waiting for this story since the day I met you.”

“In late August of that year after footfall practice, one of our players came strutting out of the shower and began bragging about how he had gotten this girl’s cherry on their first date. He said she clawed him like a wild cat, but he had his way with her.

“He even called her by name. She was a shy country girl, a rising junior in our school, and he was a prominent town boy.

“I was stunned by his arrogant gloating over such a dastardly violation of the girl. The other boys were laughing and teasing with him, but I took it upon myself to take him down.

“I called him an arrogant, self-centered rapist and told him that I hoped her father would castrate him, that I certainly would if I were her father. I embarrassed him and proved him a coward, but he never admitted his error.

“I told the coach what had happened and that I was quitting the team. How could I play on a team with a rapist? The coach eventually talked me out of quitting. He said that it probably didn’t even happen, that the boy was likely bragging, and that I would be letting the rest of the team down.

"Until my senior year, I had counted on going to college on a football scholarship, something the coach had assured me I could do. But I was through with football.

"Searching for a way forward, I decided to go to Auburn University and major in civil engineering—something that would keep me working outdoors. But my heart wasn't in it.

"I limped through my senior year, confused and bewildered. Then one night soon after I graduated, I had a profound religious awakening.

"I don't know how to explain it, except that I experienced the numinous presence of God that left me believing my mission in life was to become a voice for justice and righteousness and a servant to broken humanity.

"The next morning, I shared the experience with my parents and later with our minister. With their guidance and support, I enrolled at Samford University that fall to study religion, and thus began the formal part of my spiritual and intellectual journey.

"Soon after I entered college, I realized that I could best fulfill my mission as a professor of religious studies, not a parish minister. That led me to philosophy, anthropology, psychology, etc."

"What a powerful and interesting story, including your decision to become a college professor. Otherwise, I would have never known you."

"That's statistically true, although one never knows what the future holds. At the time of our birth, the odds that we would ever meet were staggering. But here we are sharing this day. One is lucky to stumble into such a friendship."

"You are absolutely right about that."

"Angie, this has been a good day, but it's time for me to head home."

"Truthfully, I also need to get home. I have a ton of work to do before classes, tomorrow. But what a day! What a day!"

Chapter Thirty-Two

The academic week had rolled by with no major challenges for Barsh, and as promised, he took Hannah to the farm that Saturday afternoon for a long hike in the forest. It was a beautiful fall day, and they hiked first to the granite ledge overlooking the Pacolet River, where they basked in the sun and ate a snack of dried apricots and mixed nuts.

From there, they hiked upriver until they came to a large creek, well beyond the boundary of Barsh's property. He could hear a waterfall, so they hiked up the creek to experience it. Then they returned to the farmhouse.

"Hannah, if you're interested, I'd like to start sharing some of my old records with you."

"You should know I'm interested. Why did you move your record player out here?"

"Well, Debbie's preference for television had long relegated it to a very quiet status in our den. So, I bought it out here and revived my interest in music, which is wide ranging from folk songs to opera.

"During my graduate school days at Emory, I attended various operas performed at the Fox Theatre in downtown Atlanta. Every spring, the New York Metropolitan Opera would come to Atlanta for a weeklong series of operas.

"Speaking of my Emory days, one Saturday night I ventured into the black section of Atlanta to hear Ramsey Lewis, who was playing his version of jazz in one of their night clubs. A very fine experience.

"I'll start with one of his records and then I'll introduce you to Robert Johnson, whom they say sold his soul to the Devil, one night, in order to become a successful guitarist and singer of the Mississippi Blues."

He played both records, and she responded with interest.

"I think that will suffice for, today," he said. It's time for us to head home. The next time, I'll give you some options of what to play."

"Daddy, I enjoyed the concerts at Cooper that you took me to last year. One was the Charlotte Symphony. Do you have any records of that kind of music?"

"Oh, yes, and I just had a good idea. Since you don't come out here with me, often, I'd like to buy two cassette players, one for your room and one for my study. We'll start a new collection of music recorded on cassette tapes. When we need a break from our reading or writing, we can listen to music."

"That is a good idea. Is that what Angela does?"

"Yes, and I'm confident she will let you borrow some of her cassette tapes, until you build up your collection."

He drove home feeling good about the outing. Debbie, atypically, was in a good mood and had cooked dinner. As they ate together, she inquired about their afternoon at the farm. He asked about her shopping trip to Spartanburg, and it was a good outing for her. Then he and Hannah did the dishes, while Debbie watched television.

As usual for a Saturday evening, he and Hannah worked on their poetry project in his study. She was a bit fatigued from their long hike and went to bed at her regular time without his having to remind her.

Of late, she seemed more settled and less anxious. He believed that she had gotten comfortable with his explanation of why Debbie and his intimate relationship had failed and would never be restored. Whether that was true of not, there was nothing else he could do to prepare her for separation. It was time to tell her.

Alone in his study, he followed his routine of reading and thinking, which included moments when he thought about Angela. She was spending the weekend with Catherine and her sister in Charleston, and he was confident that the visit was going well. He was also a bit envious that he was not with them.

Sunday, he hiked the Alum Cave Trail in the Great Smokey Mountains National Park. It was a special trail, and when he left for home, he committed himself to bring Angela for the experience, hopefully before Christmas break.

Over tea that Tuesday afternoon, Angela shared the highlights of her weekend with Catherine and her sister in Charleston. The visit was especially rewarding to her. She thanked him for making it happen and reaffirmed her dreams of experiencing more of the

Lowcountry. He told her about hiking the Alum Cave Trail and promised to take her at some later date.

With little further interaction between them, the academic week ended on an anticipatory note. They were both looking forward to the two field trips that he had planned for the weekend.

Saturday's field trip included Hannah, and once again, he drove the Ford pickup, so the three of them could sit together on its broad seat.

They had a fine time visiting the Cowpens Battlefield and the Tomas Wolfe Home. Then there was lunch on the Terrace Restaurant at Grove Park Inn.

On the way home from Asheville that afternoon, they visited Carl Sandburg's last home at Flat Rock. It was a superfine day for the three of them.

***

Early Sunday morning, he drove to the farm with plans to take Angela hiking on the Chattooga River Trail. After checking out the house, he waited for her on the front steps and was soon reminiscing about the last time he hiked that trail. He was all by himself with no thought of what it would feel like to have a special woman with him.

A mockingbird flew onto a branch atop a crepe myrtle and held forth with a joyful song. How poorer the world would be without the aesthetic beauty of birds and their songs, he thought.

The rumble of a car on the gravel lane caught his ear, and there was Angela easing up the lane in her Volvo. He stood to greet her, his heart beating faster. She parked beside his truck and came running to him.

"Catch me," she yelled, jumped, and locked her arms and legs around him.

"Wow! There must be something extraordinary in this country air, today."

"I love the privacy this place affords us," she said still clinging to him. "It's just the place for me to jump you, straddle-legged, on this brilliant morning.

"I'm so excited about hiking the Chattooga River Trail I thought I might get away with such a stunt. I once saw a girl do it to her lover, and ever since, I've longed for the right man to try it on. Hope that tells you how special you are to me."

"You did take me by surprise. Be assured that I will not forget the experience. And please know how much I appreciate the special attention you gave Hannah, yesterday. You are so good for her. She quotes you every time we have a poetry discussion."

"Yesterday was extraordinary, and this is going to be another wonderful day. I can feel it in my bones. I've dreamed about this day ever since I flew home from Charlotte after the job interview.

"Here's a confession. During the flight home, I relived every moment of my time with you. And I wondered if you were thinking about me as you drove back to Ashland."

"My spirit soared higher than an osprey," he said.

"You're kidding me, aren't you?"

"Actually, I was a bit depressed. I left the airport thinking it unlikely that I would ever see you again."

"But here I am, ready to headed into the wild with you."

"I hope the outing lives up to your expectation."

"Have no doubt. I'm going to enjoy this day."

She got her special bag from the Volvo, and they were on their way in his Ford pickup.

"I trust you brought music in that bag of yours."

"Oh, yes, I have music to share."

"Then enlighten and entertain me while I get us to the Foothills Trail. The last couple of miles are over a narrow gravel road, but I've never had any trouble making it. You may hear the underbody of the truck hit the gravel occasionally but have no fear."

"I have no doubt you will get us there and back."

***

From the small parking lot at the end of Nicholson Ford Road, they took the Foothills Trail west and were soon enveloped by a mixed forest of evergreens and hardwoods.

"What is this tall evergreen?" Angela asked and stretched out her hand to touch its trunk.

"That's a white pine and I'm very fond of them. We'll see a lot of them along the trail."

She gave him a big smile, and they were off again. Soon he could hear Lick Log Creek rushing down the hollow below them and stopped to identify it for her. They continued until they crossed the creek on a narrow wooden bridge and proceeded down the creek to the Chattooga River Trail, that had veered away from the river for a good place to cross Lick Log Creek.

"Angie, the Foothills Trail merges here with the Chattooga River Trail, going upriver, and then it breaks off on its own. From there it will take you to Table Rock State Park about eighty miles from here."

"Have you hiked the whole trail?"

"No, but there are access points along the way, and I've traveled several sections of the trail. We're turning left, today, but on our next visit we'll take the trail, upriver. That is if you're interested in a return visit."

"I'm most definitely interested. I never imagined how enjoyable this would be before I met you. You know what this means to me, don't you?"

"Your joy is obvious. It's essential for me to get back into the wild for a good hike, periodically, and now your presence makes the experience all the more enjoyable."

She gave him a high five, and they turned left on the Chattooga River Trail, that quickly sloped to Lick Log Creek. They crossed to the other side on another narrow wooden bridge and followed the trail to Lick Log Falls, that dropped in two tiers some eight feet.

"This is so enchanting," she said.

"The trail takes a sharp left just ahead of us, and we'll be looking down through the trees on the Wild and Scenic Chattooga River, far below us."

"Then lead the way," she said and they were off again, taking in the sights along the way.

"There it is," he said.

"Wow! What a beautiful sight. You were right about *far below us,* and this bank is almost straight down. It looks impossible to access the river from here."

"We might be able to make it, but it wouldn't be worth the effort. Further down the trail, we can get to the river's edge with less effort.

They continued down the trail until he found a place where they could access and sit by the river. He helped her down the bank onto a flat rock jutting out into the swift water. There, they sat, silently watching the currents dance down the riverbed.

"Angie, back at Lick Log Falls, I thought about Whitewater Falls. They are the highest falls east of the Mississippi River, more than four-hundred feet, and they are within easy driving distance. Would you like to go by there when we leave here?"

"Sounds like another wonderful experience for me."

"There's an observational deck not far from the parking lot. From there, we can hike down into the gorge if you'd like. Or we can save the gorge for another outing. You can make that decision when we get there."

"Thanks."

"Okay, we'll have a late lunch in Walhalla and head that way. I know a place that serves good pulled-pork barbecue. Or we can look for something else if you're not in the mood for barbecue."

"Barbecue suits me just fine."

"From Whitewater Falls, we could drive to Brevard. We'll be taking a different route, but it's a good scenic drive. Then we could ascend the mountain to the Blue Ridge Parkway, take it to I-26, and leave the mountain for home. I'll let you decide."

"You know the answer. I want to stretch this day out as long as possible. But I'm not ready to pick up the Carrick Creek painting in Brevard."

"There's no hurry about that. The painting is secured for you. Are you ready to extend our hike down the Chattooga River Trail?"

"Ready! Ready!"

They climbed back up the river bank and turned down the trail, stopping from time to time to enjoy some specific feature of the landscape. Like a good trouper, Angela followed his preference of hiking with little conversation in order to be totally alert to the sights, sounds, and smells of the wild. After hiking several more miles, he began looking for a suitable place away from the trail to take a break.

"Angie, that bluff ahead looks like a good place for us to eat our morning snack. If we take an upward angle from here, I think we can make it to the top."

"Lead off and I'll be right behind you."

They made the climb and he spread a blanket on a thick bed of leaves near the edge of the bluff with a good view of the river rapids far below. There, they sat eating dried cranberries and roasted almonds and drinking water from his canteen.

"Barsh, I don't know why this just jumped into my mind, here in this natural setting, but I'll share it with you, anyway. After our first fieldtrip, I've done a lot of reflecting on our discussion of the Catholic Mass. I've now decided that I can attend with Mother. I'll ignore the doctrine of transubstantiation and participate in remembrance of the crucifixion of Jesus, and I'll do so with no explanation to Mother or the priest."

"You won't be alone in going against an official Catholic doctrine or teaching. There are many who remain in the Church although they reject significant parts of its official dogma and teachings.

"Most Catholics in the United States, for example, do not accept the Church's teaching against artificial birth control if you can trust recent polls."

"That's true."

"Just think of all the Catholic scholars and university professors the world over. I can't imagine that they still hold to all the official doctrines of the Church. This is the twentieth century.

"I find it hard to believe that the current Pope actually believes all the official dogmas of his Church. I would say the same about most of the Cardinals, Bishops, and priests."

"Do you really think the Pope doesn't believe all the doctrines of the Church?"

"I can't imagine that he does. I find it hard to believe that any twentieth-century educated person could. But this is not something you should use against your mother. Preparing people to demythologize their faith can be a long and arduous task, even for those who are prepared to face the truth."

"You are so right about Mother. I'm learning to accept her for who she is."

"I'm pleased to hear that. Angie, I just thought about a prominent priest who demythologized his faith and remained in the Catholic Church. Do you know about Pierre Teilhard de Chardin?"

"I know nothing about him."

"He was a Jesuit priest, paleontologist, anthropologist, and theologian. He's now well known for his book *The Phenomenon of Man* that embraces human evolution. The Catholic Church, however, would not let him publish it, because its officials could not be harmonized it with the Biblical teachings about creation.

"His friends tried to persuade de Chardin to leave the Jesuit order and publish the book, but he refused to do so. So, they promised that they would see that it was published after his death, which took place in 1955. Now, his books are widely read in Catholic colleges and universities."

"How interesting and informative."

"Well, de Chardin is not alone in the effort to bring Christian spirituality in line with modern science. It's happening in both Catholic and Protestant circles, but at a snail's pace."

"Barsh, I just decided to call Mother, tonight. When I first told her that I was moving to South Carolina, she begged me to stay at Brown University. I want to tell her how happy I am with this move and how well I've been received.

"I'll say hello to Daddy before I hang up. He has always understood me better than Mother, although we were never very close. He was too obsessed with his career.

"I am so impressed with your devotion to Hannah. She is lucky to have you for a father."

"Sometimes I doubt the wisdom of my parenting. I'm beginning to think that I've kept her too sheltered, too close to me, for her own good."

"Please, have no doubt. You're the perfect father. Forgive my inquisitive mind, but I've been wondering how Debbie fits into this parental task."

"She's left it mainly to me. Back to your parents. Catherine and I will make sure they get a special reception if you want to invite them for a visit. We'll do our best to show them how pleased we are to have you on the faculty."

"I hadn't thought about that, but yes, I'll invite them down when summer rolls around."

"Please know that I will be available to help you show them the area if you need me."

"I'll definitely need your help. I can't imagine Mother coming but Daddy might. Truthfully, I hope he will come without her. He'll be most impressed with you and all that you embody.

"I wish you knew how at peace I am with myself. Just sitting here with you amid the awe-inspiring beauty of this place is so deeply satisfying."

"The feeling is mutual," he said and looked at his watch. "It's time to head back. Otherwise, we'll have to abbreviate our agenda. Your call."

"Then let us be off. I want to experience it all."

***

They left Whitewater Falls for Brevard, both pleased with the experience.

"Well, I hope the hike down into the gorge and back didn't leave you totally exhausted."

"I made it fine. I've been walking the college track three times or more a week, always with some of my students. I've never felt so energized.

"Barsh, I sometimes wonder what would have happened if we had met earlier in our lives. Do you think we would have connected?"

"Truthfully, I don't think you would have found me interesting," he said.

"That's what I was thinking about myself. I don't think you would have taken an interest in me if we had met earlier."

"I would have been fascinated with you, but I'm also certain that I would have been wary of you, the big city woman."

"Now you're teaching me how to be a naturalist among other things, and I'm enjoying your friendship more than any I've ever had.

"Fate has finally been good to me. I have a good piece of music for this moment. Are you ready?"

He gave her a thumbs-up and she played James Taylor's "You've Got a Friend."

***

Barsh exited the Blue Ridge Parkway and followed the signs to I-26, where he took the eastbound ramp for Ashland by way of Spartanburg. The whole outing had gone extremely well. They even saw a white squirrel in Brevard.

Homeward bound, his mood began to shift as his predicament began to dominate his thoughts. In spite of his effort, he could not suppress the uneasiness he felt. The line between the friendship he wanted to maintain with Angela and the love he felt in his heart had blurred too much for comfort.

"Is something wrong?" she said. "You look troubled."

"I was just thinking about Hannah," he said not willing to share his dilemma. "Sometimes I wish she were more like other girls her age."

"She is definitely exceptional. I know you're anxious to get home to spend time with her."

"That's true but this has been a good day for me."

"Yes, an extraordinary day."

Traffic on the Interstate was light. They listened to more of Angela's cassettes and talked from time to time about various subjects, until he stopped at the farm gate to unlock it. She slipped under the steering wheel. He unlocked the gate and left it open. She slowly drove them toward the farmhouse.

"How can I tell you what these field trips mean to me?" she said. "I was thinking last night about how miserable I would be if I had taken the position at Bennington.

"I would be right back in the same old rut in spite of all my good intentions to take a different path. I'm finally getting the Southern experience I've long wanted. And you . . . you are so different from the men I've known."

"Can I take that as a compliment?"

"I would walk through fire for a man like you."

"If I were a free man, I would walk through fire for a woman like you."

"Do you want to be a free man?"

"I can't go there, Angie."

"I'm sorry but I had to ask."

"It's okay. I trust you know that I treasure your friendship."

"I do know that, but you probably don't know that your friendship is better than any love I have ever known."

"That makes me sad."

"Let's forget the sad and focus on the happy. Believe me. I'm a happy woman."

She parked beside her Volvo. He apologized for not inviting her in, using Hannah as an excuse. She raved, again, about how wonderful the day had been as he escorted her to the Volvo.

"See you at Cooper tomorrow," he said.

"Yes, tomorrow," she said and left.

***

Debbie was reading a magazine when he got home. He knew immediately that she was in a bad mood when she tossed it on the coffee table.

"I guess you had a good time in the mountains."

"I enjoyed the mountains very much. How was your day?"

"It could not have been more depressing."

"I'm sorry. Would you like to go out for dinner?"

"Not really, but you can take Hannah or fix something. I've eaten some cereal."

"Daddy," Hannah said rushing into the room, "I'm glad you're home. How were the mountains?"

"The mountains were pleased to see me and made me feel right at home. Would you like to go out for supper or help me fix something?"

"I'd like a roast beef sandwich at Willard's."

"Good call, my sweet girl."

They drove to Willard's with Hannah talking all the way. She'd had a good afternoon with her writing. They ate their sandwich with potato chips and retuned home. Debbie had gone to her room and closed the door.

At Hannah's bedtime, she turned in without his having to remind her. He went to the basement for a light workout. Afterwards, he went to his study to read. Angela's copy of Denise Levertov's *Here and Now* lay before him on the desk. He resumed reading it and, again, felt the power of her poetry.

Pausing, he envisioned himself sitting in James Dickey's class at the University of South Carolina. Eureka, he whispered. Finally, he knew where he would like to spend his sabbatical.

He would enroll as a post-doctoral student in the graduate school at the University of South Carolina and begin a formal study of contemporary poetry and fiction. If he limited his classes to Tuesdays and Thursdays, he could live at home and commute to Columbia on those two days.

The house was quiet, except for the humming of the refrigerator, and he was thinking about Angela. He no longer dreaded telling her about the sabbatical. He could keep his promise to befriend her, but he would be even more vulnerable with Debbie and Hannah in Louisville.

He tried to refocus on Levertov's poetry, but he could not keep Angela out of his head. Realizing that he had lost that battle, he closed the book.

He remembered Angela's confession, earlier that day: I would walk through fire for a man like you. He now knew, without doubt, that she was ready to move from friendship to romantic intimacy.

Then the question of the day emerged in his consciousness. Could he follow his heart and still fulfill his responsibility to Hannah?

There were too many unknowns for his analytical mind and sense of duty. But he had raised the question. That was a major development in itself. He also realized the question would keep coming back until he could answer it.

It was getting late, but he was wide awake. Dreading the inevitable tossing and turning that the bed would produce, he toyed with the idea of going for a walk in the neighborhood. Then he had a better idea—self-induced exhaustion by running around the athletic track at the college.

He left a note on his desk, just in case Hannah should wake up and come looking for him, and then he drove to Cooper, where he parked beside Kimberly Hall. From there, he walked to the athletic field and ran, round and round the track, until he could run no more.

Chapter Thirty-Three

In the dream, Hannah was calling his name as she searched for him in a dense forest, but when he woke, Debbie was standing in the bedroom door, calling him.

"What's wrong?" he asked and sat up.

"It's seven-thirty. I let you sleep because I knew you left last night and were gone a long time. I woke up and went to the kitchen for something to drink. You'd left the light on in your study, so I read your note to Hannah."

"Sorry. Can you take her to school?"

"She's waiting in the car. Barsh, you must tell her about the separation. It's not going to get any easier."

"Okay, I'm ready. I'll pick her up after school and tell her at the farm."

"Don't forget to emphasize the fact that you can visit her, anytime, and she gets to stay with you during holidays and the summer."

"I'll do my best."

"While you two are at the farm, I'm coming home to talk with Davis. I have a job offer for her as a live-in maid."

"That will be a relief to me if she accepts your proposal. Do you think she will?"

"I don't know. I'm offering her a good salary with a big bonus if she stays one year. Please tell Hannah about this. She and Davis have always gotten along so well."

"Yes, I'll tell her."

"I'm sending Davis home early, and I'd like to talk with Hannah without you, when you bring her home."

"Okay, I'll drop her off and go to my office at Cooper."

"I'll be praying that Hannah responds well," she said and left.

After going to the bathroom, he went to the kitchen, poured a cup of coffee, and sat in his study. The dreaded day was upon him, and he did not feel like being around anyone, not even Angela.

Fortunately, he had no meetings or appointments. He would go straight to the farm after his eleven o'clock class and hang out there, until it was time to pick up Hannah.

***

He eased the Ford pickup away from Hannah's school and headed for the farm. The solemnity of the occasion showed on his face in spite of his effort to hide it.

"What's up, Daddy? You look worried."

"I have to talk to you about an unsettling matter."

"Is it about Mother?"

"It's about all three of us. If you don't mind, I'd like to wait until we get to the farm. We'll sit in the den and talk, sheltered from the outside world by those old log walls. As serious as this is, I can assure you that we'll all get through it."

"You're scaring me but I can wait."

"You are one in a million, my sweet girl."

They rode in silence to the farm with Barsh trying to reassure her with a forced smile from time to time. Inside the old farmhouse, he poured two glasses of cranberry juice and led the way to the den. Hannah sat on the couch and he in the rocker, angled toward her, so he could watch her as they talked.

"Hannah, you know Debbie was despondent most of last year and still has bouts of depression. You know I've been sleeping in the guest bedroom. You also know Debbie hates living in Ashland. Do you remember what city she likes best of all?"

"You told me Louisville."

"That's right. Back in March, her old boss, from the days when she lived there, called and offered her a partnership in his accounting firm."

"Daddy, I can see where this is going."

"Okay, tell me."

"She wants to move to Louisville."

"Yes, and without me. She wants a separation for a year to see how things work out. I have only one problem with her plan, because it involves you. Do you know what it is?"

"She's taking me to Louisville," she said and began crying.

He stood, pulled her into his arms, and let her cry as he held her.

"I want to live with you, Daddy."

"That's also what I want, but it would destroy Debbie's self-image of being a good mother. When people separate or divorce in our culture, the mother usually takes the children. There are cases in which the mother actually wants the children to live with their father, but they are rare exceptions. Sometimes fathers take the matter to court, but judges usually rule in favor of the mother, unless she is morally unfit or totally incompetent.

"There's no happy solution to our problem. Debbie wants you to live with her, and I want you to live with me. You can't be in two places at once. But you can be in two places, alternately.

"Debbie has promised me that you can spend holidays and the summer with me and that I can visit you at any time. I'm assuming she will want a permanent separation if things work out for her. If things don't work out for her, I hope she will move back to Ashland. Whatever happens, I will continue to be a major part of your life."

"When is she moving?"

"Probably during Christmas break."

"I don't like this one bit, but I can see I don't have a choice."

"You do have a choice. You can rebel and make Debbie and me miserable or you can make the best of it."

"I'll make the best of it. After all, I am your daughter. What did you teach me about facing the inevitable?"

"My dear sweet girl, you are the joy of my life. I have dreaded having to tell you this for months. I do hope you can understand why I waited as long as possible before telling you the bad news."

"I knew something was troubling you and now I understand."

"Here's my strategy. I'm going to treat this as if you were away at a boarding school. I'll be counting the days until you come home for holidays and the summer. I'll also look forward to visiting you in Louisville. We'll talk often by phone, and you can read me your poems.

"I'm also confident that Angela will continue working with you on your writing by correspondence and phone. I want you to have your own private phone in your room. Angela knows nothing about this, however. Please wait until I get a chance to tell her before you bring it up.

"Here's something else that I think you'll approve if Debbie can pull it off. She's going home early to ask Davis to go to Louisville as a live-in maid. If Davis accepts the proposal, she will take you to school and pick you up. And best of all, she will be home with you when you're not in school."

"I'd like that, but I'll be okay either way."

"If Davis doesn't accept the offer, Debbie will find someone who will do the job. I'm sorry, Hannah. I wish we could have done better by you. This is not what I wanted, and yet, I'm morally bound to support Debbie's decision."

"I know that."

"Now, I want you to pick out a stall for the horse that Susan is giving you. I'm contracting with someone to tear out the old partitions and build new ones. I have something special in mind for the stable you choose."

"I'm still getting a horse?"

"Most definitely. I'm also building a riding rink. And don't forget that Susan has promised to come and give you riding lessons."

"Let's go," she said and they left for the barn.

***

Following Debbie's instruction, Barsh left Hannah at home and drove to the college. The bad news was like a hard blow to her gut. It staggered her, but she managed to stay on her feet. She was definitely mature for her age, and he could not have been prouder of her.

Angela's car was still there. They'd had only one brief exchange on the stairs of Kimberly Hall as he was leaving for his nine o'clock class and she was returning from her first period class. He hurried up the stairs and stopped at her door.

"Please have a seat and catch me up on your day. I'd given up hope of getting to talk with you, today."

"There's not much I can report. I spent most of the afternoon at the farm. How was your day?"

"Quite troubling, and it started last night. You have no idea what our trip to the mountains meant to me. I reveled in every aspect of it, until I fell asleep.

"Then I woke up around midnight with a strong premonition that something was troubling you. I had a hard time settling down and getting back to sleep.

"Atypically, you had not arrived on campus before my eight o'clock class. Then you were not your usual self, when we met on the stairs as you were going to your nine o'clock class."

"I did have a bad case of insomnia last night. After Debbie and Hannah went to bed, I did my usual workout and read until bedtime. But even then, I knew it would be foolish to go to bed, so I resorted to an old tactics of inducing exhaustion.

"I ran, around and around the college track, until I could run no more. And it worked. As soon as I crawled into bed, I went down, down into that nether region of deep sleep."

"Something is troubling you, right?"

"I can't deny that."

"Please tell me what's troubling you."

"I can't now but I will soon."

"Soon?"

"Yes, soon."

"Well, that's good to hear. I need to know."

"Sorry to rush off, but I have to see Catherine before she leaves for the day."

"Can you swing by on your way back?"

"Sure. This won't take long."

Catherine listened intently as Barsh gave her a detailed report on his trip to the farm to tell Hannah about the separation. The concern etched on her face gradually relaxed as his narrative moved toward a hopeful summation.

"I am so relieved to know that part is over for you. Hannah is going to be alright and so are you. Not that it's going to be easy for either of you, but you will find a way to make the best of this."

"I trust you're right. Catherine, I now know what I want to do during my sabbatical."

"That's progress. Please tell me."

"I'd like to study contemporary poetry and fiction at the University of South Carolina. I'll schedule my classes on Tuesdays and Thursdays, so I can commute on those two days. If it's okay with you, I'd like to teach a couple of classes on the Monday-Wednesday-Friday schedule."

"This is a wonderful development. You can also continue your duties as Chair of the Division of Humanities. We'll call this a half sabbatical, which means your salary will remain the same now that you will be pursuing post-doctoral studies."

"I don't have time today, but I need to talk with you, soon, about when and how to go public about the separation and Debbie's plan to move to Louisville."

"I've already given it a lot of thought as I'm sure you have. We'll work it out together."

He thanked her for her support and left for Kimberly Hall. The place seemed deserted as he took the stairs to Angela's office.

"How was your meeting with Catherine?"

"It went very well. I'll tell you about it later. Now I have a question for you. Are you ready for our hike to the Pacolet River?"

"When can we go?"

"This Sunday. Can you meet me at the farm around ten o'clock?"

"I'll be there, ever so eager to make that hike with you. I am also excited about the dance, Saturday night. Aren't you?"

"Truthfully, I'm a bit anxious about the dance. I have to go, but I'll be back with Hannah in about thirty minutes on the pretense of picking up a book. My real objective is to invite you to join us for dinner."

"The answer is yes, and I'm buzzing with expectation."

Chapter Thirty-Four

Somewhere between Cooper College and Fern Meadows, Angela slipped from Barsh's consciousness, and the dreadful anticipation of entering his own house settled upon him. What dark mood would he find there? He parked and entered the den. Debbie, already in her pajamas, was sitting in her chair.

"Come sit with me a minute. Whatever you told Hannah seems to be working. It would have been horrible without your support. I do believe that she's going to be alright, and I'm so relieved.

"Is Davis going to Louisville with you?"

"She needs to think about it, but I believe she'll accept my offer. Will you take Hannah out for dinner? I'm emotionally exhausted."

"Sure."

He left the den for Hannah's room. She was lying on her bed.

"It's been a hard day for you, my sweet girl. Please know how much I admire the way you are dealing with this. You are far beyond your age in maturity, but that doesn't take away the pain. You know I'm also hurting."

She began to cry, and he pulled her into his arms until the crying ran its course.

"Let's go out for dinner," he said.

"I'll be ready as soon as I wash my face."

She left for the bathroom, and he went to the den to wait for her.

"We may go to Spartanburg and could be late getting home."

"That's fine, but thanks for telling me. I'll probably be in bed when you get back."

Hannah joined him and they left in the Ford pickup.

"Tell me about your conversation with Debbie. She seems to be satisfied with your response."

"I did what you expected me to do. I listened to her and told her I would be alright as long as she kept her word about you and me."

"That's our deal and I cannot imagine her going back on it. If she should, I will correct the situation, one way or another. Let's enjoy this outing. After I pick up a book at my office, we'll be on our way to Spartanburg for a good meal at Antoine's."

They rode the short distance to the college without further conversation. In spite of his forced smiles, she remained somber.

Given the mood that hung over her, he was pleased with his decision to invite Angela to join them for dinner. If anyone could distract Hannah, for a while, from the reality of the separation, she could.

"That's Angela's car. You want to say hello to her while I get my book?"

"Yeah."

"Don't forget—"

"I know not to tell her. Can I run ahead?"

"Take off."

Angela was embracing her when he topped the stairs.

"Well, do I need to tell you how pleased I am to be hugging Hannah? Such a bright moment on a rough day for me."

"Sorry you've had a rough day. We're going out for dinner. Why don't you join us?"

"Yeah, Angela, why don't you join us?"

"I'd love to join you. Can I change clothes?"

"Sure, we'll pick you up in—"

"Give me ten minutes. This is such a wonderful development."

***

Angela eased down the steps as soon as Barsh pulled into her backyard. He got out of the pickup and opened the door for her as Hannah slid to the middle of the seat. Then they were off.

"I was planning to take Hannah to Antoine's in Spartanburg? Would you like to try something else?"

"No, I'd like to revisit Antoine's."

"Daddy, we don't have to be in a hurry, do we? I'd like to stay out until midnight."

"Ah, my kind of girl," Angela said and pulled her into her arms with tender affection. "Let's think of some place we can go after dinner, and we'll gang up on your father. Two votes against one always wins, right?"

"Unless it's a school night, but if you two want a midnight outing, I can make that happen before long."

"I'm ready to put it on my calendar," Angela said.

"Do you want the three of us to plan something? Or do you want me to surprise you?"

"What do you want, Angela?"

"I'd like for Barsh to surprise us."

"Okay, I'll try not to disappoint you."

Pleased with the turn of events, he smiled at Angela, and she winked at him. Another first. She caught the quizzical look on his face and flared her eyes wide open.

"I'm so delighted to be going out that I feel like a silly girl," she said.

"Yeah, I'm glad we're eating out together."

"Hannah, I just remembered that you and Barsh are getting horses. I'm so envious. When I was twelve, I wanted a horse with all my being, but that was never in the cards for me."

"It's not too late," Barsh said. "We have six stables and enough pasture for twenty horses."

"Are you saying that I could keep a horse at your place?"

"Yes, that's what he's saying. The three of us could ride together."

"Is that right, Barsh?"

"Right as right can be."

"I can't believe this. I have a chance to own a horse."

"I'm sure Susan will give you a good deal if you'd like one of her Tennessee Walkers."

"Yes, I'd like that if I can afford one."

"Susan will work something out with you. I'll give her a call."

It was a good evening for the three of them. At least during the outing, Hannah had sublimated her anxiety about the move to Louisville. And as he expected, she carefully studied every exchange between Angela and him.

Chapter Thirty-Five

Sunday morning, Barsh left home to meet Angela at the farm. In the solitude of the Ford pickup, he relived their one dance at Cooper the night before.

Sally McCarter, one of his majors, had pulled him onto the floor for a slow dance, and other co-eds started cutting in, until Angela ended their game. Without regard for the students or faculty members in attendance, she had pressed herself against him as if they were lovers. It was an experience he would never forget.

He parked and ambled about the yard. A few minutes before ten o'clock, he walked to the gate to wait for her. Precisely on time, she turned off the highway. He waved her past the gate, locked it, and got in the car.

"Good morning, my friend," she said. "Don't ever, again, tell me that you're not much of a dancer. That was pure magic."

"Well, I don't have to tell you that I enjoyed it."

She laughed and gave him a high five.

"I'm looking forward to another good day with you," she said.

"I hope it turns out to be a good day. I don't want to spoil your mood, but I need to share a troubling development with you."

"I hope it's not as ominous as the vibes I'm feeling."

"No, it's not ominous but it's very troubling."

After parking, he ushered her into the old farmhouse.

"I made a pot of coffee. Would you like a cup?"

"I'll take a cup with lunch. Right now, I need you to share the troubling development with me."

She sat on the couch in the den, he in the rocker next to her.

"I'll start with the obvious. You know that Hannah and I typically do things without Debbie."

"Yes," she interrupted, "and I've assumed that things between you and Debbie are not ideal, although you have never complained about your marriage, like other men I've known."

"Your assumption about us is correct. That's been true for years, but now, she will be moving to Louisville before Christmas. She doesn't want a divorce, but a trial separation for a year to see how things work out for her in Louisville."

"I don't know what to say, except that I am stunned. Why would she be leaving a man like you?"

"I've told you that she's a successful accountant with her own firm, but we haven't talked about her beyond that. Let me tell you the back-story, and I think you'll understand Debbie's decision.

"She and her parents were members of the little church that I served as minister during my theological studies in Louisville. I'd drive the fifty miles to the church every Sunday, conduct the morning and evening services, and then drive back to Louisville.

"Most of the members lived on upland farms with small tobacco allotments. The tobacco they raised was the major source of their modest income.

"Debbie's family, however, owned a big bottomland farm along the Kentucky River, and they had a large tobacco allotment. They were well off by local standards.

"Debbie had finished college and was working at a prominent accounting firm in Louisville, when I arrived on the scene. One weekend, when she was home, her mother invited me for Sunday dinner.

"After that, Debbie started coming home almost every weekend. Then she started riding back and forth with me. During the week, we'd occasionally eat out and go to a movie in Louisville.

"We never talked about marriage until my final year at the theological seminary. That summer, we got married, moved to Atlanta, and I begin a Ph.D. program at Emory.

"Those years in Atlanta were extraordinary for me. My courses at Emory were excellent, and I had a teaching assistantship, which included tuition and a small stipend.

"The first year, I was a research assistant to a brilliant archeology professor from Israel who had participated in numerous excavations. The second year, I taught an introductory course to the Bible in the College of Liberal Arts. The last two years, I taught Biblical Hebrew in the School of Theology. I could not have asked for a better experience.

"Debbie hated living in Atlanta, although she had a good-paying job with a reputable accounting firm, and I managed to earn a Ph.D. without taking out a single student loan.

"I will always honor her for supporting me during those years, and I will always love her as Hannah's mother.

"Here's the problem as I see it. Over the years, I became more liberal, while Debbie remained conservative and traditional. I wanted to share my intellectual and spiritual journey with her, but she was not interested. In fact, she was frightened by my empirically based studies of the Bible and my scientific worldview.

"Please understand that I'm not belittling Debbie. She's a good woman, but she has always been miserable around intellectuals.

"Back in March, her old boss in Louisville invited her to become a partner in his accounting firm. By the time she shared that conversation with me, she had decided to give it a try. I offered to move to Louisville, but she wanted a trial separation.

"On a personal note, I can tell you that her decision stuck a hard blow to my male ego. It wasn't easy for me to come to terms with the fact that my wife was leaving me.

"The hardest blow to me, however, was that Debbie was taking Hannah with her. You know how close she is to me. Nevertheless, I've supported Debbie's decision from the first."

"Why haven't you told me?"

"I couldn't tell you until I told Hannah. Knowing the news would be devastating to her, I've been trying, in various ways, to prepare her for the harsh reality of the separation. Last week, I was able to get the whole story out."

"How is she taking the news?"

"In spite of her maturity, she's having a hard time dealing with this."

"Is there anything I can do to help her make the adjustment?"

"You can be a big help. Writing is so important to her, and you are such a good mentor. She idolizes you and needs you as a mentor."

"I will continue to work with her on her writing by correspondence as well as phone conversations if that's permitted."

"She will be pleased to hear that. Unfortunately, I lost my way trying to figure out how to prepare her for the separation, and I came up with a crazy scheme that would deceive her about the move to Louisville. I'll tell you about it later if you're interested."

"Yes, I want to know the whole story."

"Here's the worse part for Hannah and me. If things go well for Debbie during the trial separation, I firmly believe the move will be permanent."

“And you’re willing to let it play out either way.”

“What else could I do? Anyway, I immediately realized, that in addition to preparing Hannah for the separation, I had to find a solution to the professional crisis the separation would cause me.

“I felt certain that the conservative trustees and most of the local ministers would see the separation as justification for a renewed effort to get me fired. I could even imagine their rants: His own wife could not live with him.

“I knew that Catherine and Georgette would do their best to defend me, but I was tired of that battle. Now, Catherine and I are working on a plan that, if successful, will allow me to stay.”

“Well, that has elevated my sinking spirit. Can you share the plan with me?”

“Starting in January, I’ll be commuting to Columbia, two days a week, to study contemporary poetry and fiction at the University of South Carolina. Otherwise, I’ll be right here.”

“Thank God.”

“Catherine’s goal is to get me reappointed as a Professor of Humanities. If this happens, I will stay at Cooper. But there’s no guarantee that she can pull this off.”

“Just know that I will be desperately hoping that she will achieve that goal.”

“Whatever happens, I can deal with my own destiny. If I have to resign, I will find something to do. But you have no idea how devastated I was when Debbie told me she wanted a trial separation. I immediately moved into the guest bedroom.”

“May I ask a personal question?”

“Ask me whatever you wish.”

“What happens if things don’t work out for Debbie and she comes home? Will you move back into the bedroom with her?”

“No. If she comes back, she will be retreating from some failure and seeking sanctuary for Hannah. There had been no romantic intimacy in our bedroom for some time before she asked for a separation, and I have no expectation of ever restoring it. That aspect of our marriage is forever dead.”

“Surely you know that I’m in love with you.”

The silence was heavy as he studied how to answer.

“What about your vow never to get involved with another married man.”

"I made that vow before I met you. You're a different kind of married man. I trust you, because I'm confident you will tell me the truth."

"Until Debbie physically moves, I'm frozen at the level of friendship. There's nothing certain about her move.

"Something could happen here or in Louisville that would keep her from moving. If that happened, my duty to Hannah would prevail over everything else. But you must know how deeply I care about you."

"What if Debbie does move to Louisville?"

"I will still be a married man. Debbie believes that the teaching of the Bible allows her to separate from me but not for me to divorce her, and I've promised that I will not force one on her.

"Any intimate relationship that you and I could establish would likely fail you in the end."

"I'm a strong woman, and I'll be happy with you even if we aren't married."

"Are you sure about that?"

"Absolutely. I want us to move beyond friendship with all my being."

"I too would like that, but as I said, I cannot currently move beyond friendship. If Debbie does physically leave me, I will offer you my heart and all that goes with it. Damn whatever else happens. I can deal with it."

He rose to meet her as she rushed into his arms. This time she kissed him passionately until he pulled back.

"You did understand the *if* part?"

"Yes, but even a conditional promise needs an appropriate response."

"Angie, I was anxious about how this day would go, but you have given me new hope."

"And you have given me my heart's desire. This is the most wonderful day of my life."

"I'm confident our day will come, but confidence does not guarantee the future. Meantime, we can enjoy being together in our own special ways."

"Oh, yes, I love our own special ways. Barsh, when did you know I was the right woman for you?"

"I knew that first evening with you that you possessed everything I needed in a woman. The very things that were missing in my life.

"Duty, however, demanded that I rein in my heart. And as I've told you before, I didn't believe you would take the position at Cooper if it were offered to you. Even if you did, I saw no way I could untangle my bonds of duty. But I chose to hang onto your friendship because it was good for me. It's too early for me to talk about love, but please know that it's here in my heart."

"Don't worry. You've told me all I need to know for now."

"Thanks for understanding my situation. Can I assume you are still interested in hiking to the Pacolet River?"

"I am dressed for hiking and ready to go."

"Then let's get lunch started. We'll eat a little early. I don't want us to be pressed for time. Would you like to fix the salad while I'm grilling the beef kabobs?"

"With a heart overflowing with love."

"Good. But first, I'd like to show you some of the things I've made using my newly acquired earth skills."

She followed him to the green bedroom, and there, spread out on the bed, were trousers, shirt, hunting bag, gathering bag, a pouch for sharp flakes of flint for cutting, and a quiver. All were made from deer hides that he had tanned. He had also displayed the bow and the arrows that he had made.

"I still have several buckskin items that I intend to make, including moccasins, outer boots fashioned like Eskimo mukluks, a cloak resembling a poncho, and a sleeping bag."

"I'm astonished. If I didn't know you so well, I'd have a hard time believing this."

"Okay, let's get lunch underway. I'm eager to take you to a special place on the Pacolet River, a place that now belongs to me."

Chapter Thirty-Six

They sat on a granite ledge overlooking the Pacolet River. Barsh had shared with Angela his practice of musing on whatever entered his mind as he watched the currents drift by, and she wanted to try it.

"I love this place," she said breaking the silence. "Sitting here beside you is like being in paradise. Please tell me your thoughts as you watched the currents drift by."

"Don't you want to go first?"

"No, I would likely embarrass you."

"Okay, I envisioned paddling a canoe, with you in the bow, all the way to the Hampton Plantation beside the Santee River in Coastal South Carolina. It was truly a fantasy, but it was also symbolic of the fact that I'd like to travel widely with you. I want to share the world with you if our day should come."

"I know you must stick with *if*," she said, "but I'm going to believe that our day *will* come. I love the idea of traveling widely with you. Please share your vision of our journey to the Hampton Plantation in a canoe."

"I pushed off from the bank, and we rode the Pacolet currents to the Broad River. Then we paddled down the Broad to Columbia, where it joins forces with the Saluda River to form the Congaree.

"About twenty miles below Columbia, we drifted by the Congaree Swamp National Monument, the largest track of old-growth bottomland forest remaining in the United States and a wonderful place to visit."

"The Congaree Swamp National Monument," she said emphasizing the word *swamp*.

"That's the designation Congress gave the place, but swamp is misleading. The river occasionally floods the huge bottomland but then drains. Most of the land is dry for most of the year. The biodiversity of the place is amazing, and the significant thing is that it is now protected as a wilderness area.

"There's a welcome center and various hiking trails. There's also an effort underway to make the place South Carolina's first National Park, and I believe that will soon happen.

"It's on my list of places I'd like to take you hiking, but I do not wish to take you any place where you would be uncomfortable."

"The word *swamp* shot a jolt of anxiety through me, but as long as we're not wading through snake infested water, I'm good to go at your earliest convenience."

"Hopefully, we can make it before the end of this semester. If not, I'll take you next semester."

"Sounds like a good field trip to me. Now, take me back to our river voyage to the Hampton Plantation. I assume it's a special destination for you."

"Your assumption is correct. After passing the Congaree Swamp National Monument, we paddled to the confluence of the Congaree and Wateree. They form the Santee that originally spilled totally into the Atlantic Ocean.

"At the Santee-Cooper hydro-electric dam, most of the water is now diverted, by a canal, to the Cooper River that goes to Charleston, but you and I stuck with what was left of the Santee, until we docked the canoe at the Hampton Plantation and visited the old plantation house.

"Well, so much for fantasy, but this plantation is on my list of places I'd like to take you, but we'll travel to the Carolina Low-country by car and stay in the Charleston Place Hotel. Then sometime during our stay in the old city, we'll drive up the coast about forty miles to the Hampton Plantation.

"I'm amazed at the physical feat of the West African slaves who built the old rice fields of the plantation, dyke by dyke. Then they built trunks to control the flow of fresh water into the fields as needed.

"When the ocean tide came in, pushing the fresh water of the Santee to the surface, the slaves would open those trunks and flood the fields. Then they would close the trunks and the fields would stay flooded after the tide ebbed.

"The old rice fields are all in ruins, but the big house has been restored by Archibald Rutledge, who was born and reared there. The place is now a State Park.

"Rutledge was the first Poet Laureate of South Carolina. Do you know his poetry?"

"No, do you?

"I've only read his memoir *Home by the River.*"

"Then we need to read some of his poetry."

"I agree. Angie, I love Coastal Carolina almost as much as I do the Carolina mountains, and I have a long list of places I'd like to take you. For me it's a wonderland filled with natural and cultural riches. I've been visiting the Lowcountry for years and have not exhausted my list of places I want to experience."

"And you know me. I want to experience them with you."

She took his hand, kissed it, and clasped it to her breast as they absorbed the beauty of the day.

"Changing the subject," he said, "I need to tell you about a plan I've been working on for months. If Debbie leaves for Louisville by the end of this semester, I intend to spend the Christmas break in the wild, living off the land and the Tallapoosa River.

"I'll take nothing with me except the things I've made with my own hands. I want to experience what it's like to live in a state of total dependence on myself and nature."

"Wow! Only you could envision such a journey. Now I understand your focus on the old earth skills. I like your plan and will be waiting for you with open arms when you return."

"I hate to say so but we should head back."

"But we can return, right? I love this spot by the river."

"As often as we wish."

He helped her down from the ledge, and they left for the farmhouse.

"Do you realize you haven't shown me the pottery you've made?"

"It's in the barn. We can swing by on the way back."

"Does the barn have a hayloft?"

"It has a fine loft with some leftover hay."

"That gives me an image to get excited about."

"Oh, yes, that's why I mentioned the leftover hay. The feed room is another enticing place in the barn for ecstatic bonding."

"Uh . . . how does that work?"

"On top of several sacks of crushed grain."

"Okay, I'm game. I'll dream about it, too. Lead us to the barn, and I promise to be a good girl. Speaking of the barn, have you had a chance to talk to Susan about a horse for me?"

"Yes, Friday evening, and we're worked out a deal."

"But what if I can't afford one of her horses? I'll have to borrow the money."

"The money part is between Susan and me."

"I'm at a loss as what to say."

"There's nothing to say. She has four colts and five fillies that she will train next spring. From those she will pick one for herself, and then she wants us to come for a visit. We'll get our pick before she sells the others."

"I'm amazed by her generosity as well as yours."

"She's wonderful in every way and so are you."

***

Back in the den of the old farmhouse, they talked briefly about the week ahead.

"Angie, parting has never been so difficult for me, but it's time for me to head home."

"I understand the duality of your situation, but even as we separate, I anticipate our coming together again. I wish I could tell you how much I love you. But you want me to hold on to the unspoken words that swell in my heart, don't you?"

"For the time being, yes. As long as Debbie is living with me, I want us to be caring but restrained. On campus, I may seem distant, distracted, or even aloof at times.

"When we are together with Hannah, we can be playful, even a bit flirtatious. I want her to see that we are special friends, who might be well suited for a deeper relationship."

"I'll try to strike the right balance, but you know how I tend to get carried away."

"I have a surprise for you," he said. "I'm sending you home with a gift. I'll be right back."

He retrieved the Carrick Creek painting from the blue bedroom, and returning to the den, he held it before him with its back to her.

"Want to guess what it is?"

"The Carrick Creek painting," she said and took the painting. "I love it. Thank you, my dear man, but I don't understand. Did you purchase it?"

"That's the deal I worked out while you and Hannah were shopping next door. I went back that Wednesday afternoon and picked it up. I've been waiting for an appropriate occasion to give it to you."

“I could not be more surprised, and yet, it’s so you.”

“Just know that it’s from my heart. Okay, I’ll ride with you and unlock the gate. Then I’ll walk back and quickly take care of a few things.”

Angela said her goodbyes to the house, and they left in her Volvo. She stopped at the locked gate and faced him.

“Today has been wonderful beyond words,” she said, “and I will cherish it forever. My heart is overflowing.”

“It was an extraordinary day. I’m more at ease with myself than I’ve been in a long time. And you . . . you are so special I could not be more amazed if you had fallen from the night sky.”

“That is the dearest thing anyone has ever said to me.”

“See you at Cooper, tomorrow.”

“Yes, tomorrow.”

He unlocked the gate and watched her drive away. When she disappeared around the curve, he walked back to the old farmhouse.

Chapter Thirty-Seven

When Barsh woke from an erotic dream, the bedroom was still bathed in darkness. In the dream, Angela and he were making love in the green bedroom at the farm. He wished that he could will himself back into the exhilaration of the dream, but its emotional power was gone, leaving only a memory of the dream.

It was twenty minutes before his usual time to get up, but he left the bed and headed for the bathroom. Then he dressed and eased into the kitchen, where he found Debbie eating breakfast.

"I hope I didn't wake you," she said. "I'll be going to the office early and staying late this week. I have tons of work to complete before I leave for Louisville next Wednesday to look for a house. I'm sorry Davis has this week off to visit her sister in Columbia."

"Don't worry. I'll take care of Hannah."

He got a cup of coffee and sat down across the table for Debbie.

"I've decided to sell my business to Joann. If things don't work out at Dugan, Johnson and Bennett, I'll start my own accounting firm in Louisville. That's the only place I've ever been happy. I think my emotional health will improve once I get settled there."

"I assume you have thought through this carefully, and there's no turning back."

"That's right."

"Then I wish you well, now and always."

"I talked to our lawyer last week, and I think we should execute a permanent separation."

"Was that Jack Kelley's advice?"

"Given my beliefs against divorce and my intentions, he suggested that we consider a permanent separation, and that's what I'll like to do."

"What stipulations do you want?"

"They should include our agreement about Hannah. Beyond that, I want my accounting firm, which I'm selling, my savings and investment accounts, my personal things, and the furniture I told you I'm taking to Louisville. You can have this house, the farm, and your savings and investment accounts.

"You should modify your trust fund so that Hannah is now the sole beneficiary. We'll also need to change our wills to reflect the separation agreement."

"That seems fair to me. We'll both be responsible for Hannah and her education."

"I suggest we use Jack Kelly to handle the legal aspect of the separation," she said.

"That's fine with me."

"I'll call him this morning and get him started. I'll need this done before I close on a house. Barsh, I can't thank you enough for your support and cooperation."

"Please know that I will always love you as Hannah's mother even if I take up with another woman."

"Wouldn't that be committing adultery?"

"Not in my book. The permanent separation will annul our vows. The only thing left will be the legal record that prohibits me from marrying someone else. No, I will not call it adultery."

"Then I'll leave that between you and God," she said and left for work.

He got a second cup of coffee and sat in his study. His assumption about Debbie's intention had just been confirmed. She had planned, all along, never to return to Ashland, once she got to Louisville.

The good news for him was that she had finally leveled with him. As soon as the separation agreement was legally executed, he would feel free to consummate his relationship with Angela.

***

After dropping Hannah at school, he drove to Cooper and hurried upstairs. Angela had not left for her eight o'clock class, so he stopped at her office door.

"Good morning," she said with a big smile. "I trust you had a good weekend."

"Oh, yes, and you?"

"Super special. Someone slipped a letter under your door this morning. Well, I'm off to class. See you later."

He unlocked the office door and picked up the letter that Angela had addressed to *Dr. Barsh Roberts*. Settled at his desk, he read the most passionate words that had ever been addressed to him.

She concluded the letter by stating that she had carefully considered all aspects of their relationship and was ready to consummate it without any expectation of marriage. There was nothing holding her back, but she respected his need to wait until Debbie moved to Louisville.

Based on Angela's letter and Debbie's decision to execute a permanent separation, he was now prepared to move beyond friendship to intimacy before Debbie moved to Louisville. But he would wait until a firm date had been set to execute the separation agreement before telling Angela. Meantime, he would teach his classes, take care of Hannah, and mark the days.

Chapter Thirty-Eight

The following Monday morning, Barsh sat in the study with a second cup of black coffee. Debbie had left early for work. The papers for the permanent separation had been prepared, and they were scheduled to sign them at three o'clock on Tuesday afternoon. She was leaving for Louisville early Wednesday to look for a house and would not return until sometime the next week.

Dressed for school, Hannah greeted him from the kitchen door, fixed her cereal, ate it, and joined him in the study.

"Hannah, I'm thinking this Saturday might be a good time for the midnight outing I promised you and Angela. Debbie will be in Kentucky, you know."

"I'm ready."

"I'll clear it with Angela as soon as I get a chance. Don't forget that Davis is back home and will pick you up after school this week."

"I won't."

"Well, it's time for me to get you there."

***

Angela was descending the front steps of Kimberly Hall on the way to her first class, as he rounded the corner from the parking lot. She stopped to wait for him.

"Good morning," she said."

He stepped closer and whispered, "I have a major update to share."

"Out with it."

"Debbie and I are signing a permanent separation agreement tomorrow at three o'clock. Would you like to meet me at the farm Wednesday afternoon at two?"

"I will be there with a jubilant heart."

"The days of *if* and *when* are over for me. Be prepared for whatever the afternoon may bring."

"I'm packed and ready."

"You probably won't see a lot of me before Wednesday."

"Just two more days. I'm an excited woman."

She left for class, and he hurried to his office where he found another love letter from her. He read it with pleasure and locked it in the file cabinet.

It was time to bring Dean Thompson up to date. He dialed her direct line.

"Catherine Thompson."

"Catherine—"

"I was hoping you would call. How are you?"

"Actually, I'm doing much better. Can you see me between ten and eleven?"

"No, but I can see you now."

"I'm on my way. Bye"

The Dean welcomed him in her tender way, and they sat facing each other in their usual chairs. He shared with her Debbie's latest plans, and they agreed to wait until she was all set to move before telling the members of the Division of Humanities about the separation and sabbatical.

"Barsh, have you shared this latest update with Angela?"

"I just whispered it to her as she was leaving for her first class. We will soon be moving to an intimate relationship. I will be discrete. Even so, I will likely experience negative repercussions, and I'm prepared to deal with whatever happens.

"You have had to defend me too many times over the years, and I regret the burden that has caused you. Maybe I don't belong in this conservative community. The last thing I want to do is to cause you more trouble."

"Don't say that. You are the best Cooper has, to say nothing of our friendship. Thankfully, I have good news to share. Georgette has agreed to endow a Professor of Humanities. She and I are working on the details.

"This will give me the final weapon I'll need to defend you against our conservative trustees. So, please don't think about resigning."

"That is good news, very good news. What would I do without you two in my corner? I do want to stay at Cooper."

"Please keep this to yourself until you hear from Georgette."

He left the Dean's Office, picked up his mail at the college post office, and went back to his office to await his nine o'clock class. His mind was tending to business, but his heart was counting the hours until his rendezvous with Angela on Wednesday.

Chapter Thirty-Nine

Barsh waited for Angela in the farmhouse yard that Wednesday afternoon. He was dressed in a royal blue velvet jacket, a white silk shirt, and black pants. His heart responded with a faster beat at the sight of Angela's Volvo easing up the gravel lane. She parked and ran for his embrace and a long kiss.

"My dearest Barsh, I love you. I love you. I love you."

"And I love you with equal measure."

"How good it is to hear those words from your mouth."

"How good it feels to release them on this beautiful November day. Ride with me to lock the gate."

"Yes, the gate. I do like the privacy it gives us, and I've never longed for it more than today."

He kissed her again and they left in his Audi to lock the gate.

"You look stunning in that evening dress and white jacket. I assume you know the dress holds a special place in my memory. I joyously felt your sensuous body through it as we danced our one dance in the Cooper gym. I wanted to take you back on the dance floor, but knew the ramifications would not be good for me."

"Yes, I could read your mind, and I understood your reticence. Please know that I'm delighted to see that you also dressed in remembrance of that night. How long can we stay?"

"Three hours. Davis will pick up Hannah at school and stay with her until five.

"Here's the latest on Debbie. She left early this morning for Louisville to buy a house and won't be back until next week. That means I'll have Hannah this weekend. Could we do the midnight outing this Saturday?

"That would be perfect for me."

"Okay, meet us here, Saturday morning around eight. We'll have breakfast together before we take to the road. By the way, Hannah knows I've told you about the separation."

"Thanks for letting me know. I'll give her a lot of attention."

"Please do. She needs it."

He locked the gate, and they headed back to the farmhouse, brimming with love and buoyed by anticipation.

Back at the old farmhouse, she got her cloth bag from the Volvo, and they walked, hand in hand, into the den where he had champagne chilling. They draped their jackets over the back of the couch. He popped the cork and filled two glasses.

"To love as true as the North Star," he said and they drank.

"To love as true as the North Star," she said and they drank.

He set their glasses on the coffee table, and taking her hands in his, he looked into her eyes.

"Angie, I love you truly and commit myself to you and you alone."

"Barsh, I love you truly and commit myself to you and you alone."

There was slow dancing and kissing in the old den as love worked its erotic magic on them. Then he lifted her in his arms and carried her to the green bedroom, where they alternately stripped naked, one garment at a time.

***

They lay naked on the bed with their hearts slowing to a normal rhythm. He took her hand and kissed it. They were in no hurry to leave the bed, and a comforting silence settled over them that lasted for a few minutes.

"Barsh, I've never felt so totally loved."

"Nor have I."

"I assume you don't want us to go public with our relationship until you return from the wild."

"I think that will be better for us in the long run, but I will not deny our relationship even before Debbie vacates the house if the need arises.

"Just know that I am, as of this day, totally committed to you in every way. There will be negative fallout for us, but with you, I can weather anything."

"And so can I with you by my side. Do you know when you will tell Hannah about us?"

"I want her to discover on her own that there's more to our relationship than friendship. She's very observant and will soon reach that conclusion if she hasn't already. As soon as I suspect she's on to us, I'll have an honest talk with her."

"I think she's already on to us."

"You're probably right. If she isn't, she likely will be before the weekend is over. I have a special plan for our midnight outing that will certainly have her thinking about the nature of our relationship."

"I do like the sound of that."

"Angie, this wedding ring is coming off as soon as Debbie leaves the house for the last time. In spite of the law, I do not consider myself married to her. When I return from Alabama, I'd like to give you a ring to mark my commitment to you. Is that okay with you?"

"Oh, yes. You are such a romantic."

"I used to take pride in thinking I was a romantic. Then I read a biography of Faulkner and discovered the depth of the malady in his love letters. For the first time, I realized it's a sickness."

"Only if you never find your true lover."

"That's a good observation. I guess I'd lost faith in romantic love."

"My faith in romantic love was dead, dead," she said. "Then I found you at the only time in your life when you would have been open to me. How is that for a miraculous wonder?"

"I feel the same way, and it truly is a miraculous wonder for me. Let's dress and talk by the fire until we have to part ways for a while.

"I'll have to change back into my usual attire. Otherwise, Hannah won't understand why I'm wearing my fancy clothes."

"You take the bathroom first."

"Okay, I'll be out in less than five minutes."

Standing beside the bed, he looked lovingly at her naked body.

"You remind me of a refrain from the Song of Solomon: How beautiful you are, my love. Oh, how beautiful you are."

She beckoned him with her arms and he filled them, again.

***

They sat by the flickering fire in the old den as the minutes ticked toward their time of departure. He was trying to plan ahead.

"Angie, do you have commitments for Thanksgiving break?"

"No, do you have something in mind for us."

"A getaway, just you and me. Debbie and Hannah will be visiting the Whalens in Kentucky. Her goal is to close on a house and return on Sunday. We'll have four days and nights to do as we please. Would you like to go to Hilton Head Island?"

"Yes! Tell me more about the Island. I've heard it's a wonderful resort."

"That's true. It also has a significant population of permanent residents, which means the new developments are overwhelming the old Gullah culture.

"The general consensus is that it's just a matter of time before all the Sea Islands of South Carolina will be developed, and the *make-do* ways of the Gullah people will be doomed."

"Tell me about the Gullah people."

"They are the descendants of the African slaves who remained on those islands after the emancipation. Largely isolated, they developed a special culture that is now being threatened. Have you read Pat Conroy's *The Water Is Wide?*"

"No, please tell me about it."

"Our wonderful librarian, Amanda McGee, put me onto it. Before deciding to become a librarian, she taught school in Beaufort, the second oldest town in South Carolina.

"It's also the closest thing Conroy has to a hometown. The book is based on his experience of teaching a group of Gullah children on Daufuskie Island, that's located just off the southwestern end of Hilton Head Island.

"Conroy's father was a Marine fighter pilot, who was stationed at the Marine Corps Air Station in Beaufort, during Pat's last years of high school. After finishing Beaufort High, he attended The Citadel, Charleston's famous military college.

"After graduation, he came back to Beaufort where he taught at the high school for a while. He then taught the Gullah children on Daufuskie Island, until his liberal views and style of teaching got him fired.

"There's no bridge to Daufuskie, thus the title *The Water is Wide.* Conroy was astonished to learn that some of the children he taught had never left the Island, and he took it upon himself to take them to Beaufort and beyond on various field trips.

"Now it will be my pleasure to find someone to take us to Daufuskie by boat. Hannah and I have been twice. It's a good experience with dolphin sightings on the ride there and back."

"And you know me. I'll be ready to go. Has Conroy written anything else?"

"He has a novel, *The Great Santini,* published a couple of years ago. It's about a sensitive boy growing up under the demands of a violent father, who is a Marine fighter pilot. Highly autobiographical, its setting is a fictional version of Beaufort. Actually, it's my favorite coming-of-age novel with a male protagonist."

"You're ranking it above Salinger's *The Catcher in the Rye*?"

"I'm in no position to rank the two on the basis of literary merit. But in terms of story and protagonist, I'll take *The Great Santini*."

"Can I assume that the theme is about a sensitive boy finding his way in a violent environment without losing his sensitivity?"

"Yes, and that resonated with me. Fortunately for me, the violence I encountered growing up in Alabama was outside my family. I had a wonderful role model in my father, who, as you know, introduced me to the values of being close to nature.

"I also connected in other ways with aspects of male culture in the South. I had football, for example. Any red-blooded Southern boy had to demonstrate his manhood by sports, especially football in Alabama.

"Conroy's protagonist had basketball. So, neither of us was totally alienated from the male domain. But in terms of our sensibilities, we were not your typical Southern boy."

"I am very well aware that you were not a typical Southern boy. Now I want to read both books. Could I borrow yours?"

"I'll bring them to you, tomorrow. Angie, I'd like to make reservations this week for our trip to Hilton Head Island. We can stay at a beachside hotel or we can rent an oceanfront condo."

"Do you have a preference?"

"I like the idea of an oceanfront condo. It will give us total privacy, like having our own fully-furnished apartment. I know the perfect place. And here's something I think you'll like about the location. The Tiki Hut, a beach bar with live music every evening, is just a short walk up the beach. It's a favorite hangout with locals and tourists."

"Yes, let do that condo. How is the beach there?"

"Great. When the tide is out, there are twelve miles of packed sand, good for walking or bike-riding. I've covered all twelve miles by biking and by walking.

"I like to experience the beach early in the morning and late afternoon. I also like to walk the beach at night.

"There's one stretch of wild oceanfront that has not yet been developed. It's a good place to sit against the sand dunes and watch the starry sky, especially when you can catch the moon rising out of the ocean."

"You will take me to those dunes one night, right?"

"You can count on it and a lot of other good things. I've been vacationing at Hilton Head Island for twelve years, and I've always spent time exploring the Island and beyond. There are a lot of places I want to share with you. More than we could ever experience on this visit.

"If you like our Thanksgiving visit, we'll return often. Meantime, we'll meet here, whenever we can.

"If only I could stretch out this day, I would. Being no miracle worker, I have to tell you it's time for us to part ways for today. But what a day!"

"I keep repeating myself, but I can say without a doubt this has been the best day of my life."

Chapter Forty

He left the farm and drove straight home. Somewhere between the farm and Fern Meadows, his thoughts shifted from Angela to Hannah. It was time to tell her that the separation would be permanent. He parked and entered the den, where Davis was waiting for him.

"Dr. Roberts, Hannah and I have been discussing the move to Louisville. I've decided to take the offer."

"My dear woman, I will praise you all the days of my life for this decision. I am so relieved to hear this. It's going to make the separation so much easier for Hannah and me."

"Well, I'm feeling good about it," she said and left.

He called Hannah and she answered from his study, where she was working on a new poem.

"Hey, my sweet girl, how wonderful to know Davis is going to live with you and Debbie in Louisville."

"Yeah, she told me first thing when she picked me up at school."

"I hope you didn't have any bad moments at school."

"I tried not to think about the move. I focused on getting to stay with you until Christmas break."

"Good strategy. Has Debbie called?"

"About an hour ago. She made it to Louisville and will start looking for a house in the morning."

"I'm sure she'll find a suitable house in a good neighborhood."

"Whatever she does about a house will be okay with me."

"Did you tell her that Davis is accepting her offer?"

"Davis answered the phone and she told her."

"Hannah, I hate to tell you, but this is going to be a permanent move. Debbie told me that she will start her own accounting firm in Louisville if things don't work out at Dugan, Johnson and Bennett. She said categorically that she will never live with me, again."

"You were right in thinking the move would be permanent," she said without crying.

"Okay, let's talk about this. At Debbie's request, we got a lawyer to draw up a permanent separation agreement according to our stipulations. We both signed it, yesterday."

He retrieved the document from the desk drawer and handed it to her.

"This is it. You can read it anytime. The things I told you about us are now legally binding. You can spend holidays and summers with me. I can visit you at any time during the school year.

"Meantime, you and I have lots of good things to do before I have to take you to Louisville, including our outing with Angela this Saturday. We can make the best of a bad situation if we keep the right attitude."

"I'm trying to keep a good attitude."

"Trust me. This move will not keep us apart for long at a time. And here's something I want you to remember. If at any time something goes wrong in Louisville, call me and I'll be there to address whatever the trouble might be."

"What do you mean?"

"Well, suppose Debbie starts seeing someone who is unkind to you."

"Do you think Mother might start seeing someone?"

"Truthfully, I don't know what she might do. Here's my point. If things should change in any way that would make life with your mother more troubling, I will intervene and fight to get custody of you."

"That's good to know," she said and studied him as if she wanted to ask him something.

"What are you thinking about?"

"You and Angela."

"As you know from your observations, she and I enjoy a lot of the same things. We've been friends from the first, and now we're very close. We're good for each other. But whatever the future holds for us, it will not change my relationship with you.

"You've been an integral part of my life since the day you were born. On numerous occasions, I bottle fed you, changed your diaper, bathed and dressed you, rocked you to sleep, comforted you in the night when you cried, and the list goes on.

"Now you are almost twelve years old, soon to be living with your mother in Louisville, soon to be charting your own course toward independence from us. And whatever happens, I will continue to love and support you in every possible way, until my last breath."

"I know that. But I need to know about you and Angela. Do you love her? It's obvious that she loves you."

"Yes, I love her. Over the years, there have been women who have shown a romantic interest in me, even though they knew I was married, but I never let any of them get close to me. I didn't intend for it to happen with Angela but it did."

"Are you going to marry her?"

"Unless I break my promise to your mother and divorce her, marrying Angela is not an option."

"Does she know this?"

"I've been totally honest with her. As things now stand, we have three options. We can end our relationship. We can keep our relationship as it is and live separately. Or we can live together, openly, as if we were married, which is what we plan to do at some future date. I do not wish to live out my life alone."

"I think Angela is the best, and like you said, you are good for each other. I like your plan."

"That's good to hear. Angela will also be pleased to know that you approve our plan. You can tell her this weekend."

"Daddy, can we spend the night at the farm, Friday?"

"Good idea. Now that Debbie's away in Louisville, we can do whatever we'd like to do, this weekend."

"Yeah, and during holidays and summers."

"You're as right as right can be."

Chapter Forty-One

Early Saturday morning, Barsh sat in the den of the old farmhouse with his first cup of black coffee. He was thinking about Debbie, who had sounded so elated when he talked with her by phone, Friday evening. She had found the perfect house in the neighborhood where she had dreamed of living, when she worked as Henry Dugan's assistant.

The date for closing on the house was set for Friday after Thanksgiving. Once more, he had wished her success and happiness in Louisville, and she thanked him for supporting her in the move.

The sound of Hannah's feet, pattering to the bathroom, redirected his thoughts to her. The commode soon flushed, and she joined him in the den.

"Good morning, my sweet girl."

"How long have you been up?"

"Not long. Did you sleep well?"

"Finally. I was so excited about our outing with Angela I couldn't go to sleep."

"Take a pillow and you can indulge yourself with a nap while we're traveling."

"I don't want to miss out on anything you two might say. Your conversations are always interesting."

"Well, I suggest you take a pillow, just in case you get sleepy. Hannah, I'm thinking about inviting Angela to spend the night with us here at the farm. I'd hate to send her home after midnight."

"Then invite her."

"Okay, if she accepts, she can have the green bedroom. I'll sleep on the couch. We'd better get moving. I'll go unlock the gate while you get dressed. Then you can help me in the kitchen."

The morning sky was clear. It would be a good day for hiking in the mountains. He drove to the gate, unlocked it, and headed back to the house. Hannah was waiting for him at the kitchen table.

"If you'll cut up a bowl of fruit, I'll scramble the eggs. Angela should be here any minute."

"Daddy, she praises you for connecting her with nature, and she loves our outings. That's mostly what we talked about when we met on Thursday. Not our writing."

"Well, I trust this one will live up to her expectations."

"Whatever we do, we'll be together. And that's always fun."

At the sound of her car, they rushed outside to greet her. He kissed her on the cheek. She embraced Hannah with sweet affection.

"The day of our midnight outing has finally arrived," she said. "I was so pumped with anticipation last night that I had a hard time getting to sleep."

"I had the same problem," Hannah said.

He opened the door and followed them into the house. While they helped their plates, he poured orange juice for everyone and then coffee for Angela and himself.

"Angie, please sit here at the end of the table, so Hannah and I can both sit beside you."

"My, how dear of you," she said as he seated her and then helped his plate.

"Okay," he said after taking his seat, "I have a full day planned for us. Anybody want to guess what's on the agenda?"

"A hike in the mountains," Hannah said. "You did say dress for a hike."

"Yes, but where in the mountains will we be hiking? That's the question."

"Give us a clue," Angela said.

"The place is named for an American poet."

"Oh, you're taking us to the Joyce Kilmer Memorial Forest."

"That's our primary destination."

"Hannah, when I flew down for the job interview, Barsh promised to take me there if I got the job. Now he's honoring that promise and my spirit is soaring."

"Yes, and you're going to be amazed by the huge yellow poplars and hemlocks," he said.

"What else have you planned for us, Daddy?"

"Our first scheduled stop will be Highlands, North Carolina, about a three-hour drive, and much of that will be in the Carolina mountains. We'll explore some of the art galleries and have an early lunch at the Old Edwards Inn. Then we'll drive to the Joyce Kilmer Memorial Forest with at least one stop along the way.

"Not far from Highlands, we'll stop beside the Chullasaja River and do something I think you both will enjoy. I know it will be a first for you, Hannah, and possibly for you, Angie."

"Then you've done it before," Angela said.

"Once, but it will be more fun with you two. Anyone want to guess what we'll be doing there?"

"Whitewater rafting?" Angela asked.

"No, but it does involve whitewater."

"Give us a hint," Angela said.

"I'll just tell you. We're going to experience a special place called Dry Falls. Here's the fun part. We'll take a walk behind this thundering waterfall to the other side of the Chullasaja River without getting wet."

"That will definitely be a first for me," Angela said. "This is shaping up to be a great day. And it can't end before midnight."

"That was Daddy's promise."

"Don't worry. We'll be up past midnight. Angie, we'd like for you to spend the night with us. You can have the green bedroom and I'll take the couch. I know it's a late invitation, but we can swing by your place for sleepwear, *etcetera*."

"Not a problem. I accept your invitation, but I don't want to waste time going by the house."

"Let me share this," he said. "After we leave the Kilmer Memorial Forest, the most distant point on our outing, we'll take a different route back by way of Asheville and dine at the Grove Park Inn. Then we'll come back here to celebrate the midnight hour. But I'm not sharing the details, until we get back."

"I love the agenda, Barsh."

"Thanks. Unless anyone wants seconds, let us take to the road. We have things to do and things to do before we sleep."

***

The outing in the Carolina mountains had gone exceedingly well, and they were fast closing the distance back to the farm. Hannah, who was curled up with her pillow in the backseat of the Audi, had not spoken for some time. Barsh assumed she was asleep, and that validated his reason for taking the Audi over the Ford pickup with its single broad seat.

"Angie, I know you must be tired. I'm afraid my plan for today was too ambitious. I thought we would be back at the farm by nine, and it's already after ten."

"The whole outing was marvelous. I would not have missed anything we experienced."

"Daddy, I agree with Angela. Are we almost home?"

"Twenty minutes at the most. Have you been asleep?

"I've been listening to you two."

"Well, I hope we didn't bore you," Angela said.

"Listening to you two was the best part of the day for me. Daddy talks to me some when we're on a long trip, but mostly he just drives and thinks about things. You two talk about the most interesting things."

Barsh knew she was contrasting the outing with those long trips to Kentucky when there was no interesting conversation between Debbie and him.

"Well, my dear daughter, Angie and I have limited time for good conversations at Cooper. All the driving time has made this a good day for talking. We might even talk through most of the night."

"Hannah, you can count on that if I have my preference. Time after time, I've thought of something I wanted to discuss with your father, but he would be in class or in a meeting or with a student or gone for the day. Barsh, I would like to talk the whole night through. Is that possible?"

"I'm game."

"What's your plan for the midnight hour, Daddy?"

"I'm holding on to my surprise until the last minute. When we get to the farm, we'll relax around a log fire in the den. It's prepared. All I have to do is strike a match. There'll be hot chocolate for you. Angie and I will have coffee laced with a helping of Baileys."

A deep hush settled over them, except for the tires whining on the rough asphalt road. Angela reached for his right hand and held it in her lap.

Chapter Forty-Two

Half-green hickory logs were sizzling and flaring in the den fireplace of the old farmhouse. Angela and Barsh had finished their coffee lased with Baileys, Hannah her hot chocolate.

"Hannah, I'm brimming with joy to have spent this day with you and Barsh. And now I get to spend the night with you two. I thank my lucky stars that I made this move to Ashland."

"Speaking of stars, it's time to share my midnight surprise. First, I'm taking quilts form the cedar chest and making a thick pallet in the corner of the backyard away from the house.

"Then with each of us cloaked in a blanket, we're going to huddle on the pallet and let the wonders of the night sky dazzle us. Fortunately for us, this is a perfect night for stargazing."

"Let the wonders begin!" Angela exclaimed.

"Daddy. I don't have to go to bed at midnight, do I?"

"There's no set bedtime for you, but I think you should change into your pajamas. Then I can just tuck you in your bed if you should fall asleep on the pallet."

"Can I change now?"

"Jump to it but keep on your socks. Those hiking socks will keep your feet warm.

"Angie, I have sweatsuits if you'd like to change into one."

"Yes, I'd like that."

He led her into the green bedroom and pulled two sweatsuits from the armoire.

"They're too big for you, but they do have drawstrings. Anyway, they should serve us well, later tonight, when you and I have the quilt pallet to ourselves."

She moved into his arms, and they kissed with an eager passion that had tugged at them all day.

"Okay, I'll make the pallet while you change," he said.

He had already mapped out the best place for the pallet and quickly had it in place. Next, he stretched out on top of it and was pleased with the comfort it provided.

Angela and Hannah were engaged in a lively conversation when he returned to the den. He walked past them and stood with his back to the fire.

"Is the pallet ready?" Hannah asked.

"All is ready. The blankets are in the closet next to the bathroom. You two take your pick while I change into a sweatsuit."

In the green bedroom, he noticed that Angela had stripped down to skin for the sweatsuit. Her bra and panties were scattered on the bed with her hiking outfit.

He stripped likewise and clothed his nakedness with the sweatsuit. Then he let down his ponytail.

They cloaked themselves with a blanket. He turned off all the lights and led the way to the pallet.

"The night sky is truly breathtaking," Angela said. "What a perfect way to celebrate our first midnight together."

"Okay, let's see if you two can find the North Star," he said.

"I think you have to find the Little Dipper," Angela said.

"That's right, and I know the next step. Daddy taught me. He used to read me a bedtime story, every night, and one of my favorite books was *The Freedom Star.* That's what the slaves used to call the North Star, because they followed it to freedom in the North when they ran away from their Southern owners.

"I was shocked to learn that people used to own other people. After we discussed that book, Daddy told me about the practice of slavery through the ages. Do you know that the old laws in the Bible allowed parents to sell their children into slavery? The girls for life. The boys for six years, and then they would go free."

"No, that's news to me. I need to take your father's course on the Bible."

"Okay, back to the quest to find the North Star."

"Which way is north," Hannah asked and he pointed.

"I've found the Little Dipper," Angela said.

"Good for you. Let's give Hannah time to find it."

"I've found it, and there's the North Star at the end of the handle."

"Here's an idea," he said. "Let's slowly rotate clockwise and observe as much of the sky above the horizon as possible. When we get back to the Little Dipper, we can stretch out on our backs and study the sky above us."

They followed his suggestion and punctuated their observations with a lot of *wows*. Completing the rotation, they stretched out on the pallet with Hannah in the middle. Within minutes, she complained that she was getting sleepy.

"That's okay," Angela said. "Snuggle up with me and go to sleep."

"Is it midnight, Daddy?"

"Midnight has come and gone. If I'm still asleep when you get up in the morning, that will probably mean that Angie and I stayed up all night. Fix breakfast for yourself and then wake me at ten o'clock."

Angela pulled Hannah into her arms and she was soon fast asleep. Barsh carried her to the blue bedroom and tucked her in. Then he and Angela cuddled on the den couch until he felt certain that Hannah was sound asleep.

"Guess what I'm thinking," he said

"I hope it's the same thing that I am."

He stood, pulled her into his arms, kissed her, and led her from the house.

***

They lay side by side on the pallet with a blanket holding the warmth of their bodies. He reached for her hand and she rolled against him.

"Only you could have envisioned the possibilities of this night—such ecstasy on a pallet with the stars winking at us. I like the way you take care of everything."

"I guess I do have a crazy mind for details," he said and she crawled on top of him.

"Hold me tight," she said and he rocked her in his arms.

"I like the feel of things from up here."

"Then you will have the privilege of steering the ship from there on our next voyage."

"Okay, I'll take the challenge."

"Meantime, what about some scrambled eggs?"

"I'm not hungry but I'd like black coffee. I intend to stay up all night if you'll hang with me."

"I'll be right with you when the sun breaks the horizon."

***

Barsh stood with his back to the fire, waiting for Angela to return from the bathroom. The toilet flushed and she was back in the den.

"Coffee is ready," he said. "Come stand by the fire and I'll bring you a cup."

"I'll go with you as soon as I warm myself."

They got black coffee and returned to the den couch.

"I'm eager to learn more about your plan for a sojourn in the wild during Christmas break. I don't even know where you'll be staying. But first, tell me how you came up with the idea for such a unique and challenging adventure. I cannot imagine another man in the civilized world who would deliberately decide to return to the stone-age for an interim."

"The idea grew out of my struggle to deal with Debbie's decision to move to Louisville for a year-long trial separation. I was totally unprepared for that. It challenged my perception of who I was and what I should be doing with my life.

"As I told you, I could no longer see myself teaching at Cooper after the separation. Yet, I had no idea what I would do. Then several things converged in a way that got me thinking about how, as a boy, I had found strength and grace in the wild as I lived off the land by my own gathering, hunting, and fishing skills.

"From there, I came up with the idea of taking a sabbatical and living in the wild for all the seasons of one year, solely dependent upon myself and nature. This, of course, would require me to learn the old earth skills of Native Americans, which I was prepared to do."

"That's interesting. I didn't know that your original intention was to stay a year."

"Yes, I wanted to journey from our modern technological world back into the natural world of the forest, where I would live alone for one year. Cut off from the civilized world, I would examine the philosophy upon which I had built my life, and hopefully, I would return with an unshakeable understanding of my place in the modern world.

"I'm sure you're familiar with the hero's journey that Joseph Campbell describes in *Hero with a Thousand Faces.* Well, I envisioned myself as another face on such a journey."

"Yes, I'd already made that connection. What caused you to shorten your journey from a year to the Christmas break?"

"I came to my senses and realized that I could not leave Hannah to Debbie's care for a year. Yet, I still needed that journey into the wild. The primary motive remained the same, until a few days ago.

"In my struggle to come to terms with you, I chose to follow my heart and love anew. Thus, I gained the new eyes that I was hoping to acquire in the wild. Now, I simply want the experience of living in a state of total dependence upon nature and myself for a few days. If this seems like an unworthy motive to you, I will scrap the journey."

"No, you must follow through with your adventure."

"Are you sure?"

"Absolutely."

"Then I shall consider it a gift from you."

"No, you have earned the right to make this journey. It's yours to pursue, not mine to give. Now tell me where you will be living."

"There's a small cave in a high bluff overlooking the Tallapoosa River, where I camped for five days during Christmas break of my senior year in high school. That cave will be my camp. I'll fish the river with traps that I've made from split bamboo, I'll hunt rabbits and ducks with my bow and arrows, and I'll gather editable mushrooms."

"I'm stunned by the primal beauty of your vision, to say nothing of all the other things that endear you to me. I've been blindly looking for you all my adult life, not knowing the totality of what I was looking for."

"I know what you mean. We've had some influence over the direction our relationship has taken, but the big things that brought us together were products of good fortune.

"I'm as astonished to find you in the center of my life as Samson, of Biblical times, must have been when he discovered honey in the carcass of a lion."

"I haven't heard that one. Is it part of the Samson and Delilah story?"

"No, this is another story. Before meeting Delilah, he had fallen for a different Philistine woman. Once, on his way to visit her, he turned aside to examine the remains of the lion he had killed on an earlier visit.

“This is how the Biblical narrative reads: and behold, there was a swarm of bees and honey in the carcass of the lion. And he took thereof in his hand and went on eating.

“Ah, the wonder of finding something good, where and when you least expected it.”

“Honey from a lion! What a wonderful metaphor, Barsh. And it’s so appropriate for us.”

It was a night like no other for them. They shifted back and forth from the den to the love-bed under the stars. Then at first light, the lovers cuddled for the last time on those quilts and waited for the sun to break the horizon on a new day.

The Winter Is Past

"Arise, my love, my fair one and come away;
for lo, the winter is past . . ."
— Song of Solomon 2:10-11

Chapter One

Deep within an old forest in Alabama, William Barsh Roberts stood alone on a high bluff overlooking the Tallapoosa, the river of his youth. The western sky was wondrously hued by the setting sun, and for the first time that day, he thought about Angela Kundera.

When he met her nine months ago, they shared a beautiful sunset at Cherokee Falls on the Broad River in South Carolina. Since then, he had not experienced a sunset without thinking about her. Now, he imagined her fixing supper, alone, in her new house in the little college town of Ashland in Upstate South Carolina.

"Be well, Angie," he whispered as a breeze lifted his light brown hair that was cropped just above his shoulders and banded across his forehead with a buckskin strap.

Tall and physically fit, Barsh was dressed in buckskin clothes and moccasins that he had made from brain-tanned deerskins. His equipage, that he had also made, consisted of a long bow, a quiver of arrows fitted with flint points, a hunting bag, a bag for gathering mushrooms, and a pouch with sharp flakes of flint for cutting.

An experienced woodsman who was always aware of his surroundings, he caught the sound of rustling leaves. Someone or something large was coming down the watershed that he had named Bluff Ridge in his youth. He stepped in front of a large oak tree to make himself less noticeable to the unknown eyes that were headed his way.

A deer cleared the underbrush and continued toward him. At twenty yards, the buck turned broadside to proceed upriver and then stopped, nostrils flaring, having caught his scent.

He could have released an arrow for the deer's heart before it dashed off, but he did not raise his bow. Killing the deer would have been unconscionable, not because of any sentimentality but because it would have been a wasteful act. He had only to feed himself, not a clan.

It was the first day of his retreat from modern civilization into the wilds of Alabama, and his hunting bag was empty. He had, however, gathered two varieties of edible mushrooms, that afternoon.

An old woman who lived on the backside of their farm had taught him which ones were edible, and he had added that knowledge to his practice of living off the land, back during his boyhood days of camping in the wild.

There was still a chance that he might kill a duck before returning to his wilderness camp—a small cave about thirty feet below where he was standing, that he had named Bluff Cave. Otherwise, his supper would be limited to the wild mushrooms, but that would cause him no anxiety. He was confident that he could sufficiently feed himself on what he could take from the wild.

As he looked again into the western sky, the sun appeared to be dropping faster—an illusion caused by its proximity to the horizon. Twilight would soon be upon him. Then darkness would smother the last bit of daylight.

From the top of Bluff Ridge, he set out for Cedar Creek, that was about a mile downriver. Based on his boyhood experiences, he thought he might find a few ducks taking refuge for the night. If so, he was intent on killing one.

He walked at a fast pace until he approached the mouth of the creek. Then he slowed until he was taking one light step every ten seconds. Just before he was able to see the surface of the water, he squatted, waddled slowly toward the creek, and stopped. He could hear several ducks muttering to each other.

With bow fitted with an arrow, he stood and shot a male mallard as it lifted in flight. The arrow struck its back near the left wing and dropped it back into the creek, where it flapped about until he retrieved it with the aid of a long stick.

Holding its head in his right hand, he whirled the duck like a propeller until its severed body fell to the ground. As he watched the mallard jumping about in death's throes, he recalled his earliest memory of watching his mother wring a chicken's neck in the backyard of their old farmhouse.

How astonished he was by its headless dance. When the dance ended, his mother butchered the chicken for their Sunday dinner.

That was before they moved to town and bought their poultry at the grocery store, where the dirty work of butchering had been done by someone else. As a fifteen-year-old boy, he volunteered to relieve his mother of that butchering task when they moved back to the county and, once again, raised their own chickens.

It had been twenty-five years since he last killed and butchered anything, and his thoughts shifted to a discussion with the students in his course The Future of Mankind—an interdisciplinary course he had developed for the humanities curriculum at Cooper College in Ashland, South Carolina.

***

Barsh asked the students if any of them had ever killed and butchered a chicken. Not a single hand went up, but heads were shaking.

"I'm not surprised that none of you have undertaken this task," he said. "But you would if you were stranded somewhere for days with nothing to eat but a live chicken."

"Never in a thousand years," Karen McNeely said.

"I understand your strong reaction, Karen. But you do eat chicken, don't you?"

"Yes, but I'd never kill one."

"Given the hypothetical situation of the question, I can believe you wouldn't kill the chicken on the first day. But there's no doubt in my mind that you would kill and eat it, even raw, before you would starve to death."

That comment stopped all the head shaking, but no one confessed they would do such a bloody deed.

"This is one of the problems of modern urban culture," he said. "Most people now live in such artificial environments that they have little or no comprehension of what it would be like to live totally in the natural world or even on a subsistence farm.

"Most people in advanced societies have neither hunted for their food nor raised it. They are thus cut off from the process by which food arrives at stores and restaurants."

No one responded verbally, but he observed a whit of concern etched on a few faces before he shifted to another subject.

***

Refocused on his present moment in time, Barsh picked up the dead duck and dropped it in his hunting bag, where he had already placed the severed head. It and other parts of the duck would make good bait for his fish traps.

With swift strides, he walked up the riverbank to the bottom of Bluff Ridge and carefully worked his way up to Bluff Cave through a thick growth of rhododendron, that hid the cave from the unsuspecting eyes of humans.

He had accidently discovered the cave during his youthful days of exploring the wilds of Alabama. The bluff alone had challenged him to climb it and he took the challenge. Otherwise, he would never have discovered the cave.

During Christmas break of his senior year at Bradley High, he had camped there and lived off the land for five days. That was twenty-six years ago, and he was armed with a twelve-gauge pump shotgun and equipped with modern fishing and camping gear.

Now, he was equipped only with things that he had made with his own hands. With that equipage and his survival skills, he was determined to camp there and live off the land and river for ten days.

He unstrung his bow and leaned it against the cave wall. Then he removed the quiver of arrows and place it next to the bow. It was time to build a fire in the old firepit that he had built, as a boy, near the entrance of the cave. This time, however, he would be using one of the ancient techniques for starting a fire.

He gathered the needed material that he has stored in the cave, and kneeling before the firepit, he struck the flint until he had a spark on the tender. As he blew it gently, it burst into a flame. He then added small twigs, and when they flamed up, he added dead tree limbs of various size until he had a fire that would produce enough hot coals to roast a few mushrooms and the duck.

With a ceramic platter and water mug that he had fired according to the Catawba Indian tradition, he left the cave and hurried upriver to a spring of crystal-clear water, that flowed from the base of the bluff into several small pools before it drained into the Tallapoosa River. He filled the mug, drank deeply, refilled it, and then moved to the lowest pool to butcher the duck.

Kneeling there, he ripped the skin with its feathers from the duck's breast, cut it out with a sharp flake of flint, washed it in the cold water, and sliced it into small pieces, which he placed on the platter.

He put the other parts of the duck in two leather pouches with small holes cut in them. They would be the scent-bait for his two fish traps.

Finished with the butchering, he washed his hands and returned to the cave, where he was pleased to see a glowing bed of red coals under the fire.

He took a stick and pushed the un-burnt limbs to one side of the firepit. It was time to roast a few mushrooms on a hickory skewer and then the duck.

With the mushrooms roasted and cooling in a ceramic bowl, he lowered three pieces of duck over the coals. As he turned them slowly just above the hot coals, puffs of duck-scented smoke found his nostrils, whenever the drippings hit the coals.

That reminded him of Coon Peters, an old woodsman who had taught him so much about how to live in the wild. One of the best days of his youth was when he happened upon the old man, as he was roasting catfish on a skewer at a campsite in an old growth forest beside Wehadkee Creek.

When the first three pieces of duck were done, Barsh blew them cool and ate them. Pausing, he thought about his daughter, who now lived in Louisville with her mother.

He envisioned his precocious Hannah sitting at the new desk in her new bedroom. Perhaps she was writing a new poem. Or maybe she was writing in her journal about life without daily contact with him. She had promised to keep a journal and share it with him, when he returned from the wild.

It was his hope that her early journaling in Louisville would show him that she was adjusting well to the new reality she faced. On second thought, he felt certain that the recent move was causing her a lot of distress, even though she was exceptionally mature for an eleven-year-old.

He believed, without doubt, that she would be happier living with him, but that was not going to happen, at least not in the near future. He would have to make the best of the separation agreement that stipulated Hannah would live with him during summers. She could also visit him during school holidays, and he could visit her, whenever the need arose for her sake or his.

Refocusing his attention on the task at hand, he roasted the other pieces of duck. Then he ate half of them, along with half of the mushrooms. He stored the rest in a ceramic bowl to have for breakfast. His plan was to eat only two meals a day, breakfast and supper.

After rebuilding the fire from the hot coals, he sat watching the blazing flames and began to think about Angela Kundera. During his exploration of the forest that day, he had been completely absorbed in the wild beauty of the place and could not remember thinking about anyone from the time he entered the old forest at midday until the setting sun evoked a connection with Angela.

Reflecting on that observation, he raised a puzzling question. Why had his mind shifted from the world of nature to thoughts about Hannah and then Angela as he sat by the campfire?

He remembered his camping experiences as a boy. During the daytime, he forgot about the world outside of the forest. But every night as he sat by the campfire, he inevitably found himself thinking about those he loved.

In the early days, his thoughts would turn to his first love Amy Burdette. During his high school years, his thoughts turned to April Morehouse, a classmate who had captured his heart.

He had wondered why that always happened at night by the campfire, but he never came up with a plausible answer. The renewed quest, however, led him to the answer.

He had learned from his study of anthropology that the firepit was the place where the early humans would gather at day's end. There, the men would return from the hunt and the women would return from their task of gathering. There, they would eat and sleep together.

With that childhood mystery solved, he raised his water mug and silently toasted Angela. Then he began to revel in the memory of what she called their first anniversary.

***

It was a little past noon, and Barsh waited in the yard for Angela to come driving up the lane to the secluded farmhouse. Dark clouds were rolling in from the southwest, but he was thinking how lucky he was to own a second place in the country. It was the ideal place for their rendezvous—something he had never dreamed of when he bought the farm.

On hearing the car rumbling over the gravel lane, he turned to follow its progress. She parked the Volvo and ran for his embrace.

“How wonderful to be back in your arms,” she said. “I hope we don’t have to leave early.”

“I can stay until five. We’d better get inside. The rain will be here any minute. Can I help with your things?”

“If you’ll get the picnic basket, I’ll get my shoulder bag.”

They made it inside just before the downpour.

“Listen to that,” she said.

“Oh, yes, I love the sound of a hard rain drumming on a tin roof. By the way, how do you like the new gate? No more manually unlocking and relocking the old one.”

“Super special. It keeps the privacy of this place, that I love so dearly, and the remote control makes it easier for me to get to you.”

“Thanks for bringing lunch. I thought we’d eat in the den by the fire.”

“Good choice. You know what magic that room holds for me. Wouldn’t Jeremiah Keeble be astonished to see how his old log cabin has been incorporated into this farmhouse?”

“He’d be totally flabbergasted.”

“Ah, a candlelit table, a sizzling fire, and the sound of the rain on the tin roof.”

“Are you hungry?” he asked and set the picnic basket on the small table, that he had moved from the big room to the den.

“Not really. I’m calling this our first anniversary. Of course, it’s only been a week, not a year, since our long-anticipated day of ecstasy. Then there was Saturday night under the stars. And now, it’s Wednesday, again.”

She set her bag on the coffee table, slipped out of her short jacket, and stood before the fire. She was long-legged tall, gracefully slender, and her long black hair was flying high in a pony tail.

“I like your dress.”

“It’s new. I bought it with your eyes in mind.”

“Please know that you wear it well, like everything else, including my baggy sweatsuit. Saturday night was one I won’t forget.”

“I love your ingenious innovations. Your sweatsuits were perfect for our activities on the quilt pallet you made in the backyard.”

“Not a typical first night together, but the ground therapy for body and heart was beyond words. Today, we have the green bedroom. In two weeks, we’ll be on Hilton Head Island, just the two of us if all goes well. I've reserved the ocean-front condo, that I told you about."

"Hold that thought for a moment, and let's revisit the reference you just made to ground therapy. Do you realize that's only the second time you have used that expression with me?"

"Actually, I do. So, you remember the first time," he said and motioned her to the couch where they sat side by side.

"How could I forget it? It was our first outing or fieldtrip as you called it. I had already fallen for you, and after that outing, I was in love with the Southern Appalachian Mountains.

"I loved everything we did, including our debut session of ground therapy on Mt. Mitchell. Shall I recount that event just in case it has faded from your memory?"

"No! No! It has not faded from my memory. But please recount the event from your perspective."

"We had finished lunch and I was raving about the beauty of the mountains. You concurred with my summation and then said it was time for a little ground therapy.

"Although I was intrigued by the expression, I didn't know what you intended by it. Then as I watched you stretched out on your back, you said that grounding oneself, as you were doing, was good therapy for the soul and invited me to try it. And I did.

"We were lying there so close together that I could hear you breathing. God, I wanted you to roll over and kiss me, but you didn't."

"I trust you realized I wanted to do just that, but duty held my longing in check."

"You knew the expression ground therapy, in that context, had sexual connotations, right?"

"I wasn't thinking about that. It was something I often did alone. But there on the top of Mount Mitchell, I was overwhelmed by your sensual presence.

"So, yes, I knew my vulnerability and dropped all references to ground therapy on our other field trips. I now make a distinction between ground therapy for the soul and ground therapy for body and heart.

"I needed your friendship, something I thought I could manage. Truthfully, I needed your love, something I knew I could not manage at the time."

“I understand that now. But Saturday night, you took charge and showed me the ecstasy of ground therapy for body and heart. That was the best night of my life.

“Tell me truthfully, did you plan the stargazing experience, knowing that the quilt pallet would become our love-bed after Hannah’s bedtime?”

“That was my intention. The three of us would stargaze until Hannah was sound asleep in her bed, and then you and I would have the quilt pallet to ourselves.”

“Well, you certainly made a stargazer out of me, and you obviously wrote the book on ground therapy for body and heart.

“Today, I’d intended to show off my new Victoria Secret lingerie and entice you to dance with me, all but naked, before we made it to the green bedroom. I’m putting that on hold until later if you’re in the mood.”

“Oh, yes, I’m in the mood, and I look forward to the exhibition and dance, later,” he said and led her into the green bedroom.

***

Shifting his thoughts back to the moment, Barsh added several dead tree limbs to the dwindling fire. Then he cloaked himself with his deerskin poncho, and enabled only by the natural light of the stars, he made his way to the top of the bluff.

Chapter Two

Standing on the bluff above the cave, Barsh gazed into the brilliant night sky. What an awe-inspiring wonder to contemplate a universe with billions of galaxies, each with billions of stars, and everything expanding from some imaginable center.

He sat down on the thick bed of leaves and remembered the first time the paradox of infinity took hold of his mind. A fourteen-year-old boy, he was standing in the road in front of their house one night, and as he gazed into the star-studded sky, he began to wonder what was beyond the stars.

There had to be something out there that kept going in every direction, even if that something was nothingness. If that were true, then nothingness would be something. But how could something stretch forever? And even more perplexing, how could it not?

From that day forward, he always felt a sense of awe and wonder whenever he pondered the universe and his place in it. It was clear in his mind that no rationally thinking person could live complacently and self-centered.

Self-reflection had taught him that he already existed as an entity before he became conscious of himself. Thus, he viewed his existence, ultimately, as an ontological gift, and for him, the proper response to that existential truth was one of reverent awe.

He also knew that humans were social animals. New born humans depended totally on others to nurture them. Otherwise, they would die within days. The richness of one's life also depended upon the culture of the society into which she or he was born.

Based on those social and cultural truths, he felt a categorical imperative to seek and follow a path that promoted not only his own well-being but the common good of humankind and the health of the earth with its diverse ecosystems.

He did not object to individuals claiming, without arrogant pride, that they had done well with the gifts bestowed upon them, including those from the culture into which they were born. But no self-reflecting person could honestly claim to be self-made and unbeholding to anyone. Only unthinking fools could make such claims for themselves.

Barsh stood and searched the sky for the Little Dipper. On finding it, he saluted the North Star for all the times it had given him a sense of direction during his youthful treks into the forest at night.

Having checked the time table for the moon in eastern Alabama before entering the wild, he knew that in eight days it would be waxing full and illuminating the watershed ridge where he stood. When that happened, he planned to take a night walk in the forest, enabled only by the light of the moon and stars—something he had not done since he left home for college.

After more self-reflection, he returned to the cave, removed the poncho, and banked with ashes what was left of the fire—another important practice Coon Peters had taught him as a boy. That would enable him to start the fire, afresh, in the morning from the smoldering embers beneath the ashes.

Still wearing his clothes and moccasins, he wiggled into the deerskin sleeping bag, that he had made in preparation for his short sojourn in the wild. His mind, however, was not ready to shut down, and he soon picked up the narrative of what Angela called their first anniversary.

***

He and Angela lingered naked on the bed in the green bedroom of the farmhouse, both relishing the afterglow of spent desire and the joy of mutual love.

"I have an idea," she said. "Let's jump in those sweatsuits we wore Saturday night and then eat lunch. I'm suddenly hungry. Then we can talk.

"That will give us a nice interlude. I definitely want to show off my new Victoria Secret lingerie before the clock ticks down to our final minutes on this special day of togetherness."

Thus, they dressed and ate lunch. Afterwards, they sat cuddled on the couch before the sizzling log fire.

"Barsh, did Hannah have any questions about what we did after you put her to bed, Saturday night?"

"On the way home, Sunday, she asked if you and I did any more stargazing after she fell asleep. I told her that we did and she let it go at that."

"I know you are as relieved as I am that she has accepted our plan to live together in the near future," she said.

"That was a huge relief. When I shared our options based on the legal separation and told her what I wanted to happen. Without hesitation, she agreed with my choice.

"Angie, here's the latest development regarding Debbie. If she closes on the house as scheduled, she will move the week after Thanksgiving.

"Hannah is staying with me until Christmas break. I hope the three of us can spend weekends here at the farm or else take a trip somewhere."

"I'm counting on it," Angela said.

"Do you mind if we continue sleeping separately when Hannah's with us?"

"Not at all."

"Trust me. I'll find a way for us to enjoy a bit of intimacy."

"I have no doubt that will happen."

"I think you'll be pleased to learn Hannah's response to your tender affection, Saturday night. She made a point to tell me how comforting it was to fall asleep on the quilt pallet, cuddled in your arms. Just so you understand the weight of her comment, Debbie is not the cuddling type, not even with Hannah."

"Yes, I'm very pleased to learn her response. Thanks for telling me. I was so honored when you told me that she wants to be like me when she grows up. I've never known of anyone wanting to be like me."

"You've been so good for her from the first day you started tutoring her with her creative writing."

"She's a joy to work with. I'm quite impressed that she's developing a fine poetic voice at such a young age. Obviously, you had already taught her to write from her own point of view as an eleven-year-old girl. I can also see your influence in the subjects she chooses to write about as well as her sensibilities.

"I've never before had a close relationship with a preteen. Hannah is a new experience for me and I love it."

"I haven't told you this, but I believe that when Hannah gets a little older, she and I can convince Debbie to let her come live with you and me."

"Then I hope that will happen. I know it would greatly ease your parental anxiety. Perhaps, this is a good time to tell you that I have conflicting feelings about having a child of my own. But I'm not yet ready to share the experiences that led me to this position."

"Please know that you can share your feelings about motherhood with me at any time, and you will not disappoint me, whatever your feelings on the subject may be. If you don't want to have a child or children, that's fine."

"I repeat myself. You are so different from the men I've known. None of them have ever seemed concerned about me as a person."

"Then you never met the right men. Surely, I'm not an oddity."

"There's nothing odd about you. But you are different from the common lot of men I've known. I can vouch with authority on that. I must tell you that I have a lot of regrets."

"Who doesn't? Don't be so hard on yourself."

"Yes, but my regrets include my damnable story. I have never shared it nor have I been able to forgive myself for it. I try to suppress it, but if haunts me from time to time."

"Personally, I don't need to know about your damnable story, but I am concerned that you haven't been able to forgive yourself for whatever you did. If you decide to share it with me, I'll try to help you deal with it by forgiving yourself. Meantime, just know that I not only love you, I adore you."

"And I love and adore you," she said and snuggled against his chest. Do you want to guess what I'm thinking?"

"Nothing comes to mind. Please tell me."

"How much I respect you for managing our relationship so honorably. Even though you knew Debbie was leaving you, you kept me at arms distance until she asked for a permanent separation."

"Actually, I don't like the way I've handled the situation with Debbie."

"What do you mean?"

"I made a mistake by promising her that I would not force a divorce on her against her religious convictions. I was so relieved that she finally told me the truth that I didn't think through everything.

"My status of being legally married to Debbie is not fair for us. I should have responded to her request by saying that I would sign a legal separation but I would reserve the right to file for a divorce at a later date."

"I'm okay with the separation agreement. You have always been honest with me. You have never promised to marry me, and knowing your situation, I willingly and eagerly took you as my beloved. I trust you like no other man that I've ever known. Moreover, I'm in good company with this situation."

"Whose good company would that be?"

"I'm thinking of one of the leading female English novelists who wrote under the pen name George Eliot. She fell in love with a progressive thinker and philosopher. I don't remember his name, but he was already married when they met. He couldn't get a divorce under British laws at the time, so they openly lived together until his death, many years later."

"Well, that makes me respect George Eliot all the more. But I would still prefer for us to be legally married, and I intent to address the situation. At an appropriate time, I will gently try to get Debbie to agree to my divorcing her.

"I will take all the responsibility for the divorce. All I expect her to do is not to contest it. I'm willing to take the role of sinner, in her view at least, so she can have a clear conscience."

"I would dearly love to be married to you, but I'm a happy woman to have your love and commitment even if we can't get married."

"I feel the same way, but my goal now is to marry you. Changing the subject, I have plans to go to Alabama this weekend."

"Could I possibly go with you?"

"I've given it serious thought but I couldn't work it out. I do want to take you to Alabama. This trip, however, is all about my wilderness sojourn. I need to check out the area where I will be camping.

"It's been twenty-six years since I was there, and I need to make sure it's still a suitable wild place. That old forest could have been clear-cut for all I know.

"I'll also be carrying two fish traps, a holding cage, and some pottery to leave in the cave that I told you about. This means I'll have to make two long hikes there and back in one day."

"I won't have to leave until eight Friday evening, however, and I'll be back Sunday morning. We can meet here for several hours before I leave, and we can have a bit of togetherness when I get back, Sunday morning."

"That's good news. Are you ready for me to display my new Victoria Secret lingerie?

"Oh, yes."

***

The distant hoots of a barred owl pulled Barsh from his memories and he opened his eyes. The cave was pitch dark. The owl hooted again. He tuned from his back to his side and was soon sound asleep.

Chapter Three

When Barsh woke after his first night in the wild, the early morning light was leaking through the rhododendron into the entrance of the cave. He wiggled out of his sleeping bag and rekindled the campfire from the embers he had banked with ashes.

With a good fire going, he ate the leftover pieces of roasted duck and mushrooms. Then he sat by the fire and listened to the unending songs of the shoals that were such a significant feature of the Tallapoosa.

His father first took him camping on the river when he was six-years old. From then until he left home for college, he had camped and fished and hunted at numerous places along an eighty-mile stretch of the river.

From its headwaters in the Appalachian Mountains of Northwest Georgia, it coursed a crooked path into Alabama, where it passed within ten miles of where he grew up, and then continued on a southwestern course until it merged with the Coosa River just above Montgomery to form the Alabama River.

From there, the waters of the Alabama mingled with those of other tributaries until they flowed through the Mobile-Tensaw Delta into Mobile Bay and the Gulf of Mexico. He loved to read about those other rivers and the Mobile-Tensaw Delta—one of the most expansive flood plain forests in the United States.

The rivers of Alabama had all lost their pristine nature, long before he was born, but in his youth, he often wished he could have experienced them back when the Atlantic sturgeon, annually, made their way through Mobile Bay to spawn in their fresh water.

Native Americans had trapped them in fish weirs in untold numbers. And the early white settlers followed the practice.

He had read about a sturgeon, caught in the lower Tallapoosa, that was reported to weigh more than four-hundred pounds and to contain a tub of roe. Those days ended, however, with the coming of the hydro-electric dams that blocked the sturgeon from swimming up the Alabama rivers.

The lakes created by hydro-electric dams were well stocked with a variety of fish, but during Barsh's youth, blue catfish and yellows catfish were the dominant species in the Tallapoosa River itself, and he had caught both species using cane pole, rod and reel, trotline, and set hooks. Occasionally, he had also fished the river with his father when they resorted to baited wire traps to catch them.

In preparation for his sojourn in the wild, he had built two fish traps out of split bamboo, modeled after the wire ones that he remembered from his youth. This method of fishing was the only way he could envision catching fish, using only those things that he could make with his own hands, which was the test for his current sojourn in the wild.

Based on his youthful experience of fishing with wire traps, he was confident that he could catch enough catfish in his improvised traps to supplement the mushrooms, most days. The other days, he would rely on his bow and arrows to kill a duck or rabbit.

One of his first tasks after arriving at the cave had been to walk along the river bank until he found suitable places for the two fish traps. That was easy for him to do, and he soon had both in the river. They were weighted down to the bottom with an appropriate size rock and secured to the bank with a muscadine vine. Now, he was ready to bait them with the remains of the duck he had killed.

He slipped on his deerskin poncho, shouldered the hunting bag with the duck parts, and left the cave. The sky was clear but the ground had frosted over during the night. There was a cold wind blowing across the river out of the northwest, but he stuck with his task and quickly baited the fish traps.

Back in the cave, he decided to build up the fire and wait until the sun burned off the frost before taking to the woods for the day. With the flames leaping, again, he sat down in his usual place with the fire between him and the entrance of the cave. Relaxed and at peace with himself, he reviewed the next objective he had set for himself, which was to kill a rabbit.

In his explorations of the forest the previous day, he had discovered two rabbit beds. Each rabbit had bolted from its bed as he approached it.

Knowing their habits, he knew that they had likely returned to those same beds, overnight. With a mental map of where they were, he could now ease up on them for a good shot with his bow and arrow, before they bolted.

Around mid-morning, he banked the fire with ashes, strapped the quiver of arrows on his back, strung the bow, and left the cave. The frost had melted and the cold wind had died down.

He stopped at the spring that flowed from the base of the bluff, sank to his hands and knees on the dark humus, and drank from the pool of water like a deer. With his thirst quenched, he continued up the riverbank, always alert to his surroundings, always sensing the beauty of wild things.

He had traveled a good mile, when he caught a glimpse of a red-shouldered hawk before it sailed over the forest beyond his vision. Leaving the riverbank, he climbed up a hill and entered a grove of hickory trees. The ground was littered with shell fragments of hickory nuts that squirrels had chipped away with their teeth to get at the edible part.

It was obviously a paradise for squirrels and the hawk, that he had just spotted, knew it. Searching the sky, he spotted the hawk drifting about on the air currents high above the place,

He headed east through the grove with his feet rustling the thick canopy of dead leaves. Suddenly, the hawk swooped down into the far side of a tall hickory and, winging hard, flew off for some distant perch with a grey squirrel gripped in its talons.

Leaving the grove of hickory trees, he set out again for the closest rabbit bed. He knew the lay of the land and would have no difficulty finding the place. He could only hope, however, that the rabbit had returned to the same bed after foraging all night.

The woodland sloped slightly to his left toward Beech Creek about a half-mile away, and his course ran parallel with that creek, which caused him to have to jump across four small branches before he came to the vicinity of the rabbit bed. At the fifth branch, he stopped and watched some minnows darting about in a shallow pool.

The rabbit bed was located just below a sweetgum tree about a hundred yards from where he stood. Assuming the rabbit would be less likely to bolt from its bed with the small stream between them, he jumped across it and eased along the bank. As he neared the sweetgum that shielded his approach from the rabbit's eyes, he adopted a pattern of stopping briefly after every step.

He knew the rabbit was tracking him with its big ears, even though it could not see him. With an arrow fitted to the bow, he drew it to his cheek, aimed it toward the base of the tree, and took two more light steps, only to discover that the rabbit bed was empty.

He relaxed the bowstring and reflected on the situation. The rabbit might had fallen prey to a fox during the night. But more likely, it had simply decided to bed down in another place. If that was the case, the rabbit might return in a few days to this one that was well used—a sign that the rabbit had a preference to bed down in it.

As he watched a turkey vulture circling high on the wind currents, he remembered the first time it occurred to him that vultures likely drifted about, most days, on empty stomachs. Hunters definitely had a numerical advantage over scavengers. The odds of finding a live prey on any given day were much better than those of finding the carcass of some animal.

He refocused his mind on getting to the second rabbit bed that was located on the north side of Beech Creek. As he approached the creek, he stopped to admire a scattering of beech saplings.

Unlike other deciduous trees, they still clung tenaciously to their small oval leaves, now bleached to a nice shade of beige. What a pleasant sight that beige undergrowth made against the gray shades of the leafless deciduous trees.

After crossing Beech Creek on the trunk of a dead tree that had fallen across it, he soon found his way to the second rabbit bed. He eased within ten paces of the rabbit, took dead aim and released the bowstring.

The arrow hit its mark. He gutted the rabbit and dropped it in his hunting bag.

***

When Barsh returned to the riverbank below Bluff Cave in late afternoon, he was pleased to have a rabbit in his hunting bag. He had killed the rabbit with the same stoical disposition he had acquired as a boy.

It was a way of securing food in his youth, just as it was for him that day. Hunting had never been a sport for him. He abhorred that practice, especially trophy hunting.

During his explorations that afternoon, he had jumped another rabbit and made a mental map of its bed. If the need arose, he would return and try to kill it.

He had high expectations, however, that his freshly-baited fish traps would begin providing him with a steady supply of catfish, and he was eager to check them.

The rapids were singing their evening anthem as he walked down the riverbank. Just below the shoals, the river ran deep for a long stretch before turning into another stretch of rapids. This was the pattern the Tallapoosa—a stretch of rapids followed by one of quiet deep water.

The first fish trap lay in an eddy just below the rapids. He slowly pulled it up from the bottom of the river by the vine that he'd secured it with.

A yellow catfish, weighing a good two pounds, flopped back and forth in the trap. He retrieved it, walked downriver a few yards and deposited it in his holding cage, where it would remain alive until he decided to eat it.

On returning to the fish trap, he threw it back in the water and then proceeded downriver to check the second one. No catch there.

The sun was sinking low in the western sky. It had been a good day for Barsh. In addition to mushrooms he had gathered, he had a rabbit in his hunting bag and a catfish in his holding cage.

It was time to clean the rabbit and roast it and a few mushrooms, but first he would rekindle the fire that he'd banked with ashes that morning.

With the fire going, he gathered his ceramic platter and water mug, and headed for the spring. There, he filled the water mug, drank, refilled it, and eased down to the lower pool.

Holding the rabbit by it hindlegs, he remembered how easy it was to tear off its paper-thin skin, and he soon had the job done. He washed the rabbit and, with a sharp flake of flint, sliced the meat into small pieces for quick roasting.

He placed the other parts of the rabbit in two new bait pouches, that he would use to rebait the fish traps in two days. He then washed his hands and left for the cave.

The hot coals in the firepit were just right for roasting the rabbit and a few mushrooms, a task he readily performed.

According to the pattern he had set for himself, he ate half of them and saved the rest for breakfast. This was his second day of eating only two meals, breakfast and supper, and he was adjusting well to the pattern.

Having finished supper, he rebuilt the fire, and as he warmed his hands, he noticed how rough they were already beginning to look. By the time he left the wild, they would not be the well-manicured hands that Angela had praised before he left to check out the wilds of the Tallapoosa River and deposit in Bluff Cave part of his equipage for his wilderness experience.

Her cherished words were fresh in his mind, and he began to fondly reminisce about the occasion.

***

"Barsh, I love your hands," she said, as they lay naked in the green bedroom of the old farmhouse. "They know how to touch me. I also marvel at how skillful your hands are in such diverse undertakings that are so foreign to me.

"They can knap flint into arrowheads and kill deer with a bow and arrow. They can tan deer hides and make various things from them. They can make pottery like the Catawba Indians.

"During your boyhood, your hands could rein a spirited horse to your will. They could race a motorcycle over the hills and dales of northeastern Alabama.

"Now, if you will, tell me something else that your hands mastered in your youth."

"Well, they could milk a cow quite efficiently. They could plow the fields with a tractor and a horse. Those, however, are too domestic to take pride in, except there was an art to them.

"I could tell you about my tree-climbing skills, which required good hands."

"Yes, please tell me. I remember wanting to climb a tree in our backyard, but I couldn't get up to where the limbs started."

"Getting to the limbs is the hard part. But I learned how to inch my way up, pushing and pulling against the trunk with my hands and feet in what I called a bear climb.

"Then it was easy climbing to the very top. Between the age of nine and fifteen, I spent a great deal of time proving to myself that I could climb all the trees in the remnant of a forest between our house and the railroad.

"That was a short span in my life, when we lived in a neighborhood at the edge of town. I loved those tree-climbing years. My neighbor Amy Burdette often sat by cheering me on.

"Once, however, I made the mistake of trusting a dead limb on a tall poplar. It was during winter when the limbs were leafless, which meant the dead ones were hard to detect. But thanks to my quick grasping hands and a strong sap-sucking limb, within reach, I avoided the fall that would have likely broken my back."

"Wow. What a scarry story. Now I'll praise your quick-grasping hands and that strong sap-sucking limb."

"Angie, I had no knowledge of this during my tree-climbing days, but anthropologists claim that our hands are a byproduct of tree climbing. According to them, the reason we have dexterous hands is because our pre-human ancestors lived in trees before they adapted to living on the ground."

"And you concur with them, right?"

"The evidence is obvious. I don't see how anyone with an open mind could think anything else if they took the time to study the evidence.

"Right now, I'm visualizing a photo of the reconstructed fossil bones of a hand that were recently discovered in Ethiopia. The bones in this hand belonged to one of our upright-walking, pre-human ancestors that lived about three million years ago. It's amazing how much it looks like the bones of a human hand."

"I'd like to see that photo. Unfortunately, my knowledge of anthropology is rather sketchy. I need to become more informed."

"I have a good book to get you started. *Origins* by Richard Leaky and Roger Lewin. It contains a photo of the reconstructed hand I mentioned. I'll bring it by your office, Monday."

"Barsh, I love the way our conversations move in and out from intimacy to these intellectual discussions. One minute you're sexing it up with me and the next you're stimulating my mind."

"Changing the subject, how's your novel coming?"

"I'm making great progress, and as I've said before, this is by far the best writing I've ever done. I think I'll have completed a first draft by the time you return from your brief sojourn in the wild. If so, I'd like for us to get away somewhere and take turns reading it, aloud, to each other. Will you do this with me?"

"Yes, of course. Be assured that I'm eagerly awaiting that day. Are you dealing with your damnable story as you called it?"

"Early on, I decided against that, but lately, I've been thinking that maybe I should. If I do, you can read about it, and I won't have to tell you."

"Sounds like a good plan to me."

"Okay, I'll include it. After you read about it, we can discuss it, and hopefully, you will be able to help me forgive myself."

"Be assured that I will do my best to help you reach that goal," he said and looked at his watch.

"I know it time for you to get on the road for Alabama."

"Angie, I'm beginning to feel conflicted about my plan for a short sojourn in the wild. I hate to leave you for two weeks."

"You want to have that experience, right?"

"Yes, but it's no longer a necessity. That's your gift to me."

"Speaking of gifts, before I met you, I desperately needed to become the author of a best-selling novel that would put me on a book-signing tour across the country and bring devoted fans clambering to meet me.

"I would still like to have that experience, but I no longer desperately need it. That's your gift to me, so stick with your plan."

"Okay. No more second thoughts about my plan. You are so good for me in every way—body, heart, and soul.

"I like the way you put that and the same holds true for me. This is interesting. I just thought about the way Edith Wharton described how a woman is by nature like a great house full of halls and different kinds of rooms, where various people passed in and out.

"She also noted that a woman has an innermost room, the holy of holies, where her soul sits waiting for footsteps that never come. For a long time that was me. I use to think of myself as waiting in that holy of holies for footsteps that never came.

"Before I met you, men had entered my heart and body, but never my soul. After the last man, who opened the doors to my heart and body, betrayed me, I decided to lock both doors for a season or two if not for ever.

"Then I met you on what should have been an exhausting job interview. To the contrary, it was the most exhilarating trip of my life. I clearly heard your footsteps approaching the door of my soul.

"Before we got to Jackson's Steak House, you had gently opened that innermost door to my being. Not the doors to my heart or my body but the one to my soul. And I shared with you the trauma of my thirteenth summer. How an older neighborhood boy raped me. Something, as you know, I had never shared with anyone.

"That's how this all started for me. You had entered my soul before we shared our first meal. And before we parted that first night, I had also opened my heart to you and would have opened my body as well—something I had never done with any man, so quickly."

"I, too, have a confession. I immediately liked you as a person, and I was eager to befriend you without a single thought of romance or sex. Thoughts of both, however, had entered my mind before we parted that evening. Do you remember the last thing you said to me when I checked you in the hotel?"

"I know you had carried my luggage into the hotel room. I also know I didn't want the evening to end. I'm sure I said something that expressed that feeling, but I don't remember the words."

"I remember them verbatim because I was trembling when I left the room."

"I scared you?"

"No, that other kind of trembling. You said, Barsh, this has been an evening of special magic for me, and I hate to see it end. That was enough to unnerve me, but the fact that your eyes looked so yielding shook me in a way that was ineffable.

"Forgive me for using the word compassion, but my sense of compassion seemed to have mingled with romance and sexual tension—something I don't remember experiencing in that combination before. Yes, I'd experienced that erotic shiver before but nothing like that moment in the hotel with you."

"That's interesting. I never sensed that you had responded that way to me. You walked out of my hotel room without a single overture, although you were shivering for me?"

"I was drawn to you, yes, but I was by no means prepared for you. Actually, I chastised myself for being so vulnerable."

"For the record, I flew back to Providence believing that I had entered into an authentic friendship with you. There was something that pulled me to you with complete trust. That in itself was extraordinary, given my track record with men. Do you know the Persian poet Rumi?"

"One of my professors used to quote Rumi, but I haven't read him."

“Here’s one of my favorite Rumi sayings as translated by Coleman Barks: The minute I heard my first love story I started looking for you, not knowing how blind that was.

“That rings so true for me. I’d been searching for you since I was a teenager. Oh, yes, how blind the search. And how unbelievably lucky I am to have found you.”

“I like the Rumi quote, Angie. And yes, how unbelievably lucky I am to have found you.

“Sorry but I have to get on the road to Alabama. I’ll call you as soon as I check in the motel, tonight and again Saturday night. When I get back here, Sunday morning, I’ll call to let you know I’m back.”

“And I’ll rush over with open arms.”

***

When Barsh shifted from his reminiscing back to the moment, the campfire was barely flickering. He banked it with ashes, slipped into his sleeping bag, and was soon asleep.

Chapter Four

Barsh woke from deep sleep to the loud cawing of a crow. What a delightful alarm clock, he thought. Lying there listening to the crow, he judged it to be perched in one of the tall oaks at the edge of the bluff above the cave. The cawing soon stopped, and he assumed the crow had taken wings.

It was his third day in the wild, and he felt refreshed after a good night's sleep. He crawled out of the sleeping bag and rekindled the fire.

With it blazing again, he ate the leftover rabbit and mushrooms, while he anticipated another day in the forest. He had a yellow catfish in the holding cage and intended to cook it that evening. So, he wasn't concerned about killing any game.

His objective was to explore the forest, upriver, beyond where he had previously hunted. If there was an occasion to kill a rabbit or duck, he would take it. Otherwise, he would just enjoy exploring the forest.

Finished with breakfast, he banked the fire with ashes, strung the bow, strapped the quiver of arrows on his back, and left the cave. Although it was early morning, there was no frost on the ground like the previous day.

After drinking his fill at the spring, he hiked up the river bank to Beech Creek and then followed it upstream to the dead tree that had fallen across it. There, he paused for a moment to admire a tall sycamore tree on the opposite bank. Then he walked across the fallen tree to the other bank and continued on a northward course parallel to the river.

Near the top of the next watershed, he noticed a lot of heavy scratching among the leaves. Soon he came upon a scattering of what he took to be turkey droppings under a big oak.

Ah, a turkey roost, he thought. On closer examination, he concluded that some of the droppings were fresh and resolved to return to experience a rafter of turkeys on their roost, during his planned night walk.

As he descended the northside of the watershed, he saw a Cooper's hawk riding the air currents high above the trees. He watched the hawk until it drifted out of view, and then continued his exploration of the area.

At length, he came to a big creek, and following his habit of naming those he did not know, he named this one Hawk Creek in honor of the Cooper's hawk he had just seen.

He turned upstream and continued until he found a place where he could cross by jumping from one big rock to another. Pausing for a moment before crossing, he detected the faint sound of a waterfall further up the creek. He definitely wanted to check it out but decided to do so later.

After crossing the creek on the rocks, he followed it back to the Tallapoosa River, where he sat on the trunk of a fallen tree. After enjoying the natural beauty of the place for several minutes, he heard the rustling of leaves near the mouth of the creek. Silence and then more rustling.

He recognized the pattern. A bird was scratching among the leaves for worms and bugs. He waited, hoping to catch a glimpse of the bird, and his patience paid off when a white-throated sparrow came hopping from the underbrush.

The sparrow took wings and he continued up the river bank until he came to a thicket of alders. As he stopped for a moment to consider whether to enter the thicket or hike around it, he watched a vulture descend into it.

Catching a glimpse of its red head, he knew that turkey vultures typically soared, alone, in their search of carrion. Based on his experience, the vulture's descent could only mean one thing. It had found its lunch. Driven by a bit of curiosity, he decided to enter the thicket and check out the scene.

There in the midst of the alders was a dead deer and a turkey vulture. The vulture flapped off a few yards and turned to watch him as he approached the deer.

Some hunter had shot the mature buck through the stomach, and the rest of the story was easy to reconstruct. Wounded, the deer had dashed away, and the hunter had been unable to track it to the alder thicket, where it died from hemorrhaging, perhaps as far as several miles from where it was shot.

Barsh left the scene, so the vulture could do what nature had fashioned it to do, and continued his exploration of the forest until it was well past noon. Then he headed back for Bluff Cave by a different route.

***

It was late afternoon when he got back to camp, and he was pleased with his long trek through new areas of the old forest that stretched along the east bank of the Tallapoosa River. Not once did he draw the bow with the intent to kill something.

He did, however, jump three rabbits and made mental maps on the location of each of their beds. If the need arose, he was confident that he could kill one or more of them.

Before entering the cave, he decided to check the fish traps. The second one yielded two blue catfish. He dropped one in his hunting bag to eat for his next two meals, deposited the other in the holding cage with the yellow catfish, and returned to the cave.

After rekindling the fire, he set out to fill his mug with spring water and clean the blue catfish.

When he returned to the cave, the fire was still blazing, so he sat before it, waiting for sufficient red-hot coals to roasted the small pieces of fish and a few mushrooms. In due time, he roasted them, ate half of them, and stored the rest for breakfast.

Satisfied with his supper, he built up the fire and sat before it with his mug of fresh spring water. Lifting the mug, he toasted Angela and began reminiscing about their rendezvous after his trip to Alabama to check out the terrain surrounding Bluff Cave to make sure it was still suitable for his planned sojourn and to deposit some of his equipage in the cave.

***

A bit weary and hungry, Barsh parked the Ford pickup at the farmhouse. He had driven non-stop from Alabama without breakfast. He hurried inside to call Angela.

"I'm back," he said.

"Splendid! What time did you get up?"

"Three o'clock. Are you ready for some country air?"

"I'll be there in twenty minutes if I don't get stopped for speeding."

"I left the motel with a cup of coffee, and I didn't stop for breakfast. Will you join me?"

"I've already eaten but I'd like coffee."

"The coffee will be waiting for you and so will I. Love you. Bye."

He built a fire in the fieldstone fireplace in the den and stood there praising whoever had decided to incorporate the old log cabin into the farmhouse. With the fire blazing, he started the coffee. There was deli ham in the refrigerator, and he decided to make do with a sandwich and a glass of V-8 juice, rather than scrambling eggs.

Finished with the sandwich, he arranged in a large vase several cuttings of holly that he had brought back from Alabama. Then he ambled about in the front yard as he waited for Angela.

It was a beautiful morning, just perfect for their planned hike through the forest to the Pacolet River. A turkey vulture drifted about over the north pasture. He walked to the back of the house, where he scanned the horizon in all directions.

There was no hawk, a-wing, as he had hoped to see, but there was a large white bird perched in the top of the tallest oak beyond the fence line of the pasture. If it had been closer to the coast, he would have assumed that it was a great egret. Puzzled, he went inside for his field glasses.

With those in hand, he walked to the edge of the yard and focused on the white bird. It was a snowy owl—only the second one he had ever sighted.

The splendid creature was far south of its normal winter range. He knew, however, from various field guides to birds that they occasionally drifted further south than usual for the winter.

At the sound of Angela's car, he returned to the front yard. Their faces beamed with bright smiles as she parked the Volvo. He opened the door for her, and she moved quickly into his open arms. They kissed tenderly.

"What's up with the field glasses?"

"I'll show you," he said and led her to the edge of the backyard. "Scan the trees beyond the pasture and tell me if you see anything unusual."

"There's something white in one of the trees. Is that a bird?"

"Yes, and it's south of its normal range. Take a good look at it with the field glasses and tell me what you think."

"Is it a hawk?"

"It's a snowy owl. I was just a boy when I first saw one. Unlike my grandmother Roberts who thought its rare appearance was a bad omen, I'm hoping this one will spend the winter with us, and if it does, it will likely return to that same tree from time to time to roost during the day. Owls are night creatures, as you likely know."

"I do know that, and I'm joining you in hoping it winters with us. If it does, maybe we can find a painting of one to hang in the den to remind us of my first winter in the South with you."

"Yes, I'd like that."

They gathered her things from the car and went inside. He poured coffee and ushered her into the den, where they stood with their backs to the fire.

"Look," he said pointing to the large vase of holly on the credenza. "On my way out of the wild, late yesterday, I took those cuttings from a holly tree less than fifty yards from the cave where I'll be staying. You can take the arrangement home with you if you'd like."

"Yes, and I'm keeping them until you return, even if they wither. I was pleased to learn, when you called last night, that the cave and wilderness area were still suitable for your sojourn."

"Fortunately for me, nothing had changed since I camped there during my senior year of high school, except that the area has been restocked with deer and turkeys."

"Thanks for leaving Alabama in the wee hours of the morning, so we would have time to hike to the Pacolet River."

"I'd promised to take you there, again, and today seemed like a good time. We can have lunch, of a sort, on the granite ledge overlooking the river.

"I'd like to introduce you to my typical lunch back when I would be out hunting all day in my youth. Sardines out of a flat can, hoop cheese, saltine crackers, and an apple.

"Feeling a bit nostalgic when I left the motel for Bluff Cave, yesterday morning, I stopped at a country story and bought those items. That's what I ate for lunch as I sat on the bluff above the cave and listened to ceaseless songs rising from the shoals of the Tallapoosa River. I also bought enough to share with you if you're game."

"I've never eaten sardines, but to paraphrase Ruth of Biblical time, I'll go wherever you go and eat whatever you eat."

"You're my kind of woman, Angie, not because of that submissive parody of Ruth but because of your openness. You can give and take on an equal footing with anyone, and I love that about you."

"That's how I feel about you," she said with an adorable smile. "It just occurred to me that you must be exhausted. You've hardly had time to rest or sleep since you left me, Friday evening. Wouldn't you like to take a nap before we hike to the river?"

"I'm fine. Let's sit on the couch and talk awhile. Here's an update for you to consider. Last week, I made a pallet in the hayloft. If that image still interests you, we can try it on our return from the Pacolet River."

"Have no doubt, my dear. I am so ready to try that pallet."

"And so am I. Now, tell me about your Saturday."

"There's not much to tell. I spend most of the day writing. Otherwise, I was thinking about you and dreaming about our Thanksgiving getaway to Hilton Head Island.

"This Wednesday, we get to sleep together all night in a bed for the first time. That will be another splendid milestone for us. Then we'll have Thursday, Friday, Saturday, and most of Sunday, all to ourselves."

"I trust you know that I've also been dreaming about that."

"Here's a small confession that will give you a smile. Don't' know why it jumped in my mind, but it did. I'm a reformed cat woman."

"Please tell me the story."

"My years of living in an apartment were, for the most part, lonely years. You know the story of the struggling, would-be novelists.

"I bought a neutered cat to share the apartment with me. Then I took the cat to my new apartment in Providence, when I started graduate studies at Brown. Back in June, Bow-Boy died, and I decided to begin life in Ashland without a cat. Here I am in the deep South with no interest in owning another cat."

"I like your cat story. You know I'd love you, reformed cat woman or not."

"I have no doubt. And what an amazement to feel so totally loved."

***

Breaking away from his reminiscing, Barsh realized that he had been unconsciously playing in the fire with a stick, something he liked to do as a boy. He tossed the stick in the fire and decided to leave for the bluff above the cave. But first, he needed to tend the fire or it would be dead before he returned.

With the fire roaring again, he slipped into his deerskin poncho and eased into the darkness, where he waited for a few moments for his eyes to adjust to the faint illumination of the starlight. Then he made his way to the top of the bluff to stargaze and ponder whatever came to mind.

Chapter Five

Barsh left the cave early on his seventh day in the wild. He had decided to visit an old campsite that was located upriver at the mouth of Corn House Creek. His best guess was that it would take him at least until noon to hike there. There would be creeks to cross, and he would have to search for places to cross without wading the cold water.

Driven by nostalgia, he hiked north through the forest with a zestful purpose, but not at the cost of enjoying the forest as he trekked along. About mid-day, he reached the mouth of Corn House Creek. As he stood and watched its clear waters mingling with the dingy currents of the Tallapoosa River, he recalled the unforgettable day when he, just six-years old, first stood on that bank.

His father had taken him on his first overnight camping trip. Two of his father's friends had camped with them. They caught catfish on a trotline that they'd strung across the river with the aid of an old wooden bateau.

As night fell upon the camp, his father cooked catfish, cornmeal fritters, and potatoes in a large cast-iron skillet. It was Bash's first supper in the wild and one that he enjoyed recalling.

About every two hours, they would check the trotline and deposit the catch in a holding cage that was submerged in the creek. Between rounds of checking the trotline, the men told stories about their youth. Some were funny and some were tragic. Occasionally, they would pass a quart jar of white lightning for a swallow. And Barsh was processing it all to the limits of his ability.

Long after his regular bedtime, he rolled up in a quilt and drifted off to sleep under the stars, while the men were still talking. That experience had aroused feelings he could not describe. He would later understand them as the call of the wild.

Exhilarated by his memories, he walked up the creek to the old campsite. Surveying the place, he couldn't square it with his memory. The area around the firepit had been cleared of the old trees. He remembered looking up through them at the stars before he drifted off to sleep.

As an older boy, he had occasionally camped there with his friends, always with satisfaction and always the leader of the pack, just as his father had been. Twenty-five years had spilled over the dam of time since he last slept there.

If there was one creek that he honored above all others, it was Corn House Creek. He had fished and hunted along its banks over a range of twenty miles. He bowed slightly in reverence to the place and in homage to his father who had introduced him to life in the wild.

On the way back to Bluff Cave, he decided to swing by one of the places where he had previously jumped a rabbit. He found the rabbit hunkered down in its bed and eased within striking distance.

He and the rabbit stared, eye to eye, for a brief moment before he stoically released the arrow that hit it mark. He gutted the rabbit and dropped it in his hunting bag.

As he headed for camp, he resolved never to kill another rabbit, deliberately. Since entering the wild, he had killed two ducks and three rabbits to supplement the catfish he caught in the traps that he had built, and that was enough to satisfy him.

He had two catfish in the holding cage and plenty of mushrooms stored in the cave. All he needed was to catch another catfish in one of the traps. That would give him two meals a day until he broke camp.

***

The day was yielding to twilight, as Barsh entered the cave with the butchered rabbit. The coals were just right for roasting it and a few mushrooms, and he began the task in a mood that he could not quite label.

In his youth, he had stoically killed numerous rabbits for food without an ethical thought. Now, he was satisfied with his resolve never to kill another rabbit, deliberately, and yet, he felt nostalgic about those times he had eaten fried rabbit with milk gravy and hot biscuits that his mother had cooked on a wood-burning stove in their old farmhouse.

As usual, he ate half of the roasted rabbit and mushrooms and stored the rest for breakfast. Settled back by the fire, he lifted his water mug and toasted Angela. Then he breathed a prayer of well-being for her and Hannah. He could only trust that they were well.

Tired from all the hiking that day, he stretched out on his back to rest awhile. With no intention of doing so, he fell asleep and then woke with a start after a short nap.

He rebuilt the fire and sat there thinking about the night Angela's father was hospitalized. It was the Monday before Thanksgiving, and he and Hannah were in his study when the phone rang.

***

"Barsh, forgive me for calling you at home, but Daddy has been hospitalized with a heart attack."

"I'm so sorry, Angie. What does the doctor say?"

"He thinks they have stabilized him and will probably do open-heart surgery. Mother wants me to come home and I don't know what to do."

"Let me come over and we'll work it out."

"Yes, please come. I need you."

He explained the situation to Hannah and Debbie and then drove into Angela's backyard. She was standing in the kitchen door as he entered the screened back porch.

She beckoned him and he held her in his arms for a few moments. Then she led him into the living room where they sat together on the couch.

"Do you think I should go home?"

"I would go if I were in your situation. What are your reservations?"

"You and our Hilton Head Island trip, I suppose. I was so looking forward to it."

"We can make that trip at a later date. This is a family crisis and deserves our first attention. I totally support your going. I'll take you to the Charlotte Airport and I'll pay for your flight."

"What will you do if I go?"

"Don't worry about me. I'll check off some books from my reading list, while feeling lucky to have you in my life."

"Okay, I'll go but I'll pay for the flight."

"I need to help you with this, so please let me. You can call the Charlotte airport, tonight, and make a reservation with my

American Express Card. I can take you to the airport early in the morning or anytime in the afternoon."

"I'll do an afternoon flight so I can teach my classes in the morning."

"Okay. I'll find someone to cover your classes until you return, so don't worry about anything down here. Sketch some lesson plans for the week if you can."

"Yes, I'll do that. How shall we communicate?"

"I would call every day if you parents knew about us. Since they don't, I'd like for you to call collect at the farm between four and five. You can also call me at Cooper or at home if the need arises."

"Do you want me to tell my parents about us?"

"I'll leave that up to you."

"Then I'll probably wait," she said after pondering the situation. "But here's something I'd like to do on this visit. I want to review my life story with them, including my deepest aspirations and disappointments. Then I can tell them that I've finally found my place in the academic world, that I'm writing with confidence and high expectations, and that I have a whole new set of special friends.

"And you know what? After I share my story with them, I'm going to ask them, separately, to tell me about their lives before they married. I have no idea what they wanted out of life when they were young."

"That's a great idea. I wish that I'd had the forethought to ask my parents to share their stories with me. Okay, are you ready to call about a flight?"

"Do you know which airline would best serve me?"

"You know me. I even have the number," he said and gave it to her along with his American Express Card.

"You're the best. No one takes care of the details like you."

Angela called the airport and reserved a flight for 3:15, Monday afternoon. She then called her mother, who was much relieved to hear that she was coming home.

"Well, that was easy enough, thanks to you. Is it too late to cancel the reservation for the condo at Hilton Head Island?"

"I'll call tomorrow. They'll probably charge me unless they can rent it on short notice, but don't worry about that. I've already gotten my money's worth just by anticipating our time there."

"I can't tell you how disappointed I am that we won't get to go."

"We're going. It's just a question of when. While you were on the phone, I came up with a new timetable for my short sojourn in the wild.

"I'll turn in my semester grades sometime Wednesday afternoon on December the thirteenth and hit the road for Louisville with Hannah. After I leave her there, I'll drive through the better part of the night, spend a few hours in a motel, and be at Bluff Cave by noon on Thursday.

"The day before Christmas, I'll leave the forest, drive to Louisville, and spend Christmas Eve in a motel with Hannah. Christmas morning, I'll head for Ashland and be home by mid-afternoon. Then we'll go to Hilton Head Island for a nice getaway if all is well with you father."

"That sounds wonderful, but I think you're giving up too much of your planned wilderness experience."

"Ten days will be sufficient for my objectives, and I really want to take you to Hilton Head Island before the January Interim."

"You are the dearest. Now that I have things under control for my trip home, let's have a glass wine."

They left for the kitchen where she poured the red wine and handed him a glass. They toasted each other and returned to the couch.

"Okay, let's set a date for our trip to Hilton Head Island, so I can make the new reservations, hopefully in the same condo. I should get back to Ashland on Christmas day in time to make it to the condo that night or we can go later. What would you like to do?"

"I'd like for us to spend Christmas night at the farm. That's where we committed ourselves to each other, that's where we consummated that commitment, and that's where I'd like to spend my first night in a bed with you. Right there in the green bedroom. Two lovers, alone with each other without so much as another human being nearby.

"I'll prepare our first Christmas dinner and we'll eat it before the old fireplace in the den. Then I'd like for you to take me to Hilton Head Island the next morning."

"What do you want to do about the New Year's Eve party that Georgette is hosting?"

"That's a tradition for you, right?"
"I've been going for five years."
"Then let's come back in time for the party."
"Okay, that suits me."

***

The campfire was still burning bright when Barsh broke off his reminiscing. He cloaked himself with the deerskin poncho and made his way to the top of the bluff. There, he communed with the stars and pondered the ontological mystery of being until he was ready for his sleeping bag.

Chapter Six

After a good night's sleep and an adequate breakfast, Barsh was refreshed and ready for another day in the forest. He had decided to revisit several of his favorite places along the river and left the cave without his bow and arrows.

One place on his list for the day held such exceptional beauty that he had named it Cathedral Cove. Huge deciduous trees stretched high above the leaf-blanketed ground with their branches intermingling like a dome. A spring of crystal-clear water gushed from a small bluff and flowed through the cove into the river.

He was in no hurry to reach the place and stopped frequently to enjoy the scenery or watch a bird. On reaching the cove, he lingered, once again, as he absorbed the essence of the place.

It filled him with such a sense of ontological wholeness that he had no analogy to describe the experience. The best he could do was categorize it as the pure joy of being.

When he left Cathedral Cove, he trekked further north along a bank of quiet water until he reached a stretch of rapids. There he sat on the bank and listened to their anthems for a while. With a deep sense of wellbeing and much anticipation for the agenda he had set for himself later that night, he left for Bluff Cave.

***

After a supper of roasted mushrooms and catfish, he made his way to the top of the bluff. The astral luminosity of the cloudless night sky, untainted by any artificial light, awed him. He bowed his head in a gesture of reverence to the unfathomable Ground of Being—a designation for God that he had borrowed from Paul Tillich.

The moon, that was waxing toward fullness, would soon be overhead. When that happened, he would leave the bluff above the river for a night walk in the forest.

After a twenty-five-year hiatus, just to experience, again, such a walk would be good in itself, but he also hoped to experience, for the first time, a rafter of turkeys on their roost. On his second day in the wild, he had discovered their droppings beneath a huge oak tree, and he was confident that he could find the tree with the aid of the light from the moon and stars. He could only hope, however, that the turkeys would be roosting in the tree.

Meantime, he stretched out on his back on the thick bed of leaves to await the moon's closest journey overhead. Thus reposed, he reviewed his short sojourn in the wild.

Using only tools that he had made with his own hands, he had been able to sustain himself with several varieties of mushrooms, catfish, rabbit, and duck. The natural beauty of the place, the solitude, the reflections and meditations, however, were at the heart of this journey, and they had all nourished his soul. A deep sense of contentedness welled up in him.

In due time, the moon was beaming down on the terrain that he wanted to cover, and he walked northeast along the watershed that he'd named Bluff Ridge. The hollows to the south drained into Cedar Creek and those to the north drained into Beech Creek. And both creeks drained into the Tallapoosa River.

There was little underbrush along the ridge, and the luminosity of the night sky made for easy walking without stumbling over any obstacle. He paused occasionally to study the aesthetic beauty of the moonlight on various deciduous trees that had shed their leaves for the winter—each one with multi-formed boughs stretching out into various formations.

As he studied the moonlight on the gray bark of a tall hickory, he heard an animal pattering through the leaves. It was coming up from the north hollow, and if it kept its course, it would cross the ridge just above him.

He immediately ruled out a rabbit. They traveled in hopping spurts with a lot of stops. He thought it was likely a possum—a common night creature of the Alabama forests.

There was a breeze blowing down the ridge toward the river, which gave him hope that the keen nose of the animal would not detect his scent and scurry back down the hollow. Its feet kept pattering through the leaves.

It was a fox, probably a red one, although his eyes could not detect its color. He watched the sly creature, until it became aware of him and dashed off.

Although he had a mental map of the way to the turkey roost, the landmarks were not as easy to find at night. His first task was to find the dead tree that had fallen across Beech Creek. That was the nearest place for him to cross it. From there, he would have no trouble finding the turkey roost.

He remembered the huge sycamore tree on the opposite bank, just below the place where he would cross the creek. That would be a good landmark for him. Its gray-white bark always caught his eye when he passed near it during the day, and now he would get a chance to study it in the moonlight.

He left Bluff Ridge and eased through the forest toward Beech Creek. As soon as he heard the gurgling creek, he walked upstream until he saw the tall Sycamore.

The glistening moonlight on the tree created an astonishing sight. Standing here, taking in the experience, he wondered if any artist had ever tried to capture such a night scene on canvas.

Relieved that he had found the crossing point with such ease, he walked the trunk of the fallen tree to the other side and was soon standing beneath the turkey roost. He counted eleven turkeys, huddled about in the big oak.

They would be easy targets for him to kill with his bow and arrows, but he would not need to make that kill. Pleased with his night walk to the turkey roost, he headed back to camp.

The cold night air had chilled him by the time he entered the cave, and he quickly stirred the smoldering coals in the firepit to a red glow and then added tender and dead tree limbs until the flames danced with welcomed heat. He hovered close to the flames until he was warm and then sat in his usual place before the fire.

It was likely past midnight, and he tried to envision Hannah in her new bed in Louisville. Although he had never seen her sweet slumbering face in that bed, he knew it was bathed by the faint glow of a nightlight. She did not like to sleep in the dark. Fortunately, he had seen her new bedroom and could imagine her sleeping there in her favorite position.

"Be well, my sweet girl," he whispered.

The blazing fire had worked it magic on his cold body. Now he would have to wait for it to die down so he could bank it. Although it was late, he was not sleepy.

Shifting his thoughts to Angela, he assumed that she was asleep in her bed—a bed that had also felt the weight of his body together with hers on one occasion. That was the Sunday after Thanksgiving, and he began to reminisce about that special evening with her.

***

Barsh waited in the Charlotte Airport for Angela's flight from New York City as the clock ticked toward 5:20 that afternoon. Inevitably, he thought about the first time he waited for her in that same room back in April. Back then, he was deeply burdened by the fact that Debbie was leaving him, and he was not pleased that the responsibility for picking up Dr. Angela Kundera had fallen on him.

In his judgment, her visit for a job interview would likely be a waste of everyone's time. He could not imagine her leaving the urban centers of the North for small-town Ashland and a small liberal arts college like Cooper.

That assessment was not the first time he had misjudged a situation, but he had never been so astonished by the unforeseen turn of events this one produced. The idea that he would soon bond himself to Dr. Angela Kundera in romantic love was beyond his imagination at that time. But there he was waiting for her to return to his arms.

Someone announced the arrival of her flight, and he found a good place to watch for her. The passengers streamed into the waiting room, but no Angela. There was a break in the flood of people pouring through the door, and then a woman carrying a baby emerged with Angela following her. He waived and they rushed into each other's arms.

They collected Angela's luggage and left the airport. The Charlotte traffic was heavy and they rode in silence for a few minutes. At the first break from constantly shifting the gears of the Audi in the stop-and-go traffic, he took her hand and kissed it.

"I've only been gone six days and yet we have so much to catch up on. Did Debbie close on her new house?"

"Yes, everything went well. She now owns a fine house in the upscale neighborhood, where she had dreamed of living when she moved to Louisville as a young college graduate. She and Hannah got back about an hour before I left to get you."

"Is she still planning to move this week?"

"She will be leaving early Thursday morning. I'm taking the day off so I can be home, until the moving van leaves with her things."

"How is Hannah dealing with this?"

"I've never seen her as despondent as she was when they got back this afternoon. Debbie, however, was as happy as I've ever seen her. That pleases me. She deserves her own happiness. Truthfully, I'll be relieved when she leaves. I'm tired of all the duplicity.

"Catherine and I have agreed that it's time to inform everyone in the Division of Humanities about my situation. I have called a meeting during the lunch hour on Tuesday. Catherine will be there to confirm my narrative about Debbie's decision, back in March, to move to Louisville without me. She will also explain my half sabbatical that will start next semester.

"Catherine's role in this meeting is at my request. I don't want anyone thinking that you are the cause of Debbie and my permanent separation. Be prepared for how you want to respond if anyone asked if you already knew about the move."

"You always think ahead and I like that. Our colleagues have obviously noticed my adoration of you. Can I tell them the truth?"

"Yes, of course. Our early friendship was very noticeable and undoubtedly raised questions about us. Now the playing field has shifted, and I will be showing more affection for you around our colleagues."

"And you should know that I'll love that."

"Angie, while you were away, I made a firm decision to divorced Debbie. In early January, I'll consult with Jack Kelley, the lawyer we used to draw up the separation agreement. She trusts him. Hopefully, he can help me make the case that a non-contested divorce is the only fair recourse for me, and it will place no blame on her.

"I'll be disobeying Saint Paul's admonition against divorcing my wife. She will remain innocent and can quote him as giving her permission for the separation.

"The stipulations of the divorce will be the same as the separation agreement. The only difference being that I will be free to marry you."

"I like your decision and the gentle way you intend to deal with Debbie. But whether the divorce happens or not, I'm sticking with you until my last breath."

"That was also my resolve, but I'm now determined to divorce Debbie on equitable terms, whether she consents or not."

"Do you think you can get the divorce this winter?"

"Yes, I'm quite optimistic about that."

She did not respond immediately and he knew she was pondering something important.

"Based on your optimism about a quick divorce, I just came up with an idea. What would you think about keeping our current arrangement until after the divorce? I know you have concerns about adverse reactions from the trustees that could endanger your position at Cooper if we start living together while you're a married man."

"That's a good idea in more ways than one. The conservative trustees would definitely be unhappy to learn that their professor of religion was living with a woman other than his wife. Unfortunately, they view my position more as that of a minister than a professor.

"Since Debbie will be living in Louisville and I will be seeking a divorce, we can spend time with each other, every day, without having to keep it a secret. We also have the farm for private getaways."

"This is definitely the best course for us," she said.

"Let me focus on getting us onto I-85 South and then I want to hear more about your trip home."

The southbound traffic on the Interstate was flowing in a steady stream, but he spotted a slight opening and gunned the Audi into the flow. At the first safe opportunity, he smiled at her and she returned it. He felt whole and revitalized in body, heart, and soul.

"You are a gift from heaven, my dearest Angie. My joy gage is bubbling at one-hundred percent."

"Ditto, as you like to say."

"Okay, please share with me all the details of your trip."

"It was clearly my best visit home. When I got there, Mother and Daddy were anxious about the open-heart surgery that the doctor had scheduled. For once in my life, I think my presence was comforting to them.

"They seemed to sense my newfound peace and happiness, even before I told them how wonderful everything was going for me. Thanks again for sending me home."

"That was an easy call."

"The open-heart surgery went well, as I told you by phone, and they were feeling optimistic when I left.

"The idea of asking them, separately, to tell me their story before they married worked wonders in strengthening my relationship with them, especially Daddy. He's even talking about visiting me as soon as he regains his strength."

"Can I assume you're excited about that?"

"Most definitely. Okay, I'll jump to the most significant part of Daddy's story. As a young man, he dreamed about earning a Ph.D. in history and become a college professor, but family responsibilities forced him to drop out of college after two years. I had no idea that he had once dreamed of being an academic but had to settle for the business world. I now see him with new eyes."

"Empathy is a good thing," Barsh said.

"Fortunately, Daddy is finally retiring after devoting most of his life to one insurance company. I suggested that he take advantage of retirement and revive his interest in history. He said he would think about it and thanked me for suggesting it.

"I didn't tell him about us, but he took note of the fact that I kept talking about you. He was obviously curious about our relationship, but he didn't ask me.

"If you're wondering why I didn't tell him, it's because of my past history. After he learned about my last disastrous affair, he told me that I didn't know how to pick a man, that I always jump into an intimate relationship too soon.

"I have no doubt, however, that he will be most impressed with you and also approve our plan to get married, even though you are not a Catholic. Of course, my commitment to you does not depend on his approval, but I would like to have it."

"I totally understand."

"I was more cautious around Mother. She would definitely be distraught if she knew I was marrying someone who was not a Catholic. I talked about how well things were going for me and how happy I was at Cooper."

"Did you gain any new insights about her?"

"Did I ever! She was the fifth child of a large Catholic family. Her father was a hard worker but there was never enough income to meet the family needs. Mother's older siblings had to work to help support the family while she, as an adolescent, took refuge in the Catholic Church.

"The nuns saw her as a potential novitiate and managed to convince her that she had been called to serve God in their order. Her mother, however, derailed that dream and made Mother go to work as soon as she was old enough.

"Marrying Daddy, I think, was Mother's second choice for escaping the drudgery of living with her parents. After marriage, her primary goal seems to have been to rise to middle class status on Daddy's back. That gave her sufficient time to be a devoted Catholic, who seldom missed a service in the local church.

"This revelation gave me a better understanding of Mother. Now, it's more obvious to me than ever that she and Daddy were not a good match. But I can't complain about that. If they hadn't married, I wouldn't exist."

"And here you are the love of my life," he said.

"I love you, love you," she said, "and I am so ready to put some action behind my words as soon as we get back to my little house in Ashland. I have an ache to take you for the first time in my bed."

"Then I'll do my best to relieve your ache."

They made the trip back to Angela's house and soon retreated to her bedroom. Knowing they had but a short window of time before he had to leave for home, they utilized the time exceedingly well, before shifted back to a verbal connection.

"Could you have possibly missed me as much as I missed you?" she said as he dressed.

"Have no doubt, but a couple of hours with you has more than compensated for those few days. I'm now ready for the week ahead, although things are going to be hectic for me through Thursday."

"I understand, so don't worry about me."

"The good news is that you, Hannah, and I will now be able to spend the weekends together, until I take her to Louisville. Other than one obligation, the three of us can set our own agendas from Friday afternoons until Sunday evenings."

"What obligation?"

"Have you gotten to know Sarah Love?"

"Yes, and she's a trip."

"She will have a painting on exhibit at the Greenwood Arts Center during the month of December. It's a state-wide juried competition, and she's excited about making the show. One of her former students is a member of the Greenwood Artist Guild, and she raves about the talent of the local artists and the status of this annual exhibit.

"Sarah has invited me to the reception and awards ceremony. I'm fond of her and promised I would attend. I've attended most of the recent exhibits where she's had her work. Remember the Inn on the Square in Greenwood?"

"Yes, a lovely place."

"You, Hannah, and I could attend the reception and spend the night there if you'd like."

"I'll be packed and ready to go."

"If I reserve a suite or two-adjoining rooms, would you mind sharing one with Hannah?"

"Not at all."

"Of course, there will an opportunity for you and me to have a bit of privacy, once Hannah goes to sleep."

"I have no doubt. Sounds like a wonderful weekend in the making."

"That's my expectation. And here's my plan for sleeping arrangements after I start the divorce proceedings in January. Hannah will have her room and we will have ours."

"I like your plan. Thanks for sharing it."

Chapter Seven

Barsh woke to the sound of wind rattling the rhododendron bushes that guarded the entrance to the cave. It was the 22nd of December, Winter Solstice, the shortest day of the year. The sun had traveled as far as it would go from the earth and would now turn back and give the earth longer days until the Summer Solstice.

As he lay in his sleeping bag, he reminisced about his studies of the Ancient Near East. The Winter Solstice was the most significant day of the year for the people of those early civilizations. It was their New Year, and they celebrated it with various rituals—some of them included death and resurrection themes.

This Winter Solstice also seemed like a day of turning back for Barsh. For the first time since entering the wild, he was thinking about his return to civilization, and the first order of business he had set for himself was to divorce Debbie, so he could marry Angela.

He crawled out of the sleeping bag and rekindled the fire. As soon as it was blazing, he left to check the fish traps. The sky was mostly clear, but a strong wind was blowing from the southwest. The first trap was empty, but there was a blue catfish in the second one. On the way back to the cave, he added it to the catfish already in the holding cage. Those two catfish and a few mushrooms would feed him for the last two days of his wilderness experience.

Back in the cave, he thought about Hannah as he ate the leftovers from supper. This was her tenth day in Louisville, and he could not help but wonder how she was doing. During their last moments together, she told him not to worry about her, that she would be a big girl, that she had Davis to keep her company and that Angela had promised to call.

His thoughts soon shifted back to the agenda he had set for the day. He wanted to revisit Hawk Creek and explore its upper reaches, especially the waterfall that he could faintly hear whenever he crossed the creek by jumping from one large rock to another. He banked the remains of the fire and left the cave without bow and arrows.

As usual, he took note of things as he hiked through the forest. Not far from the cave, a white-breasted nuthatch flew into an oak tree, only twenty feet away. He watched it claw-hang its way down the trunk, head first, as it searched for various insects in the crevasses of the bark. With the image of the nuthatch stuck in his mind, he decided to focus on birding until he reached Hawk Creek.

During his daily hikes, he had sighted quite a number of different species of birds, although he had not consciously followed the practice of birders, who stopped frequently and waited for birds to come to where they are.

His decision to follow that practice proved to be a good one. By the time he reached Hawk Creek, he had sighted a diverse array of birds, including two species that he had not previously seen on this sojourn in the wild—a mountain bluebird and a ruby-crowned kinglet.

As he continued up the bank of Hawk Creek, the sound of the waterfall continued to intensify. Then he was there. Beautiful, just beautiful, he thought as he stood below the waterfall that dropped a good fifteen feet into a clear pool.

He sat down on the leafy bank with a deep sense of gratitude that Hawk Creek had remained such a pristine place. From the river to the waterfall, there was not a sign of human disturbance along its banks.

After considering possible names for the waterfall, he chose Angela Falls. Then, he took note of the number of days until he would be with her. In three days, dear Angie, he whispered.

Leaving the waterfall, he headed back to camp for an early supper in order to watch the sunset from the bluff above the cave and then to reflect on the Winter Solstice.

****

Barsh got to his special place on the bluff about thirty minutes before the sun would disappear from his vision, far beyond the Tallapoosa. There were a few clouds in the distant horizon. All the better for the sun to paint the sky on its descent.

He remembered his first sunset with Angela. He had picked her up at the Charlotte Airport for her job interview. On the way to Jackson's Steak House, he learned that she loved waterfalls and offered to take her to Cherokee Falls before dinner. She readily accepted his offer.

He had casually noted that they might get there in time to watch the sun paint the western sky with its weeping descent into the netherworld. Surprisingly, he was moved by her response to his comment: Ah, an intellectual who can still experience the world, mythopoetically. I like that about you. Among other things, I should add.

The sun was now painting the Alabama sky with the boldest of reds, and he was longing for Angela. It was the second time that day he had felt a deep longing for her, and he knew he was almost ready to complete his wilderness experience.

The temperature was dropping, but there was no wind. He was comfortable in his deerskin poncho and began to reflect on the efforts of humans to determine the relationship of the celestial objects to the earth.

He knew the fundamental discoveries that had marked the journey and freely acknowledged that he had contributed nothing to it. He was the beneficiary of the findings of a host of astonishing people, both known and unknown, who had advanced astronomy down through the years.

He thought about the early human clans, scattering over the earth. It seemed obvious to them that both the sun and the moon were circling the earth in predictable motions.

He assumed that shepherds of early herding societies were most likely the first to discover that the stars were also moving in relation to the earth. He imagined them studying the stars, night after night, as they watched over their herds throughout the year. Then one night, someone noticed that a certain group of stars had moved to a new location in the night sky and shared the discovery with a sense of awe.

The same story, no doubt, occurred among various people at various time, and thus humans began plotting the movement of the stars until several different cultures had discovered the twelve signs of the Zodiac. If he remembered correctly, it was the Egyptians who first refined their celestial observations until they developed a solar calendar of 365 days.

For a moment, he thought about Stonehenge and regretted that he had not found a way to work in a visit to that special place during his only trip to England. There had been too much to do and too little time. Hopefully, he would get a second chance to tour England, this time with Angela and Hannah.

Then he thought about the things he did experience in England, including the cuneiform “flood tablet” from the Gilgamesh Epic, that was housed at the British Museum in London. How he had stood before the glass case and praised George Smith who first translated the flood story on the tablet.

He refocused his thoughts on the New Year Festivals in the Ancient Near East with their myths and rituals of dying-and-rising gods based on the cyclic nature of the year. What a debt he owed to his graduate school professors who introduced him to the British Myth and Ritual School of thought and to the form-critical studies of the Germans and Scandinavians.

The combination of both schools of thought had guided so much of his research on the Hebrew scriptures of the Bible. He could only believe, however, that his major professors would be disappointed to learn that he had shifted his focus from Biblical research to more generalized studies.

He would always credit them with helping him find the grounding and perspectives that were essential for his teaching career. But they were always looking backward, trying to uncover more and more of the past. For him the past was significant primarily as prologue.

As soon as Barsh became a professor at Cooper, he heard the prophetic call to address the pathologies of modern civilizations. Responding to that call, he began to introduce interdisciplinary courses into the humanities curriculum.

One of those new courses was the Future of Mankind. He recalled one of his recent lectures in that class dealing with the question of sustainability and found himself reliving that hour with his students.

***

“Without doubt,” Barsh said to his students, “we are polluting and destroying vast areas of the natural world because of our consumer-driven economy. The people running most corporations seem to be motivated by insatiable greed with little concern for the common good or the natural environment.

"Moreover, people in general are committed to the pursuit of economic power that will enable them to buy bigger houses and more things. Neither the producers nor the consumers seem to care about the destructive effects their actions are having on the natural world.

"Think about the majority of people you know. Do you see a healthy balance in their lives between the pursuit of things and the pursuit of knowledge, wisdom, and the aesthetic power of the arts? I don't and I doubt that you do.

"I see greed and the dogged pursuit of economic power as two of the major pathologies of modern humanity. And it's clear to me that the poisonous fruits of these pathologies will be calamitous if we don't change our ways. I'm reminded of a prophetic vision recorded in the Bible:

> I looked at the earth,
> and it was waste and void;
> and at the heavens,
> and their light was gone.
> I looked at the mountains,
> and they were quaking;
> all the hills were swaying.
> I looked, and there were no people;
> every bird in the sky had flown.
> I looked, and the fruitful land was a desert;
> all its towns lay in ruins.

"This vision is recorded in the book of Jeremiah. But don't think that it and the other prophetic visions of the Bible, whether dystopian and utopian, were proclaimed as if they were set in stone by God to be fulfilled at some predetermined date. The Biblical prophets believed, as I do, that the future course of human history depended, in large part, upon the collective choices of the people of the earth."

"Dr. Roberts," John Jackson broke in, "my preacher claims that when every prophecy in the Bible comes to pass, time will end and there will be a new heaven and a new earth. He definitely believes that all Biblical prophecies are set in stone and will be fulfilled in every detail. What would you say to him?"

"I'd tell him to read the book of Jonah."

"I don't get it," Jackson responded.

"Do you know the story of Jonah?"

"Yeah, God told him to go to Nineveh and tell those wicked people that He was going to destroy their city. But Jonah was rebellious and sailed away for some other place. Then God sent a storm that terrified the sailors and they cast lots to find out who had caused God to send the storm. The lot fell on Jonah and they threw him into the sea.

"Then God sent a whale that swallowed Jonah, alive. After three days and nights in its belly, the whale spit Jonah up on dry land. After that, he obeyed God's original command and went to Nineveh and prophesied that God would destroy their city in forty days."

"Okay," Barsh said, "what happen after Jonah delivered that prophecy?"

"I don't remember."

"Does anyone remember?" Barsh asked and no one responded. "Well, here's the rest of the story. The people of Nineveh repented of their evil ways. Then God decided not to destroy the city. And how do you think Jonah responded to this?"

He paused for a response but the class was silent.

"Jonah was so mad that God had changed his mind about destroying Nineveh that he wanted God to take his life."

"Why?" someone asked.

"The people of Nineveh were enemies of the Hebrews, and Jonah wanted God to destroy them. That's why he first refused to go to Nineveh and proclaim the message. He knew God would change his mind if the people repented and changed their way."

"Dr. Roberts, you don't believe this happened, do you?" someone asked.

"For me, this story is a parable. It's also relevant to what I was trying to get across. There is a way that leads to destruction and there is a way that leads to sustainability.

"Our contemporary prophets are telling us that modern civilizations are headed down the wrong road, and I agree with them. We have to start thinking about sustainability and that in terms of the common good or we're going to be in big trouble."

***

Breaking from his reminiscing, Barsh returned to his reflection on the advances in astronomy. He thought about Copernicus and Galileo and their views on the heliocentric nature of our immediate universe.

How their discovery negated so many religious beliefs of yore that were set in the mythology of a three-story universe. For most ancients, there was heaven above where God or the gods and other divine beings dwelt, the earth in the middle where mortals lived, and the netherworld below where the dead resided in a devitalized form.

Barsh could not think of Galileo without remembering how the Catholic Church had forced him to recant his views. What a damnable document he was forced to sign.

Fortunately, there were no more Catholic and Protestant Inquisitions that could result in people being put to death. Still, there were too many intolerant dogmatists of all faiths who refused to be informed by scientific data.

In Barsh's view, it was way past time for all religions to demythologize their dogmas and focus their teaching on how we should live together here on this earth. Although that was not happening for the most part, there were a few within the various religious institutions who were challenging their people to reimagine God and religion.

As Barsh stood to leave the bluff for the cave, he resolved to continue his academic efforts to challenge his students to reimagine God and religion. Yes, he wanted to become a humanities professor, but he would not abandon his commitment to teaching religion courses. Too many people were still devoted to a religious system that blocked them from accepting many of the empirical discoveries of science.

Chapter Eight

With the fire blazing again in the cave, Barsh sat before it in a reflective mood. What struck him at that moment was the fact that the function of the campfire had changed for most humans during the course of history. For the paleolithic family, it was their gathering place, the place that pulled the family together. Now, it typically marked the campsite of a few people, men and boys more often than not, who journeyed forth from their homes to reconnect with nature on various levels for a short spell.

His current sojourn in the wild was fast coming to an end, and he was thinking about his house in Ashland, South Carolina—the place where his family had regrouped, almost daily for thirteen years. But never again would he regroup there with his wife and daughter as a family unit.

Twenty-three days ago, his wife Debbie left that house at daybreak for Louisville, Kentucky, with no intention of ever returning. Huddled before the campfire in the cave, he began to reminisce about the events of that day.

***

After driving his daughter to school, he returned home and waited in his study, until the moving van rolled in at the appointed hour. Ready to put life with Debbie behind him, he freely joined two men in carefully loading her things.

By early afternoon, that job was done, and at his request, the two men helped him move the furniture from the guest bedroom into the master bedroom. He was finished with sleeping in the guest bedroom in his own house.

He thanked the men, wished them a safe drive to Louisville, and watched the moving van leave the driveway. He then ate a light lunch and read, until it was time to pick up Hannah at her school.

He left the house and drove the same route that he had taken many times but never in quite the mood that had overtaken him. Truthfully, he was glad that Debbie and her things were gone, but he was sad that Hannah would soon be living with her in Louisville.

That sadness suppressed him, even more, when he saw his despondent daughter waiting in the pickup zone. He stopped at the curb and she slid into the seat beside him.

"Hey, my sweet girl, I've had a hard day. Did you?"

His day wasn't really that hard. His hope was that Hannah would share hers if it had been.

"What was hard for you, Daddy?" she asked with tears welling in her eyes. "You don't miss Mama, do you?"

"No, I'm actually relieved that she's gone. For months, I've tried to wear a public face like everything was okay between us.

My colleagues were shocked when I told them the truth. What was hard for me, today, was the inescapable fact that your days of living fulltime with me are numbered.

"In just two weeks, I'll drive you to Louisville to live with Debbie. My only relief comes from knowing that we'll exchange a few visits and then you will be back here for the summer.

"Don't forget that I'll be back in Louisville on Christmas Eve, and we'll spend the night in a motel. Then I'm flying you and Davis home before the end of January. In February, I'll be there to celebrate your twelfth birthday, and I'll likely return several more times before your school year ends.

"Putting that aside, I'm all for making this a good father-daughter night."

"Me, too."

"What would you like us to do for dinner? I can cook something or we can eat out?"

"Let's eat at home. I want to help you with dinner."

"Suits me. Then we'll discuss some possibilities for the weekend. Angela's meeting me at the farm at noon tomorrow. Then we'll pick you up at school."

"Are we spending the night at the farm?"

"Unless you have a better idea."

"No, I'd like that."

They drove in silence until they were back home in Fern Meadows. He parked the Ford pickup in Debbie's old place in the garage beside his Audi.

"Okay, brace yourself for the starkness of four empty rooms. This is not the same house you left this morning."

He followed Hannah into the den from the garage. She stopped to take in the emptiness.

"It makes me want to cry," she said.

"Crying is okay," he said.

"I didn't know she was leaving the paintings."

"The paintings are mine and were not negotiable."

"Like the books."

"Yes, of course, the books are mine. Here's something I can now tell you about this house. Angela and I have decided to make it our home. I gave her this option, not knowing if she would want to live here or not. She does and that means you'll be coming home to your old room."

"That's good news."

"Yes, it's good news for you and me. Angela and I will refurnish the empty rooms, but your room will always be your room. It will not change unless you want to change it.

"When you come back this summer, you'll have the option of redoing it. You can pick out any furniture you might want."

"Right now, I like my room as it is. But I might want to change things, later."

"That's fine. Just know that you have dominion over your room and I have dominion over my study. Beyond that, I intend to let Angela refurnish the house anyway that pleases her."

"Yeah, other than my room, your study, and the basement where we work out, we don't care about the house. Right?"

"You are ever so right, my sweet girl. I'm having grapes and water. What would you like?"

"I'll take the same."

They sat silently in his study and ate their grapes. Barsh forced a smile at her a few times. Hannah gradually relaxing a bit.

"Okay, my sweet girl, let's think ahead. Like I said, Angela's meeting me at the farm a little after noon tomorrow. We'll pick you up after school and go back to the farm. What would you like to do for the rest of the day?"

"What are the options?"

"We could eat dinner in Spartanburg and go see a movie—something the three of us have never done. There's a new movie playing that should interest you. *The Lord of the Rings*. Like you, Angela likes Tolkien's books, so I'm confident she would like to see the movie."

"Oh, goodie, let's do that. What about Saturday?"

"We could spend the day at the farm unless you would prefer something else. The three of us have never spent a whole day there. The last time Angela and I walked in our woods, I took her by a patch of cedar trees of various sizes.

"She jumped at the idea of cutting one and putting it up in the farmhouse. Would you like for it to be our only Christmas tree or do you want us to get another one for here?"

"A Christmas tree in our empty den would make me cry. Just one for the farmhouse."

"Okay, that's what we'll do."

***

Barsh shifted from his reminiscing and sat watching the smoldering coals in the firepit. It was time to bank them, but the sleeping bag did not seem the answer for the disquietude that had overtaken him. Thinking that a short stint down by the river might help settle his mind, he fed the fire with a few dead limbs and left the cave.

He eased his way down to the river bank, where he sat watching the rapids that were illumined by the moon's silver light. As he had hoped, he found their endless songs to be relaxing and was soon totally absorbed in the moment.

Somewhere in the forest behind him, the loud hoots of a barred owl seemed to declare that all was well in its world. Trusting that the same held for those he loved, he made his way back to the cave, where he sat warming himself by the fire.

As he thought about his return to Ashland, he began to reminisce about his last weekend with Hannah and Angela, when they attended the reception for the December exhibit at the Greenwood Arts Center.

***

As soon as they entered the large gallery, that was filled with people in a festive mood, Sarah Love came rushing over to greet them.

"This is a pleasant surprise, Angela," she said and embraced her. "Thanks for coming."

"It's good to be here."

"Barsh, I've been on the lookout for you and Hannah. Now I'm delighted that you brought Angela."

"Let's start with your painting," he said. "I'm eager to see it."

"I have good news. I won second place. And someone has already bought the painting."

"Congratulations!" Angela said and Barsh echoed her.

They followed Sarah to the painting—a large piece entitled "Down by the River."

"What a splendid painting," he said.

"Yes," Angele said. "I love the impressionistic way you've painted the trees along the river bank."

"Angela, you probably don't know this, but Barsh is responsible for my interest in painting trees. He showed me prints of Emily Carr's enchanting paintings of trees in British Columbia and asked if I'd ever painted trees. Of course, I had not. That was the beginning of my interest in painting trees, including the yellow poplars and hemlocks in the Joyce Kilmer Memorial Forest."

"No, I didn't know that, but I've seen your painting of the yellow poplars that Barsh bought. He also took Hannah and me to see those magnificent trees."

"That's interesting. I had to go there on my own. Barsh, there's a large painting of a lone woman journeying forth into a forest on a starry night that I think you'll like."

"Please show me," he said.

"It's on the opposite wall," she said and pointed to it.

The lower horizon in the painting was black, but the night sky was filled with brilliant stars that illuminated a massive oak that had shed it leaves for the winter. In the foreground, there was the backside of a woman walking alone in that forest. Her hair was long and black, and she was wearing a red robe. Barsh assumed the woman was Native American even before he read the title "She Walks Two Worlds."

"You like it, don't you, Daddy."

"Very much and it's priced within my acceptable purchase range. I think we should buy it. What do you think?"

"Yeah, let's buy it."

"Good choice," Angela said.

"Hi, I'm Amy Allen," a young woman said as she approached them. "Do you like my painting?"

“I’m quite taken by it. Your hair is so like the woman’s. Are you Native American?”

“My mother was Cherokee and I’m proud of my heritage.”

“And you should be,” he said and introduced the group.

“Amy, I love your painting,” Angela said.

“Thank you. It’s one of my older paintings. For some unknown reason, I decided to exhibit it for the first time this year.”

“How fortunate this is for me,” Barsh said. “I’d like to buy it.”

“Wonderful. I’ll find the curator and we’ll settle things. You can pick up the painting when the exhibit comes down.”

Just so, the transaction was soon completed.

“I think we should celebrate with a glass of wine,” Sarah said. “There’s punch for Hannah.”

After they’d visited the wine table, he noticed that Sarah had edged Angela aside for a private conversation. He assumed that she was questioning her about her relationship with him.

Angela was soon at his side, again, and they set out to study the rest of the paintings. A stunning portrait of a pre-teen girl soon caught his eye. It was not for sale, so he assumed it was probably commissioned.

“Hannah, look at this,” he said. “I love this portrait.”

“It’s nice,” she said.

“I’d like to meet the artist. Amy, do you know Denise Wildsmith?”

“Yes, give me a minute and I’ll find her.”

Amy retuned with the artist and proper introductions were made.

“Denise, I love this portrait. Would you be interested in doing one of Hannah?”

“I’d love to paint Hannah. The two girls seem to be about the same age. Can you bring her for a sitting or do you want me to work from photos?”

“Photos. I have a suggestion. Let’s meet at the Inn on the Square after the reception. We have a reservation there for the night.

“The entrance is such a grand room with couches and chairs. And there’s an accessible bar. I think it would be a good place for us to socialize.”

“Yes, and I’ll take some photos of Hannah.”

"Amy, Sarah, would you like to join us?" Barsh asked and they both did.

Later, they gathered in the large lobby of the Inn on the Square for a lively and joyous time. And Denise took lots of photos of Hannah in various poses.

When the group dispersed, Barsh led the way to their two-adjoining rooms, where they conversed in his room, until Hannah's bedtime. In the adjoining room, Angela let her choose which bed she preferred and waited while she changed into her pajamas.

"I like sharing this room with you, Hannah. If you should have a bad dream in the wee hours of the night, just crawl in my bed and snuggle up with me."

"I like this arrangement," Hannah said.

"Okay, let me tuck you in. Barsh and I have a lot to talk about. This will be our last weekend together, until he returns from the wilds of Alabama. Sleep well. I'll close the door so our conversations won't distract you, and I'll try not to wake you when I come to bed."

***

The memories of that last weekend with Angela and Hannah had filled Barsh with deep anticipation of reconnecting with them. His brief sojourn in the wild had been good for him, but in one more full day, he would be ready to leave the forest and begin a new chapter in his life.

"Be well, my dear Hannah and Angie," he whispered. Then he banked the fire and crawled into his sleeping bag.

Chapter Nine

Standing on the bank of the Tallapoosa River, Barsh watched six ducks flying upstream in the early morning light. It was December 23th—the last full day of his excursion into the wild.

He pulled his last fish trap from the bottom of the river onto the bank. It contained a large blue catfish, that he released back into the river. The holding cage already held one that would suffice for his last two meals.

Pleased with the success of his two fish traps, he carried them back to the cave, where he stashed them, although they would likely rot without ever being used again. That would be fine with him. They had already served him well.

He left the cave with the primary objective of visiting a campsite from his youth that was located miles downriver. The sky was clear, the weather was mild for December, and he was hiking with purpose and a joyful heart.

Knowing that he would have to cross Cedar Creek, the largest stream between him and his destination, he set out for a place that he had named Three-Rock Pool in his youth. On reaching the place, he paused to admire the beauty of the pool that was created by three huge boulders.

On arriving at the pool, he was tempted to strip naked and bath himself. He certainly needed a bath. On second thought, he decided against it, because he would have to dress in the same buckskin outfit that he had worn for ten days.

Overhead, islands of puffy white clouds were drifting in from the east. He caught sight of a small hawk above the forest beyond the creek and watched it until it alighted in the top of a tall poplar on the opposite bank. After a few minutes, the kestrel flew across the creek just above the pool and disappeared.

Barsh descended the creek bank, crossed over on the boulders, ascended the other bank, and travelled southwest on a course that placed him near the river. There was little underbrush among the tall hardwood trees and he walked at a good pace.

Late that morning, he came to a place on the Tallapoosa that he had known as Heflin's Ferry, although the ferry had disappeared before his time. In his youth, he would park his Ford pickup near the end of the road and hike down-river about a mile to a spring, where he would camp in the open air.

With memories afresh, he hiked through the woods to his old campsite, that he had named Camp Heflin. A thick bed of leaves had all but hidden the firepit that he had built, but his knowing eyes could still detect the outline of the stones that he had use to line it.

A hickory sapling was now growing in the firepit. Grow tall and feed the squirrels with an abundance of hickory nuts, he whispered to the sapling.

The nearby spring was still bubbling crystal-clear water that trickled into the Tallapoosa River about thirty feet away. He knelt beside the little pool and drank his fill.

Back at the firepit, he sat, facing the river, and reminisced about his boyhood days of camping there. At night with the fire blazing before him and bullfrogs bellowing up and down the river, he would find himself dreaming about April Morehouse.

She was the new girl in his freshman class at Bradley High and had captured his heart, almost from day one. The year he turned seventeen, she had showed considerable interest in him, even visited him at their farm to see his quarter horse Thunder.

He, however, had gotten entangled with a married woman, while her husband was fighting the communist in Korea. It was not a love affair, but a sexual affair. She had pulled him into her life to help her get through some of her lonely nights.

Based on his ethical code, that sexual entanglement prohibited him from seeking a courtship with April. Meantime, a prominent town boy made a move on her and they became sweethearts.

After her husband returned home, Barsh dated a few girls, but April remained his dream girl all through high school. He was in his first year of college before he realized that she was not the girl that he needed for a lifetime partner. She would have bound him to that little town, for life, and trapped him in its conservative perspectives on things.

Turning from those thoughts, he reminisced about how his experiences had gradually prepared him for Angela Kundera. As a young man, he would not have been drawn to her. But how perfectly she seemed to match his needs at midlife. Would that assessment ever change with time? Could time change his love for her or hers for him? The questions broke into his consciousness, but he dismissed them with no further analysis.

There was a faint rustling of leaves between him and the river that pulled him back into the moment. A rufous-sided towhee was foraging the leaves, and he watched the fascinating bird until it flew away.

Standing, he looked into the sky for the sun and judged the day to be about noontime. He surveyed the place for a final time and left for Bluff Cave.

***

Finished with his last evening meal in the cave, Barsh added several dead limbs to the fire and sat down before it. As his thoughts turned to Angela, he visualized her preparing dinner in her little house near Cooper College and then eating alone at her kitchen table.

Letting his mind go wherever it wanted to go, he was soon reflecting on the few times he had been with her in that house. They were always with the nagging constraint of time hanging over his head. On every occasion, he'd had to say, "Sorry, but I have to go."

If all went well, that would change in two days. For the first time, there would be no rush for him to leave her house.

Next, he reminisced about his first rendezvous with Angela in the house in Fern Meadows after Debbie moved to Louisville.

***

He had just finished averaging his students' semester grades, when he heard Angela's steps in the hallway. He stood and watched as she entered his office. As always, she exuded a disposition that elevated his spirit.

"Have you finished the grading?"

"Yes, I'm ready to take them to the registrar's office. Give me ten minutes and I'll be back."

"And I'll be eagerly waiting for you."

"Hopefully, I'll be able to tell Catherine goodbye, while I'm over that way. I promised her I'd stop by."

"Please tell her I send greetings," she said and walked across the hall to her office.

He gathered up his paperwork and took it to the registrar's office. Then he stopped by Dean Thompson's office. Her door was closed, and her secretary was talking on the phone. He knew Catherine was in conference with someone or working on something important. Otherwise, the door would be open. He hesitated a moment and then turned to leave.

"Wait, Dr. Roberts," her secretary said. "Dean Thompson asked me to interrupt her if you came by."

She knocked gently on the door and announced his presence. Catherine rose, greeted him warmly, gestured for him to sit, as usual, so they were facing each other.

"I assume you've finished your grading," she said.

"I just dropped the final grades at the registrar's office."

"Do you realize this will be the first time in years that you and Hannah have not eaten breakfast with me the first Saturday of Christmas break? I'm very fond of traditions, but sometimes they must be broken for good reasons. And you have a good reason this year."

"I used to think I had a good reason for this short journey into the wild, self-centered though it would be. Now, I don't really need it. Angela is more than adequate for anything that was missing in my life.

"She insists, however, that I stick with my plan. I think she's afraid that if I don't take advantage of this opportunity, I'll regret it, when it's too late, and blame her. But I would never do that."

"No, but Angela doesn't yet know you as well as I do. Personally, I'm glad you're taking this unique journey. My guess is that you do need it. And like you told me earlier, it's now or never."

"Thanks for always supporting me, Catherine. You are and will remain a vital part of my life as long as we both have breath. When I return, we'll work on creating new traditions."

"And I'll look forward to them."

"Angela asked me to give you her greetings," he said as he stood to leave.

"I hope you want worry about her while you're gone. Georgette and I will make sure she has a bit of social life. Have a good trip, Barsh."

"And you have a good Christmas break."

He hurried back to his office, retrieved his brief case, locked the door, and joined Angela who was locking her office door.

"Did you see Catherine?"

"Yes, I'm pleased to say. She assured me that she and Georgette will see that you have a bit of social life, while I'm gone."

"My goal is to work like the devil on the novel. But I'll accept their invitations. There will never be a substitute for you, however."

"I don't have to go, you know."

"Yes, you need to go for both of us. But, oh, what a wonderful day it will be for me when you return."

"Make that a wonderful day for us."

"For us, always."

They walked silently to the parking lot and left in Barsh's Audi.

"Do you realized this is the first time you and I have left the college together, since I moved here? I mean in the same car."

"I'm very conscious of that. Fortunately for us, this is a new day. We are now a public couple."

"When people query me about our relationship, I unabashedly tell them that we are now an item. Don't forget to go by the house, so I can get my bag.

"I'm looking forward to a new first. More explicitly, I'm primed for our first love session in our house as you now call it."

After retrieving Angela's bag, they drove straight to Fern Meadows. He parked in the garage next to his Ford pickup and closed the garage door.

"Welcome, to our house," he said as he ushered her into the empty den. "Remember you can furnish the empty rooms as you choose, but I like the idea of using your furniture. We can also have someone rip up the carpets and replace them or install hardwood floors. Now, let's take a quick tour of the place before we settle down.

"Oh, before I forget it, I'm giving you a set of keys for the house. They're on the kitchen table with a remote control for the garage. Don't forget to take them.

"I'd like for you to pick up my mail every few days if you don't mind. You can leave it on my desk."

"No, I don't mind. Would you mind if I occasionally used your study to do some editing on the novel, just for a change of pace?"

"Please use my study anytime."

"One more question. What if I'm working late in your study and decided I'd like to sleep over?"

"The house is now yours as much a mine. Use it anyway that please you. I've told my closest neighbors that you might be coming and going. No one will be alarmed."

"Thank you," she said as he led her into the dining room.

"This room and the living room would make a good study for you. Your choice."

"I like the idea of keeping a formal dining room—something I've never had. I'd like for us to host formal dinners parties as well as cocktail parties."

"Then that's the way we shall entertain, and you can furnish the dining room with any style of furniture that pleases you."

"We'll choose something that we both like," she said and they moved to the living room.

"Oh, yes, I'd love to turn this into my study."

"Good choice. What would you think about building floor-to-ceiling bookcases along the far end of the room?"

"I'd like that a lot, and there's room to create a cozy sitting area for four people."

"Let me show you the master bedroom," he said and led her down the hall to the open door. "This room is now furnished with the furniture from the guest bedroom—Debbie's move to Louisville having left it empty.

"Here's my story. I'd been sleeping in the guest bedroom for almost a year, so I was eager to get myself back in the master bedroom of my own house, even though I would be sleeping by myself. I'll move it back if you prefer yours for our bedroom."

"No, I like the queen-sized bed. As you know, mine is a double bed, so we'll put my bedroom furniture in the guest bedroom."

“Angie, we have about two hours before I pick up Hannah and head for Louisville. Let’s make roast beef sandwiches and talk in the study, while I anticipate the presentation you will make in our master bedroom.”

“All I’ll need is a few minutes with my big bag.”

They fixed sandwiches in the kitchen and shifted to his study, where he ushered her to his chair at the desk.

“I also need a fresh image of you at this desk,” he said and sat in the chair facing her. “Yes, I see more than a wife and professor. I see a brilliant novelist.”

“Thanks for believing in me.”

“I totally believe in you, and here’s a copy of my new Last Will and Testament to back up my words.”

“Wait a minute. I don’t want to think about your Last Will and Testament. Is this trip more dangerous than you’ve been telling me?”

“No, no. I would have changed my will to include you even if I were not leaving for the wilds for a few days. It’s just a precaution against the uncertainties of life. I will be at far greater risks on the highway than camping in Bluff Cave. We’ve committed ourselves to each other, and I consider you my wife, regardless of what our state laws have to say about us.

“The law would give you nothing if something fatal happened to me before we are married. I’m in a position to leave you something if I should die before that happens, and a will is the only way that I have of making sure that you get what I would want you to have.”

“I’ve already taken care of Hannah by creating a trust in which she is the beneficiary. I think I told you that the funds for the trust came from the insurance settlement with the trucking company whose driver was responsible for the death of Mother and Dad.

“As detailed in my will, you’ll get this house, my annuity, and my investment and savings accounts. You’ll also have a living interest in the farm, but after that, the farm is to be sold with the proceeds going to the trust. That stipulation is because I used funds from the trust to buy the farm.”

“You are a generous man and I’m grateful that you care about my wellbeing.”

He then shared his strategy that, if successful, would get him to his campsite by noon the next day. It involved rigorous driving with only four hours of sleep in a motel.

"Couldn't you get there a little later and get more sleep?"

"I have a lot of things to do before nightfall, including gathering mushrooms and killing a rabbit or duck for supper. I can make it on four hours of sleep. Please don't worry about me."

"I need a hug," she said and they stood there in a tight embrace that soon shifted to a passionate kiss.

"Give me a few minutes," she said and left for the master bedroom.

He quickly cleaned up the kitchen and then waited in the study.

"Come and take me," she called and he did.

Afterwards, they lay side by side silently holding hands with pure contentment. Then they began to share their tender thoughts, and from there, the conversation branched out in various directions as the clock ticked away their allotted time. Each shift in the conversation seemed natural if not essential for their last time together before his journey.

"Sorry to say so, Angie, but we need to get dressed. By the time I get you back to Cooper, it will be time of me to pick up Hannah and get on the road to Louisville."

***

Breaking from his reminiscing, Barsh banked the last flickering flames of the fire and wiggled into his sleeping bag. Given his intention to rise early, he needed to get to sleep and he did, most likely for the last time ever in Bluff Cave.

Chapter Ten

Barsh woke long before daybreak in the pitch-dark cave, where he lay for a moment in his buckskin sleeping bag. He was ready to leave the wilds along the Tallapoosa River.

Rising to embrace the day before him, he rekindled the fire for the last time and ate the leftover fish and mushrooms. Finished with breakfast, he retrieved his backpack that had set undisturbed for ten days and began to transition from the physical culture of the stone age back to that of the modern world.

He removed his buckskin clothes and sponged off with a bath cloth that he had packed for the task. Other than washing his face and hands without soap or bath cloth, he had not bathed since entering the forest.

He applied a generous amount of lotion to his chapped hand, dressed in the hiking outfit that he had worn into the forest, combed his tangled hair, as best he could, and fixed it in a ponytail. He retrieved his wallet, car keys, wristwatch, and flashlight from the backpack.

Except for his buckskin clothes, water mug, bow and quiver of arrows, he had decided to leave everything else in the cave. It was time to bid the cave good bye.

The fire had burned down to a few flickering flames. He smothered it with ashes and left.

The sky was clear and luminous with stars. The moon, however, was well into its westward journey, so the landscape was dark. With the aid of the flashlight, he hiked through the forest with purpose and a good sense of direction.

The day was dawning when he reached John Hicks' old farmhouse at the edge of the forest where he had parked his Audi. He had also parked there during his first camping experience at Bluff Cave during Christmas break of his senior year at Bradley High.

Mrs. Hicks, now widowed, lived alone in the old farmhouse. She had remembered Barsh from those days and granted him permission to park in her backyard, again.

The light was on in the kitchen. After depositing his things in the trunk of the Audi, he knocked on the back door.

"Come in, my good man. You're just in time to have breakfast with me."

"Thanks, but I've already eaten. I would like to use you phone if I may."

"Yes, of course, you can use the phone. Barsh Roberts, you know I wouldn't charge you anything for parking your car, while you were camping by the river. I couldn't believe my eyes when I open the Christmas card you gave me. Nobody's ever given me that kind of money."

"Freely given. I need to make a long-distance call, but I'll call collect."

"Come right on into my parlor," she said and led him to the phone.

He dialed the operator and placed a call to Angela.

"Oh, my dearest Barsh, I've been up, drinking coffee and waiting for this call. How are you?"

"I'm fine. I just got to the farmhouse I told you about. How are you?"

"Feeling super fine now that we've connected by phone. How was the wilderness experience?"

"Very good. I look forward to telling you all about it, when I get home. What's the latest on your father?"

"He's doing very well. We had a long conversation, yesterday, and I told him about us."

"How did that go?"

"I couldn't have been happier with his response. He's looking forward to meeting you."

"That's good news. What about your mother?"

"Daddy's going to lay the groundwork for me. Thanks to you, I now know how to deal with Mother."

"Any urgent news I should know?"

"All is well. Hannah and I have had a lot of good conversations, including one last night. She's on cloud nine as she awaits your visit."

"I'd call her but she likely still asleep. Will you please call her later this morning and tell her I'm on my way to Louisville?"

"My pleasure."

"I'd also like for you to call Catherine and give her an update."

"That's already on my agenda. We also talked last night, and she asked me to call her as soon as I heard from you. She and Georgette have been very good to me, during your absence."

"I can't wait to see you, tomorrow."

"Oh, yes, tomorrow! Do be careful on the road."

"Love you. Love you. Bye."

"And do I ever love you. Bye."

He thanked Mrs. Hicks and left. Feeling exuberant, he drove with a determined effort to complete the drive with as few stops as possible. But there was so much for him to think about along the way. Not only were he and Angela starting a new journey, he was taking a half sabbatical starting in January and would be commuting to the University of South Carolina in Columbia on Tuesdays and Thursdays.

He had signed up for a course in modern poetry with a professor he knew nothing about, and he was okay with that. The prize for him, however, was getting accepted into James Dickey's creative writing course on poetry. He had heard Dickey took delight in his own poetry but knew nothing about how he conducted his class or critiqued the work of his students.

Barsh was mentally tough and could take criticism. In his field of religious studies, he could run with the best and that would help protect his ego as he struggled to sharpen his creative-writing skills.

He felt certain that whatever corpus of poetry he might write it would contain poems about nature and the ecosystem. It would also include poems that focused on social issues as well as narrative poems that focused on some of his seminal experiences.

The idea of becoming a poet had thus become very pleasing to him. He could see that it would give him a voice that extended beyond the classrooms at Cooper College.

The drive to Louisville went well. There were no accidents or roadworks to delay him, and he got to the motel within twenty minutes of the time he had calculated.

As soon as he checked into his room, he called Hannah to tell her that he would pick her up as soon as he showered and dressed for the evening. She was jubilant and asked him to hurry.

Chapter Eleven

When Barsh turned into the driveway of Debbie's new house, Hannah was sitting on the front steps. She stood and waited for him to park.

"Daddy," she cried as she ran for his embrace.

"My sweet girl," he said as he scooped her up in his arms and carried her to the steps, where they sat side by side.

"I've been waiting for you."

"Sorry it took me so long. After I called you, I called Angela. Then I took a long shower that I much needed. Now, I need to hear how you're making out."

"Okay, I guess. I read and write a lot. Most afternoons, Davis and I go for a walk in the neighborhood. I look for birds along the way, and she talks about the big houses. One day, she took me to the library and I checked out a load of books."

"That's good. I want you to keep reading all kinds of books. Have you visited your new school?"

"Mother drove me by. The buildings are nice."

"I'm hoping you'll have good teachers who will recognize your abilities and challenge you."

"Don't worry, Daddy. I can deal with living here as long as I can stay in touch with you."

"That's a given. Now that you have your own phone, we can have private conversations as often as we wish. And we can talk as long as we wish."

"Are you still planning to fly Davis and me home in January?"

"Oh, yes. Let me say hello to Debbie and Davis, while you get your things. Then we'll be off on our own."

"Daddy's here," she yelled from the foyer and ran to her room.

"We're in the den," Debbie responded.

The den furniture was arranged just as it had been in the house in Fern Meadows. Debbie was sitting in her big platform rocker and Davis was sitting in what used to be his big stuffed chair.

"Hello," he said, nodding to each woman.

"Hey," Debbie said.

"You're looking good, Dr. Roberts. No noticeable wear from your camping trip."

"It was actually very good for me. How are you making it in Louisville?"

"Good, so far. It's not bad at all up here. Don't know why I was dreading the change."

"Hannah tells me that the two of you enjoy afternoon walks in the neighborhood."

"She's right about that. And I like the car y'all bought me. I'm learning how to drive to places. Next week, I'll learn how to drive to Hannah's school."

"I'd like to fly you and Hannah down the last weekend in January if that suits you."

"I'll be packed and ready."

"Will that be okay with you, Debbie?"

"That's fine with me."

"Thank you. How are things at the firm?"

"Very good. I'm happy and the partners all seem pleased that I'm here. Henry is constantly telling me how glad he is to have me back. He does seem lonely, however. I guess he's still missing his wife. I don't think I told you that she died last year of congestive heart failure."

"I'm sorry to hear that, but I'm glad you're happy," he said as Hannah entered the den with her bag. "I'll have Hannah back by 7:00 in the morning. Is that too early for her to open her presents?"

"No, I'll be up."

"Good. I'll be heading straight for Ashland as soon as she opens her presents. A good evening to you both."

***

He took Hannah to a restaurant that he remembered from his days at the theological seminary. They talked about his experiences in the wilds of Alabama and the agenda facing him when he got home. On leaving their table, he stopped at an empty booth across the room.

"Hannah, the first time I took your mother out on a date, we ate dinner here in this booth and then went to a movie. At the time, I don't think either one of us realized that we were not a good match. But I would do it all again, just to have you as my daughter."

Hannah did not respond, but he could tell she was thinking about their marriage. He paid the cashier and they left in a rather somber mood.

"I've never doubted that you love me, Daddy. Still, it's good to hear you say you'd do it all again, just to have me as your daughter. As you're always telling me, words have magical powers for good and evil."

"Just remember that I'm partly responsible for the separation. Honor Debbie as your mother and try to understand her."

"I'm trying but it's hard."

"You're in a boat that I never had to row, so I can't say I know how you feel. I do remember that my father expected me to do tasks on the farm that I'd never done before nor had I watched anyone do them. I had to learn on the job, while he was at work.

"According to Dad, responsibility is the first step toward manhood for a boy. And I managed to earn his respect in a lot of ways. By the time I was seventeen, he and his friends were deferring to me on decisions about hunting and fishing. I guess I'm trying to say that I trust you will somehow manage to navigate the rough waters before you."

"I can do it, Daddy."

"That's my girl. Now, let's enjoy this Christmas Eve."

***

Back in the motel, he plugged in the lights of a small artificial Christmas tree that they had just bought at a strip mall.

"I'm calling this the make-do Christmas tree of 1978. Maybe you can write a poem about it."

"It will serve its purpose, Daddy."

"Yes, it will," he said and they both placed two presents beneath it.

"Daddy, I feel bad that the books you ordered for me to give Angela didn't come before we left Ashland."

"Don't be. That delay is going to work out just fine. When the college bookstore reopens the first of the year, I'll pick up the book and wrap them for you. Then I'll create a special occasion to give them to her. As you know, she really likes the practice you and I recently adopted of giving each other only two books for Christmas and focusing our giving on various charities.

"Okay, it's poetry time, and then you can open one of my presents and one of Angela's. I want you to save the other two for Christmas morning."

Hannah retrieved her notebook, and they sat facing each other. First, she read a poem she had revised since the move the Louisville.

"I like its new slant, Hannah. I just thought about what Emily Dickinson said: Tell all the truth but tell it slant. Revising is usually essential for good writing, and I'm pleased to see you doing so."

Next, she read a new poem and he responded to it with appropriate praise and one constructive suggestion.

"I'm working on another new poem, but I'm not ready to share it."

"Ah, my sweet girl, it's hard for me to comprehend the literary feats you have achieved at your age. I have no recollection of writing anything other than answers to test questions at your age.

"I'm sorry to say that I was twelve before I started reading books other than my school books. That's the year, I discovered a series of novels about five young men who would shun the frontier settlements of eighteenth-century America and roam the vast virgin forests of their day.

"Like Native Americans, they could live off the land, and they loved the freedom of living independently in the wild. What I liked most about those books was the descriptions of vast virgin forests teeming with game and pristine creeks and rivers brimming with fish.

"I envied those five young men for being able to experience such unspoiled places of nature, and I lamented the fact that I was born too late to do so. Still, I felt the call of the wild, and in my own way, I took refuge in various patches of wildness whenever I could. Well, with that said, I think this would be a good time to give you my first Christmas present."

He gave it to her and she ripped off the paper.

"*The Eyes of the Woods* by Joseph A. Altsheler," she read out loud. "Is this one of those books you just told me about?"

"You got it. I know you can't identify with Henry Ware, the leader of the pack, but try to envision me reading it at twelve."

"This is going to be fun," she said. "Now, here's my Christmas Eve book for you. I had help choosing it, and I'm sure you can figure out who helped me."

He unwrapped the book, *The Poetry of the Negro: 1746-1970* edited by Langston Hughes and Arna Bontemps.

"What a marvelous choice. You could not have chosen a better book for me."

"Angela says this is a collector's book. You won't find most of these poems in the standard anthologies of American poetry."

"Then I'm indebted to both of you."

"You'll have to wait until you and Angela exchange gifts to open this one," she said and gave it to him.

"Well, it's heavy. Does that mean it has a lot of photos?"

"Lots and lots."

"Then I'm guessing it all about birds."

"You are on the wrong trail, Daddy."

"A travel book, maybe?"

"I guess you could call it a travel book but not a typical one. It's part of a big surprise that involves Angela. She wants to explain everything to you."

"Then it must be part of some series, right?"

"Yes, and that's all I can tell you."

"Okay, I'll open it with Angela, tomorrow. Just know you've aroused my curiosity. Here's Angela's present for tonight."

Hannah ripped off the paper and read aloud, "*Complete Poems of Robert Frost*. Great. She knows I like Frost's poems. Daddy, I like the way the three of us share things."

"Speaking of sharing, I need to share a decision I've made about Debbie and me."

"Does it affect me?"

"No, it's about the legal status of your mother and me. I can no longer accept the fact that we are legally husband and wife. The marriage is dead, and I want a legal acknowledgment of that truth.

"To achieve that status, I've decided to divorce Debbie with the same stipulations as the separation agreement that we executed. Debbie will always be your mother and I will always be your father. Nothing will change for you in that regard.

"At first, Debbie wanted a trial separation for a year, and I accepted that, hoping that she would come back if things didn't turn out well for her here in Louisville. Then she wanted to make the separation legal and permanent.

"When I introduced the question of divorce, she pleaded with me not to force a divorce on her, so I promised that I wouldn't divorce her and agreed to a permanent separation. I now realize that was a big mistake for me."

"But Daddy, why would she think a permanent separation is okay but divorce isn't? Like you said, either way the marriage is dead."

He retrieved the Bible that the Gideons had placed in the motel and turned to a passage in I Corinthians.

"Okay, in Biblical time, Jewish men could divorce their wives, but Jewish women could not divorce their husbands. Saint Paul changed that for Christians. This is what he wrote to the Christian in the Greek City of Corinth: To the married I give charge, not I but the Lord, that the wife should not separate from her husband (but if she does, let her remain single or be reconciled to her husband) — and that the husband should not divorce his wife.

"Debbie believes that this passage is God's will for all marriages, but I don't. I understand this passage to be based on Saint Paul's assumption that the world, as it was known then, would be radically changed during his lifetime with the return of Jesus the Messiah."

"What does that mean?"

"Saint Paul and other Christians of his day believed that after Jesus was crucified, he rose from the dead with an immortal body and ascended to Heaven, where he sits on a golden throne at the righthand of God. They also believed that Jesus would return to earth during their lifetime to establish the Kingdom of God on earth.

"Those who were still alive, when that happened, would be immediately transformed from mortal beings into immortal ones, the dead would be raised from their graves with immortal bodies, and a new world order would be established here on earth. In that new world order, there would be no marriage and there would be no more children born, ever."

"Well, that didn't happen in Saint Paul's time," Hannah said. "That's why you don't believe you have to follow his teaching about divorce, right?"

"You've deconstructed the situation, precisely. Divorce is the best solution for most failed marriages, regardless of what Saint Paul wrote. And both women and men should be able to get one. I don't want to hurt Debbie, but I need to divorce her, so I can marry Angela.

"First, I'll try to convince her to release me from my promise and let me proceed with a non-contested divorce. The onus, if there is one, will be on me. If that doesn't work, I'll proceed with the divorce, anyway."

"I think that's the right thing for you to do, Daddy. Will you talk to Mother about this tomorrow?"

"No, but I'll talk to her sometime in January, so let keep my decision to ourselves until then."

"Does Angela know?"

"She knows and looks forward to marrying me. It's getting late, and we need to get some zzzz's. I was up long before daylight and I need a good night's sleep."

"I'm ready."

***

Barsh lay in the bed next to the motel window, but he couldn't shut down his mind which was jumping all over the place. Soon he was thinking about the conceit for a poem he had worked out, late one night in the cave as the campfire flickered before him.

He eased out of bed and soon had a draft of the poem. He silently read it, twice, and was pleased with his effort.

He lifted his eyes from the poem to study Hannah who was slumbering peacefully in her bed with the light from the cracked door of the bathroom illuminating her face.

She would be twelve-years old in less than two months, and for eleven years, they had celebrated Christmas Eve with Debbie at their home in Fern Meadows. There was always an abundance of food and drink and a real Christmas tree with presents heaped beneath it.

Although this Christmas Eve had ended in a motel room without Debbie and the usual trappings, it was a good reunion for Hannah and him, and they had managed to live in the moment most of the evening. Now, he had just finished the draft of the second poem he had written, since his failed attempts in college.

Back in November, on his way to check out Bluff Cave and the surrounding forest along the Tallapoosa River, he had passed an old abandoned farmhouse that rekindled the memory of a tragedy that had befallen the family who lived there, a tragedy that he had gotten pulled into as he happened to pass by as an eighteen-year-old boy.

On returning home, that experience of carrying a dead black boy in his arms and sharing his mother's deepest sorrow would not let go of him until he fashioned it into a narrative poem. With a bit of anxiety, he had shared the poem with Angela, and she had nothing but high praise for it.

Given the subject matter of the new poem, "This Land," he decided that he would read it to Angela at the Indian Shell Ring on Hilton Head Island, during their upcoming getaway.

***

Barsh woke early Christmas morning, took a long shower, and dressed in clothes that had been stored in the trunk of his car. They were a bit rumpled but what did he care.

He examined his hands. The nails were now neatly trimmed and cleaned. The skin looked better but was still chapped from being exposed to cold weather for ten days. He rubbed them with another heavy application of lotion.

It was still early but he decided to wake Hannah. His intention was to leave Louisville before eight o'clock that morning, and he wanted to spend as many waking minutes with her as possible. Standing beside her bed, he softly called her name until she opened her eyes.

"Christmas gift," he said. A greeting he had learned as a child from his father.

"Christmas gift," she said and sat up on the side of her bed.

"My sweet girl, this is my twelfth Christmas morning with you. For eleven of them, you were the best gift in our house in Ashland. The same will hold true in Debbie's house, today. Unlike those other Christmas mornings, I feel sad because I have to get on the road back to Ashland."

"Sadness is a part of life. Those are your words, remember?"

“I do remember. While we’re on the subject, I have a request. After you and I have breakfast and I take you home, I want to hang around until you open your presents.

“Then I want us to say our goodbyes in the den. The image of you waving from the front porch, as I drove away last time, haunted me all the way to Alabama.

“I’ll motion for you to come give me a hug. Then as I’m telling Debbie and Davis goodbye, I want you to go back to your presents, pick one up, and give me a big smile. That’s the image of you I want to take away from this Christmas.”

“Request granted.”

Chapter Twelve

The drive from Louisville had gone well with only one stop for gas, a restroom, and water. His pulse quickened as he took the I-85 exit for Ashland and weaved his way across town to his house in Fern Meadows.

Angela had left him a note on his desk next to the mail that she had collected during his absence. He read the endearing note and called to tell her that he was home and would be leaving for the farm within forty minutes. Relieved and joyous, she promised to be there right behind him.

Finding nothing in the mail that needed his attention, he packed for one night at the farm and five nights on Hilton Head Island. After a quick shower, he dressed for the reunion with Angela and left for his farm.

He felt good to be driving again on those county roads. Even before Angela entered his life, he had found a renewed sense of wellbeing whenever he headed for the farm that he'd purchased that summer. For many reasons now, he treasured the place that Jeremiah Keeble first settled in the late eighteenth century.

He turned off the county highway onto his private drive, opened the gate with a remote control, and drove down the long lane to the old farmhouse. After checking out the house, he built a fire in the old fieldstone fireplace. Then he left the house and ambled about in the backyard.

At the sound of Angela's Volvo on the grave lane, he hurried around the house. She parked and rushed for his embrace.

"How good it is to be back in your arms," she said.

"How good to have you back in my arms. I have no intention of ever again leaving you for twelve nights."

"That's music to my ears. If you'll take the big box with the food, I'll take my tote bag. We can come back later for the other things.

"Hello, dear house," she said as they entered.

"What can I fix you to drink?" he asked as she refrigerated some of the food. "I brought gin and tonic to add to my stock of wine for today as well as for Hilton Head Island."

"And I brought champagne. What are you having?"

"I'm having a glass of Merlot."

"Then I'd like the same."

"To us," he said as he lifted his glass.

"To us," she responded and they eased into the den, where they stood with their backs to the fire.

"Our first days of uninterrupted togetherness have finally arrived," he said.

"Just you and me with so much to share. Where do we start?"

"Let's do a bit of catching up and then we'll be in the moment."

"You're the only man I've known who doesn't rush the moment."

"When I was a boy, the anticipation of a camping trip was almost as enjoyable as the trip itself. That doesn't hold true when it comes to you. But the anticipation has its own rewards."

"I could not have said that better. Let's sit on the couch. I'm eager to hear more about your journey in the wild."

"It was definitely a lifetime experience."

"I hope you had enough time to achieve your goals."

"The timespan was just right. I now know what it's like to live only by my wits, my handmade equipage, and the resources of nature. If I'd stayed any longer, I would have started spending most of my time longing for you."

"Ah, that's so dear of you to say that."

"As you might assume, I reexamined and reaffirm my determination to keep the issues of ecology and sustainability as integral parts of my teaching and advocacy.

"If I can develop any creative skills at writing poetry, that will give me a way, beyond the classroom, to promote these issues. I'll also share some of the seminal experiences of my life as well as address some of the existential issues of our existence."

"Based on the esthetic power of your first poem, I'm confident that will happen, and I want to be right with you in this new endeavor. I decided last week that I want to renew my interest in writing poetry. I don't think I have another good novel in me, but

I know I have lots of poems to write. I can envision us traveling the circuit and doing joint reading at libraries and colleges."

"That's an interesting vision and one that I like."

"Together, we'll make it happen. Now, tell me about the rhythm of your days in the wild."

"During the day, I'd hunt if I needed food. Beyond that, I would roam the forest with total abandon. I was typically in the moment without a single thought about you or Hannah or anything beyond the forest. Occasionally, I'd experience something that I wished I could share with you. Otherwise, I was in the moment.

"Down by a pool of crystal-clear spring water in late afternoon, I'd butcher into small pieces a duck or a rabbit or a catfish. Back in the cave, I'd roast the pieces, three at a time, on a hickory skewer over hot coals. I'd do the same with editable mushrooms that I'd gathered during my treks through the forest. Then I eat half of what I roasted and save the rest for breakfast."

"Did you always have something to eat?"

"I ate two meals every day as planned."

"I should have known that you could provide for yourself, but I have to admit that I worried a bit about you. Now tell me what you did at night."

"After supper, I always spent time sitting in the cave by the campfire and reminiscing about you. Of course, there were times when I would also think about Hannah and wonder how she was making it in Louisville.

"Then I'd typically leave the cave and make my way to the top of the bluff, where I'd sit under the stars and ponder the wonders of the Universe or contemplate the evolution of human cultures in terms of some of the major problems we're now facing.

"One night when the full moon was high overhead, I took a long walk in the forest with only the light from the night sky. That was something I had not done since my youth.

"Three sightings made that night walk exceptional—a fox, a rafter of turkeys roosting in a big oak, and the moonlight in a tall sycamore tree.

"As I studied the moon's silver light on that sycamore, I wished you were there to share that moment with me. I also wondered if any artist had ever tried to capture such a sight on canvas.

"That was quite a night for me. Have you ever been on a night walk in the forest without any artificial light?"

"No, but with you as my guide, I'd like to try it."

"Okay, we'll do it. One night when the moon is full and the sky is clear, we'll walk to the granite ledge overlooking the Pacolet River and huddle there for a while.

"Oh, I just thought of something that might interest you. As I was exploring a creek far from camp, I discovered this beautiful waterfall. Knowing neither the name of the creek nor the waterfall, I followed my old habit of giving them names. In my mind, there's now a pristine place on Hawk Creek named Angela Falls."

"Oh, my dear man, how I love the way you elevate me in your world."

"Okay, it's time for you to wow me with your accomplishments during my absence."

"First of all, I wowed myself by finishing a draft of my novel, and I'm now ready to share it with you. Later tonight, I'd like for us to take turns reading it, aloud. I'm not interested in correcting typos or improving sentences. I'll do that later. You can help me analyze how it flows, chapter by chapter, as we read. Are you with me?"

"Count me in as you would say. I'm so looking forward to this."

"When we get to Ava's damnable story, I want you to read that section, silently. Then you can respond."

"Just know that I'll read it with compassion and understanding. Hopefully, I'll be able to help you forgive yourself."

"What a great moment that would be for me."

"Angie, I have something to show you. I will be right back."

She was standing before the log fire when he returned. He opened his hand. It was an engagement ring made of white gold with a blue sapphire on each side of the solitaire diamond.

"How beautiful! I love it, love it."

"It's okay with me if you want to wait until the divorce before I give it to you."

"No, I want to wear it as a promise ring on my right hand. After the divorce, it will become an engagement ring and you can move it to my left hand."

"Speaking of such things, I told Daddy this morning about our plan to get married. He was so pleased to hear the good news and said he's definitely coming to the wedding, but he doesn't think

Mother will come with him. I'll tell you more about my latest conversations with my parents over dinner. Right now, my finger is begging for the ring."

"My dearest Angie," he said after kneeling before her, "I give you this ring as a constant reminder of all the promises I've made to you."

"It's just beautiful, Barsh. I can't wait to show it off. Changing the subject, how's your anticipatory status holding up?"

"I think one slow dance will shift me from an anticipatory status to a ready-to-go status."

"And I'll be sizzling right along with you."

"Do you mind if I shed this jacket? The better for my body to feel your body"

"You've taken the words from my mouth. And take down the ponytail if you don't mind. The better for my hands to grasp your hair."

***

The sun had set and the natural light in the green bedroom was getting dim as they lay naked on the bed.

"What are you thinking about?" she asked breaking the silence.

"I was thinking about the fact that I've owned this bed for seven months but have only slept in it once. That was by myself back in early summer.

"I'd worked hard all day on my wilderness equipage. I was pleased with my work and for some unknown reason I wanted the spend the night in this old farmhouse. So, I call Debbie and she had no objection.

"After I finished supper, I walked about in the yard at twilight. The moon was hanging low in the western sky. When darkness enveloped the place and the stars came out, I went back inside and took a shower.

"With the intention of reading late into the night, I settled on the couch with E. O. Wilson's latest book, *On Human Nature*. I was so tired, however, that I marked my place after a couple of hours and went to bed.

"I don't recall ever thinking about that night before now, but my memory of it is very vivid. I was a troubled man and slept fitfully.

"What can I say? Time changes everything for better or worse. Fortunately for me, the change was for better. I'm now at peace with myself and bonded with you."

"Ditto for me, as you like to say."

"Thanks for choosing the farm for our first night of sleeping together in a bed," he said.

"There was no competition in my mind. I'm getting a bit hungry. Are you ready for my Christmas dinner?"

"Yes. I'm ever so ready for our first Christmas dinner together."

***

Barsh moved a small table and two chairs from the big room into the den. Angela spread a white linen cloth and set the table. He added a candle and lit it.

"This is such a lovely setting for our first Christmas dinner," she said. "If you'll pour the wine, I'll set out the food, buffet style on the big table.

He poured the wine and watched her spread the food.

"Angie, you've prepared a lovely feast."

"Catherine helped me plan it, Southern style. If you like it, we'll make it our tradition."

"Yes, let's make it our tradition."

Soon they were eating and chatting about whatever popped into their minds.

"Now, tell me about the conversations with your parents," he said.

"I called them around nine Christmas Eve. Mother answered. She'd just returned from church and told me all about the service. Next, as I knew she would, she asked if I'd been to Mass. To her rejoicing, I had, although I couldn't remember the last time that I'd been to Mass on Christmas Eve. Anyway, I credit you for this one. But I do like the priest. He's young. Probably just ordained.

"As Mother and I were ending our conversation, Daddy interrupted to say he wanted to talk to me. He's now showing such an interest in me—the daughter he had neglected most of my life. It's as if he suddenly cares about the woman I'd become.

"This morning, he called and we had a long conversation. He wants to visit me in February. But Mother won't likely be coming. Actually, I'm hoping he comes by himself."

"I look forward to meeting your father."

"And I'm eager for you to meet him. Barsh, you've had two nights with little sleep and two days of hard driving, and I have a lot on my agenda for us tonight. I'm thinking that now would be a good time for you to take a power nap, right here on the couch. I'll wake you in twenty minutes, so you won't feel groggy."

Without objection, he complied with her request.

Chapter Thirteen

Kneeling at the edge of the couch, Angela softly called his name. Even so, Barsh woke with a startled stir.

"Well, I certainly took a deep dive into the realm of slumber. You were right about my needing a nap. Thanks for indulging me."

"And thanks for your determination to be back here with me on this Christmas day."

"I would have had it no other way. When I was growing up, Christmas was always a big social day for my family. After breakfast, we rushed off to Granny Roberts' farm for the rest of the day. Her whole clan would be there. The adults were exceptionally merry and paid special attention to us kids.

"There was no church service, unless Christmas fell on a Sunday. If that was the case, we'd head for Granny's after the morning service and spend the rest of the day with her. Again, the mood was merry and the focus was on family."

"Contrary to your family tradition," Angela said, "my mother, out of fear that we would minimized the miraculous birth of the Christ child, suppressed what should have been a happy day of rejoicing with gifts from Santa.

"This Christmas, however, begins a new tradition of social joy. I'm ready to exchange presents. You sit tight and I'll gather them from the Christmas tree."

"According to Hannah, I'm in for a nice surprise."

"I think so, thanks to a suggestion by Amanda, our excellent librarian," she said and handed him a beautifully-wrapped book.

"Thank you," he said, tore off the wrapping paper, and read aloud, "*The North American Indian, Volume I* by Edward S. Curtis. This is wonderful, Angie. You could not have given me a better book."

"I'm pleased to be the one to give you the first of the twenty-volume set. Now, you see the Amanda connection, right?"

"Back in the fall, she told me that Curtis' books were now available in reprints, and I intended to buy all twenty volumes when I returned from the wild.

“Can you imagine Curtis spending thirty-five years on this project? I so admire people who devote the best years of their life to some meaningful project.”

“I join you in admiring such people. From what I’ve learned, those dedicated people often died with little admiration or attention after a lifetime of significant work.”

“You are so right. I’m afraid that may have happened to Curtis. Amanda could not find a single biography of him. All she could find was the information about him in the re-publication material about his books.”

“Well, maybe the re-publication of his books will inspire someone to write his biography,” Angela said.

“I hope so. But I’ll be able to learn a lot about him, just by reading the books. More importantly, I’ll learn more about Native Americans.

“What I like about this series is that each book contains photographs from several different tribes that Curtis took and developed as well as information on their traditional cultures. He typically had an ethnologist with him to help document the culture.”

“Yes, I noticed that. Okay, here’s Hannah’s second present. As you’ve assumed by now, it’s Volume II of the set. She agreed to let me be the one to surprise you. The two of us are committed to buying the other eighteen volumes for you over the next few years.”

“How dear of you two. I like your idea of spreading them out. The better for me to read them as they come my way. Thanks for helping Hannah. She was quite excited about joining you in this endeavor.”

“It was my pleasure.”

“I also owe you a big thanks for helping her gift me *The Poetry of the Negro.* I’m delighted to have the anthology.

“The history and culture of Native Americans and African Americans are very different from each other, and both are totally different from any other ethnic group in the United States. No other ethnic group has been treated as horribly by white individuals and mobs. The same holds true for the way they’ve been treated by Federal and State Governments.

“As important as it is to have books like these that Curtis produced, it’s even better that Native Americans and African Americans are now telling their own stories.”

"On those points, I'm in complete agreement with you. Here's your other present."

"Don't you want to open one of yours?"

"Not until you open this one. Get ready for quite a shift."

He unwrapped the book and silently read the front cover, *The Gospel Singer: A Novel,* by Harry Crews.

"I don't know Harry Crews."

"This one is the first of his novels, and I'm confident you'll find it interesting. As a professor of religious studies, you know about hypocrisy but not likely in the form Crews gives us in *The Gospel Singer*."

"I definitely know about hypocrisy and I'm sure I'll enjoy reading the novel. Give me a synopsis."

"The protagonist is *a hypocritical freak.* He was born with good looks and an exceptional voice for singing gospel songs, and he used those gifts to get himself out of poverty in South Georgia and into the arms of a lot of different women. His gospel-singing tours were all hypocritical acts, but to his credit, he eventually owns up to his freakish exploitations."

"A hypocritical gospel-singing freak. Okay, I'm moving *The Gospel Singer* to the top of my reading list."

"Just so you know, Crews, a native of South Georgia, has made a reputation for himself by creating unusual freaks in his novels. There's also another freak in this novel. This one with a physical birth defect, and I'm sure you'll be amused by the way he capitalized on the distortion he was born with."

"You're giving me a book about two freaks whose lives must be connected in some way."

"You got it. And you'll admire the way Crews connects their lives."

"Well, we certainly have plenty of freaks in the South."

"Just like every section of the country. But as someone has said, Southern writers don't mind parading their freaks before the world."

"Well stated. Now I'm trying to imagine what birth defect Crews gave the other freak. You want to tell me?"

"The character goes by the name of Foot, because he was born with a twenty-seven-inch foot. But here's Crews' genius. Foot follows the Gospel Singer's crusades because he can draw the same crowds to his show, that features his freakish twenty-seven-inch foot."

"That is a stroke of artistic genius. Yes, I'm moving the novel to the top of my reading list. Thanks for choosing both books, Angie. You know me well."

"You're welcome. And yes, I'm getting to know you well because you open yourself to me. So, what did you choose for me?"

"Two Southern novels, both set in Alabama. One in North Alabama and one in South Alabama. Both won the Pulitzer Prize. I hope you haven't read them. You told me you could only remember reading three novels set in Alabama—*To Kill a Mockingbird*, *Ollie Miss*, and *Train Whistle Guitar*."

"That's true, but as you know, Alabama now has a special interest for me, so thanks for your thoughtfulness in choosing books to enlighten me about your native state."

"This one was published first," he said and gave her the present.

She tore off its wrapping paper and read aloud, "*The Store* by T. S. Stribling. No, I haven't read it. Now, it's your turn to give me a synopsis."

"It's a good overview of what life was like for blacks and whites of all classes in the Post-Reconstruction South, that started in 1880.

"Farming was mostly done by sharecroppers, both white and black, and they typically owed their souls to some store that provided, on credit, everything they needed until the new crops were harvested and sold—sometimes for less than what they owed the store. Thus, the well-chosen title of the novel.

"It's set in the North Alabama town of Florence. I should warn you that there's not a white Southerner in this novel who does not view African Americans as inferior to whites.

"You will also see that African Americans are beginning to realize that there was no hope for them to be integrated into white Southern society nor for them to receive just treatment under segregation. That was true even if they looked more like white people than black people. Thus, you will see the emergence of the idea that the only road to a better life for them was the road north.

"Thankfully, that is beginning to turn around. I know a few African Americans who have moved back to the South and intend to stay.

"Do you know H. L. Mencken's sever indictment of Southern culture, which he called the Sahara of the Bozart? I think it appeared in *The New York Evening Mail* in 1917."

"Yes, I know it well and *indictment* is a good way to describe the article."

"Well, a lot of it rings true. He correctly traces the cultural decline of the South to the devastating and lingering effects of the Civil War, but I wish he could have been a bit more empathic for us. Almost everyone had a hard time surviving. But the blacks suffered most of all.

"Far too often black men lived a short life because of the South's damnable Jim Crow culture. God, the horrendous history of lynching as well as the exploitation of black prison laborers to name two examples.

"The people who contracted with the prisons for black laborers didn't give a damn about them and treated them worse than most of their predecessors treated their slaves."

"Why was that?"

"They had no financial loss if they over-worked and maltreated them, even unto death. They could simply contract with the prisons for replacements with no upfront expense.

"Back to *The Store*. I was pleased to learn that it won the Pulitzer Prize in 1933, and I took that as evidence that there was some cultural literacy in the South, around the time of my birth."

"You're right," she said. "The Southern Literary Renaissance, that started in the 1920s, was an extraordinary achievement. And Southern authors are still writing great books. I'm very pleased that I chose to do my graduate studies in Southern literature."

"And so am I. Otherwise . . . you know the story."

"Thanks for choosing this novel and for the synopsis. I'm moving it to the top of my reading list, unless you think I should start with the other novel you chose."

"Stick with your decision and read this one, first," he said and gave her the other novel, T*he Keepers of the House,* by Shirley Ann Grau.

"Splendid. This one has been on my list of Southern novels I need to read. I'm thinking Grau is from New Orleans. Please refresh my memory."

"You're right. She was born in New Orleans but spent most of her youth in South Alabama before moving back to New Orleans. The book won the Pulitzer Prize in 1965. I like the fact that it covers seven generations of the same family, all living out their lives in an everchanging house.

"As you get near the last keepers of the house, you'll encounter some race mixing that's more than white men siring children with black women. You'll meet a keeper of the house who took his colored live-in-maid, north, and secretly married her, after the death of his white wife. When the interracial marriage was revealed after his death, the burden fell on his white daughter by his first wife.

"Big trouble for her, no doubt," she said.

"Yes, big trouble. White men could get away with having black mistresses, but they could not get away with marrying them."

"Could white women get away with having a black lover?"

"There was no way that would be tolerated. If it ever happened without a lynching, it happened secretly.

"Shifting thoughts, I was stunned to learn from this book that there were slave owners in North Alabama who were outright slave breeders. They made their money not by farming with slaves, but by breeding female slaves and selling their children.

"I'd never heard of this before I read Grau's book, and I was outraged by it. If it were true, I needed to know, so I turned to Catherine. She knew about the practice, especially in States like Virginia and Maryland.

"Congress had passed legislation prohibiting the importation of slaves. That was in the early nineteenth century when there was a growing demand for additional slaves in the Deep South. Slave breeders were thus responding to the slave economy. Damn those people and all who will do anything for the almighty dollar."

"The book sounds like another informative read for me. Thanks for choosing these special novels for me. The big bonus is that I'll get to discuss them with you."

"I definitely know the terrain of these two novels and look forward to our discussions. Yet, I probably would not have read either book if they had not been set in Alabama. I'm still rather ignorant about Southern literature, but with your help, I intend to remedy this.

"Perhaps, I should tell you that the slow pace of both novels will likely be a bit tedious for you, although I didn't mind. I appreciated the details."

"Don't worry. I'm confident I'll find them rewarding."

"Angie, I don't understand people who don't read books. Do you?"

"No, they're beyond my comprehension. How could anyone with free access to a library live without curiosity and interest in things beyond their own experience but accessible in books?"

"I've packed several relevant books to share with you during our trip to Hilton Head Island. Our reading priority, however, will be your novel, and I'm ready to get started anytime."

"Thanks. I definitely want to get started tonight. But first, I'd like a stroll in the yard for fresh air and a bit of star gazing on our first Christmas night. Then I'll take the first turn reading my novel."

"And I'm ready for both."

***

After tending the fire, Barsh stood with his back to it and waited for Angela to get the manuscript from the green bedroom. This was a moment he had eagerly anticipated. He would soon be learning more about his beloved Angela as they read her autobiographical novel.

"Three-hundred-and-seventy-eight pages of good writing if I do say so myself," she said as she entered the den. "Please hold them while I shift these books from the coffee table."

"Feels like I'm holding a pot of gold," he said.

"I would love to have a best seller, but I've accomplished my goal of writing a good novel. Now, if a major publisher will take it, I'll be happy with whatever royalties that comes my way."

"I like your attitude. This is a major accomplishment, and I'm honored to share your joy."

"You are most definitely entitled to share my joy and whatever comes my way as a result of the novel. You are a major part of the story, although fictionalized quite successfully, I think. First, let's celebrate with champagne, and then I'll read the first chapter."

They left for the kitchen, where he popped the cork and then toasted her. On returning to the den couch, they settled into the warm glow of the champagne. In her own sense of timing, Angela sorted out the first chapter and set cross-legged on the couch. He moved to the rocker and sat facing her.

"The two chapters I sent you back in the summer were drawn from my youth. That's where I started writing after visiting Cooper, back in April. Those chapters actually come later in the novel as flashbacks. The opening chapter is the setup for Ava's first mid-life crisis."

With that explanation, Angela read the first chapter as Barsh listened intently without interrupting her.

"I'm very impressed, Angie. The opening chapter is well-crafted in every way. I was drawn into Ava's life almost as quickly as I was into yours."

"Maybe that because Ava is me at that stage of my life. After graduating Columbia University, as you know, I worked in advertising for ten years, just to support myself.

"Nights and weekends, I'd pound the keys of my typewriter. My only compensation as a writer, however, was the publication of a few of my poems and short stories in literary journals. My two novels were repeatedly rejected by publishers.

"There were no critiques, just standardized rejection letters. So, like Ava, I kept revising and submitting them to other publishers, until an editor harshly declared that there was no way I could salvage what I considered my best novel, that he got numerous manuscripts every year that told the same story.

"That was a horrible blow for me to absorb. For almost ten years, I'd been traveling down a dead-end road. I quit writing and that left me with nothing good to do, when I wasn't working. Depressed, I could no longer tolerate my lonely life and that lead me down a new kind of dead-end road.

"You'll learn about that in later chapters. I regret my behavior during those days, but I now own them."

"So, you didn't commit what you call an unforgivable behavior on that dead-end road, right?"

"Your assumption is correct. That happened later during my graduate studies at Brown University."

"Angie, I'm eager to know what catapulted you from that dead-end road into academia. Are you up to telling me? Or do you want me to wait until the novel takes me there?"

“I’ll tell you. I began to review my life back when I was an adolescent and retrace the experiences that led me to want to become a novelist.

“You know about the trauma of my thirteenth summer, how an older neighborhood boy raped me. After that, I took refuge in novels. During my freshman year in high school, my wonderful English teacher put me onto the novels I needed and continued to do so, until I graduated high school.

“I admired her more than any person I’d ever met. Based on those memories, I decided to quit my job, enroll in graduate school, earn a Ph.D. with a focus on Southern Literature, and become a college professor.”

“I like your story and look forward to seeing it fictionized in Ava’s life.”

“Thanks. Now, I’d like for you to read chapter two. I’m ready to hear my words coming from your mouth.

“By the time we finish discussing the second chapter, I think I’ll be ready for bed. Tomorrow will be another big day for us. I can’t wait to experience some of the things you’ve told me about Hilton Head Island and the Lowcountry.”

Chapter Fourteen

Barsh and Angela had finished breakfast at the farmhouse, except for their second cup of coffee, that they were sipping with contentment.

"I like sharing the kitchen with you," she said. "You certainly know how to cook an egg omelet."

"Maybe the old saying about two cooks in the kitchen isn't always true."

"Not if one of them is a man like you. I'm looking forward to our cooking breakfast together at the condo on Hilton Head Island?"

"So am I. But one morning, I'll take you to Sun Rise Café on Broad Creek for their eggs Benedict. That's something I don't cook."

"Nor do I and I'd love that experience."

"If you agree, I'd like for us to use the leftover ham to make sandwiches for lunch on a few outings that I have in mind."

"Yes, I'd like that."

"Other days, I'll take you to one of my favorite eateries for lunch. Evenings, we'll dine out. There's a multitude of excellent restaurants for us to choose from.

"Here's the rhythm that I've typically followed on previous visits to the Island. I like to be on the beach in early morning and late afternoon. From mid-morning until late afternoon, I like to be out and about on the Island and surrounding areas. I also like to take to the beach at night. But I'll always defer to your preference on what we do on this trip."

"That's good of you. But I'm trusting you to lay out the options. When we get to the Big Apple, I'll assume that responsibility."

"Okay, here's a decision we need to make this morning. There are two places, Francis Beidler Forest and Mepkin Abby, that are not far off our route to Hilton Head Island. As I've said before, I think you would enjoy both of them. If you'd like, we could visit one going and the other returning."

"Yes, I'd like that, so you decide which one we'll visit today."

"Then we'll swing by Beidler Forest, this morning. We'll still make it to the condo with plenty of time for the beach this afternoon. I suggest we prepare a light lunch to share while we're exploring the place."

"It's a swamp forest with some giant cypress trees that we can experience from a boardwalk, right?"

"You have a good memory. No wading through the swamp water required."

They prepared a light lunch, cleaned up the kitchen, packed their things in Barsh's Audi, and got on the road. Angela took the occasion to read more of her novel to him.

After she finished reading a new chapter, they discussed it. Then she would play a few songs from one of her cassettes to rest her voice. Occasionally, they would forsake the novel and music to converse about some topic of interest.

When they reached the visitor's center at Beidler Forest, they spent time getting Angela oriented on what to expect. Then they headed out on the boardwalk.

They were in no hurry and enjoyed sharing their observations with each other. A little over halfway around the boardwalk, they stopped to admire a giant cypress that was more than a thousand-years old.

"This is the oldest living thing I've experienced," Angela said.

"Can you imagine being rooted to the same spot on this good earth for a thousand years?" he asked.

"No, I'm glad to be walking upright on my own two feet, to say nothing of getting about in various modes of modern transportation."

"What about the thousand years? Doesn't there seem to be something wrong with the order of things, when trees outlive humans? We're supposed to be the crowning glory of creations."

"I've often thought there were things wrong with the order of human life, but I've never raised that question."

"Okay, what's on your list?"

"Well, everywhere you look there's some group classification, where some people are on top and other people are on the bottom. In your old South, there was a culture based on the slavery of Africans. Then one based on racial segregation. In Hinduism, there's the caste system with the untouchables at the bottom with no chance of social mobility during their lifetime. Sociologists divide those of us in the United States into lower, middle, and upper classes with subdivision in each, although they do allow for some social mobility.

"My biggest personal struggle, however, has been with the male-female divide. Why should males dominate?"

"They shouldn't. It's well past time to change that dynamic. I cannot imagine a time, however, when humans will run out of social problems. And now we have major environmental problems looming on the horizon.

"In one way or another, we're always in a state of agitation and conflict. I'm proud that you and I have chosen to pursue truth and enlightenment in the struggle against ignorance and prejudices. But this, in itself, is a form of elitist egoism. Have you gotten to know Dana Lightfoot in the music department?

"Somewhat. I hear he's an extraordinary pianist."

"There's no question about that. His recitals are fantastic. You'll get to hear him in his spring concert. Here's the point I want to make. At a party, I once heard Dana call Homer McTeer a Neanderthal.

"I assume you know that Homer is one of our social science professors. He's an educated man with a reputable Ph.D. Yet, Dana measured the gap between his sensibilities and Homer's to be so insurmountably broad that he labeled him a Neanderthal. And he wasn't joking. I suppose intellectuals and artists are always susceptible to some form of egotism."

"You're right, Barsh, but you and I don't flaunt our intellectual egotism. And we certainly don't claim any rights for ourselves beyond those due to all people."

"True, and I guess that's the best we can do. Let's eat lunch on this bench. I'm hungry. Are you?"

"Yes, and what a delightful place to eat."

He slipped off the backpack and spread the lunch between them. They ate in a contemplative mood with frequent glances at each other and the magnificent cypress.

"Thanks for bringing me to this special forest, Barsh. I'm so pleased to be experiencing it with you."

"My pleasure. When we get on the road, again, I don't think there's much to interest you along the first stretch of I-95 South, so you can set our agenda—your novel, music, or chatting. But things will change when we take the Coosawhatchie exit."

"Well, the word Coosawhatchie is enough to stir my interest. Just let me know when it's coming up."

***

After they took the Coosawhatchie exit onto highway 462, Barsh began commenting on the changing scenery of the Low-country, and Angela listened with interest. He soon slowed for a caution light at a place named Old House and then turned east down a narrow dirt lane for a brief stop at the Heyward Family Cemetery.

As they walked about in the cemetery, he gave a short narration on the Heywards and their Old House Plantation. His focus was on Thomas Heyward Jr, a signer of the Declaration of Independence, who was born on the plantation and buried in the cemetery.

"If he had not embraced slavery," Barsh said, "I would hold Thomas Heyward Jr. in highest esteem. He was prominent in state and national politics, a Revolutionary War hero, a notable lawyer and judge.

"He is described as one of the most honest, intelligent, and fearless men of his day. But he was horribly flawed by slavery, although he likely thought that he was following God's plan for advancing civilization, which goes to show how easily we can be deceived or deceive ourselves.

"That's my judgment about planters and slavery, and I'm sticking to it. It's relevant for most of the historical places we'll visit on this trip, so you know my feelings even if I don't express them every time that I show you something related to those olden times."

"I knew you felt that way, but I like the way you just summed it up. You noted that Thomas Heywood Jr. spent most of his adult life in Charleston. Any chance, he was one of Du Bose Heyward's ancestors?"

"That's my understanding. So, you've read Du Bose Heyward's novels."

"Only *Porgy*. What about you?"

"I've read *Porgy* and *Mamba's Daughter*."

"Do you think I should read *Mamba's Daughter*?"

"In many ways, I found it interesting. For example, Heyward divided the African Americans of Charleston into two basic groups—those who have worked in close proximity with white people (maids, for example) and those that haven't.

"He also makes note of the different ways in which African Americans interacted with Southern whites and whites who had moved to Charleston from the North. Their psychological strategies for manipulation the two groups of whites for their own limited goals were different and speaks well for their intelligence."

"Well, with those two things alone, you have convinced me that I need to read *Mamba's Daughter* in order to boost my credentials as a specialist in Southern literature."

Leaving the graves for the saltwater marsh a few yards away, Angela touched her first live oak and exclaimed about its beauty. He promised to take her, on a future trip, to see the famous Angel Oak on Johns Island, that was reputed to be fifteen-hundred-years old.

"This is good," he said as they approached the marsh. "The tide is out, so there will be a lot of hard-packed sand on the beach for us to tread after we check in the condo. That hard-packed sand is also good for biking.

"A lot of our activities will be determined by the ever-changing time-table for the ebb and flow of the tide. I always buy a copy of *The Island Packet* for the changing time for high and low tides and to see if there are any special events that might interest me."

"Then the tides call for a mood of relaxed flexibility, right?"

"Well stated. Here in the saltwater marshes, the ebbing tide exposes a special mud rather than sand. It's called pluff mud and it has a distinctive smell."

"So, that's what I smell."

"Yes, and you likely find it unpleasant. But Lowcountry residents, who've been away, can't wait until that pungent smell reaches their nostrils and rejuvenates their soul."

"Well, the scent of pluff mud hasn't yet captured my soul. But I have already fallen in love with the natural beauty of the live oaks, all draped in Spanish moss, which you tell me is neither moss nor Spanish. I'm also taken by the saltwater marshes."

"I had the same reaction when I first encountered pluff mud. For the most part, we won't experience it that much, but we'll get to enjoy the live oaks and the marshes, extensively. Some of the saltwater marshes are so expansive they'll astonish you. Okay, are you ready to head for Hilton Head Island?"

"Ready! Ready!"

They left the Heyward site and drove non-stop to the rental agency for the condo. Barsh checked in and bought a copy of *The Island Packet*.

"The next stop will be our condo," he said and headed east on Pope Avenue.

"Can you imagine how excited I am," she said.

"Perhaps as excited as I am. That's Coligny Beach, straight ahead. We're almost there."

At the traffic circle, he turned right onto South Forest Beach Drive.

"Here we are," he said as he pulled into the parking lot and cut the engine.

"Looks inviting. I'm pleased that it's not one of those monstrous condos."

"We can thank the Island's building code for this. Let's take the food and I'll come back for everything else."

They took the elevator to the second floor with smiles and excitement.

"Oh, I love the décor," she said after they entered the big living-dining room.

"Yes, it's appealing. Let's check out the view," he said and led her through the sliding glass doors onto the deck that overlooked the beach and the Atlantic Ocean.

"This is wonderful. You chose well."

"You enjoy the view and check out the condo, while I bring in our things."

"Let me help you."

"Thanks, but there are carts and I can bring everything in one trip."

When he returned, Angela was coming out of the master bedroom and beckoned him into her arms. They embraced and kissed.

"Have you hatched a schedule for the rest of this day in that dynamic brain of yours?"

"I have a tentative one, which you can amend. Let's get something to drink and I'll share my thoughts."

With drinks in hand, they settled on the couch.

"Okay, lay it out for me."

"After we rest a bit, we can take a long walk on the beach. I'm thinking north, possibly as far as Folly Creek that divides the Island's twelve-mile beach. If so, we'll pass the dunes that buffer the last strip of wild oceanfront that, no doubt, will all too soon be spoiled by condos.

"During our summer visits to the Island, I've often walked up the beach at night to sit against the edge of those dunes. One night, I heard a barred owl hooting its prophecy about the dangers of spoiling nature.

"I couldn't see the owl, but it seemed to be settled in a huge live oak that looms just beyond the dunes, so I named the place the Dunes at Owl Oak. I'd like to take you there one night to watch the moon rising from the ocean. But first, I want you to experience those dunes this afternoon if you're game."

"Yes, I'm eager to do that. What do you have in mind after the Dunes at Owl Oak?"

"When we get back here from our beach walk, we can test the comfort of the king-size bed."

"Perfect timing," she said with a smile.

"After that, I'm proposing dinner at Quarter Deck located in a development named Sea Pines Plantation. After dinner, I'm suggesting that we climb to the top of Harbor Town Lighthouse that's located next door.

"It's not a real lighthouse but a tourist attraction. It is, however, a good place to do a bit of night gazing. We'll be able to see any traffic on the Intracoastal Waterway, the north end of Daufuskie Island across the way, etc.

"Back here again, we can read more of your novel plus whatever the night might bring. Amendments are in order."

"No amendments needed."

And just so, their first day on Hilton Head Island unfolded.

Chapter Fifteen

Angela had so enjoyed her first visit to the Dunes at Owl Oak that she wanted to settle into them and watch the sun rising from the Atlantic Ocean—something she had never experienced. There they sat cuddled on a blanket.

The sky was clear. A light breeze was blowing south, and gentle waves were breaking near the shore. A rosy hue along one stretch of the horizon signaled where the sun would rise.

Sandpipers were rhythmically rushing in and out with the flow of the surf. Ring-billed gulls were crying to each other as they flew hither and yon.

"Angie, that's a brown pelican riding the air currents at its favorite height above the surf. This is the way it fishes. When it spots a suitable fish near the surface of the ocean, it will divebomb out of the sky with its huge beak leading the way. I've never seen them surface with an empty beak."

"I'd like to see that."

"You will before we leave the Island. Look, the sun's glow is getting brighter."

They watched silently as the sun gradually cleared the ocean's horizon and climbed into the sky.

"What a gorgeous sight," she said and snuggled under his arm and into his chest. "Such a beautiful first for me, and such a good way to start our first full day on the Island.

"There are twelve miles of beach," she said, "but this is the only strip of wild oceanfront that hasn't been developed. Naturally, you took notice of it, singled it out for yourself, and named it the Dunes at Owl Oak. I'm a lucky woman to be sitting here with you."

"Well, now that these dunes have a place in your memory, that makes me a lucky man. Obviously, it's the isolation and natural background of these dunes that make them my favorite place on the beach.

"If I sit against the dunes anywhere else on the Island, I have a hard time blocking out the houses, condos, and hotels behind me. It's like I'm sitting in someone's backyard.

"These dunes feel so different. They feel like they, along with the beach, belong to the ocean, which they do. If you have the money, you can buy an oceanfront house or condo, but the dunes and the beach don't come with it. They belong to the ocean. So, I like all twelve miles of the beach, even when a stretch of it is packed with people and bordered by houses, condos, and hotels."

"But you love this stretch best of all, and I'm excited about coming back, Thursday night, for the moonrise above the ocean. That will be another first for me."

"Anyone getting hungry besides me?" he said and pulled her on top of him as he leaned back against the dunes.

"Here?"

"No, I'm thinking breakfast. A good kiss will suffice in that department for the time being."

Thus, they left for the condo but soon turned aside to check out a catamaran that was safely harbored at the edge of the dunes beyond the reach of the tides. There was a trail, nearby, that ran inland through the undeveloped woods. Barsh also noticed marks in the sand where the owner had obviously pulled it to and from the ocean.

"I've never sailed on a catamaran, have you?" he said.

"No, nor any sailboat."

"Our colleague Mike Littlejohn has a thirty-foot sailboat on Lake Norman, just west of Charlotte. He's taken me a few times. He's actually taught me how to manage the big wheel without losing the sail. Have you gotten to know him?"

"I just know who he is. As yet, I've had no dealing with him."

"This spring, I'll get him to take us sailing if you're interested."

"Yes, I'd love that, but I think I'd be afraid to sail on a catamaran. Nothing but this canvas to ride on. I hope that doesn't disappoint you."

"Oh, no," he said, but he had already imagined a different kind of sailing, with her, on the canvas of that catamaran, late one night, while it was still stashed near the dunes. That was something he thought she would embrace, although he didn't share it at the time.

***

Back in the condo, they had finished breakfast and were sitting on the couch with a fresh cup of coffee. Barsh looked at her with a devoted smile, which she returned.

"Want to guess what I'm thinking about?" she said.

"Give me a clue?"

"It's something we have yet to discuss."

"Sorry, but that doesn't help."

"A date for our wedding. What are your thoughts?"

"I believe I'll have the divorce before March. We'll have a week off, you know, for spring break in mid-March. If you're ready, we could get married then, and I'll take you to Rome for our honeymoon. Otherwise, I think June would suit me. It's your decision, however, and you don't have to decide now."

"My first reaction favored March, but then I thought about all we have to do. Now, I'm thinking there's something special about a June wedding."

"I agree. But take your time deciding and consider everything."

"Thanks. I will."

"Angie, most visitors to the Island typically focus on playing golf or sunning on the beach, but there's much more on the Island that I would like to share with you. I'm also thinking about several excursions off the Island, later in the week."

"I'm with you all the way."

"Good. I'd like to spend the better part of today in the Sea Pines Forest Preserve, one of my favorite places on the Island. It contains a beautiful forest with hiking trails, three freshwater lakes, an oyster shell ring created by Native Americans four-thousand years ago, and an old rice field from the antebellum period, that was created from an inland marsh by African slaves and then cultivated by them."

"Sounds wonderful. Where is it located?"

"The same development where we dined last night."

"Sea Pines Plantation?"

"Yes, but I wish they'd left off the word plantation. It did incorporate two or three of the historical plantations that occupied the southern end of the Island. Still, the word plantation has so many negative connotations.

"It was the first gated community on the Island and the model for the others. Charles Fraser, the developer, bought the property from his father who had bought it for its timber.

"I admire the way Fraser designed the development to preserve as much of the environment as possible. And I especially honor him for setting aside six-hundred acres to create the Forest Preserve.

"We'll drive through the major areas of the development, so you can see the them during the day. Then we'll take to the trails of the Forest Preserve."

Working together, they prepared a light lunch and left the condo. Barsh took the ocean gate entrance into Sea Pines Plantation and drove toward South Beach with an occasional exploration of one of the side streets to view some of the oceanfront houses.

He noted that when he first visited the Island in the late 1960s, the oceanfront houses were rather modest. Since then, a significant number of them had been demolished and replaced with multimillion dollar houses, a trend that he was sure would persist.

They were soon walking on South Beach with its expansive view across Callibogue Sound to the southern end of Daufuskie Island. Below that island, vast saltwater marshes stretched to the southwest down to the Savannah River.

To the south, the northeastern tip of Georgia stretched to the Atlantic Ocean. There was a huge tanker on the southern horizon headed for the Savannah River, where it would dock upriver past the old city and unload it cargo.

"Angie, this is the best place on the Island for us to catch the sunset. Next place would be the top of the lighthouse at Harbor Town. Third would be the shrimp dock at Hudson's Seafood Restaurant on Skull Creek as you look west across Pinckney Island.

"I definitely want to take you to Hudson's for dinner one night. It's the oldest and probably the best-known restaurant on the Island. What would you think about going tonight?"

"I'd love it."

"Okay. We can come back here, perhaps tomorrow evening, to watch the sunset. Then we can eat at one of the nearby restaurants at South Beach Marina Village. Salty Dog Café is popular. They have inside dining or we can dine on the outside deck overlooking Calibogue Creek."

"I'm voting for the deck."

"Then the deck it is."

They left South Beach and took a different route through the western side of Sea Pines Plantation to Baynard Ruins Park. There they read the historic marker and examined the tabby ruins of the big house and slave cabins.

Leaving the ruins, Barsh took the shortest route to the road that would take them well into the Forest Preserve. As he eased along the last paved road that followed a lagoon to the entrance, he stopped to point out a great blue heron.

It was standing at the edge of the water as it waited for a fish to swim within reach of its sharp beak, that was well adapted to a small head and long neck that was folded against its breast. The heron, spooked by their lingering, took to air with its six-feet wing-span gracefully fanning its way down the lagoon.

"What a huge graceful bird," she said. "And the way it flies with those long legs stretched out behind like that."

"Great blue herons are fairly common here and fun to watch," he said as he continued along the lagoon. "They typically find a good place to fish and wait patiently for something good to come to it."

"By contrast, the snowy egret is typically on the move along the water's edge, as it searches for something plump for the taking. It's a beautiful white-feathered bird with a long black beak, black stilted legs, and showy yellow feet.

"We'll likely get to see them, along with great egrets, when we get to the lakes in the Forest Preserve. The snowy egret and the great egret are both big white wading birds that people often confuse. Last year, I saw a painting by a local artist with the title 'Snowy Egret' that was actually a great egret."

"So, you have to notice features other than the color of their feathers and size, like yellow feet and black beaks."

"You got it."

They turned into the preserve and eased along the sandy road, until Barsh parked near a picnic shelter on a narrow strip between the two lower lakes.

"Angie, these lakes have names, but in my mind, this is Middle Lake. That is South Lake. I'll show you what I call North Lake before we leave the Forest Preserve. It's by far the largest.

"On several previous visits, I've seen a huge alligator sunning on that little island in Middle Lake. I once paddled a kayak out toward the island for a better view of that alligator.

"It was bigger than the kayak, and when it slipped into the water and eased my way with its eyes just above the surface, I quickly turned back and took the canal to North Lake. That was a fun day of kayaking for me. Do you like kayaking?"

"I have yet to try it but I'm game."

"We'll add it to our list of things to do this summer. I know a place that rents kayaks and there are a lot of good places to kayak down here.

"Let's ease along the trail on the eastern side of South Lake. We should see yellow-rumped warblers in those wax myrtles, just ahead. They forage in quick spurts, so it hard to watch them with field glasses. But we'll likely get to see their yellow rumps when they take flight away from us."

They did see several of them, both foraging and in flight before they left the lake side and took the trail to the oyster shell ring.

"Here we are," he said.

"Yes, I see it."

"I don't think of this as a holy place, but it's semi-sacred to me. I once thought about taking one of the oyster shells but decided they all belong here."

"And this shell ring dates back four-thousand years?"

"That what the archeologists say, but they don't know for certain why it's here. Some say Native Americans lived in the center of the circle, seasonally, ate their oysters, and threw the shells around the edge of the camp. Others say it was created specifically for ceremonial purposes."

"Do you have an opinion?"

"The circle seems a little too ragged to have been built strictly for ceremonies, so I lean toward the campsite view. But I can also see that it would make a good place for their ceremonies"

"Then it may have served both purposes."

"Yes, I agree. Just think, the indigenous people who left this oyster ring never dreamed that the day would come when a strange people from a distant land would settle on this Island. Nor had the Escamacu ever dreamed of such a day when the Spaniards first discovered about 2,000 of them living here in the early 1500s.

"One of the major themes that I find in Native American literature is the unrequited sense of loss that they carry for the land their ancestors were driven from. My new poem is about the route it took me to become more aware of the extent to which that loss still haunts them.

"The conceit came to me one night during my short sojourn in the wild. I'd banked the fire in the cave and crawled into my deerskin sleeping bag. As I waited for sleep, I juxtaposed my experience of first hearing about the massacre of the Creek Indians at Horseshoe Bend, only thirty miles down the Tallapoosa River from where I was camping, with my recent reaction to reading *Ceremony* by Leslie Silko.

"Christmas Eve, I wrote the poem in the motel after Hannah had gone to sleep. I thought this would be a good place for me to read it to you."

"Yes, please stand on the shell ring and read it to me?"

He took a blanket from his backpack and spread it for her. As soon as she was settled, he took a stand on the shell ring and read the poem.

Angela stood and started clapping. He walked into her arms and they held each other with tender affection.

"I love the poem. It is so you. So honest and straightforward."

"I have no idea whether or not it has any literary merit," he said. "I can only say that it has value to me."

"Literary merit is, more or less, in the eye of the beholder, as they say. For me, your poem has both substance and literary merit. And I like the conceit. Would it be published in one of the top tier literary journals? Probably not. Nor have any of my poems been published in them. But it's a good poem.

"There are so many forms and styles of contemporary poetry, and it's obvious to me that you are on your way to developing your own distinctive style."

"Thanks. That's my objective."

They stretched out on the blanket with their bodies stilled by an almost sacred feeling for the place. White puffy clouds eased along on the southwestern wind currents, as they lay for a few minutes without speaking.

"Barsh, I like the distinction you make between ground therapy for body and heart and ground therapy for the soul. The mystical experience of being one with this place for a moment feels serenely redemptive for my soul in spite of the horrendous ways Native Americans have been treated."

He squeezed her hand without commenting, and they continued to absorb the place for a while. How good it felt to be sharing it with his beloved soulmate.

"Are you ready to experience more of the Forest Preserve?"

"Yes, but what a special experience this oyster shell circle has been."

They backtracked to the car, where they took a trail westward that included a section of boardwalk over Vanishing Swamp. During the rainy season, the place turned into a swamp, but it stayed dry most of the year.

That day, it was somewhat swampy with lots of standing water. About halfway across it, they stopped at a live oak that was leaning away from the boardwalk.

"Angela, see that green growth on top of the limbs of this live oak? That's not moss, but a species of fern. They call it resurrection fern. Any idea why?"

"Nothing comes to mind."

"In a dry spell, it turns brown and dries up like it's dead. But when the rain comes—"

"Oh, I see where you're going. When it rains, it turns green as if resurrected from the dead."

"You got it."

Beyond Vanishing Swamp, they came to the edge of the old rice field of Lawton Plantation and took the southern trail that paralleled it. When they came to a tower that was built for visitors to get an overview of the place, they climbed it and gazed across the old rice field.

"This abandoned rice field takes us back to the age of the planters and slaves," he said. "It now stands as a testament to the African slaves who built it.

"I don't know whether or not Charles Fraser consciously created the Forest Preserve here in order to preserve the remains of this old rice field and the Indian oyster shell ring. But from my point of view, he could not have chosen a better place on the Island to create a Forest Preserve."

"I now see why this place is so special to you—its natural beauty and the relics created by the two ethnic groups that interest you the most. But the old rice field doesn't look like what I'd imagined. It looks like a shallow lake that's all grown up with cattails and such."

"Yes, but more than a hundred years ago, they grew rice here. And as far as I know, this was the only barrier island plantation that grew rice.

"The other plantations on this and the other barrier islands grew cotton—sea island cotton which had a long fiber that was in much demand. The rest of the rice plantations, and there were many of them, were located beside coastal rivers and creeks or on river islands, where the full tides could push the fresh water into the fields through specially designed trunks.

"The tides could not do that here. So, they obviously pumped the needed water for this field from the three-freshwater lakes on the Island. I've often wondered but have not been able to find any information on the type of pump they used before the invention of steam engines.

"My guess is that they were powered by slaves on treadmills. My mind keeps going to the drawing of such a treadmill in Charleston. This one provided power for grinding corn. And the treading was done by slaves who were sent there by their owners to be punished. It was an alternative for whipping them for some unacceptable behavior.

"What a hell of a task that would have been for the slaves of this plantation if my conjecture is correct. Of course, it was in the owner's best interest to rotate the treader.

"Let sit here on this bench and I'll tell you the story about a young woman from Connecticut who lived on this plantation for about six months during the early years of Reconstruction."

"Is this the lady who wrote letters to her sister?"

"The very one," he said and they sat side by side on one of the railing benches. "When the Union Army captured Hilton Head Island in 1861, the planters fled inland and, in so doing, left behind a thousand or so slaves. That meant the U.S. government had responsibility for the former slaves and the plantations.

"The Union general in charge of the Island put out calls for benevolent organizations in the North to send teachers and other forms of aid for the freedmen as they were called. This set the stage for the story of Eliza Summers.

“She and her friend Julie, also from Connecticut, responded to the American Missionary Association’s call for teachers who were willing to teach the newly freed slaves. They were accepted and sent to Hilton Head Island in January of 1867. Upon arrival, they were sent here to the Lawton Plantation, where they lived alone in the big house with no other white people within miles.

“The two women did have one scary night, when a drunk freedman slept down stairs, while they hovered in their bedroom upstairs. Other than that scary night, it’s obvious from Eliza’s letters that she and Julie trusted the colored people, implicitly.

“Colored people. That’s what she called them in her letters. The children and adults apparently held the two women in high esteem. They were constantly bringing them gifts of oysters and other good things to eat.

“Once, the two women arranged for six colored men to row them to Daufuskie Island to visit a plantation that was noted for its flower gardens. As she writes in her letters, they were enchanted by the beauty of the gardens.”

“Speaking of Daufuskie Island,” Angela said. “I did read Pat Conroy’s *The Water is Wide* while you were in Alabama and liked it a lot. I always turned to it whenever I needed a break from working on my novel. Now, I’m looking forward to reading his debut novel, *The Great Santini.*

“I’ll be interested to get your response to *The Great Santini.* Since our earlier discussion of it, I’m been thinking about making it one of the books I’ll give Hannah on her twelfth birthday in February.

“It will give me a segue to a discussion about her coming of age. I’ll be able to learn what she knows and what she needs to know. I doubt that Debbie has talked with her about the changes facing her as she become an adolescent.

“That sounds like a great idea. I wish my father or mother had had that talk with me.”

“Angie, would it be okay if I tell Hannah that she can talk to you about any further questions she may have about the journey she’s facing?”

“Absolutely. And thanks for sharing this. Sometimes, my interruption of your narration turns out to be quite fruitful. Now, please take me back to Eliza Summers’ experiences here. Is the big house where she lived still standing?”

"No, neither it nor the slave quarters have survived. They were located on the back side of the Island near Broad Creek, a large tidal creek that almost cuts across the Island. It ebbs and flows with the Intracoastal Waterway. There was no bridge to the Island back then and the inland waterways were major courses of travel and transportation.

"According to Summers, there were about fifty slave cabins in the quarters. That's what they called the area that contained the slave cabins near the big house.

"She also writes about attending religious meetings in their praise house, but she doesn't describe the meetings or the important place that the praise house played in their lives. It was a place where they could practice their own understanding of the Christian faith without a minister or any outside leader.

"One of the unique things about the services at the praise house was a shuffling dance that they called the shout. You couldn't cross your legs in the shout. That would be dancing or so I've heard them say.

"I don't know of any praise houses that are still active. I do know, however, that they continued to be an important component of Gullah life, long after the development of black churches.

"Well, that's my story of the Yankee woman who once lived on this place. Her letters were published only recently in *Dear Sister*. A couple from Connecticut discovered them in the family's old farmhouse after visiting Sea Pines Plantation."

"That's a good story. Thanks for sharing it."

"My pleasure. Are you up to seeing more of the Forest Preserve?"

"Lead the way," she said.

They had a fine time birding on their way to North Lake, where they decided to rest at a good spot near the edge of the water. There, they sat on a blanket and ate their lunch.

"Your story about Eliza Summers is still dancing around in my head. A Northern woman journeying into the old South to live for a while among the freedmen on a rice plantation.

"Now, here I am, another Northern woman who has journeyed into South Carolina, but unlike her, I have no intention of ever moving back to the North, unless you should move there with me."

"Together until the end, north or south, that's my commitment. Angie, I just thought about another Northern woman with connections to rice plantations, but after they had fallen into ruins.

There's a place up the coast beyond Charleston and just above Georgetown, known in the plantation days as the Waccamaw Neck. I'd like to take you there, hopefully this spring, to experience its natural beauty, its history, and something fairly new—Brookgreen Gardens that were created on an old defunct rice plantation by a Northern woman and her husband."

"And you know me. I'll be ready to go. Give me an introduction."

"The Waccamaw Neck is a strip of land bound on the east by the Atlantic Ocean and the west by the Waccamaw River. By the early 1800s, it had been divided into thirty something plantations, each one stretching from the river to the ocean, and they were all very prosperous rice plantations.

"I have a book that opens a telling window on that place, *Down by the Riverside: A South Carolina Slave Community* by Charles Joyner. But that's another story.

"Around 1930, Archer and Anna Huntington bought four of those Waccamaw rice plantations, including Brookgreen. They were from New York City. He was an industrialist and philanthropist. She was a sculptor.

"They built a winter home, Atalaya, near the beach. It's laid out in Moorish fashion with an inner and outer court, where she spent countless hours chiseling marble into splendid sculptures.

"Here's the good part of their story. They turned Brookgreen Plantation into Brookgreen Gardens for her own sculptures as well as those they collected. Today, there's a grand host of wonderful sculptures, some breath-takingly mammoth, that are integrated into beautiful gardens.

"Brookgreen Gardens now claims to have the largest collection of American figurative sculptures in the country. It's a magnificent place and open to the public."

"Anticipation is already buzzing in my head. You know I came looking for a Southern experience. You're making that happen beyond my expectations. But you, William Barsh Roberts, have filled me with a love I've never known."

Chapter Sixteen

After returning to the condo from the Forest Preserve, they settled on the couch with a cup of green tea. Angela was filled with appreciation for the things Barsh had shared with her and referenced several of them in their light conversation before turning to the Civil War.

"Barsh, since I know so little about the Civil War, I'd like to hear your take on it."

"I'm not an American historian, but yes, I'll share my perspective with you.

"Let's start with the philosophy behind the secession of the Southern States and the formation of the Confederacy. Like the founding father of the United States, I agree that people have a right to exit old political unions and form new ones if they have a just cause. That was the very principle that the Colonies use to declare their independence from England.

"In my judgement, the Southern States did not have a just cause for seceding from the Union. There were significant regional differences, but I do not believe the Southern States would have seceded if it were not for slavery.

"I can say categorically that there was no valid justification for slavery. Thus, I see no valid justification for the secession of the Southern States and the formation of the Confederacy. It was a horrible mistake, and I fault the Southern States for seceding.

"General Ulysses Grant was only half right, however, when he asserted that the Confederate cause was one of the worst causes for which people ever fought. The South fought, with justification, to defend its homeland from the invading forces of the Union.

"While I fault the Southern States for seceding without just cause, I do not fault them for defending their homeland against the invading Union Army. From their point of view, it was the War of Northern Aggression.

"Zealous South Carolinians did fire the first shots of the war on Fort Sumter, but they considered that Union Fort a part of their homeland. The matter should have been resolved through negotiations, and the State officials of South Carolina had appointed a commission to do that.

"The Union definitely brought the war to the Confederacy with the primary mission of bringing its states back under Federal control. Whereas, the South never had any ambition of conquering the North and bringing it under Confederacy control.

"So, I fault the Union for two things. First, I see no moral justification for the Union to sacrifice hundreds of thousands of its own people to conquer the Confederacy and to kill hundreds of thousands of Southerners in the process. Second, I see no moral justification for the brutal way the Union ravaged the land and people of the Confederate States.

"Additionally, the short period of Reconstruction was a failure for blacks and whites.

"In spite of all the horrors of the Civil War and its aftermath, I do find two good outcomes—the abolition of slavery and the restoration of the Union.

"Unlike many Southerners, I have never lamented *the lost cause.* Moreover, I don't think Confederate soldiers should have been memorialized with statues. This, by the way, was also Confederate General Robert E. Lee's position.

"There's no way you can separate the dedication of those memorials from Southern declarations of white supremacy. Catherine has shared with me the speeches given during the dedication of some of the Confederate Statues here in South Carolina. They are saturated with proclamations of white supremacy.

"Both the North and the South paid a horrific price for that war, but the South, more so. It has taken the South a century to begin to heal from the curses of slavery and the devastation of defeat. Okay, my dear Northern woman, that's my take on the Civil War."

"Please know that I like your take on the War. Thanks for sharing it."

"As always, it was my pleasure. Are you ready for a walk on the beach?"

"Ready, ready."

They walked south this time and soon had the beach to themselves, except for the birds. Sandpipers rushed along the shore with their busy little feet tripping ahead of the breaking waves. A few gulls stood sentry near the dunes. Those a-wing seemed to be showing off their flying skills. Brown pelicans rode the air currents north, likely heading for their roost.

Coming back up the beach, Angela scanned a scattering of sea shells until she found two that she liked. She only wanted a few to commemorate their first visit to the Island.

Back in the condo, they dressed for dinner and were off to Hudson's Seafood Restaurant on Skull Creek. As planned, they got there in time to watch the setting sun paint the western sky with a splendid array of colors, but notably a dark red.

Barsh was pleased to see how charmed Angela was by the old shrimp boat that was moored at the dock and how she wondered what a shrimper's life was like. She was saddened to learn that it was getting harder, by the year, for them to make a good living from the sea.

Those were the same reactions he had when he first learned the story, but he had kept his thoughts to himself. He knew Debbie had no interest in the shrimpers and Hannah was a mere child. How lucky he felt to have Angela by his side to share his feelings.

They ordered fried oysters, that the waiter advertised as having been harvested from local waters and processed by the Bluffton Oyster Company—a place on the May River that Barsh had visited several times.

Once he watched a black man putter up to the landing in a bateau loaded with his harvest of oysters. The Gullah-speaking man told him that he'd been making that trip down the May River to the oyster beds for twenty-six years—rowing there and back in the early years before he bought a five-horse-powered outboard motor for the bateau.

Barsh and Angela enjoyed themselves at Hudson's and left the restaurant delighted with the experience.

***

Back in the condo, they cuddled on the couch like young lovers. Barsh was pleased with the way the day had gone and was looking forward to more of Angela's novel.

"What a wonderful day this has been," she said breaking the silence.

"Yes, another wonderful day with you."

"We're coming to the dark place in the novel—my damnable story that I've given to Ava."

"And I'm ready to put that behind us," he said."

"I'll read until I get to that part and then I'll give you the manuscript."

She left to retrieve the manuscript and he shifted to the big stuffed chair, so he would have a good view of her as she read. He had already learned that Ava had become entangled in an affair with Dr. Quinton Shifflett, the major professor of Southern literature at Brown. As she progressed through the graduate program, he had agreed to become the faculty advisor for her doctoral dissertation.

He was ten years older than she and was married with grown children. In wooing Ava, he told her that he and his wife were estranged and that he was divorcing her.

Ava had heard the same story from other men but, nevertheless, fell for it, assuming there was more honor among academic men than the business men who had wooed her.

Angela returned and settled on the couch. She looked stressed as she began reading. Things continued to go well for Ava and Dr. Shifflett, until she had completed about half of her dissertation. Then Ava began to doubt his intention to divorce his wife.

He had not even hired a lawyer. With growing disgust with the affair, she decided to end it and prepared herself to confront him the next time they met to get his critique of her latest work on the dissertation.

At that point, Angela handed Barsh the manuscript. He smiled at her and began to read.

> "Quinton, you have no intention of getting a divorce, do you?" Ava said with outward boldness but inward trepidation.
>
> He stared at her long and hard without opening his mouth.
>
> "I take your silence to mean *no*," she said, seized with mounting anxiety.
>
> "Take it, however, you will," he said.
>
> "I loved you but you deceived me. I will hold you in high esteem as a literary scholar and I will never fail to

honor you for directing my dissertation, but our relationship is no longer working for me."

This time, he stared at her and then responded.

"Then you'll have to find a way to make it work if you want to graduate from here with a Ph.D. Unless I sign off on your dissertation, the committee will not approve it."

"Would you do that to me?" she said and stood to leave.

"Try me. I'll be at your apartment Wednesday evening, as usual, expecting you to receive me as if this conversation had never happened."

Barsh stopped reading and looked at Angela. Tears were trickling down her face. He moved quickly to her and tenderly embraced her.

"That's what my dissertation advisor Jacob McFarland did to me. I became his sex slave for five months, but I had to act like I was his lover. I hated myself for doing that and I haven't been able to forgive myself."

"Damn that bastard Jacob McFarland," Barsh said. "Damn any man who would abuse a woman."

"Believe me, Angie, I could not love you more than I do this very moment, and I don't blame you for taking that horrendous abuse to achieve your academic goals. If I'd been in your shoes, I would have done the same thing."

"Are you sure."

"Yes, and as soon as I graduated, I would have exposed the bastard and then I would have forgiven myself."

"Maybe that's part of my problem. I wrote McFarland a degrading letter, but I didn't expose him.

"I knew he would claim that I had consented to the sexual affair. Moreover, another professor had recommended me for a position on the faculty at Brown, and I didn't want the matter to interfere with my getting the position."

"I totally understand your situation. It's not too late to expose McFarland, and I will help you develop a strategy to do so."

"Yes, I need you to help me with this. I thought I could bury it in my unconsciousness, but I was wrong. Now that I've told you, I have to do something about him."

"I think you should use a lawyer to convey your experience to University officials with a copy to McFarland, and I know just the man to help us."

"Thank you. Thank you. I'm already feeling like I can forgive myself and put it behind me, once I expose the bastard.

"I'll also have to revise my novel and let Will help Ava expose her advisor, Quinton Shifflett.

"Barsh, will you find a time to finish reading Part Two by yourself? Then there's only good stuff. You'll get to see how I've depicted the fictionalized you. What a joy it was to write those chapters."

"Yes, of course. You should know I'm looking forward to those chapters."

"I trust they will please you. Has the tide ebbed, yet?"

"The tide is ebbing. Are you ready for a night walk on the beach?"

"I'm so ready, and then I need your brand of intimacy to reassure me that your love has not diminished."

"Have no doubt. My love for you has not diminished one iota. Actually, I had planned something new for us, tonight, but it can wait if you're not in the mood."

"Out with it, my good man."

"I've been imagining a new therapy for soul as well as body and heart. Remember the catamaran, stashed in the dunes, that we explored this morning?"

"Oh, yes, lead the way."

"Are you sure you're up to this, right now? The catamaran should still be there, later in the week."

"No delay needed. First, we'll nourish our souls and then our bodies and hearts.

"I'm taking a couple of blankets, one to lie on and one to cover us. I'm also changing into my sweatsuit. You might want to change into a skirt."

"I have the perfect skirt and a loose sweater. Bra and panties be gone."

***

They walked north on the beach until Barsh spotted the catamaran.

“Well, here we are.”

“How I love the way your mind works. While I was expressing my fear of sailing this thing on the ocean, you were thinking, yeah, but I’ll bet you would jump at an opportunity to try catamaran therapy for body and heart on its taut canvas.”

“Truthfully, I did think about the possibility of the experience, although I didn’t make that bet about you.”

“Well, I did jump at the opportunity. I need your intimate affirmation like never before.”

As Barsh had expected, they had the place all to themselves, and their experience on the catamaran was memorable in every way.

Chapter Seventeen

Thursday morning, Barsh woke early and eased out of bed without waking Angela. As she had requested, he finished reading Part Two of her novel.

Ava had endured the role of a sex slave that her dissertation advisor Quinton Shifflett had coerced her into. After graduating with a Ph.D, she wrote him a hostile letter breaking all relationships with him and damning his soul. In spite of her raging anger, she kept his sexual abuse to herself.

On the recommendation of one of her women professors, the university offered her a non-tenured position in the English Department and she accepted it. After two years of disquietude, she applied for a professorship in several Southern colleges, got an offer from one in Upstate South Carolina, accepted it, and moved South.

The commode flushed and Angela soon appeared in the bedroom door. The sheer fabric of the gown she was wearing was alluringly revealing.

"Good morning," she said with a big smile.

"And a good morning to you," he said and stood as she walked toward him with her short gown swaying slightly with each step.

"I trust you slept well," he said.

"My dreams were so scrambled I can't describe any of them. But I feel fine."

"That's good to hear. You certainly look gorgeous."

"Thank you. How did you sleep?"

"Very well. I'm ready for another good day with you. Are you ready for a light breakfast of juice, coffee, and bagels? I'm thinking Sunrise Café for a good brunch. My taste buds are calling for their eggs Benedict."

"Sounds good, but I can wait on breakfast if I've read your eyes."

"You've definitely read my eyes. But if I were a bull and you were a cow, my eyes would tell you nothing."

"I don't get it. You'll have to explain that to your city woman."

"It was just something that my monkey mind grabbed from the bag of my past experiences."

"Then there's a story behind your quip and you must share it with me later," she said as they headed for the bedroom.

***

That beautiful moment of afterglow seemed to linger as they lay naked in bed. He pulled her hand to his lips, kissed it, and eased it back on the bed, where he gently held it as they conversed about various things. Then he issued a second invitation for breakfast.

"Ready! Ready! You take the bathroom, first, so you can fix the bagels while I take my turn."

"Do you want yours with cream cheese and apricot jam?"

"Please. That's a new jam to me and I like it."

After they finished breakfast, they moved to the balcony. The sky was a Carolina blue. The Atlantic Ocean was rolling in, wave after wave. A few people were already on the beach. One woman was throwing pieces of bread into the sky for the hovering gulls.

"Which way are we walking this morning?"

"I'm thinking south, since we're going north this evening."

***

After an enjoyable brunch at Sunrise Café, they left for the condo.

"Angie, I just thought of a good place to take you—Red Piano Art Gallery. Among other things, I'd like to show you paintings by Walter Greer, who's considered the Island's first resident artist of notability. His large paintings of the Island's natural beauty are wondrously rendered."

"Can we go now?"

"Sure. Here's an oddity of mine I'll share. If I didn't have a Jesus complex about possessing expensive art, I'd certainly own one of Greer's large nature paintings."

"So, your Jesus complex governs the way you spend your money?"

"Probably not enough, but yes, it does to some degree, especially earnings from the trust. I spend that only in ways that I know my parents would approve.

"I know the farm is a luxury. Even so, my parents would approve my purchase of the farm with money from the trust.

"They gave me the gift of living on a farm in Alabama during my high school years. Then they sold it and moved to Georgia during the second semester of my freshman year at college. I consider the Jeremiah Keeble place as their re-gifting me with a place in the country."

"I like the way you think about the trust fund. What else would your parents approve?"

"Travel to experience the world. But not a Walter Greer painting. So, I purchase good art from starving artists, which is a good deed that I can also enjoy.

"Speaking of which, I want to stop at Red Piano Too Art Gallery, when we get to St. Helena Island on Saturday. Some of the paintings there fall within the range of my art budget, and I'd like to buy a painting to commemorate this trip. There's also a gallery in Bluffton that I want to visit tomorrow. It too has paintings in my price range."

***

They both enjoyed the paintings on display at the Red Piano Art Gallery, especially those by Walter Greer and Ray Ellis. Then they returned to the condo, relaxed and happy.

"Well, this was another special morning," she said. "Sex before breakfast, a beach walk, eggs Benedict at Sunrise Café, and a visit to the art gallery.

"Are you up for more of my novel? Only good stuff, now."

"Yes, then I suggest we take a nap before dinner? The moonrise is late tonight, but fortunately the tide will be out. We'll have no trouble walking to the Dunes at Owl Oak to experience the moonrise."

"I'm so looking forward to another first-time experience."

"Angie, I'm wearing my sweatsuit. You might want to wear the same outfit you wore last night. The moon might give us permission to shift from beach therapy for the soul to a session of beach therapy for body and heart."

"Oh, yes, and I'm putting my money on the moon's permission for that."

***

They left the condo late that night and walked north on the hard-packed sand. Barsh was in a silent reflective mood but feeling serene, just to be there beside the calm majestic Atlantic Ocean with Angela.

The fact that it could and did frequently shift to an uncontrollable, destructive force never once entered his mind that night. On reaching the Dunes at Owl Oak, he spread a blanket next to them, and they sat facing the ocean.

"Over the last twelve years, I've often sat alone here at night and enjoyed the solitude of this place. In all those years, I never once dreamed that I'd one day share this place with a woman like you. But here we are waiting for the moon to rise above the ocean with a special wake shimmered straight to us. Look. There's its faint glow on the horizon."

"I see it," she said and snuggled against him as the glow turned brighter and the moon slowly rose from the ocean.

"Wow! That was beautiful. You were so right about the moon's wake. I like the way it's shimmering straight into our eyes as if we were the center of its attention."

"Yes, and when we leave for the condo, its shimmering wake will follow us all the way and give us the illusion that it has singled us out for its attention."

"Now, let me query it about our interest in a session of beach therapy for body and heart. Good news! It just told me that it would not object, since we are so in love with each other."

"Will this be a first for you?"

"My very first. The idea occurred to me as we settled in the dunes here before sunrise on Wednesday. I remembered how deserted the beach was here late at night. And just as I expected, we have the place to ourselves with the moon now watching over us. This night belongs to us. We have no one to answer to but ourselves."

Chapter Eighteen

Following their late-night visit to the Dunes at Owl Oak, Barsh and Angela had gone to bed with no intention of rising early that Friday. As usual, however, they woke early and in a joyful mood. They ate a hearty breakfast, which they prepared together, and then moved to the couch, where he shared the agenda that he had prepared for the day.

"Before we take to the road, I'd like to brief you on a significant Civil War battle that took place on the north end of the Island. Take a look at this artist's sketch of how the Union warships looped, around and around, Port Royal Sound as they repeatedly shelled Fort Walker on Hilton Head Island and Fort Beauregard across the way on Saint Philips Island.

"After being bombarded for about two hours, the Confederate forces abandoned Fort Walker and retreated to the mainland. As I mentioned earlier, the planters also fled to the mainland. I'm sure they took their house slaves as well as those who managed their horses and carriages. The rest of the slaves, numbering about a thousand, were left behind.

"The same thing happened on a number of neighboring islands that had fallen under the control of the Union Army. The administration of the abandoned slave, now called freedmen, became known as the Port Royal Experiment, which included white teachers from the North like Eliza Summers and her friend who taught them at the Lawton Plantation here on Hilton Head Island.

"The reason the Union Forces set out to capture this island so early in the war, a feat they accomplished on November 7, 1861, was to build a naval base here, which they did at Port Royal Sound.

"It was a part of their larger strategy to blockade shipping to and from the Confederate States. During the Civil War and Reconstruction, the U.S. maintained an occupational force of twenty to thirty thousand. They also built their own little town on the north end of the Island and named it Port Royal. The freedmen also built their own town, nearby, and named it Mitchellville."

"I remember your telling me about Mitchellville, when we were discussing Zora Neale Hurston's *Their Eyes Were Watching God*. Are either of those town still standing?"

"No. After Reconstruction, all of the Union troops withdrew and the population drastically declined. I've heard that those who remained on the Island started salvaging lumber from the buildings of Mitchellville and Port Royal, until there was nothing left of either place. Next, wealthy Northerners began to buy the plantations for hunting preserves.

"When the resort developments started in the 1950s, there were only about 300 blacks and fewer whites living on the Island. The blacks lived on their own small subsistence farms. I've heard some of them call that pre-development era *the make-do days*."

He paused and laid the history book on the coffee table.

"I'll say it again, I love the way you share with me the history of the places you take me."

"Always my pleasure. Now, I'll like to take you to the mudflats at Port Royal Sound. Shall we get on the road?"

"Ready! Ready!"

Barsh drove north on the William Hilton Parkway, the only road onto and off the Island. When the Parkway turned west toward the bridge and mainland, he turned right and took a series of back roads. The last one came to a dead end, and he parked on the edge of the road. There was nothing but trees and bushes before them and on both sides of the road.

"There's a trail just behind us on the right side of the road. It will take us to a sandy beach for dry walking and viewing the mudflats, shorebirds, and Port Royal Sound."

"Then lead the way, my dear man."

They took to the trail, which was clear walking until they got near the beach. Then they had to work their way through a thick tangle of wax myrtle bushes.

"So, this is Port Royal Sound, where the battle for the Island took place."

"The very place. Let's walk east toward the ocean as far as Fish Haul Creek, and I'll tell you a story about one of my visits to this place. We'll search the mudflats for birds as we go."

"I now understand why this place is called the mudflats."

"They actually extend much farther as the tide ebbs to its lowest point. Look. There's an oystercatcher."

"What a long red bill."

"Good for opening oysters, mussels, and such," he said as it took flight, and they continued walking down the beach. "Okay, this is Fish Haul Creek. At low tide, you can wade across it. But not at high tide.

"Late one afternoon two summers ago, I was standing here just past high tide, when a man and a woman rode up on bikes and were alarmed that the creek was unpassable. Visitors to the Island, the couple were staying at the oceanfront hotel in Port Royal, a gated development that starts on the other side of this creek.

"The woman became hysterical because they didn't know how to get back to their hotel. The man told her they could push their bikes across the ebbing creek. I warned them that the water was too deep and as dangerous as a riptide. Then I took them to the trail that you and I came in on and told them the roads to take to get back to their hotel.

"My point to the story is that sometimes, when we go to a new place, we do stupid and even dangerous things because of our ignorance. As a boy, for example, I'd gone swimming in the ocean several times before I learned about riptides.

"I now know what to do if I'm ever caught in one. But during my first experiences in the surf, I would have done the wrong thing by swimming against the riptide. Looking back on my life, I know I've luckily escaped more than one life-threatening situation based on my ignorance."

"The point of your story is a good one. I'm sure I've also narrowly escaped fatal mishaps because of my ignorance."

"Okay, it's time to bid the mudflats goodbye. Our next stop is Pinckney Island National Wild Life Refuge."

***

They sat on a blanket on a grassy bank overlooking a freshwater lake and ate their picnic lunch. Earlier, they'd seen a hooded merganser paddling away from the edge of the lake and then taking flight, as they approached the place. There were several gallinules and coots that continued to paddle about without concern about their presence.

"Pinckney Island is such a lovely place to enjoy nature," she said. "I feel grateful for those who made this island a refuge for wildlife."

"Gratitude is definitely the right feeling. Otherwise, this island would already be another gated community with a few golf courses. For the future of the earth's biosphere, we need to set aside much more land as wildlife preserves."

"You've made a believer out of me," she said and stretched out on her back. "Join me for a bit of ground therapy for the soul."

He studied her face for a moment. She seemed at peace with herself and the world, and he stretched out beside her.

"Well, your baked ham has served us well for our outings. Tomorrow, we'll eat lunch in Beaufort, a lovely little town. If I were freely locating to the Lowcountry, I think I'd like to live there."

"I trust you know you've got me excited about experiencing the place."

"Here's something I forgot to tell you. I noticed in yesterday's *Island Packet* that there's a jazz combo playing at the big hotel in the Palmetto Dunes development. Would you like to dress up and dine there tonight?"

"Sounds like a great way to start the evening. But right now, I love the tranquility of just being here with you."

"The next time we vacation down this way, I'll show you more beautiful places on this little island. In addition to the trails that we experience today, there are several more trails branching off on the western side that are worth exploring.

"One leads to the site where an old plantation house once stood—a reminder that the Island has an agricultural history. In fact, it's named for an important planter, Charles Pinckney, who married an even more significant planter, Eliza Lucas.

"I only know enough about Eliza Lucas to know that she was an exceptional South Carolina woman for the 1700s. She was educated in London and developed a special interest in botany and philosophy, which was certainly atypical for women of her day.

"If I remember correctly, she was managing, at the early age of eighteen, three of her father's plantations that were located between Beaufort and Charleston.

"One thing that I do remember is that she figured out how to grow indigo in the Lowcountry, and that became a major cash crop for the planters before the Revolutionary War.

"I read somewhere that she copied all the letters she wrote in a book that was passed down through her descendants. It's now a major source for understand life in the Lowcountry in the eighteenth century.

"I don't know if her letters have been published, but I'm sure I would find them interesting. But like almost all of the prominent people of the South in her day, she was flawed by the exploitation of African slaves."

They lingered beside the freshwater lake on Pinckney Island for a while longer and left for the little town of Bluffton located nearby on the May River. After they crossed the bridge to the mainland, he pointed out a gated community named Moss Creek.

"Angie, a former student from Cooper lives in this development. She married a prominent lawyer down here and teaches biology at Sea Pines Academy. We drove by the backside of the campus when we visited the Forest Preserve. Although she was a biology major, she took several of my classes and has kept in touch with me.

"She's taken me to lunch on several of my visits to the Island. Two summers ago, she invited me to go kayaking with her. Half of the Moss Creek Development is surrounded by saltwater marshes with several tidal creeks, and we kayaked through them. I had a great time.

"I was also impressed that the developers of Moss Creek set aside a small island and some lowland acreage as nature preserves. They also created two tidal lakes—something I'd never seen before."

"You are a lucky man to have such ongoing relationships with your students."

"That's an advantage of teaching at a small college. You will soon experience the same extended bonding with some of your students."

"I hope so. Anyway, I'm looking forward to kayaking with you when next we return."

"There's a woman on Broad Creek who rents kayaks and teaches people how to paddle them without flipping over. She will also teach you how to get back in the kayak if you do turn over. I've kayaked with her and I'd like to get you started under her tutelage."

"Sounds like a good plan to me," she said.

Barsh drove by the major points of interest in Bluffton, including the Oyster Factory. They made only one stop and that was at an art gallery. He bought a large painting of a beach scene on Hilton Head Island that they both admired, and then they headed back to Hilton Head Island.

"Where do you intend to hang the painting?" she asked.

"It's yours to hang wherever you'd like."

"How dear of you. I'll treasure it forever as a reminder of this getaway."

"Angie, would you indulge me for a sentimental moment."

"Of course, what do you have in mind?"

"Hannah and I have always made at least one stop at Hilton Head Ice Cream Shop. You'll never eat better ice cream, and it's made right there."

"Then get us to Hilton Head Ice Cream Shop. My tongue is ready for a good workout."

He looked at her and they both smiled.

"You do lick you ice cream?" she said.

"I usually get a cup. But today I'm getting a cone."

They enjoyed their stop for ice cream and then returned to the condo.

Chapter Nineteen

It was late afternoon, and Angela was reading, aloud, from the last chapter of her novel, as Barsh listened intently.

"Last page," she said and then read it.

"Angie, I love your novel, and reading it together has been an extraordinary experience. First, I've never participated in an oral reading of a novel. This was so satisfying that I'd like for us to make it a practice to read to each other excerpts from the books we're reading."

"Yes, let's make it a practice."

"Second, I never dreamed I'd someday love a woman who has been so brilliantly reflected in a novel. Once I'm drawn into someone's life, even if it's fictional, I'm emphatically engaged in their struggles. I would have been rooting for Ava even if the novel had been written by someone that I knew nothing about."

"Thanks. That's what an author wants to hear."

"Your literary skills in telling the story are superb. Flawless, I'd say. I have no doubt your novel will find a good publisher."

"Again, I thank you. Your judgement means everything to me. As I've said, I'm very pleased with the novel, and I do have high expectations for it. Now, tell me what you thought about the way I depicted the fictional version of you."

"Well, you made Will Robinson a likable man. So, yes, I like him and I'm honored to be reflected in the novel. Our actual journey to date has been fantastic and my aspirations for us reach to the moon."

"Speaking of the moon," she said, "I say *wow* to last night's session of beach therapy for body and heart. That experience is in my memory bank for keeps—the image of your face looking down into mine with the moon framing you. I don't have the words."

"Nor do I have the words, and it's also in my memory bank for keeps."

"Back to my novel," she said, "you're telling me your honest feelings, right?"

"Absolutely. Nothing but the truth. The novel is excellent on so many levels. Of course, I was moved by the time-to-love-anew theme.

"You also deserve the highest praise for writing about a woman's devastating experience with her dissertation advisor. Fiction is a good way to make people aware of different forms of sexual abuse."

"Just know that you take on the novel has reinforced my own assessment of it. And I thank you. Now, I'd like to take a shower and get ready for dinner and some good jazz."

***

Dinner at the hotel was excellent and the jazz combo afterwards at the bar was superb. Playful and relaxed, they returned to the condo and sat together on the couch.

"Barsh, our outing this evening was just what I needed—the food, the music, the dancing."

"I'm pleased to hear that. I certainly had a great time. I've been thinking about where we might dine tomorrow on our last evening here for this trip. Two places came to mind—an excellent steakhouse and a superfine Italian restaurant. I'll defer to you if you have a preference."

"My choice would be to go back to Harbor Town for dinner at Quarter Deck and, afterwards, enjoy the view from the top of the lighthouse."

"Then that's what we'll do. What about a bit of night gazing from the balcony before we settle in for the night?"

"Good idea. Then you must explain the quip about your eyes versus those of a bull."

"As you wish. It dawned on me after I made the quip that I was noted for that kind of wisecrack in response to whatever was going on around me, during my high school days. But when I went off to college, I shook off or suppressed that kind of witticism. I became too damn serious about everything. I credit you with reviving some of my old quirkiness."

***

They stood on the balcony and took in the night scene. The beach was deserted. The tide was full and calm. They could see the lights on Tybee Island, Georgia. Without their coats, they soon felt the chilled night air and returned to the couch.

"Okay, time for you to tell me why your eyes would tell me nothing about my sexy display if you had the eyes of a bull."

"Here's my *if story*. If I were a bull and you were a cow in my herd, you could parade your naked sex before my eyes all day, even raise your tail to give me a better view, but you would never arouse me through my eyes.

"Simply stated the sexual stimulation for a bull is that special scent that it smells when a cow is in estrous or *in heat* as I would say in my youth.

"So, if I were a bull and you were a cow in heat, I'd flare my nostrils for your erotic scent, curl my upper lip, and quickly *service* you. I'd repeat that act a number of times over the next few days. Then I'd pay you no attention for more than a year.

"In about nine months, you'd have a calf and nurse it until it was weaned. You would do that without any help from me. You would need me only when you were in heat, and that's when I would need you. Sex for us would be strictly for reproduction."

"Well, you expressed that quite graphically. Now, tell me about your eyes."

"Fortunately, evolution has created a different kind of sexuality for humans, primarily because women need help raising the children who are born helpless and remain so for years.

"The ability for us to have sex at any time is clearly an evolutionary adaptation to aid human bonding, and in the process, sexual stimulation for the male shifted from smell to sight and touch."

"So, you're saying evolutions has engineered human sexuality, unlike cow sexuality, for purposes other than reproduction."

"Yes, that's obvious to those who have studied the situation."

"Then why does the Catholic Church oppose artificial birth control?"

"Because they're behind the times. I knew the difference between the sexuality of humans and other mammals from observations as a country boy, but I didn't know how to express it, until I recently read E. O. Wilson's *On Human Nature*. This is Wilson's third book on what he calls sociobiology, the effects of evolutionary biology on social animals.

“A world authority on ants, Wilson’s first book on sociobiology was *The Insect Societies*. Next, he extended that study to the social behavior of vertebrates in *Sociobiology: The New Synthesis*. And now, he’s expanded this type of study to us in *On Human Nature*. There’s much to learn from Wilson’s studies.”

“Will you share more of Wilson’s thinking with me in the days to come?”

“Yes, of course. I’ve also recently learned about a new book by Donald Symons entitled *The Evolution of Human Sexuality*. I intend to order a copy and read it sometime next year. According to the reviews, Symons is definitely on the right course. And that course is in line with the studies of E. O. Wilson.

“The special sexual capacity that we have as human beings has also opens us to all kinds of opportunities for destructive behavior such as rape, child molestation, sexual trafficking, and promiscuous behavior.

“These are ethical concerns for everyone, including the Church, but not artificial birth control. Decisions about when to have sex for mutual pleasure and when to have sex to produce a child are two totally different decisions.

“I want to marry you in order to share all aspects of life with you, including sex. As I’ve said before, I’ll follow your lead on the question of children.

“Although I don’t need another child, I’m definitely prepared to have one or more, even at my age. And among other things, age and health are both considerations that couples should always factor into their decision about having or not having a child.”

“Artificial birth control has been a part of my life, since I became sexually active,” Angela said. “But having no philosophical perspective of my own, the Catholic Church’s teachings against it occasionally aroused a sense of guilt. No more. Thanks for giving me this new perspective. Now, I need to test your eyes.”

“I’ll make you a bet. The very sight of your display will produce a positive response in me in less than one minute.”

“Oh, my! Now, I’ll have to blame myself if I fail the minute test.”

“Put your money on my eyes and have no worry.”

“Then stay here until I reappear in the bedroom door.”

He sat facing the bedroom door. A few minutes ticked down, and there in the doorway, she presented herself. Rising to the occasion with every step, he walked into her beckoning arms.

Chapter Twenty

Early Saturday morning, they left Hilton Head Island to visit several nearby islands to the north. The weather was fair and they were contented, although noticeably conscious of the fact that it was their last full day in the Lowcountry for this trip. Their conversations along the way were sparked by the scenery, both natural and manmade.

"I can't believe how expansive these saltwater marshes are," she said. "They seem to stretch for miles."

"They actually do. Here's an important fact about the Lowcountry that we're driving through. Twenty-five percent of all the saltwater marshes on the East Coast are located right here in Beaufort County.

"The food chain for so much of sea life starts in saltwater marshes like these. That fact, alone, demands that we protect them from all forms of pollution. Human greed, however, seems to care nothing about the conservation of nature."

"You are so right. I've long concentrated on other destructive aspect of human greed, but I credit you for making me more aware of its effects on nature."

"It's a never-ending struggle, and most days I think greed has the upper hand. But today, you and I will enjoy a fairly good blend of natural and human-made environments."

"Knowing you, I have no doubt you have created an interesting agenda for us. Last night, I asked you to wait and surprise me with your agenda for today. I'm now ready to hear it."

"After we cross the Broad River, which is just ahead, we'll travel as far east as possible by car, and in so doing, we'll experience parts of six islands before we head back this way.

"Red Piano Too Art Gallery is located on St. Helena Island. We'll be driving right by it, and I'd like to make that our first stop. Hopefully, we'll find another Lowcountry painting that we both like. I think you'll enjoy the place even if we don't find something to buy.

“Among other things of interest, we’ll see prints of the primitive art of a well-known local Gullah man. He painted on pieces of tin, wood, anything he thought suitable to paint on.”

“Yes, that will certainly interest me.”

“After visiting Red Piano Too, our next stop will be Hunting Island State Park. Okay, we’re leaving the mainland. Look to your right down Broad River. You can see almost down to Hilton Head Island.”

“My, what a beautiful view.”

“You can’t tell it from here, but on the north side of the river, there’s one island after another all the way to the Atlantic Ocean.”

“And we’re experiencing parts of six of them.”

“Yes, we’ll also drive close to the causeway to several other. If I remember correctly, there are more than sixty islands in Beaufort County. That’s not counting what they call hummocks, tiny islands with a few trees.

“When we exit this bridge, we’ll be on Port Royal Island. Typically, I would head straight for the little town of Beaufort, founded in 1712.

“The oldest surviving house was built in 1719, and it’s built on the same lot where the Yemasee Indian burned its predecessor in 1715, during the Yemasee War. I think I told you about the Yemasee War when we were discussing books by William Gilmore Simms. Anyway, Beaufort is a jewel of an old town.”

“We will be visiting Beaufort, right?

“It will be our last stop on the way back from the Atlantic Ocean. We’ll have a late lunch at Plumbs—a small restaurant on Bay Street that parallels the Beaufort River. If the weather is still fair, we can eat on the porch overlooking the river, which is part of the Intracoastal Waterway.

“I’m skirting Beaufort, this morning, so I can take you by Parris Island, home of the Marine Corps Recruit Depot. They allow visitors on the Island, and we’ll take advantage of that on another visit. Sometimes you can see the cadets doing marching drills.

“There’s also a museum that includes both military and cultural facets of the Island, including a short-lived settlement of French Huguenots led by Jean Ribault, who is something of a folk hero down here. That was in the fifteen-hundreds, but I don’t remember the exact date.”

"It all sounds interesting, and I'll look forward to that visit. Tell me about Hunting Island State Park."

"It's a small barrier island that fronts the Atlantic Ocean. We won't spend much time there, just enough for you to see the beach and the expansive view from the lighthouse. Unlike Harbor Town Lighthouse, this one is the real thing. You'll also see what the ocean can do to a barrier island."

"And you know me. I'll be soaking up both experiences."

***

They had climbed the stairs to the top of the Hunting Island Lighthouse and were slowly making the circle around the viewing deck to take in the whole expanse. The sky was blue except for a few white clouds drifting in from the southeast. Two brown pelicans rode the air currents north, searching for fish they could divebomb and catch in their big beaks.

"The view from here is just stunning," Angela said. "But the beach is so different from the one at Hilton Head Island. Why are all those dead trees on the beach?"

"Beach erosion. Those trees were once rooted on the bank of this island. Then the ocean gradually ate the land away, until some of them fell right where they were rooted. Others are still standing out on the beach, dead but still standing. It's just a matter of time before the ocean takes them down.

"This is one of the things I wanted to show you. How the ocean is eating away at the Island. One day, it will claim this lighthouse unless they move it or re-nourish the beach."

"How would they re-nourish the beach?"

"The last time we vacationed on Hilton Head Island, I read an article in *The Island Packet* about a long-range plan to re-nourish some of the beaches by pumping huge amounts of sand from the ocean bed onto the beaches. Don't know how that will work but that's what I read."

"Wouldn't the ocean wash the sand away, again?"

"That's what I'm thinking. So, you give in to the ocean's encroachment or engage it in an ongoing battle.

"Look up north to that most distant shore. That's Edisto Island. The coastal land south of there is call the ACE Basin after its three rivers—the Ashepoo, Combahee, and Edisto. There are efforts underway to transfer as much of that coastal land as possible into a National Wildlife Refuge. Hopefully, that project will continue with great success."

"Are there any islands south of here?"

"Yes, there's Fripp Island, which has been developed into a gated community. The Sea Island Parkway, that we drove here on, ends there at the security gate, just after you cross the bridge. When we leave here, we'll drive there and stop at the Visitor's Center just for the experience if you'd like."

"Suits me."

***

They left the Visitor's Center on Fripp Island and began retracing their way on the Sea Island Parkway.

"Our next stop is Fort Fremont at Lands End on St. Helena Island. This will be a good place for our morning snack."

"Is this the Confederate Fort that you told me about when we were at the mudflats?"

"No, that was Fort Beauregard on Saint Philips Island, just east of St. Helena Island. Fort Fremont was built during the Spanish-American War. Remember the caution light at Frogmore?"

"Oh, yes, and Red Piano Too Art Gallery. What a special place. I love the painting you bought of the Gullah Oysterman with his bateau brimming with just-harvested oysters.

"We now have two paintings to remind us of our first getaway to the Lowcountry. What about the caution light at Frogmore? You were going to tell me something before I interrupted you."

"That's where we take the road to Lands End. From that light, it's about ten miles. During the plantation days, cotton was the major cash crop on St. Helena, and we'll pass field that date back to those days, although no one grows cotton there anymore.

"More recently, they turned to truck farming, especially raising tomatoes and shipping them to various markets. But even that type of farming is dying out. I know of one defunct packing house on St. Helena.

“The Lands End road will take us by the Penn Center. We’ll stop there on the way back from Fort Fremont. It’s one of my favorite historical places in the Lowcountry. I think you’ll understand why, once you view the museum exhibits.

“The Penn Center was originally a school for freed slaves and has a long history of serving blacks in the area. Its current mission is to preserve and promote Gullah culture.

“Last fall I attended one of the programs of their annual Gullah Festivals and just happened to sit by a woman from New Jersey. She grew up on St. Helena but her parents moved them north when she was a teenager. She is so proud of her heritage that she rode a bus from New Jersey to get back for the festival.

“If the Gullah people have an island where they’re still a major force, it’s St Helena. And hopefully, it will stay this way and escape being developed into gated communities.”

“That’s also my hope, and I’m definitely looking forward to visiting the Penn Center.”

***

They sat on the leaf-covered ground beneath a live oak near one of the concrete walls of Fort Fremont and ate their snack.

“Angie, the last time I was here, this place seemed desolate and forlorn, a wasted human endeavor. Now, I’m much more aware of the trees and the expansive view of Port Royal Sound from the north side, and my senses want to romanticize it.”

“That’s interesting. I romanticized the place immediately because of the natural surroundings, and I know that’s because of you—the only person in the world who would want to bring me here. Perhaps you did the same, today, because of our connectedness.”

“You’re obviously right. Look, those are boat-tailed grackles. The brownish ones are females. The black ones with the long tails are males. I guess the long tails are all about attracting a mate. But they look dysfunctional in other regards. They seem to slow them down. I guess attracting a mate is more important than swift flight for the male grackle.”

“Does that mean the female gets to choose her mate?”

“It looks that way to me. My guess is that the females can fly faster than the males, unless they want to get caught.”

"That's an interesting observation. A lesson on the sexual evolution of humans versus bulls and cows, yesterday. Boat-tailed grackles, today. Two quick lessons on sex by way of evolutionary biology."

"That's just an amateur guess about the grackles. I'm not an evolutionary biologist, but I know how they think.

***

The visit to the Penn Center was special for both of them. At the museum, Angela gained new graphic visions of slavery and reconstruction in the Lowcountry. At some of the exhibits, she was almost overcome with emotion. She also enjoyed talking with one of the Gullah docents.

On leaving the museum, Barsh drove by one of the Penn Center houses where Martin Luther King Jr. stayed a few times, during the troublesome years of his civil rights crusades. The Penn Center was one of the few places in the South where he could gather for planning sessions with blacks and whites without fear of being attacked by racist whites.

Next, they ate lunch at Plumbs in the old town of Beaufort. The weather was still fair, so they dined on the porch and watched the traffic on the Intracoastal waterway. Then they toured the historic area known as the Point where most of the antebellum houses were located.

That evening they returned to the Quarter Deck at Harbor Town for dinner. Afterwards, they climbed the stairs to the top of the lighthouse and enjoyed the view from there, before leaving for the condo.

"Barsh, this has been the best getaway I could have ever imagined."

"And does that ever ring true for me," he said. "Are you ready to begin shifting thoughts toward tomorrow?"

"As a matter of fact, I was just thinking about welcoming the New Year at Grove Park Inn. If all goes as planned, another dream of mine will become a reality. But we still have one more night in the condo that has served us so well."

And what another splendid night it was for them.

Chapter Twenty-One

Sunday morning, they left Hilton Head Island. Angela was in a joyous mood and started one of her James Taylor cassettes. When it got to "Carolina in My Mind," she began to sing along. That was the first time that Barsh had heard her lovely singing voice. The song ended and she paused the cassette player.

"Do you remember when I first played this song for you?"

"How could I forget? In keeping with my promise to introduce you to the Carolina mountains, I was taking you to Mount Mitchell."

"Yes, and at your request, I'd brought along some of my favorite music to keep us company. Not that I needed anything other than you.

"I wasn't thinking about the possibility of winning your love. My hope was to establish as close a relationship with you as possible. From the very first, I had sensed that a friendship with you would be good for me.

"Later, I even though I might share my damnable story with you at some point. I kept thinking that you might be able to help me come to terms with what I had done, but I kept putting it off because I was afraid it might turn you against me.

"Sharing that dark secret with you turned out to be so redemptive. I feel rejuvenated, like I'm sitting on top of the world to use an old saying."

"Your joy is obvious and contagious. I can also tell you that I'm more optimistic than I've been in years. Now, my most urgent task is to divorce Debbie in an amicable way. I'm beginning to think she will accept my plan. So, my mind is free from worry."

"That's good to hear. Are you ready for more of James Taylor songs?"

"Most definitely and please sing along. You sing so well."

"I often sing when I'm driving by myself. Today, I feel totally uninhibited with you. So yes, I'll sing along. But first, a question for you regarding our getaway.

“How many people do you suppose have every tried your superfine duo of catamaran and beach therapy for body and heart?”

“I would assume they’ve been practiced rather often, wouldn’t you?”

“I’m going to think our experiences were exceptional.”

“Well, they certainly were to me. And now my monkey mind has been toying with the notion of adding surf therapy for body and heart, when we return this summer, if you’re game.”

“Tell me how that would work.”

“We would need a fairly calm surf, just a gentle swelling of the waves on a deserted beach. I’m thinking the Dunes at Owl Oak, late one afternoon. We would wade into the surf until we’re a little past waist deep. You would strip off your bikini bottom and wear it like a lei, lest you should lose it.”

“Now I get it. Then I’ll lock my arms and legs around you for an ecstatic ride in the surf. Yes, I’m definitely open for such a session on our next trip to the Island.”

“Then we’ll try it. Look how dark the sky has turned. I think we’re in for heavy rain, any minute. But I have no complaint. We had perfect weather for our getaway. The threat of rain, however, has caused me to reconsider our visit to Mepkin Abby.

“My primary interest in showing you the place on this trip was to see if you thought it might be a good place for your mother to attend one of their retreats. If so, it might help us entice her south. Unless you’re eager to go, I suggest we drive straight to the farm and rest up before Georgette’s party.”

“I’m all for going straight to the farm.”

“Good. I’ll call the Abby soon and ask them to mail us information about their retreats.”

***

They were back at the farm early that afternoon—a bit stiff from the drive but looking forward to the evening. After settling in, Barsh called Hannah to let her know they were back at the farm and to give her an update on their plans for the next three days. As far as he could tell, she was adjusting fairly well to life in Louisville, and he felt somewhat relieved as he handed Angela the phone.

After Angela hung up the phone, they talked about Hannah and discussed ways to keep a good check on her. Then they decided to take a nap.

On waking from the nap, Barsh eased out of bed and made a pot of coffee. Back in the den, he poked up the fire, which would consume itself by the time they left for the New Year's Eve party that Georgette Wingo was hosting.

In the past, he had always attended alone. Although Debbie was always invited, she had no interest in the gathering. This year, he and Angela would be attending as a couple, and she would likely be the center of attention. The commode flushed and he was pleased that he wouldn't have to wake her.

"I'm having coffee before I dress for the evening," he said. "What can I fix you?"

"I'll have coffee with you."

"I'll be driving, so you don't have to be cautious about what you drink."

"Coffee will be good. We have a long night ahead of us with two parties. I've also adopted your position of having no more than one acholic drink per day, unless it's a special occasion. Then I'll indulge myself without overing doing it."

As they drank their coffee in the den, he shared some of his previous experiences at the New Year's Eve parties that Georgette had hosted. Then he gave Angela brief sketches of the guests he expected to be there.

"Can I be candid and open with these people?" she asked.

"Absolutely. They will be interested in learning about you, so be yourself. Let's pack for our stay at Grove Park Inn, and then it'll be time to get dressed."

Chapter Twenty-Two

Angela was the center of attention at Georgette's party as Barsh had expected she would be. A little before nine o'clock, they left with lots of good wishes.

"What a great party," Angela said as he drove away. "You were right. They all seem to like me. Margaret Randolph promised to call next week and settle on a date when we can join them for dinner. How do I handle that?"

"Just as if we were married. Presume upon me and work out a date with her. I will always accept any commitment you make regarding us. If I should have a conflict, you can call back and reschedule. If it's something that doesn't interest you, you can delay your response until you check with me. We'll create a conflict by planning something the two of us would like to do."

"I like your stance on this and you must adopt it when it comes to your response to invitations for us. Now, would you like for me to read Georgette's card?"

"Sure," he said and turned on the overhead light.

She opened the envelope and began reading the card, aloud.

Dear Barsh,

As you know Catherine and I have, for some time, discussed how I might best benefit Cooper with a significant endowment gift. Recently, she asked me to consider endowing a Professor of Humanities, and I knew she had you in mind as the first appointee even before she shared that with me.

I have worked out the details for endowing the Georgette Wingo Professor of Humanities. There is an understanding that you will be the first appointee before the end of this academic year, but let's keep it to ourselves until the official announcement.

I've loved and admired you since the day we met, and now I'm glad that Angela has joined our circle. Wishing you both the best as you journey into the New Year.

Love,
Georgette

"Wonderful!" he said. "This is good news for us. I don't have to be concerned anymore about the trustees trying to fire me."

"Did you really think they might fire you?"

"I knew the matter would continue to be pressed by one group of trustees. I also knew Catherine and Georgette would defend me to the limits of their power. Now, they have the weapon to shut down any grumbling.

"My opponents on the board will not likely attack me as long as I'm not their professor of religion. As I've said before, they view that position more as a minister than a professor.

"With the new appointment, I'll still be teaching my favorite religion courses. More significantly, I'll be able to develop more inter-disciplinary humanities courses. This is something Catherine and I have been wanting and now it's going to happen."

"I know of no one more qualified for this honor than you."

"Thanks, my dear woman. Once, I get beyond the divorce, you and I will be running free."

"You're not anticipating any problems with the divorce, are you?"

"No, I have no worries. It's just that I don't know how long it will take. I'm now in a good place, even if it should get stretched out a bit. How do you feel about our situation?"

"I'm quite contented with our status and excited about being on our way to Grove Park Inn for two nights."

"Have you given any thought to what you'd like to do tomorrow?"

"I'd like for you to take me back to Mt. Mitchell. After we take in the view from the observation tower, I want you to spread a blanket on that same spot where we ate lunch on our first field trip. Just to sit there and reminisce about that first visit."

"Okay, and this time I'll be sure to kiss you."

"Truthfully, I'm now glad that you held yourself in check, so honorably. That kept the suspense boiling in my blood until it finally happened."

"I just thought about something we could do while we up that way. You haven't met Eleanor Meredith, but she and her husband Guy are dear friends. Her nephew Ben Long has mastered the old-world art of creating frescos.

"He has frescos in two Episcopal Churches that are located just off the Blue Ridge Parkway not far beyond Mt. Mitchell. One church is in West Jefferson and the other in Glendale Springs. If the weather is fine and the churches are open, we could experience more of the Parkway as we drive north to experience the frescos."

"Is there any way you can find out if they're open?"

"Thanks to Eleanor who put me onto the frescos, I have the phone number for each of the church caretakers. I'll call them in the morning."

"You're always prepared. I do hope the churches are open."

"Me, too. While we're in the planning mode, let's think about an agenda for Tuesday. I have two suggestions for you to consider.

"We can sleep in, enjoy breakfast at the hotel, and head back to Ashland. Or we can have an early breakfast and visit the Biltmore Estate."

"Since we both have a lot to prepare for our new academic duties," she said, "I like the first option, but I'd like to visit the Biltmore Estate this spring. Can we do that?"

"Yes, of course. I actually prefer a spring visit. The expansive grounds, especially in the spring, nourish my soul. I enjoy them more than the mansion, that they say is the biggest private house in the United States.

"In my opinion, no one needs a house that large. The first time I experienced it, my mind jumped back to the days when tepees and igloos where sufficient for some people."

"Then I'll look forward to visiting the Biltmore Estate this spring. Meanwhile, I have a good selection of music for this New Year's Eve. Are you ready?"

"Oh, yes, bring on the music."

***

They checked into their room at Grove Park Inn and were pleased that the windows opened to the west. He had requested such a room but was not guaranteed one. The drapes were open, and they looked out on range after range of mountains that were dimly lit by the stars.

"What a marvelous way to end this year and welcome the new one," Angela said.

"Marvelous is the right word. It's eleven-thirty-two. Let's join the party in the Grand Ballroom?"

The place was filled with a crowd of merry people. He found a table, seated Angela, and headed for the bar. Returning with two glasses of champagne, he toasted Angela for bringing a joy to his life like nothing he had ever before experienced. She, in turn, toasted him for the same thing.

Soon the televisions were blaring the countdown at Times Square in New York, and they counted along with the crowd. Then they welcomed the New Year with a tight embrace and gentle kiss.

After enjoying the Grand Ballroom for a while, they found a bar in one of the new wings of the hotel that featured a pianist. There, they enjoyed the sense of pure togetherness, as they soaked up the music with a margarita.

When the pianist started playing "A Moment Like This," he reached for Angela's hand and led her onto the dance floor. After the music ended, he kissed her gently, tipped the pianist, and led the way to their room. There they watched the other undress. Their movements were almost casual, but their eyes were engaged and their pulses were rising.

***

As usual, they lay naked on their backs with no desire to leave the bed or turn their thoughts away from the other. Then Angela broke the silence.

"Just think of all the good things we've experienced in the past seventeen hours. That's how long it's been since we woke this morning on Hilton Head Island. I just counted them up. What an amazing day this has been. I hope you aren't sleepy?"

"No, not at all."

"Good. We can sleep late, right?"

"As late as you wish."

“This togetherness around the clock has been such a joyful experience. But now, we only have tonight, tomorrow, and tomorrow night. Then it’s back to Ashland and our separate beds for the night, until the weekend. Sleeping without you is going to be more difficult than I had imagined.”

“Do you want to go back to our original plan and move in together?”

“No, I’m just trying to tell you how special this uninterrupted togetherness has been. We’ll get to spend quality time together every day, until our wedding.”

“And we’ll spend weekends sleeping through the night at the farm or in a hotel if we’re traveling. I definitely want to take you to Highlands, North Carolina, for a weekend. Speaking of plans for the future, have you thought any more about a wedding date?”

“Since we both have a busy schedule for the rest of the school year, I’m now committed to June.”

“Good decision.”

“I’ve checked the calendar and June comes in on a Friday, so what would you think about the next Friday, June 8?”

“Perfect. Have you given any thought to where you’d like to have the ceremony?”

“The farmhouse is the only place I’ve thought about. What are our options?”

“The farmhouse would suit me. The college chapel would also be appropriate if you’d like a formal setting.”

“I’d prefer a simple service at the farmhouse with just a few people in attendance. Hannah and Davis, of course, now that we’ve settled on June. Then Catherine and Georgette and Daddy. I know Mother won’t come.”

“Sounds just right to me. What would you think about getting Peter, the college chaplain, to officiate?”

“Yes, there’s no better choice than Peter. Could we compose our own ceremony?”

“Sure. Peter will approve that.”

They dressed in their sleepwear and settled on the loveseat, where they talked late into the night. Sleepy-eyed but contented, they finally went to bed, intent on sleeping late. And they did for the first time.

After a leisurely breakfast at the hotel, they enjoyed their return visit to Mount Mitchell. Then they continued the drive north on the Blue Ridge Parkway to the Virginia State line with several other stops along the way, including the two Episcopal Churches with Ben Long's frescos. Both churches were open, and they were impressed by the beauty of the frescos and the art behind them. That evening, they experienced some of the nightlife in downtown Asheville and then reveled in another night in Grove Park Inn.

Tuesday, they returned to Ashland, energized and ready to focus on the demands of January.

Chapter Twenty-Three

With vigor and purpose, Barsh and Angela had successfully dealt with the tasks they faced in January. He had gently persuaded Debbie to accept an uncontested divorce and had engaged Jack Kelley to start the legal proceedings. Everything was on course for the court to grant the divorce in early February.

Angela had written a letter about the way Jacob McFarland, her dissertation advisor, had sexually abused her. Barsh had engaged an appropriate lawyer to send it to the Dean of the Graduate School with a copy to the offender.

She was asking for nothing more than a confirmation that the Dean and Chair of the English Department had met with McFarland and discussed the matter with him. Three weeks later, she got a response affirming that her request had taken placed. McFarland, as expected, had denied her claim.

Angela accepted the news in a good mood. She had forgiven herself and was ready to put the matter behind her.

The contractor that Barsh hired to make the changes to the house in Fern Meadows had successfully completed them. Angela had picked out new furniture for the dining room and her study. It had been delivered, and they were pleased with both rooms.

The two courses that he was taking at the University of South Carolina were going well. He had established good relationships with both professors. The students seemed to be fond of him, the mature man in the class, and they occasionally inviting him to join them for lunch or coffee.

Angela's January Interim course had gone well. She had finished editing her novel and submitted the manuscript to four literary agents in New York.

As he had promised, he flew Hannah and Davis down on the last Friday in January. He picked them up at the Charlotte Airport that afternoon, and they were both happy to be on the way back to Ashland. Sparked in large part by his questions, they chatted all the way to Davis' house.

He and Hannah then headed straight for Angela's, where the three of them enjoyed the dinner that she had prepared. Afterwards, they talked in the living room for a while, and then he took Hannah home.

As soon as they entered the house, she ran to her room and stretched out on the bed. He casually followed her.

"How does that feel, my sweet girl?"

"Good. But I'll feel even better if you'll read me one of my old children's books."

"Do you have a preference?"

"You pick one, like the old days when I was your little girl."

He picked out a Madeline book and pulled the desk chair beside the bed. As he read the story, he occasionally glanced at his dear daughter, who had closed her eyes. He assumed she was reimagining the illustrations.

"Thanks, Daddy. There's still magic when you read to me. Now, show me the changes you've made in our house. I like the hardwood floors in the halls and dining room."

"Let's start with the den, where I've made a lovely addition. A wonderful portrait now hangs in a prominent place. I hope you like it because it's there to stay."

She ran ahead of him, and when he got there, she was studying the portrait that Denise Wildsmith had painted.

"What do you think?"

"Isn't the painting prettier than I am?"

"No, no. The artist did a masterful job of capturing you just as you are. Now, I plan to get Denise to do a portrait of Angela. That was a lucky night for me in Greenwood when I met her and Amy Allen.

"Amy's painting now hangs in the big room at the farm. Here's a bit of good news. Amy has invited Angie and me to join her for a Lower Cherokee Pow Wow, this summer. They're the South Carolina Cherokee.

"They've never lived on a reservation, but they're now organized with their own chief and gathering place. I'm looking forward to their drumming, chanting, and dancing. I trust you'll want to go to the Pow Wow with us."

"Yes, I want to go."

"Good. Did you notice the new furniture in the dining room?"

"I glanced at it, but what good is that dining room?"

"It now has a purpose. Angie and I intend to host formal dinner parties after we're married. And on special occasions, just the three of us will eat there. What do you think about that?"

"Sounds good. Definitely different. We never ate there with Mother."

"Okay, let's take a look at Angela's new study," he said and led the way.

"I like it, Daddy."

"Here's a question for you. Would you like to refurnish your room?"

"Maybe later, but I'm fine with it now."

"Just know that you can refurnish your room, anytime."

"What about the den and guest bedroom?" she asked.

"As soon as we return from our honeymoon, we plan to move Angela's furniture into those two rooms. Let's sit here on the loveseat and think about our agenda for the weekend.

"The focus this weekend is on you, so you get to set the agenda. If you'd like to take a daytrip, just name it."

"Let's work out in the basement and I'll think about tomorrow while I'm peddling. Then I want us to talk in your study like we used to do on Friday nights."

After working out in the basement, they returned to his study with plans to talk late into the night.

"Daddy, I'd like to spend Saturday at the farm with you and Angela, maybe hike to the Pacolet River, and then dine at Jacksons' Steak House that evening. I'd also like for the three of us to spend the night back at the farm."

"Good decision. She and I spend most weekends there, working on various projects, taking hikes to the river, and so forth. I can also tell you that we now share the green bedroom."

"And why not?" she responded as if she assumed they were.

It was a special weekend. There was still a definite bond between Barsh and Hannah that he did not believe would ever be broken, but she was somewhat less of a Daddy's girl, which he took to be a good development.

Chapter Twenty-Four

Late Wednesday afternoon of February 7, the court granted Barsh a divorce on the same terms that he and Debbie had agreed to in the legal separation. Much relieved to have the divorce, he headed for Kimberly Hall to share the good news with Angela.

As he drove toward the college, he found himself thinking about Debbie and her life in Louisville. Henry Dugan's wife had died a little over a year ago, and Barsh could not help but believe that had something to do with the older man's efforts to entice Debbie to join his accounting firm as a junior partner. If so, he might try to start a romantic relationship with her.

He would be pleased for Debbie if it happened. That would, however, bring a step-father into Hannah's life if it led to marriage. Oh, hell, he thought, I'll deal with that if it happens.

He parked beside Kimberly Hall and rushed upstairs to Angela's office.

"I have the divorce," he said.

"Halleluiah!" she said and rushed into his open arms.

"Are you ready for the shifting of the ring?"

"Yes! But I want to do it at my place."

They drove to Angela's in separate cars and entered her house, hand in hand.

"I'm confident you know how you want to do this," she said.

"Oh, yes, I'd like for you to sit on your corner of the couch. I have so many beautiful images of you sitting there, and I want to add this one."

He followed her into the living room and watched her take her place.

"That's good," he said and kneeling before her, he took the promise ring from her right hand. "Angie. now that I'm a free man and you have agreed to marry me, I shift this ring to your left hand as a symbol of our engagement. I love you from the depth of my heart, and I eagerly await the day I can claim you as my wife."

"Barsh, I will proudly display the ring as a symbol of our engagement. I love you from the depth of my heart, and I eagerly await the day I can claim you as my husband."

They both rose for a tight embrace and kiss. Then they eased into the kitchen where he popped the cork. Returning to the living room, they cuddled on the couch and drank their champagne.

"Since we're now engaged," he said, "I'd like for us to take Catherine and Georgette to dinner at the Ashland Hotel as soon as possible."

"Yes, I'm ready to share the good news with them."

"What about tonight if they're available on short notice?"

"Suits me."

"Okay, I'll call them. What about seven o'clock?"

"That's good," she said and he called.

Both women accepted the dinner invitation and his offer to pick them up.

"I have work to do that's calling me home, but I'll be back for you no later than 6:30."

***

The dinner at Ashland Hotel had gone well with several pleasant interruptions as prominent citizens of the little town stopped to greet Georgette or Catherine. Wednesday evening was a favorite time for these worldly folks to dine out, while the faithful were attending prayer meetings at the local churches. Barsh did a lot of standing while she introduced him and Angela with the good news that they were engaged to be married in June.

"What a pleasant outing this has been," Georgette said. "I thank you two for sharing this special occasion with Catherine and me."

"It feels good to be officially engaged," Barsh said. "Angie and I are looking forward to entertaining you two at our home in Fern Meadows and at the farm."

"And we're look forward to those events," Georgette said and they left the restaurant.

***

Barsh walked Catherine to the door of her house, bade her good night, and returned to the Audi with a big smile. From his perspective, the outing could not have gone better.

"Well, what do you think?" he asked.

"A splendid evening. Could we go to your place before you take me home? I can't stay long. I have a lot of work to do tonight, but I need a bit of intimacy on this very special day."

"The need is mutual," he said, kissed her hand, and headed for his house in his Audi.

"Are you prepared for your classes at the University tomorrow?"

"We're studying some of Richard Wilbur's poems in Contemporary Poetry and I'm ready."

"I bet you like his poems."

"I do like his poems. So far, my favorite is 'Advice to a Prophet.' Do you like it?"

"Oh, yes, and I would have guessed it was your favorite. What about your class with Dickey?"

"Fortunately, I have until next Tuesday to complete another poem for him and the class to critique. But I'll be prepared for them.

"Most of the students either don't know what they're talking about or they're trying to make points for themselves with Dickey. So, it's easy to ignore most of their negative comments. But I do seriously consider some of them.

"The process of having my poems critiqued in an academic setting is good for me. This, of course, in addition to your critiques. I'm learning when a poem needs additional work, and when I need to stick with what I've written."

"I like your attitude, and you are definitely on the road to becoming a good poet."

"I don't know about *good,* but yes, I'm making progress. I certainly made the right decision to study at the University this semester.

"Oh, here's some good news. I'll be back at Cooper, fulltime this fall. Catherine has approved my plan. Being with you is more important to me that using the rest of my half sabbatical."

"That's music to my ears."

"I wish I could be on campus with you, tomorrow, as word of our engagement spreads to colleagues and students."

"I'd like that, too. Would you like to have lunch in the cafeteria, Monday, since none of the faculty will be eating there Friday?"

"Yes, we'll even dine at the faculty table, and we can start eating lunch in the cafeteria on Monday, Wednesday, and Friday if you'd like."

"Yes, I'd like that."

Barsh pulled into the garage and closed the door with the remote. They stopped in the empty den for a long embrace and then moved to her study where they sat on the loveseat.

"After I left your house this afternoon, I called Debbie at her office to tell her that the judge had approved the divorce. To my surprise, she seemed relieved.

"I also asked if I could visit Hannah a week from Friday and she was fine with that. Hannah's birthday is the following Monday.

"Then I called Hannah. She was excited to learn I will be there to celebrate her birthday. Of course, I told her the court had granted me the divorce, and she was pleased that you and I can now get married. I'll tell her about our wedding plans during the visit."

"We have a lot to be thankful for," Angela said. "Do you think you can handle me after a day like this?"

"I'm totally prepared for you."

Chapter Twenty-Five

On returning from his eleven o'clock class that Friday, Barsh heard Angela talking with someone. He recognized the other voice as Sharon Whittaker, one of his favorite students and decided to greet her.

"Hey, Dr. Roberts," Sharon said with a big smile. "Congratulations on your engagement. I can't imagine a better match than you two."

"Thanks, Sharon. Can't say I deserve a woman like Angela, so I'll say I'm a lucky man."

"Don't be fooled by his modesty, Sharon. He knows I adore him to the very marrow of his bones. I'd say that I worship him, but he'd call that idolatry."

"Oh, yes, he definitely would. I remember how he expressed it in his Faith, Knowledge, and Selfhood course. Love becomes idolatrous when one's life is totally vested in the beloved. Like when someone's child or spouse dies and she or he no longer has a reason to live.

"But you can't love anyone too much as long as you love her or him as a mortal creature. That means true love must transcend any individual. Therefore, transcendent love is also an affirmation of the Eternal Ground of Being."

"Well stated, Sharon. I'll bet you excel in his courses."

"You're right about that," Barsh said. "Sharon's the kind of student who makes you proud you chose to become a professor."

"Well, thank you for the compliment, Dr. Roberts. I'm returning a book I borrowed from Dr. Kundera. You obviously taught her your system of loaning books to students."

"I can affirm that," Angela said. "Just a moment and I'll find your card."

Angela handed Sharon the notecard she had signed with the name of the book, the date she borrowed it, and her phone number. They wished Sharon a good weekend and crossed the hall to his office to share lunch before he left for Louisville to visit Hannah.

"I'll start the tea," he said, "if you'll break out the sandwiches that I made with my simple recipe for tuna salad—solid white Albacore, Duke's mayo, chopped walnuts, and raisons. I trust you eat tuna. I also brought apples."

"Yes, I like tuna, and thanks for sharing lunch. I know you're anxious to get on the road."

"You're right. But I also need to spend these moments with you. How did your morning go?"

"Very well. I'm immensely enjoying my new status of being engaged to you."

"The feeling is mutual. My colleagues are going out of their way to congratulate me."

They sat facing each other in the two comfortable chairs in front of his desk as they ate and shared their thoughts. Then it was time for him to go. They hugged and kissed and he left. She stood at the window and waved as he drove away.

***

The drive to Louisville was Interstate all the way, and Barsh made good time by pushing the Audi just beyond the speed limit. The porch light was on, when he pulled into the driveway.

He was pleased that Hannah was not waiting on the steps as she had been on his first visit. He rang the doorbell and almost immediately he heard her running to answer it. The door opened and she jumped into his arms.

"Ah, my sweet girl. How I love you."

She did not respond verbally but clung to him a bit longer before leading him into the den, where Debbie and Davis were watching television.

"Greetings," he said. "I trust you ladies are well."

Debbie responded by tilting her head and raising an open hand.

"I'm managing okay for a woman away from her home," Davis said.

"Well, it's good to see you, and thanks for all you do. Debbie, I'll have Hannah back by eight Sunday morning."

He took Hannah's small bag, stashed it in the backseat of the Audi, and they were off.

"Would you like to stop for something to eat?" he asked.

"Only if you want to. I'm fine."

"So am I. We'll have birthday cake when we settle in. How did things go for you at school this week?"

"Some old stuff except for my English class. I like the teacher. She praised my writing skills on last week's exam."

"That's good. Have you shared any of your poems with her?"

"Not yet, but I'm thinking I might."

"That's up to you, of course. I brought two new poems to read to you. Do you have any?"

"I've been working on one this week but I don't like it."

"Then my advice is don't fret about it. It's okay to put a failed effort in a special file. Returning to it later, you may come up with a new conceit that will salvage the poem. Then again you may not."

They checked into the motel and Barsh called Angela for a short conversation. Then she and Hannah talked for a few minutes.

"Angela said she was envious that we're going to Mammoth Cave, while she'll be all alone in Ashland. Why didn't you bring her?"

"That's a good question. One that I also asked myself."

"And what was your answer?"

"Anxiety, I guess. I was afraid Debbie might not approve, and I don't want her to put any restrictions on my visits to see you."

"I have news about Mother and Mr. Dugan. He took her to dinner after church last Sunday. Mother drove Davis and me home. He picked her up and they ate out."

"Well, that is stunning news. You can be certain that Angela will be with me the next time I visit you. She definitely wanted to come."

Okay, let's start celebrating your twelfth birthday with some cake. You know me. I'm no legalist, so February 23 is just as good for celebrating your birth as February 26, the day you were born. Ready for some chocolate cake from Ashland Bakery?"

"That's my favorite as you know. What are we drinking?"

"What else but my concoction of punch? I brought everything I need right here in this box. If you'll put the candles on the cake, I mix the punch."

Finished with making the punch, he lit the candles and sang the happy birthday song to her. She closed her eyes, made a wish, and blew out the candles in one big puff.

He served the cake and poured punch for them. They enjoyed both and glanced often at the other with contented smiles.

"Do I get my presents tonight?"

"I'm giving you one tonight and the other tomorrow night, so we can talk about them. But I'd like for you to save Angela's for your birthday. She wants you to call sometime after you open them, so she can share why she chose them."

He gave her one of his presents. She tore off the wrapping paper and studied the front cover of the book, *The Memory of Old Jack,* a novel by Wendell Berry.

"Have we talked about Wendell Berry?" he asked.

"Not that I remember."

"Think of your mother's parents and their farm along the Kentucky River, just a few miles above where if flows into the Ohio. About six more miles up the Kentucky from your grandfather Whalen's farm, there's a community named Port Royal.

"Wendell Berry was born on a nearby farm and he has remained attached to that area. I think you could even say that land is sacred to him. He continues to care for a section of it as a farmer.

"While Berry has reclaimed his role there as a farmer, he is also a well-known poet, novelist, and essayist, who has held visiting professorship at major universities. One of his major concerns is the proper use of land and how we should treat the environment.

"These are issues you and I are both concerned about, but the reason I chose *The Memory of Old Jack* is to help you understand your grandfather Whalen's attachment to his farm in that region of Kentucky and to give you insights into your mother and grandmother.

"They remind me so much of Old Jack's wife and daughter, neither of whom felt any attachment to the land. If Mrs. Whalen outlives Mr. Whalen, I confident that she will sell the farm and move to Louisville, although she is quite capable of managing it. Should Debbie inherit the farm, she will undoubtedly sell it."

"Mother seems to hate that farm. It's almost as if she's ashamed she grew up there. Am I right in thinking that?"

"You're very preceptive. Hannah, *The Memory of Old Jack* won't be an easy read for you, but I do want you to finish it. Would you like a brief introduction?"

"Yes, but I'll finish it because that's what you want."

"The setting is a fictional version of Port Royal that Berry has named Port William. Old Jack, the protagonist, is ninety-two-years old. The time is one day in 1952, the last day of his life. But on this day, his memory takes him back across the years.

"Early on in the book, he remembers a day when he is eight-years old. He's approaching the old farmhouse, a place where a sense of loss seems to linger. That loss includes two older brothers, whom he hardly remembers, and his mother. The brothers rode off to join the Confederate Cavalry, never to return. His mother died soon afterward of grief.

"That sense of loss followed Old Jack down through the years. After his own marriage failed, he basically surrendered that house to his wife and daughter. He ate his meals there and slept alone in a small room above the kitchen. Other than that, he spent most of his life outdoors or in the barn, until he moved into a boarding home in the little town of Port William

"The woman, whom Old Jack had wooed as a handsome young man, soon discovered that she could not love a farmer who worked the soil. He was often dirty and soaked in sweat. He was too coarse and earthy for her, although he was a man of integrity who made an adequate living from the land.

"She had grown up in the nearby town on the Ohio River and wanted him to be a respectable business man, who owned and managed several tobacco farms that were worked by tenant farmers. After her attempt to push him in this direction failed, she rejected him and focused her attention on their daughter."

"I see what you mean, Daddy. It sounds just like Mother's family."

"Unfortunately, the pattern repeated itself with Debbie and me. She also rejected me because she couldn't embrace who I am. With her, however, it was my intellectualism and liberalism."

"Daddy, Mother and I have nothing in common. But I love you just the way you are. I can't imagine having any other father."

"That makes me a lucky man to have a daughter like you. But sometimes, I think that I've kept you too close to me, that I've sheltered you from the world too much, that I should have sent you out to play and run with the neighborhood children."

"But I didn't want that. Like you've said, I'll find my way in the world and it will be a good one. I'm glad you chose *The Memory of Old Jack* for me."

"If you don't understand something, make a note about it. We'll discuss it when next we talk. Well, it's getting late, but there's time for a little poetry before we call it a day."

Chapter Twenty-Six

The outing that Barsh had planned for Hannah that Saturday went exceedingly well. They had fun experiencing Mammoth Cave, but best of all, they had good conversations.

Back in Louisville late that afternoon, they ate at the café where they had dined in December and then settled in for the night at the motel. They had just finished eating a big slice of Hannah's birthday cake, when the phone rang.

"I'll bet that's Angela," he said. "You want to answer?"

"Yeah."

He watched Hannah's beaming face as they talked. Then she said good bye and handed him the phone.

"Barsh, I couldn't wait any longer to tell you my good news. The very literary agent I wanted to represent me called this morning. She loves my novel and is eager to be my agent. She claims to know the perfect New York publisher for it and is confident she can get a quick decision from them to publish it. I said, yes, and she's mailing me a contract."

"How wonderful, Angie. I'm looking forward to celebrating the good news with you, tomorrow."

"I'd like to celebrate at our house in Fern Meadows, as you now call it. I'd also like to spend the night there for the first time, even though it will be Sunday and I have an eight o'clock class Monday morning."

"I'm with you all the way."

"Then I'll be there, waiting for you with champagne."

"Splendid! I should be back around three o'clock."

"Drive carefully. Love you! Love you! Bye."

"Love you! Bye."

"What's the good news, Daddy?"

"A New York literary agent has just agreed to take Angela as a client, and she's ecstatic as she should be. She's written an excellent novel."

"What's is about? Can I read it?"

"The main character is a fictional version of Angela, so the novel recounts the major facets of her life. She has changed the details significantly, however, so people wouldn't know what's fictional and what's autobiographical. It's definitely an adult novel, but I think you'll be ready to read it by the time it's published.

"Speaking of reading, are you ready for the second book I chose for you?"

"I'll get it," she said and unwrapped Pat Conroy's *The Great Santini.*

"This is my favorite coming-of-age novels with a male protagonist. You are fast approaching your own coming of age. I don't know what obstacles you'll have to overcome in addition to the separation and then the divorce of your parents, but they won't be the same as those of the protagonist of *The Great Santini*.

"Like Conroy, his primary obstacle on the journey to manhood was a harsh and violent father, who had dubbed himself The Great Santini. The real Great Santini was a flying trapeze artist. Conroy's father was a daring Marine fighter pilot, but also an abusive husband and father.

"Hannah, I've tried to teach you about the world and how to get along in it, but there's no substitute for experience. Of course, you'll make mistakes as everyone does. You'll learn from them, however."

"Don't worry, Daddy. I probably know more about coming of age than you think I do."

"That's most likely true. Can I assume you know about puberty and the changes that will soon be taking place in your body as you move from childhood to adolescence?"

"The basics, yes, from the school nurse. Not mother."

"Do you know that boys will soon be trying to have sex with you?"

"I know that, Daddy."

"Do you know about birth control?"

"No."

"Well, you should. There are various methods of birth control. I'll mail you a good book on the subject. You can also talk with Angela about all issues related to adolescence and womanhood.

"You're far too young to be thinking about having sex. I just want you to know how to take care of yourself whenever that happens.

"Deciding when to have sex and when to have children are two separate decisions that you'll have to make. Please make them deliberately with knowledge and forethought."

"Don't worry, Daddy. I'll read your book on birth control and get myself informed. It's also good to know I can talk to Angela."

"One more parental admonition. You should choose when to have sex. If anyone tries to force himself or herself on you, resist with all your ability. Scream and fight back. Then call me immediately, even if the person should threaten to do bad things to you if you tell. I will address the matter, swiftly and judiciously.

"When you grow up and get married, only you should decide if you want to have children and when to have them if you do. Discuss this with your beloved before you get married, and don't marry anyone who's not in agreement with you."

"I'll remember your advice, Daddy. It sounds good to me. I know the course I want to take. I want to be a college professor like you and Angela. And I want to be a poet."

"If you stick to that course, you'll be an excellent poet and professor. But even in academia, there are hurdles and hazards to negotiate."

"Did you have to negotiate them?"

"Hurdles, yes, but not hazards."

"Did Angela?"

"Yes, and she has given her protagonist the same type of hazard that she had to deal with in graduate school. At a later date, you'll get to read about it. Ah, my sweet girl, I'm trying to prepare you, not scare you."

"I know that, Daddy. I don't have to go to bed now, do I?"

"No, what would you like to do?"

"Let's take turns reading poems to each other like we used to do. I brought the anthology you gave me."

"Good idea."

Around eleven that evening, Barsh suggested that they should call it a day. She agreed and soon drifted off to sleep, as he sat nearby thinking about his visit, that would end after breakfast the next day.

Chapter Twenty-Seven

It was almost three o'clock, when Barsh pulled into his driveway and parked. He assumed that Angela had parked her Volvo in the garage beside his pickup truck, so he headed for the front door. As he opened it, he heard the keys of her typewriter clicking.

"I'm home," he announced lest he startle her.

"Welcome home, my love," she said and rushed from the desk in her new study into his arms.

"How sweet it is to come home to you, here. And you, now, with a New York literary agent. I'm impressed but not surprised. Congratulations."

"What a special afternoon this has been for me as I waited for you to return. I've been working on a new poem. You, no doubt, need a bathroom."

"Yes."

"Then go. I'll fix a snack. You can pop the cork and we'll celebrate my good news, here on the loveseat."

They kissed again. Then he left for the bathroom and she for the kitchen. Returning from the bathroom, he opened the champagne and poured two glasses.

"To the future New York Times best-selling novelist, Angela Kundera," he said and they drank.

"My hopes are not that high, but I do believe I've written a good novel that will be well received by a lot of readers and, hopefully, will be well reviewed by critics. I'm so pleased with the changes I've made since we read it, aloud, to each other after your return from the wilds of Alabama.

"You know that I could not have written this novel if you had not become a part of my life. Obviously, I've dedicated it to you. We'll be married before it's published, so the authorship will carry your last name. I like the sound of Angela Kundera Roberts."

"That's up to you. Angie, I have no doubt that it will be successful. If the publisher doesn't underwrite a book-signing tour for you, I will. And I'll travel with you as your biggest fan."

"You're willing to finance a book-signing tour for me?"

"Absolutely."

"Then I'll accept your generous offer, if the publisher doesn't finance one." she said and they returned to her study with the champagne and a tray of snacks.

"I have a bit of interesting news about Debbie," he said. "Hannah told me that Mr. Dugan, the senior partner in the firm, came by after church, a week ago, and took Debbie to lunch."

"Well, that is interesting news. Tell me what you make of that."

"I've believed all along that he had a personal interest in her, when he invited her to join his firm. I'm not surprised by his action. But I'm not sure whether Debbie felt obligated to go with him or wanted to go. I hope it's the beginning of a romantic relationship that will lead to marriage.

"I know the minister of the church they both attend. He and I were in the same pastoral counseling class during my theological studies at Louisville. We were among the minority of the students who believed that divorce is the best option for most failed marriages.

"If Debbie is interested in a relationship with Mr. Dugan, he and the minister can likely convince her that there would be no theological problem with them getting married."

"Should that happen, I believe it would be good for her and possibly for us. He is a lot older than Debbie and has grown children and two small grandchildren.

"I can't imagine that he would be looking forward to having an adolescent under his roof. If I'm right, there's a good possibility that Debbie will let Hannah live with us. Of course, I have no intention to cut her out of Hannah's life. I'll make sure they maintain a proper relationship if Hannah ever comes to live with us."

"Then I, too, am hoping for the same development. Changing the subject, I'm pleased to tell you that Daddy is planning to visit me. He has a reservation to fly to Charlotte the first Friday of March. Then he'll have to fly back to New York, Sunday afternoon."

"Wonderful. I'll help in any way you want me to, including picking him up at the airport."

"Thanks, I definitely want you to help me with that."

"Are you disappointed that your mother isn't coming?"

"Truthfully, I'm relieved, but I'm so excited about Daddy's visit. I believe you two will become good friends, now that he has taken a deeper interest in me, his wayward daughter.

"My older sister is Mother's pet. Their religious piety is hard for me to deal with. But thanks to you, I'm learning patience and tolerance."

"I understand the situation with your mother and commend you for accepting her for who she is. Once you learn the strategy, you can love her and still be yourself. I'm confident I'll get along well with your father and I'll love your mother even if she rejects me."

"Who know, Mother might even take a liking to you," she said and kissed him passionately. "The champagne and snacks have put me right where I need to be. That means I'm ready for us to take care of a different appetite."

"And so am I."

***

On returning to Angela's study, they focused on plans for spring break that was less than a month away.

"Angie, I'm open to anything you would like to do during spring break. New York. New Orleans. You name it."

"Both are on my list of places I want to visit with you, but not for spring break, unless you're eager to go."

"I have nothing special in mind except to please you. Just tell me what you'd like to do, and I can probably arrange it."

"What I'd really like to do is to start the break with at least three quiet days at the farm. Just you and me with no schedule to meet, except our own."

"Sounds great. What next?"

"I'd like for you to choose some place in the South that we haven't visited and take me there for two or three nights. Then back to the farm for the rest of the break."

"Okay, I'll offer you several options. The first is Nashville. As you know, we can now visit Susan Halford anytime and pick out our horses. Hannah wants me to pick out hers, since she knows nothing about horses."

"Let's do that. No other options needed for me."

"Good I'll call Susan to be sure that's a good time for her."

Barsh called Susan and that date worked for her. Then the two women talked for a while.

"I like her," Angela said. "She wants to take me to the store where she buys her riding accessories. According to her, I must have authentic riding boots—those made specifically for horse women. Riding pants, too."

"You'll definitely be impressed by Susan and all her horse-related skills and stuff."

"I have no doubt, although I'm overwhelmed by the challenge of becoming a horse woman."

"No one will judge your progress as you start down this road, step by step. You get to set your own goals, and your comfort will always be on my mind."

"Thanks for that reassurance. You always indulge me. So, here's another request. I'd like for us to cook our first dinner in our house. I brought everything we'll need."

"Yes, I'd like that."

***

The alarm clock buzzed. Barsh, already awake, rolled over and turned it off. Angela stirred and he turned against her.

"Good morning," he whispered.

"And to you. I feel like a hibernating bear awaking from a good winter's sleep. So happy to be alive and to wake up in bed with you, here in this bedroom. How are you?"

"Couldn't feel any better."

"Thanks for pampering me with this much-anticipated sleepover. I won't make it a habit."

"Whatever pleases you. Since you have an eight o'clock class and I don't, I'll fix breakfast while you get ready."

"Then I'll accept your offer."

Chapter Twenty-Eight

They were waiting at the Charlotte Airport for Angela's father. Someone announced the flight's arrival and people began to stir. As the passengers began to stream through the gate, Angela could hardly contain her excitement.

At first sight of her father, she waved to him. He smiled and she rushed into his open arms. Breaking the embrace, she introduced Barsh and they cordially exchanged greetings.

"What a joyous occasion, Angela. I've never seen you looking so radiant. The South has been good for you. Dare I hope for a shot of optimism from this Southern trip?"

"You're a handsome man with a keen intellect. Always a smart dresser. If you'll open yourself to the agenda that we've planned for you, I promise you a double shot of optimism from this trip."

"Open myself, huh? Okay, I'll take the challenge."

"That's what I hoped you would say. We're taking you to our favorite restaurant near Ashland, unless you're ready to eat now."

"No, I'm fine."

"Angie, if you'll help John retrieve his luggage, I'll get the car and pick you up at the curb."

"Thanks," she said and they parted ways

He parked the Audi at the curb, where they were waiting, stashed the luggage in the trunk, and they were on the way to Jackson's Steak House.

"Barsh, it's good of you to help Angela reconnect with me. She'd been independent so long that I'd given up on a strong reconnection with her. Now, she's welcoming me with open arms."

"Just know that I, no less than Angela, am pleased that you chose to make this trip so soon after your surgery. We want to introduce you to friends, the college, and a bit of local history, but we're also mindful that this is still recovery time for you. Please tell us if you're not up to anything we suggest."

"Ditto, to what Barsh said, Daddy."

"I'm slowly getting my strength back, so I'll probably be up to whatever you've planned. I'm disgusted at myself for the unhealthy lifestyle I'd drifted into, but I've resolved to take better care of myself. Just hope it's not too late."

"You can do it, Daddy. I hope you'll share your thoughts about the future you want for yourself. Barsh and I have suggestions for you to consider, including more time in the South. But we'll talk about that later. Are you ready for the big news?"

"Yes, what's the big news?"

"We've chosen the 8th of June for our wedding."

"That is wonderful news. May God bless you both with happiness until death do you part."

"You will be here for the wedding, right?"

"I'll be here if there's any possible way."

"I know Mother will be displeased that I'm marrying a divorced man who isn't a Roman Catholic, but I'll forgive her. Barsh has taught me to love her as my mother. That means loving her as she is, not what I'd like for her to be. I hope she'll come down for the wedding, but I'm not going to worry about it."

"You are obviously right about her. I've little, if any, influence on her. But I'll do my best to bring her with me."

"Thanks, but don't fret about it. Just make the case that she should be here for me and let the decision be hers."

"I've tried most of my life to please her, but rarely succeeded."

"Well, Daddy, it's time for you to make decisions that please yourself, whether they displease her or not."

"Believe it or not, I can now say I agree with you. Yes, I'm feeling a bit more optimistic about my future, already."

"I'm glad to hear that. Now, let's enjoy some music as Barsh drives us to Jackson's Steak House. This is what we do when we're on the road. We divide the drive between good conversation and good music."

"Will you give me a short introduction to the music? I'm sorry to say I've not given music a decent place in my life."

"I'll start with this cassette featuring one of our favorite jazz pianists, Ramsey Lewis. Do you know his music?"

"I know nothing about him."

"He was born in Chicago in . . . I think it was the mid-thirties. This is all instrumental jazz—piano, bass, and drums. Just let yourself sink into the rhythm. I'll only play a few pieces before switching to Mozart's piano concertos. Then I want to tell you about my first visit to Cooper last April to interview for a position on the English faculty."

"I eagerly await your story, since it was obviously a good visit."

"The very best."

They silently enjoyed the jazz trio and the piano concertos for a stretch, and then Angela stopped the cassette to tell his father about her visit to Cooper last April.

"Daddy, slide over behind Barsh, so I can see you. That's good. First, I have a question for you. Do you know how I got interested in Southern literature?"

"I have no idea, although I've actually wondered about it."

"But you never asked me."

"I'm sorry about that and a lot of other things in our relationship. You don't have to forgive me, but please know I'm determined to do better by you."

"Relationships are a two-way street. I haven't been a good daughter. But I do credit you with understanding and approving of me, somewhat. That was my assessment, although you never really told me."

"I do believe I understood you, and I've always appreciated who you were. I didn't know how to be any closer to you, and that's another regret."

"Thankfully, you and I are now on a good course. Okay, here's how I got turned on to Southern lit. It started when I first read Harper Lee's *To Kill a Mockingbird,* during my thirteenth summer. I kept wishing that I could have been Scout at her age with a father like Atticus. Sorry, Daddy."

"I understand. I knew you loved the book and that inspired me to read it. I also wished I could have been Atticus."

"That's interesting. I had no idea you'd read it."

"Well, I did. I found the book after you left home for college.

"Then perhaps this will interest you. When I reread the book in graduate school, I found myself wishing I could marry a man like Atticus. Miracles of miracles! I'm now marrying a better man than Atticus, because Barsh chose to love anew when he lost his wife.

“Barsh’s wife Debbie didn’t die like Atticus’ wife. She insisted on a permanent separation that left him in a worse situation. He had a wife but only legally. Now, he has corrected that by getting a non-contested divorce, so we can get married.”

“That speaks well of you, Barsh. Do you have children?”

“A twelve-year-old daughter who lives with her mother in Louisville.”

“Daddy, Hannah and Barsh have an even better relationship than Atticus and Scout. She and I also have a great relationship that started with our love of creative writing. She’s a fine poet for her age, and Barsh arranged for me to tutor her at the college, early on, before the sparks started flying between him and me. Now, I’m tutoring her long distance.”

“I know it must be difficult for you, Barsh. Your daughter living in Louisville.”

“It has caused me a lot of anxiety, but I think Hannah’s adjusting fairly well. At least, I don’t see any major problems looming on the horizon.

“Debbie and I have joint custody of her with amicable terms. She lives with her mother in Louisville during the school year. During summers, she’ll live with Angela and me. She also gets to visit us during holidays. And I can spend weekends with her whenever that seems appropriate.”

“I commend you for creating an agreement that doesn’t shaft anyone. That doesn’t seem to happen often in failed marriages.”

“Okay,” Angela said, “Here’s the basics of my first visit to Cooper College. You know my failed attempts to become a famous novelist and how I retreated to graduate school with the goal of becoming an English professor.

“There I was last winter, thirty-seven-years old, trying to put behind me another failed relationship, while teaching in a non-tenured track at Brown University.

“I’d earned a Ph.D. with a focus on Southern lit, and I had never spent any time in the South. It was time for me to get a Southern experience, and fortunately, Cooper College was looking for a specialist in Southern lit.

“I flew into Charlotte just like you did, and there was Barsh waiting for me. He was open and candid as he talked about Cooper and himself.

"Soon, I found myself in the presence of someone I felt was totally trustworthy. Before we parted ways that night, I'd told him things about myself I'd never before shared with anyone.

"Although everything about the visit went extremely well, I was afraid they wouldn't offer me the job, perhaps, because I wanted it too much. My Catholic rearing troubling me, I guess.

"As a backup plan, I'd asked Barsh if we could correspond whether or not I got the job. I needed to correspond with him about my new interest in philosophy and religion, which were his major fields of study.

"He graciously accepted my request. Fortunately, I got the appointment, and we began to correspond about intellectual things. By the time I moved down, we were good friends.

"I knew nothing about his marital problems, and he knew nothing about my wounded heart and crushed soul. Love and questions of intimacy never entered our conversation, until last November when Barsh told me that his wife had asked for a separation.

"Then we discovered our mutual love. And here we are totally committed to each other and eager to get married."

"What a beautiful story, Angela. Listening to you, I made a surprisingly harsh decision about your mother. I'm giving her an ultimatum. If she doesn't come to your wedding with me, I'm going to divorce her."

"No, Daddy, I don't want her to come unless she comes with good will."

"I'm doing this for myself, not you," he said. "She's been married to the Catholic Church, long enough. I'm tired of sleeping in the guest bedroom."

"You're right about Mother. Barsh has taught me the error of such behavior. To love God, in truth, we must also love our neighbor as we love ourselves. That means loving this world as we find ourselves in it. To devote oneself wholly to a transcendent God is false devotion.

"Don't use the wedding against her. Give her an ultimatum base on the guest bedroom, not whether she will come to the wedding. It's time she quit ruining your life."

"All right, I like your reasoning."

"Here's something for you to think about. Georgette Wingo has invited us for dinner at her house, Saturday evening. She's bold and wonderful, to say nothing of being a multi-millionaire with an apartment in the Big Apple.

"Widowed, she came back from New York several years ago and now lives in the house she grew up in. Flirt with her a bit and see if you can put a twinkle in her eyes. Then go home and find yourself a perky widow or divorcee if Mother doesn't want you in her bed.

"At your age, you don't even have to divorce Mother unless you want to. Tell her you've found a woman who wants to share her bed with you and you've decided to share it. Just be honest with Mother and the woman."

"Do you really believe that, Angela?"

"Wholeheartedly."

"What do you think, Barsh?"

"I'm in complete agreement with Angela. I know what it's like to sleep in the guest bedroom. But like Angela said, be honest with your wife and the other woman if that's the route you take."

Angela righted herself in the front seat and they fell silent. Traffic on Interstate 85 South was thinning out, and Barsh was feeling good about the interaction between Angela and her father.

After a few moments of silence, Angela played a varied selection of music until they arrived at Jackson's Steak House. Dinner was a pleasant time for them. Her father queried them about various things, and they agreed on the agenda for his visit.

***

After breakfast at Angela's on Saturday morning, they took her father on a short tour of the college that ended in Barsh's office.

"Daddy, imagine how impressed I was when I first noticed both the depth and the breadth of Barsh's reading, based on this collection of scholarly books.

"As I surveyed this section, I noticed Ernest Becker's *The Denial of Death* and was so intrigued by the title that I asked Barsh for a synopsis. Bottom line, I've now read the book and recommend that you read it."

"Okay, give me a synopsis."

"It's about the various ways humans attempt to escape their mortality. Strong meat as they say. That's the way I remember Barsh explaining it to me."

“Then I shall add it to my reading list.”

“Take my copy home with you,” Barsh said. “Keep it as long as you like.”

“Thank you. One of my new resolutions is to start reading again, especially about the American Revolutionary War.”

“I have two excellent books to get you back into the subject, if you don’t already have them. Henry Lumpkin’s *From Savannah to Yorktown* and *The Revolutionary War Memoirs of General Henry Lee* edited by his son General Robert E. Lee.”

“No, I haven’t read them.”

“Then take mine.”

“I will. So, Lumpkin’s book focuses on the British plan to shift the war from the North to the South. I remember that much from my college days, but I don’t remember General Henry Lee’s role in the war.”

“George Washington was so impressed with Lee’s early exploits in the war that he gave him his own Legion made up of cavalry and dragoons. Washington then assigned Lee’s Legion to General Nathanael Greene after he was given command of the American forces in the South.

“Both books will keep you in South Carolina most of the time. More Revolutionary war battles were fought here than any other State.”

“Then I’ll start with Lumpkin’s overview and then I’ll enjoy Lee’s first-hand accounts of the war.”

“Here’s a note that might interest you about Lee. He wrote the memoirs in debtor’s prison. After the war he overinvested in western land and found himself unable to repay his debts.”

“That is interesting. Angela, what a joy it is to be with you and Barsh.”

“Anybody ready for Cowpens Battle Site?” Barsh asked and got affirmative answers.

***

Angela’s father enjoyed the visit to Cowpens National Battlefield. He had known nothing about the battle and was captivated by the movie depiction of it.

He left Cowpens championing a newly-gained hero, General Daniel Morgan, who had devised a brilliant strategy to trap the cocky Colonel Banastre Tarleton and his British forces. The victory was swift, and Tarleton had to flee for his life.

Her father was shocked to learn about the brutality that Tarleton and his British forces had inflicted on the patriots in South Carolina. He had never heard of the expression "Tarleton's quarter," which mean no quarter, because he kept slaughtering the patriots who had surrendered during the Battle of the Waxhaus.

After a pleasant lunch at Ashland Hotel, they took her father to Barsh's house in Fern Meadows and then to the farm. He especially liked the farm, and Barsh offered him free access to it. He could come anytime and stay as long as he wished. At Angela's suggestion, they took him back to her house, so he could take a nap before Georgette Wingo's dinner party.

After a refreshing nap for her father, they attended Georgette's party, which turned out to be a big success. She and Catherine fussed over him and treated him like an old friend. He, in turn, did his best to charm them. Angela had never seen him so exuberant.

Back at Angela's, Barsh bade them goodnight and returned to his house in Fern Meadows. The whole day could not have gone any better.

***

After brunch at Angela's Sunday morning, Barsh took her and her father to the Visitor's Center of Kings Mountain National Military Park, where Southern patriots known as "Over-the-Mountain Men" won a major victory over British loyalist forces. Again, her father was impressed and excited to learn about another major Revolutionary War victory by the patriots.

Then they were off for the Charlotte Airport for her father's flight back to New York. The flight was on schedule and he was gone. The two lovers walked hand in hand to the car. It was midafternoon, and they were both ready to get to their respective houses and prepare for the demands of the coming week.

"Well," Angela said, "that exceeded my wildest dream for a good visit from Daddy. I've never seen him in such a happy mood."

"It was a good visit. Your father's a good man, and I will be honored to have him as my father-in-law."

"You'll be pleased to know what he said about you this morning as we drank our second cup of coffee. After first praising you, he told me that you are the son he's long wanted."

"Yes, I'm very pleased to hear that."

"I trust you know I've missed our regular weekend intimacy," she said. "What shall we do first when we get home, work or play?"

"We both have a lot to do, so here's my suggestion. I'll take you home and leave. We'll work into the night. Then you'll call me when you get to a stopping place for the evening, and I'll come over and put you to bed with a lot of love."

"Ah, that's perfect."

Chapter Twenty-Nine

It was mid-March, Barsh and Angela had spent the first three days of spring break at the farm. They loved such days together when they could set their own agenda. Early Tuesday morning, they left for Nashville to visit Susan and Terry Halford.

"I've been thinking about the day my parents moved from our Alabama farm to Macon, Georgia. Are you ready to hear about one of the saddest days of my life?"

"Yes, please share it with me."

"It was early spring of my freshman year at Samford. Late that Friday, I'd driven home in my Ford pickup to sleep, for the last time, in the farmhouse my great-grandfather had built. Dad had already sold the tractor, the livestock, and my horse Thunder.

"My good days on that farm had abruptly ended. That was sad enough, but nothing compared to saying goodbye to Susan, the next afternoon.

Before the moving van got there Saturday morning, Susan rode up on her horse and stayed until the end. I think I told you her family's farm joined ours on the north side. She put Dan, her beautiful Palomino, in the barn lot and removed the saddle as she often did when I wasn't saddled up and ready to ride with her.

"When the moving van pulled away that afternoon, Dad and Mother soon followed. That left Susan and me, all alone.

"I told her that I'd like to saddle Dan for her before I left for Birmingham, that it would be my last time to saddle a horse in the foreseeable future. With her consent, I saddled him and led him from that lot.

"There we stood facing each other, not knowing how to say goodbye. Tears began to trickle down her face, and then she began to sob. I dropped the reins and held her in my arms for the first and last time.

"I told her that, although our riding days were over, I'd never forget them. That the images of her riding beside me with her auburn hair dancing with Dan's gait were burned into my memory. That I would remember her as the most beautiful girl I'd ever seen.

"Not knowing what else to say, I told her of my determination to become a college professor, and that meant I had a long journey in academia ahead of me. Ten years or probably more as a student. Then I rambled on about how she would grow up and find her place in the world and it would be a good one.

"I tried to get her to let me foot-lift her into the saddle, once more, and watch her ride away. But she refused to leave before I did. I told her goodbye and drove away with her holding Dan's reins. That's my sad story."

"Now, I understand why you're so glad you've reconnected with her, and I'm happy for you. I hope Susan and I will become friends."

"She's a good woman, and I'm confident she's looking forward to becoming friends with you, just as I was eager to become friends with Terry. I have no doubt that this visit will go well for all of us."

"I hope you're right. I'm certainly eager to do my part."

"Don't worry. We'll all have a good time. What about some of your music?"

"Coming your way with a surprise, I think."

***

They were warmly received by Susan and Terry and they settled on the deck that overlooked the big barn, several other outbuildings, and the rolling pastures that were dotted, here and there, with Tennessee Walkers. There were hors d'oeuvres and drinks, but best of all, there was pleasant conversation, including Susan's stories of her horseback-riding days with Barsh.

That evening, the Halfords took them to dinner at the country club. There was delicious food, more pleasant conversation, and dancing. The four of them were in a joyous mood that followed them back to the Halford estate and lasted until bedtime.

After breakfast and a bit of relaxing in the den the next morning, they headed for the barn lot for Barsh and Angela to pick a horse that best suited them. In deference to their youthful riding days, Susan wanted Barsh to go first.

He chose a solid black gelding, the biggest and most spirited of the group. Susan then acknowledged that she had already guessed he would choose that one, and in her judgment, it was the best one for him.

Angela asked for help with her selection, and Susan described the characteristics of two fillies that she thought would be good for her. Angela then chose the black one with a white star on its face, because she thought it made a good match with Barsh's horse.

Barsh then chose a brown filly with white socks for Hannah. It was sleek and a bit undersized for a Tennessee Walker. Once again, Susan approved his choice.

At his request, Susan saddled her black stallion and led him to the mounting block. After calming him for a moment, she explained to Angela that she would put him in his flat foot walk for one round in the riding rink and then urged him into that special running walk that Tennessee Walkers are noted for.

She mounted the stallion and off they went. What a special sight it was for Barsh to watch her put such a powerful horse through those two gaits with such ease.

Finished with her demonstration, Susan stabled the horse and they returned to the house where they relaxed for a while in the den. Then Susan took Angela shopping.

While the women were out shopping for Angela's riding boots and pants, Terry and Barsh discussed several topics of interest. They were both well versed in anthropology, Terry more so in physical anthropology and Barsh in cultural anthropology.

A retired physician, Terry was not a church-going man nor a student of the finding of modern scholarship on the Bible, but he was impressed by Barsh's scholarship and his perspectives on existential issues.

When the women returned, it was obvious that they had forged a strong bond of friendship. Each was awed by the special talents of the other, that were so different from their own. Yet, each looked forward to learning from the other.

Susan promised to spend a week at the farm when she delivered the horses. She would give Angela and Hannah riding lessons, and Angela would introduce Susan to some of her favorite Southern novelists. And to everyone delight, Terry decided to come with Susan when she delivered the horses.

***

After two nights and a full day, Barsh and Angela left for Ashland in an exuberant mood and high expectations of the Halfords' visit in June.

"Now, that was Southern hospitality, second only to yours," Angela said as they drove away.

"They are indeed a gracious couple. We'll have to think of something special to do with them when they visit us."

"Yes, we must and we will. This was a good trip all around."

"A very good trip. Susan and Terry both like you. It's also obvious to them that I adore you and that I've found a good woman.

"Susan was concerned when I first told her about the failure of my marriage to Debbie, and she shared some of Terry's experiences with his first wife. Not only was she a bad match for him, she was wild and treacherous.

"Obviously, I'm pleased that Susan and Terry love and respect each other. They both deserve a good mate."

"I agree with your judgment about their relationship."

"Can you also see why Susan would not have been the best match for me?"

"Actually, I can see that now that I've been with her. You both are very special but also very different beyond your love of horses. It's a matter of the whole package, of having the things each mate needs from the other. That's the hard part of the search. It's more than physical attraction. That was there for you as Susan matured, right?"

"You are so right. There were times when I found it hard not to take advantage of the fact that she loved me. On my visit in the fall, she confessed that she would have submitted to my every wish back in our youth.

"Thankfully, my moral compass kept that from happening. Even as a young man, my romantic heart told me, intuitively, that I should keep searching for my beloved. I say intuitively because I could not have expressed it in words. And you're probably thinking what happened to my romantic heart when I decided to marry Debbie."

"Not really. But now that you've mentioned it, what did happen to it?"

"I think my spiritual and intellectual quests had caused me to abandon my romantic heart. For the first time, I was in a position to get married. I needed a wife and Debbie was available. That may be an oversimplification, but something along those lines happened."

"Now that you've expressed it that way, I can see parallels in my early response to Jacob McFarland. For the first time in my life, I was ready for a husband and he told me that he loved me and would soon be able to marry me."

"Well, I'm both able and ready to marry you."

"I have no doubt about you. Changing the subject, do you really think I can learn to ride my horse?"

"I have no doubt. You're not aspiring to ride a stallion. Your filly is quite docile. We'll take our time getting to know our horses as they get to know us. We could not have finer horses for our needs.

"Trust me, Susan will help you in a step-by-step process, until you'll be riding with ease, confidence, and joy. First, she'll get you comfortable just riding in the saddle with her leading the horse. Once you learn how to move with the horse with no fear of falling off, you'll be ready to learn how to rein it to your command."

"Okay, that is reassuring."

"Thanks to Susan who gave me a fine set of plans for a riding rink, I intend to have it ready before she brings our horses. I know a contractor who will build it, and I'll set up an appointment with him next week. Do you know how excited I am about getting my second horse? This one a Tennessee Walker."

"Actually, it's beginning to register with me, and I know of no one more deserving."

He took her hand and kissed it. The Audi hummed down the Interstate. The sky was clear, and a few trees were budding along the roadway. Just so, the spring break unfolded and energized them for the tasks they would face in the weeks ahead.

Chapter Thirty

It was the last Thursday in April, and Barsh left the University of South Carolina with his spirit soaring like an osprey in early spring. James Dickey had just applauded his latest poem. He was even a bit lavish with his praise.

As usual, Barsh was eager to get back to Angela and pushed the Audi, just beyond the speed limit. The miles kept rolling away, until he eased into Angela's backyard. He parked beside her Volvo and bounded up the steps onto the porch as she opened the kitchen door.

"How good to see your smiling face," she said. "Can I assume Dickey liked your poem?"

"Well, as you can see, I'm a bit full of myself. Yes, the poem got a good response from everyone. It even got an ovation from Dickey."

"Well, it certainly deserved one. Congratulations."

"Thanks. How was your day?"

"I've had a fine day," she said, fixed him a glass of iced tea, and led him to the couch where they sat side by side.

"I had an interesting phone conversation with Daddy, last night. He told me that I had redeemed his life. That his seemingly worthless life now seemed worthwhile. That he would do it all over, just to have me as his daughter.

"When I hung up the phone, I began weeping—my tears mingled with sorrow and joy. Then I found myself reevaluating my position about becoming a birthmother.

"Based primarily on your devotion to Hannah and my observations of how she has enriched your life, I was already having positive thoughts about motherhood.

"Then as I examined my soul after Daddy's confession, I decided that I'm now mentally and emotionally prepared to become a birthmother. But I haven't yet committed myself to having a baby. You haven't changed your mind, have you?"

"No, no, that decision is still yours to make."

"I can wait awhile before I decide, right?"

"Yes, but at our age, I don't think it wise to wait more than year."

"I agree with your judgment. I'll soon be ready to discuss the pros and cons with you, and then make a decision.

"I know there's no guarantee that I can get pregnant and have a normal baby. I also know that's not essential for my happiness. Whatever I decide, I'll be happy as long as I have you."

"Just know that we're fortunate to have options to accommodate your maternity if you have a baby."

"I haven't thought about that. Please share my options."

"You can take a leave of absence for as long as you wish without a salary. Or you can take a reduced teaching load with a reduced salary."

"I like the idea of a reduced teaching load. What would you recommend here?"

"One option would be to teach two courses on a Tuesday and Thursday schedule. On those two days, we could arrange our schedules, so I could take care of the baby while you teach your classes.

"I'd like that option very much. How would a baby effect the book-signing tour you promised me if I get my novel published?"

"We'll take the baby with us. I'll take care her or him while you're signing your novel, and I'll do the same when book clubs and literary groups start inviting you to discuss and read from the novel."

"Yes, I can envision that working quite well. We could also take the baby with us if we follow through on our plan to start doing joint poetry reading. I'll manage the baby while your reading, and you can while I'm reading.

"Thanks for sharing those options. They are all very good. Shifting subjects, I'm excited about our plan to visit Hannah in Louisville this weekend. This should be a good weekend for the three of us."

"That's my expectation. I've been thinking about things we might do on Saturday, including a visit to The Oriental Institute Museum in Chicago. They have an extraordinary collection of ancient artifacts from the Fertile Crescent.

"During my Master of Theology studies in Louisville, my professor of Biblical Archeology took our class on a field trip to this museum, and it was an extraordinary experience.

"Sounds like a good trip to me. Do you think Hannah would enjoy it?"

"Definitely. I've shared memories of my visit, and she was very interested in what I had to say about the exhibits."

"Then let's go."

"Okay. It will be a demanding day, time and energy wise, but well worth it in my opinion."

"I'm totally on board for making the trip. Are you ready of supper?"

"Sure, then I have work I need to do at home, but I'll come back and put you to bed if you want me to."

"Oh, yes, I love the way you put me to bed."

Chapter Thirty-One

Barsh left Cooper at noon that Friday and drove to Angela's, where they ate a light lunch and left to visit Hannah in Louisville.

"I assume you chose the Ford pickup so Hannah will be sitting on this broad seat with us, when we leave for Chicago in the morning."

"Your assumption is correct."

"You always think ahead, as I've said many times."

With a heart overflowing with love, he took the ramp to I-85 North to Charlotte, the first stretch of the seven-hour drive to Louisville. They stopped several times, including one for a fine dinner in Lexington, Kentucky.

They picked Hannah up around eight that evening and then checked into a motel, where he had reserved two adjoining rooms. The three of them were in a jovial mood and discussed various topics, both serious and trivial.

Hannah was especially excited about getting to visit the exhibits from ancient Sumer and shared with Angela the experience of listening to Barsh read the Gilgamesh Epic to her when she was ten.

Angela had heard about the epic, but didn't know much about it. Hannah shared her take on it, and Barsh commented on the connections between it and two Biblical stories—the tree of life in the garden of Eden and Noah and the flood.

At Hannah's bedtime, Angela followed her into the adjoining room and waited for her to change in her pajamas.

"If you have a bad dream or get scared, come wake me and I'll stay with you until you got back to sleep."

"Don't worry about me. I'm not afraid to sleep in this room by myself. Daddy has securely locked it."

***

Early Saturday morning, they left for Chicago. Together on the broad seat of the Ford pickup, they talked and laughed and listened to music in cycles during the drive up.

After spending most of the afternoon at The Oriental Institute Museum, they left for Louisville. Hannah had been so impressed by the experience that she kept bringing up various aspects of the exhibits that had captured her interest.

It was late when they got back to the motel. They were tired but pleased with the way the day had gone. They relaxed for a while and then went to bed.

After breakfast Sunday morning, Barsh and Angela took Hannah to Debbie's and headed back to Ashland. They talked about Hannah and the changes they could see in her. In their judgment, the changes all seemed healthy and appropriate for her age. Then Angela wanted to talk about Hannah's response to The Oriental Institute Museum.

"I'm sure you noticed Hannah's positive response to the museum. I must tell you that I had the same positive response. It gave me a visual window on those ancient cultures—something I did not have. Now, I'm questioning our honeymoon plans."

"Would you like to change them?"

"Only if you concur. I consider the Christmas getaway our true honeymoon. Nothing could have been better for me. We had our first extended period of intimacy, and I so enjoyed Hilton Head Island and the Lowcountry.

"I'm now thinking our trip to Rome should be an educational experience for the three of us. Could we go back to Hilton Head Island for our official honeymoon, and then the three of us go to Rome, later?"

"That would please me, immensely, as long as it's your preference."

"It's definitely my preference. If Susan can bring our horses as soon as we return. I think Daddy will stay at my house until she delivers them. I would love for him to see my new horse. He knows how I wanted one as a teenager.

"I'll call her tonight. How long would you like to stay at Hilton Head Island."

"Right now, I'm thinking five nights, rather than the week we'd planned for Rome. Is that long enough for you?"

"That's fine with me. I'll call tomorrow and reserve us a place, hopefully in the same oceanfront condo we stayed in during our Christmas getaway."

"Splendid! As you say, there's much more down there you want to share with me."

"True, ever so true. In addition to the things I've mentioned, I think a daytrip to Savannah and environs would be good for us. After exploring the old city, we could have lunch on River Street and then find a bench where we can watch the traffic on the Savannah."

"Next, I'll take you to Fort Pulaski National Monument and then Tybee Island. Coming back from the Island, we'll visit Bonaventure Cemetery. Do you know the poet, Conrad Aiken?"

"I know his poetry but little about him. Does he have a connection with Savannah?

"He was born there. His father was a physician. His mother was a Yankee who got caught up in the social life of the old city—constantly giving and attending parties, much to the displeasure of her husband.

"When Conrad was eleven, his father shot and killed his wife. Then he killed himself. Young Conrad was there in their house when that happened."

"Oh, my God, what a tragedy. What happened to Conrad?

"Relatives in the North took him in. Late in life, he moved back next door to the house where he was born. He died in Savanah and is buried in Bonaventure Cemetery.

"There's a bench beside his grave that looks out on the Wilmington River and the saltwater marshes. The epitaph on his grave is very unique—Destination Unknown.

"Conrad once noted a cargo ship headed up the Savannah River that interested him, and he looked up its destination. The log read Destination Unknow.

"Oh, I love that story. Let's sit on the bench and take turns reading, aloud, some of his poems."

"That's a wonderful idea. On a past visit, I sat there alone, silently pondering my somewhat sad destination. This time, I'll be married and my mood will be a happy one."

"Have no doubt that I'll be bubbling over with happiness."

"Angie, let's shift back to our wedding plans. How shall I dress since we're having it at the farm? I have a black tuxedo, but I will buy or rent whatever you'd like for me to wear."

"If you're letting me decide, I'd like for you to wear your tuxedo."

"Of course, I'm letting you decide."

"I've bought a light blue evening dress—my preference over a traditional wedding grown at my age."

"Ah, my bride to be, I can imagine how stunningly beautiful you will look. I'm very pleased with our wedding plans."

"So am I. I don't even care anymore that Mother won't be in attendance as long as Daddy is there."

"He'll be with us unless there's an unforeseen problem. If that should happen, we can postpone the wedding until he can come."

"Then I have no worries. I trust you know I cherish the way you typically honor my feelings, and I don't take your deference for granted. I realize you're strong enough of mind and soul to defer to my needs without feeling diminished. And I'm grateful. I also know that if you have a strong interest in something else, you will let me know, right?"

"We understand each other very well."

The drive back to Ashland was tiring. Angela would grade her student's papers for a while and then stop to talk about something that occurred to her or to listen to music on one of her cassettes. After arriving at her house, they parted ways early to rest and get ready for the week ahead.

Chapter Thirty-Two

The month of May had rolled by with lots of special activities. Barsh was appointed the Georgette Wingo Professor of Humanities. There was a bridal luncheon for Angela. Then graduation ended the academic year on another high.

The day of the wedding broke, bright and fair. Barsh woke early and eased into the bathroom. Atypically, he deferred his shower until after breakfast and left for the kitchen in his pajamas.

On his way, he stopped at Hannah's bedroom door and watched her for a moment as she slept peacefully. What joy he felt to have her back home for the summer.

With his first cup of coffee, he sat in his study. How blessed he was to have Hannah and Angela balancing the center of his heart. Bowing his head in reverent awe to the unfathomable Ground of Being, he whispered a prayer for strength and wisdom to be the father and husband that would not fail them.

He soon heard Hannah's pattering feet coming down the hall. The sound was so familiar that it almost erased the months she had been living with Debbie in Louisville.

"Ah, my sweet girl, how I love to hear your pattering feet coming down the hall to find me in the study. I hope you slept well."

"I did. And you?"

"Oh, yes. Let's review the agenda for today and next week, and then we'll eat breakfast. Would you like some juice, now?"

"No, thanks."

"Okay. After breakfast we'll dress for the wedding and wait for Davis. She'll leave her car here and ride with us to the farm. A few friends will begin arriving a little before ten o'clock.

"I'd like for you to be my watch dog. When Angela and her father drive up, you'll announce their arrival to the rest of us. Then you'll manage the record player as I've rehearsed with you. Everyone will shift into their places for the ceremony that Angela and I have streamlined.

"We wrote our own vows, which were quite elaborate, but then decided not to use them in the wedding. Instead, we privately recited them to each other and filed them away for future journeys back to this extraordinary year for us. Thus, the ceremony will be short and simple. Those present already know the depth of our love and commitment.

"We've also designed this gathering as a joyous celebration for a very select few. There will be champagne punch, wedding cake, dancing, and just being together. Cecilia Moorhouse will be there to take photos.

"As the noon hour approaches, the guests will leave the farm for the wedding luncheon in the private dining room of the Ashland Hotel. You and Davis will ride with Catherine and Georgette. Angela and I will change into our travel clothes. Then we'll join you at the hotel.

"After the luncheon, Angela and I will leave for Hilton Head Island. Catherine will take you and Davis back to our house. Davis will stay with you until we return. Angela's father will stay in her house.

"We're eager to get back and be with you and Mr. Kundera, so we're only staying five nights. The first thing we'll do when we get back is move Angie's things into our house. I've already made arrangements with the movers.

"Susan and Terry are bringing our horses the next day. They're staying a week, so she can give you and Angie riding lessons. Mr. Kundera is also stay for that week. Questions?"

"Why did you change your plans about going to Rome for your honeymoon?"

"That was Angela's idea. After our trip to The Oriental Institute Museum in Chicago, she decided we should make Rome an educational trip for the three of us. We assumed you would like to go with us."

"Yes, but won't I be in your way?"

"No! No! We're not looking for nightlife that would exclude you, and I'll reserve a two-bedroom suite at a good hotel."

"Do you have plans for any other trips this summer?"

"We're also thinking about a trip to New York."

"Am I invited?"

"When you're living with us, you will be a part of our trips, unless you prefer to stay home. You'll have that option and Davis can stay with you. Okay, it's time for breakfast."

***

Catherine and Georgette were the first to arrive at the farmhouse. Barsh and Davis helped them bring in their things from the car. As promised, Georgette brought a beautiful cloth for the long table in the big room as well as a lovely floral arrangement. She also brought everything needed to make and serve the champagne punch. Catherine brought a wedding cake, serving plates, flatware, and napkins. The two women set to work and soon had everything in order.

Barsh ushered them into the den, where the furniture had been pushed to one side. There, they sat talking about what a blessed day it was. Peter, the college chaplain, was the next to arrive. Then Cecilia came and began taking a few candid photos. As the hour approached ten o'clock, Hannah kept watch for Angela and her father.

"Here they come," she yelled from the front door.

Peter and Barsh took their places. Hannah started the wedding march record.

All eyes were on Angela as her father escorted her into the room. She was dressed in an ankle-length, light blue evening dress that gracefully caressed her slender body. Her neck was unembellished, but her radiant face was adorned with dangling sliver earrings. Her silky black hair was put up in a fashionable statement.

Peter nodded to Hannah and she stopped the record player.

"This is a blessed moment, dear people," Peter said, surveying the room and motioning the group to be seated.

"Barsh, do you stand before me to take Angela as your wife?"

"I do."

"Angela, do you come to take Barsh as your husband?"

"I do."

"In the presence of God and these witnesses, proclaim to the other your vows of commitment and then seal them by exchanging rings."

"Angela, I love you. I cherish you. I adore you. I promise to be faithful to you in all of love's callings."

"Barsh, I love you. I cherish you. I adore you. I promise to be faithful to you in all of love's callings."

"Angela, wear this ring as a seal of my love and all the promises I've made to you, since first I knew I loved you. Wear it as a sign to all that I have taken you as my wife."

"Barsh, wear this ring as a seal of my love and all the promises I've made to you, since first I knew I loved you. Wear it as a sign to all that I have taken you as my husband."

Then holding hands, they smiling at each other, as Peter said, "By the authority vested in me by the State of South Carolina, I pronounce you husband and wife. May all your days be blessed."

They embraced and kissed tenderly. Hannah started a slow dance record, and the newlyweds gracefully danced into the center of the room.

***

Around two o'clock, Barsh and Angela were showered with rice and shouts of best wishes as they left the Ashland Hotel. They were on their way to Hilton Head Island, where they would honeymoon in the same oceanfront condo that they had stayed in during their Christmas getaway.

"I'm a satisfied woman, my dear husband. Happy and satisfied."

"And I'm a satisfied man, my dear wife. Oh yes, I'm happy and satisfied."

"Here we come, Hilton Head Island, full of passion and with expectations for a super good time," she said.

Angela took his hand, pulled it into her lap, and settled into a deep silence. Assuming she was reflecting on something momentous, he honored her silence and shifted his mind into its philosophical mode.

He was keenly aware of his good fortune to be traveling the road of happiness in midlife. Like every enlightened person, he had experienced the existential dread inherent in the uncertainties of life. He knew, all too well, that a torrential flood could roar down upon him at any moment and wash him from the road of happiness.

Be that as it may, Barsh firmly believed that nothing could ever cause him to regret choosing to love anew.

About the Author

An Alabama native, Frederick W. Bassett holds four academic degrees, including a Ph.D. in Biblical Literature from Emory University. During a twenty-one-year tenure at Limestone College, he served as Professor of Religion and Philosophy, Chair of the Division of Humanities, and Vice-President for Institution Advancement.

He then enjoyed a twenty-one-year residency at Hilton Head Island, where he served for four years as the Director of Development at Hilton Head Preparatory School. After his sons graduated Prep, he became the Executive Director of the Hilton Head College Center and then the Director of Hilton Head Horizons, an Elder Hostel Program.

Toward the end of his academic career, Bassett turned to creative writing with much satisfaction. He is the author of two books of "found poetry" that he created from Biblical lyrics—*Awake My Heart: Psalms for Life* and *Love: The song of Songs*. His poems have been widely published in literary journals and anthologies. He also has two published books of poetry—*The Horse Dreamer* and *The Old Stoic Faces the Mirror: A life in Poems.*

Bassett has two sons, Jonathan and Michael, who are academics. Now retired and widowed, he lives in Greenwood, SC, near Jonathan and family.

www.ingramcontent.com/pod-product-compliance
Lightning Source LLC
Chambersburg PA
CBHW060526310726
48982CB00002B/446

* 9 7 8 0 5 7 8 2 8 1 2 4 7 *